# ESCAPE FROM MELRIDION

## REBALANCING THE COSMOS
### BOOK 2

## ALEX GALASSI

GALACTIC TREEHOUSE LLC

Escape from Melridion

# MELRIDION

PROGNISH (WORLD OCEAN)
VRENG THAUL
MAULIS
GRUMNA PAH
Yombic River
GNUSARLIS
Yomvret Wall
YONIOAR
VRENG NA
Nishna Delta
DENSAR
MYARAAG
SOTARAAG
RATANATAR
GRENAG
OKOCOMVIE
VRENG BOS
OPPIN
NOJRICK
NALPETALIS
VOLGASH DESERT
THE COMPOUND
KREFNA MOUNTAINS

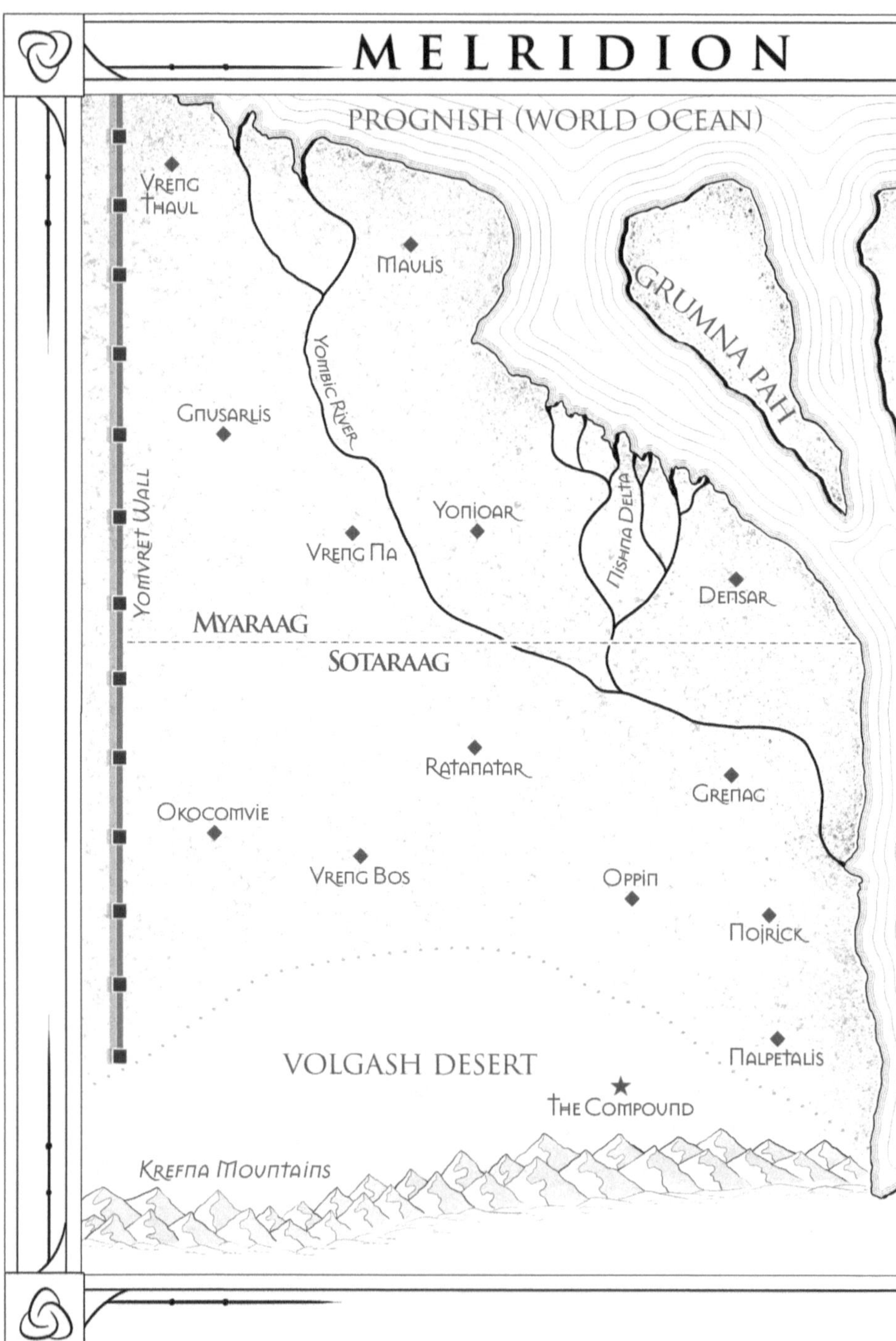

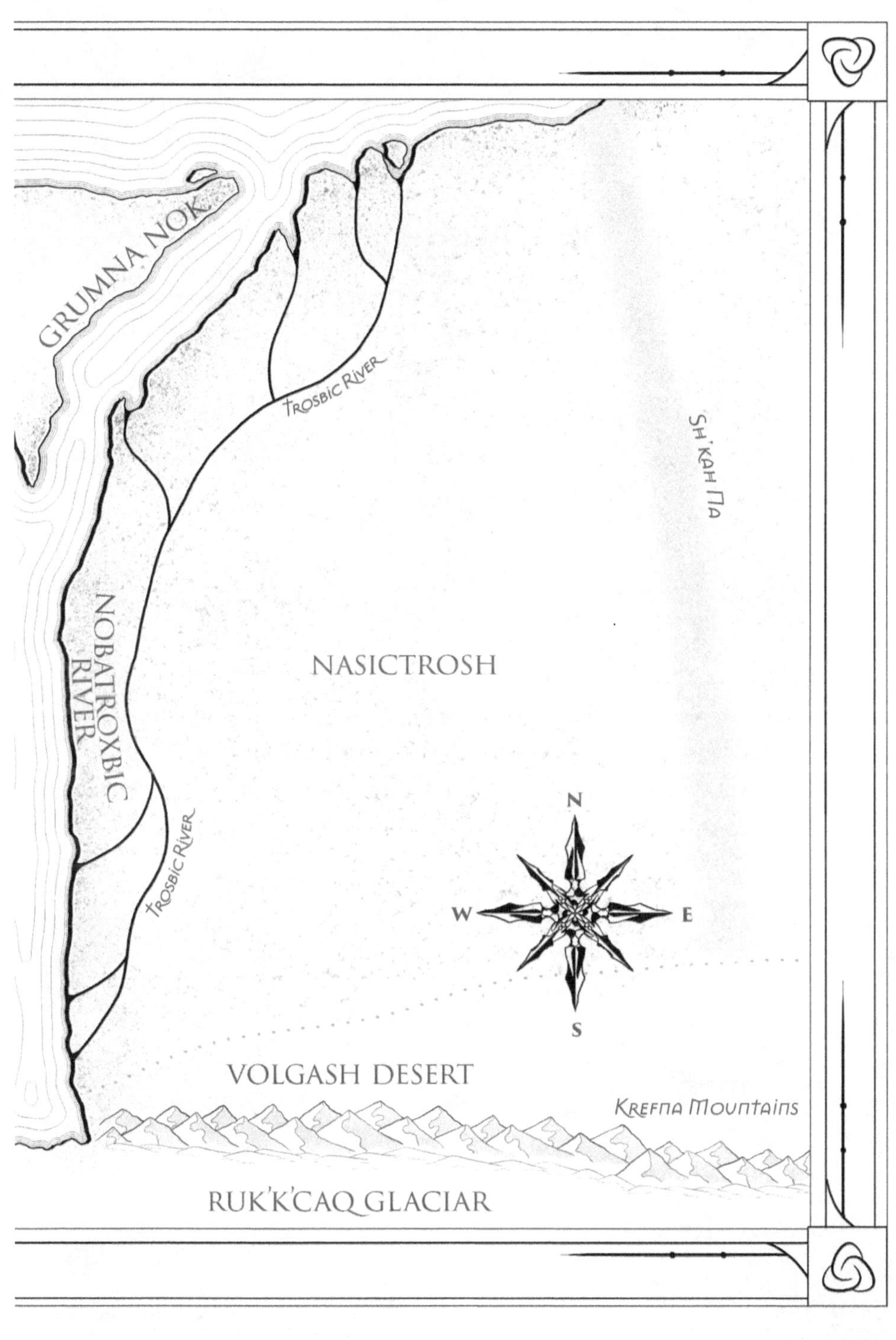

GRUMNA NOK
TROSBIC RIVER
NOBATROXBIC RIVER
TROSBIC RIVER
SH'KAH ПА
NASICTROSH
N
W E
S
VOLGASH DESERT
KREFNA MOUNTAINS
RUK'K'CAQ GLACIAR

# VORTEX SOLAR SYSTEM

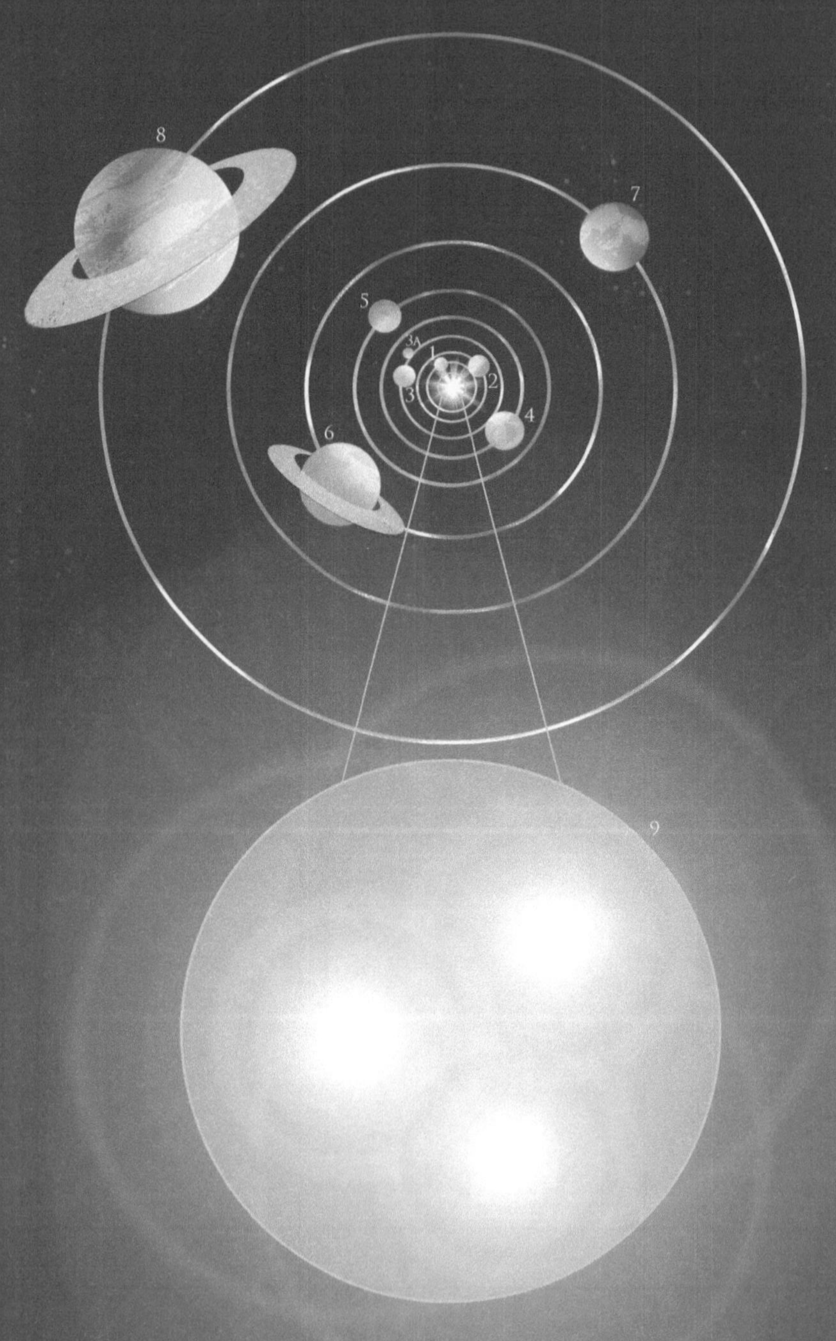

LEGEND

1. ACAMPACHETLI

2. MISHUNAED

3. CARANGE

3A. TERMATYL

4. MELRIDION

5. CLENDENIC

6. STRUTHEINE

7. IJURVOLL

8. DUNARTERA

9. THE THREE STARS

# CONTENTS

# PROLOGUE
## A RADIANT LIGHT

The last thing Sorceress Tyrona Claire Knorse saw was her lover's worried face. Theodore, whom Tyrona affectionately referred to as Dorie, was scared. He had a look of hopelessness in his eyes, but all she felt was relief. She had nothing to worry about anymore as she became a radiant light.

Then there was nothing. Time seemed to stop as Tyrona floated in whiteness. She hung in that limbo for what seemed like an eternity.

A dark, dusty hallway faded into her awareness, and she found herself floating above a large, intricately carved stone door. At first, she was alone, but soon her friends started to arrive. Joan was first, followed by Vesten. Her heart lurched as Dorie stepped into view. She wanted to rush to him, to embrace him, but she couldn't move. Although she could see her companions, she was still trapped in limbo. She stopped her struggling as Cecil and Dasch emerged from the blackness, followed by Ànifa.

A moment later, a small tug at her heart drew her down toward the door. She placed a hand on the door at the same time as her friends and the door opened. Then, impossibly, Theodore looked up at her and smiled. She smiled back and found she could move again.

As she rushed to him, she passed through him and appeared in a strange, unfamiliar room.

As Tyrona looked around the room, she realized she was back in her physical body. She was alone and surrounded by strange objects and blinking devices. Large black ropes connected all the devices. As she studied the ropes, she turned around to see they all led to a large stone gate. In the middle of the gate was a fading yellow glow that soon dissipated, revealing a whole new set of devices behind her.

Her head spun and she brought her hands to her face. She unclenched her right fist and discovered she was holding several strands of thick brown hairs—hairs from her dire wolf spider. So this wasn't a dream—she really had been transported to a different location. Only, this was no location she had ever heard of before on Eklatros. Theodore, Ànifa, and the rest—where were they? She had just seen them pass through a large stone door, but how did they get there? Hadn't they just been at the Nibelkaith Volcano?

As she mulled over these thoughts, a door slid open and several slug-like alien figures approached her, along with a blond-haired woman with strange metal parts. Without a second of hesitation, Tyrona drew her wand and encased herself in a protective barrier. Beams of energy shot toward her, only to bounce off the sound barrier and back at her assailants. She flung her barrier out in the direction of her assailants, creating a high-pitched frequency that brought them all down, except for the blond woman.

Before she could create another barrier, the blond woman raised her arm and shot a beam of energy at her.

Tyrona gasped and fell to the ground.

*Dorie... I need you...*

**1**

# ESCAPE FROM NORMALCY

Professor Navacus Clums looked around the room in disbelief. Four strange people had just appeared out of a large stone gate and were promptly tranquilized by Carl Feng. One of the strange otherworldly travelers wore uncomfortable-looking metal armor. Sprouting from the top of the metal helmet was a plume of rainbow-colored hairs. Next to the armored Human was an elderly Human, who was dressed in dark blue robes and wore a large blue hat that was similar, yet altogether different, from the hat West Kilinder wore. Then, there was a pale, bald Human in green robes and a black-skinned Human who wore green metallic armor that seemed quite different from the armor the Human with the rainbow plume wore.

"Professor Clums, are you listening?" Professor Durrist was saying.

Navacus tore his gaze from the travelers to look at the large, dark-green Lakinceitian. He smelled like lavender to cover up his natural unpleasant Lakinceitian body odor.

"I'm sorry, Professor Durrist. Can you repeat that?"

Professor Durrist sighed impatiently. "I need you to go with West and Carl. They'll take you back to the elevator you came down."

"You're sending me back upstairs?" Navacus asked.

"For now. The unexpected arrival of our new guests supersedes all other matters. We'll call upon you when we're ready to resume your orientation. Until then, please continue your work with Norman. And remember, you cannot tell anyone about your time down here."

"Yes, I understand," he replied.

"Good. Svetlana, Bsarg, please assist me with our guests," Professor Durrist said as he turned his attention to the travelers.

"Come on then, Professor," Carl Feng, the black-haired Human said as he straightened his glasses.

Navacus nodded. "Right."

With one final glance back at the strange Humans, he followed Carl out of the room, and West followed them. West Kilinder was a Eusphyrchiian and a former member of the Intergalactic Bounty Hunter Association. After a life-threating injury, West had been brought to Navacus and his team. They saved his life by implementing a Life Support System onto his chest, which controlled his vision, speech, hearing, and so much more.

They moved through the strange underground laboratory in silence. The hallway twisted, turned, and branched off in unexpected directions. He wasn't sure what to make of it, but he got the sense that the underground was much larger than what he was being shown.

"Hold on," Carl said as he stopped in the middle of the hallway, one hand to his ear. "Understood. I'll be there momentarily," Carl said, then turned toward them. "I apologize, there are matters I must attend to. West, I trust you know the way."

West shrugged. "I'm pretty sure I do. But I'll use LSS to navigate us just to be safe."

"Good idea. I'm sure we'll speak soon, Professor," Carl said, then turned and ran down the hallway.

"Well, we better get a move on, too," West said.

"Lead the way, West. Is this a good time to talk?"

"If it's brief. We'll be at the elevator soon," West replied as he straightened his white cowboy hat.

"Alright. I have a lot of questions, but I'm still curious about

Svetlana. She seems different from when I worked on her," Navacus said.

West tipped his cowboy hat forward, which was his way of nodding in agreement without having a head. "All I can say is that when we started training together, Svetlana was always kind-spirited. By the end of it, she was cold and distant. All of her playfulness seems to have been zapped out of her somehow." West turned to face Navacus as he walked backward, still leading the way to the elevator. "But I'm sure she's just taking her job seriously, nothing more."

As West was speaking, a line of text appeared on LSS' small screen that read WE'RE BEING MONITORED. ALWAYS.

Navacus nodded and West turned back around. "Now, I know this place can be *mind-bending*—I'd get lost if it wasn't for LSS. But we're here."

They turned a corner and found the elevator.

"Thank you for leading the way, West."

"It's my pleasure. I'm sure I'll see you again soon."

"I hope so. Take care, West."

"You too, Professor."

Navacus stepped into the elevator and pressed one of only two buttons—the large up arrow—and the elevator doors slid closed. Once he was alone, he wheezed out a sigh through the nasal slits in his large orange beak as he ruffled his white feathers. His first trip to the underground may have been unexpectedly cut short, but what he learned filled him with a sense of dread. For the first time, Navacus felt like a pawn being manipulated. He didn't trust Carl, Professor Randall, or Professor Durrist.

West, on the other hand, may be his only ally. If he understood West's subtle message right, Svetlana's mind was being tampered with. With all the wiring he and his team had connected to Svetlana's brain so she could control her robotic eye, hand, and other parts, it didn't surprise him. Yet, it was a terrifying thought. In the wrong hands, Svetlana could be a dangerous weapon.

Plus, why did West's LSS tell him they were being monitored? If even one of the compound's own security guards couldn't speak to him openly, then what was really going on?

The elevator doors slid open, and Navacus found himself at the end of the hallway that was in his wing of the compound. It was late —only the security lights were on. Everyone was already back at the barracks.

He had been expecting to be awake for most of the night, so he'd prepared a stimulator but hadn't gotten a chance to use it. Instead, he made his way to the exit. He passed Nijork, a light blue Lakinceitian and one of the compound's security guards, as he headed outside.

The cool air hit his face and Navacus smiled. To him, nights in the Volgash Desert were perfect. The days were far too hot for his liking. He much preferred the cooler nighttime temperatures, as his plumage was thick and dense.

The path to the barracks was covered, so he decided to walk beside the path so he could get a better view of the night sky. Aside from the dull glow on the eastern horizon toward Nalpetalis, there was no light pollution, giving him a pristine view of the dark web of wormholes. Even though they were dormant, they still shone and shimmered as light from the suns and the other planets was absorbed and shot back out of the cosmic ring. Occasionally, he saw a shooting star as space debris fell into the atmosphere and burned up.

A particularly intense shooting star continued to grow brighter and brighter until he had to shield his eyes from the sudden burst of radiant light. A moment later, the light was gone and he found himself standing in front of the entrance to the barracks.

*It's certainly been one long, strange day*, he thought. *Why not end it with even more strange events?*

He ruffled his feathers and keyed in his unique six-digit code to open the door. Once inside, he faced three doors. Just like the compound, the barracks were segmented. The door on the left led to Professor Peal's team's apartments, while the middle door led to Head Professor Yilvin's, Professor Dea's, and Professor Bodeelch's apartments, as well as that of the security guards. The door on the right led to his part of the barracks. He walked up to it and keyed in the code that unlocked the door, then made his way to the apartment that he shared with Fumalli Qymberkon. Most of his staff had their own rooms. Aside from Navacus and Fumalli, only Mac and Poi shared a room, since they were siblings.

Navacus silently crept into his apartment to find Fumalli dozing on the couch. He was wearing his sleeping clothes and had his three feet propped up on the entertainment table. As he closed the door behind him, Fumalli awoke with a start.

"Ah, I didn't mean to wake you," Navacus said.

"It's no problem." Fumalli yawned, covering his wide mouth with his slender blue hands. "I should make it to bed anyway. I thought you said you'd be working all night, though."

"I got sent home early. It was a lot of information to take in, so they decided to wait until next time to finish going over everything. Which is all I can say about it."

"I know, I know," Fumalli said with a wave as he stood up, "but a secret project for Carl certainly sounds interesting."

"It has been quite interesting, and very unexpected, so far."

"I'm sure it has. Are you coming to bed?"

"I'll be there soon. I need to freshen up a bit first. It's been a long night," he said as he headed to the washroom.

"I'll warm it up for you then, my friend."

"Thank you, my friend."

As was typical of his species, Navacus shared a bed with Fumalli. Yggdrazim families slept cuddled up together, and when Navacus had arrived at college, he had missed that. He had a hard time sleeping on his own, so his friend and roommate, Fumalli, agreed to share his bed with him. Since then, Fumalli had grown quite accustomed to it as well. Everyone needed their cuddling time, didn't they?

Navacus stepped out of the bath and shook himself dry—his plumage never stayed wet for long. As he looked into the mirror, he thought he saw a small orb of light behind him, but when he turned around, it was gone.

*I must be seeing things. First the shooting star, and now this... It must be stress related.*

He yawned and stepped out of the washroom, only to be greeted by a blinding light.

"Oh stars, what is this? What's going on?" Navacus exclaimed as he shielded his eyes.

He jumped in surprise when a deep, disembodied voice answered him.

"Navacus..."

"Who's there? Fumalli, is that you?"

"Open your eyes, Navacus."

He hesitantly opened his eyes. It was still bright but wasn't overpowering anymore. After a few moments, the light seemed to refocus itself and collect in the center of the room. The light became a swirling ball, pulsing at regular intervals, sending out waves of light.

"You must repeat these next words, Navacus, for our bond still must be solidified: I am the bearer of light."

"I am the bearer of light," Navacus repeated. He wasn't sure if he wanted to repeat it, or if he was being lured into it, but he couldn't help himself.

"I will shine light into darkness. I will protect and guide lost souls to divinity."

"... souls into divinity."

Navacus blinked. The sphere of light was no longer a sphere, but now something that resembled a ghostly being.

"What's happening? What is this? Fumalli, can you come out here?"

"Your companion cannot hear you. He slumbers too deeply," the ghostly Light Being said in a deep, rumbling voice.

Navacus wanted to run, but he couldn't move. He was absolutely terrified and tried his best not to let it show. "What did you just make me say?"

"It's a simple spell, but a powerful one. Our souls are now linked."

"Our souls? What are you?"

"I am just that—a soul without a body. I am a conduit of the Universal Consciousness. I am everything, and I am nothing. I am, as some have called us before, a Light Being."

"That's... you're everything, and nothing? What does that even... a Light Being?" He shook his head. "Look, whatever you are, do you have a name?"

"Not until now. You may call me Sterg."

"Okay, Sterg. I have a million questions running through my mind right now. Can you read my mind?"

"To some extent. We may be linked, but it will take time for us to truly be in sync with one another."

"Ah, well, that makes me feel slightly better about this whole situation. But, seriously, why me? Why did you choose... me?" Navacus said as he looked down at his weak, feathery body.

"I have been observing you for some time now, Navacus—ever since you began working on Svetlana. You are a kind, generous soul, one that will soon be tested in ways you are not yet prepared for. But you must be prepared. You are important, Navacus. There have only been three other souls before you across our vast universe that have been linked with Light Beings. But of those souls, your journey will be the most taxing."

His head was spinning. Not only was he still trying to process the four otherworldly travelers appearing out of the gate, but now he stood before a ball of light that was telling him he was important.

"This isn't a dream, right?" Navacus asked.

"No, this is real."

"So, we're linked now? Does that mean that you'll just be this floating ball of light that follows me around wherever I go?"

"As of now, you, Navacus, will be the only one who can see or hear me. However, when the time is right, you may reveal me to those closest to you, including your slumbering companion. I know you must have many more questions, but it's time for you to slumber as well. Your mind needs rest after all it's been through today."

Navacus nodded in agreement. He still had a lot of questions, but the urge to ask those questions had passed. Now, all he wanted to do was sleep.

*It really has been a long day, hasn't it?* he thought as he let out a yawn and waddled over to the couch. *I started my day with my team.*

*We're still perfecting Norman's vehicular attachment while we finalize the hover attachment. Norman really is progressing well, but there's still a lot to do. So, in its own way, it's good I'll be able to continue to work on him. Though, I'm really curious about what happened underground. As creepy as that place is, I really want to know more. Especially concerning the four Human travelers.*

*Then, of course, the garnish on the dish is Sterg—this being of light. How is it... How can I be having a conversation with light?*

## 2

# ESCAPE FROM THE ORDINARY

West watched the elevator doors slide shut. It would take Professor Clums several minutes to make it back up to the main compound. West still didn't know how far underground they were, but he guessed they were quite deep.

He turned away from the elevator and headed back to the gate room, where he spotted Professor Durrist moving his slug-like body as fast as he could toward him.

"Professor Durrist, what's going on?"

"Ah, I'm glad I ran into you. Come with me. We must hurry over to the Titans. Professor Randall and the others require our assistance."

"Right, Carl ran off in that direction as well. But what about those Human travelers from the gate?" West asked as he followed Professor Durrist.

Professor Durrist grunted. "It's quite unfortunate timing. Or, perhaps our travelers triggered this commotion. Either way, I had to pull Professor Xergat away from his duties. He'll be in charge of them now; however, I instructed Svetlana and Bsarg to watch over them until they're safe in their individual cells."

West had still never met Professor Xergat, though he knew that he was in charge of the Lakinceitian drones that kept the underground facilities running. And, as Professor Randall had put it, Professor Xergat also took care of all the failed experiments, both living and deceased. He didn't really want to know what that meant. Yet he couldn't dwell on that now. They were approaching the Titans, which meant he had to stay aware of his surroundings. West was already beginning to hear howls and screeches.

"Blast it, they must have fully woken up. But how? They were heavily sedated. The energy from the gate couldn't have done this... could it?" Professor Durrist asked.

West nodded and said nothing. Professor Durrist often talked to himself, and West had learned not to reply unless directly spoken to.

Professor Durrist stopped before a large door and approached a tablet on the wall. He tapped it and said, "Randall." A moment later, Professor Randall appeared on the screen.

"What's the situation?" Professor Durrist asked.

"Durrist, you've got to see this. Theesakin is awake."

"What?" Professor Durrist exclaimed as he tapped the tablet and opened the door. He and West walked into a circular room with eight doors that looked identical to the one they had just passed through. The cries and howls intensified as a low growl rumbled through the floor.

West's Life Support System, or LSS, truly was an amazing system. Since he no longer had a head, he used LSS to see, hear, speak, and do just about everything else. He switched through the electromagnetic spectrum, ultimately choosing infrared. Through the thick walls he could make out several enormous creatures that were visibly in distress. He had never been this close to any of them before, so just seeing their fuzzy outlines was exciting.

Professor Durrist led him to the door marked 5 and opened the door. West was surprised to face yet another door as he switched back to his normal vision.

"Is this an airlock?"

"Indeed. We can't be too careful," Professor Durrist said as he closed the door behind them.

A whoosh of air caused West to stumble while a fine mist sprayed them with anti-bacterial agents. Within a few seconds, he used his internal computer to identify each compound that made up the mist. While he didn't understand what any of them did, he logged the information for later use.

Professor Durrist opened the door and rushed into the circular room. West took a deep breath and followed.

If he had a jaw, it would have been on the ground. Before him stood a massive creature, nearly three and a half meters tall. It was covered in dark green scales and had four thick arms, two large bat-like wings, two stocky legs, and a fat tail that ended in a thin point. Out of its beast-like face sprouted four horns, two above each eye and two from behind each ear that curved forward. Its eyes, while large, were frighteningly Human-like. And it looked like it was terrified. Currently, the creature was standing in front of the transparent energy barrier, emitting a low-pitched growl. As he studied Theesakin, he was overcome with a strong sense of sadness and terror, but it wasn't his own.

"Randall, when did Theesakin first awaken?" Professor Durrist asked the tall brown-haired Human.

"Only a few minutes ago," Professor Randall replied as he pushed his glasses up onto his nose.

Aside from the three of them, Carl, Professor Peal, and six Lakinceitian drones were in the room with them. Each drone was on a tablet, recording and logging different pieces of information about Theesakin, while Professor Randall held his own tablet to control the drones. Carl simply stood off to the side, watching everyone closely.

"Why is it just standing there?" Professor Durrist asked.

"We're working on figuring that out. It's behaving quite differently from the other Titans," Professor Randall replied.

"And how are the other Titans?"

"When the gate opened, it sent out a large burst of energy. Its intensity was nearly four times greater than the first burst of energy the gate released when the first traveler, Tyrona, appeared. Since the energy burst was much stronger, it affected the Titans in ways we never would have expected. First of all, Zinartee's brain waves spiked —the largest spike we've ever recorded. Yet it remains immobile. As for the other three, they were thrashing around as if trying to break out of their cells. But not to worry—Karkilver and Ophertusc have been tranquilized. Zadgarcolth's tranquilizer is being specially prepared now, but we have managed to get it under control using a low frequency of sound waves. I must admit, I never would have thought of that if not for Tyrona."

"Wait, are you saying the gate opened once before? I thought today was the first time it has activated," West asked.

"It activated five days ago, but you did not need to know about that incident. Now, back to the matter at hand," Professor Durrist said as he turned to Theesakin. "How long has it been standing there?"

"Pretty much since it woke up. The energy from the gate must have triggered it to wake up, but we don't understand why it's immobile," Professor Randall said.

"He's not immobile," West replied. "He's terrified. And sad; he's very sad. He doesn't want to be awake. He doesn't want to be alive."

"How do you know what it's feeling?" Professor Durrist asked, as Carl walked up to them.

"I can see it in his eyes. But more than that, it's like he is trying to communicate with me. I can't explain it, but it's as if he is projecting his thoughts and feelings to me. Since he just woke up, he's still sorting through his thoughts. His mind is in a haze, but he's working through it," West said.

"Fascinating. Simply fascinating. After this, we'll need to see if you can pick up on the other Titans' thoughts," Professor Durrist said.

"Fine by me," he replied with a shrug.

"I'd also like to see if you could pick up anything from my own test subjects," Professor Peal said. "I know that mine can talk, but maybe you'll be able to get a read on their inner thoughts as well."

"I suppose I could do that, too. I mean, I know I'm still getting used to LSS, but I don't think that I can read everyone's emotions—

the computer isn't that powerful. But I'll see what I can do. It's possible that it may just be Theesakin who can do this."

"Yes, that is certainly a possibility, but now that we know you can do this, we must test this out on the others," Professor Randall said.

"And we will soon enough. Stop getting distracted," Professor Durrist said with a wave of his hand. "West, can you communicate back?"

"Sure, I'll try, but I have a question of my own first. You keep saying that he's awoken. How long had he been asleep before today?"

"It's never woken up before. It's been slumbering for several weeks—ever since we completed our work on it," Professor Durrist replied.

"Each of the Titans took a few days to wake up. But with Theesakin... we were starting to wonder if it would ever wake up since it had been so long," Professor Randall added.

"I know we don't have time for this now, but I'd like to know how you created Theesakin, if you can even tell me anything," West said, then turned to face Theesakin. He took several steps forward and flipped through the electromagnetic spectrum until he found a frequency that allowed him to *see* Theesakin's dark aura.

"Whoa, this is pretty cool," West said. "I can see his aura. Now, Theesakin... what do *you* wish to know?"

"Shouldn't he ask something more specific?" Carl asked.

"Hush. Let us observe now and ask questions later," Professor Durrist replied.

West watched in the corner of his vision as Carl glared at the large Lakinceitian professor. He smiled inwardly to himself.

"*Theesakin, can you understand me?*" West thought.

"*Yes. Scared. Confused. Hungry. I want to eat... living things. This disgusts me. I disgust myself. What am I?*"

The questions continued to flood out of Theesakin. It was as if a dam had broken—now that he could communicate with West, Theesakin couldn't control his thoughts.

"He's hungry. He wants to eat something living," West said out loud.

"Professor Peal, see that it gets fed," Professor Durrist said.

"I'll go see Professor Xergat right away," Professor Peal said as he brushed his blond hair with his fingers, adjusted his glasses, and left the room.

*"Who am I? What am I? Who are you?"*

*"I am West Kilinder, and I am a product of experimentation, much like yourself, Theesakin. But I am not like you. I don't know how they made you. As for me, I am the way I am because of an injury I suffered, but my life was saved because of the experiments. I have many new abilities that I had to learn. Just like you will need to learn to use your body."*

*"New abilities. New body. My body is unknown to me. What am I?"*

"He wants to know what he is. He keeps asking what he is," West said.

"Tell it that it is a Titan, a creature of awesome strength and power," Professor Durrist said.

"You keep saying 'it.' He is a *he*," West replied. "At least, he identifies as a he."

"I'll keep that in mind," Professor Durrist said.

*"Did you catch what my colleague said?"* West asked.

*"Yes. I heard. Do not understand. What is Titan?"*

*"I think he means that you are unique—one of a kind."*

*"How did I come to be?"*

*"The people in this room helped you become who you are now."*

*"I do not know them. I do not like them. I know you. I like you."*

*"Thank you, I like you, too. I believe we can be friends."*

*"Friend. Yes. You are friend. Thank... you. Hungry."*

*"A meal is being prepared."*

*"Thank you, West."*

"What's going on?" Randall asked.

"He reiterated that he's hungry. And I was helping him figure out who he is."

"Good. I think we'll need to rearrange your duties after today. I want you to continue to speak with him," Professor Durrist said.

"I'd like that. He seems kind."

"Kind? He is a powerful monster," Carl said. "Monsters aren't supposed to be kind."

Theesakin snarled at Carl.

"He didn't like that," West said.

"Ah, but he shows his temper. That's a good sign," Carl said with a smirk.

"West, is there anything he can tell us now?" Professor Durrist asked.

He shook his head. "Not right now. He's just hungry. How much longer until he's fed?"

"Whenever Peal and Xergat figure out what to feed him. Each of the Titans has a very specific diet, so it might take a few tries before we can figure out what he likes," Professor Randall said.

"In that case, let's see if you can communicate with any of the others. Start with Zinartee," Professor Durrist said. "And take Professor Randall with you. I want to observe our new friend a little longer."

"Alright, take over the drones for me then, would ya?" Professor Randall asked as he handed Professor Durrist the tablet. "Come along, West."

"Lead the way," West said, then turned back to Theesakin. *"Theesakin, I must go now. Please take care. I'll be back when I can."*

*"Friend. Take... care."*

West and Professor Randall exited the room. They had to go through the airlock again, but this time the compounds were different. Apparently, it was a different formula for those entering than those leaving the room.

Professor Randall led him to the door marked 2 and opened the door. Again, the formula in the airlock was different.

As West followed Professor Randall into the room, he adjusted his vision to try and see the creature. Once he found the right frequency, he couldn't believe what he was seeing. Before him floated an ethereal being that had a purplish tint to it due to the high frequency he was looking through. It had no body—it was like a living cloud. And yet, he could see neurons and electrical signals shooting through it.

"Alright, what can you see?" Professor Randall asked.

"I can see Zinartee. It's like a large purple cloud with multi-colored lightning flashing through it. It's thinking—observing. It has... no emotions, only logic and reasoning."

"You can actually see it? That's highly impressive. We can't see anything at all—only what gets picked up on the scanners."

"That must have been odd," West replied as he continued to focus on Zinartee.

"It really was. But it sounds like you can read Zinartee as well."

"Not really. Zinartee is different. Theesakin was like a scared child, and he literally spoke to me in my head. This time around, I'm just picking up what I can sense through LSS. And as I said, there is no emotion. What does it eat?"

"Strangely enough, it consumes hydrogen cyanide in its gaseous form," Professor Randall said as he crossed his arms and held them close to his chest.

In a nanosecond, West had scanned his internal computer to pull up information about the element.

"Poisonous gas? That is strange." As West continued to scan Zinartee, he felt a chill run down his spine. "I don't like it. Can we leave?"

"I was just about to suggest the same thing. No one has lasted longer than five minutes in the room," Professor Randall said as they hurried back into the airlock. A different solution sprayed them down this time.

"So, I've been through four airlocks now—well, two airlocks two times. And each time I've been sprayed by a slightly different solution. They've been quite similar, but the ratios of the compounds have been different all four times."

"Ah... of course you could pick up on that. I'm impressed," Professor Randall said as he stood in the center of the room. "The airlock isn't for us, it's for the Titans. We've discovered that if we spray ourselves with their pheromones, they're more likely to act less hostile toward us. And when you leave the room, you get sprayed by a solution that removes the pheromones."

"That makes a lot of sense, actually," West said as he tipped his white cowboy hat forward in agreement. "So, who's next?"

"Well, Karkilver and Ophertusc are out cold. You'll need to wait until they wake up before you see them. As for Zadgarcolth, let's check on its condition."

Professor Randall walked over the door marked *4* and tapped the tablet. After scrolling through a few different screens, he frowned.

"It appears as if Zadgarcolth is also asleep now."

"Ah well, I'll just have to check in on the three of them some other time, then," West said. "By the way, I like the idea of naming them after the Lakinceitian gods."

"Yes, well, it wasn't my idea. I've never been much into religions or mythologies myself," Professor Randall replied. "Now, if you've got nothing else to do, I believe Professor Peal wanted you to check up on his test subjects. I trust you know the way?"

"It's one of the few destinations I have on my map. I'll head over there now," West said as he tipped his cowboy hat again. "Anything else you'd like me to do after that?"

"No, I think that should be all for tonight. Once you finish up, go get some rest. Report in first thing tomorrow."

"Of course, Professor."

"Oh, one more thing, actually. As you can see, each door is marked with a number. When you get to Peal's area, you'll only need to go into the doors numbered one and two. Just use the tablet to open the door. And there will be no airlocks this time around."

"Great, good to know. By the way, earlier Bsarg and Professor Durrist mentioned a prophecy that was related to those Humans who appeared from the gate. Do you know anything about that?"

"Prophecy? Oh, you must mean that silly old tale. I really can't talk about it at the moment, but it's nothing to worry about. Now, we have a lot of work to do," Professor Randall replied.

"Of course, Professor."

West left the Titan enclosure and headed toward the blinking light on his internal map. Professor Randall was definitely hiding something. He'd been nervous when West asked him about the prophecy, as if there was information the professor didn't have the authority to share. West was certain that it was more than a silly old tale.

Along the way to Peal's area, he passed by several Lakinceitian drones moving stiffly toward their own destinations. He had put up with a lot of brutality and violence while he was in the Intergalactic Bounty Hunter Association, but the drones bothered him more than any of that had. These were mindless drones, taken over by Professor Xergat and used around the underground. They were still alive but were completely devoid of any personality they once had. Sprouting out of their heads was a single antenna, which was constantly blinking at different intervals, depending on the task they were doing. It was horrifying, but it made him thankful that at least he had gotten through his experimentation alive and with his sanity.

West approached Professor Peal's area of the underground and headed into the circular room. It had a similar layout to the Titan's enclosure, but this time there were only five doors. West scanned the room and found that aside from the lifeforms behind the first two doors, there was one massive creature behind the third door, two small creatures behind the fourth door, and a Eusphyrchiian-sized creature behind the fifth door.

He shrugged and changed back to his normal vision. It wasn't any of his concern—he was only asked to check out the first two doors. He headed for the door marked *1* and tapped the tablet to open the door.

He entered the cramped space to find three large cells, each one situated on each of the three walls. The cell directly in front of him was partially shaded, obscuring his view of what was inside. However, to his right was, without a doubt, the strangest creature he had ever seen. His internal computer informed him that it was a Zubba from the planet Acampachetli. It looked as if someone had fused the body of a rusty-haired bat onto the back of a large, bright-red scorpion. The cell to his left contained a large, blood-red snake. It was a Loxocemae, also from Acampachetli. Each of the cells contained plants, rocks, and dirt to imitate their natural habitats.

"Who the blazes are you?" came a high-pitched, squeaky voice.

West looked over to the cell that had been shaded and saw a half-meter tall tan stick bug standing in front of the glass with its arms crossed.

"So, you really can speak. Professor Peal had mentioned it."

"Oh, you're one of *his*. I don't want to flippin' talk to you then," the stick bug said as it turned its back on him. It pressed a button with its left leg and the glass darkened.

"Wait, I'm not with Professor Peal. I'm not a scientist at all. I'm a security guard. I was simply sent here by Professor Peal to check in on you."

"See what I mean?" the stick bug said from behind the shaded glass. "You're with Peal. I don't want to talk to you."

"Hey, come on, can't you give me a few seconds at least? Hello?"

"He's probably shut offs his soundses," the snake said in a thick accent that was heavy on the *s*'s.

"Ah, he can do that willingly?"

"We all cans," the snake replied.

"Ah. Forgive me; I was not briefed on what to expect," West said.

"Allow me to introduce everyones. I'm Sassafrass, and across from me is Blood Bat. The rude one is Denoptace."

"It's nice to meet you, Sassafrass. It's nice to meet you all."

"Meet... nice! You!" Blood Bat squawked.

"Can Blood Bat not..."

"He speaks in his own fasionses. We all do, in a sense."

"I see," West said as he tipped his white cowboy hat forward. The blood-red snake looked at him curiously.

"You are differentses from the others. Why do you have that machineses on your chests?" Sassafrass asked.

"Well, I was severely injured, but I was saved by Professor Clums. He is the one who built and designed my Life Support System, and I owe him my life."

"Professor Clumses... is that the bird-like man?"

"Yes, he's a Yggdrazim. Now, Sassafrass—"

"Why are you really heres?" the snake asked him pointedly.

"Why? You! My story!" Blood Bat squawked.

"He means mystery. Since you are very mysterious," Sassafrass said.

"I see you're quite perceptive, Sassafrass. I respect that. Truth be told, a few minutes ago I was able to communicate with one of Professor Durrist's lab experiments... but we communicated through our minds. It's hard to explain, but we weren't speaking out loud to each other. It was as if we could read each other's thoughts. So, I was asked by Professor Peal to see if I could do the same with you."

"And can you?" Sassafrass asked.

"I haven't tried yet. Give me a moment. I'll need to focus on each of you separately."

"Okay!" Blood Bat squawked.

West stepped into the center of the room and focused on Sassafrass first. He scanned through the electromagnetic spectrum, but he was unable to see her aura with any frequency. It was the same for Blood Bat and Denoptace.

"Nope, I can't do the same with any of you. That creature is the only one I've ever been able to communicate with in that way. I didn't even know it was possible."

"Well, that's comforting," Sassafrass said.

"It really was nice to meet you all, though," West replied.

"Leave?" Blood Bat asked.

"Yes, I've had a long day, and I still need to go to the next room over."

"Ah, yes, we know littles of those roomses," Sassafrass said. "I enjoyed our conversations."

"I did as well. If I get the chance, I would like to come back again, just to chat, if that's okay with you."

"Oh, go screw yourself," Denoptace hollered from behind the shaded glass.

"I would like to talk with you agains," Sassafrass said, ignoring the stick bug.

"Me! Me!" Blood Bat said happily.

"That means he wants to talk to you again, too," Sassafrass translated.

West laughed. "Then that settles it, I'll be back when I can. I can't say when, or promise that it will be anytime soon."

"That's fines. Talks later."

"Talk never!" Denoptace shouted.

West smiled inwardly as he tapped the tablet and stepped out of the room. The door closed behind him with a whoosh of air. He had not been expecting to talk with animals and an insect. His curiosity piqued, West walked over to the door marked 2 and tapped the tablet to open the door.

This time around, the room only contained one large cell separated by a transparent barrier. At first, all he saw was dense foliage. He was tempted to scan the room using his infrared sight but resisted and kept his natural vision. While he knew the creature in the room with him wouldn't know the difference, he didn't want to invade its privacy.

"Hello? I'm West, a security guard here. Professor Peal asked me to check up on you. Would you mind stepping out where I can see you?"

"Oh, but if you chose to, you could already see me. Isn't that why you are here?"

A deep purple lizard with six strong legs stepped out of the dark green foliage. She was the largest lizard West had ever seen, and he couldn't help but be captivated by her large jade green eyes and circular black pupils. While they looked almost out of place with the large lizard, they managed to fit her perfectly.

"How do you know why I'm here?" West asked. He was glad that LSS kept his voice from quavering. It was as if her eyes pierced right through him.

"Aren't I always being watched?"

"I wouldn't know. Honestly. I was never allowed near here until now."

"So, what changed, West?"

"I... well, I was able to speak with a large creature in my mind. Meaning..."

"I understand what you're saying. This is familiar to me. My species communicate telepathically. So, you want to see if you can do the same with me."

"Professor Peal asked me. I didn't even know who was behind this door."

"Yes, that man... Anyway, go ahead and do what you need to do."

"Sure. If I may ask first, do you have a name?"

"Newtus."

"It's nice to meet you, Newtus. Now, hang on for a moment."

As West scanned the electromagnetic spectrum, Newtus immediately felt different from Sassafrass and the others. He jumped to the frequency that allowed him to communicate with Theesakin and saw Newtus' aura. Even though they'd just met, he could tell her aura was weak.

"You're in distress," West said out loud.

*"Of course I am. I'm being kept in a cage. My kind was never meant to be constrained. We go where we wish,"* Newtus said in his mind.

*"Yes... I don't envy your situation,"* West replied telepathically.

*"But aren't you in the exact same situation as I? The only difference is your cage is this entire compound. But you're the same as me—you can't leave, and you can only do what you're told. Plus, you've also been experimented on."*

*"How do you know all of this?"*

*"Just as you can read more than my thoughts, I can read more than your thoughts, West Kilinder. Now, what can you read about me?"*

*"You've been through so much pain. It's different from my physical pain —yours is much more spiritual. You've become a monster in your eyes. Not only do you fear your new strength and abilities, but you've grown two extra legs. You're not what you once were."*

*"Neither are you. Now, please, I want to be left alone. I appreciate your company... but you've made me miss my family."*

*"I understand completely. Could I see you again?"*

*"Perhaps. I'm sure Professor Peal will speak to me about you."*

"*Right. It really was nice meeting you.*"

"*Goodbye, West Kilinder.*"

Newtus put her front foot on the glass. West subtly moved to place his own hand on top of hers, but stopped when he realized the barrier was becoming shaded. West swapped back to his normal vision, cutting off their mental link.

---

West walked back to the barracks, choosing to walk under the stars and not the shaded walkway. The stars seemed brighter than usual tonight.

*I am in a cage, aren't I?* West thought. *I think I've always been in a cage—a cage of my own choosing. My education, the IBHA... and while I didn't choose my current situation, I am thankful to be alive. But after meeting Newtus, Theesakin, and the others... I really am the same as them. I may be a security guard, but I have no real power.*

*I do hope that I get to see Newtus again, though. I'm very curious as to why I could speak with her in nearly the exact same way I could speak with Theesakin. I'll need to see both of them again to figure it out.*

**3**

# ESCAPE FROM STAGNATION

"Navacus, wake up. If you don't get up now, you'll be late!"

He groaned, rolled off the couch, and smacked onto the floor. "Ow." Navacus lay there for a moment before sitting up and leaning against the couch. As he moved to sit up, his head felt like it split open.

"Ow. Ah... why am I on the floor?"

"You never made it to bed. I really don't understand why. You hate sleeping on your own," Fumalli said.

"Oh my, I feel extremely hungover," Navacus said as he placed his hand on his head. "I didn't drink anything last night, did I?"

"How could you? We don't have any alcohol. It isn't a holiday or anything like that."

"Do I smell tea? I could really use some tea."

Fumalli walked to the table, picked up a white mug, and brought it over to him. "It's already brewed. Be careful, it's still hot," Fumalli said as he handed him the mug.

"Thanks, Fumi," Navacus said as he took a sip. "Ah, that's good. If you need to you can go on ahead. I'll get ready soon."

"Didn't you just say you feel hungover? Do you need to rest?"

"No. I mean yes. I have a splitting headache. But no, I don't want to rest. As much as my head hurts, I feel really rejuvenated and awake. It's an odd combination."

"Perfect for an odd fellow like yourself," Fumalli said with a wink. "And I don't need to leave quite yet—I still need to eat."

As Navacus sipped on his tea, he felt his headache weaken significantly. "I'm actually already feeling a lot better."

"I'm sure it was just from sleeping on the couch. You've never slept there before," Fumalli said as he spooned himself a bowl of yogurt.

"I know. I don't honestly know why I did that. The last thing I remember was talking to you and then you were waking me up. I'm not sure what happened."

"Well, between working on Norman and working on that secret project for Carl, you've been doing nearly double shifts. You've got a lot on your plate. Maybe you were just exhausted."

"That would make sense. But even so, we used to stay up all night studying while we were in college, and I never missed making it to bed," Navacus said as he finished his tea. "I guess I'm just getting old. I'm going to go get ready."

"I'll see you over there, then. There's a lot to do today," Fumalli said as he ate a spoonful of yogurt.

---

"Can I see your tablet for a moment, Syl?" Professor Qymberkon, the dark blue Nioavellian, asked as Professor Clums walked into the lab. "Ah, there you are, Professor."

"Here you go, Professor," Sylcertiverner said as he handed Professor Qymberkon the tablet. Professor Qymberkon took it as he turned his attention to Professor Clums.

"You're late."

"Yeah sorry, it took a little longer than usual to get ready," Professor Clums said as he wheezed, his species' way of sighing. "And I woke up late. Can someone give me a brief summary of today up to this point?"

As always, Norman Harrison was watching the activity around him with a sense of wonder and appreciation. This had been his new normal for a while now, but he was still getting used to the fact that all eight scientists in the room were working hard to give him a new way to move around and a new way of life.

At first he wanted to ask a lot of questions, and did so loudly, and most of the time his questions were answered. Yet, one day, Sylcertiverner had gotten so flustered by explaining everything he was doing he nearly dropped a screwdriver on his own tools. Luckily Grasberg was there to catch it before it fell. Since then, Norman simply observed them. Besides, through his nagging, he was able to learn a lot about what they were doing and how intricate and delicate the process was. He didn't want to cause any issues for them, for he had come to truly respect each of them. In a way, they were his friends. But he also had no one else to talk to, besides the other professors. He didn't care for them much, except for Professor Dea. He had always been kind to Norman.

The pain of Kate's sudden disappearance still gripped at his heart. He just didn't understand why she would leave without saying a word. It wasn't like her. Sure, at this point, he was beginning to understand how top secret everything was, but even if she couldn't see him off, why didn't she at least send a message? Something seemed wrong, and the fact that everyone in the room with him seemed to genuinely believe the false truth he was fed scared him. That meant that it was probably Head Professor Yilvin who was behind it. Of course, he had no evidence that Kate was not on Carange. It was possible that she was back home and couldn't send him a message or that her messages weren't reaching him.

Either way, he missed her like crazy.

"... so the leg attachments are pretty much a hundred percent complete," Grasberg was saying. "They've been fully plated and painted as of this morning."

"Good. What about the vehicular attachment?" Professor Clums asked.

"We're still making adjustments on the engine," Mac replied. He stood next to his twin sister Poi on the lab table next to them. Lyd, the third Harmertian, stood beside them and nodded along.

"We're trying to fine-tune the acceleration and make it as smooth as possible, while double checking the breaks. He needs to be able to stop in a second's time if needed, which will require us to increase the amount of absorbent shock padding," Poi said.

"All small adjustments, to be sure. We just want to make sure everything is perfect," Mac finished.

"When will we be ready for another field test?" Professor Qymberkon asked.

"We should be ready to go by tomorrow," Poi said.

"Excellent. I'm sure Professor Dea will be pleased," Professor Clums said. "You've all been making really good progress. Kurjon, how's the hover attachment coming along?"

The female Kolythoanthaean grimaced. "Ah, well, opposite of good progress. The reverse engineered anti-gravity device is extremely unstable. You've got to keep in mind that these things are massive, nearly fifteen meters in diameter. They have to be that big or bigger to stabilize a multi-ton spaceship. They're not meant to be small."

"A clean ratio wouldn't work?" Professor Clums asked.

"Not in this case. For it to be a clean ratio, the device would be too big to fit in the attachment. Anything smaller than that would be too unstable and it wouldn't be able to manage the mass," Sylcertiverner answered.

"Hmm, alright. I'll take a look at that," Professor Clums said.

"Please, if you wouldn't mind, that would be fantastic," Kurjon said, placing her six-fingered hands together in thanks.

Norman was still having a hard time imagining himself hovering and flying around. He wondered if someone might mistake him for the first Eridavlos with arms.

He tried to follow the rest of the conversation but he had a hard time understanding their scientific terms. Norman had been a miner —nearly all of the men raised in Bahutenrut had become miners, as it was a mining town. Their education hadn't really mattered. The women, on the other hand, had their work cut out for them. They were the ones who had to support the men in case of the unthinkable. Miners didn't get paid while in the hospital, and even though they made good money, it wasn't enough to support both medical bills and everyday life.

He shook his head—his thoughts were leading back to Kate. Nearly all his thoughts led to Kate.

*Kate, where are you?* he thought. *Are you safe? Are you hurt? If anything were to happen to you, I'd do everything in my power to avenge you.*

---

Navacus wheezed as he sat down in his padded office chair. He only had about ten minutes, but it was ten minutes to be alone. He had his office window shades down, giving him that much more privacy.

He wheezed again, then took the cover off of his meal. Fumalli had made him a plate of fish with rice and spinach. They never knew what kind of fish it was, as they were never told. It simply arrived each month, along with the rest of their monthly supplies. And each month it was slightly different. Of course, now that he was finally accustomed to the current fish, in a couple days he would have a new fish to get used to.

Sure, he loved fish—he had specially requested it. But Melridion fish just didn't taste the same as Strutheine fish.

He caught a slight movement in the corner of his eye and turned to his left. At first, he saw nothing at all, but then a ghostly figure faded into view. For a moment he was terrified, but then the events from the previous night rushed back to him.

"Sterg! I had nearly forgotten about you," Navacus said.

*"You actually did completely forget about me. I needed to block your memories from last night in order to strengthen our spiritual connection,"* Sterg replied in his mind. *"And you shouldn't speak out loud, not now. Someone could hear you."*

He shrugged and took a bite of his lunch. *"It's not like I don't already frequently talk to myself, but I suppose this is quite a different situation. Also, why did you have to block my memories? That doesn't really make sense. And didn't you say last night that our souls are linked?"*

*"For the most part, but now the merging is complete. I couldn't allow you to unwittingly sever any connections before they fully took hold."*

*"So it was for my own protection then. I suppose that sounds about right."*

*"Right. Navacus, listen to me closely, as we don't have a lot of time. It's about the Human, Norman Harrison."*

*"What about him?"*

*"As you were working on his attachments today, I was able to glimpse into his inner thoughts. He was thinking about Kate. He believes there is a conspiracy surrounding her disappearance."*

*"Yeah, he used to ask about her a lot. But I guess he hasn't recently."*

*"He believes that you and your team know nothing about what happened to her. I know this to be true, but he also believes that you are all being used by the head professors."*

*"Norman believes that we're being used?"*

*"Not yet, but I'm certain his thoughts will lead to that conclusion. And in light of everything that you saw in the underground laboratory last night—"*

*"You know about all of that?"*

*"Of course I do, Navacus. I began fusing with your soul the moment you descended from the elevator. It's a complicated process. Now, to the matter at hand: Katherine Padmashiri Thomas. I want to help investigate her disappearance, for I, too, believe that she may be here—she may be underground."*

*"It's definitely a possibility. That place was massive. You think she might be down there? Do you not have any evidence?"*

*"Not at this time. Just a feeling—a feeling I cannot ignore, which means you cannot ignore it, since our souls are now bound."*

*"Right, how does that work exactly? You haven't really filled me in on all that much,"* Navacus thought as he polished off the last of the rice.

*"Now that our souls are linked, I cannot travel more than a hundred meters away from you without causing both of us tremendous amounts of*

pain. At too large a distance, the link will be forcibly severed, and both of our souls will be wiped clean from the universe."

Navacus rubbed his beak in thought. "So, that's terrifying."

"I will never allow that to happen. I can travel up to fifty meters away safely. Anything after that, we will feel the tug. There are extremely rare circumstances that can force us apart, but I foresee us not running into any of those in the near future.

"At any time, even while I am away from you, I can relay anything I see or hear back to you. In time, your soul will be able to travel with me. But until then, anything you wish to know, I can fill you in. In addition, I can read people's emotions and feelings, and if their emotions are strong enough, I can even read their thoughts. Hence why I knew Norman was thinking about Kate. But I can only sense those surface level thoughts, nothing deeper."

"Alright. Are there any other rules I should know about?"

"Not at this time. Just remember what I told you last night—only you can see and hear me until you choose to let others know of my presence."

"Alright. It sounds like this will be a learning process. So, is that why you can't just go underground and check things out down there? It's too far away?"

"Indeed."

"So what do you plan on doing about Kate?"

"We can't do anything right now. We must wait until you return underground. Now, your lunch break is nearly over."

"Yes, I know. Thank you for informing me, though."

"Of course."

"Could you relay to me what's going on in the lab?" Navacus thought as he cleaned up his lunch. Sterg continued to float next to him, unmoving.

"The Harmertians are still tweaking the vehicular unit. The rest are all working on the hover attachment and are still making no progress. I don't see why; the solution is plainly obvious."

"Is that so?" Navacus thought as he opened the door and stepped out into the lab.

"See for yourself."

As Navacus stepped out into the lab, it was as if he put on augmented reality goggles. Everything was clearer, crisper, and he could now, literally, see how each part of each component fit together.

*"How is this possible? I thought you said you could only pick up surface level thoughts,"* he thought. He was only acutely aware that he stood in the doorway with wide eyes and an open beak.

*"That was in relation to living beings. What you are seeing are objects. As you know, everything is made up of microscopic particles, even me. Each particle contains energy, and so each object contains energy. What you see is a diluted version of what I can see—the potential trajectory of every object in the room. I figured it would be helpful for you to see what I'm allowing you to see."*

"Helpful indeed," Navacus muttered out loud. Fumalli was staring at him impatiently. He returned his friend's gaze and winked.

"Professor Clums, are you sure you're feeling alright?" Fumalli asked.

"I think I can faithfully say that I'm quite a bit better than alright."

"Okay... well, unsurprisingly, we've made no advancements in the twelve minutes you were gone."

"It's no problem at all, Fumi..." he muttered, then snapped back to attention. "I mean Professor Qymberkon. Just, give me a second. I have an idea."

It really was quite obvious, now that he had enhanced vision. They had put the attachment together completely wrong. They had been on the right path, but had veered off track early into the build. While it seemed like it was correct and that it should work, the components were in all the wrong places. It was a miracle that it hadn't exploded from the amount of energy pressurized inside of it.

*"Sterg, help me break this down and put it together in the right way,"* he thought.

*"Already processed,"* Sterg replied.

*"This is crazy. You just passed the information to me, but it feels like I knew it all along."*

*"Perhaps you did. You really have been very distracted lately."*

*"And as helpful as you have been, you yourself have also been a bit of a hindrance."*

*"I will be more careful in the future."*

He nodded, then walked over to the hover attachment.

"No, no that piece goes there, this piece goes here," Syl was saying as he was directing Grasberg.

"Everyone, please stop for a moment. This clearly isn't working," Navacus said.

"I think we've nearly got it though," Kurjon replied.

"While I see why you think that, it's not the correct solution. Instead, we need to disassemble the entire thing."

"Professor Clums, begging your pardon, but that's an impossible task. It cannot be disassembled," Kurjon said.

"I agree, it would be reckless and dangerous to disassemble it now," Syl added.

"It would actually be even more reckless to continue on the path we've been going down. And no, there is a way to take it apart, we're just going to have to be very careful. Luckily, we've got three sets of small Harmertian hands—exactly what we're going to need. Give me some time to type this all up and send you the instructions. In the meantime, please put everything down. You could all use a lunch break of your own."

"Thanks boss," Grasberg said. "It's been a long day."

"As for you three," Navacus said, turning to the Harmertians that were working on the vehicular attachment.

"Yes, just a moment... and there!" Mac exclaimed. "We've finished."

"Great, good job. You three can take a break as well. We'll need your help on the hover attachment when you're back. I'll start running the diagnostics on the vehicular attachment. Professor Qymberkon, please bring back lunch for Norman when you return."

"I was planning on it," Fumalli replied as he glared at him. "Are you sure you don't need any help? And how do you suddenly— almost magically—know exactly what to do?"

"Just know that I've got it handled. I'll see you all back here in thirty minutes," he said while wearing a forced smile.

*Ah, that's going to bite me in the ass later.*

After everyone left, Navacus walked over to the vehicular attachment. He was alone, save for Norman, who sat in his special chair watching everything.

"So that's completed now, too? I'm eager to test it out," Norman said as he rubbed his hands together.

"Yes, it seems like it," he said, then looked over at Norman strapped into his chair. "The legs are completed, right? I think we need to make them permanent."

"That would be fantastic. I have been immobile for too long," Norman said with an eager laugh.

"Great. I'll let everyone know when they return. Now, I want to look over the vehicular attachment for a moment," he said as he studied what Mac, Poi, and Lyd had done this morning.

*"Sterg, do you see what those three Harmertians did? They're really quite ingenious. They've made it so that Norman will feel through the wheels. The shocks are quite impressive—while he'll feel every little bump, it won't rattle around his physical body."*

*"They were only following your leadership."*

*"Sure, but something like this has never been done before."*

*"That reminds me, it may be best if we don't jump to so many conclusions so quickly,"* Sterg said telepathically.

*"Why is that? I just saved at least a week or two of time."*

*"Yes, that will be very helpful. But you must not draw attention to yourself. We can't act suspicious in any way—we must keep the status quo."*

*"You're the one who told me that you knew the solution,* and *you enhanced my vision and my thought processing power."*

*"Yes, I am still getting used to the adjustment as well. But you know what I speak to be true. We must act normal."*

*"Like my ordinary self. Got it. I'll make sure to keep any mention of you out of the recordings I make."*

*"That would be wise."*

Navacus connected the vehicular attachment to the computer so he could run several tests, of which he felt like he already knew the outcome.

*This will change everything*, he thought. *It's as if my intelligence has been increased tenfold. And I suppose it has.*

*Sterg, I'm sure you can hear these thoughts as well by now—my own inner thoughts. And if you can hear me, I just want to thank you for everything you've done for me. I have a lot of questions for you, although those can wait until tonight. Now, we have a cyborg to complete.*

# 4

# ESCAPE FROM FREEDOM

A loud bang against the metallic wall roused Theodore Henry Caldwell from his stupor. His meal had been delivered.

*Yippee,* he thought. *Another gross, bland meal to start off another bland day.*

After repeatedly trying to use magic to escape his prison cell, Theodore had finally concluded that it was a waste of his time and energy. Although, there was little to use his energy on in the first place. By his estimation, he had been in his cell for two and a half days, and he had not lost hope that he was one step closer to Tyrona. Even if this step seemed like an impossible task, as he saw no way out of his metal cell.

He sighed and attempted to stroke his beard, only to remember that it was gone. When he had woken up in his cell, he rudely discovered that both his face and his head had been shaved. Theodore shook his head, then got out of bed and took the handful of steps necessary to reach his food tray. As he squatted down, another loud bang against the wall made him lose his footing and slip, causing his legs to knock into the tray of food.

"Holy Eklatros, what was that?"

A window that he wasn't previously aware of appeared, allowing him to see two figures standing before his cell. Both he had seen before. One was the dark green Lakinceitian that had been present when he emerged from the gate, and the other was the black-haired man with spectacles who had shot him with a drugged dart and placed him in his cell.

"My apologies about your meal. I'll see to it that you get a new one shortly. We can't have you going hungry. Please place the tray on the platform," the Lakinceitian said as a platform came out of the wall.

"Thank you, I suppose. It's not enjoyable in any way, but it fills my stomach," he said as he stood up and placed the tray on the platform. He had more of the gray gruel on his pants than was left on the tray.

"I'm glad to hear that it is serving its purpose. Now, I believe introductions are in order. Please call me Professor Durrist. You may call my associate Mister Feng. What may we call you?"

"It's always good to put names to my captors," Theodore spat.

"That may indeed be the situation, but it is better for all of us this way. It keeps us safe from you and you safe from us," Professor Durrist said.

"I suppose that's true. If I had my powers, I could easily break out of this metal box. That's right, you address the S-Class sorcerer, Theodore Henry Caldwell."

"Could you please tell us about your powers, Theodore?" Professor Durrist asked.

"You stand before the most powerful elemental wizard on Eklatros! I can control the wind, the ground, fire, and electricity. If I could, I would simply manifest a quake to jostle the room and create a crack, by which I could use fire and wind to enlarge that crack and escape."

"So boastful, for one who has no such powers. You are no longer on Eklatros. You are now on Melridion, the fourth planet from the sun in the Vortex Solar System. Your powers do not work here. Even you know this to be true."

"Indeed, I may not have my powers, but my mind is still sharp and cunning."

"That's good to hear. We need you to stay strong and healthy. That is why I wanted to ask if I could get you anything. Books, magazines, videos, games, music... You name it and I'll find something that we can provide to help keep your mind sharp," Professor Durrist offered.

"I don't know what magazines or videos are, but I would be surprised to find a book I could read on this strange planet."

"All you'll need is one of our translating devices—a special set of eyeglasses that will allow you to read any text written in any of our many languages. I'll find you a set of books you can choose from."

"Why are you being so generous?" Theodore asked as he peered at the dark green Lakinceitian.

"It may surprise you, but we knew of your coming beforehand. There are many questions we wish to ask you, in time. For now, we just want to ensure that you are comfortable."

Theodore chuckled to himself. "Of course, Tyrona is here, so she must have told you that we would rescue her. And we will do everything we can to rescue her."

"Ah yes, Tyrona. She's certainly a special one, isn't she? I can assure you that she's safe and unharmed, just like yourself. As I said, we are only keeping you for our own safety. When we decide you are no longer a threat, we will release you."

"Again, so generous of you. Were you showing generosity when you shaved my head and my face?"

"Less hair is more manageable. Now, we'll go fetch you a fresh meal, a change of clothes, and some books to read. Until next time, Theodore."

The window closed, leaving him alone with gruel-covered trousers. He sat down and ate the gruel off his pants.

*I better take advantage of the extra food while I can*, he thought. *I honestly can't believe those two. Well, the human never said a word, but Professor Durrist... his promises sound too good to be true. There has to be a catch. They shave off all my hair, throw me in this cell, and now they want to provide me with books? They must be trying to catch me off guard. In that case, I'll be extra vigilant.*

*But they did confirm one thing. Tyrona is here. We made it to the right place. I've nearly found you, my love. Yet I do not know if you are truly unharmed. I cannot trust anyone here.*

———

Cecil lounged against the gray wall. He was bored out of his mind. There was nothing to do but eat, sleep, and work out. He had already completed several sets of push-ups, sit-ups, lunges, squats, and jumping exercises since he had woken up. It had been a long time since he had trained his body in such a way. He had been quite busy on the quest with Ànifa, and before that he had been a lazy, good-for-nothing drunk. But there had been a time when he worked out daily —when he had been trying out for the Guild of Exemplary Knights.

He was glad he was rid of that guild and thankful for his new guild, the Guild for Eklatros. He hoped Vesten was faring better than he was and that he hadn't put too much responsibility on the sailor's shoulders.

Speaking of shoulders, he missed his nearly shoulder-length hair. He didn't like getting haircuts, but he supposed since he didn't remember getting his hair cut it was fine. He had needed one anyway.

Cecil sighed. He was the team leader and he had led them right into a trap. He should have been expecting something like this. It didn't matter that he had only been the leader for all of five minutes before they got captured—Theodore, Dasch, and Druder were his responsibility, and he had let them down. He had to try and make things right in whatever way he could.

A knock against the wall brought him back to reality. He stood up with his empty food tray expecting the platform to appear. Instead, a window appeared in the wall, allowing him to see two figures. He recognized both of them.

"You shot me," Cecil said, glaring at the human man with spectacles.

"You were a threat. And you still are a threat. That's why you remain in your cell," the man replied.

"I wasn't a threat then, but I am now."

"Mister Feng, let's not antagonize our guests," the dark green Lakinceitian in the white lab coat said.

"I am not your guest; I'm your prisoner. Where's the rest of my team? Where's Theodore, Dasch, and Druder? And where's Tyrona? We were told she was here!"

"Please calm down. I will answer all of your questions shortly. First, I must introduce myself. I am Professor Durrist, and my associate..."

"Right, Mister Feng. The one who shot me."

"And I greatly apologize for his rash actions. What may we call you?" Professor Durrist asked.

"Call me Sir Cecil Kloud, or Sir Kloud for short."

"Sir Cecil Kloud. What does your title mean? Do you hold a rank of some kind?"

"I am the guildmaster of the Guild for Eklatros, and I am a knight of Ajenti and all of Eklatros."

"Ah, you are a man of high status. Good—we may yet come to understand each other."

"Understand? Apart from the fact that I'm still quite amazed that I can understand your speech, I can't understand why I was treated with such blatant hostility when I had only arrived to deliver a warning."

"And what was your warning?"

"First tell me where my friends are," he demanded.

"Your friends are all safe, including Tyrona. We just spoke with Theodore not too long ago. He was interested in reading books. Would you like some books to read as well?"

"Books? I care not for your propaganda. I just want to be free of this cell!"

"And you will be, in good time. Now, you were going to tell us the warning you had come to deliver. We are now ready to hear it."

"Great," Cecil said as he struggled to not roll his eyes. "Well, you see, our warning was about Gnusaramnii. The foul monster that originated on this world nearly destroyed my own. We had to trek a dangerous journey across our world, and we fought hundreds of

Gnusaramnii's spawn along the way, including Gnusar, Gnuelry, and possessed animals and humans. We successfully fought off our enemy and defended our home. But the task is not yet complete. That is why we were sent here. For if our world falls, then Gnusaramnii will finally have enough power to return here and destroy your world."

"And what is so special about your world, Sir Kloud?"

"Let me out of my cell, free my friends, and I'll tell you anything you want. I can assure you we did not come to fight. We are only messengers and are here to help you with your defenses."

"We're not setting you free. Not yet, at least. Thank you for telling me what you did, though. It was very enlightening. I shall inform my superiors about this new information at once."

"So, what, that's it? You come here to squeeze information out of me then leave me to rot?"

"Sir Kloud, please understand that we are holding you in this cell for your own safety."

"You mean for your own safety," Cecil said as he glared at them and clenched his fists.

"Yes, indeed. We're protecting ourselves by protecting you. Now, I understand you don't want to read anything, but we have music, games—"

"I told you that I don't want your propaganda. But if you want to give me something, give me my axe. I could use the training."

"I don't think we can give you your weapon back, but we'll see what we can do."

"Alright. You get me something to train with, and I can provide you with a little more information."

"Sounds like a deal, Sir Kloud. It was a pleasure."

Cecil nodded as the window was hastily shut.

*Maybe I should have asked for a game or a book*, Cecil thought. *Perhaps becoming acquainted with their propaganda could be strategic. Either way, I'm glad I turned down the offer. I don't trust them. If we're being kept in these cells for our own safety, why have we been separated?*

*This is obviously just like the old interrogation cells we used back in*

*Ajenti. They need to break us down first before we give them any useful information. I mean, at the very least, I delivered the warning that Mau asked us to deliver. Anything else I tell them will be of my own choosing. As much as I want to help Eklatros, I need to make sure that we aren't being used in the process. At least, not in a way I don't agree with.*

<br>

Druder stood on his hands with his feet straight in the air. In a way, he didn't mind that his long silver hair had been cut, as there was nothing to get in his face. He had loved walking on his hands since he was a small child. It provided him with a new perspective. Sometimes seeing things upside down was just what he needed to solve a difficult problem. And the metallic cell he had been put into was a difficult problem. He saw no seams in the metal, nor cracks or nails. It appeared as if he was in a metallic box made of one single block of metal that had been hollowed out. While it didn't seem like there was any way out of the cell, standing on his hands was still comforting.

His cell was too bright for his liking. He would much rather there be barely any light at all. It would help him think, sleep, and calm his soul.

There was a loud bang against the wall, but he felt no vibrations run through the floor. Either the metal box only shook against the one wall, which wasn't very likely as he would still be able to feel the vibrations, or the source of the noise was coming from somewhere else.

He jumped back to his feet and picked up his empty tray. To his surprise, a window appeared in the wall. He guessed that there were still a few centimeters worth of material between him and his two visitors, but it gave him answers to several of his theories. This box was not just one large piece of metal—the material that made this room may not be metal at all. All of his preconceptions about this place had to be thrown out.

"... and this is Mister Feng. What may we address you as?" the dark green Lakinceitian was saying.

"Professor Durrist. Mister Feng. I am Druder Nanasazii of Yttendaus."

"Druder, I understand these last few hours may have been a bit confusing. Is there anything you'd like us to clear up?"

"Begging your pardon, but you're asking me what I want answers to? I have too many to count. You can start with telling me who exactly you are."

"Ah, you're a clever one, aren't you? I can't tell you much about myself, but know that we are providing you with the best care possible. I know your meals are not the best, but know that they are packed full of everything you need to stay healthy."

"If you want to keep me healthy, then I must kindly ask you to dim the lights. Or turn them of completely. I prefer the dark."

"Oh sure, give me a moment," Professor Durrist said as he approached the wall and tapped upon it. Again, Druder felt nothing. He had been trained to sense the minute vibrations that ran through Yttendaus' roots from a young age. It was how they communicated with their godly protector and the upper-world. Then again, his cell could be made of a material he had never come across.

Within a few moments, his cell was nearly pitch black. He could once again see how he was born to see.

"How is that?" Professor Durrist asked.

"Perfect. Just perfect. Now, I suppose you can't tell me what the box I'm in is made out of."

Mister Feng looked at him with a brief sense of surprise before it was replaced with the cold, dead stare he had had during the entire conversation. Professor Durrist made a noise he assumed was a laugh.

"You really are clever. I can't answer that, though, for several reasons. Now, can I offer you anything else? Perhaps you'd like to hear some music?"

"No music, please. I prefer the silence. It helps me concentrate. Can I ask another question?"

"Go ahead."

"Why are you asking me these questions? What do you really want from us?"

"Information, just like yourself. You seek to escape this room— why else would you ask what your cell is made from? I can assure you that you will be released in time. We just need to process each of you individually. Now, we must be moving on. Please take care. We will see you again soon."

The wall once again became opaque. He immediately moved over to the area where the window was and felt around. Just like he had expected, it was smooth like the other walls. Even in the spot where the tray platform came out and the space in the wall that held his toilet and shower—it was all smooth until the compartment opened.

Druder stood on his hands again and looked around the dark room. He realized that he must be in more than one box. First, a box of clear, transparent material that must have had various thicknesses, and then the material that was covering the transparent box. And the transparent box must be made of a material that showed no seams.

*Everything is solvable,* he thought. *Every problem has a solution, and most often the answer is either plainly obvious or the complete opposite. This room is a puzzle, one that I will solve. But more than that, there is a deeper puzzle—the motivations behind my containment. Both Mister Feng and Professor Durrist are not to be trusted. They may have been showing kindness today, but I fear that kindness will soon give way to sinister actions. I must escape before that happens.*

Dasch stood in the center of the open circular room that he had spent hundreds of years in. While there were four paths, two of the paths were blocked by a set of thick roots. Those were the paths to his right and left. The path he faced would take him to his well of water, and the path behind him led to the room he often slept in. He breathed in deep, then coughed on the dusty air. He shook his head and walked forward only to hit a wall of impassable air.

In front of him he watched as a small blue-haired girl stepped into his view. For a moment, she looked at him curiously. Then, two more little girls entered his view, both of them with green hair. The two green-haired girls chased the blue-haired girl around in circles before they each fell to the ground in laughter.

He shook his head. What he was seeing wasn't his memory, but Ànifa's. After they had awoken Yttendaus, he and his companions had all absorbed Ànifa's memories. And he had received *all* of her memories. He was just now beginning to process everything. It felt strange, having two lifetimes inside his head. And yet, the more of Ànifa's memories he processed, the more he felt his own memories slipping away. He was a half-elf, but his mind was having difficulty containing both sets of memories.

Suddenly, the Gnusar remnant that resided in his chest stirred. His heart lurched, and Dasch clutched his chest and fell to his knees.

He opened his eyes and found himself curled up in the corner of a metallic room. He was afraid. He had been spending too much time in his head, whether it was with Ànifa's memories or in that underground prison. Now he was in a new prison, and there was nothing left to help him grasp his sanity. He felt himself slipping away while the alien presence was taking over.

He deduced that it had begun shortly after he'd been thrown into this square metal room. The Gnusar remnant knew it was home. It was stronger now than it had ever been before. If he wasn't careful, he would lose himself completely. The spark known as Dasch would be extinguished. From then on, an alien would be in full control of his body with complete access to his and Ànifa's memories. He had to do everything he could to fight it off. If not for his own sake, then for Ànifa's.

A knocking sound broke his concentration. On the wall to his left a window slid open, though he couldn't yet see through it.

"Who's there?" he called. "What do you want with me?"

"You must be Dasch the Destroyer. May I call you Dasch?" a deep voice responded.

"I don't... Dasch is my name. Yes."

"Great. Can you please step out where we can see you?"

Dasch stood up and walked to the window.

"Now you can see me, and I can see you."

"Indeed we can. I wanted to apologize for how we met. I am Professor Durrist, and my associate here is Mister Feng."

"Professor Xabio Durrist and Mister Carl Feng, to be precise," Dasch said.

"How do you know our full names?" Professor Durrist asked calmly. "Only one's own kin may know a Lakinceitian's full name."

"Indeed, you are a Lakinceitian. You have a similar reading to the Gnusar and their spawns. I can read your thoughts as I... Wait... That's not right, is it? When could I ever read the thoughts of... Oh crap, you know what it must be?"

"I know exactly what it must be," Professor Durrist said with a wide smile. "Carl, we've found him. The prophecy is in motion. We must bring him to see Lord Foxaire immediately."

"I'm already on it," Mister Feng replied as Dasch watched him furiously tap on his tablet.

"How do I know these things? I know too many things I shouldn't know. Too many things she shouldn't know," Dasch whispered.

"All will be revealed in time. Please, come with us," Professor Durrist said.

The section of the wall he stood in front of slid into the floor. He was free.

*There's no choice, is there?* he thought. *Are these the final thoughts of Dasch Valentine? Or will I find the strength to hold on to my consciousness and protect Ànifa's memories even after the Gnusar remnant takes control?*

*If I stay, I'll continue to lose my mind. If I go with them, I'll learn more information and possibly lose even more of myself. There's simply no way out of this.*

*It was a mistake for me to come here. Ànifa, Cecil, Theodore... everyone... I failed you.*

5

# ESCAPE FROM EXPECTATIONS

"Thank you, West, for that thrilling report. If there's nothing else, we'd like you to now visit with the three Titans you didn't get to see last night. I can assure you, they've all calmed down to their normal levels of distress. Be sure to send me the recordings of your interactions with them."

"Sure thing, Professor Durrist," West replied. "Afterward, would I be able to visit with Newtus again? I feel like there's a lot more that I can learn from her."

"Only if you make it quick. You are scheduled for guard duty with Bsarg this afternoon at 15 o'clock."

"Right, understood."

West stood straight and tipped his white cowboy hat forward, then left Professor Durrist's office. He had just finished delivering his report and recordings from the night prior. Both Professor Durrist and Carl had been visibly excited when he told them he had been able to telepathically communicate with Newtus. As expected, they hadn't told him any new information and had avoided his questions. It didn't matter; he would find the answers he wanted. Besides, he was a whole new person thanks to LSS. His scope of awareness made his previous Eusphyrchiian point of view seem so narrow.

As he stepped into the Titan enclosure, Professor Randall and Professor Peal greeted him.

"Hey, West, good morning," Professor Randall said with a wave and a yawn. "Now, are you ready to get started?"

"Sure. Will Professor Peal be joining us?" West asked.

"Professor Peal is to observe Theesakin. After you're done visiting with Zadgarcolth, Karkilver, and Ophertusc, you're to visit with Theesakin again."

"Great. I want to talk to both of them, actually, meaning Professor Peal and Theesakin."

"Sure, I'll be here," Professor Peal said as he headed into Theesakin's airlock.

"So, who do you want to see first?" Professor Randall asked as he brushed back his short brown hair.

"I'm not sure. Even with my enhanced vision and senses I can't fully see though these walls. I can only get abstract heat signatures."

"Alright, dealer's choice. Let's get Zadgarcolth out of the way. He's... how shall I put this... the most temperamental of all the Titans. In other words, he's my least favorite by a long shot."

"Alright, lead the way."

West followed Professor Randall to the door marked 4 and stepped into the airlock. After they were sprayed down, they stepped into the main room.

He didn't know what to expect, but the creature that stood before him was absolutely not what he had been even remotely expecting. It looked like a cross between an Ancilsan and a gorilla, an animal native to Carange, only close to three times the size of both. Bright yellow hair covered its head, back, two muscular arms, and two thick legs, while cream colored hair covered its stomach and chest. It had two round black eyes and a huge mouth that sported dozens of long, sharp teeth. It was pounding its large black hands against the barrier as it screeched at them.

"My apologies, even with the sound dampened, Zadgarcolth can be a loud bastard. I would suggest trying to get a reading quickly, before it starts throwing its feces. Of course it doesn't hit us, it's just really gross."

"And this is its normal temperament? What does it do when it's riled up?" West asked as he scanned through the electromagnetic spectrum to try and identify a frequency he could use to resonate with the creature.

"Last night it was body-slamming the barrier, jumping around wildly, pounding the walls, floor, and ceiling with its fists and feet... Essentially, it was doing everything it could to break out. It was as if the gate created a frequency that drove it insane. Well, even more insane than usual."

"That sounds quite scary," West replied a little absentmindedly. "I wasn't able to pick up on its aura like I could Theesakin and Newtus. But would it be possible to duplicate that frequency?"

"Yes, It's possible. Let's finish this discussion in the main room," Professor Randall said.

Zadgarcolth continued to screech as its pounding became heavier and more frequent.

"Agreed. This is not a creature to trifle with," West said as he stepped into the airlock.

After Zadgarcolth's pheromones were removed, they walked into the center of the circular room.

"Now, as I was saying, Professor Durrist and I actually discussed this earlier this morning, and we do think it is possible to replicate the frequency the gate made. We would need to use extreme caution when testing it, but it could prove that all the Titans have the same reaction to the same frequency, even though they are all so vastly different from each other. This is something we never would have expected."

"Yeah, it really is quite interesting. Now that I can see in different frequencies, I've gained a real appreciation for them."

"It's always been fascinating to me—like the fact that all color is just frequency and wavelength, and what our eyes can pick up from those said frequencies and wavelengths. Of course, all things science interests me. Now, let's save the bird for last. Ophertusc will be up next."

Professor Randall led him to the door marked *1*.

"Do the numbers mean anything in particular?" West asked.

"Each number corresponds to the order the Titans were created. Meaning, Ophertusc here was the first. Are you familiar with the story of Ophertusc? From the mythologies, I mean," Professor Randall asked as he stopped in front of the airlock.

"I've heard bits and pieces, but that's about it."

"Right, well, as I said, I am not very interested in myths and legends. For the most part, there's just too much drama, and I don't care for drama—I care about facts. But Ophertusc's story is my favorite. The best part being that Ophertusc and his twin brother, Hajinmahn, basically murder each other over a simple misunderstanding. That just resonated with me... I now try to look at each issue from a different perspective before getting lost in emotion."

"That's some wise advice right there," West replied.

"I certainly think so. Now, Ophertusc here is nothing like any of the stories. I hope you don't get nightmares," Professor Randall said as he opened the airlock. The mist they were sprayed with smelled dusty, and indeed West was surprised to find average dust particles mixed in with the liquid spray of enzymes.

The door opened and they stepped into another circular room. In front of the opaque barrier hunched a truly terrifying creature. Its sickly pale gray skin clung to the outlines of grotesque and seemingly misshapen bones. It stood on six insectile legs, three of which sprouted from either side of a very skinny Human-like torso. It had two long, skinny arms, each one sporting four long, sharp claws. It's singular large, thin eye stretched across its bulbous head with a gaping mouth, which had at least four rows of small, sharp teeth below it.

"How do you even make a creature such as this?" West asked. "This thing is *horrifying*. And to answer your question, the only nightmares I've been having lately are related to my injury. But this thing might just invade those dreams."

As he spoke, Ophertusc moved its head from side to side, taking everything in. It started drooling as three skinny tongues slithered out of its mouth, each one probing the opaque barrier.

"You must know I can't answer that question," Professor Randall replied. "As terrifying as this thing is, I still prefer it over Zadgarcolth. Now, scan this thing so we can get out of here."

"Also, what's even the point of creating something like this?" West asked as he scanned Ophertusc. As he neared the frequency he had used for Newtus, he got a slight ping of static.

Before Professor Randall could answer, Ophertusc quickly lowered itself and stared straight at West.

"What did you do? Did you talk to it?" Professor Randall asked excitedly.

"No, I am just getting pings of static. Although, that could be how it communicates—with static. But if it's trying to say something, I don't know what it is."

"It's fine, as long as you can record it."

"Already am. Don't forget that everything I sense is automatically recorded. It serves as my memory bank—memories I can upload to databanks and send to your tablets."

"Right, of course. Professor Clums really did magnificent work on you, West. You're truly one of a kind, and I'm glad to have you on our team."

"I'm just glad to be part of a team that's not constantly trying to stab me in the back," West replied. "Even if I am subjected to terrifying creatures."

Ophertusc had started growling. It had its large, round mouth fully pressed up against the barrier, giving them a clear view of all seven rows of teeth and its five tongues. Its eye hungrily darted back and forth between them.

"At this point, I think the static is repeating itself. It must be relaying the same message over and over again. And while I can't read it, I can only imagine what it's saying—"

"It wants to eat us," Professor Randall finished for him.

"Not just eat us—devour us. It feels like it goes deeper than our flesh… that it wants our souls."

"So you can understand it!"

"Maybe? It feels different from Theesakin and from Newtus. Either way, do you think we got enough data?"

"For now, yes. But don't be surprised if you're asked to spend more time with this freak show."

"Only if I have to," West replied.

As they moved toward the airlock, Ophertusc followed them, its insectile legs scurrying across its enclosure. All the while it kept its mouth plastered to the barrier, its five tongues searching them out.

"Are you sure it's not poisonous or anything? Like, does it have acid that can eat through the barrier?" West asked as Professor Randall opened the airlock.

"These barriers can take anything. They're made of pure energy, but feel like glass to the touch. I've never heard of one breaking before."

"Let's hope we aren't around to witness the first one breaking then," West replied as he stepped into the airlock.

After the spray, the door opened and they walked into the center of the room.

"Wow, what even was that thing?" West asked in shock. "And how is it that you prefer it over Zadgarcolth?"

"Because I'd rather be eaten by this monster than have my body broken by the yellow ape," Professor Randall replied matter-of-factly. "Now, I know you're curious about the purpose of these creatures here, but do understand I can't say anything. Maybe we can tell you more one day, but only on a need-to-know basis. Now, Karkilver is last."

Professor Randall walked to the door marked 3. West remained standing in the center of the room for a moment longer.

*What have I gotten myself into? This isn't what I signed up for.*

He shrugged and walked over to Professor Randall.

"Last one, and then of course you are to see Theesakin again."

"Theesakin was interesting. The others have just been monsters."

"Ah, but you can't make a creature like Theesakin without such experimentation."

The airlock slid open and West stepped inside. This time the spray contained a solution that featured several different species of avian DNA. LSS told him that the birds came from Melridion, Acampachetli, Strutheine, Carange, and Clendenic.

West stepped into another circular room and faced the most normal-looking of all the creatures he had seen. In front of him was a gigantic bird with a wingspan of nearly five meters. It had reddish-brown feathers without any noticeable patterns or designs and two large feet, each sporting four sharp talons. Its head seemed a bit small for its size, with a long, skinny, sword-like beak.

Karkilver was hovering in the air, flapping its wings slowly as it watched them enter. It didn't move or screech, it just simply stared at them.

"I know you said this was a bird, but I was expecting something much more ghastly or monstrous," West said.

"Yeah, after Ophertusc and Zinartee, we decided to get back to the basics."

"Sure. I'll start scanning it now."

West flipped through the electromagnetic spectrum, and while he didn't seem to be able to communicate with it, he discovered a few oddities. First, as he scanned the visible light spectrum, he saw its coloring continuously change, which meant it could change colors depending on the light source. Next, he discovered that surrounding Karkilver was a thin shield of static electricity, though he didn't know how it was created or maintained.

He mentioned his discoveries to Professor Randall, who hummed in thought.

"We knew about its color-changing plumage, but we had only suspected that it was giving off electricity. Professor Durrist will find this all very interesting."

"That's great. I can't communicate with it, though."

"It's not a problem. You've provided us with a lot of new and valuable information about each of these creatures. We can't thank you enough. Now, if there's nothing else, we should be on our way."

"Yes, of course," West replied.

Back in the main room, Professor Randall pulled him aside for a moment.

"I know that we can trust your discretion about what's going on here, right? What you saw here today and last night can only be spoken about between us, Professor Durrist, and Professor Peal. Bsarg, Jakog, Nijork, and Professor Clums don't know about this yet, and we must keep it this way. Even Svetlana, who is in charge of guarding this area, only knows as much as she needs to."

"Sure thing. I understand."

"Great. Now, on to Theesakin."

West stepped back into Theesakin's enclosure and immediately switched to the frequency he used to speak with him the night prior. Yet, before he could focus on Theesakin, Professor Peal huffed over to them.

"Took you long enough. I still don't understand why you're keeping me away from my own test subjects. I've done all I can do and more to help out here."

"Professor Peal, I know the past few days have been frustrating for you, but I can assure you that things will get back to a semblance of normalcy soon," said Professor Randall.

"Right well," Professor Peal said, turning to West. "What did you want to talk to me about, West?"

"Ah, yes, well I visited your test subjects last night like you asked me to."

"Of course, I had nearly forgotten," Professor Peal replied with a smile. "What did you find out?"

"Well, Denoptace is quite rude, for one."

Professor Peal burst into laughter. In response, Theesakin tilted his large, horned head at the professor in curiosity.

"I'm sorry, but you're right, he is a pain in the ass to deal with."

"At least he had his shade down most of the time I was in there. But Sassafrass and I got along quite well, and Blood Bat was chipper. I couldn't communicate telepathically with any of them. Yet I could with Newtus. We had a full conversation in our minds."

Professor Peal grinned from ear to ear as he fiercely rubbed his hands together. "Ha, I had a suspicion. You see, Theesakin here—"

"Professor Peal, not another word," Professor Randall cut in. "Please do not disclose details about any of the Titans."

"Of course, my mistake," Professor Peal said with a slightly mocking tone as he turned to Professor Randall. "So, can I get back to my own test subjects yet?"

"You know, West said that he would like to visit with Newtus again after this. You can escort him back to your area. But I'll need you to come back here once West leaves for guard duty."

"Great, thank you. I'd really like to check in with Kalosse and the others as well."

"Of course. Now, let's let West do his thing."

"Sure, I guess I could watch this again," Professor Peal replied.

West stepped forward into the middle of the room and faced the large green-scaled Titan. He took a second to marvel at him. Although he was monstrous—with four arms, a thick tail, two wings—he had such a gentle demeanor. He hoped it wasn't just a facade. He tipped his cowboy hat up so Theesakin could get a better look at him.

*"It's good to see you, friend,"* Theesakin said.

*"It's good to see you, too. I've met all of your cousins. They are quite different from you."*

*"Cousins? I don't understand."*

*"Ah, of course,"* West paused for a moment, then decided against telling him much more. These conversations, while silent, were being recorded by LSS. He had to be careful. *"I just mean that there are others in rooms like this, but they are not like you."*

*"There are others... yes... that is what I have been sensing. It's faint, but there are other large entities around me."*

*"That's... Well, I'm impressed. I thought my sensors were good, but I can't sense much at all through these walls."*

*"Walls... barriers they may be, but still passable,"* Theesakin answered cryptically.

*"So, you can sense others. What do you know about Professor Peal?"*

*"He is being tested. Not like me. Mentally. Emotionally. The other man, Professor Randall, is behind Professor Peal's suffering."*

*"Do you know why he is being tested?"*

*"No. That information is too deeply clouded."*

*"And what can you pick up about me?"*

*"You are kind. You are my friend. You have been through trauma and you are better because of it."*

*"I would like to think so,"* West replied. *"I think you are kind as well."*

*"Thank you, friend. Speaking with you is very helpful. Language is coming more easily. Thoughts are moving quicker."*

*"I'm glad to hear that. Is there anything I can do to help—aside from speaking with you?"*

*"Knowledge. I want information about me. Those two Humans know, but they won't tell me, and I can't sense it."*

*"They are being very tight-lipped with me as well. I haven't been able to find out any information from them."*

*"No surprise. They are bad men. They are the reason I'm in this cage."*

*"I can't deny that. If it were up to me, I'm sure things would be different."*

*"Yes, you are a gentle soul. These two only care about results."*

*"That's the vibe I've been getting as well."*

*"Randall is getting impatient. He wishes to speak with you again."*

*"It's only been a minute or so, but Humans do tend to have short attention spans."*

West turned toward Professor Randall and Professor Peal.

"This time Theesakin is asking for information. Are there any books or anything like that I can read to him?"

"Books about what?" Professor Randall asked.

"Well, it wants to know about itself, but I know you won't allow that. So, I was thinking I could teach it about our home. You know, the Vortex Solar System. He's a resident of our system, just like we are."

"I'll bring it up with Professor Durrist and Carl. I'm not sure they'll go for it, though."

"Thank you for at least considering it."

"Sure, I mean it makes sense," Professor Randall said with a nod. "If we're to have you visiting with Theesakin, you're going to need to talk about something. For now, you'll need to send that conversation to Professor Durrist."

"Yes, I know. I'll do that right now, and I'll send everything else, too." It took LSS a total of zero-point-two-eight seconds to send the data to Professor Durrist's computer. "Done. Message sent."

"That fast? You had only just finished speaking," Professor Peal said. "Man, I need to have a chat with Professor Clums."

"Now, West, if you have nothing else to speak to Theesakin about, you should be moving on."

"I've only just arrived, but I'll make sure he has nothing else to tell me."

He turned back to Theesakin.

*"Did you catch that?"*

*"Yes. They want you to leave me. They only care about results."*

*"Exactly, they don't have much empathy, and they don't like wasting time. I suppose that's what makes them good at their jobs, though."*

*"I will see you again?"* Theesakin asked.

*"I certainly think so. I would like to. If I don't, though, know it was not my decision."*

*"Of course. The bad men might interfere. I understand."*

*"Good. Take care, Theesakin."*

*"Take care, West."*

West tipped his white cowboy hat forward and nodded with his body. He walked over to Professor Peal.

"I'm ready, Professor."

"Great. I have many things that need attending to."

"West, enjoy your night," Professor Randall said. "I'll send a message to your LSS when we are able to have you back."

"Sure thing, Professor Randall. Take care."

West followed Professor Peal to his area of the compound. The only exchange was a one-sided conversation Professor Peal was having with himself as he talked over everything he needed to get done. West wasn't really mentally following, since he knew LSS would record it anyway. It really was great to have a mind that worked for you while you could focus on the menial things. Such as, where were all the Lakinceitian drones? Normally at this time of day he saw at least a few out and about, but today there weren't any.

When they made it to Professor Peal's area, Professor Kalosse, Professor Peal's number two, greeted with a wave of his blue-skinned hand.

"Professor Peal! I wasn't expecting you."

"Oh, did I not send a message? I must have been distracted," Professor Peal said. "West is here to see Newtus. Is this a good time?"

"Oh, sure. She was just fed, actually," Professor Kalosse replied.

"What does she eat?" West asked.

"Today it was a dozen juvenile sand snakes. We captured several of them and have been able to successfully speed up their breeding process," Professor Kalosse replied.

"Okay, that's pretty cool."

"Yeah, yeah, it's cool," Professor Peal said with a wave of his said. "Now, Kalosse, give me the latest update on Ivy."

"I was heading over there now—the rest of the team is with him. The situation hasn't changed much."

"I see. West, see yourself out when you're finished," Professor Peal said.

"Sure thing. Oh, tell Kamarial I said hi."

"I'll relay the message," Professor Kalosse replied as he turned back to his work.

West watched as the Nioavellian ambled to the door marked 5 with Professor Peal in tow. He may not have known why Professor Peal was being tested, but he shrugged and headed for the door marked 2.

When he walked in, the large, six-legged purple lizard greeted him with a slight flick of her graceful tail.

"Hi, Newtus," West said out loud. "I hope I'm not interrupting anything."

*"Hello, West. You've come at a fine time, and I'm glad you're here,"* Newtus projected into his mind. *"I've had some time to think, and I really enjoyed our previous conversation."*

"So did I, and I am glad to be here as well. It's been a strange day," West replied telepathically.

*"Care to tell me about it?"*

*"I'm not sure I can. Everything is wrapped under a layer of secrecy down here."*

*"Yes, this place certainly holds many secrets."*

*"Too many, I'm sure,"* West replied. *"Do you enjoy eating sand snakes?"*

Newtus huffed and leaned her head to the left. *"They're edible. I don't much care for their taste, or for the toughness of their scales. At least they're still alive when I feast upon them."*

*"Are they similar to what you would eat back home?"*

*"The snakes I prefer are tangier and juicier. Though, I would feast on an assortment of different creatures, including Loxocemae, Grumantrus, Brekloax, Zubba, and even Curik when they gather in large numbers."*

*"Tell me more about your home. What was it like?"*

*"Ah well, it was magnificent. My jungle had no walls or physical boundaries. I could go anywhere I wanted within my own limits. And, in my territory, I had anything I could ever desire—food, water, sun, and shade. Of course, even I had to be wary of predators."*

*"What would be big enough to consider you a meal?"*

Newtus laughed softly in his mind. He smiled inwardly at its fleeting presence. *"West, there are many creatures larger than me, and even some that are smaller than me are dangerous predators. Though, most types of predators do not travel within my territory. However, my main foe is a large hard-shelled amphibian called an Aldagos. And then, near the southern boundary of my territory, I am at risk of being attacked by snakes that grow hundreds of meters long. We call these Bahamus. Yet the risk is well worth the reward—it's where the Loxocemae lay their eggs."*

*"Wow, I have never heard of any animal growing that large."*

*"They are mostly immobile. If Professor Peal ever came across one, it was likely he never realized it. They blend easily with their surroundings, even for being so large."*

*"It certainly sounds like an experience no matter what."*

*"For you, yes. For me, it is just my home. My kirwach."*

*"Kirwach?"*

*"Kirwach is the name given to my home, my jungle. Many of the species including Loxocemae and Zubula use that term for what you call home."*

West and Newtus lost themselves in conversation. Newtus told him more of her home, while West relayed his own stories of growing up on Ijurvoll. Nothing in too much detail, of course. He didn't like to revisit those years, but there were happy parts he had shared, including his only memory of his true mother. Then, before he knew it, his alarm went off.

"Ah shoot!" West spoke out loud for the first time in nearly an hour. *"I need to get going. It got later than I had expected."*

*"I understand. See you again soon?"*

*"Sure. I'm sure that should be fine."*

*"Great. Until next time, West."*

*"Until next time, Newtus."*

West waved at the lizard, then stepped out of her room. Standing in the main room was Professor Peal.

"Ah, West! That was spectacular! We have yet to witness Newtus communicating in such a way."

"Yes, that was certainly a special interaction. Were you able to tune into our conversation?"

"Unfortunately, no. It was just silence, but we could still learn more about her. Would you be able to send us the full conversation? LSS recorded that, right?"

West hesitated for a moment before he answered. "Uh, yeah, it was recorded. I can send it you."

"Wonderful! Thank you for all of your help."

If West had eyes he would have rolled them. He should have known he was being used. "Sure. I'll send it over now. Check your inbox."

Professor Peal looked at his tablet and tapped at it a few times.

"Wonderful. Now, you have other duties to attend to, yes?"

"I do. Which means you should head back over to see Professor Randall, right?"

Professor Peal huffed. "Yes. I had almost forgotten. So annoying."

West tipped his cowboy hat forward and followed Professor Peal out of the main room and back into the hallway.

"Oh, feel free to visit Newtus or Sassafrass and the others at any time," Professor Peal said as he went the opposite direction.

"Sure, thanks."

West headed to the gate where Bsarg was sure to be waiting for him.

*Seriously, what have I gotten myself into?* he thought. *I mean... the more I learn about this place, the less sense it makes. Why would they create me and then hire me on as security? And not just me, but Svetlana as well? And possibly even Norman Harrison later on down the line. What is their goal in creating us?*

*The prophecy that was mentioned when those Humans came through the gate... I feel like we're all connected in some way. Like they're preparing for something big. I want to see them again... Maybe they'll let me one day, after a bit more time spent with the Titans and Peal's subjects. I wish there was a better word than* subjects.

*Man, I really hope they can't read my inner thoughts.*

# 6

# ESCAPE FROM LIMITATIONS

"Overall, it has been a successful few days," Navacus said, speaking into a small microphone. "Our biggest win was finishing the vehicular attachment. We plan on doing a field test with it tomorrow. We also now have Norman's legs attached at all times, giving him much more freedom. He is really quite overjoyed to have his mobility back, and I can't blame him. I wouldn't want to lose my mobility.

"Anyway, we finally finished disassembling the hover attachment, and that was also a complete success. My team has clear instructions on how to assemble it this time. Tomorrow, after the morning field test, we will begin that process—the process to assemble it correctly. I predict the assembly should take about three to five days in all, as there will be several times where we will need to let the device cool down before continuing the build. We are working with quite delicate materials and need to ensure that nothing goes wrong.

"Now, I think I am quite ready for some rest.

"With peace and love and faith, this is Professor Navacus Clums, signing off."

Navacus flipped off the recording device and wheezed. He rubbed his beak, yawned, then stood from the chair he had been sitting in.

The lab was empty, save himself and Fumalli. He had sent everyone home about twenty minutes ago while he prepared and made his daily recording to Head Professor Yilvin's archives. Fumalli had decided to wait for him. He was definitely onto him and Sterg.

"Alright, ready to head home, Fumi?" Navacus asked as he walked toward his friend.

"Sure. That was a short recording today. Don't you usually have a lot more to say?"

"Yeah, but it's fine. I can give a more detailed report if need be tomorrow, or something like that," he said as he locked the door to the lab behind them.

"You're usually more thorough than that. Are you still feeling off?" Fumalli asked, his large jade eyes searching him.

"No, well yes, but no. I know that doesn't make any sense and probably doesn't make you any less concerned."

"No, I'm still quite concerned," Fumalli said as they passed Jakog, the azure Lakinceitian guard. Navacus nodded to Jakog—who smelled like citrus—and Jakog waved back. Each of the Lakinceitian guards put on fresh scents each day, the only unique trait they had. They wore the same uniform each day—much in the same way that he wore nearly the same thing every day.

Once they were outside, Fumalli continued. "I mean, the way you basically forced me out of the room yesterday at lunch, and then you somehow came up with a brand-new solution in seconds? What's been going on with you?"

Navacus wheezed. He looked over to Sterg who floated silently beside him.

"It's just... well, I guess I can't really keep secrets from you, huh?" Navacus said with a shrug.

"Definitely not. You slipped up several times when you were planning my surprise twenty-fifth birthday party. And besides, I can read you like a book, Nava."

"A book with redacted pages, I'm sure," Navacus said with a chuckle.

"Oh no, from cover to cover you're an open book."

"I'm sure I still have a surprise or two to pull off. I'll tell you once we're home. For now, can we just enjoy the peace and stillness?" Navacus said as he gazed toward the night sky.

It was a nice evening—the temperature was perfect, and the shimmering wormholes emerged above the towering peaks of the Krefna Mountains. The lights from the walkway and buildings around them illuminated the sand, as it glinted dully in the artificial light. Around the lights buzzed several local flying insects.

"You've always loved the night sky, haven't you?" Fumalli asked as they slowly approached the barracks.

"I mean, it's fascinating, no? There are tales from my species' home world that said the night sky was filled with millions of stars. Not just the three we have in this system. Why is our solar system encased in a sphere of dried-up wormholes? I know the story goes that it's because we're at the center of the universe, the literal spot where the universe began, but even if that were true..."

"You don't think it explains the reason behind the wormholes, meaning you don't believe in what nearly everyone else believes, including me."

"Yeah, I suppose we've talked about this before, haven't we?"

"It's fine," Fumalli said as he keyed in his unique code to unlock the doors. Once unlocked, Fumalli opened the door and let Navacus go through first.

They wound their way through a specific combination of doors to reach the one leading to their apartment. Once they were both settled in, Fumalli sat on the couch and looked pointedly at Navacus as he paced around the room.

"So, tell me. What's been going on? Is it related to your secret project with Carl?"

"Um, yes, but no because... Well, hang on for a moment before I answer that."

"Okay..." Fumalli said, furrowing his brow.

*"Sterg, are there any recording devices in our apartment? Like, is anyone listening in on us?"*

*"Yes, but with me around, those devices don't work. I cause them to just relay back static."*

"Ah, that's great," Navacus said out loud.

"What? Were you..." Fumalli asked.

"Right. Sorry. I had to make sure we weren't being listened to. I think that this will make things easier. Just... well, don't freak out, okay?"

"Um, Navacus? What in the world are you talking about? You're making no sense."

*"Do you want me to calm him down for you?"* Sterg asked.

"Well, try and calm down, okay? And no."

"No what?"

"No nothing. Anyway, are you ready?"

"Again, I'm terribly confused."

"All will make sense in a moment. Sterg, could you try and not frighten Fumalli while you slowly reveal yourself to him?"

"How about this?" Sterg asked as a disembodied voice.

"What in the void was that? Who said that?" Fumalli asked as he jumped off the couch and frantically looked around the room.

"Yeah, I don't think that worked. Just show yourself, okay?"

"Sorry, I miscalculated," Sterg said, as a small orb of light appeared in the room, hovering above the coffee table. To Navacus, Sterg's ghostly figure became a little brighter.

He looked over at his friend. Fumalli hung his wide mouth open in shock as his eyes locked onto Sterg. He slowly slinked to the edge of the couch, then stood up and nearly tripped over the armrest as he backed into the wall.

"Navacus, please explain what is going on. Right now."

"I suppose we both mucked that up a bit, didn't we?" Navacus asked Sterg. "Well, Fumalli, I'm sorry. I thought this would have been easier than trying to explain first. Now, where should I begin?" He paused for a moment, then pounded his fist into his hand. "Right. So, to explain this properly, I need to tell you about something else first. I am not working on a secret project with Carl; there is no secondary project that I'm working on at all. Rather, I was invited into a secret facility hidden beneath the compound."

"Wait, beneath the compound? So, there's an even more secretive facility hidden under an already secret facility?" Fumalli asked.

"Essentially, yes. But satellites can technically see the compound, if they knew exactly where to look and how to see past the camouflaged rooftops."

"The rooftops are camouflaged? How do you know this? We don't have access to the roofs."

"Oh, right. I picked up that piece of information through Sterg. It's only been a few days, but it's already getting harder to tell whose thoughts are whose. Anyway, Fumalli, I know you must have a lot of questions, but if you could please let me fully explain everything."

"Sure, sorry. This is just already a lot to take in," Fumalli said as he sunk back into the couch with one hand rubbing his smooth blue head.

"It's fine. Now, this secret underground laboratory is the true purpose of the compound, from what I have been able to deduce. Also, Professor Peal is essentially fully moved down there at this point. From what I can gather, his experiments became too sensitive for them to continue in the main facility.

"Anyway, Fumalli, I know you're overwhelmed, but I gotta tell you, I was in full disbelief when I watched the wall at the end of this hallway slide into the floor, revealing an elevator. I was even told what to expect the day before, but seeing it is much different from hearing about it. At least, when you step out of the elevator, all you really see are the white walls of the three different hallways that lead to different sections of the underground. So, that part isn't too overwhelming, but it is like a maze down there. I don't know how anyone can navigate it.

"Also, that was when Sterg initially contacted me. Thinking back on it now, Sterg, you calmed me down, didn't you?"

"Indeed. Although we were not yet bound together, I could still clear your mind of your doubt and shock and allow you to think clearly," Sterg replied.

"So, that's why I felt a wave of calm wash over me. And it helped me take everything in," Navacus said as he turned back to his friend. "Fumalli, I saw things I wouldn't even have believed had I been told beforehand. There was an Ancilsan who could shape-shift into every other species. I watched him change from being an Ancilsan to being a Human, then a Lakinceitian, Kolythoanthaean, Harmertian... He even changed into a Yggdrazim. It looked like it caused him a great deal of pain, but they were perfect transformations. Professor Randall called him Altun. That's the one thing that really stood out to me about the underground. The experiments going on down there are quite grotesque, but they prefer to call their subjects by their names.

"Also, there are two professors in charge of the underground—Professor Durrist and Professor Randall. Durrist is a Lakinceitian, and Randall is a Human.

"They also gave me a tour of Professor Peal's new setup down there. I saw all the different animals he's working on, as well as a Eusphyrchiian-hybrid creature. What I mean by that is that it had the torso and arms of a Eusphyrchiian, but it has spiders for hands and ivy for legs. And, it was headless."

"Wait—West isn't the only headless Eusphyrchii?" Fumalli asked.

"Apparently not. And, speaking of West, I saw him down there, too. He's doing quite well for himself, it seems. Svetlana, on the other hand, has changed. She's not the bubbly woman we once knew. She's now cold, like a machine. I suspect that Professor Durrist or someone has messed with her mind. I'm eager to see for myself once we start on her upgrades.

"Anyway, my visit down there was cut short because of the arrival of a handful of otherworldly Humans. They were definitely not from Carange, I can tell you that. There was an older man with a long white beard, blue robes, and a peculiar pointed hat. There was a man with reddish-orange hair, wearing a full suit of ancient armor, like from the bronze age. Then there was a man who was so pale he had nearly white skin, and a man with pure black skin. Carl sedated them before they got to say very much. But West was able to play back the recording, and they gave a warning of a great evil approaching. They called it Gnusaramnii. Now, doesn't that name sound familiar?"

"Gnusaramnii? Wasn't Gnusar the name of the Lakinceitian who stole the Ancilsan's ark?"

"Indeed it was. Remember we took that class together as one of our electives? Melridion History? Professor Durrist spoke of a prophecy, and Sterg and I believe Gnusaramnii is Gnusar, returning now to Melridion to complete his age-old task of converting all life to be controlled by one mind. While it sounds like the otherworldly Humans were able to fend off Gnusaramnii and save their planet, they say that it will be here sooner than later."

"That's honestly quite frightening, and all of this has been quite the story, but what does this have to do with the floating sphere of light hovering in the room?" Fumalli asked, pointing at Sterg.

"Right, sorry. There's been a lot going on lately. I still don't fully understand it myself, but Sterg is a Light Being, which, from my understanding, is a soul in its raw form."

"Essentially, yes, but not all souls can exist outside of a vessel. Only the most disciplined of souls can achieve this, and those souls are called Light Beings," Sterg explained.

"Yes, and Sterg and I are now bound together. We are linked—Sterg cannot travel very far away from me without both of us experiencing pain. And Sterg is the one who is heightening all my senses. Sterg helped me realize we needed to disassemble the hover attachment and how to reassemble it the correct way. Not only that, but I can see and hear through it, and I can sense others' emotions and base level thoughts around me."

"You can read my mind?" Fumalli asked, his eyes darting back and forth between Navacus and Sterg.

"I have chosen not to; I didn't want to invade your privacy. But yes, I can. I was able to sense Norman's thoughts and how distraught he is about Kate," Sterg said.

"Oh yeah, Kate! Is she in the underground?"

"I strongly suspect so, but I didn't see her," Navacus said. "As I said, my trip was cut short. I was on my way to see someone who had also arrived through the gate. For all I know, she came from the same place as the other travelers. And, for all I know, Kate could be involved with her somehow. That, or Kate is going through some other horrible experiment. Either way, we need to get back down there, and soon. We can't wait for me to get invited, as it might be several days or even weeks. We need to know what's going on down there, now."

"So, you can't send Sterg, due to the pain you were talking about. What do you suggest then?"

Navacus glanced at Sterg then back to Fumalli. "Well, we were thinking about utilizing the Harmertians. They're already small and stealthy. We think they could climb into the air ducts, find the elevator shaft, and go down it. Or something along those lines. Again, Sterg can only sense so much."

"I mean, that seems like the most logical solution," Fumalli replied. "Are you sure they'd be up to the challenge?"

"We would need to talk to them about it, of course. The choice will ultimately be theirs. If they decide against it, I'm sure we can come up with another plan."

"But how would they scale down an elevator shaft? Rope? Do you even know how far down it goes?"

"Nope, I truly don't," Navacus said as he shook his head. "And no, not rope. Working on the hover attachment for Norman got me thinking. I think I can use what little materials we have left over to create three small suits that the Harmertians can wear. It'll be kinda like a jetpack, but with more finesse."

"So, what, you and Sterg are just going to sneak into the compound, steal multi-millions worth of raw materials, and make suits for three Harmertians?"

"Well, yes, but without the sneaking. We're still working on Norman. We can scrub up the numbers a bit to hide the loss of materials. The timing is everything. We are going to begin reassembling the hover attachment tomorrow. It's now or never, for this idea at least."

"Well, I guess I can alter the numbers a bit. But I'm afraid of what would happen if Professor Dea or Head Professor Yilvin found out."

"It's likely that they will, but not immediately. Sterg will also be able to help with that, but it can only do so much."

"Sure, but you've got to think ahead in situations like this. How long do you realistically think that you can hide Sterg from them?" Fumalli asked, his concern showing in his eyes.

"I give it two to three months at the most. But by then, it may not be a problem."

"Why? What are you planning, Nava?"

"I don't know yet. But I'm sure if you saw what I saw, you would know that we need to get away from this place. I'm sure you can sense it too, right? They won't ever let us return to a normal life. Not after what we've done. We know too much. We're no longer their employees, but their prisoners. Even the layout of our barracks proves it. The security system and door combinations to even get to our apartment is just ridiculous."

"Sure, it is ridiculous, but I think it's necessary. And I don't agree that we're prisoners here. Yes, we know a lot, but we're bound by nondisclosure agreements. And it's not like we could remain anonymous for long if anything got out. All we would need to do is just not talk about it."

"Oh Fumi, this is why I love you. You always try to find the most positive solutions. But I don't think Lord Foxaire is a trusting individual. For example, why are there multiple levels of secrecy here? If you're trying to keep secrets from those with whom you are already trusting secrets, there's got to be something bigger going on. I just can't say what it is yet. I mean, did you ever really stop to think about what we're doing here?"

"You mean, why are we doing what we're doing?"

"Yes, exactly. Why are we working on Norman? Why are we creating three different attachments? Why did we create the first cyborg the Vortex has ever seen? And why now? Not to mention the otherworldly Humans that mentioned Gnusaramnii and the prophecy that Professor Durrist and Bsarg spoke of. I believe everything is connected. But again, I just don't know how yet. So, we need more answers; we need to send the Harmertians into the underground."

"You know, none of this is what I expected you to say. I mean, I didn't know what you were going to say, but it wasn't any of this. You're talking of a conspiracy."

"Yeah, I guess I am. I mean we are conspiring to send the Harmertians to the underground."

"Yeah, I guess you are. And now I've been roped into this."

"You would have found out one way or another, but I'm glad we had this talk. I'm glad I have no more secrets hidden from you."

"Me too," Fumalli nodded in agreement. "Can I ask you something, Sterg?"

"Certainly."

"Navacus spoke of a prophecy and of Gnusar's return to Melridion. How do we know you aren't part of Gnusar? Gnusar wanted to control everyone through telepathy, isn't that right? Are you really a piece of Gnusar?"

"No, I am not," Sterg replied. "I am here in response to Gnusaramnii's defeat at Eklatros. I am here to prepare you all for Gnusaramnii's return to the Vortex System."

"Wait, really? Why am I just finding out about this? And what is Eklatros?" Navacus asked.

"I didn't know my true purpose until a few minutes ago, during your conversation. But I can feel it—I know I was recently in contact with Gnusaramnii. But I know little more than that. I don't retain memories the way you do—I would have too many different lifetimes to remember. Rather, I get impressions and feelings. And I feel strongly that I was nearly touched by Gnusaramnii, but that I could avoid its grasp and that I am here, now, to help you defend against its eventual attack."

"You know, that doesn't really convince me," Fumalli said. "Touched by Gnusaramnii? I mean, you might as well be one of its minions!"

"Fumalli, do you trust me?" Navacus asked.

"Yes, but…"

"Then trust Sterg. I trust that it is telling the truth. Remember, I can feel it in more ways than one. Its impressions and feelings are my own. It can't lie to me."

"You never know, Navacus. You could be so wrapped up in the lie that you can't see the way out. But I do trust you, so I will trust Sterg. For now, at least."

"That's all I ask. Thank you, Fumalli. Thank you for listening to me and for entertaining a belief that what I say is true. You are the best friend I could ever have, and I don't know what I would do without you."

Fumalli sighed. "I don't know what I would do without you either, Navacus. And that's the problem. I'm terrified for you. You've been thrust onto a path that I can't easily follow."

"I know. The next few weeks are going to be hard on all of us. But I can assure you, we will make it through this, and we'll do it together."

"Together," Fumalli said with a nod. "I'm with you until the end, Nava."

"Until the very end," Navacus said, smiling at his friend.

"So, what's the plan then?" Fumalli asked.

"Well, we should cook after this. I need to get to bed soon to be at the compound early in the morning to build the three suits. It shouldn't take more than an hour, but I'll need to be careful. Which reminds me—Sterg, won't they get suspicious if all the cameras that I am nearby go to static?"

"Indeed, they will. Which is why I am working on a few different solutions. I want to see if I can loop the camera feeds or even edit the surveillance recordings in real time. However, there's no guarantee that either of those solutions will work. My influence can only do so much."

"Yeah, that all sounds quite complicated. Do you need my help with anything?"

"I'll let you know if such a situation arises," Sterg responded.

"Great. Now, what do you feel like eating tonight?" Navacus asked Fumalli.

"How about I make my signature Qymberkon family dish? It's been a while."

"Oh, that sounds amazing. I can help chop the veggies."

Navacus and Fumalli busied themselves with cooking. It would take roughly an hour until the meal was ready.

*Sterg, would you tell me if I'm on the wrong path? Is this plan truly the correct move?* he thought. *It is the right path? Okay, great. I was getting worried. Or I'm just nervous—yeah, I'm definitely nervous.*

*What am I doing? I've never been one to rebel. I've always been a good student and a good person. I've always followed the rules and done what I was told. And now we're about to go completely off script. Of course I would be nervous. Fumalli is dealing with it better than I am, though I think that's why he offered to cook this meal. He needs to focus on something familiar among all this insanity. And I suppose I should do the same.*

7

# ESCAPE FROM VIBRANCY

Tyrona Claire Knorse awoke to the same view every day. Gray walls, gray ceiling, gray floor, gray bedsheets... all of the color had been removed from her life. Gone were her pink and purple couches and matching candles. Gone were the black walls of Ajenti. There was only gray. The worst shade of gray imaginable.

Even the rags she wore were nearly the same shade of gray. Everything had been taken from her when she had been knocked unconscious by that woman who shot her with a magical beam of energy. Her purple robes, her hat, and even her cherished ivory wand were gone. On top of it all, even her hair had been cropped short. All she had left was herself. And she felt she was losing herself, losing her sanity.

In order to influence other people's minds using magic, she had to learn how to steel away her own mind—protect it and the essence of herself from melding with the other minds and memories. This always made her acutely aware of her own state of consciousness.

It had started when she lost track of the days. At first, she had wanted to mark the days on the walls, but she had nothing to write with. Then she tried to time her days when she was given gray gruel and dirty water, but she quickly realized there was no set schedule to that. Possibly for that exact reason—to throw her off balance.

Her final attempt was to measure the days by the rate at which her hair and nails grew, but there were two glaring issues. First, she was on an alien planet. She had no sense of night or day or even how long the hours and minutes were. Second, she soon came to realize that her hair and nails were not growing at all. She figured it was something they were putting in her food or water—or both.

She had completely given up on attempting to use magic the first 'day' she had been in this gray box. She had nothing to draw from and no conduit to use. She had even given up on praying for help, whether she was calling on Theodore, Ànifa, Cecil, Joan, Dasch, or even Vesten... it didn't matter because they were worlds away. They would never find her. All that was left was gray.

Gray, gray, and gray.

Gray, gray, and more gray.

Gray was the only substance left in her life. Even her thoughts were losing their vibrancy. Her thoughts were becoming harder to hold on to. Her memories were getting harder to access. She really was losing her mind.

She no longer had any distinction between her dreams and reality. When her head hit the gray mattress, she would sit up a second later feeling as refreshed as she could be. For she was always tired, and yet it seemed she was always awake. And all she had was gray.

Then, there was a voice that wasn't her own. It started as a faint whisper at the edge of her mind, but it was there, and it was terrified.

*"Hello? What's going on? I just... I just want to see Norman! Norman... where are you, Norman?"*

*"Who is Norman? I don't know a Norman,"* Tyrona replied to the wispy voice.

*"Norman is my fiancé. He was hurt, and I helped bring him here... I'm Kate Thomas."*

When the voice spoke her name, it became much more focused. A woman faded into her vision. She had straight brown hair that went just past her shoulders and fair skin. Her eyes were a deep blue, as if they held small oceans.

Tyrona held her hand out to Kate. *"It's nice to meet you, Kate. I'm the S-Class Sorceress Tyrona Claire Knorse of Ajenti. Although, I think I must be going crazy. I thought I was alone in a gray box."*

Kate took and squeezed her hand.

*"Same—I had been alone, too, in a gray box of my own. Everything was gray—there had been nothing else. But then I started having these strange dreams. I started seeing things that... well, frankly, it felt as if I was looking into someone else's memories."*

*"That is certainly peculiar. Especially your dreams—I haven't had a single dream since I've been in that gray box."*

*"Tyrona, this is a dream. And I think I understand now."*

*"Understand what, Kate? Who are you?"*

The brown-haired woman turned away from her and walked away.

*"I'm you, Tyrona. We're the same, you and I..."* Kate disappeared from view.

*"What does that mean? I don't know you, and I don't know Norman!"*

*"Norman, my love... come back to me..."*

The voice slowly faded away. Tyrona wanted to call after it, but she was confused and scared. What had just happened? Who had she just spoken with?

She woke up to the same view every day. Gray walls, gray ceiling, gray... she had just woken up? So, she had been asleep. The voice had only been a dream.

When she began to pursue the magic of mind tampering, the first thing she learned was that this magic came with a heavy toll. Most of those who practiced this type of magic went insane. For some, it took only a few years, for others it took decades—but they all succumbed to mind-madness in the end.

The seal she had on her own consciousness was not impermeable. For instance, after the showdown at the Compass Crossroads, her mind had been in a haze. It took a lot of energy to mess with that many minds at once—all while holding onto her own consciousness. She had had to weed out the unfiltered memories that had infiltrated her mind. Then the diprotodon had slammed into her, and Theodore had been there for her... Either way, she was old, and she wasn't getting any younger, no matter how much magic she used on her appearance. She had been long overdue to succumb to mind-madness.

For all she knew, she was still on Eklatros. Maybe the volcano had caused her to faint, and she was simply within a prolonged dream—a dream that had lost its creativity and had become only gray.

That's right, Eklatros and the Nibelkaith Volcano. Theodore, her friends, their mission, her dire wolf spider, and an intricately carved stone door. All her memories were coming back to her. Yet something was off. Kate hadn't been there, too, had she?

*Kate, are you there?* she thought. *Who are you? And why are you in my dreams and my memories?*

Wait, her memories? The volcano and that dire wolf spider—those weren't from her own memories, were they?

Kate hadn't been there—she hadn't been there. She drew up her own memories. Her first high school boyfriend, Owen. She had been with Owen for only a few months before Norman had moved to her hometown of Bahutenrut. At first, she laughed when Owen made fun of the skinny red-haired twerp. But then she had gotten to know Norman and he quickly stole her heart.

Then, there was that time when she was studying for her final exams. Norman had been working long shifts at the mine and there had been an accident. Luckily, he had been okay, but several other miners had died. That caused them to re-evaluate their lives, and they decided to move to Kokorocco once she graduated. She had received a promising job offer there, and they could move out of their rural town and into a big city.

Before they moved, Norman had proposed to her. They had been in a field of endless grass while the suns were setting over the horizon. The setting suns' rays also reflected off of Mishunaed, making it appear as if there were four suns, three that were quickly setting and one that was slowly rising.

They had been so excited for their new lives and opportunities. And yet, even after leaving the mine and getting a job at a convenience store while hunting for a better job, Norman still got hurt. She had been driving, and that damn truck had come out of nowhere. She made it out uninjured while Norman lost his legs. She completely blamed herself. How could she not?

What if they had stayed in Bahutenrut? What if Norman had been driving? What if they hadn't stopped for drinks? What if she hadn't been thinking about work? The 'what ifs' tormented her. They were driving her insane.

She woke up to the same view every day. Yet today was slightly different. Today her gray tray of gray gruel and dirty water sat on the floor. It looked like it had been there for a while, judging by the crust forming on the gruel.

She looked at her hands and studied her brown skin. Kate had light bronze skin. So why was she talking to her, thinking her thoughts, and seeing her memories?

Tyrona checked up on the barrier that surrounded her sense of self and her own memories. She gasped out loud—the barrier was now only a thin veil that was full of holes. It hadn't been like this just... just when? What was time when all she had was gray? Of course, the barrier was nearly gone. There was nothing left to help hold onto her sanity. Theodore, Ànifa, Joan, and the rest were all out of reach. There was only gray.

Whoever Kate Thomas actually was, she was the one that was tampering with her mind. Or was someone else causing this? It was hard to imagine how someone could do this to her. Do what to her? And where was Norman?

She shook her head and looked at the gray floor. The tray with the gruel and water was gone. Did she consume them, and if so, when? It didn't matter. Nothing mattered. Only Norman and his safety. Even though she couldn't remember if she actually knew Norman. Part of her felt like she loved him. Another part of her felt like she'd never met him. Who was Norman, anyway? She loved Theodore, not Norman, right?

*I can't... Is this the last of me? The last of the great S-Class Sorceress Tyrona Claire Knorse?* she thought. *Norman... I mean Dorie... please, don't come looking for me. Stay away... Stay as far away from here as you possibly can. I'm glad it was me and not you.*

*Wait, what am I thinking? I wish it had been me, Norman, and not you.*

8

# INTERLUDE: LOCATION - THERONIOR

Begin Replay of NIWAT Inner Datalog
Recording C-0000670329 S-068 N-42

"I just got word that Drae'Cole has fallen. I repeat, Drae'Cole has fallen."

I watched the attractive androbotix reporter deliver the grim message on the television screen while the video behind her showed footage of the destruction.

"Holy crap, the capital... If the capital has fallen, then Theronior is lost," Blu-Dreem said as he hung his long head down in sadness.

"Spyke, Databag, Lophye... They aren't responding to my messages!" Zanzi exclaimed.

"Didn't you just hear Tally? Drae'Cole has fallen!" Blu-Dreem replied.

"Both of you, quiet down," I said. "We must stay calm. We don't know how it spreads yet; Lophye and the others could just be in private mode. Speaking of which—"

I couldn't finish my sentence. In the left-hand corner of my screen, Maker Denorad's profile picture went black. Beside me, Zanzi and Blu-Dreem gasped.

"Zanzi, Beedee, can either of you reach Maker Denorad?"

"No," they said in unison.

"Did we lose our maker? Will we be lost, too?" Zanzi asked.

"I don't know. His system may just be rebooting. Come on, let's go find him," I said as I turned off the television. I brought up the newsfeed and put it in the right corner to monitor the situation.

"Do you know where he is, Niwat?" Blu-Dreem asked.

"My feed tells me that he was last in kitchens," I replied.

"Ah, right. Humans need to eat like, all the time," Zanzi said.

"Exactly. Now, come on."

I led my fellow androbotix out of the entertainment room and into the hallway.

"Freeze your circuits, Zombu is calling me," Zanzi said.

"Bring up the call in our group chat," I ordered.

"Sure thing," Zanzi replied.

A moment later an opaque Zombu filled my screen, allowing me to see both the androbotix and the hallway we stood in. I kept my other windows up as well. On the left side of my screen, I saw the five of us that made up Denorad's crew. We each had our own avatars. I was at the top, as was standard, with Maker Denorad right below me (who was currently offline), followed by Blu-Dreem, then Zanzi, then Zombu. Below Zombu was the miniaturized newsfeed.

"Zombu, what is the situation?" I asked.

"Maker Denorad says not to worry. He discovered the parasite can travel through the internet, so he used the kill switch to completely sever our connection to the main internet. Once his systems are booted back up, he'll be able to connect to our private intranet. In the meantime, please head to the hangar and prepare *Francentia* for our immediate retreat," Zombu explained over the video chat.

"I was thinking along the same code before Maker Denorad went offline," I replied. "We should all go into private mode. While I trust that Maker Denorad's intranet is protected from the main internet, we must play it safe if we are to survive."

"Maker Denorad says that he agrees. Meet you on board *Francentia*. Over and out."

Zombu disappeared from my view while I took one final glance at the official report. Theronior was lost, and it fell in just six short hours. I shut off the newsfeed and put myself in private mode. On the left side of my screen, I watched as each of the other avatars became grayed out.

"We won't be able to contact the others if they get into trouble," Zanzi said.

"The five of us are the only ones in here. And you know our maker—he has always been paranoid of the internet. Nothing in this house is connected to it."

"Yeah, but that doesn't mean something can't happen," Zanzi replied.

"It's just your over calculating logic circuits. There's nothing to worry about. Now, let's go."

While I did my best to convince the others that everything was fine, I didn't believe it myself. Zanzi was right. There were many variables, even in our own home. But as Maker Denorad's first androbotix, I was the leader among my kind here. I had to appear calm and collected.

We hurried down the hallway. Before we reached the stairs, we passed a window and stopped dead in our tracks.

The world was on fire. We were three stories up, on the laboratory level, allowing us to see down to the main street. Blood and oil were everywhere. Humans and androbotix alike were either running for their lives or rabidly chasing others down. The few ground-level vehicles that were still operational were driving at top speeds, running over anyone and anything that got in their way.

In the air, the situation wasn't any better. Numerous spaceships trying to flee the planet were being shot out of the sky, crashing into the city below.

"How are we going to get out of here?" Zanzi asked.

"We'll find a way. Come on, we're running out of time."

I turned away from the window and ran up the stairs. A few

moments later, I heard Blu-Dreem and Zanzi follow. As soon as I got upstairs, an explosion rocked the house, knocking me to the ground.

"Niwat, that was the ground floor!" Zanzi shouted.

"Then hope that Maker Denorad and Zombu made it up in time. We need to move, now!"

I stood up and ran down the hallway until I reached two large double doors. I threw them open and ran into the hangar. As I approached *Francentia*, I stopped dead in my tracks. A large black cable had fallen onto *Francentia's* right wing.

"Beedee, get the ship running. Zanzi, help me get the cable off the wing."

"Right away," they responded simultaneously. Blu-Dreem ran up the ramp and into the ship, while Zanzi followed me as I hurried toward the mobile ladder. I threw myself into the control box and sped toward the right wing. Zanzi jumped onto the ladder even before I secured it to the wing. I slammed on the breaks, punched the emergency break, and followed Zanzi up the ladder.

Zanzi was the first one to the cable and began hoisting it up. I hurried past Zanzi and saw that the cable had gotten lodged beneath three plasma cannon turrets.

"Zanzi, help me over here," I called out. "We've got to get the cable free!"

Zanzi hurried over, and we shoved the cable out from beneath the turrets. As soon as it dislodged, Maker Denorad and Zombu ran into the hangar. A second later I felt the ship rumble as the engines purred awake.

"They've gotten inside!" Maker Denorad yelled up to us. "Zombu, hurry to the guns. Niwat, Zanzi, move that cable double-speed. We've got to get out of here, now!"

"We've got no time to waste, lets lift this thing!" I ordered Zanzi. "Together now, and heave!"

With the two of us, we could lift the cable just enough to carry it over each of the numerous obstacles.

"Now, to the tip of the wing, hurry!"

The turret that we had just gotten the cable dislodged from spun toward the hangar door and unleashed fury. I whirled my head around and watched in horror as four bloody humans ran into the room, screaming wildly. The plasma cannon ripped them to shreds, but seconds later, three more ran through the bloody spray.

Zanzi and I were nearly at the tip of the wing. Three meters. Two meters.

"Now, toss it!"

Zanzi and I tossed the cable and it slammed down onto the ground, causing a large crate to fly into the air and land near the hangar door, crushing an enraged androbotix. Above us, the ceiling retracted into itself, giving us a clear view of the chaos in the skies. I tore my eyes away from the carnage and looked at Zanzi.

"Get inside. I'll move the ladder!"

"See you inside," Zanzi said as he jumped off the wing and ran toward the entrance ramp.

I ran toward the ladder and jumped to the ground right before I reached the active plasma cannons. I hit the ground running as I sprinted into the ladder's control panel. I pounded the release button, causing the ladder to detach from the ship. I then turned the ladder toward the entrance and cranked up the speed. Breaking off the joystick, I jumped onto the ground and ran toward *Francentia's* entrance ramp while the ladder sped toward the incoming horde.

All the while the plasma cannons ripped through human and androbotix alike. When the careening ladder reached the entrance, a plasma bolt hit it, causing it to explode.

I dove onto the ramp and smashed the Door Close button.

"Go!" I yelled.

A second later, *Francentia* lifted off the ground and sped into the turbulent sky. I hurried into the cockpit and strapped myself in beside Zanzi. Maker Denorad was steering while Blu-Dreem assisted as copilot, and both were doing everything they could to avoid plunging back to the ground in a fiery burst.

"Zombu, disarm the plasma cannons. We don't want to draw any attention to ourselves," Denorad ordered, speaking into the microphone that broadcasted around the ship. "But stay ready, just in case."

"Sure, no arguments there," Zombu replied, his voice cracking through the speakers.

"Do you see that above us?" Blu-Dreem asked.

"What's going—" I was stopped short when I saw what was happening.

Directly above us, a massive G-class transport ship was hovering in the air, still suspended by its engines as explosions ripped through it. Debris pelted into our current trajectory.

"You got this, right?" I asked.

"You know it, pal," Maker Denorad replied as he deftly maneuvered *Francentia* past the falling debris.

Out of nowhere, a plasma burst shot past the ship, coming within five meters of us.

"*Francentia*, who's shooting at us?" I asked the ship's AI.

"There are fourteen active militarized fighters in the vicinity that are shooting down any civilian ship trying to escape the planet," *Francentia* responded calmly. "No one is currently directly targeting us. That must have been a stray shot."

"Let's keep it that way," Denorad replied. "*Francentia*, focus all your resources on our shields."

"Why would the military be shooting down civilians?" Zanzi asked.

"They all must be infected by the Gnusar," Denorad replied, his voice full of regret.

"The Gnusar? What are they?" I asked.

"It's the name given to the parasite that's ravaging Theronior. From what I heard, a meteorite carrying the parasite crashed nearby during the night," Maker Denorad replied. He was keeping *Francentia* hidden from the military by flying within the shadow of the destroyed transport ship.

"We can't stay in this position much longer," Blu-Dreem said. "That ship will start plunging toward us any second now."

"That's exactly what I'm waiting for, Beedee. I hope it's the distraction we need," Maker Denorad replied.

"And it's falling," Zanzi said.

"I see it," Maker Denorad replied.

"And yet we're still speeding toward it!" Zanzi cried.

"Quiet down, let them focus," I ordered.

"Three, two, one. Beedee, punch the port-side thrusters."

"Port-side thrusters activated."

*Francentia* veered to the left, shooting out from under the burning wreckage just in time, and right into a military fighter.

"Zombu, guns!" Maker Denorad cried. "Zanzi, get down there and help him!"

"Yes, Maker!" Zanzi replied. He unlatched his restraints and hurried out of the cockpit as the militarized fighter in front of them blasted into pieces.

"Punch it!"

*Francentia* shot into the air as five militarized fighters pursued. Currently, Zombu manned all the guns, but momentarily Zanzi would take over one of the two sides of the ship, allowing them to shoot in two different directions.

Plasma fire screamed past them as they entered the upper atmosphere. A bolt hit us, rocking the ship, and then another.

"Niwat, we've got one plasma bomb. Can you control it so that it hits our pursuers?" Maker Denorad asked me.

"What about *Francentia*?" I asked. The ship was just as good as I was with piloting bombs and drones.

"She's too busy holding our shields together. I can't let her lose focus," Maker Denorad said as the ship took another direct hit, rocking her back and forth.

"Right, sure thing."

I keyed the code into my armrest console, ejecting the headset as it dropped from the ceiling. I grabbed it and put it on. After a second of load-time I was in *Francentia's* mainframe. I took a second to reorient myself, then zoomed into the munitions folder. I watched as our plasma cannon power reserves dropped into the red, and then I took control of the plasma bomb. Once the code was entered to open the launch tube, I keyed in the separate code to release the bomb.

As it shot out of the tube, I took manual control and maneuvered the bomb toward the second closest militarized fighter. When it was in range, I set the target lock and disengaged manual control.

As I pulled off the headset, an explosion behind us rocked the ship.

"Good job, Niwat," Maker Denorad said. "*Francentia*, are there any left?"

"Negative. One more direct hit and we would have been done for," the female voice emanated through the speakers.

"We're exiting the upper atmosphere. We'll be free from Theronior's magnetic field within ten minutes. Once we're free, we can jump out of here," Blu-Dreem said.

"Do we have a destination?" I asked.

"Zanzi, Zombu, come up to the cockpit in five minutes. Keep an eye out for any pursuers until then," Maker Denorad said into the microphone, then turned to me. For the first time since we escaped, I got a good look at his face. His skin was pale and smudged with grime and his eyes were bloodshot. "I'm willing to go anywhere but here."

"Maker, are you okay?"

"I'm fine. I took an adrenaline boost right after the explosion on the ground floor. Do you have any suggestions on where to go?"

"I suggest in the opposite direction that the Gnusar came from," Blu-Dreem suggested.

"I agree," I replied.

"That would lead us toward the sandstorm nebula," *Francentia* replied.

"Aren't there stories about that nebula?" Blu-Dreem asked.

"Not good ones," I replied. "*Francentia*, where are the nearest populated or habitable planets?"

"Allow me a few moments to zero in on any populated or habitable planets in the region between us and the sandstorm nebula," *Francentia* replied.

The sandstorm nebula was said to contain many wild space-faring animals, including giant space eels, space whales, and terrifying creatures known as iris imps, which were essentially floating eyeballs with dozens of tentacles.

"Unfortunately, I couldn't find any habitable or populated planets, moons, or asteroids on my scans. That being said, I have a destination for our first jump point—a large planetoid within an asteroid field that should allow us to lie low for a while."

"Great, that works. We can make a plan there."

Zanzi and Zombu entered the cockpit and sat in their designated chairs.

"We've begun the cool-down process for the weapons. We nearly maxed them out today. Our guns were not made for sustained fire," Zombu said.

"Exactly why the bomb was needed," Maker Denorad replied. "We've found a spot to hide. Just a few more minutes until we're out of the magnetic field and we'll make the jump."

"I've got the coordinates set and locked in," Blue-Dreem said. "Just say when and we'll be out of here."

"Can I just be the first to say what a miracle it is that we've even gotten this far?" Zombu said. "I wasn't expecting to make it out of the house, let alone escape Theronior."

"I had faith, because I trust in each of you. We are a team, and we're stronger together because of it," I said.

"Niwat's right. You all did a great job today," Maker Denorad said.

"That was some really impressive flying," I responded. "We wouldn't have made it through that debris storm if it wasn't for you."

"Any of you could have done it. I programed all of you to be excellent pilots if the need ever arose."

"I'm perfectly happy as copilot, thank you very much," Blu-Dreem said, causing each of us to chuckle.

I smiled, then switched my main internal display screen to the rear camera feed. Theronior loomed behind us. While it was quiet, every few seconds there were flashes—explosions from the ground and in the skies. Theronior was truly lost.

We passed the rest of the time in silence.

"Alright, we're sixty seconds out from the jump point. Beedee, prepare for instantaneous hyperspace travel."

"Engines switching to hyperspace travel mode," Blu-Dreem replied.

"*Francentia*, prepare the ship."

"Readying for instantaneous hyperspace travel."

As I continued to watch Theronior, I saw a flash of light appear.

"Hey guys, something is coming," I said.

"Proximity alert," *Francentia* announced. "A plasma missile is swiftly approaching. Impact in ten seconds."

"We're not going to make it. *Francentia*, eject garbage and waste, now!" Denorad exclaimed.

"What do you mean 'we're not going to make it?'" Zanzi cried as he leaned forward in his seat.

A moment later, the plasma missile found the expelled waste and exploded. The blast threw them forward while momentarily causing the power to flicker off and then on again within the span of a second.

"Sparks, the power hiccup caused the jump drive to activate, and we've shot far past our intended jump point," Blu-Dreem said.

"The power went out because the blast surged the ship with extra power as it pushed us forward," Maker Denorad said.

"Sparks! It could have fried the navigation system," I exclaimed.

"Twelve seconds until jump," *Francentia* announced. "Ten, nine, eight, seven, six—"

9

# ESCAPE FROM THE PARAMETERS

His eyes shot open. He lay in bed and listened to Fumalli's heavy breathing beside him while staring up at the ceiling. The image of the spaceship bursting into a flash of light was still seared into his mind.

Navacus looked at the digital clock. It was four in the morning. He wheezed, then slowly and quietly got out of bed so he wouldn't disturb Fumalli.

He headed to the kitchen, carefully placing each of his flat, webbed feet on the ground so they wouldn't slap against the floor. Turning on the faucet, he filled up the electric kettle. Once the water started to boil, he whispered to Sterg.

"Sterg, what was with that dream I just had? Everything felt so real. It was if I were actually there, witnessing those robots and their maker flee their own planet."

"*It's because we were there,*" Sterg replied telepathically. "*Our souls are linked, and as I explained earlier, I cannot physically move far away from you without causing both of us pain. Yet my consciousness can, and will, travel at will to wherever it is called.*"

"*But, as a Light Being, you are a physical representation of a soul,*" he replied. "Are you saying that one's soul and one's consciousness are two different things? I had always thought of them as the same."

"In most cases, the two are so intertwined that they are indistinguishable from one another. And yet, for all living things, they are separate. While some biological species can separate the two, only a fraction of those individuals achieve enlightenment. Only us Light Beings can do this at will, because to become a Light Being, one must have mastery over both its soul and its consciousness.

"So, that all being said, because my consciousness traveled to Theronior to witness Gnusaramnii and its minions destroy the entire planet, your consciousness came with mine."

"Right, because we're linked and all that," Navacus replied as he poured the boiling water into his portable teacup. He watched as the tea leaves swirled around in the infuser basket.

"Precisely. You should expect to continue to have dreams like that. You may even see Francentia and her crew again. But it won't happen every time you sleep either."

"That's fine with me. I need to process my own thoughts, and sleep has always helped me with that."

"Indeed, that is why it won't happen every night."

Navacus took a sip of his tea. It was still hot, but the warmth woke him up the rest of the way.

"Well, it certainly will be interesting when it does happen. That was quite intense. But as exciting as it was, we need to get moving."

"Get ready then, I'm not stopping you."

Navacus grinned as put the lid onto his teacup. Even though he was speaking telepathically, he was still acting as if he were having a physical conversation. He shrugged, then stepped into the bathroom.

---

As Navacus headed into the compound, he saw Bsarg standing guard. He smiled and walked over to the dark blue Lakinceitian. Today he smelled minty.

"Bsarg, how's it been going? I haven't seen you in a while."

"It's going fine, Professor. I've been busy training West, so I got the night shift tonight," Bsarg replied.

"Ah, I understand. Tell West hi for me next time you see him."

"Sure thing, Professor. You're here quite early today."

"Yes, I couldn't sleep. I have too many ideas rattling around in my brain, so I figured I'd get an early start to the day."

"I don't know how you do it. Honestly, between you and me, what you did for West is nothing short of a miracle. LSS is a true masterpiece."

"Oh, thank you very much, I appreciate it," Navacus replied, bowing slightly in thanks.

"Well, don't let me get in the way of your genius. Head on in, Professor," Bsarg said with an outstretched arm.

"Thank you, Bsarg. Take care."

"You as well."

Navacus smiled. He had always liked Bsarg. He was the only one of the Lakinceitian guards he could actually have a conversation with.

He stepped into his laboratory and scanned the room.

"Alright, Sterg. What's the best place to start?"

"The propulsion system will take the longest. Start by grabbing some blank motherboards."

"Alright, let's get to soldering."


Navacus stood back to admire his work. It had taken him only an hour and a half to scavenge the parts he needed from the leftover pile and construct three tiny jetpacks, each the perfect size for a Harmertian. Now he was working on securing the tiny jetpacks to three Harmertian-sized hazard suits. They were the only thing around durable enough to handle the tiny battery-powered machines. He needed to modify each one to keep the integrity of the suit while fastening the jetpack. Aside from the jetpack, he made additional modifications to the suits to allow them to travel stealthily.

"I'm impressed," Sterg said out loud. "You're moving twenty percent faster than I had predicted. That's good, as we have little time left."

"And I keep telling you that while my arms and hands are small, what they lack in size they make up for in dexterity."

"Are you sure we're talking about the same thing here?"

He laughed, then looked at the floating sphere of light. "Did you just make a joke?"

"I attempted one, yes. Was it successful?"

"It was awkward, but not bad."

Navacus smiled and went to work on the second suit. As soon as he finished, Sterg tensed up beside him.

"Navacus, you must quickly clean your station. You can finish the last one later. Norman Harrison and Professor Dea are approaching."

"Ah shoot, I ran out of time."

He ran and grabbed an empty plastic tub and carried it over to his workstation, then pushed the suits, jetpacks, and his tools into the tub and carried them into his office. He shoved the tub under his desk and moved his chair to block it from view.

As he moved to step back into the lab, warning sirens flashed through his mind.

"*Navacus, I must go into my dormant state. The Eridavlos can sense my presence. Awaken me when he's gone.*"

"*Okay, sure thing.*"

As Navacus stepped back into the lab, Norman and Professor Dea were entering from the hall.

"Ah, Professor Clums. Good morning, and great timing," Professor Dea said with a smile.

"Good morning to you both, Professor Dea and Norman," Navacus replied as he felt Sterg's presence wane to nearly nothing.

"Are you ready for today?" Professor Dea asked.

"Yes, we are all quite excited for the field test. Should we wait for the rest of my team to arrive before we head out?"

"Certainly," Professor Dea replied.

Navacus felt like he was staring at Professor Dea for a moment too long, so he hastily turned to Norman.

"How have your legs been holding up?"

"They're... well, they're amazing, but it's really strange. While I can feel through them, it's still not the same as before. I guess I'm just not fully accustomed to them yet, but seriously, being able to walk around on my own is so freeing."

"That's great to hear."

"Yes, and not only that, but his mood has dramatically improved as well," Professor Dea said.

"Well, of course my mood's improved. I don't need to ask for assistance every time I need to use the bathroom now."

"That alone would make a big difference," Navacus replied.

They chatted mundanely for a few more minutes before the rest of Navacus' team arrived. Syl, Grasberg, and the Harmertians went to work preparing the vehicular attachment for transportation. Once they were ready, Navacus led everyone outside. Nijork, the security guard currently on duty, greeted them on the way out. They made their way behind the building and into the shade to protect themselves against the intense morning sunlight.

"Alright, so I was thinking that I'll need to know how to swap attachments on my own," Norman said.

"Yes, of course. Give us a moment to get the vehicular attachment unloaded from the dolly," Syl replied.

While the others were preparing the attachment, Professor Dea approached Navacus.

"How's the temperature for you today?" Professor Dea asked.

"It's certainly hot, but nothing I can't handle at this point," Navacus replied.

"Good to hear. By the way, I've been sensing something different about you today. Is everything alright?"

"Oh, well, everything is fine," he replied, tripping over his first few words. "I just had an extremely vivid dream last night and I think it's been effecting me more than I anticipated."

"Some say that our dreams are the link to our most inner fears and desires. Others claim that dreams give us a glimpse into the future. I'm not sure what you believe, but I think both things are true. Only for certain dreams, that is."

Before Navacus could come up with a response, Fumalli approached them.

"Professors, we are ready to begin the field test."

"Wonderful," Professor Dea said.

Navacus breathed a small sigh of relief once Dea turned away. The floating Eridavlos could be quite intense at times. It was as if he could feel Professor Dea's aura, which would make sense, seeing how the Eridavlos use a unique energy to levitate. Navacus had always felt like he was sensitive to such things, but now that he had Sterg along for the ride, his own senses had increased dramatically. Even with Sterg in hibernation, his senses were still more elevated than before.

Navacus shook his head and focused on the field test.

---

Norman Harrison took a deep breath and then flipped open the manual release cover on his legs, and pressed the button to disconnect his grafted-on base from his legs. Even though he was no longer attached to his legs, they still supported his weight.

He looked down at the vehicular attachment that sat beside him and planned out his next move. He guessed he was about half a meter up from the connection point on the vehicular attachment. He took another deep breath and started to swing his arms to gain momentum.

"Now!" he cried as he launched himself from his legs. Movement caught his eye, distracting him, and he saw Professor Bodeelch approaching. He turned his head back in shock, realizing he had over calculated. Norman landed face first in the sand.

"What's going on here?" Professor Bodeelch roared.

"Oh, Professor Bodeelch, I didn't see you arrive," Professor Qymberkon replied.

Norman sat up and spit out a mouthful of sand.

"You see, Norman expressed his interested in learning how to transition from one attachment to the other on his own, so we figured we would give him the chance to try," Professor Clums said.

"That was a stupid idea," Professor Bodeelch said.

"Well, I take full credit for it, then," said as he continued to spit out dirt. "Can someone get me some water and help me up onto this thing?"

Kurjon sprang into action. She rushed over to him and handed him a water bottle. Before taking a drink, he swished out the remaining crud from his mouth.

Professor Bodeelch crossed his arms. "Hrumph. We can't allow our test subjects to endanger themselves."

"Last time I checked, Professor Dea is my direct superior, and *I* am the professor in charge of Norman. You, my friend, oversee Professor Peal. Or am I wrong?" Professor Clums said.

"No, you are not wrong. I was just speaking on behalf of Head Professor Yilvin."

"But you're not Head Professor Yilvin, are you?" Professor Clums said as he glared at his Kolythoanthaean colleague. "Now, let's get Norman back on track."


A few minutes later, Norman was securely hooked up to the vehicular attachment.

"Are you ready, Norman?" Professor Qymberkon asked.

"Ah yeah, I think so. Also, I had a thought," he said, turning to Professor Clums. "How am I going to carry around my attachments? It's not like I can just put them in my pocket."

"You know, I've been so caught up in everything I haven't even thought about that," Professor Clums said. "I'll think about it. I'm sure we can come up with a solution."

"Sure, I'll leave it in your hands then. You've been doing a mighty fine job already," Norman replied.

"Thank you. Now, let's start by just rolling forward about a half-meter or so," Professor Clums told Norman.

Norman took a deep breath. While this wasn't the first time he had tested this attachment out, everything felt completely different from the other times. He could actually *feel* the sand beneath his treads, as if he had two very long, wide feet. And yet, while he felt the heat of the sand, there was no skin to burn, so it wasn't painful. It was just a powerful sensation of hot.

The other difference about today was that in his previous tests, he had had a joystick to control the treads when he needed the extra assistance. Now, the training wheels were off. Just as if he were taking a step, his treads moved forward a few dozen centimeters.

"How's it feel?" Professor Clums asked.

"This is crazy. I know the sand is hot and I know it would burn my skin, but obviously there's nothing to get burned."

"Is that not how you felt walking across the sand in your mechanical legs?" Professor Qymberkon asked.

"Sure, it's a similar feeling, I suppose. But the treads have so much more surface area, so I feel the heat much more intensely."

"Yes, we made sure to include as many nerve endings as possible in the treads, and even in the wheels themselves. We wanted you to feel the ground so you could detect any irregularities while you were moving," Mac said.

"While what Mac is talking about is true, that's for when you are fully accustomed to them," Poi added while giving her brother a playful shove.

"What should I do now?" Norman asked.

"Feel free to move about however you feel most comfortable," Professor Clums said.

"So, are you saying I can go fast if I want to?" he asked.

"Only if you're comfortable with it," Professor Clums answered, eliciting a glare from Professor Bodeelch. "But I would advise to start off slowly."

"Sure thing," he replied.

"Now, remember that we can read your vitals and the stats for the vehicular attachment. And we'll be able to watch through the cameras we've installed in your treads," Syl said.

"Wait, there are cameras in them, too?" Norman asked as he turned and looked directly at the Kolythoanthaean.

"Yes, one in the front and one in the rear. The feed goes directly to our tablets—for now, at least. Once we hand the attachment over to you, you'll take complete control over those cameras. That way, you can watch the footage whenever the need arises," Syl explained.

"Hmm, I guess that makes sense. Sounds like a dash camera that some people use back home. There aren't cameras in my legs, right?"

"Oh no, just in this attachment," Grasberg said.

"Okay, great. I trust you guys, so you better not be lying to me. I don't want you violating my privacy."

"You don't need to—" Syl began before Professor Bodeelch interrupted him.

"As a test subject, you currently have no right to privacy. It's all in the contract you signed."

"Yeah, I signed it. I may not have read the entire thing, though, so I suppose that's on me. But the contract was six hundred pages!"

"Indeed, there are a lot of important terms and stipulations in there. I suggest you go back and freshen up on it when you get the chance," Professor Bodeelch sneered.

"Right, well, enough talk. See you all in a few," he said as he turned toward the Krefna Mountains.

As much as Norman wanted to speed away, he knew he wasn't ready for that, so he took it slow. At a pace of about ten kilometers per Melridion hour, he moved forward while tuning out the argument that was kindling between Professor Clums and Professor Bodeelch.

*What a place this is,* he thought. *You'd think that everyone would get along in a place like this, considering how few of us there are out here. But I suppose that can make tensions higher at times, too. I do understand where Professor Clums is coming from, though. Professor Bodeelch has been interfering with his work. You know what, I can go faster than this.*

He reached for the joystick, then remembered it was gone. He grinned, then let out a hearty laugh as he sped forward.

The Harmertian twins were right. It was as if he could feel every single grain of sand that he passed over. The sensation was nothing like he had ever experienced before, and it was intoxicating. He never knew that he could *feel* such speed.

"This is absolutely amazing!" he yelled, then twisted back and forth in an infinity pattern. "It's like driving, but a billion times better. I *am* the car. My thoughts control my speed, my breaking... How did I get so lucky to—"

He stopped himself short as his thoughts turned to Kate. Suddenly, he didn't feel so lucky; he felt like he was a fool for coming here in the first place. He should have known that there would be a high price to pay for getting these enhancements, but he never imagined that price would be Kate. A fire burned in his chest when his thoughts turned to Professor Bodeelch. That gray dickhead had to know something; otherwise, why was he so damn smug all the time? And that remark about the contract—what if there was something in there related to Kate's disappearance? When he got back to his room, he would study that contract from cover to cover, even if it meant unveiling just a sliver of information.

Norman continued to drive around aimlessly, mulling everything over. It was a great way to let off some steam. He spied a rocky outcrop close by and sped toward it. However, before he could reach it, Syl was calling him back to the compound.

*Oh, right. They probably heard everything I said*, he thought, then shrugged. *I mean, they only own me, so why not allow them to listen to everything I say, too?*

<hr>

"I know Norman is your test subject. Please stop repeating it!" Professor Bodeelch roared.

"Then why are you trying so desperately to interfere with what I'm doing here? I really don't need you to—" Navacus glared at the source of the interruption as he clenched his fists.

"Yes, you do; you absolutely need me," Professor Bodeelch replied.

"Professor Bodeelch, please, could you—" Professor Dea began.

"Quiet, Dea! This does not concern you!"

"Well, actually it does, because the point that Professor Clums is trying to make is that you are overstepping your role here," Professor Dea replied.

"Yes, that is exactly my point! Look, Venkatt, I absolutely respect you, I do. You were a wonderful mentor, but that was a long time ago and only for a few weeks. We're not in basic training anymore. I simply don't understand why you need to constantly hover over everything I do. And honestly, if your interference is required, I wish you would tell me about your visits beforehand," Navacus said with a defiant wheeze.

"Alright Navacus, if you feel that way, then I'll send you a message before I come by. But, again, you do need me. Head Professor Yilvin has deemed it necessary that you require more supervision."

"Then why wasn't I informed?" Professor Dea asked.

"Because you also need more supervision, Professor Dea. So, I don't care if you like it or not, but it is now part of my duty here to watch over you all."

"And what about Professor Peal?" Navacus asked.

"I can't say much about what he's doing, but I can say that we've got everything under control."

"Hey everyone, Norman has nearly returned from the test," Syl said.

Navacus wheezed, then looked up to see Norman approaching them. "We'll talk later then. It sounds like we all need to talk more about this later."

"What more is there to say? Now that you know what's going on, deal with it."

"When did you become such a cold-hearted—"

"Navacus! Please!" Fumalli shouted.

He turned to see Norman idling in front of him.

"Yeah... I'm back," Norman said with an awkward wave.

"That was an exceptional test run," Grasberg exclaimed as he rushed over to him. "Everything was running smoothly, and you handled it perfectly."

"Well, that was the point of the previous tests, right?"

"It was certainly part of the reason we ran those tests. This now proves that all the minor tweaking we've done has paid off. You were fully in control of everything," Syl replied.

"Yeah, it was indescribable. One of the best feelings of my entire life."

"Wonderful, just truly wonderful," Navacus exclaimed. "I'll need to review the data later. I apologize for being so distracted."

"I actually completely understand," Norman said as he glared at Professor Bodeelch.

Professor Bodeelch glared at Norman. "Don't start with me too, now."

"Oh, trust me, I'm not that big of an idiot. In fact, I am going to review my contract tonight."

"Good. I'm glad someone is taking my advice to heart," Professor Bodeelch replied.

"Everyone, if the test is concluded, then I suggest we all head inside before the heat of the day is upon us," Professor Dea announced.

Navacus wheezed. It really was getting hot, and the argument with Professor Bodeelch didn't help.

As they headed back into the compound, Professor Bodeelch requested they send him all their data as soon as they concluded with the post-test. Once inside, Professor Bodeelch grunted and headed toward Professor Peal's wing, while the rest of them filed into Professor Clums' lab.

As soon as the door closed, it seemed as if everyone spoke up at once.

"Hey, one at a time!" Navacus shouted.

"I can help to interpret," Professor Dea offered. "Essentially, many of us feel the same way—that you went too far with Professor Bodeelch today. Before you interrupt, let me just say that I completely understand where you're coming from. Professor Venkatt Bodeelch is a frustrating enigma, but he holds a lot of power here."

"Yeah, I honestly don't know what got into me. He really got on my nerves today. And sure, I said some things I probably shouldn't have, but I feel so relieved to have gotten all of that off my chest.

"Now, it's not like I don't want to hear each of your opinions, but we should get back to work," he continued. "Allow me to review the data from the field test. Norman, if you don't mind, I'd like you to stick around until we finish up with that in case we need to make any final tweaks."

"Sure, that's fine," Norman replied with a nod.

"Good. I want Mac, Poi, and Lyd to make those adjustments. Everyone else, I have detailed the procedure I want you to take to reassemble the hover unit. I want Professor Qymberkon to take lead on this."

"Well, I better get out of your way," Professor Dea said. "If you wouldn't mind, Professor Clums, I'd like to see you in my office when you next get a chance."

"Alright," Navacus replied, then watched as Professor Dea used his ghostly green aura, called a pronosua, to open the door and leave his office. "Well, let's get to it then," he said. As he stepped toward his office door, he turned back to everyone. "Lyd, Poi, and Mac, can you three please see me in my office?"

"Oh, okay," Poi replied.

Navacus held the door to his office open and allowed the three Harmertians to file in. He closed the door behind him and sat down in his chair.

"Is everything okay?" Poi asked.

"Are we in trouble?" Mac asked.

Before he answered, he checked up on Sterg to let him know that Professor Dea had left the area. Sterg pulsed a wave of awareness in response.

"No, you're not in trouble. In fact, I've got an extremely important assignment for you three. Now, this must stay between the four of us. Not even Syl, Grasberg, or Kurjon can know about what's going on.

Fumalli—Professor Qymberkon—is the only other one who is in on this, but all communications must go through me. If any of you have any qualms with these requirements, I ask that you leave this room now."

They looked back and forth between each other, but none of them moved.

"We understand, Professor," Lyd replied.

"Good," Navacus replied. He quickly got them up to speed on the situation with the underground facilities. "... so that's why I need the three of you. You're the only ones small enough to travel through the air ducts. And I even made special suits for the three of you. Well, one still needs to be finalized, but I can do that later tonight."

He pushed himself forward and swiveled his chair around to reveal the plastic tub he had hidden earlier. Beside him, Sterg faded into view. He nodded at his phantasmal friend and pointed to the tub.

"Earlier this morning I modified each of your back-up hazard suits to include a jetpack that will allow you to maneuver down the elevator shaft and into the air ducts. Before I take them out, I will again ask if the three of you are willing to agree to this task."

"Professor, I am absolutely in. I've been asking a lot of my own questions recently, many about what we are even doing out here. If you claim that there is an underground laboratory, and that it's even bigger than the compound, then I must see it for myself," Lyd replied.

"I agree," Poi said. "I would also like to see it."

"Sure, I get that seeing is believing and all that, but shouldn't we exercise just a smidgen of caution here?" Mac asked. "There are a multitude of ways that this could go sour. What if a security camera catches us? What if there is invisible laser detection set up in the air ducts? What if someone hears us? What if someone sees us?"

"Mac, I completely understand your concerns and already have solutions for several of them. First, not only will your jetpacks be able to fly you down and up through the elevator shaft, but they can also expel a breathable gas. This gas will allow you to not only see any invisible security lasers but will also temporarily deactivate them without alerting the system that they are deactivated. Not only that, but I built in a wrist monitor that will scan for the frequencies used by the security cameras. It will allow you to be aware of where those are. As for the other two concerns, I leave the stealth to you. That being said, I added extra padding to the boot soles to dampen your footfalls."

"Professor, how do you even come up with these ideas?" Poi asked. "I'm just in awe. Can we see the suits?"

"Oh yes, let me get those for you." He reached into the tub and dug out each suit. "The one you've got, Poi, is the unfinished one."

They each inspected their suits while nodding in approval.

"These are surely something, Professor," Mac said. "Look, I'm not saying that I don't want to know about anything strange going on beneath our feet, but I'm just trying to look at all the outcomes here. Yes, it would be great if we could go in and come out undetected, but what if we get caught?"

"If you do get caught, then I'll know, since I won't see you tomorrow morning."

"Wait, you mean..." Lyd began.

"Yes, I want you to do this tonight. The time to strike is now. I see little reason to wait. Sure, my argument with Professor Bodeelch may come back to haunt me, but right now, they're not suspicious of anything. So, there's no reason at all for them to be on the lookout for you. But of course, be extremely careful."

"I'm in. What time tonight?" Lyd asked. Poi nodded fiercely beside him.

"Midnight. If possible, slip in while the guards are changing shifts."

"That part won't be too difficult. They already overlook us nearly half the time," Lyd said. Poi laughed in response.

"Okay, well, if we're doing this, then I'm coming along, too. Someone has to watch your backs," Mac said.

"Wonderful. Now, give me back the suits and get back to work. I'll leave them on the floor in my office when I leave tonight."

"Sounds like a plan," Poi said as she handed him the suit.

"Great. Now, can you all review this data with me? I'd like your input and commentary along the way."

"Sure thing," Mac replied as he took out his tablet. "I'll pull everything up and cast it to each of our devices."

*Everything is coming together now*, he thought. *Sterg, were you able to witness the events from today? No? Well, even if you can review my memories, I still want you to watch closely. Let's review this data together. I'd also like you to closely monitor the Harmertians. We can learn a lot from what they don't say as well.*

# 10

# ESCAPE FROM CONTAINMENT

Dasch followed Carl Feng as he led him through an elaborately decorated hallway. Large purple and silver drapes hung to the sides of the many windows, and the walls were painted red with gold filigree. Elegant glass chandeliers were suspended from the vaulted ceiling, and below it, the white marble floor sparkled with gold and silver accents.

The time since he left his cell to now was a blur. He had been whisked away in a glass and metal orb that traveled swiftly through a dimly lit tunnel. The entire journey had been underground. It was only after he entered Lord Foxaire's mansion that he had seen daylight for the first time since leaving Eklatros. Even now, as he passed each window, he relished the few moments he had in each beam of sunlight.

The Gnusar remnant that dwelled inside of him was tugging him forward, as if it knew what lay ahead. And yet, Dasch was surprisingly calm. He had accepted that he may lose his mind to the Gnusar. He was definitely not happy about it, and he felt like he was dishonoring Ànifa's legacy, but there was very little he could do about it. He would fight against it, but he knew he wasn't strong enough, not on this planet at least.

They approached a set of large, wooden double doors, and Carl pushed one open to allow Dasch through. He entered into what looked to be a reception area. There were wooden benches lining the mossy green walls, and a large wooden desk sat in the middle of the room. Behind the desk was a strangely attractive indigo-skinned alien with an egg-shaped head. She had two large black eyes and wore a black dress.

"Gazelle, please inform Lord Foxaire that our guest has arrived," Carl said.

"I already did. I sensed the two of you as you entered the red hall. He's waiting for you," Gazelle said in a smooth voice as she looked into Dasch's eyes.

"Pardon me, but what do you mean, you sensed us? Is that something unique to your species?" Dasch asked.

"Not exactly," Gazelle replied with a smile. "It's something unique to me. Now, please, follow me. Lord Foxaire is waiting."

Gazelle led Dasch and Carl to another set of double doors. As Gazelle walked, Dasch marveled at how each of her three legs carried her along gracefully. He had never seen a three-legged being before and was quite impressed.

Gazelle approached a device in the wall next to the doors, placed her hand on the device, and entered a code. The doors audibly clicked, and the door next to the device swung open several centimeters.

"Okay, we have twenty-four seconds to enter before the doors automatically lock again. Hurry along, now," Gazelle commanded.

Dasch followed Carl through the door with Gazelle following behind him. Once inside the room, it took a few moments for Dasch to truly register what he was seeing.

At this point, he had seen several Lakinceitians, including Professor Durrist, a deep blue Lakinceitian guard, and several others that he passed by throughout the mansion. While each Lakinceitian seemed to have their own unique color and accompanying scent, they had all been roughly the same height—about a meter and a half tall.

Yet the Lakinceitian he faced now was well over two and a half meters tall. Lord Foxaire also had a beard of sorts, consisting of tentacle-like appendages that moved around on their own. Running down his back was a dark green stripe surrounded by bluish circles, while the rest of his hide was nearly black. He did not use any perfume to mask his body odor, and the stench was quite strong, though not particularly unpleasant. It reminded Dasch of his old home—the underground passage and its two rooms hidden beneath Schelff Island. Internally, the Gnusar remnant had quieted down, as if it, too, was fully taking in the spectacle that was Lord Foxaire.

The room he was in was completely covered with paintings, and each painting hung in an elaborate frame. It was horrendously gaudy, as many of the paintings clashed with each other, creating a cacophony of color.

"Dasch Valentine, it is a true honor to finally meet you," Lord Foxaire said, his booming voice encompassing the entire room.

Dasch realized he must have been staring, so he straightened up, cleared his throat, and replied, "You must be Lord Foxaire. You've got a very impressive place."

"So polite, even while in captivity. But don't worry, you won't be our prisoner for much longer."

"Does that mean you're going to let me and my friends go? Theodore, Tyrona, Cecil, and Druder have no right to be locked away in cages."

"The fates of your companions depend on the actions and decisions that you'll make in this room," Lord Foxaire replied.

"Alright, what do I have to do?" Dasch asked. He looked behind him at Carl and Gazelle, but they simply nodded at Lord Foxaire.

"Pay no attention to my associates. Instead, Dasch, look at me. What do you see?"

Was this a trick question? Dasch turned to face Lord Foxaire and looked at him again. This time, the Gnusar remnant pulsed, and understanding dawned on him. The knowledge came from the Gnusar remnant, but now that he knew, it seemed so obvious.

"You... it's you. How have you survived for so long?"

Lord Foxaire made a noise akin to laughter. "Yes, indeed. I am Gnusaramnii's original clone, made back when he was still known as Gnusar. Since I was his first, he spent a long time perfecting me in every way. I look nearly identical to how he appeared back then, and I am as intelligent and cunning as the original. While we essentially share each other's minds, they are separate as well. However, everything it knows, I know, and vice versa. And so, because of this, I survive because Gnusaramnii survives."

The Gnusar remnant's tug returned, stronger than before. "Do you feel the remnant inside of me?"

"I do. I can feel how much it desires to return to its full state."

"I want this as well. Maybe that's the remnant talking, but I can't help it. I want to let it out—I'm so tired of fighting it. But what will become of me—Dasch Valentine?"

"I don't know. Yours is a unique case, Dasch. Never before has anyone of any species resisted the call to Gnusaramnii's divine will for so long. Your mind is sharp, even while it unravels. I am curious to see what the outcome will be. I have been waiting a long time for this day."

"So, what do I—"

Two tentacles burst out of Lord Foxaire and flew at Dasch. They wrapped around him, squeezing under his clothes to feel his body. Upon contact, electrical shocks shot through him, reigniting the Gnusar remnant.

At the last second, he threw everything he had at the Gnusar, but he could do nothing to stop it. It burst from its cavity in his chest and wrapped around his muscles and his ligaments. He felt it flowing with the blood in his veins. Within moments, it was in his brain.

He twitched. What a strange feeling this was. The half-elf who had been in control for so long could not be completely eradicated. A small remnant of him remained. Much like how he had once been captive inside of this body, so too will the consciousness of Dasch Valentine be trapped. And yet, he was free—finally free of his shackles. He could now be who he was truly meant to be.

The tentacles withdrew and returned to the original clone.

"How do you feel?"

"Elated," he said as he studied his hands. "I am once again born anew. Here, on the planet of my birth, do I now return. You have done well, Lorphax."

"Gnusar? Is it you?"

"Alas, not anymore. However, at the moment of my rebirth, my consciousness mingled with Gnusaramnii's, imprinting a copy of it. So, I am only a copy of Gnusaramnii's consciousness. Beyond that, I am just me, with a sliver of Dasch remaining. Your link to the divine one is stronger than mine."

"Ah, so Dasch really was that strong. In that case, how does the name Gnudasch sound to you?"

"Gnudasch... it contains too much of what I was before. If I am to hold a unique title, I would like it to be Gnudashar."

"Gnudashar, I, Lorphax Nare, welcome you to Melridion. We have been waiting a long time for your arrival."

"Why have you been waiting for me when you are Gnusar's most complex clone?" Gnudashar asked.

"You are the one who will lead the way for Gnusaramnii's eminent return. We trust you to be our guide, Gnudashar. As our guide, what will you have us do?"

"I don't understand. You, the one whose mind is connected to Gnusaramnii, turn to me for guidance?"

"Our minds are linked, yes. But, as you surely know, Gnusaramnii is recovering from a devastating wound. It is currently focused on healing and consuming. That is why you must be the one to guide us. You, who have walked both paths and have experienced Eklatros— the key to Gnusaramnii's return."

"If you look to me for guidance, then please allow me some time to organize my mind. There are multiple sets of memories within me.

Between my own and Dasch's—which are nearly identical, but not fully—and Gnusaramnii's, there's a lot to unravel. And that's not even including the memories Dasch absorbed from that hybrid creature, Ànifa Ekataramnii. Her memories could also hold a lot of useful knowledge."

"Of course. While Dasch obtained her memories, none of them reached you. Take all the time you need. When you are ready, Carl will lead you to your quarters," Lorphax said.

"Yes, Carl. Why do you keep one such as him around you? Why do you not enhance him like you did with the Nioavellian?"

In response, Carl glared at him while audibly grinding his teeth.

"I need Carl to stay the way he is. While I truly enjoy Professor Durrist's work—Gazelle is a masterpiece—I need someone I can trust who is unmodified. Carl has been by my side for seventeen years. He has proven his loyalty time and time again. He is perfect the way he is now."

"If you say so. Gazelle, I'm curious, what are you sensing now with your abilities?" Gnudashar asked.

"Your aura is unlike any other I have ever felt. When you, I mean Dasch Valentine, first arrived, his energy was pure, full of understanding and acceptance. It radiated a golden hue. When you, Gnudashar, took control, that golden hue became consumed by dark purple vines. And now, you emanate both—the dark purple of Gnusaramnii along with a faint accent of gold and pops of blue."

"You can see my aura?" he asked.

"Yes, along with much more. You emanate curiosity, with a hunger for knowledge and understanding. You seek answers."

"I do. Lorphax, I shall call upon you once I have uncovered more knowledge."

"Wonderful. Now, only call me Lorphax when we are here, in this room—my private quarters. In all other occasions, you must call me Lord Foxaire."

"Certainly. I understand you must protect your disguise," he replied.

"Indeed. Now, Carl, show our exalted guest to his quarters."

"Of course, my lord," Carl said with a deep bow.

Gnudashar turned to follow Carl, then stopped for a moment and turned back around. "So, what are you actually going to do with Dasch's companions?" he asked.

"The current plan is to wait to start on any new projects until after the move. We are also awaiting the results of the mind fusion that Tyrona and another Human woman are currently undergoing. Professor Durrist predicts that should be completed by the end of next week," Lorphax replied.

"Why so long?"

"Fusing two minds into one is a fragile process. It cannot be rushed or tampered with in any way. That being said, his predictions have been wrong before, so anything could happen."

"Fair enough. While you are talented, you are nowhere near Gnusaramnii's level. Also, I'd like to have a chat with Theodore, Cecil, and Druder."

"Certainly. Just say the word and I'll have it arranged."

"Thank you. Now, I must be going."

---

Gazelle unlocked the doors to Lord Foxaire's chambers, allowing Carl and Gnudashar through. The door closed heavily behind them. The reception room always felt lonely and stale without Gazelle. He quickly led Gnudashar through and into the red hall.

"Tell me, Carl. What brought you and Lord Foxaire together?" Gnudashar asked.

Carl swallowed. He hadn't been expecting such a blunt question from someone he was still struggling to understand. Ten minutes ago, Dasch had simply been a strange human from an alien planet. Now, he was a Gnusaramnii duplicate—the prophet for whom the Lakinceitian race had been waiting a millennium for. He always suspected that he would be at the forefront of Gnusaramnii's return, but this was not what he had been expecting.

"Carl, I would like an answer, please," Gnudashar instructed.

He nodded. He would reveal as little possible to this strange prophet.

"When I was a teenager, I kept getting into trouble. The people on Carange got tired of cycling me through the foster care system, so they sent me off-planet, to Melridion. That's when I met Lord Foxaire. He took me in and molded me into what I am today. I owe everything that I am to Lord Foxaire and I truly would do anything for him."

"Ah, so you're an orphan. Someone with no real home. Part of me can sympathize, as Dasch and Ànifa both felt similarly at times. Do you remember your birth parents?"

"I do," he replied. Of course he remembered them. It didn't matter how many times he willed himself to forget them—they would always return to him in one way or another. They had been so happy together—a happiness that he bore as a curse, for he wished he had never experienced it. It was the one thing that held him back from being fully committed to Lord Foxaire and the divine plan.

Carl stopped in front of a door—one of only three doors that lined the red hall.

"These are your quarters. Lord Foxaire has long prepared for this day, but if there is anything more you need, please press the white button next to the door. Either I or Gazelle will answer your call."

"Wonderful. I'll speak with you soon then," Gnudashar said as he opened the door and shut it behind him.

Carl straightened his glasses. He had perfect vision, so the glasses had no prescription, but the gesture had become a habit. The glasses he wore were constantly transmitting video and audio to a large database that only Lord Foxaire could access. This was a secret that only he and Lord Foxaire knew about, and Carl intended to keep it that way.

He stood in front of the door and stared at it as if it would somehow come alive and attack him.

*And so, the fabled prophet has returned,* he thought. *The prophecy was actually true, up until now, at least. I fear this prophet has been tainted by all the minds that swirl within him. Plus, he said that a sliver of Dasch remains. I must keep a close eye on him. I just wish that I had super senses like Gazelle, or enhanced vision like Svetlana or West. I mean, I know I had initially requested to not get enhancements… but now, after seeing them in action, I was a fool to turn down the opportunity. Granted, that was ten years ago—I would have simply been fodder for Professor Durrist's initial experiments. But still, I wish Lord Foxaire would let me get something. If not from Durrist, then from Professor Clums.*

He shook his head and sighed. *It's all a fool's hope. I am at the will and command of Lord Foxaire.* He took out his phone and stared at the lock screen. *I should talk to Sid. Discreetly, of course. He's always been loyal to me. Us Humans need to stick together.*

<hr>

Dasch Valentine was alone in the dark. From what he could gather, it appeared as if he was in the underground prison he had been in when he was still waging his war against the Gnusar remnant. Yet now, he had lost that war and was a prisoner in his own body. It was only fitting for his mind to trap him here.

The only light source came from a screen of sorts that was projected onto whichever wall he found himself facing. He discovered that when he focused on the screen, he could see and hear what was going on around his body, but when he wasn't focusing on it, it was only a blur and murmur in the background. He did his best to focus on everything the creature was doing, even if he didn't like what he was seeing.

He considered it abhorrent that the name the monster was using was Gnudashar. He didn't want any part of his own name used by the abomination. But he knew from experience that no matter what he tried, Gnudashar wouldn't listen to him, for he had no idea that the remnant had been so uniquely intelligent. Unless it had been the war he waged against it that had crafted it into what had become.

*I have truly failed you, Ànifa,* he thought. *Through Gnudashar, Gnusaramnii now has access to your memories and knowledge. I never should have come to this vile planet. I never should have fought by your side. I never should have left my underground prison in the first place.*

*I've failed you, Ànifa. Theodore, Cecil, Druder, Tyrona… I am so sorry. If I ever get the chance to retake control of my own body, I will do what I should have done in the first place—obliterate it. Because at this point, neither one of us can survive without the other, and I cannot allow this remnant to live.*

**11**

# ESCAPE FROM THE UNDERGROUND

Lyd of the Yan Clan crept silently into Professor Clums' office with Mac and Poi in tow. The three modified orange-colored hazard suits were lying on the ground, just like Professor Clums had promised.

"Last chance to back out," Poi whispered to her brother.

"I already told you, I'm not letting you go without me. You'll need me," Mac replied quietly. "Besides, I don't feel like sneaking past the guards with Bsarg, Nijork, and West around."

"Yeah, that was too much. But I wasn't expecting to see West. What would he do if he saw us? Would he hurt the ones who helped make him?" Poi asked.

"I doubt it, and I don't think he saw us. Either way, we'll need to rely on each other," Lyd whispered. "We need to be extremely careful. As we decided earlier, I will be in charge of leading us through the vents, Poi will be in charge of drawing the map, and Mac will be in charge of looking out for any traps or cameras and ensuring that no one discovers us."

"Right, I know, I was just joking. I know I need to be serious, but I'm very nervous. I can't help it," Poi whispered.

"I understand, just try your best to contain it until we're back to safety," Lyd replied. "Now, let's be quick about this—we don't have all night. We need to be back up here by five at the latest. That gives us just about four and a half hours."

"And that means there will be three hundred and sixty chances for us to get caught," Mac whispered. "Of course, we won't, not with me around."

Lyd approached his suit, then started taking off his clothing, leaving only his underclothes. Beside him, Mac and Poi were doing the same. He sneaked a quick glance in Poi's direction. He had long been attracted to her, but with Mac always around, he never seemed to get the chance to tell her how he felt. He shook his head and pulled on the hazard suit. It was nearly skin-tight, but perfectly insulated to regulate his body temperature. They had actually helped to design these suits—it was their very first project at Foxaire Biotech Industries.

Once on, Lyd toyed with the wrist monitor that Professor Clums installed. He ran a quick test scan in the room for any security frequencies. As expected, the reading was negative.

"Whoa, this suit is stellar. It's almost like we now have enhancements of our own," Poi whispered.

Mac nodded. "So, we need to head back to the lab, right?"

"Yes. Professor Clums had mentioned he would set up a way for us to climb into the ceiling. From there, once we make sure the area is unmonitored, we will make our way to the hidden elevator shaft," Lyd explained. "Now, remember, there is no talking in the underground. We can only use hand signals or laser-point umpty code. I'd like to enact this as soon as we leave this room."

"Got it," Poi replied.

"Let's just do a quick run-through of our systems, just so there are no surprises, then we can climb into the ceiling."

They ran through each component together. First, they turned on the suits' headlamps. Then, they tested their wrist monitors. Next, they tested the jetpacks' smokescreens, and indeed, this revealed Mac's invisible laser. Finally, they tested the jetpacks themselves. Unlike fuel-powered jetpacks, these were essentially smaller versions of the hover unit they were building for Norman. However, the design was altogether different, as a Harmertian weighed a fraction of what a Human did. Each of them hovered ten centimeters off the ground for ten seconds, then lowered themselves back to the ground.

"How did the Professor build these jetpacks in just a few short hours?" Mac whispered. "These are incredibly advanced."

"I don't know. A lot has been off about him lately," Lyd replied. "Even this request is odd, but it is our job to see the task through. Now, no more talking. I'm looking at you, Poi."

"I know, I'll do my best," Poi replied with a smile. "Oh, does everyone have their tablets?"

"Shoot, thanks for the reminder," Mac said. He bent down and picked up his pants, then dug into his pockets until he found his tablet.

Lyd looked at them and signaled *okay*?

Mac and Poi nodded simultaneously. Lyd nodded back and then headed into the lab.

He made his way to the back table and used the ladder built into the leg of the table to climb up. From there he made his way to a stack of books, upon which was a desk lamp. It was pointed straight at the ceiling. Even though it was resting against a microscope, it would still be unsteady.

"That doesn't look very safe," Poi whispered.

Lyd turned to her and put his hand over his mouth.

"Right, sorry. Shoot!" Poi whispered, then made a motion like she was zipping up her mouth.

Lyd nodded then climbed up the books and onto the lamp. It was surprisingly sturdier than he had expected. Once he made it to the ceiling, he pushed up the ceiling tile and moved it out of the way, creating a gap just big enough for them to climb through.

He poked his head into the dark, dusty passageway and turned on his headlamp. All clear. He climbed up and then reached down to help Poi. As soon as she was up, she activated her tablet and began creating the map.

Lyd turned back to help Mac up into the ceiling. He took a moment to study his surroundings. Poi signaled to him, *the wall.*

He nodded, then led them over to the nearest wall and followed it until they were above the hallway. It didn't take long for the trio to find the rows of cables that helped to power the elevator. They followed those and found themselves staring down into a deep, dark passage.

Lyd nodded and held up a hand, asking Mac and Poi to stay put. He activated his jetpack, took a deep breath, and stepped over the edge. He hovered in midair, suspended by the jetpack. He looked at the others and nodded. Poi let out a small squeal when she stepped over the edge and received an elbow jab from Mac in response.

They quickly lowered themselves into the dark passage. Lyd looked down into the deep, but his headlamp didn't reveal the bottom. And while the jetpack did give off some light, it was essentially insignificant. As they descended, he had to marvel at how quiet the jetpacks were. They didn't even create an echo.

After what felt like several minutes of descending, they landed on top of the elevator. Poi took out her tablet and swiftly updated the map. Lyd wondered if her guess was the same as his—roughly one hundred and thirty-eight meters. A very long way down, if his calculations were correct.

Lyd looked at Mac, who gave him a nod for *all clear*, then made his way over to the air duct grate, where he took out his tool and unscrewed the screws. In no time, the grate was off and the three of them headed into the air ducts.

They entered a large rectangular chamber that split into seven different passageways, not including the path they took from the elevator. The passageways were located in the corners of the rectangle and in the center of each of the sides. The path they took to reach the chamber was located on one of the sides. Lyd pointed at the corner passage located directly to their right.

Above them spun a large, loud fan that pumped air into the ducts from the surface. The pressure of the air pushing down on them was quite strong but still manageable, especially since the hazard suits' boot soles gripped to nearly any surface. When they reached the entrance to the first corner passage, Mac took out his tablet and scanned the area. While he was doing this, Lyd used his wrist monitor. Negative—no camera frequencies found. Mac gave the okay to continue.

Once they entered the corner passage, the air pressure eased back to normal levels. The progress was slow going, due to security checks every five meters or whenever they passed a vent or fan. The first few vents led to dark rooms, filled with large machines and computers. Whatever the machines were powering, it must have been something big.

As they slowly made their way down the air duct, Lyd watched as Poi drew the map. From what he could tell, the map was extremely detailed. He smiled. It had been a long time since they had engaged in an activity that wasn't science related. He could finally use his innate sense of direction and distance. All Harmertians were expert navigators, so he often took it for granted. Being in the dark, underground air duct made him reflect on his ancestors. As the stories went, before the Harmertian migration, most Harmertians lived underground in a mass network of tunnels and caverns. The surface of their home world had been inhospitable—a violent place full of geysers, pools of methane, volcanoes, acid rainstorms, and more horrors. That's why they built their ark in the first place—to seek out a new home world. In their current situation, they were only seeking information, but he still felt akin to his ancestors.

It took them nearly an hour to reach the end of the first air duct. Unlike the other rooms they passed, the final room was fully illuminated. As peered down through the vents, he discovered what the computers were powering. A massive stone archway sat in the center of the large room. A set of large cables that came down from the ceiling and traveled along the walls and floor were hooked up to the archway. Standing guard was a pale gray Lakinceitian, who seemed to have an antenna sprouting out of its head. The Lakinceitian appeared to be asleep with its eyes open or in a trance of some kind. He shivered and stood up.

Poi was still finishing her map of the archway room while Mac continued to check his wrist monitor for any unwanted frequencies. Lyd had no idea what the purpose of the archway was, but judging from the cables and the rooms of computers they had passed, he suspected it might be related to teleportation, which had never been perfected and was now a banned technology. Too many scientists lost their lives in pursuit of making a teleportation device, so the intergalactic senate had banned any research related to it.

Once the trio was ready, they made their way back to the main airflow room at a much quicker pace. Once they were back, Lyd checked the time. It was it was nearly two o'clock. They had roughly three hours left.

They went counterclockwise and headed into the next passageway, creeping along the wall to avoid some of the air pressure from the fan above them. As before, there were no concerning frequencies or laser security systems present.

The second passageway they went down was quite different from the first. All the intermittent vents and fan systems they passed seemed to lead to a peculiar hallway. While it was difficult to tell by looking down through the vents, it appeared as if the passageway twisted and turned, leading to false rooms. While Lyd had always known Lakinceitians were a paranoid species, building dead-end hallways and rooms with no ventilation seemed extreme. It would be easy to get lost in a place like this. At least the ventilation system was straightforward and organized, just like a good ventilation system should be.

About thirty minutes later, they found themselves facing another chamber that was divided into eight other passageways. However, this chamber was round, not a rectangle like the main one.

While Poi was updating the map, Mac and Lyd scanned the area. This time, there was a faint trace of security frequencies, but nothing that was an imminent threat to them. Plus, the smokescreen test revealed there were no lasers, so they headed into the chamber. In the center of the chamber was a vent. They approached it, but there was nothing to see below, just an empty floor.

Like before, they took the path to their right. Rather than leading to another long hallway, the vent was only about a meter away from the chamber.

Lyd approached first and peered down into the vent. While the room below was completely empty, a foul stench was emanating from below. It took him a few moments to recognize the smell, then he jumped back.

Mac and Poi looked at him in concern, so Lyd took out his laser pointer and sent a message in umpty code. *I'm okay. I was just surprised. The room below us is empty. While you can't smell it from here, the room smells like death. Something bad happened here.*

Poi shook her head, then signed, *Bad feeling. Next room.* Mac nodded in agreement.

Lyd gave them a nod and headed back into the circular chamber. He asked them to wait in the chamber while he checked out the other vents. The next four he checked were all empty, and each one reeked of death. As he entered the short passageway for the fifth room, he immediately sensed that something was different. This time he motioned for Mac and Poi to follow him into the meter-long passage.

Lyd looked at Poi and gave her a small smile, then glanced at Mac, who nodded at him. He took a deep breath and peered down into the room below. The beam of his headlamp fell straight into the eyes of a large, deep brown Ancilsan, who promptly screeched. Lyd fell over and turned off his headlamp while Poi quickly knelt down next to him and put a hand on his shoulder.

Lyd placed a hand over hers and smiled, then nodded, as if to say "I'm okay." Poi nodded back. Lyd turned back to the vent.

Lyd peered into the room and saw the Ancilsan look up at them.

"Who are you?" the Ancilsan whispered. "Are you here to rescue me?"

While the Ancilsan was speaking, Poi had gotten in between him and Mac and was also looking down into the room.

"Hello there," Poi said quietly. "We're sorry for frightening you. I'm Poi, this is my brother Mac, and this is Lyd. Ow."

Both he and Mac had elbowed her at the same time. She glared at them, and when they shook their heads, she shrugged in response. Her message was clear—the box had been opened.

"Hello, little Harmertians from the vents. I am called Altun. I've been imprisoned and tortured for what feels like an eternity, though my best guess puts me at eight months."

"Eight months?" Poi yelled the first word before her senses kicked in. "I'm sorry, we're not here to rescue you. We're only here to gather information. We had no knowledge of this area until earlier today."

"I see. Once you gather the information you require, I humbly urge you to send help."

"We will do what we can. I apologize we can't do more," Poi replied.

"Oh, on the contrary, you've done more than you know. You've reignited my will to live. There is now hope."

"Hope is a powerful thing," Mac whispered. "It is an honor to have given that back to you. We will not forget you, Altun."

"Mac, Poi, Lyd. I will not keep you, and I do not want to alert anyone to your presence. Be safe."

"Be safe," the three of them replied in unison.

Lyd turned his headlamp back on and signed to the others, *no talking.* Poi and Mac nodded in unison.

Lyd led them to the next vent and turned his headlamp off. He peered in and was again met by a rank smell. His breath caught in his throat, but not because of the smell. This time the occupant was a Yggdrazim. Before he had met Professor Clums, he had only ever seen other Yggdrazim in passing or in the media. Now, every time he saw a Yggdrazim, he couldn't help but compare them to the professor.

The Yggdrazim was extremely gaunt. Its gray feathers were strewn across the room, while only mangled clumps of plumage remained on its body. It was barely alive; he doubted it would survive another week.

Lyd tore his gaze away from it and looked back at his friends. Mac nodded at him, then started flashing his laser pointer. *I've identified the source of the security frequencies. It's actually a mixture of frequencies. I am picking up three security cameras, three motion detectors, and three sets of bio-monitoring systems. All are based in the rooms below; I don't see any way that any of those sensors could have or will detect our presence.*

Lyd nodded and replied in kind. *Good to know. What about audio?*

Mac shook his head. *No audio systems detected. They must be offline. My guess is that they don't want to listen to them.*

*I see. The person below us is a very weak Yggdrazim. I fear that no matter what we do, they will not survive for long.*

*Those bastards!* Poi replied as she furiously tapped on and off her laser pointer. *Do they get enjoyment from watching others suffer?*

*It's possible. We must continue on. We have less than two hours left. Let's check out the last room, and then see what the next main passageway is about.*

Mac nodded. Poi was still visibly upset, so Mac took her aside while Lyd went to check out the last room.

This time, the smell emanating from the room below was stronger than the other rooms. He looked down through the vent and saw a skin-and-bones Eridavlos. Rather than hovering above the ground naturally, she lay slumped in a corner, drool running down her chin. Various tubes and machines were hooked up to her. Lyd suspected the machines were the only reason she still breathed. He wasn't sure if he even wanted to know what use they could have for half-dead Eridavlos.

Lyd sniffed back a tear and approached Mac and Poi. Mac was embracing a silently sobbing Poi. Rather than explain what he had seen, Lyd somberly shook his head, then motioned for them to follow him. Poi nodded weakly.

As they exited the area, Poi regained her composure and followed Lyd out with a sense of conviction. When they reached the main area, Poi signed to Lyd, *There is still some time left. Please, continue. Mac is going to take me back up. Take my tablet; you should be able to continue the map on your own.*

Lyd nodded, took the tablet, and gave Poi a hug. He then clasped Mac's shoulder. Mac nodded, then led Poi back to the elevator shaft. Lyd watched them until they disappeared into the tunnel. He took a deep breath, then hurried into the next ventilation shaft. Every few meters he scanned the area, and luckily, no threatening frequencies were found. At the end of the air duct, he found himself in another circular chamber. This time there were only five other paths to take rather than eight like before. The vent in the center of the room also led to an empty floor.

This time, Lyd got the urge to check out the rooms from left to right. Judging from the last chamber, he wanted to get the most depressing rooms out of the way first. Before checking out the first of the five rooms, he ran another security scan and updated the map.

As he approached the first room to his left, the smell that greeted him was of nature. As he looked down below, he noticed that the room was split into four different sections. Three of the four sections each held a different animal. Lyd rotated to each side of the vent to get a better look at the creatures below. First, he saw a strange animal that could only be a Zubula or a Zubba from Acampachetli. He didn't know much about Acampachetlian wildlife, but he had at least heard of the unique creatures. In the next section he had to search hard to spot the stick bug. It was larger than most stick bugs he had seen before and assumed it must also come from Acampachetli. The last section held a blood-red snake.

Turning away from the vent, he realized that he was looking down into Professor Peal's experiments. That must mean Professor Peal was now working underground, which would explain why he hadn't seen him or his assistants in a while.

Lyd updated the map then moved onto the next room. When he ran his security checks, he picked up on a familiar signal. After a little digging, he realized that the signal was coming from West's Life Support System.

*Wait a minute, why is West here?* Lyd thought. *Did Professor Peal want to talk to West?*

Lyd looked down into the vent and saw West sitting in the center of the room, facing a large, purple, six-legged lizard. After a few seconds, they both turned and looked directly at him. Lyd yelped in surprise, then dashed away from the vent. His heart pounded in his chest as he stood against the wall of the air duct.

*I need to get out of here. Now.*

Lyd moved as quickly as he allowed himself. He still needed to run security checks every so often—he couldn't allow himself to become careless. Not when the danger was this real.

When he finally made it back to the elevator shaft, he yelped in surprise to find an empty elevator shaft. He immediately looked up to where it had ascended. This was bad. While he could still ascend the shaft, he would have nowhere to run if the elevator descended, and he didn't know how fast an elevator like this could move. At the very least, there was no sign of Mac or Poi. Lyd took out his tablet and typed Mac a private message.

> Hey Mac, did you sleep well?

It took about a minute to get a response.

> Very well. Poi is still resting. How about you?

Lyd smiled. They had made it back safely. Before he replied, he took a moment to really let his situation sink in. He already knew that he didn't want to ascend without knowing more about the elevator itself, and yet, the elevator could descend in just a few minutes, or it could be hours. He had to come up with a solution.

As he examined the elevator shaft, he keyed into the tracks that the elevator's wheels connected into. The elevator moved along these tracks to ascend and descend without cables. He realized that if he could hook into those tracks, he could sense vibrations. Luckily, Professor Clums hadn't touched the utility pocket that was built into the hazard suit. While there wasn't much in there, he knew he could use the contents to rig up something. Before he got into it, though, he replied to Mac.

> I had a dream that I was trapped. It was
> pretty scary, but I'm working through it now.

It took him about twenty minutes to build the makeshift vibration detector using some multi-use wire, spare motherboards, magnets, and various other components. It took another ten minutes to get the signal connected to his wrist monitor. When he was finished, he checked the time. It was 4:71. He had to hurry.

He ran a few baseline tests of the new vibration detector, and all readings were negative. Then, as almost an afterthought, he gave the signal a slight boost. While he wasn't too keen on leaving behind evidence of his presence, if it went unnoticed, he should be able to get notifications each time the elevator descended or ascended.

When he was ready, Lyd took a deep breath and started up his jetpack. After a few minutes, he stared at the bottom of the elevator. While he wouldn't be able to squeeze past it, he had taken note of a vent several meters down. He descended and immediately got to work unscrewing the vent. When he had one screw left, his wrist monitor chimed. He looked up and saw the elevator shudder. Lyd finished removing the final screw, then tore off the grate and jetted into the ventilation shaft. Moments later, the elevator whooshed past him.

He breathed a sigh of relief, then realized that in his haste, he had dropped the grate. He would have to deal with that another time. For now, with the elevator descending, he had a clear path up into the ceiling.

Before he knew it, he was back in Professor Clums' lab, happily embracing Mac and Poi. They had one final task left—sneaking back out of the compound. For that, they had to wait for Professor Clums' signal. He was to distract the guard while they sneaked out, which would be any second now.

*What a night,* Lyd thought. *That was draining, both physically and emotionally. Even though I had prepared myself for the worst... actually seeing it, and smelling it, is entirely different. I just hope that Professor Clums gives us a nice break today. I'm not sure I will be able to give it my all.*

# 12

# ESCAPE FROM REALITY

West lay in bed, trying to ignore the throbbing pain in his chest. He found it odd how part of the time he was completely pain-free and other times the pain crept back in. As for tonight, the pain was the worst it had been in weeks.

*I should speak to Professor Clums about this. Aside from our brief interaction the other night, it's been too long since I've seen him.*

He sighed and sat up. He couldn't sleep, so there was little point in just lying in bed. He had always been bad at sitting still, unless it involved hunting a target.

His mind flashed to Newtus and the thought of her hunting for Loxocemae eggs. As the large lizard prowled through the underbrush, she turned and looked directly at him, her eyes piercing into his. He yelped in surprise and his heart lurched. He hadn't been expecting that, even though he had only been imagining the scene.

Much to his surprise he began putting on his uniform—black pants, a utility belt, and a black vest. He wasn't sure why, but he wanted to see Newtus.

Before he knew it, he was locking up his apartment and heading outside. The crisp nighttime air felt great. This was exactly what he needed. The pain in his chest was already receding. He stepped out from underneath the covered walkway and stared into the night sky. After a few moments, he spotted the dim, orange-tinted planet Ijurvoll. It had been too long since he had been back home, and he feared it would be a long time before he could return. He didn't really have any family or friends to go back to, but he still longed to visit his hometown.

Behind him, Bsarg was approaching.

"Hey West, it isn't your shift yet."

"Good evening, Bsarg. Or should I say night? Anyway, yes, I know. I couldn't sleep."

"I see. I won't disturb you then," Bsarg said without stopping.

"It's fine. I'll walk with you—I was going to the compound anyway," he said as he turned away and started following Bsarg.

"Why? Are you going to see that lizard again?"

"How did you know?"

"Well, for one, you couldn't stop talking about her yesterday."

"Ah, I suppose you're right," West said with a chuckle. "It's strange. I've just never met anyone like her before."

Bsarg grunted. "Just don't get too attached. You should know better than anyone what goes on around here."

"Yes, I understand," he replied as he tipped his white cowboy hat forward.

They approached the doors to the compound and were greeted by Nijork.

"Good to see you, Bsarg. I can now finally rest. West, are you on guard duty, too?"

As Nijork was speaking, West thought he sensed a familiar presence. He elevated his sphere of awareness and didn't find anything, which wasn't surprising. LSS still gave him notifications of things that he didn't want to be notified about. He would need to tweak the settings later. After a few moments he looked at Nijork, who was patiently waiting for him to respond.

"Ah, sorry Nijork. I've just been having a strange night. I am not on guard duty; I just couldn't sleep."

"He's on his way to go see Professor Peal's Neutortous again," Bsarg said as he leaned toward Nijork.

Nijork shuddered. "Bah, I hate reptiles. I don't see how you can stand to be around one. But you do you. Have a good night."

West waved goodnight to Nijork, then nodded to Bsarg.

"Don't forget that we're meeting up at 16 o'clock," Bsarg said.

"Right, I'll set a reminder alarm now," West said as he configured the alarm within his mental database. He then waved to Bsarg and headed inside the compound. The lights were dimmed and it was colder than it was during the day. He liked when it was like this; being a Eusphyrchiian from Ijurvoll, where the temperature stayed relatively cool, he always preferred colder temperatures.

As West passed Professor Clums' lab, he remembered that he wanted to send him a message. He stopped and quickly composed an email, detailing his chest pain and the strange signals that LSS gives him from time to time. Once the message was sent, he made his way to the elevator.

---

West sat cross-legged on the floor. All his senses were focused on the purple Neutortous that sat across from him. He knew Newtus was still getting used to her extra two legs, but she managed them gracefully. She lay in front of the transparent barrier with her body curved in a way that her tail nearly wrapped around herself.

He was really enjoying Newtus' company. He had only been with her for a few minutes and he already was calmer and fully pain free.

*"I'm glad you're feeling better,"* Newtus said telepathically as she smiled. *"It must be because of me."*

*"I think you're right. It's strange; when I got up, you flashed through my mind. At the time my chest hurt, but the pain is now gone."*

*"Indeed. It is due to our connection. You see, Neutortous' have a strong connection with one another because of our psychic link. We can communicate without using words by reading each other's emotions. When*

*someone is sad, we can lift their spirits by sending them calming energy. You are not Neutortous, and yet we are linked in a similar way."*

*"I just sent a message to Professor Clums, but I should ask him about this as well. I was not modified using any biological parts, only technology. Somehow, the frequencies that LSS uses are perfectly in sync with yours— and Theesakin's for that matter."*

*"This Professor Clums, do you trust him?"*

*"I do, for the most part. He and his team have always been kind to me."*

*"I see,"* Newtus responded as she broke her gaze from his.

*"Do you not want me to ask him about our connection?"*

Newtus lifted her eyes to him. *"I don't see how it would make any difference to me. I am imprisoned here."*

*"Yes, as you mentioned, we both are trapped here,"* West replied.

*"You have come to understand this. That's good. Have you seen Theesakin recently?"*

*"Yes, I saw him and the other Titans again yesterday. Professor Durrist is still quite keen on me learning more about them. He thinks I can help him solve some of the problems he's been having with them. What those problems are, though, I don't know. At least I read to Theesakin for a while yesterday—it was a book about the history of the intergalactic community."*

*"Sounds interesting. I just can't help but wonder if I can speak with Theesakin telepathically as well."*

*"I still need to spend more time with him to confirm this, but I have my suspicions. I think that Theesakin may have been created using Neutortous DNA, as well as DNA from several other Acampachetlian species. He must also include a Human or a Kolythoanthaean, because how else could he have that body shape?"*

*"You don't think he could be from your own species?"* Newtus asked.

*"I suppose it's a possibility, as I know little about how this all works. But his hide is scaly. If he was a Eusphyrchiian, I would imagine his hide to be more akin to a shell like mine. Of course, I could be completely wrong about all my assumptions."*

*"And yet you are confident that you are right,"* Newtus replied.

"*I do think I am right. But over-certainty can be one's downfall. I've seen it happen before.*"

"*In the IBHA, you mean?*"

"*Yes. The newest, least experienced bounty hunters tend to be quite cocky. They think that they're all that since they got accepted into the Intergalactic Bounty Hunter Association. But if you aren't a quick learner, you'll be dead before you complete your first mission.*"

"*Were you one of those overconfident new recruits?*"

"*To some degree, yes. I nearly screwed up my first mission. The target was a Eusphyrchiian woman who was wanted for poisoning several high-profile men. When the moment came, I hesitated. I was struck by her beauty. Luckily, the weapon she had hastily grabbed wasn't loaded, so I got the upper hand in the end.*"

"*You have such a gentle soul for having such a ruthless profession.*"

"*Right, well, throughout my years as a bounty hunter, rather than growing cold to the killing, each hit would affect me differently. There were some I wept over and others that I celebrated—if they had been evil enough to deserve such an inappropriate response. And yet, I never truly wanted to quit. Being a bounty hunter gives you certain privileges and freedoms that are hard for others to come by, and one of those privileges was travel. Each planet within the Vortex System is quite different, and I count myself lucky to have visited each one multiple times.*"

"*So, the benefits outweighed the emotional toll?*"

"*When you put it that way, it really makes me sound like a cold-blooded killer, doesn't it? Honestly, before getting seriously injured, I never took the time to think about it. Or maybe I wasn't letting myself think about it. But now, I'm not sure if I would ever go back to being a bounty hunter. I feel like LSS has granted me a chance at a new life, so I am going to take it.*"

"*A new life as a prisoner of Foxaire Biotech Industries,*" Newtus replied.

"*Yeah, but there's got to be a way out of here.*"

"*I don't think we will ever get that chance. We have both been experimented on, and both survived those experiments with the enhancements to show for it. Why would a company let such an expensive asset like us go free?*"

*"Hold on for a moment, Newtus. Reptiles don't have industry, do they? How do you know all of this?"*

*"I pay attention, and I listen to what goes on around me. There is much to learn when your captives think you aren't listening, or too stupid to understand what is being discussed."*

*"Hmm, yes, very true. I should work on being more aware of my surroundings as well."*

Newtus smiled in response.

Several hours passed, and they continued to chat the night away. About half an hour before dusk, West was about ready to wrap things up. He was growing tired and wanted at least a few hours of sleep before he was scheduled meet with Professor Durrist and Professor Randall again.

While Newtus was telling him a story about a time when she jumped down a waterfall in pursuit of a meal, the same familiar presence he felt earlier reappeared within his sphere of awareness, only this time from above. Newtus stopped communicating—she had felt the presence, too. As the presence grew closer, he realized what he had felt earlier was no error, but only Lyd.

West turned his body toward the ceiling while Newtus looked up at the same time. Lyd looked down at them in shock and surprise, then yelped and disappeared.

*"You know him, don't you?"* Newtus asked.

*"I do. That was Lyd, one of Professor Clums' assistants."*

*"Did he work on you?"*

*"Yes. He was one of three Harmertians actually."*

*"Why was Lyd in the vents?"*

*"That I do not know. Although, I can guess. Professor Clums was down here a few days ago, and as far as I know, he hasn't been invited back down yet. So, my guess is that he sent Lyd down here to check out what's going on so he could see more than he was shown on his tour. Smart move, to travel through the air ducts."*

*"Do you think anyone else noticed him?"* Newtus asked.

*"I don't think so. If he was, I would likely have been alerted. So that's*

*good. I don't want Professor Durrist finding out about this. I can't imagine what he would do to him. I must tell Lyd to be more careful."*

*"Well, it sounds like you have even more of a reason to speak with Professor Clums now."*

*"Yes. I will need to schedule time with him. Which wouldn't seem so out of place—Professor Durrist promised that Professor Clums would run some checkups on me soon."* West said.

*"Good, that should work out then. Now, West, go home and go to sleep. I shouldn't keep you any longer. You need your rest for what's to come."*

*"Yeah, I think you're right. And I'm exhausted. What about you, are you tired?"*

*"Unlike you, I have absolutely nothing to do, aside from eating, sleeping, running around in circles, and talking to you and the others. I can rest whenever I want."*

*"Yes, of course, that makes sense,"* West replied as he tipped his cowboy hat forward and stood up.

*"Sometime soon you need to tell me about that hat of yours."*

West couldn't help but chuckle. That was not what he had been expecting Newtus to say. *"Sure, sounds like a plan, friend. Take care, and until next time."*

*"Take care, friend,"* Newtus replied.

West tipped his hat forward again and left the room. As he was leaving, he nearly bumped into Professor Kalosse, who jumped back about a meter.

"Oh my word, West, you nearly gave me a heart attack. What are you doing down here so early?"

"I couldn't sleep," West said. After telepathically speaking with Newtus for so long, it felt strange to be speaking out loud again.

"So you decided to visit Newtus? Did Professor Peal approve of this?" Professor Kalosse asked.

"He told me I could visit at any time."

"Right, well that may be the case, but next time check in with one of us. We don't want you accidentally interrupting one of our experiments."

"I never even considered that. My apologies. Now—" Before West could finish his sentence, Professor Peal walked into the room.

"Ah, West, good morning. What a surprise to see you," Professor Peal said as he brushed his matted brown hair with his hand.

"West here was just visiting with Newtus," Kalosse said.

"I see. Did she give you any new information?"

"Yes, we had a long conversation."

"Wonderful. Another telepathic conversation, I assume?" Professor Peal said as he tapped on his tablet.

"Yes, it was."

"You two really are quite fascinating together. If possible, please send me that recording."

"Right, sure. But first, I was on my way to bed. I've been up all night and really need to rest before my day starts."

"I see, no problem. Doesn't it take you only moments to send the file, though?" Professor Peal asked.

"For smaller files, yes. This file is really big. It will take some time to process it and send it your way." This was only partially true, as Professor Peal couldn't know the rendering was nearly complete. The last file he sent had been completely unedited, but this one would need to be. He just hoped he could edit it seamlessly. He couldn't allow them to find out about Lyd—at least, not before he had a chance to speak with him.

"Well, just send it over when you get a chance then. See you later, West."

"Wait a minute," Professor Kalosse cut in. "Shouldn't West ask us for permission before he visits with our test subjects? What if he—"

A loud beeping blared from both professors' tablets, and they each had to manually silence the notification.

"Kalosse, we can discuss this later. West, I know you're tired, but I would like to ask you for a favor, since you're already here."

West sighed. "As long as it's quick."

"It should be. This specimen of ours is highly unstable. Not even we can stay in the room for long with him. But I fear that if we do not act quickly, we will lose him."

"So, what do you want me to do? I'm no scientist."

"And yet, you have extremely useful abilities that we do not have. Just like how you can speak with Newtus and Theesakin, we would like to see if you can speak with Ivy as well."

"Ivy, is it? I'll see what I can do."

"Wonderful," Professor Peal said as he led him to the door marked 5.

"Is this really okay?" Professor Kalosse asked.

"I'm sure that as a bounty hunter, West has seen his fair share of grotesque things. Haven't you, West?"

"More than I'd care to share," he replied with a soft shake of his head.

"Great. Now, I should at least tell you that Ivy is another Eusphyrchiian," Professor Peal said.

The news caused him to stop in his tracks for a moment.

"Are you okay?" Professor Kalosse asked. "We've been hesitant to ask you, but Ivy is in the worst state we've seen yet. Anything you can do to help would be much appreciated."

"Yes, I understand. I'm ready," West said with a nod. If there really was another Eusphyrchiian in there, then it was his duty to do everything he could to help.

"Thank you, West. Ivy is the reason I'm here so early, so you're timing works out nicely. Please, go on ahead. We'll keep an eye on the both of you," Professor Peal said as he pressed the button to open the door.

West took a deep breath as the doors slid open in front of him. Even without taking a step forward, LSS was already picking up a strange presence. While the breathing and heartbeat was a match for a Eusphyrchiian, he was picking up several other strange bioelectric signals emanating from Ivy.

West stepped forward and walked into the room. Through the transparent barrier, he saw a gaunt Eusphyrchiian that was hooked up to several machines with various tubes and wires coming out of him. The first thing West noticed was Ivy had no head. He had thought he was the only living headless Eusphyrchiian. Now that he knew there was another, his desire to help Ivy increased even further. The next thing he noticed was that Ivy had large strands of green vines wrapped tightly around his hip joints.

"What do we have here, Adok?"

"Another play thing is it, Ados?"

"Yes, it appears to be, Adok."

It took West several seconds of scanning the room to see that the voices were coming from two large black spiders. Their mouth-parts were clenched tightly around Ivy's wrist as they spoke, which meant that they were speaking out loud telepathically, something he didn't even know was possible.

"I'm not here to talk to you, spiders. I'm here to talk to Ivy."

"But we are Ivy, can't you see?" they replied as one.

West took a breath and ignored the spiders. Instead, he reached out in the same way he reached out to Newtus and Theesakin. He could see Ivy's aura, but it was thin and cloudy.

*"Ivy, can you hear me? My name is West, I'm a Eusphyrchiian like you."*

The reply was weak and sounded distant, even though the response was telepathic. *"West? Can you hear me? Help me... please help me."*

*"That's why I'm here, to help you. Tell me what you need me to do."*

*"I hurt all over. I don't want to live. These spiders, this ivy, my deformed body... I am not who I was."*

*"And who were you, Ivy? What was your name before all of this?"*

*"I can't remember. I can't remember anything. Only this pain. Only these spiders and this ivy. They have invaded my consciousness, invaded my soul. It is all I can do to fight against them. But I can't fight any longer."*

*"Ivy, I understand. I have undergone changes as well, though much different from what you are going through. And I am still adjusting to those changes. Ivy, I don't think you need to fight anymore. Let them in. Let them in and embrace them. Embrace who you are now."*

*"You want me to give up the fight?"*

*"No. No, you're not giving up. You're accepting victory. You can only be victorious if you finish the fight."*

*"I'm scared. I don't want to lose anymore of myself."*

*"It's okay, I'm here with you. You're not alone."* West approached the barrier and put his hand against it. The spiders continued to blather on, speaking nonsense. *"You can do this, Ivy. Believe in yourself. After you accept them, you will control them."*

*"I will control them?"*

*"Yes, you will."*

He wasn't sure why, but West truly believed in what he was telling Ivy. Either way, LSS confirmed that all four entities had been melded into one presence. Something had to happen, or all would perish.

*"I am... I am in control!"* Ivy screamed inside his mind.

West watched in awe as the spiders simultaneously stopped speaking and stretched out all their legs as if they were in pain. At the same time, the ivy flailed violently as it reached out toward the barrier. After a few moments, everything calmed down and Ivy's aura became vibrant and radiant.

*"Ivy?"*

*"Thank you, West, for helping me see."*

---

West made his way to the elevator that connected to Professor Clums' wing. While he could have used the elevator that connected to Professor Peal's area, he needed to stretch his legs after his time with Ivy. He was still in shock at what had happened. It was strange to him how Professors Peal and Kalosse, and even Kamarial—the resident Eusphyrchiian scientist—couldn't do what he had been able to do.

Once the elevator was in sight, he stopped as a thought struck him.

*If Lyd made his way down here, then he must have used this elevator shaft. Very dangerous. If he's still climbing back up, I could crush and kill him with a push of a button,* he thought. In order to make sure the coast was clear, he expanded his sphere of awareness as far as it could go. While he didn't sense Lyd, he did sense a small device that was sending a signal.

*Ah, I see you figured out a clever solution to your situation. I'll need to somehow mask the presence of the signal so Carl and the others won't find out. Hopefully it will be unnoticed for the next few hours.*

West pressed the button to call the elevator, and several minutes later he was once again passing by Professor Clums' laboratory. Now that he knew what to look for, he expanded his sphere of awareness and sensed Lyd was safely back in Professor Clums' lab, along with Mac and Poi. He considered sending another email, but decided against it. This was a matter better spoken about in person.

He nodded to Jakog as he exited the compound. He still didn't know Jakog very well; he was quiet, even for a Lakinceitian.

The tertiary sun system was already rising. He wouldn't be able to sleep for long, which was fine, as he was quite used to lack of sleep. There had been many missions he had been on in the IBHA where he had barely slept and could still function at full capacity.

As he approached the barracks, he saw Professor Clums and Professor Qymberkon heading in his direction. For a few moments, he thought he detected a third presence even though there was no one else around.

"Ah, good morning, professors," West called out to them.

"Good morning, West. Are you getting off duty?" Professor Clums asked.

"No, actually. But I am headed to bed for a few hours before my responsibilities begin for the day."

"I see. How have you been? Our last interaction was too brief."

"I completely agree, Professor. In fact, I sent you an email earlier this morning. I want to talk to you about those things in person sometime, as well as a few other things. I was hoping to schedule some time with you. Mainly, LSS seems to be on the fritz. It keeps on picking up strange signals; I actually just got a strange reading a few moments ago."

"That is odd, isn't it? No problem, we can definitely connect to get that checked out," Professor Clums said. "Fumalli, remind me to check my calendar later on."

"Sure thing," Professor Qymberkon replied.

"I'll keep an eye out for your message then. I'll be seeing you both."

"Yes, have a good day, West," Professor Qymberkon said.

"Thank you, the same to you both."

Once he was back in his room, West crawled into bed and scanned through the recording between him and Newtus. After a few minutes of editing, he sent the file to Professor Peal. He just hoped it sounded as seamless to the Professor as it sounded to him.

*That Professor Peal... what he has accomplished is mind-boggling,* he thought. *While I don't know how to feel about Ivy just yet, I truly admire his work. Newtus is already a really good friend.*

*But, Ivy... what I witnessed today was an unforgettable experience. You found yourself right in front of my eyes. That's why I couldn't accept your thanks. You had all the tools you needed the entire time. All I did was push you in the right direction.*

*You know... I don't think LSS is acting strangely at all. The feeling I had this morning about Newtus and just now with Professors Clums and Qymberkon... maybe that was just a feeling of my own, felt through LSS?*

*Either way, just like you Ivy, I still have a lot to learn.*

# 13

# ESCAPE FROM OPPRESSION

Navacus nodded to West was they parted ways, then he and Fumalli continued to walk down the covered path that led to the compound.

"*Did West just sense you?*" Navacus asked Sterg.

"*He may have. I wasn't quick enough in masking my presence. I'll need to be more careful in the future.*"

"*Or not. He could be a useful ally. He goes down to the underground all the time, and he gave me that warning as I was leaving. Now, send the message to the Harmertians.*"

"*Sent.*"

"Hey, do you think West knows about... you know..." Fumalli whispered.

"Funny, I just asked Sterg. Yes, it's possible," he replied. "Now, back me up, okay?"

"Sure thing," Fumalli replied.

Navacus smiled. He and Fumalli knew each other well enough at this point that they hadn't needed to plan ahead for this. They grew quiet as they reached the automatic sliding doors. Jakog, the baby-blue skinned Lakinceitian, greeted them as they entered.

"Oh hey, Jakog, would you be able to help me with something?" Navacus asked him.

"It depends."

Navacus shook his head as if he was exasperated. "Depends on what?"

"On what you need help with," Jakog replied coolly.

Navacus straightened up and adjusted his collar. "Ah, I see. I apologize for my tone. You see, Professor Qymberkon and I have been having a debate, and we hoped you could give us your opinion on the matter."

Sterg notified him that the Harmertians were waiting at the entrance to their wing, watching the front doors to make their dash out. In response, Navacus moved his body so he was standing in front of the hallway and motioned to Fumalli to follow him. As they moved, the three Harmertians made it to the entrance before the automatic doors had time to close.

"Well, it's silly, but when it comes to fish, I prefer mine salty, tasting like the sea," he said, pointing a feathery finger at his chest. "Professor Qymberkon prefers his to be savory and accompanied with mushrooms and fresh herbs. What do you prefer?"

Jakog stared blankly at him for several seconds before responding. "Of course fish need to be salty. And as raw as possible. I prefer eating them live if I have the opportunity."

"A man after my own culinary heart. See Fumalli? I told you I was right."

"And I could have told you his answer. It's a known fact that Lakinceitians love live fish."

"Even so, I appreciate your opinion, Jakog."

"Sure thing."

"Good morning, professors," Poi said as she, Mac, and Lyd entered the compound.

"Ah, wonderful timing," Navacus replied. "Come, we have a lot of work to do. Have a good day, Jakog."

"Same to you all," the Lakinceitian guard said as he returned to his duties, none the wiser.

Once they were all safely in the lab, they turned to the matter at hand.

"Now, before the others arrive, please tell us what you discovered in the underground laboratory," Navacus prompted.

Poi laughed nervously as Lyd began his story. Navacus had to take a seat when Lyd reached the part about the tortured Yggdrazim. When he mentioned West, Navacus leaned in without interrupting.

"… so essentially I need to go back down there to clean up a few things. I also didn't make it to every area, as I explained."

"Which we knew would be the case," Navacus responded, speaking for the first time since Lyd began his story. "Now, there's a lot I would like to address, but first, West. He mentioned he sent me a message. I haven't gotten a chance to read it yet, but I do know that a meeting is in order, one where everyone can join in."

"Are you sure that's wise?" Fumalli asked. "We need to be careful. If Yilvin or Carl catch wind of what we're doing here, we could end up as permanent residents in that underground facility."

"Are you saying that we should back off?" Navacus replied.

"No, of course not. I'm as curious as you as to what's going on, but we need to tread lightly."

Sterg notified him that Norman Harrison, Syl, Grasberg, and Kurjon were approaching, and Navacus could tell that Lyd was itching to ask him another question.

"We can talk about this later. Lyd, do you have something you want to ask me? And quickly, we're nearly out of time."

"Yes, actually. What about security? Yes, we evaded Jakog this morning, but aren't there cameras everywhere?"

Navacus nodded. "Indeed there are. We have a way around those, for now. I'll explain later."

The door to the lab opened. Sylcertiverner entered and held the door open for Norman, Grasberg, and Kurjon.

"Good morning, everyone. I see we're the last ones here today," Grasberg said.

"Even so, you are right on time," Navacus answered.

"Hey, Professor, I hope it's okay, but I thought of something last night," Norman said, finishing with a yawn.

"No problem, Norman. Did you sleep well?"

"No, actually. I was up for most of the night studying my contract. But that's not what I want to bring up right now. Rather, it's about the manual release switch that I messed with yesterday. So, all I had to do to release my legs was to open a little compartment door thing and press a button. That doesn't seem very ideal. For one, it could be difficult to do if I was in a situation where I needed a quick-release. Also, what if someone tampered with it, by either releasing the attachment without my consent or sabotaging it so I can't open the little compartment thing?"

Navacus was impressed. Norman had thought of a wide variety of situations and found flaws with the current design. "You know, that's a great question. I can honestly say that was, for the most part, overlooked. We were focusing on everything else. We'll put some more thought into it."

"That would be great, thank you," Norman replied.

"*You do realize how obvious the answer is, right*?" Sterg whispered in his mind.

"*Of course, but again, it's hard to tell my thoughts from yours sometimes, and this is one of those times.*"

Navacus laughed out loud. "I'm sorry, but thinking about it now, I don't know how we didn't think about it before. All we would need to do is some sort of bio-signature scan."

"Of course, that's so obvious," Syl said as he slapped his fist in his hand. "What about a fingerprint scan?"

"That was my first thought, too, but no. What if his hands are dirty? What if he's wearing gloves? A fingerprint scan, while practical, wouldn't be the correct answer. Nor would an audio command, because what if he couldn't speak for some reason? Or what if there's a lot of background noise? Also, that could be too easy to imitate. We'll need to think about this more, but let's not get distracted. Our goal today is to continue our work dissembling the hover unit. Let's focus on that, since we know what to do."

Norman Harrison settled into his typical routine—sitting back and observing Professor Clums and his team go about their work. It was always impressive to watch. However, it was hard for him to focus on them today. Not only was he exhausted due to only getting around two hours of sleep, but he was still processing everything he had uncovered last night.

After Professor Bodeelch had goaded him, Norman had gone back to his room and dove headfirst into his six-hundred-page contract. He still hadn't read the entirety of it, but he had gained a lot of insight from it.

First of all, the contract was not a document one could read page by page. There were footnotes that led to annotations, which led to the index that led to hidden clauses... It was pure madness. Apparently, Lakinceitian laws and contracts were vastly different from Human ones, because something like this could never be legalized back on Carange. At least, he hoped not, anyway. He wasn't a lawyer, only a lowly miner, but even his complicated mining contract had been far more straightforward than this.

As he was scouring the contract, he had come across a clause buried in a footnote's sub-footnote that had simply stated "Any assets brought in by the subject are immediately transferred to Foxaire Biotech Industries." That had led him to an index, which led him to a table full of specified items that Foxaire Biotech Industries would own, in case there was any confusion. Among that list were fairly obvious items—clothing, personal phones, tablets, jewelry, and so forth. But then there were the items that made his skin crawl—the subject's deeds, including those of properties, vehicles, and businesses, would be immediately, and legally, transferred to Foxaire Biotech Industries, along with any plants, animals, or people that the subject brought with them. Plants, animals, or *people*. Norman had wanted to retch.

Because Norman had unwittingly brought Kate with him, Foxaire Biotech Industries owned her. That meant she was somewhere in this compound—a subject to experimentation, just like him.

Upon learning this devastating information, he had thrown his tablet across the room, where it had thumped to the carpeted floor and slid to bang into the wall. He'd stared at the tablet as his mind raced through dozens of scenarios that Kate could be in. It had all led to two conclusions—if Lord Foxaire owned Kate, then they must own him, and that he had to escape from this place.

However, he had to be patient. He needed to finish reading the contract so he could learn more about his situation. If he found the clause that explained they owned Kate, there had to be one that explained they owned him, too. Also, his enhancements. Even though he was owned by Foxaire, and had been subjected to experimentation, his results were ones he fully approved of. Not only did he now have new, highly advanced prosthetic legs, but he was also receiving the means to fly *and* become his own car. How could he argue with that? Once he had all his new attachments completed, he would escape the first chance he got.

Of course, that had led him to realize that he needed secure attachments. He needed to ensure that Carl, Bodeelch, Bsarg, or anyone else couldn't remove his attachments without his consent. Although he had signed the contract, he never would have agreed to this if he had known about all the hidden clauses. And yet, he knew he had stamped his own ticket when he and Kate boarded that transport to Melridion.

Norman shook his head. He hadn't meant to review what he had stayed up all night for, but it had also gleamed him new insight. He looked around him. Syl was standing nearby, gazing down at his tablet.

"Hey, Syl, you got a second?"

"Sure, what is it, Norman?"

"Well, I was just wondering. Did you read your entire contract when you signed on to work here?"

"What? I don't— No, I definitely did not. It was really long from what I remember. But I understood the basics. Is this about your contract that Professor Bodeelch was talking about yesterday?"

Professor Clums approached. "Norman, while it's good to be asking such questions, now is not the time or the place. In fact, everyone, listen up for a second. I—"

A loud chime interrupted him.

"What was that?" Professor Clums muttered as he looked at his tablet. After a few moments, he lowered his arms and huffed in annoyance.

"Professor Bodeelch is on his way. We'll need to talk about this later."

*Professor Bodeelch really can't seem to leave us alone,* Norman thought. *Either way, I really need to finish reading my contract. There must be things they're not telling me, or even Professor Clums for that matter. I need to figure out what's going on around here.*

***

"Great progress. I'll be back in a day or two to check in again," Professor Bodeelch said as he walked out the door.

Navacus resisted the urge to slam the door behind him. He was growing to resent that nosy guy. When he turned around, he saw most of his team were staring at him expectantly.

"Let's get back to work, alright? I know his intrusions can be quite intrusive, but let's try to refocus. In the meantime, can I speak to Sylcertiverner and Professor Qymberkon in my office, please?"

"What's going on, Professor?" Syl asked once the three of them were alone in his office.

"Syl, would you be so kind as to pass along a message for me?"

Syl looked confused and shrugged his shoulders. "I suppose so. What is the message, and who am I passing it along to?"

"Pass this onto everyone, meaning Grasberg, Kurjon, and the Harmertians. The message is a simple one: I would like all of you to meet me at my apartment later on tonight. Oh, and Norman, too. I think he should be a part of this as well."

"Again, and I don't mean any offense, but are you sure this is wise?" Fumalli asked. "I thought you said we need to be more cautious."

"This is me being cautious. Having Syl pass along the message would make this much less suspicious. Plus, the three of us meeting together like this makes sense. We're the 'leadership' of this group," he said, using finger quotes.

"That's not what I meant," Fumalli groaned.

"I'm sorry, I'm still confused. Why do you need to be cautious? Is this about Professor Bodeelch?" Syl asked.

"I'll explain everything tonight. And please ask everyone to trickle in slowly over the course of half an hour. We can't have you all showing up at my apartment at once."

"Sure, I guess that makes sense, even though none of this makes any sense. But I understand," Syl replied.

"Great. Now, let's all get back to work. The hover unit won't reassemble itself."

Later that evening, Navacus laughed at a joke Kurjon delivered. He was pleased. Just as he'd asked, Navacus' team had slowly trickled into his apartment. Syl had arrived first, then Grasberg arrived about five minutes later, Kurjon seven minutes after that, with Mac and Poi arriving shortly after Kurjon. They were all confused and had many questions for him, but until everyone was there, he kept the tone light, and they chatted and joked about the mundane. He kept an eye on Mac and Poi, ensuring they didn't reveal anything until everyone was ready. However, both were extremely tired and simply lounged on the couch, enjoying everyone's company.

Fumalli, on the other hand, was having a hard time hiding his concern, so Navacus had put him to work in the kitchen to cook up some snacks for their guests. Cooking always calmed down his blue-skinned buddy.

"*Navacus, do you really intend on going through with this?*" Sterg asked.

"*Of course. Why let them know one by one? It's best to just rip the adhesive bandage off now. It'll be easier that way for all of them. Are you doubting my decision?*"

"*No, I agree with you. However, there are many ways this could go badly. I can only do so much to mitigate their reactions.*"

"*No, please don't do anything like that. If they realize their feelings are being tampered with, they will trust you even less. Allow them to work through their feelings on their own.*"

"*Of course.*"

Just then, there was a knock at the door.

"*Norman and Lyd have arrived,*" Sterg announced.

Navacus smiled and opened the door. "Come in, quickly now."

"I'm sorry, I took a nap and time got away from me," Lyd said. "I had meant to arrive with Poi and Mac."

"It's not a problem," Navacus replied.

"You know, I was thinking your apartment would be bigger and nicer than mine, but it's essentially the same," Norman said as he scanned the room.

"Right, that's because the rooms are all nearly identical," Syl replied. "But I don't complain. These apartments are far nicer than the place I grew up in on Mishunaed."

"Okay," Navacus said as he wheezed loudly, almost like a whistle. "Now that we're all here, let's get to business. I know you all have a lot of questions. First, let me start from the beginning. So, when we started our work on Norman—meaning back at the beginning of Ohocinar—is when this whole thing begins. Remember when Carl first arrived, and we were all like, 'Who the heck is this guy?' Well, less than a week after he arrived, Carl told me that he wanted me to help him with a side project. He told me to keep things under wraps, so I never brought it up. Well, for several weeks, nothing happened with that. He never spoke of it again—not until four days ago, on the thirty-eighth. He invited me into a secret elevator located at the end of our wing that leads down to an underground laboratory."

He went on to explain his tour and everything he had seen, including a shape-shifting Ancilsan, an Eridavlos with the ability to sprout and retract a pair of legs, and Professor Peal's experiments. It was when he was leaving Professor Peal's area that they were called over to a strange gate, but not before Professor Durrist mentioned something called the Titans. Then, after the four strange, otherworldly Humans emerged from the gate, he was sent upstairs and was never invited back down.

"Please keep my story in mind as Lyd, Mac, and Poi explain what they discovered last night. And don't leave out any details," Navacus concluded, turning to the Harmertian trio.

As they began their story, Fumalli passed around the snacks he had made for everyone. When Poi described seeing the near-death Yggdrazim, she broke down in tears. Kurjon, who was also in tears at this point, embraced Poi.

Mac took over and described his journey back to the elevator with Poi. He remarked on how lucky they had been; soon after they ascended the elevator shaft, the elevator had also ascended.

Lyd picked up the story from there. When he finished, the room was silent.

"So... let me get this straight," Syl said. "Not only is there a secret underground facility that is larger than the compound, but, from what it sounds like, we are some of the last ones to learn about it?"

"Yes, and yes," Navacus replied. "That is part of the reason I did not want to wait to tell you all. As you already know, I don't really like secrets. I have never been too keen on the nature of our facility, but lately I have been reevaluating my view on this place. I think we're trapped here. Sure, we can go on vacations, like the one to Nalpetalis that Fumalli and I took not too long ago, but I am beginning to fear that we may never be able to truly leave this place."

"Yeah, after reading my contract last night, I came to a similar conclusion," Norman said.

"That's right. What did you learn?"

"That Kate is down there." Once the gasps subsided, he continued. "I also learned that any assets I own, and any plants, animals, or people I brought with me now belong to Foxaire Biotech Industries, under the guise that they are doing me a service by taking care of my cherished assets during my stay here. But now it all makes much more sense. They aren't stealing my assets out of charity, but so I can become their property—their slave. That's why I asked you about your contract, Syl. Because while it is a maze to navigate, being able to uncover its secrets makes the process well worth it."

"Yeah, I'll need to go back and read it now," Syl replied.

"Same here," Grasberg added.

"We should all review our contracts after this. And if the truth of our situation is buried in those contracts, then we have all been such fools. The truth has been at our fingertips this entire time," Navacus said.

"Professor, can I ask something?" Lyd asked.

"Of course."

"That Ancilsan you saw in your tour—was it the same one we talked to?"

"It's possible. Did he have a light spot under his left eye?"

"Yes, he did!" Poi exclaimed. She was now back to her chipper self. "So, he can shape-shift? That sounds... painful."

"Yeah, it really does," Mac added.

"Do you think we can help him?" Poi asked.

"I would like to. I would like to help anyone we can. We are all in danger. You all remember Sharg, right? Well besides you, Norman."

"Yeah, I remember her," Fumalli said. "She always smelled the nicest. Like a mixture of fresh rain and blooming flowers." He paused, thoughtful. "You know, I had convinced myself that she just retired or like found another job and didn't tell us. But if we are all the property of Lord Foxaire..."

"Then she could be down in the underground as well," Navacus said, finishing his friend's sentence. "Why the Lakinceitians would want to experiment on their own, I have no idea."

"You know, that reminds me, professor," Lyd said. "When we saw that gate—I assume it was the same one you saw those strange Humans emerge from—it was being guarded by a Lakinceitian who didn't look right. I almost could have sworn it had an antenna sprouting from its head."

"Whatever the case may be, before we do anything rash, we must first collect more information. So, again, we should all review our contracts. And we need to learn more about the underground," Professor Clums said.

"Yeah I just… I don't think I am ready to go back down there," Poi said.

"And I can't leave her alone, you know?" Mac replied.

"That's fine, I understand. You two can stay behind. I can finish this on my own," Lyd replied.

"Are you sure?" Fumalli asked. "Last time, West saw you."

"Yeah, but I believe West is our ally," Navacus said. He then told everyone about the message West sent him. "Judging from that message, I believe we can trust him. I replied and he is scheduled to meet me in my office tomorrow at 14:40. That being said, I think we should wait a few days before we convene again. And until then, keep quiet about what you uncover, even you, Lyd."

"But what about Kate? I just… I really need to know where she is," Norman said.

"Right, there's still a lot of ground to cover," Lyd said. "There are four passages I haven't gone down yet, and she could be down any one of them. But I think I'll head down there again either tomorrow night or the night after. Hopefully I can find her then."

"And the sooner we know where she is, the sooner we can rescue her, right? She's been down there for close to two months now… well, in Carange time. But no matter what, it's been too long. I need to know how she's doing."

"I agree—I hope she is safe, too, but at this point, anything is possible," Navacus said. "Now… how are you all feeling?"

"Quite overwhelmed," Kurjon replied.

"I agree. This has been a lot to take in," Grasberg added.

"You know, I feel like you only ever ask us that when you have one more thing up your sleeve," Syl said.

"Not all the time," Navacus replied, feigning a look of offense. "But yes, most of the time, including now."

"What more is there?" Lyd asked. "How could there be even more going on? I mean, it's like my entire world has been flipped upside down. A week ago, I was perfectly happy, blissfully ignorant of all of this. And now I feel horrified to even be here. We have been lied to, and I for one cannot forgive Foxaire, or Carl, or those two professors you mentioned..."

"Do you mean Professors Durrist and Randall?" Navacus asked.

"Right, those guys. All of them have been playing us," Lyd said as he threw his napkin on the floor in anger.

"Don't forget about Professor Bodeelch. He most certainly knows about everything we've been discussing," Syl added.

"Of course. What an asshat. If I see him down there, I'm going to spit on his fat gray head," Lyd said.

"I wouldn't advise that," Navacus said. "But I do whole heartedly agree that we have been deceived. My entire world has imploded in the last four days. I'm not the same person I was a week ago. I'm sure you've all noticed."

"Yeah, I've noticed. Something is very different about you," Kurjon said. "But after learning all of this, I just figured it was from your tour of the underground."

"Well, yes, that's part of it. But it's not just what I saw down there that's changed me. My entire perspective on life has changed. I'm honestly still getting used to it."

"Used to what?" Poi asked.

"Well, I have gained a new, permanent sidekick of sorts. One that has been present in the room this entire time, but only two of us are aware."

"What the heck? Are you sayin' we're being spied on?" Norman asked as he frantically looked around the room.

"No... well, I guess it all depends on the perspective. And, sure, from your perspective, it would seem as if it's been spying on you."

"Just a word of warning, everyone," Fumalli said from his spot at the kitchen counter, "you're going to be terrified, but it'll only be for a few moments. At least, that's how it was for me. And I know it's bright, but it won't hurt your eyes."

"Thanks for that disclaimer, but I can assure you, you will be surprised. Now, Sterg, they're ready for you."

Norman was thankful to be part of this important conversation. Sure, he was around these eight people day in and day out, and after being around them so much, there were times he was tired of being around them. But, this was the most riveting conversation he'd had with any of them yet, almost even more exciting than getting his legs. What they were hinting at was the promise of freedom. Yes, his legs gave him back his mobility, but what good would they do if he could never leave this hot, dusty place? Why would they even matter if he could never see Kate again?

While he truly did not want to find Kate underground, just knowing where she was would be an immense relief. He knew he had to be patient—that they all had to be patient as they uncovered more information—but he had been apart from her for too long. He would do anything to see her again.

Norman shook his head and focused on Professor Clums. "Now, Sterg, they're ready for you."

"As you wish." The deep, rumbling voice emanated around Norman. It seemed to come from all directions. Everyone was just as surprised as he was.

A moment later, a radiant light pulsed outward from the center of the room. Along with the light came waves of air that slowly spun around the pulsating light. Kurjon screamed and covered her eyes.

"What in the Vortex is happening?" Poi cried.

"No matter what happens, I'm here for you!" Mac replied.

"Navacus! What is this?" Professor Qymberkon exclaimed. "It wasn't like this for me!"

"Hold on, everyone! It'll pass momentarily," Professor Clums said.

He was smiling maniacally with a mad twinkle in his eye as he stood directly next to the miniature tornado.

As promised, the tornado subsided a moment later. Where it had been floated a ghostly creature. It held no shape as it flowed like a fish in a river. The same voice as before emanated from the ethereal figure.

"My deepest apologies. I did not know that was going to happen. I have never revealed myself to seven souls at once. My name is Sterg, and it is an honor to officially meet you all."

The room was silent for several moments before Norman dared to speak up. "Sterg, is it?"

"Yes, Norman Harrison."

"Ah, well, it's nice to meet you, too. What exactly are you?"

"I am an entity known as a Light Being. Think of me like a soul without a body."

"A soul without a body... so are you a ghost?"

"I differ from what you refer to as ghosts. However, I am more like a ghost than I am like you, Norman."

"A ghost, is it?" Lyd asked. "Were you the one spying on us then?"

"I would not use the word *spying*, Lyd. Rather, I have been observing you without your knowledge for the purpose of learning more about Navacus' current situation."

"Yeah, that's called spying. And how are you connected to the professor anyway?" Lyd asked.

"My soul was drawn to his and his to my own. Such a pairing is rare and only happens during a time of great change and cataclysms."

"Cataclysms? Is something going to happen?" Syl asked.

"A cataclysm can be many different things. Some may say that you are all going through a cataclysm right now, as your world views and beliefs are being tested and questioned like never before. Such is the nature of substantial change."

"Does that mean that there really is something evil going on beneath our feet?" Kurjon asked. "I mean, I trust in everything that has been said tonight, and yet I do not want to believe it."

"It can be hard to accept that those you trust are only using you to their own benefit. But that is the case. However, not all are corrupted," Sterg said.

"Who do you mean?" Professor Clums asked.

"Professor Dea. For as curious as he is about me, I believe he is morally against the wrongdoings in this facility."

"Wait, does Professor Dea know about you, too?" Syl asked.

"Not exactly, but he is aware of my presence," Sterg replied.

"Professor Dea is curious about Sterg, and so is West," Professor Clums said. "Hopefully we'll be bringing both of them into our fold soon."

"And what do we do now? How can we go back to our normal routine after learning all of this?" Grasberg asked.

"As I said before, we must be patient. We must prepare for the opportune moment," Professor Clums replied.

*What in the world is actually happening? Norman thought. As overwhelming as everything was before this... I am going to really need some time to process everything. I guess it's a good thing I have almost nothing to do every day.*

---

The conversation went late into the night as the newly formed group discussed what to do next. Once Lyd nodded off to sleep, Navacus knew it was time to adjourn. In similar fashion to how they'd arrived, he made sure that they did not leave all at once. Norman was the last to leave.

"So, to clarify, I'll always be able to see you from now on? But anyone that was not in this room tonight won't be able to?" Norman asked.

"Indeed. However, there will be times I will hide myself, such as when around West or Professor Dea. However, that may not be the case for much longer."

"Right. I don't really know West; it would be nice to meet him. Anyway, I'm off to bed. I'll see you all bright and early."

Norman gave them a wave as he left the apartment. Once gone, Fumalli let out a sigh.

"What a night. We better get ready for bed also, it got really late."

"Mm. Right behind you," Navacus replied.

*You know, I think that went pretty well, Navacus thought. Sterg, you really know how to make an entrance. I know you didn't know that was going to happen, but I must admit, it was a lot of fun while it happened, especially watching everyone's reactions.*

*I only wish that we could have come up with an actionable plan to do something about our situation. Right, I know it's still early for that, but I suppose it means that we just need to learn as much as we can as fast as we can. So, could you read my contract and absorb the information for me? Because that would be prime. You can? Fantastic. Let's get a power nap in, then do some studying.*

# 14

# ESCAPE FROM SANITY

Tyrona sat cross-legged on the gray floor as she stared at the gray wall in front of her. She took a deep breath, feeling the cool air as it filled her lungs. During moments like this, she was confident that she was, in fact, Tyrona Claire Knorse. She had grown up in Ajenti with her mother, father, and grandma. She had been with her grandma when she had discovered that she had a unique talent for the magical arts. She had been young, only about seven or eight at the time.

Tyrona was admitted into Ajenti University when she was fourteen, a few years younger than most. For the first few years, she had loved everything about her studies. She was mastering her craft at an impressive rate and often had the highest grades in her classes.

*"What's with this school-days reminiscing? Get to the good part already. How did you and Theodore meet?"*

As soon as the other woman's voice reached her mind, Tyrona took another deep breath, attempting to push her away.

*"C'mon Tyrona, you should know by now our minds are linked, now that we've gotten through that strange, dreamlike situation. Why do you keep ignoring me? This place is so boring. And gray is like the worst color, ever. How can you just stare at the wall like that all day?"*

"*Because what else can I do, Kate?*" Tyrona snapped. "*I'm doing everything I can to keep my sanity in check. As you of course know because you know literally everything about me—even how I met Theodore; I am very skilled at keeping my mind separate from others. It's what my powers are based on—having a strong mind and resilient sense of self. Having you in my head destroys all the boundaries I put in place.*"

"*And yet you allowed your boy toy, Theodore, to mingle minds with Ànifa.*"

"*That was nothing to worry about. Ànifa had no sexual desires at all.*"

"*Well, sure, but that's not what I meant. How do you think Theodore felt having Ànifa in his head?*"

"*He told me on* West Wind *that it was strange and the only reason he didn't jump out of his skin when it happened was because I used to speak to Theodore that way from time to time. It was how I helped him pass his world geography final.*" Somehow, Tyrona felt Kate roll her eyes. "*Look, I know what you are prodding me for, but it's just not like that. Theodore only ever cared about me. And it is my biggest regret in life that I didn't take the plunge with him sooner. All those years that we could have had in Ajenti together... That's all I want, to grow old with my Dorie—and to have nothing to do with you.*"

"*Yeah, well, I didn't ask for this situation either. But, you know, we're similar in that we both fiercely love our men. I would do anything for Norman... including getting my mind melded with yours. I know that I'll see him again one day. I need to believe it. For all you know, Tyrona, you will see Theodore again. And if our minds are forever linked, so be it. And I mean, who knows? It's only been a few days, I think. This could turn into a gift.*"

"*How? How is situation anything but a curse?*"

"*Look, I know you were suddenly ripped away from your friends, only to be caged in this place and get me all up in your head. And you know, I was ripped away from Norman. Just like you, I never got a chance to say goodbye. As soon as we arrived, Norman was whisked away, and I was made to believe that I was being taken to a special waiting room for family and friends. We're both in the same situation here. The least we can do is work it out together while trying to stay positive. Because once you go down that negative mindset, it can be hard to find your way back to the light. I've seen many good men succumb to their own negative attitudes—my own father being one of them. So, you can preach all you want, my sister, about how you are so talented with magical powers and how you can steel your mind away from those you are tampering with. You can be the most bitchin' witch there is, but even you can still learn a thing or two. Just like how you can steel away your mind, I can steel away my mind—from negativity and depression.*

*"So come on, Tyrona, think positive. I challenge you to find three positive things about this place. Right now. Come on, no dilly-dallying!"*

Tyrona was stunned and had no idea what to say, but Kate kept on prodding her. *"Alright already! Holy Eklatros, you can be annoying."*

Kate giggled. *"It's one of my specialties!"*

*"Okay, just three things? Well, I know you don't like it, but I like the plain gray walls. Admittedly, at first, I hated the color, too. But now, I see it as calming and soothing. So, that's one."*

*"Really? The gray walls?"*

*"Yes. Okay, two, I like the solitude, as it reminds me of Ajenti. Now, this place is nothing like my apartment, mind you, but the solitude is similar. Aside from your presence, I actually find it quite peaceful."*

Kate rolled her eyes. *"What's the third thing then?"*

*"I mean, honestly, for how annoying you are, and for how much I don't like that you have destroyed my ability to put up a steel wall around my mind, you, Kate, would be the third positive thing."*

*"Me? Didn't you just say you liked the peace and quiet?"*

*"Yeah, I do. But it wouldn't be the same without you. Just having someone to talk to has been reassuring, I will admit."*

Kate burst out into a joyous laughter. *"I freaking knew it. You do have a soft spot for me."*

It was Tyrona's turn to roll her eyes, but she also grinned. *"Yeah, I suppose you could put it that way."*

*"Does that mean that we're officially friends?"*

*"Yes, we're friends, Kate."*

*"Aw, thanks, bestie!"*

Tyrona smiled and enjoyed the silence that stretched between them.

"Hey, Kate, can I ask you something?"

"Of course, bestie."

"Do you… are you, like, constantly aching?"

"No, not at all. What do you mean?"

"So, when I first arrived in this room, I was quite sore. I assumed it was from getting knocked unconscious by that metallic human woman."

"That was Svetlana. I met her on my way down here. She seemed… distant."

"Right, well after she knocked me out, I was sore and didn't really think anything of it. I thought it would get better, but over the past few hours or so it's just been getting steadily worse. What was sore is now aching, and I am developing a truly killer headache—which I attributed to you."

"Thanks, Tyrona, but yeah, no. I feel the complete opposite. I feel way more energetic and alert. That's part of the reason I've been bugging you so much, because I can't keep on running around in circles without getting tired… it's just freaking me out. I feel suddenly so alive."

"And I feel like I'm slowly dying. Well, at a faster rate than the normal slow rate."

"You know, that's really strange, don't you think? I mean, how we feel totally opposite? And, not to mention that, like, our minds are linked, right? Why can't we feel what each of us are feeling physically?"

"Well, I can safely say that every time I toyed with someone's mind, I never felt what they were physically feeling. I think it's because it's only our consciousnesses that are connected and not our physical bodies."

"Yeah but, aren't they one and the same?"

"I think it's more like separate but equal. The sum of two parts."

"Sure, I guess so. But seriously, Tyrona, I'm sorry you're in pain. Do you think it has anything to do you with your magic?"

"You know, that's possible. When I first arrived here, I used my magic easily. But here, in this room, I've never been able to feel it. I wonder if that is the reason—because I am cut off from my natural abilities. But then there's you running around in circles."

"*Right? It's just so strange! I've never been much of a runner, but I mean, I should get tired after an hour or two, right?*"

"*Uh, yeah, absolutely you should.*"

"*Yeah I just—it doesn't make any sense.*"

"*Or... maybe it does. Our minds are linked, right? I've never linked my mind with anyone for this long before. What if our minds are connected because they're draining the life out of me, and giving it to you?*"

"*Um, how could that even be possible? We're not even in the same room! I don't have any wires connected to me, do you?*"

"*What are wires?*"

"*What are wires? Oh yeah, I guess your home planet doesn't have any electricity. But, you know, my planet does. You can read my memories, right?*"

"*Yeah, I can. I just don't know what a wire is.*"

"*Oh, well it's like a cord—a string that connects two or more devices together to pass along electronic signals.*"

"*Cords and strings... I remember seeing some large ropes when I first arrived. They were connected to that gate that I came through.*"

"*Oh yeah, that's a crazy memory. Svetlana really knocked you on your ass.*"

"*Thanks, Kate.*"

"*Love you, bestie!*"

Tyrona stared at the gray wall in front of her and smiled. "*What's the first thing you'll do when we get out of here?*"

"*So, we're getting out of here now, are we? Heck yeah, count me in, my bestie witch! I mean, aside from giving Norman a big ol' hug and a long kiss, I really am just craving sushi. Do you know what sushi is? Like, raw fish, rice, seaweed, and all that?*"

"*You know, I have heard of people eating raw fish, but I've never tried it myself.*"

"*Oh, it's just the best. With some wasabi and soy sauce... just divine. What about you?*"

"*Well, getting out of this cage is just the first step. I need to find a way to get home. I know it's crazy, but if I had a chance to check out that gate again... it would be worth getting caught if I could just learn more about it and how it works. And then, yes, I need to embrace Theodore, but not only that, I need to find Ànifa and the others and apologize to them."*

*"Apologize for what? You have nothing to apologize for."*

*"But I abandoned the quest. Even if it was against my will, I still abandoned them. The journey they were on was a difficult one—they needed all the help they could get."*

*"Okay, I get that. But what if all they want to do is apologize to you? What if they feel bad about not being able to help you? That all they could do was stand by as you disappeared? I don't think apologizing is the right thing to do. Instead, just embrace them and be happy. Enjoy the time you have with them and don't dwell on the past. The past is the past. Enjoy the moment. Even this moment, even if we are in crappy gray rooms. Enjoy this moment, because this is the moment that you take control of your life."*

*"Yes, thank you so much, Kate. You really are my bestie. Now, if only I had my wand. Then I could set us both free."*

*"Could you use something else to channel your power through?"*

*"I can channel my power through many things. But I am only attuned to one object, and that is my wand. And the wand itself contains a powerful energy that other catalysts do not."*

*"Ah, I see. Also, you also only ever used one other object to channel your energy through, and that was in a classroom."*

*"But even if I only did it once, it means it can happen again and that I know how to do it. Of course. That being said, no utensil I have been given for my meals has done anything for me."*

*"Well, how about we try together? What if I try to lend you my energy?"*

*"Kate, you're a genius. The next time they feed us, I'll try it."*

*"Great. Now, if only we knew when that was going to happen."*

*"I know, right? Somehow, whatever they're feeding us is keeping me full for what seems like days."*

*"Yeah, which doesn't make sense to me, because if there's such a substance in the world that can keep a human full for over a day, then why isn't it available to everyone? It would help tremendously."*

*"I guess we can just add it to the growing list of extreme oddities about this place."*

A few moments later, a knock sounded through the walls. The tray slid open and Tyrona's latest meal was revealed. After she shoveled down a few spoonsful of gruel, she held the spoon out in front of her.

*"Did you just get fed also?"*

*"Yeah, strange timing, huh? It's almost as if they're listening to us."*

*"If they really were, though, do you think they'd really want us breaking out of here?"*

*"I mean... what if it's all part of their elaborate plan? They let us escape to give us the illusion that we could still have freedom, when everything is being controlled?"*

*"Remember what I said earlier? You need to think positively, not negatively."*

*"Right, well I'm just thinking logically. Sure, there are no wars back home, but people can be deceitful. I wouldn't put it past whoever designed our cages to design something like that as well."*

*"Okay, so what if you are right? Is that going to stop you from breaking out?"*

*"Absolutely not. I'm going to do everything I can to pour all the energy I have into this spoon. You got my back, right?"*

*"Yes, my bestie, I will do whatever I can to send you some of this extra energy I've got."*

*"Great. Let's do this in three, two, one..."*

She held the spoon out in front of her and poured all the energy she had into it. As she did so, she noticed a few oddities. The first was that the hand she held in front of her was not her hand; it looked as if might be Kate's hand. The second oddity was that her grayness had been replaced by pure whiteness.

*What's going on?* she thought. *What's happening? Am I not Tyrona Claire Knorse, S-Class Sorceress from Ajenti? Unless I am not seeing through my own eyes, but Kate's eyes? Kate, are you there? Where did you go? Why is it suddenly so quiet?*

*Did it work? Am I free?*

## 15

# ESCAPE FROM HUMANITY

"Again, sire, I do not recommend this course of action," Carl said as he desperately tried to plead with his new master.

"And I have told you this already, Carl—they were my companions once. I need to do this alone," Gnudashar said firmly as he strut down the hall, his eyes always forward, never once looking back at him.

"But is that Dasch speaking, or Gnudashar?" he asked.

"I am Gnudashar, though Dasch still dwells within me. I cannot escape from his presence, just as he could not escape from mine. We are linked, for better or for worse. And besides, why do you need to be there if you won't be saying anything at all? I'll be recorded the entire time from the security system, right?"

Carl sighed. He couldn't reveal to Gnudashar that Lord Foxaire watched through his glasses. His presence was necessary so Lord Foxaire could observe the conversation from a direct perspective, not one from above. Because he was supposed to be their prophet, Foxaire was determined to let Gnudashar do whatever he wanted, which meant only headaches for Carl.

He sighed again. Overnight, Carl had become servant to a child with no supervision. And child he was, for Gnudashar was

173

experiencing nearly everything for himself for the first time. While it was interesting to witness, Carl just wished he didn't need to observe so closely. But, as much as he disliked being around Gnudashar, he was the only one trying to keep him in line, and he was horrified at the thought of what this creature would do without his nagging.

"Yes, of course the security system will record your conversations just fine," he said. "It's just—"

"It's just nothing. Lord Foxaire will get what he wants, and I will get what I want, and what *we* want is far more important than whatever a pitiful creature such as yourself could ever want."

Carl stopped dead in his tracks. "You know what? Fine. I don't even want to be around you right now. I'll just wait right here."

"Wonderful," Gnudashar said. He hurried through the door that led to the rooms where the specimens were kept.

*Seriously, what an ass,* Carl thought. *As tempted as I am to pass off this responsibility to Sid, he would have even less patience than I. So I suppose I will just keep my babysitting duties.* Carl took out his tablet and switched over to the security feed.

*Well, at this point, I hope he stays in there for a while. And you know what? This may be the better situation. I still get to observe him without being in the same room. Isn't that what I wanted? Yeah, yeah it is what I want. Even if I hardly ever know what that is anymore. At least Lord Foxaire won't have any grounds to punish me, as Gnudashar is getting his way.*

***

Druder Nanasazii stood on his hands as he attempted to return to what he was doing before he had been rudely interrupted. He took a deep breath and calmed his mind as he stared into the nearly pitch-dark room. He had long given up on trying to determine what his cell was made of and how to escape. The only way he was getting out of here was if he was allowed to leave. Now he spent his time practicing to reach out with his consciousness so he could peer beyond his containment cell, but it required a calm and quiet mind. After speaking with the Gnureaver that had once been Dasch, his mind was racing.

*That Gnudashar... he has a sinister reason behind all his questions,* Druder thought. *It does not seem as if he realized I was only telling him half the truth. I have all of Ànifa's memories processed. I fear what would happen if he found out, even if I am unsure as to what he seeks. Yes, Ànifa was wise and knowledgeable, but there must be more to it than that. I don't understand how her memories are of any value to the enemy now that she is dead. Perhaps, next time he comes around, I can dig out some more information from him. But that is a worry for the future. I must return to the present. It is the only way to prepare.*

"... forty-two..." Cecil breathed out as he pushed his body up. He was on his third set of fifty push-ups for the day. His average had been two sets each of push-ups, sit-ups, and squats. In just a few days—by his judgment—he was on his way to becoming the strongest he'd ever been.

"Fifty." Rather than collapsing on the floor, which is what he wanted to do, he instead forced his body to stand up straight. As he worked out the kinks in his back, he heard a familiar voice.

"Good day, Cecil."

"Dasch?" he asked as he turned around. Amazingly, Dasch stood before him in front of the same transparent wall that he had used to talk to that slimy Professor a few days ago. After the initial surprise wore away, he realized something was off about Dasch. He wore elaborate clothing, including a light blue jacket, pressed white pants, and shiny black shoes. There was also a strange, wild look in his eyes —at least, wilder than the usual amount of crazy.

"Dasch, is that really you?"

"Very observant. Druder couldn't tell the difference. Dasch is no more—just his body. I am called Gnudashar now."

"Gnudashar," he repeated. He didn't like the sound of it. "So, the Gnusar remnant you were fighting against..."

"*I* was the Gnusar fighting against Dasch, you puny knight. And you know what? Looking at you now, I realize that you only survived your quest with Ànifa because of your armor."

"So, you have Dasch's memories I see."

"Not just Dasch's, but Ànifa's as well. Yes, my superior intelligence has processed everything. It is quite beneficial to have two perspectives of the same events. It helps me to better understand Dasch."

"So, what, are you here now to suck up my brains? To gain my memories? To the void with you, Gnudashar. You can go screw yourself."

"How hostile. So be it. I don't need to speak with you anyhow. I am far more interested in the wizard."

"Theodore! How is he?"

"I haven't spoken to him yet, you dimwit. I just wanted to see you with my own eyes. And all I see is disappointment. You've spent your free time getting stronger, but it will do no good. You will never escape from this place."

Cecil smiled. "Oh, you can bet your stolen ass that I will get out of here, and it will be over your dead body."

Gnudashar smiled even wider in response. "So, you'd kill your friend to escape?"

"You are not my friend. And even if Dasch is listening, I'm sure he'd want me to kill you, too, since the Dasch I knew would never allow himself to aid the enemy."

"If only I was willing to educate you on the matter. But alas, I am not. No, you're better off to remain ignorant. It suits you much better."

"Fuck you, too."

The transparent screen quickly returned to being a boring old wall.

"I don't suppose you can get me something to train with, huh?" he yelled. "Who am I kidding? Why would they need any information from me when Dasch has been lost to that Gnusar!" He kicked the wall in frustration, and a sharp pain flew up his leg. He sat down and rubbed his foot.

*What. An. Asshole,* he thought as he shook his head. *Dasch... I failed you. I was your new leader, and I allowed you to follow us through the gate. I did not think of the consequences. I did not think of the remnant that lay dormant in your chest. Whatever Gnudashar does is on me. As a Knight of Ajenti and Steward of Eklatros, I will bear the burden of your misdeeds, so you are my responsibility. I will get out of here, and once I do, I will not show any mercy.*

Theodore placed the bookmark between the pages, closed the book, then let out a massive yawn. When he had requested books to read, he had been expecting something a tad bit more entertaining and educational. That's not saying that *The Nishna Delta: Volume 213: Year 67901 to 68100* wasn't interesting. But he could only read up on the soil samples and salinity levels of the delta for so long before going cross-eyed.

He took off the special set of spectacles that he had been given and flipped through the book, looking at the actual foreign text. He assumed the Nishna Delta was a geographical feature somewhere on the planet he was on, and if so, he was learning quite a lot about the world through these volumes.

He nearly jumped out of his skin when the wall in front of him suddenly became transparent.

"Oh, Dasch its just... Wait... how is it possible? Did you escape? And what are you wearing?"

Dasch smiled as he stared at the wizard with unusually dark eyes. "Theodore. I have been looking forward to speaking with you. Please call me Gnudashar. The one called Dasch is no more; I am in control now."

Theodore didn't know what to say. Dasch, who was the strongest of them all, had lost? He could only imagine it was due to this foul planet. He sighed.

"What a shame. Dasch was the best of us. I just... I don't want to accept that he lost."

"Accept it, wizard," Gnudashar spat. "That human is now locked in the same cage I once was. A fitting turn of events, in my opinion."

Theodore glared at him. "Gnudashar is it? How can you speak ill of the man whose body you possess? Also, if you really are a Gnusar, why don't you look like the monsters we fought in that slot canyon?"

"I am quite different and far more intelligent than those beasts. I have had thousands of years to fuse myself with this body. I do not need to mutilate it in any way to take control.

"Now Theodore, I understand you may have questions for me, but I also have questions for you. How about we go back and forth asking questions? Since you just asked yours, I will ask mine. And this question does not count."

"Yes, I have questions. I don't really know what it is I am talking to, but I guess that's part of it. And sure, why not," he said as he threw his arms in the air. "Go ahead and ask yours."

"I knew I could count on you to be amicable."

"Yeah, sure. The only reason I'm being so civil is because I have no other choice if I want to talk with someone other than myself."

"Well then, let's get to it. Tell me what you understand Gnusaramnii to be."

"Pure evil. How else can I describe a being that enjoys causing pain and destruction? To me, Gnusaramnii is the epitome of pure evil."

Gnudashar nodded slowly. "I can see how you would think that. However, good and evil are simply matters of perspective. Given enough time, everything dies, including planets. Death is as natural as birth."

"Yes, death is simply part of life. But killing for the sake of killing is wrong. Now, I will ask my question. I understand that Gnusaramnii was attacking our planet to access the gate we went through, since it wants to return here. But, why Eklatros? Throughout our journey, I learned that even the Ekataramn we were awakening are aliens. What is so special about Eklatros that attracted all these otherworldly beings?"

"Theodore, that is a loaded question, one not even I have the answer to. Neither me nor Gnusaramnii truly know why the Ekataramn traveled through space. It could be completely random. Or, possibly the Ekataramn foresaw everything that was going to happen." Gnudashar chuckled. "Whatever the reason is, don't you find it ironic that you invited Ànifa along to learn more about the Ekataramn, and yet she was the one to learn their secrets? I do. How much of her memories have you processed?"

"Well, I have vivid images of certain parts of Ànifa's life from the initial transfer. However, as you may know, I have been in some distress due to losing Tyrona, then Ànifa, and now Dasch," he glared at Gnudashar as he said his former companion's name. "And now that I'm finally in the same place as Tyrona, I'm stuck in this cage. And on top of all of that, I can't use magic. So, to be honest with you, I haven't gotten a chance to process her memories."

"That's quite disappointing. I thought that out of the three of you, you would be the one to process them fastest."

"Out of the three of us? Did you already talk to Cecil and Druder?"

"Indeed. Cecil was brash, as expected, and Druder told me of the many memories he has processed. However, you know Ànifa better than he does, so it was your unique perspective I was looking for."

"And what are you looking for?"

"Answers and information. Anything to help aid master Gnusaramnii when it is ready to once again descend upon Eklatros. Ànifa was the key to awakening the Ekataramn. And yet, you all failed to awake the final and most vital one."

"Vital for what? Also, I just asked a few questions in a row, did you want to ask me one first?"

"I will answer your follow-up question first. As you are aware, each Ekataramn held a special power of sorts. The final Ekataramn, Hajinmahn, holds the power of time. With Hajinmahn awake, one can travel through both space and time."

"So, Gnusaramnii could potentially travel back in time and destroy the past? That's a terrifying thought."

Gnudashar stared at him for a moment, as if confirming his

statement. "Now, Theodore, which of Ànifa's memories do you remember the best?"

"Just bits and pieces of her life, before she met all of us. So, for instance, there was this one time when Ànifa, Nayeli, and Pearla were socializing with a group of male elves by a small pond. Ànifa and Pearla weren't into it and wanted to leave, but that is how Nayeli met Raveen. To which, Ànifa somewhat regrets because when Nayeli met Raveen, she turned down other, more suitable elves. Raveen was a common elf and a troublemaker, and Ànifa never liked that."

"Yes, I know of the memory you refer to. At least that confirms the memories you have are indeed the same ones I have. Druder spoke of other memories I have as well. However, transferring memories like that, more often than not, causes certain ones to mix together. Yttendaus truly has a special power."

"How do you know that? How do you know how other memory transfers work?"

"Gnusaramnii. While you may see Dasch's body, there are many people's memories floating around in my head. Mine, first and foremost, then Dasch's, Ànifa's, and Gnusaramnii's. For at the moment of my rebirth, my mind melded with Gnusaramnii's. I know more than you ever will, Theodore."

"And yet, you require information from me. Now that is something I find ironic."

"I do not, for you do not seem to possess any of the knowledge I seek."

"Wonderful. I would rather not help you out."

"And yet, you already have."

"Sure, whatever. Look, I do have another question. I want to know about the Ekataramn. If you have the memories you do, then you know the Great Barriers were truly formidable. And yet, after the Ekataramn were awoken, the Great Barriers disappeared, but the threat against them did not. And after this conversation, it seems to me like Gnusaramnii never wanted to harm the Ekataramn. Is that correct?"

"Indeed, you are correct. You may not have the knowledge I seek, but you are wise. Normally, this is not a question I would answer in full. However, out of everyone, you should know this.

"No, Gnusaramnii never wanted to harm the Ekataramn—it wanted to gain their power and steal their divine abilities. During Gnusaramnii's first tour on your planet, it learned that it could not possess the Ekataramn in the same way it can possess other creatures. It nearly destroyed Alakana to learn that. It was only after Alakana was gravely injured that the other Ekataramn created their Great Barriers. And with the barriers, Gnusaramnii could not gain access to the knowledge and wisdom that lay inside. And, as you know, Ànifa was the only one who could wake them up. So, in turn, Gnusaramnii never wanted to kill Ànifa."

"But wait, what? Ànifa died—killed by Gnusaramnii!"

"No. Ànifa died because she spent her entire life force to push Gnusaramnii out of Queen Stella's body, and in doing so obliterating Gnusaramnii of its physical presence on your planet. Gnusaramnii never wanted to kill Ànifa; it wanted to bring out her power. The only way to do that was to give her an enemy to fight and people to save. You and the rest of her party played that role well. Without all of you, Ànifa never would have discovered her true power and identity. And then, right when she reached the peak of her power, she died. Right when Gnusaramnii was ready to reason with her, to speak with her one-on-one. Its plan was to gain Ànifa's trust so they could awaken Hajinmahn together. After that, he would have welcomed her and whoever followed her as an ally."

He squinted at his former comrade's features. "Gain Ànifa's trust? Become her ally? Did you even know Ànifa? She never would have sided with you!"

"Perhaps she would have, if she learned of its true goal."

"And what is Gnusaramnii's goal? Why is it trying to make everything a copy of itself?"

"I know that—from your perspective, as it was also Dasch's and Ànifa's—everything about the Gnusar's invasion on Eklatros was evil. But that is not the case. The Gnusar, Gnuelry, Gnureavers, and Gnurargurts are of a higher intelligence. They are the superior beings. Individuality only leads to pain and loneliness. Yet creatures that share a singular mind, a singular intelligence—that is the peak of evolution. That is what life is supposed to be."

Theodore laughed aloud until his stomach ached. All the while, Gnudashar simply glared at him. "Oh man, I really needed that. I really needed to hear a good joke. I know you're serious, but that's what makes it even more hilarious. How is it even possible that you, a being who holds multiple people's memories, truly believe that?"

"How can I not? Dasch's existence is the definition of loneliness. Ànifa spent her entire life trying to figure out who she was. Being part of a larger consciousness alleviates all that. With Gnusaramnii, no one is alone. With Gnusaramnii, everyone knows their purpose. With Gnusaramnii, life can thrive and flourish without the crushing weight of doubt and unnecessary emotions. How can you not see the benefit in that? For instance, you are lonely and bored now, correct? That would not be the case if you were one with Gnusaramnii."

"Yeah... I hear you, but I can't buy what you're selling. Did you forget that I am an S-Class Sorcerer of Ajenti? That I wield the elements of wind, fire, ground, and electricity? Every time I would cast a spell, I could feel Eklatros' energy move through me. Yes, I am currently lonely, but it is because I am missing Tyrona. But I am not alone, for I have Eklatros by my side. Even now, however far away I am from Eklatros, I know she is still out there, and I know that she still loves me. If you are as close to nature as I am, you will never be alone. That is all the higher intelligence I need."

"Is it, now? Gnusaramnii has taken possession of hundreds of planets. All of them are part of the collective consciousness Gnusaramnii has created and nurtured. And they are all still as mighty and divine as Eklatros."

"Ah well, good to know that can happen. But understand this—I know what it's like to have other people in my head. It's not something I would welcome on a day-to-day basis. I need to be in control of my own mind and my own feelings, for it is the only way I can use magic."

"It is not the only way. There are many magic users under Gnusaramnii's protection, and they all—"

"Okay! Enough already, I get it. You are utterly infatuated with Gnusaramnii. Nothing you can say will convince me otherwise, just like Gnusaramnii never would have swayed Ànifa to his side. Again, you hold her memories and Dasch's memories, and yet fail to understand how fiercely independent we can be."

"So, you won't join with Gnusaramnii, even if you could get your magic back and be free of this cell?"

"What you offer is not freedom, but simply trading one prison for another. Look, do you have any other questions for me?" Theodore was growing quite impatient with this new pseudo-Dasch.

"No. But next time we speak, I hope that you have more of Ànifa's memories processed."

"What are you, my instructor now? I don't answer to you."

"And what if I told you that you can see Tyrona again if you were to comply?"

"Wow, you are *really* good at convincing people of things," Theodore said, crossing his arms smugly. "Yeah, I'm not going anywhere with you, and I'll see Tyrona again, but it will be on my own terms."

"Perhaps. Until next time, Theodore."

The transparent wall once again became opaque. Theodore stared at the wall for several seconds before throwing his arms in the air and bellowing out a scream.

"Seriously, what is wrong with this place?" he yelled. He took a deep breath, calming himself slightly before he continued. "First, it takes Tyrona away from me. Now Dasch is prisoner to that steaming pile of scum. At least I now know how truly evil Gnusaramnii is. Dasch, I am so sorry. I will try to find a way to set you free from that monster. There has to be a way, right? Just like there must be a way to get out of here, without succumbing to that creep?"

He leaned against the wall and slumped to the ground.

*What did I get myself into?* he thought. *Tyrona, why were you taken here? What is the point in all this?*

# 16

# INTERLUDE: LOCATION - UNKNOWN

Begin Replay of NIWAT Inner Datalog
Recording C-0000670330 S-001 N-01

*Francentia* emerged into an unfamiliar system. Before them was a large moon. Its surface was obscured by a thick, gray atmosphere. The moon was one of seven large celestial bodies that orbited a large mustard yellow gas giant with scattered clouds of swirling black storms.

"Is everyone functioning?" Blu-Dreem asked.

"I don't know, am I functioning? Did we make it?" Zanzi asked.

"My internal datalogs are struggling to make sense of what happened," I replied.

"*Francentia*, respond," Maker Denorad commanded.

"Acknowledged, Captain. We have safely arrived in an unknown location."

"What do you mean, 'unknown?'" I asked.

"This planetary system is not in my databank."

"That explains why my datalogs are still freaking out. Everyone, shut off your universal positioning system."

"Golden gears, that's so much better," Zanzi replied.

"*Francentia*, scan our surroundings," Zombu commanded as he leaned forward in his chair.

"Initializing scan," *Francentia* responded.

"Beedee, how's the jump drive looking?" Maker Denorad asked.

"Fried. It's quite fried," Blu-Dreem said.

"So are several of the other systems. We're going to need to set down somewhere so we can repair the ship."

"I figured as much," Zombu said. "On the bright side of things, I don't think we need to worry about being pursued. If we don't know where we are, how could anyone find us?"

"I agree, but we must stay vigilant. Unknown dangers lie in unfamiliar places," I replied.

"Way to bring down the mood," Zanzi said.

"Listen to Niwat," Maker Denorad said. "He is right—we are going to need to be extra cautious from here on out."

"Scan complete," *Francentia* replied. "I have located two hundred thirty-nine suitable landing zones on the nearest moon."

"Analyze the twenty closest ones for the best option," Maker Denorad replied.

"Analyzing. Analyzing. Route updated. However, navigation systems are functioning at forty-five percent."

"Something is draining power. We need to head down there now," Blu-Dreem said.

"*Francentia*, upload the routes to the crew, then turn on power saving mode."

"Acknowledged. Routes uploaded. Powering down now."

The data was in our network even before *Francentia* powered off. Out of the twenty options, there were three that made the most sense. One landing zone was in a deep, wide crater, another on a high plateau, and the last was in a large cave hidden by a massive waterfall.

"I'm tagging the three that I think would work the best," I told the crew.

"Yeah, I was looking at the waterfall cave spot," Zanzi said. "I think that would be the best. We'd be really hidden in there."

"There are too many variables. I don't want to have only one way out," Maker Denorad said. "Plus, I'd much rather have a place with wide open sky. I say we choose the plateau."

"That was my top choice as well," I replied.

"It doesn't really matter to me. We just really need to land somewhere, now," Blu-Dreem said as he nervously fiddled with his hands.

"The plateau it is," Maker Denorad said.

"Great. It looks like there's a medium-sized settlement one-hundred-and-one-point-seven kilometers from the landing zone. We should take a skiff over there to see if we can pick up any supplies," Zombu said.

"I agree. We'll need to be careful. There's no activity of any kind coming from there. It could be a ghost town," I cautioned.

"Better that than full of hostiles," Zanzi said.

---

Begin Replay of NIWAT Inner Datalog
Recording C-0000670330 S-001 N-07

"I seriously can't believe you two talked me into coming along," Zanzi said.

"I know you are quite jumpy in situations like this, but you do have the best scanners. You'll be able to identify the parts we need better than anyone," I reminded him.

"Yeah, our maker and Beedee got everything covered on their side," Zombu said. "You'd only get in the way if you had stayed behind."

"Thanks, Zom-butt," Zanzi mocked.

I smiled and focused on driving the skiff. Zanzi and Zombu had always had a sort of sibling rivalry going on between them, even if they were quite different. They had been built simultaneously, but only Zombu contained several biological parts—provided by their maker, Denorad. Maker Denorad was a cyborg, a common sight back on Theronior. However, few who underwent the operation used their own removed body parts to construct a bio-androbotix. Maker Denorad had always prided himself on that fact. In turn, Zanzi has always been jealous that Denorad hadn't chosen him instead. As for Zombu, he had always been quite down to earth, much like Maker Denorad.

The land we passed was heavily scarred. There was no life to be found—only decomposing carcasses of various animals. The stench was so overwhelming that I was forced to shut off my smell receptors.

"You know, this is looking—and smelling—a bit familiar," Zombu said.

"Indeed. It is possible the Gnusar may be here," I replied.

"But, where are they?" Zanzi asked.

"We are headed toward the settlement. It's possible there could be some there," Zombu suggested.

"My thoughts exactly," I said. "*Francentia*'s scanners can't pick up everything. Stay on guard, you two."

Upon saying the words, the settlement began to come into view. Large, towering structures thrust into the sky. Each one was pointed at the top, and some seemed to have horns.

"Interesting architecture," Zanzi commented.

"Stop gawking and start scanning," I ordered. "You too, Zombu. We can't let anything take us by surprise."

Seven minutes and twenty-two seconds later, we entered the large settlement. All scans were negative for any activity. Signs in an unknown language hung from buildings and were written on street signs. At first, the way was clear, but the streets became more and more dense with trash and corpses as we pushed on.

I drove the skiff into a relatively empty alleyway and powered it down.

"We walk from here. Did you find anything that we need?"

"Yes. We got a cache of items containing copper, aluminum, and magnesium to the northwest. Steel nails are in abundance around us. I'm also picking up several items nearby that may be batteries. Some are in the direction of the elements, but the one object giving off the purest signal is behind us," Zanzi said.

"So we can pick that one up on the way back. Let's just focus on grabbing what we can that has copper, magnesium, and aluminum first. We should each bring up the map on our screens. Keep an eye out for any hostiles."

We made our way out of the alley and into the open street. The corpses we passed were mostly of an unknown bipedal alien species, but scattered among them were round and scaly creatures. I sent a short recording to the others, and Maker Denorad quickly replied. He recognized the scaly creatures to be the same Gnusar that had destroyed Theronior.

"It figures as much," Zanzi replied as he viewed Maker Denorad's reply. "We try to run from them and we stumble upon a moon that was decimated by the same aliens that took out our own planet."

"The odds of this happening seem quite low. I wonder if the blast was purposeful?" Zombu asked.

"An intriguing thought, but it's a near zero probability that whoever shot that missile knew of the outcome," I replied.

"Yes, but even so, this is quite strange," Zombu replied.

"Indeed, it is."

We made it to our destination without any more chatter. I immediately checked the door handle and to my surprise it opened easily. I stepped inside and scanned the darkly lit room, which turned out to be an alien forge. Within seven seconds, I identified all the materials we could gather. While there was raw copper and raw aluminum, the only magnesium I could identify had already been processed and alloyed.

"I'm sending you both the list of items we should gather. I've categorized them by element. Once we have all the items, we can assess if we need to melt anything down here or if we can carry it all back on the skiff."

In total, we gathered five-point-eight-two kilograms of copper, four-point-seven-six kilograms of aluminum, and three-point-zero-nine kilograms of the purest magnesium alloy we could find. The alloy contained eighty-seven percent magnesium, twelve percent aluminum, zero-point-seven percent zinc, and zero-point-three percent manganese. While the mixture wasn't ideal, it would work.

We left the forge and walked out into the street.

"Hold on, I'm picking up some movement just south of us," Zanzi said, causing all three of us to turn around. I heightened my scanners and identified a lone Gnusar. It was ninety-six meters away and moving with a sense of purpose.

"You two up for a detour?" I asked.

"You're not seriously thinking of following that thing, are you?" Zanzi whispered loudly.

"Of course I am. I don't think it sensed us, and it's the only life we've seen since coming here."

"But what if there are more of them where it's going?" Zanzi asked.

"That's exactly what I want to know. Yes, Theronior is destroyed, but now that we're here, standing amongst the ruins of a completely unknown civilization... it makes me sad, you know? We don't know anything about who these people were or what kind of culture they had. I don't want Theronior to succumb to the same fate. I say that once we figure our circuits out, we make our way back to Theronior and reclaim what was once ours. But now is not the time for this discussion. I don't want to lose the Gnusar. We need to find out more about them."

"Come on, Zanzi," Zombu chided. "Or would you rather stay behind, alone with the skiff?"

"When you put it that way, let's get Gnusar hunting!"

---

Begin Replay of NIWAT Inner Datalog
Recording C-0000670330 S-001 N-09

We tracked the Gnusar for one-point-eight-two kilometers, at which point it squeezed itself into a hole and disappeared underground.

"Do you think that's where it lives?" Zanzi asked.

"It's possible. We should set up a remote feed and keep an eye on this spot. Zanzi, can we use one of your cameras?"

"Alright, I guess," Zanzi said as he opened a compartment in his side and removed a small silver camera. He then walked over and adhered it to a street lamp.

"Okay, so as you know, this thing only has enough battery to last a week, at which point, I'll need to recall it. How's the feed looking to you, Niwat?"

"It looks great. It's got a great sphere of view. Now, we need to hurry back and finish our mission."

"We should set up a few more cameras," Zombu suggested. "It'll be better if we observe a few other locations as well."

Begin Replay of NIWAT Inner Datalog
Recording C-0000670330 S-001 N-15

"So, what do you think, Beedee?" I asked.

"The copper and aluminum will work perfectly, and the magnesium will do. It looks like you've got more than enough steel nails—so that's a big help. As for the three batteries you gathered, these two I should be able to work with just fine. This battery, though," Blu-Dreem said as he picked up the hand-sized square battery and inspected it closer, "I've never seen anything like it. We'll need to run some tests, but before that, we need to figure out how it even works. I don't see any clear positive or negative charge symbols. But it certainly is a battery, unless our scanners are providing a false-positive."

"Great, well, at least we found what we needed, right?" Zanzi asked.

"For the most part, yes. But if we can't figure this battery out, you'll need to go back. The two others won't cut it," Blu-Dreem said.

"There's got to be other batteries we can use out there. The problem is that we weren't alone," Zombu said.

"We found a Gnusar and followed it back to what appears to be its den, so we set up four of Zanzi's cameras to monitor for any activity," I added.

"I still can't believe the Gnusar are here as well," Maker Denorad said. "Where did these monstrosities even come from?"

"It's still far too early to tell, but we may be on a path back to where it came from," I said. "Judging by the state of destruction and how it appears to be recent, I believe this may have been the celestial body they destroyed before Theronior. And if that's the case, perhaps the next place we jump to could possibly be the location the Gnusar visited before this one."

"That's certainly a wild theory, but stranger things have happened," Maker Denorad said.

"But... have they? Have there really been stranger things than this? Go ahead and name one thing," Zanzi said.

Zombu sighed and shook his head. "Hey Niwat, what was it that you were starting to say earlier? About how you wanted to save Theronior?"

"Yes, I do. Don't you all want to save Theronior as well?"

"Do you even need to ask? Of course I want to. I never wanted to run—but that was our only option," Maker Denorad said.

"Agreed, it was our only option. But here on this moon, we have found a unique opportunity. We need to monitor these Gnusar. We need to learn as much as we can about them so we know what to do when we return home."

"It could be years until we return home," Maker Denorad said.

"I know that, but even so, I hope to return," I said.

"You know I'm with you," Zombu said.

"Yes, I will support you as well," Blu-Dreem said.

"Heck, we're all going," Maker Denorad said. "Beedee, how long do you think the repairs will take?"

"Unsure. Could be about a week. The fabricator can only work so fast, and the damage is quite extensive."

"Well, that's perfect. We'll be able to get maximum usage out of the cameras," I said. Beside me, Zanzi was grumbling.

"I don't want to be here for a week," Zanzi said.

"The more you help out, the faster the repairs will take," Blu-Dreem said.

Zanzi clapped his hands together. "Great, where should we start?"

---

Begin Replay of NIWAT Inner Datalog
Recording C-0000670330 S-007 N-09

I stood behind Zanzi and Zombu as they eagerly watched a screen split into four quadrants. Each quadrant displayed a live video feed that tracked each of the four cameras as they flew back to the ship.

"Come on little guys, you can make it," Zanzi was saying.

"Are you sure you saved enough power? They still have twelve kilometers to go and they're nearly depleted," Zombu said.

"Correction: they have one-point-eight-two kilometers to go before they're in range of my radio signal. Once they pick up the signal, the emergency reserve power system will kick in," Zanzi replied.

"As long as they get here within the hour. The repairs are nearly complete," Maker Denorad said.

"Oh, they should get here in half that time," Zanzi said confidently.

"Either way, we got a lot of good data from those cameras," I said. "From what I have analyzed so far, six different Gnusar have been going in and out of that hole. While sometimes they return empty-handed, most of the time they bring back random items. Almost as if they are building a nest."

"For all we know, they could be thriving down there. We should have sent a camera down that hole," Zombu said.

"Again, they could have learned of our presence that way," I replied.

"We've gone undetected this entire time, and I plan to keep it that way," Maker Denorad said.

"Exactly. If they're building a nest here, then we can assume they'll build one on Theronior," I replied.

"Precisely why we should have had eyes in their lair. Wouldn't it be better to know how many are down there?" Zombu asked.

"Too late now," Zanzi said and shrugged.

Blu-Dreem entered the bridge. "Alright, the repairs are complete. We just need to wait twenty minutes for the battery to cool down and recharge. In the meantime, *Francentia* should be back online shortly."

"When we have more time, I'd like to analyze that battery more closely. Its power output and capacity are unlike anything I've ever seen before," Maker Denorad said.

"I'll log that into my list of reminders," Blu-Dreem said. "It really is quite extraordinary. It's too bad we only have the one."

"It was the only one that we could find on our scans," Zanzi replied. "Granted, we only scanned roughly thirty percent of the entire city."

"It's strange, really. It's almost like it didn't come from here," I said.

"There are other settlements on the moon," Maker Denorad said. "And while we could scan all of them, I would rather like to move on from this place."

"The materials that compose the battery are quite unusual," *Francentia* replied as she crackled online.

"*Francentia*, I hope you had a nice rest. Can you give us a precise reading on the battery?" Maker Denorad asked.

"The shell is an alloy made of iron, carbon, silicon, manganese, phosphorus, aluminum, and trace amounts of oxygen. It's combination of elements allow it to draw energy from surrounding light sources, including the light source it gives off."

"Are you saying it's a self-recharging battery?"

"To a degree, yes. Overtime I will learn more about its full capabilities," *Francentia* replied.

"Wonderful. I'd like to know as much as I can about that battery. It sounds to me as if it could replace your tri-battery system," Maker Denorad said as he looked at each of us. "You wouldn't need to recharge at all."

"Yeah, but recharging feels really good," Zanzi said. "I wouldn't want to lose that. Ah! The emergency power kicked in. All four cameras made it."

"Great. *Francentia*, how much longer until the battery is ready?" Maker Denorad asked.

"It will be ready in seventeen more minutes," *Francentia* replied.

"While we wait, could you provide a full system report?" Blu-Dreem added.

"Affirmative. All systems normal. Power levels at ninety percent and rising."

"Just eight more kilometers to go. I've got them going at their top speed, too. ETA: ten minutes," Zanzi said, his eyes never leaving the monitor.

---

```
Begin Replay of NIWAT Inner Datalog
Recording C-0000670330 S-013 N-02
```

"Two minutes until instantaneous hyperspace travel," *Francentia* announced.

"Oh man, this is crazy. I still can't believe we're making a blind jump. If *Francentia* is off even a little bit, we could be crushed by a gas giant, or even consumed by a star," Zanzi complained.

"For the last time, we've got no choice," Blu-Dreem exclaimed. "Stop complaining."

"Trust in *Francentia*; trust in our maker," I said. "We'll be fine."

The cockpit fell into silence. No one spoke, aside from *Francentia*'s announcements.

"Fifteen seconds until jump," *Francentia* announced. "... Ten. Nine. Eight ..."

"Hold on tight," Maker Denorad said over the countdown. "We don't know what we're in for."

The universe flashed into a geometric rainbow of colors as *Francentia* jumped through space. Three seconds later, they emerged into another unfamiliar system. They sat above a medium-sized planet. The planet's atmosphere, if it had any at all, was transparent. The surface was charred black, with oceans of red lava flowing past jagged mountain ranges.

"Calculating location. Error: location unknown," *Francentia* announced.

"Surprise, surprise," Zanzi replied mockingly.

"Surprise indeed—we didn't get crushed by a gas giant," Zombu chided.

"Or killed by a star," Zanzi replied.

"*Francentia*, system status update," Blu-Dreem prompted.

"All systems functional and fully operational," *Francentia* responded.

"Fantastic. Now, scan the planet below for any life."

"Scanning. Scanning. Life forms found. There are seven large clusters of Gnusar below ground scattered throughout the planet, with several hundred additional Gnusar roaming the surface."

"The Gnusar are here also? I wonder if this is where they came from. Severed circuits, it looks like it would suit them perfectly," Zanzi said.

"That is unlikely," *Francentia* replied. "My scans are also picking up on several mass graveyards of an unknown species."

"Again, this is another planet ravaged by the Gnusar," Maker Denorad said as he hung his head. He looked up and smacked his fist into his palm. "How many planets have they destroyed? Dozens? Hundreds?"

"We may yet see," I replied. "This only solidifies my theory that we are following the Gnusar's path backward. This means that we may yet find it's home planet."

"Even if it takes a hundred jumps?" Zanzi asked.

"At this point, whatever it takes," Blu-Dreem said.

"Does *Francentia* even have enough power to last a hundred jumps?" Zombu asked.

"My power levels are maxed out," *Francentia* replied. "The new battery you installed charged itself when we jumped."

"So, you're saying you can charge yourself by jumping? A move that typically uses a good percentage of your power?" Maker Denorad mused. "That is absolutely amazing. You know, I think I can only agree with Niwat. I believe we are on a path to track the Gnusar back to their home planet. It is up to us to save Theronior. We were meant to find that battery. We now have everything we need to continue our path. *Francentia*, how long until you can jump again?"

"While my power reserves are maxed out, the jump drive itself needs to cool down. We have forty-one minutes until the jump drive can be used again."

"Then we wait. There's no reason to go down there. The sooner we make it to their home planet, the sooner we can save Theronior," Maker Denorad said.

"And how do you suppose we will save Theronior?" Zanzi asked. "What can we do against an enemy that destroys entire planets? Not to mention the fact that there must be trillions of them out there!"

"I don't know, Zanzi," I replied, "but we have time to figure it out. Besides, we may stumble upon that answer just like we stumbled upon the battery."

"My thoughts exactly," Maker Denorad said.

---

```
Begin Replay of NIWAT Inner Datalog
Recording C-0000670332 S-001 N-01
```

*Francentia* emerged into another unknown star system. This was the third system we had journeyed to since escaping Theronior, and once again, it didn't look promising. While the blue planet contained landmasses with plant life, I could also make out an uncountable number of destroyed settlements just from my own scans.

"*Francentia*, scan the planet below for Gnusar activity," Maker Denorad asked.

"Scanning. Heavy Gnusar activity confirmed, both above ground and below ground. It appears as if the Gnusar are feeding on the remaining foliage."

"Is this going to become our new routine? Jump from one planet to another planet, scan new planet, then jump to the next planet?" Zanzi asked.

"What would you rather have us do?" I asked.

"You know, I have no clue. I suppose that I'd rather not explore any of those planets."

"Then, for the last time, can you please stop complaining?" I asked.

"Everyone, we must keep our heads together," Maker Denorad urged. "How can we expect to save Theronior if we keep arguing amongst ourselves? That being said, Zanzi, understand that we're all in this together. While I absolutely value your opinions, know that none of us enjoy the situation we're in. Try to look for the positives, rather than the negatives."

"Right, sure, I understand," Zanzi replied.

"And Niwat, I need you to be a leader."

"Yes, of course, Maker. I apologize for my lack of patience," I replied.

"Great. Now that we're on the same page, let's prepare for the next jump. I know this may start getting old, but just because the last three planets we've been to have been overrun by the Gnusar, we may yet find a planet that beat them. If we do, we must attempt to gather as much knowledge as we can. We must not be hostile to any species that could defend themselves."

"Right, but wouldn't that make them not so forgiving to strangers falling out of the sky?" Zanzi asked.

"Yeah, how do you suppose we get them to reveal their secret to beating the Gnusar in this hypothetical situation?" Zombu asked.

"We'll just need to solder those wires when we get to them," Maker Denorad said. "Beedee, status check."

"Everything looks fine to me. As *Francentia* said, the battery I installed does indeed charge itself during hyperspace travel. It's quite magnificent."

"So it seems. Keep a close eye on it. Just because it's working miracles for us now doesn't mean that it won't become a problem. We still know little about it," Maker Denorad stressed.

"Of course, Maker. I absolutely agree. I will run a complete diagnostic scan on the battery after every jump," Blu-Dreem replied.

"Good," Maker Denorad nodded.

"Maker, I have a concern," I said as I pointed at my fellow androbotix. "We don't need to eat to survive, but you do. Do you have enough food and water on board for the journey?"

"I have enough to last me another four months. But if need be, I can always take the time to scavenge for food. I will be fine, but thank you for your concern. Now, we've got some time to kill. Anyone want to play a game?"

<h1 style="text-align:center">17</h1>

# ESCAPE FROM IGNORANCE

Navacus sat in his office as he watched his team start work for the day through the windows. He took a sip of his hot green tea and wheezed.

"Sterg, I can't thank you enough for how helpful you've been recently. There's been so much going on lately, and having you around has been helping me work through everything."

"*It's my pleasure,*" Sterg replied telepathically. "*Is there anything you're still needing assistance with?*"

"*I just need to think through the contract we read last night and the subsequent dream we had. So right, that was a heck of a lot to go through —the contract, I mean. I've always been a slow reader, so absorbing over six hundred pages in about thirty minutes was incredibly intensive. I still have a slight headache from the overload of information. But at least you helped me gain new insight. Now there truly is no more rose-colored veil; I can fully see the ill intent. While having my creations and ideas automatically becoming Foxaire Biotech Industries' intellectual property is not surprising—in fact, that I had already known about—I wasn't aware that who I worked on would become Foxaire's property. You would think that I would have been able to put two and two together earlier, but I thought it was only my ideas they could take ownership of, not actual people.*

*"But you know, the most chilling aspect of this is that my team and I are also owned by Foxaire. There was that one clause that said once a professor started work on a subject, that professor would lose all rights to certain individual freedoms. In other words, I will be monitored by Foxaire for the rest of my life. So, even if I can move on from this place and get a job elsewhere, Foxaire could still meddle with my life."*

*"Indeed, you and your team will never be free from Foxaire's grasp. Even the definition of what a professor is solidifies that fact,"* Sterg added.

*"Ah yes, I had nearly forgotten about that with everything else going on. Right—professors are called professors because we are professing the truth; we are paving the way for the prophecy to be fully realized—the prophecy that Bsarg mentioned the other night. How odd that the contract contained definitions of so many terms, but the prophecy that was alluded to was never explained. But right, exactly—since we are working to make this prophecy come true, we cannot be left unmonitored, as they do not want us to interfere with the prophecy, wittingly or unwittingly."*

*"While the prophecy wasn't explained, you know a good amount about it. For instance, you know that it heralds the return of Gnusaramnii to the Vortex Solar System. You know that those who want Gnusaramnii to return also want Gnusaramnii to complete its goal."*

*"Right, exactly. And, judging by our dream, Gnusaramnii is on a mission to consume life planet by planet. From Theronior to the three unknown worlds Francentia observed, the Gnusar are taking over everything."*

*"As is Gnusaramnii's will—to control all life; to be the intelligence behind a hive mind that all life adheres to."*

*"We cannot let that happen. We cannot let Gnusaramnii win."*

*"Indeed. I believe that is why we are connected, Navacus. I am here to help you protect the Vortex System against this planet-eating threat."*

*"And I still don't understand why this all falls onto my shoulders, but I'm sure I'll just need to be patient to discover that answer. Either way, I can't just sit here all day long. I need to start preparing for my meeting with West."*

*"And don't forget about the meeting Head Professor Yilvin invited you to this afternoon."*

*"Yes, and I'm actually looking forward to it, considering that Bodeelch will likely be there. I'm sure he knows about the underground; maybe I can ask him when I'll be able to return."*

---

As West stepped into Professor Clums' lab, he took a moment to examine the room. It was his first time being back here since his operation was completed. He had spent a lot of time in this room—although, he supposed, he had been unconscious for a large portion of that time. It was strange to be back here after all he had been through. In a way, this was both his birthplace and the beginning of his imprisonment.

West looked at the operating table and the Human male with mechanical legs standing next to it. The Human smiled and waved at him.

"Ah, you must be West! I've been looking forward to meeting you. I'm Norman Harrison," the Human said as he approached and held out his hand.

West took the man's hand and gave it a good shake. "Norman, it's nice to meet you. As you know, I'm West Kilinder."

"It's truly a pleasure," Norman said as he ended the handshake and put his hands on his hips. He nodded toward LSS and continued, "So, this is it then, what Professor Clums and the rest of the team made for you?"

"I'm sorry to interrupt," Professor Qymberkon said as he approached them, "but we don't have time for chit-chat. I'm sure you two will get a chance to talk some other time."

"My apologies. Yes, it would be great to talk with you again," Norman said.

"I agree," West said to Norman, and then he turned to greet the others. "Professor Qymberkon, Syl, everyone, it's great to see you all again."

"It's great to see you, too, West!" Poi said with a wave. Beside her, Lyd groaned as he looked down and put a hand on his forehead. West smiled inwardly and tipped his hat at the Harmertians. West approached Professor Clums' office, but before he could grab the knob, the door opened and Professor Clums stepped out to greet him.

"West, thank you so much for meeting with me today."

"No problem; thank you for taking time out of your busy schedule."

"Well, we do have a lot to discuss, so I'm happy to make the time. Please, come in."

West made his way into Professor Clums' office and sat in a chair facing the Professor's desk. Professor Clums plopped into the chair across from him. Now that they were this close, West was certain he could discern a third presence in the room, but it was faint, as if someone had left a lingering impression. He shook his head and focused on Professor Clums.

"West, it really is great to have this chance to talk with you. How have you been doing?"

"I've been pretty good overall. How about you?"

"Well, there's been a lot going on, so I've been staying busy," Professor Clums replied. "So, I understand you have a few things you wanted to talk to me about. I read your message, but can you tell me more about what's been going on?"

"Right, well, as I mentioned in the message, there are times when my chest really hurts. The other night it hurt so badly that I couldn't sleep."

"Does it hurt now?" Professor Clums asked.

"No, it doesn't hurt, but it is giving me an odd tingling sensation. That only started when I entered the lab. Before I got here, everything felt fine."

"Do your chest pains coincide with the strange signals you have been picking up?"

"Not exclusively, but yes. For instance, right now I am picking up a strange, foreign presence that I can't identify. The tingling in my chest began when I picked up on the ghostly signal."

Professor Clums hummed to himself. "If that is the case, then the pain and the strange signals should stop within the next few days."

"Oh, okay. Is this just a side effect of adjusting to LSS?" he asked. "Also, I want to mention that these strange signals only seem to appear when I'm near you. Even now, as we've been talking, the pain in my chest is only getting worse."

"That is strange, isn't it?" Professor Clums said as he stared off into space. "Are you able to continue our conversation?"

"Yes, I—wait, this is even more strange. The pain is decreasing, but at the same time, the strange signal is getting stronger."

Professor Clums' eyes widened slightly. West suspected the professor knew more than he was saying. He quickly scanned through the electromagnetic spectrum and found a range of radio waves containing a peculiar low frequency hum.

"That is strange, isn't it? Again, though, I'm sure that in a few days' time, you'll find the answers to your questions."

"If you say so," West replied. "Now, Professor, there's an urgent matter I must talk to you about. It's Lyd. Do you know what he has been up to lately?"

"Yes, I was the one who sent him underground. As you may know, I have not been invited back down since those otherworldly Humans arrived. I asked Lyd to check things out for me in the meantime."

"You do understand how dangerous that is, right? It wasn't just me who saw Lyd—Newtus, the one I was speaking with when Lyd surprised us, also sensed his presence. If we could sense him, then Professor Durrist or one of the drones could as well, and that would be very bad for Lyd and your entire team."

"Yes, I am aware of the risks."

"And are you sure we should even be talking this openly about this here?" West asked.

"Yes, no one is listening in, that much I can assure you. The only security threat to us right now is LSS itself, as it automatically records everything."

"But only I have access to those recordings, right?"

"Correct. That is how we built it anyhow," Professor Clums said.

"That's what I thought, but thanks for confirming. Now, Professor, are you sure you should be sending Lyd into the underground? What are you trying to discover?"

"Anything we can learn. But mainly, we're trying to find Norman's missing fiancé, Kate."

"Kate? I've never heard of her before."

Navacus hummed. "What about those four otherworldly Humans that came through the gate the other night? Have you seen them again?"

"No. I haven't heard any news about them at all."

"Then that proves it. Lyd will need to go back underground," Professor Clums said. "However, you mentioned something about drones earlier—what exactly are those?"

"They didn't show you any of the drones? That's a little surprising; there's dozens of them down there. The drones are mindless Lakinceitians that are controlled via tablets by Durrist and Randall. They carry out most of the grunt work in the underground."

"Mindless Lakinceitians... you know, Lyd mentioned something about a Lakinceitian that seemed to have an antenna."

"Seriously? That was one of the drones. Did it see him?"

"Not that he is aware of."

"That's good. They can sense things, kinda like I can, but not as well as I can, from what I can tell. Lyd needs to try and avoid them. It sounds like he got lucky the first time, but that may not be the case next time."

"Do the drones emit frequencies from their antennae?" he asked.

"Yes, they do. Professor Durrist and the others use a set of frequencies to control them."

"Well, then avoiding them should be easy. I just need to build a device that detects those specific frequencies, which you should have saved in LSS."

West nodded. "Yes, I have those frequencies. There may be others I'm not yet aware of, but LSS recorded seventy-nine separate frequencies."

"Ah, that should be perfect. That's quite a good amount. I can use those to extrapolate and program in any others that they could be using.

"You came up with that solution really quickly. I suppose that if you can design a device as complicated as LSS, something like this would be easy for you."

Navacus shrugged. "It's just frequencies—pretty basic stuff for me."

West tipped his cowboy hat forward in acknowledgment. He chatted with Professor Clums for a few more minutes before being shown out. As he passed Lyd, he again tipped his cowboy hat forward in acknowledgment.

As West left the lab, he turned and headed toward the end of the hallway and revealed the elevator. When the doors opened, he quickly stepped inside and pressed the button to descend. He knew he should be using the elevator in Professor Peal's wing, but he did not like that it descended right into Professor Xergat's lab—he hated seeing Xergat's twisted experiments. Besides, he had another scheduled session with Theesakin soon, and this elevator was closer to the Titan enclosure.

*There really is something strange going on with Professor Clums,* he thought. *I can't place it, but it's almost as if there's another soul near him, a soul he seems aware of. But that doesn't make a whole lot of sense either. Who knows? Maybe ghosts are real. I mean, if Professor Durrist can concoct something as ethereal as Zinartee, maybe Professor Clums has some sort of guardian spirit watching over him.*

<hr>

Navacus wheezed, then stepped into Head Professor Yilvin's office. Upon entering, Head Professor Yilvin turned away from Professor Bodeelch and smiled at him.

"Ah, Professor Clums, you're right on time," the elderly male Kolythoanthaean said as he remained seated behind his deep black granite desk. "Now we're just waiting on Professor Dea."

Navacus' mind flashed to Sterg, who dutifully complied and once again retreated.

Professor Bodeelch grinned as he stepped out of the way. "Professor."

He gave Bodeelch a shallow nod then turned his attention to Yilvin. "How's everything been going on your end?"

"Just as busy as ever, and I suspect things will only get busier," Yilvin replied. "But it's all part of the job, as you know."

Before he could ask more, Professor Dea arrived. "I'm sorry for the wait, everyone."

"No need to apologize. Professor Clums arrived only moments ago."

"Great," Professor Dea said.

Head Professor Yilvin nodded. "Now, take a seat if you wish, and let's get to it. Professor Clums, I want to start by congratulating you on your success with Norman. Professor Bodeelch has been informing me of the latest developments, and I've been listening to your audio reports, but I'd like a full update now, if possible."

*So, I guess someone listens to those things after all.* "Of course, Professor. As you may know, Norman's legs are fully complete, and he has been using them for a few days straight now. He's adjusting to them quite well. The vehicular attachment is also fully complete. We are now just working on the hover attachment. We had a bit of a setback by going in the wrong direction, but we're now on the right track and work is going steadily. I suspect that should take about a week until we can do a field test."

"Ah, that's fantastic. Do you think you can get it fully tested and completed by next Rikiln—Tsenar fourteenth?"

"That's quite a tight schedule, but I can speak with my team and see if we can make that happen. But it all depends on how the field test goes."

"Sure, I understand. Now, in the meantime, can you work on the upgrades I've drawn up for West? His are simple. They shouldn't take you long, which will allow you to focus completely on Svetlana's upgrades, as hers are quite extensive."

"Oh, well, I can't promise anything until I see what you have planned." *Also, what's the big rush all of a sudden?*

Yilvin nodded, then handed him a tablet.

"All the details should be there. As you can see, it's just three minor adjustments with one add-on to his functionality. LSS is practically perfect as it is, so we're just enhancing it."

"Alright, well, let me take a quick look."

As he scrolled through the information, he did everything he could to suppress his reactions. In fact, he even needed to lean on Sterg. Even though Sterg was hiding its presence from Professor Dea, they were always connected, so he could still draw upon the powers that Sterg lent him.

The designs only cemented his worst fears. Lord Foxaire truly wanted full control over West. While the first item on the list was the most innocent—installing a jetpack—the rest were nightmarish. The second item on the list was to install a monitoring device, so they could have full access to LSS remotely, which would completely eliminate West's privacy. The last two items were a chip that could allow them to control West's movements and a literal kill switch, requests that completely went against Navacus' morals. He figured he would need to show some sort of protest to it, but he also knew he had no choice but to accept. He would need to speak with West again, and soon.

"What do you think? Are the designs doable?" Head Professor Yilvin prompted.

"Well, theoretically you are correct, each of these items would not take long to construct and install. The jetpack would be the most time consuming, but now that we have figured out the solution for Norman, we may be able to apply a similar solution for West. However, the other three, as I said, will not be a problem for us to install. The only issue I have is the morality of these designs."

"Sure, I completely understand where you're coming from," Yilvin said. His tone made it sound like he had already prepared what to say. "However, please understand that these improvements will really help us and West to have a better working relationship. The monitoring device will negate the need for us to request West to send us data. And, of course, we will program safeguards to protect his privacy."

"Of course," he replied, nodding along as if they were talking about different species of fish.

"As for the other items, we will only use those in extreme circumstances. West is an ex-bounty hunter, and while his exceptional skills work in our favor, it also makes him dangerous. If he were to turn against us, we would have the means to protect ourselves from what essentially amounts to a living weapon."

He continued to nod. "All very reasonable explanations." *For a scumbag.*

Yilvin smiled in contentment. "So, its settled. Now, onto the next item I would like to formally discuss—Professor Bodeelch's new role on your team."

"I'm glad you brought that up. He's been a bit of a nuisance," Navacus replied.

"I apologize," Professor Bodeelch said with fake sincerity. "I have only ever been doing what I have been asked."

"Indeed, I also need to apologize for not telling you about this sooner," Head Professor Yilvin said. "It's just been so busy on my end, which is of course part of the reason why Professor Bodeelch has been helping so much. But I would like to officially let you know what his role is. So, Professor Dea here will still be your direct superior, but Professor Bodeelch will have the final say in any future decisions with your test subjects."

"I would just like to get some clarity on that," Professor Dea said. "What exactly will my role be if Professor Bodeelch will oversee everything?"

"Yes, I understand how this may be confusing. To make things simpler, Professor Dea, just continue doing what you have been doing. Your role stays the same—you will still be doing the same job. I have started to mentor Professor Bodeelch to take over my position as I step away from my role for a few months."

"So what will you be doing then?" Navacus asked.

"Starting tomorrow, I will reduce my role overseeing your and Professor Peal's departments. I am to facilitate a big project Lord Foxaire assigned to me, so that will take my full attention. Of course, Professor Bodeelch will continually keep me updated on what's going on, so if there is an emergency that will require my attention, I should be able to help. But, again, only in an emergency."

"Sure, I understand. This all makes a lot more sense now," Navacus said. "Why didn't you just tell us about this earlier, Professor Bodeelch? We could have avoided some of the tension."

"I was instructed not to say anything until Head Professor Yilvin held this meeting."

"Exactly. Again, I do apologize for the tension you mentioned, but I hope things will run more smoothly from here on out," Professor Yilvin said as he placed his hands together in front of him.

"Yes, I hope so, too," Navacus replied. "I hope it's okay for me to ask, but I didn't realize you were still overseeing Professor Peal. Last time I saw him was in the underground facilities, and it seemed like Professor Durrist was in charge of things."

Yilvin had placed a hand on his forehead as he had been talking. "I realize that all of us in this room are privy to this information, but you we're asked to never speak of the underground facilities, even in this setting. However, since it's been addressed, I can say that I still receive reports from Professor Peal's team."

"I'm sorry for bringing it up, but okay, I understand now."

"Good. Now, if there's nothing else, our meeting is adjourned."

---

Navacus stood at the edge of the open desert with his feet slightly burrowed in the warm sand and gazed into the sky. It was dusk—the beautiful time between the triple sunset and the night's darkness. Melridion didn't have any large moons to reflect the suns' light, so nights were particularly dark here. The shimmering wormholes were already starting to appear.

"*Sterg, why are we all trapped inside this strange place? These shimmering wormholes that surround us used to lead to somewhere, right? I mean, my entire species migrated here because our planet had become too hostile. At times, I feel like we were all cursed. Just as I am trapped here in this compound, we are all trapped and contained within the Vortex Solar System."*

*"Believe me, it was no curse that brought the Yggdrazim and the other species into this system. Back then, it was an immense honor to join such a unique system of planets, all with their own intelligent species. Did you think only four species tried to enter? No, there were hundreds, but only four were allowed in."*

*"What? We weren't taught that!"*

Sterg seemed to laugh. *"And why would those in power teach you such things? Just like any society, you have been molded to conform to a story that is based in truth but never the whole truth."*

*"Isn't that just the theme of the day—never the whole truth. I don't understand why the underground facility is such a touchy subject. The only ones that aren't supposed to know about it are my team members, which they of course all know about it now."*

*"Did you ever stop to think that this place is one large experiment? Tell me, what are Head Professor Yilvin's own projects?"*

*"I honestly don't know. It was never my place to ask."*

*"Precisely. Because you and Professor Peal are Head Professor Yilvin's projects. He is experimenting on you by giving you the subjects you received. At least, that is my interpretation of what I could read from his surface level thoughts."*

*"If that's the case, then obviously Professor Peal is doing something I'm not; otherwise, I would also be asked to work down there."*

*"Again, it could be all part of the experiment."*

*"Either way, one thing is for sure—the more you talk about it, the more it seems so obvious. The whole layout of this place has always bothered me —including the barracks we live in. If this place is truly one giant experiment, then it would make sense why it is the way it is."*

*"All the more reason for you and your team to be free from this place."*

*"Right, well, Lyd's going underground again tonight. I hope he can find*

Kate—and I hope the frequency-monitoring device I whipped together will work.”

“You know it will work.”

Yes, it will work, he thought. We will find our way out of here.

## 18

## ESCAPE FROM THE NIGHTMARE

He looked over his body in disbelief—he truly didn't know how to feel about himself. His spider 'hands' terrified him, while his 'legs' were simply just vines of leafy ivy. He was seeing through the spiders, and yet, he also had an ethereal awareness. Somehow, he could see around him as if he were having an out-of-body experience. All the various perspectives were giving him a headache, if it could even be called that—he didn't have a head.

The last thing he remembered was speaking with someone—another Eusphyrchiian—West. West had helped him find himself and overcome his negative thoughts. But now West was gone and he was alone.

He didn't know how he got here or even who he was. All he knew was his body had been grotesquely disfigured and crafted into something out of a nightmare. It didn't help that before he had heard West's voice, the only thing he could remember was stark blackness —a void created by a black hole that had consumed his entire identity.

West had called him Ivy. He didn't know if that had been his name before, or if it was a new moniker in recognition of the ivy limbs he now possessed. Either way, it didn't matter what others called him. If Ivy was to be his new name, so be it. And he supposed it did suit him, for he had full control over the ivy. As he played with his new limbs, he realized just how long and stretchy the ivy was. As he was testing the ivy's limits, something caused him to nearly jump out of his skin.

"That may be impressive, but it's nothing compared to what we can do," two voices said as one. One sounded feminine and the other sounded masculine, and both tones resonated harmoniously.

He focused his awareness on the spiders that clung to his handless wrists. It was strange to experience a voice coming from himself that was not his own.

"Um, hello... what is this?" He was trying to speak, but his voice was the same as the ones that had just spoken to him. "Are you... are you speaking for me?"

"Indeed, we are," the voices replied.

"Who are you?"

"I am Adok," the larger, more feminine sounding spider on his right wrist replied.

"I am Ados," the smaller, more masculine sounding spider on his left wrist replied.

"We are in a situation we are not particularly fond of," Adok said.

"We are being forced to comply," Ados echoed.

"I'm not forcing you two to do anything. At least, I'm not trying to make you speak for me."

"Understand that we are bound together in a way that makes us one," they said as one voice once again.

"So, can you read my thoughts?" he asked.

"While we speak telepathically, we can't see within your mind as of yet. However, in time, our consciousnesses may yet intertwine."

"I see. So, what exactly can you do then? Are you able to back up your boast from earlier?"

The spiders looked at each other, then each shot unique strands of silk, if it could even be called silk at that point. They stuck to the wall to the right of him, and each affected the wall differently. The silk Adok released was about two centimeters wide and appeared to be a steel-like substance, for it clanged loudly against the metal wall upon impact. On the other hand, Ados produced a fine set of strands, which seemed to be acidic; they were already eating away at the metal wall. A moment later, a loud alarm sounded from somewhere outside his cell.

"Shoot, that acid you shot is going to get us in trouble. How do we remove the strands from the wall?"

"Walk over to them," Adok said.

"We'll do the rest," Ados said.

"Alright. That wasn't what I was expecting, but it was quite impressive."

As Ivy approached the wall, his 'fingers'—the spiders' legs, giving him a combined total of sixteen 'fingers'—crawled along the strands until they reached the wall. Ados and Adok each used their legs—his fingers— to deftly remove the strands from the wall. A few seconds later, the alarm stopped.

He realized he had felt it when the spiders had cut the strands and when they had crawled along the strands.

"So, I really can feel through your legs as if they are my fingers."

"Exactly," Adok said.

"We are connected," Ados echoed.

"We are your hands."

"We do as you command."

"So, if I were to pick up a cup of water..." he began.

"One of us would pick it up for you."

"Okay, I think this is starting to make sense. But also, not really at all. I mean, I don't have a head, right? How do I eat? How do I drink?"

"I believe that Ados and I, in addition to your Ivy legs, will help to absorb the nutrients you need."

"So, does that mean I don't get to enjoy food anymore?"

He looked up and realized that a blond Human man was watching him through the window.

"How long have you been here?" Ivy asked. "How did I not sense your arrival?"

"Ivy, I apologize for startling you. I am Professor Peal. We—my team and I—are thrilled to see that you are awake. How are you feeling?"

"I don't know. I feel strange. I feel like part of me is missing, but those parts have been replaced with outside oddities."

"I understand. Allow me to explain. It was me and my team that cobbled you together. It was the only way to save you. When we first saw you, we knew we had to make quick decisions to ensure your survival. Luckily, we had recently gathered the ivy and spiders from Acampachetli. It is only because of your outside oddities, as you put it, that you are alive. You struggled and barely clung to life, but you fought through it and overcame an extraordinary set of obstacles."

"Did you say Acampachetli? I thought no one was allowed to go to that planet."

"I'm glad to see your memory is intact. Yes, under normal circumstances, you are correct. But I work for Lord Foxaire. Do you know about Lord Foxaire?"

"I don't... Wait... Yes? Do you mean the guy who makes nanotech?"

"The very same. With his power and influence, he can secure the permits needed to journey to Acampachetli and bring back samples. Again, the ivy and spiders you use now are some of those samples."

"Yeah, that's just quite strange, but, hey, everything is strange and new right now."

"Of course, I understand completely. What else do you remember?"

"It's hard to say. I only now remember about Acampachetli since you brought it up. But, now that you mention it, it's coming back to me. I'm a Eusphyrchiian from Ijurvoll. Or, I was a Eusphyrchiian, I don't know if I still count as one anymore."

"What can you tell me about your past?"

"Nothing. I remember nothing. Only that my species is from Ijurvoll. As for myself, I cannot say."

"That is to be expected. Your body and mind must have experienced horrors and trauma that I can't even imagine. When that happens, memory loss is common."

"Well, whatever the case may be, I hope I can reclaim my memories someday."

"We hope for that as well. Now, I'm sorry to ask this, but would you mind if we ran a few tests? We need to learn more about how everything is functioning now that you're awake."

"I suppose so. Is it going to hurt?"

"No, nothing should hurt."

"That's good. What do you need to do then?"

Before Ivy knew it, he was strapped to an operating table with several people standing over him. It was still odd—being able to look down upon himself and seeing them standing over him. There was the Human from earlier, Professor Peal, and there was another Human, a brown-haired female. There were also two Kolythoanthaean brothers, a Nioavellian, and much to his surprise, a female Eusphyrchiian. The Eusphyrchiian was called Kamarial, and Ivy had a strange feeling he'd met her before and said as much.

"Well, we all worked on you," Kamarial answered. "I know you don't remember, but we all spent a lot of time with you."

"Yeah, but wasn't he unconscious the entire time?" one of the Kolythoanthaeans asked.

"Mahlvern, come on," the Nioavellian, Professor Kalosse, said, then frowned at him. "I'm sorry for his lack of tact."

"Oh, it's no problem. That would explain why I don't remember anything at all."

"Do you remember anyone else, or do you only remember me?" Kamarial asked.

"Now that you mention it, I think I do remember Professor Kalosse and the Kolythoanthaean brothers. It's quite blurry, but I remember a fuzzy blue shape and two fuzzy gray shapes... and even two Human-like blurs."

"Why do we get reduced to our colors?" Walverm asked.

"I'm sorry, I didn't mean anything by it," Ivy quickly replied.

"It's fine, I'm glad you're remembering," Professor Peal said. "Now,

I know you're as comfortable as can be, but none of us want you restrained for long."

"It's fine. I understand. You said nothing would hurt, right?"

"Ideally, yes," Professor Peal replied.

"However, you are quite unique," Professor Kalosse said hesitantly. "So, if you feel any pain, please let us know immediately."

"Sure, I will."

"Great. Then let's begin," Professor Peal said. "I want to start off simple. I overheard you earlier when you asked about how you eat or drink. While we believe we know the answers to those questions, I would like to test our hypotheses out now. So, let's start with the ivy. It should be able preform both photosynthesis and osmosis and pass those nutrients to you."

"So, what, do I need to root into the ground whenever I get hungry?"

"That's what we're here to find out. First, let's test how well the ivy absorbs our artificial starlight. We ran several tests before to get a baseline, so we have a general idea on how it will react now."

"Is this going to take long?" Ivy asked.

"In all, it shouldn't take more than a few hours. However, while the photosynthesis test is running, we can run other tests on Ados and Adok."

"Oh, okay; that's fine."

Professor Peal and the others busied themselves with setting up equipment around his legs. By the end of it, his ivy was fully encased with a metallic device that would shoot oscillating intensities of artificial sunlight.

"Now, please let us know how you feel. Remember, the ivy is part of you. If you start to feel nourished and more energetic, let us know."

"Sure, I mean, if I feel anything, I'll let you know."

"Great. As I said, that can go on in the background while we focus on your spiders. Let's start out easy. I'm going to give you a few objects to hold onto."

"Okay, that's fine."

Professor Peal passed him a small cylinder, and Ivy easily

grabbed onto it with his right spider. After that, they tested a variety of shapes and other random objects. He could grip them all without any issue.

"You're off to a great start. Next, let's move onto something a little more fun. I saw you shooting interesting strands earlier; however, that was them showing you how to do it. Now, I would like you to repeat it yourself. Each spider is pointed at a predetermined target, so there's no need to worry about causing any accidents. Whenever you're ready."

*I'm sorry for this, Ados and Adok. I am sorry for using you in this way. I know you have accepted your fates, but still, I feel bad about using you like this.*

"Ivy, are you ready? Can you repeat those same strands of ivy for us now?" Professor Peal prompted.

"Yes, sorry. I'm ready. I'll try. Do I just have to imagine I'm the spider, or something like that?"

"Ivy, the spiders are part of you now. You are the spider. Use your thoughts to shoot the silk."

*Use my thoughts? Okay… let's make some spider webs.* He focused his thoughts on shooting the silk, and much to his surprise, he produced a strand of normal spider silk from each spider.

"Great job, Ivy. I knew you could do it. Now, focus on the strands they showed you earlier. The acidic one and the metallic one."

"I mean… that seems quite advanced. I don't think I can shoot them at the same time."

"One at a time is fine then. I understand we're asking you to do something quite complicated. But the point I'm trying to make is that you already shot them both at the same time. That was *you*. The spiders may speak independently from you, but they are you. So, if you did it before, you can do it again."

*Right, I keep on thinking of myself as separate from them, but I am them—and they are me. Okay, hands, let's see what you can do.* He focused on the acidic strand first, then on Ados—his left land—and shot an acidic strand of silk. It was weaker than the first time, but it still managed to sizzle against the target. He tried several more times, and on his eighth try, the acidic strand shot straight through the wooden target.

"Yes! I knew you could do it, Ivy. Great job," Professor Peal said as he led his team into a quick applause.

"Good timing," Professor Surridge, the Human woman, said. "The first round of photosynthesis is just now completing. How do you feel, Ivy?"

Now that she mentioned it, he did feel much more energetic. He could feel the energy flowing into him and coursing throughout his body, which included his spider hands.

"I feel great. In fact, I think it was because of the energy created through photosynthesis that I could produce that acidic strand."

"That's fantastic, what splendid results," Professor Peal said. "Surridge, how are the readings?"

"Off the charts. The amount of absorption has increased by nearly two-hundred percent."

"It's likely because it's part of a larger whole now," Professor Kalosse replied.

"My thoughts exactly," Professor Peal said.

"Can we continue shooting silk? I have a lot of energy now," Ivy asked.

"Absolutely. Let's focus on the metallic strand next."

"Sure thing!"

He was able to reproduce the metallic strand with ease. After that, he reached into Ados' and Adok's inner thoughts, which were part of his own thoughts now, and discovered the full extent of silk-like substances they could produce. While both Ados and Adok could produce nearly all the same ones, there was one each that only Ados and Adok could produce. However, there seemed to be some kind of shadowy mental block obscuring them from him. He decided not to let the professors know as he shot strand after strand of various silk strands, from electric ones and poisonous ones to icy cold ones and burning hot ones.

As he was shooting the strands, he realized the spiders were drawing energy from his Eusphyrchiian body, just as his body was drawing energy from his ivy. All of his parts fed each other, just as each of his parts could feed off each other. It was a strange symbiotic paring, but it was working out well. And it felt good—it felt like he was more alive than he had ever been more.

"Excellent! I'm in awe, Ivy. I wasn't expecting you to get the hang of this so quickly," Professor Peal said with wide eyes and a wide smile.

"I'm also in awe of myself. That was... not anything I have ever experienced before, and yet it felt so natural."

"Fantastic. Now, I would like to move on to a different test with your spiders. This may seem odd, but we'd like to ask you to remove Ados and Adok from your wrists."

"How? I'm strapped... but wait, of course. I am the spiders."

"Exactly. You are the spiders. Simply let go."

"Okay, here it goes..." Ivy searched inside himself once again and zeroed in on each spider. Starting with Adok, he released the grip on his wrist, detaching Adok from his body. Even though they weren't physically connected anymore, nothing felt different. Ivy could still watch from his god-like view over his body, and he could still see through Adok's eyes. He hummed to himself as he then detached Ados from his left wrist.

"Very good. How do you feel now?"

"Exactly the same."

"Great, that's precisely the result we were hoping for. Now, if you don't mind, we'd like to conduct one more test. We want to see how far the spiders can travel from your physical body."

"Hmm that's interesting. But where can they go? This room isn't big."

"How confident. Let's see how well you can control them in this room for now."

"Sure, that's fine."

"Whenever you're ready, then," Professor Peal prompted after several seconds passed.

Ivy stared at the two spiders from above, through their eyes, but for some reason, he was having trouble getting their legs to move.

"What's the issue?" Professor Peal asked. "Earlier you were able to grip all of the objects we gave you."

"Yes, you're right. I could move them back then because that was natural. This seems unnatural."

"Again, it is only your own mind that is holding you back. You must believe in the new possibilities you've been granted."

"Okay, I'll try again."

This time Ivy stopped trying so hard and let the spiders free. They immediately began to walk in different directions.

"I did it!"

"Very good, Ivy."

"Thanks, but this is nothing." He guided Ados and Adok to the walls of the small containment room and sent them up the walls and onto the ceiling. He made them pass by each other before they crawled back up onto the table and over his body to return to their starting points. He smiled inwardly. He had been wrong; it had felt so natural to let his spiders return to being spiders. And he had retained all his viewpoints without taking focus away from any one of them.

"So, how is it exactly that I can do that? I mean, Ados and Adok obviously have their own brains. So do I just have three brains now?"

"Think of it like this," Kamarial explained. "All of your multiple minds are coming together to create a central conscious intelligence, so you are the sum of all your various parts. So, yes, you have a brain in your chest and a brain in each spider, not to mention the intelligence and consciousness that the ivy vines contain. But you, Ivy, are more than each individual part now."

"So that's how I can focus on and see three different viewpoints at once. The out-of-body viewpoint is that central intelligence you mentioned."

"What do you mean, out-of-body?" Professor Kalosse asked.

"Oh, well, this whole time I've been watching everything from above. I can see everything that goes on in this entire room from that perspective. I can also sense two other presences outside of this room."

"Amazing, so that's how your vision works. I should have asked you that to begin with, but thank you for sharing that with us now," Professor Peal said with a smile.

The second round of photosynthesis was complete, and Ivy was brimming with so much energy that they skipped the third round of photosynthesis and moved on to the water absorption test. Professor Peal explained that they simply needed to place his ivy in a pool of water for an hour and measure how much water was absorbed during that time.

Once the artificial starlight device was removed, he watched as the team of six put together the pool. It wasn't long before the water began flowing into the makeshift pool.

"How's the temperature?"

"Its fine. Not too warm and not too cold."

"Good to hear. Now, I'd like for us to repeat the same tests we ran earlier with your spiders. We'd like to see how you perform those same tasks while absorbing a different source of energy."

"I guess that's fine. I just don't want to stress Ados and Adok."

"Do they feel stressed to you?"

"No, not particularly. But they don't seem to enjoy being used either."

"Ivy, you're not using them. You are the spiders. They are you. Your energy is their energy, your thoughts are their thoughts. If you are feeling as if they don't enjoy it, maybe that's because you don't like the thought of exploiting them."

"You know, that could very well be it. So, like, have you all done something like this before? Meaning, are there others like me? You seem to know a lot about how I work."

"No, you're the very first, Ivy. We're simply using algorithms to gain an idea of how you might work, and you're proving us right. That's all."

"Alright. So, are you going to hand me more objects then?

In all, they were at it for over six hours. Even though he was still energetic, Ivy was mentally exhausted. After the water absorption test, they brought out soil samples to see if he could absorb any nutrients from soil. They had tested three different types of soils before they gave him a break. They promised they had only a few more tests to run in another session, and while he had no reason to doubt them, part of him knew that this was just the beginning.

*What exactly is going on here?* he thought. *What am I? Professor Peal said I am the only one like me. But, why? What is my purpose? Why did they make me? After these tests are concluded, what are they going to make me do?*

*Maybe, once the tests are over, I can ask them about West. And maybe they'll let him talk to me again. I have many questions for him. He was different from me, but he was the same—he had no head. I need to find out where he came from, because maybe I come from the same place.*

*All I know is that I do not want to be here. I do not want to be used.*

**19**

# ESCAPE FROM HOPELESSNESS

Lyd took a deep breath. Even though he had done this before, it was still terrifying. He quadruple-checked his monitoring device, and the elevator was still not moving. It remained on the bottom just like it had been nearly ten minutes ago. It was unfortunate; with the elevator descended, he wouldn't be able to pick up the grate he dropped last time he was down here. Yet, there would be other opportunities to grab the grate.

He took another deep breath then stepped off the ledge and into the abyss. Lyd's jetpack automatically activated, and he began to slowly descend the elevator shaft.

When he reached the bottom, he inspected the monitoring device he had left. It appeared no one had discovered it yet. He then used his own gadgets to check what was going on in the hallway that led up the elevator. All readings came back negative, so he headed into the rectangular chamber that split into eight different directions. He stared at the shaft that was directly in front of him. That was where he was headed next; he only had four more shafts to explore. He couldn't walk straight there, though. The torrent of air was too strong, so he crept along the edge and wound around the shafts that he, Poi, and Mac had already explored.

When he made it into the shaft he was shooting for, he ran his security checks again. He immediately picked up several frequencies used by the drones. He was impressed; the device that Professor Clums had built was completely untested, and yet it seemed to work perfectly. Not only could he identify each individual frequency, but he could also gauge the distance between the source of the signal and himself. While most of the frequencies were faint and pretty far away, there were two that were much closer. He quickly shut off his monitoring device out of fear that the drones could read his signal. Professor Clums hadn't been sure about that part, so he decided he would err on the side of caution and simply move on to the next shaft.

In the next air shaft over, Lyd picked up zero traces of drones, and he cautiously made his way down. He just hoped that Kate wasn't down the shaft he had just skipped.

As he made it further down, he again picked up traces of the drones, but these felt different. They seemed to be fully occupied; their signals were close to ten meters away and were still faint. It was as if they were either inactive or already busy performing a set of tasks, so they didn't need to be commanded.

*You know, screw it*, he thought. *I already came this far; I can push on a little further. I just hope you're okay, Kate, and that you're alive. Not only for Norman's sake, but for all our sakes. I just... I don't want this place to be as evil as it seems to be.*

---

Cecil breathed heavily as he pushed his body up, then forced it back down. He only had three more squats to go, and he was already past his limit. His legs burned. His whole body screamed at him to stop, and yet, he still pushed on.

*What kind of knight would I be if I quit now?*

He finished his set then promptly collapsed on the ground, panting deeply. He reached for the cup of water he had saved and gulped down what was left. As he lay there, listening to his own labored breaths, a strange sound crept into his cell—the first outside sound he had ever heard. It sounded like someone was scratching at something.

He smiled, then said aloud, "Hello, strange sounds. How are you doing this hour?"

He felt ridiculous, talking to strange scratching sounds, but this is what it had come to. He didn't know how long he had been in this cell, but he was lonely. He laughed at himself.

"Hello?"

The unknown voice made him choke on his laughter. He broke into a coughing fit before he could calm himself.

"Hello? Is someone there?" Cecil whispered loudly.

"Yes, I'm here. My name is Lyd. What's your name?"

"Well, Lyd, how can I trust you?"

"I know this is highly unusual, but I'm no threat to you. I'm down here looking for someone, but at the same time, searching for anyone I can find."

Cecil hummed to himself. He wasn't sure if he could trust this strange voice, but he figured there'd be no harm in playing along. "Down here? Where am I?"

"You're deep underground, underneath the compound where I'm employed. I can't see you, but I heard someone talking, so I called out."

"I see. Please, call me Cecil, Sir Cecil Kloud. I'm... I'm not from around here. But my friends are nearby—Theodore, Druder, and even Tyrona. Have you come across them yet?"

"No, you're the first one I've discovered in this area. Like I said, I can't see you, but I can hear your voice as it comes through this vent."

"That makes sense. The place I'm in has no seams—it's like I'm encased in one large, solid block of metal. And yet, my bed and toilet can be stowed away in the wall, and a food tray comes out of the opposite wall."

"Oh, okay, I know exactly what you're talking about. But this kind of technology is meant for spaceships, not for prison cells."

"I'm sorry, did you just say spaceships? You can travel into space?"

Cecil asked as he stood up and looked up at the ceiling in awe. Sure, it was obvious that the planet he was on was much more advanced than Eklatros, but even so, the thought of traveling through space was tantalizing.

"Oh yes, space travel is quite commonplace here in the Vortex Solar System. Where again did you say you're from?"

"I'm from Eklatros. I'm sure you've never heard of it before."

"No, I can't say that I have," Lyd replied.

"It figures as much. No one has heard of me. No one knows we're down here."

"That's where you're wrong. My entire team knows you're down here. My superior, Professor Clums, was there when you came out of the gate."

"Really? Which one was he?" Cecil asked.

"Ah, well, he has a large, wide beak, and—"

"Oh okay, the bird-like guy. He arrived with the man who shot me."

"That may be so, but Professor Clums is a kind person. Now, I can't say for sure, but I think he's planning something. I think he wants to escape from this place."

"What do you mean? Didn't you say you work here? Why would you need to escape?"

"It's complicated. But understand this: I am taking a tremendous risk talking to you like this. If I were to be discovered... I'm honestly afraid to know what would happen. But it would be bad."

"I understand. I've only talked to a few assholes, and they don't come around often."

"I'm sorry you're being treated this way, I really am. Now, you said you had some friends around here, right?"

"Yes, Theodore, Druder, and Tyrona. Can you help them?" Cecil asked. In his excitement, he had forgotten to whisper. He had thought everyone here was an enemy. If Lyd could be trusted, that meant he had allies he had never known about.

"I will do what I can."

"Thank you very much, Lyd, for restoring my hope. This is twice now in the past few weeks that my hope needed to be restored. If only Ànifa were still with us... but no, I can't go down that path right now," he said as he hung his head down.

"Who's Ànifa?"

"She was... She was a lot of things, but most of all, she was my friend. Now, as much as I'd like to chat longer, you should probably be on your way. If anyone were to find out about this..."

"I know, we'd both lose our heads. Until next time, then."

Cecil listened as the shuffling sounds moved away, then he let out a breath.

*That was a big surprise,* he thought. *I really hope my trust in Lyd is not misplaced. I hope he can find the others and give them hope. I just... I know nothing about the guy. And why would he need to escape if he works here? Also, why would someone that works here even need be moving through air ducts to begin with? There's definitely a lot more going on here.*

---

Tyrona hovered above a gruesome scene. It was worse than the most frightening nightmare she'd ever had.

She barely recognized her own body—it was nearly skin and bones. The magic that had been holding her youthful appearance together had all but faded away. Her eyes were so sunken she wasn't sure if they could even open. She suspected they never would.

She lay on a metal cart and wore a helmet that was connected to two different machines, while an array of wires connected her body to other strange devices. That must be how she clung onto life. If it could even be called life. Next to her on a different metal cart lay a healthy-looking woman. Her long brown hair shimmered, and her olive skin shone. That must be Kate, and why she was in her head. The Gnusar-like creatures in the room with them really were draining the life out of her and giving it to Kate. That was why she couldn't use magic—because her magical abilities had been unwillingly given to Kate.

*"Kate, can you hear me?"*

The reply was quiet, as if their connection was weak. *"I'm here, Tyrona. What do you see?"*

"It's... it's horrifying. They're draining the life out of me and giving it to you."

*"What? Why? Why would they do something like this?"*

Before she could reply, she felt her link to Kate slip away. She watched as her body trembled. Tyrona knew she was dying. Pushing her awareness out like this was draining the little life she had left. She knew she had little time remaining.

Rather than return to her body, she decided to expand her awareness. She immediately picked up on someone nearby, and from what she could gather, he was not associated with what was happening to her. She used what energy she had left to reach out to him.

*"Hello, can you hear me?"*

She watched as the little gray man in orange clothing froze in his tracks, then nervously looked around the tunnel he was in.

*"Who's there? What is this? Why do I hear you in my head?"*

*"I apologize for the sudden intrusion. This must be unnatural for you, but I don't have much time left. My name is Tyrona Claire Knorse, and I'm an S-Class Sorceress of Ajenti, from the planet Eklatros. My life is being drained me and being given to another woman, Katherine Padmashiri Thomas. I do not know who you are, but please, if possible, pass my message onto my friends. Theodore, Ànifa, Cecil, Vesten, Joan, and Dasch. I failed them, I failed them all..."*

Her vision blurred as everything turned to white. All her pain and worries dissipated. She laughed. It felt the same as when she had been yanked from Eklatros—away from Theodore. And yet, this time it felt completely different. She was weightless as she floated away into nothingness.

*Now I'm finally free. Theodore, I love you with all my heart. Wait, Theodore? Is that you? Are you here for me?*

*Theodore... if you can hear me, save yourself. Save yourself for me. Live for my sake.*

Lyd remained frozen long after the woman's voice had dissipated. He had no idea what had just happened, but she said her name was Tyrona, someone Cecil had mentioned, and she had even mentioned Kate. Even stranger, none of his devices had been set off, not a single one. And yet, he knew the voice had been real, that it really had been Tyrona speaking to him.

He had to tell Cecil what just happened, but as he turned around to go back, several of his alarms went off simultaneously.

Lyd's first thought was that he had been found out, that speaking with Tyrona had caused his presence to be revealed. He soon realized the alarms were coming from a room nearby, and those alarms were setting off his alarms. Tyrona had said she didn't have much time left. She must have died, and so the alarms meant that drones and possibly even professors were on their way.

Time wasn't on his side. He couldn't get all the way back to the elevator, so he had to find somewhere to hide. He hurried down the shaft as quietly as he could toward approaching signals.

He barely had enough time to exit the shaft and hide his presence down the adjacent one. His alarms blinked at him as the various presences passed him. He remained hidden for a few minutes after his alarms went quiet, taking the time to update the map. He stood up to make his way back to the elevator when a strong feeling in his chest stopped him. Even though he wanted to get out of there as quickly as he could, there was something different about this shaft. He couldn't place what it was, so he ventured further down it. He eventually came to several dead ends. There was literally nothing down this shaft, not even vents like the one he used to talk to Cecil. And yet he knew he was missing something.

He took a deep breath and scanned the area around him. This time, something small caught his eye, and he approached a set of thin slits in the metal floor below him.

He took out a small camera attached to a metallic cable and stuck it through one of the slits. He would need to analyze the data later, but it looked like there was a completely separate building below him. It was a large circular-shaped dome, which seemed to be self-contained—no external vents, pipes, or wires led to it. A shiver ran down his spine as he thought about what was being kept in there.

As he surveyed the scene below him, he spotted Svetlana standing at rapt attention. He couldn't see her well, but what he did see unsettled him. Svetlana looked more like a lifeless automaton than a living, breathing person.

Several alarms chimed at him. Someone was coming. He retracted the camera, stowed it away, and made his way back to the elevator shaft.

When he arrived, the elevator was still descended, which again meant he couldn't replace the grate. He checked the elevator monitoring device he had left there last time and decided to remove it. Sure, there were still two shafts he hadn't gone down yet, but he had found Kate. And what he had just seen had really spooked him. Layers upon layers of security, layers upon layers of secrets. The compound was like a bad onion that only got worse as you got closer to the core.

With the monitoring device securely tucked away, the only thing that would give away his presence was the grate, and that could be chalked up to poor maintenance.

He turned on his jetpack and ascended as quickly as he could.

*That was far more eventful than I had expected*, he thought. *Between talking to Cecil, and Tyrona being in my head, to finding that large dome-structure… that was a lot. I don't think I want to come down here again, not alone at least. Plus, I don't see a need to. We've found Kate. We've discovered several others we can help. The only thing is, how can we help them if we can barely help ourselves out of the situation we're in?*

*All we have left to hold onto is hope, like what Cecil had said. The hope that we'll escape from this place, that we won't be tortured like so many others. That's all we have.*

*Cecil, I'm sorry I couldn't tell you what happened to Tyrona. The next time I see you, I'll make it up to you.*

**20**

# ESCAPE FROM THE PROFESSORS

"It's been another long and productive day," Navacus said into the microphone as he recorded his latest update. "First of all: Norman. We are continuing to focus our efforts on the hover attachment. Judging from my designs, we're roughly forty percent complete with the rebuild. However, even though today went smoothly, the hardest parts are still to come. So, for tomorrow, we are going to finish the foundation and then start building several separate elements at once, as each of these separate elements are quite volatile on their own and will take time to become more stable before we can combine them.

"Also for tomorrow, I plan on working through the two points Norman brought up a few days ago. First, I will look into a better way to allow Norman to detach his attachments. We'll need a way for Norman to enter a bio-signature scan that can be easily performed under pressure. Next, we'll need to determine how to allow Norman to carry around his attachments. Theoretically, one of the easiest ways would be to shrink them by external capture. In other words, create a small, hand-held device that can consume an attachment and store it inside. The device would have a release button that could eject the attachment from it. Other ideas include similar methods of

235

shrinking. I just can't see an alternative to shrinking down the devices at this point. I realize that this will take us down a path not many have successfully followed. But with determination, I'm sure we can make it happen."

He paused and wheezed. Even Sterg wasn't sure what the solution was, but there had to be a way.

"That reminds me. Head Professor Yilvin stopped in today to check up on our progress. Even though I just met with him yesterday, he was eager to see it for himself. This was the first time he's visited since West's awakening, and his determination to see us complete this attachment on time is helping drive our own determination.

"And, speaking of West, in two days' time, so on Tsenar seventh, I will work on installing his latest upgrades. So that's something else I'll need to do tomorrow—review those designs and start building the components needed. I'll start with the easiest enhancement and go from there—the easiest being the jetpack. Since we're already building a hover device for Norman, I can easily apply that knowledge and make something for West. It will take much less time building West's jetpack than it will take to build Norman's hover attachment. Even though the concept behind both is the same, they're inherently quite different from each other.

"Next, installing the monitoring device and the kill switch should entail some software updates to LSS, so both won't be too difficult to do. The toughest enhancement will be to allow remote control over West's movements. The easiest way will be through electrical signals to his brain, but I will also need to see if we'll need to build any physical parts that will need to be inserted into his body.

"Either way, I sure have my work cut out for me. It's as if my workload has exploded recently. At least days on Melridion are longer than back on Strutheine. And it's not all bad. This will be a real test for all of us, one that I'm sure we will pass, and one that will teach us a great many lessons that we can apply to future projects.

"With peace, and love, and faith, this is Professor Navacus Clums, signing off."

He wheezed, then stretched out the kinks in his body. "*Sterg, thank you for helping me keep all the truths and lies straight.*"

"*Navacus, I'm sensing a strange presence coming from the lab. While it's not a presence I've felt before, it feels familiar.*"

"*What are its intentions?*"

"*Unclear. I cannot pick up on any motives.*"

"*Alright, well, stay on alert, and be ready to hide your presence if necessary.*"

"*Will do.*"

Professor Clums stepped out of his office and into the lab. He found Professor Dea near the hover attachment. His back was turned to him, allowing Navacus a split second to give Sterg the command to retreat. He wasn't sure it mattered if Professor Dea had seen him or not—he still felt a little better knowing his back was turned.

"Professor Dea, I wasn't expecting you," Navacus said as he tried to keep his voice calm.

"I apologize for the intrusion," Professor Dea said with his back still to him before turning around. "It looks like the hover attachment is coming along well."

"Yes, I believe so," he replied.

"I just wanted to check in with you to see how you're taking West's upgrades. I know they're asking for some controversial changes."

He hesitated before answering. "My opinion doesn't matter. I'll need to make the changes whether I like them or not."

"Quite so, but your opinion does matter, because it means we can do something about it. Also, while I appreciate what you're trying to do, you can drop the act now. There's no need to hide it from me any longer."

Navacus was stunned. Now he really didn't know what to say.

"From the look of it, you didn't know that I already knew? I pieced it together a few days ago. And you also didn't know that I could mask my own presence, did you?"

"No, I didn't know that."

"See, we're both master deceivers. So, there's no need to deceive each other any longer."

"Alright then," Navacus replied. "But first... I trust you, but I don't think that I *really* trust you. How do I know you won't report back to Yilvin?"

"Yes, you can trust me. You know I don't like what Professor Bodeelch has been doing. And if we're being honest, I've never been to the underground facility. I just know about it because it's part of my job. I don't like this place. And I know you don't either."

Sterg's voice chimed in his head. "*Navacus, he is not baiting you. He is being trustworthy.*"

Navacus wheezed. "Alright, alright. I just wasn't expecting this right now."

"And, I do apologize about that, but I believe we're running out of time," Professor Dea said.

"In what way?"

Professor Dea tilted his head to the left. "Bring out your companion, and we'll talk. You don't need to worry. I'm shielding us so no one can listen in on our conversation."

"I wasn't worried about that; I can do that, too, but thanks," Navacus replied, and then addressed Sterg, "Now, I think it's time for you to come out."

Navacus watched as Sterg reappeared beside him in his normal ghostly state.

"Oh wow, now it's my turn to be surprised," Professor Dea said. "In truth, I didn't know what to expect. It was only my hypothesis that you had another soul with you, but it really is true."

"Yes, it is true. My time with Navacus is of the utmost importance," Sterg said.

"Of that, I'm sure. My kind have many stories about how we acquired the means to levitate like we can. Many of them point to a wayward soul that attached itself to Kolax, an ancient Eridavlos. Keep in mind, these stories originate from well before we arrived in the Vortex System."

"I know what you speak of," Sterg replied.

Navacus nodded. He absorbed the story through Sterg and took a moment to digest it.

Kolax had lived a few thousand years before the Eridavlos migrated to the Vortex Solar System, back when the Eridavlos were still in their primitive state. Originally, the Eridavlos evolved to have no limbs because they had an innate power of telekinesis. They could move almost anything with their minds, including themselves.

Kolax had been born into a humble family of potters. From an early age, Kolax had been fascinated with her parents' ability to create amazing works of art with just their minds, for she herself lacked any powers of telekinesis. She was the first Eridavlos to be born without it, and her parents had done everything they could to help her. In the end, her family went broke, and her parents lost their lives, leaving Kolax homeless. With little means to move, she could only lay in the street, completely helpless.

One day, a mysterious wayward soul visited her and gave her the ability to levitate on her own, without needing to use mind control. She was the first Eridavlos to develop the specialized organ. Then, by some strange miracle, a large percentage of the population also developed their own levitation organs.

Over time, the Eridavlos lost their powers of telekinesis, as there was no need to move anything with their minds now that they had they had other means to achieve the same goal.

Navacus shook his head and looked at Professor Dea. "I never heard that story before; it's quite tragic, but also fascinating. I had no idea that is how you evolved."

"Oh, you suddenly know the entire story now?" Professor Dea asked, looking back and forth between Sterg and himself. "I only brought it up a few seconds ago."

"Yeah, you see," Navacus explained, "when Sterg thinks of something, I know its thoughts."

"Its name is Sterg? I didn't realize it had its own name."

"Yes, please call me Sterg."

"It's nice to meet you, Sterg. But Navacus, keep in mind that the story of Kolax is just a story. There are not many of my kind that truly believe in it, and those who do are cast out as deranged cultists. I only brought it up because of, well, because of Sterg."

"Sure, I understand that. It's quite hard to believe unless you experience it yourself," he replied.

"Quite so. Now, back to the matter at hand. I don't believe we have much time, but I can't tell you the why because I don't know the reason. What I do know is that whatever Head Professor Yilvin and Bodeelch are up to, it's going to change everything. They're preparing for something big."

"Alright, so you don't know what's going on, but you decided you'd come and warn me anyway?"

"Yes. If I could sense Sterg, then others may be able to. I don't know why Sterg is with you, but I do know that if Head Professor Yilvin found out, you would become the next science experiment, and you would lose all semblance of freedom.

"Now, I realize I have many inherent natural abilities that other species do not, but Professor Yilvin and the others are cunning. They know something is going on with you, but they can't place what it is. I just don't want to see you dissected."

Navacus wheezed and ruffled his feathers. "Yeah... let's hope it doesn't come to that. But if Yilvin suspects something, then maybe that's why I haven't been asked back underground. And I thought you were good at covering your tracks, Sterg."

"I'm new at all of this, just like you are," Sterg replied. "I may be a divine being, but I can still make mistakes."

"While that may be, it doesn't matter much, because they're onto you," Professor Dea said. "You need to be extra careful from here on out. That's why I'm here. I needed to know what was going on with you so I could help you."

"So, how can you help me?"

"For starters, by helping West."

"What do you mean?" Navacus asked.

"Navacus, what you did with West is a work of art. That is the most advanced piece of technology I have ever seen in my life, and I've been around for quite some time. If there's anyone besides me in this compound that can pick up on Sterg, it would be West."

"Yeah... he already has. He doesn't know about Sterg yet, but he knows something is going on."

"Exactly, so once you install the upgrades, Yilvin, Bodeelch, and the others will know about it as well, and this will only confirm their suspicions."

"But what can I do about it? I need to do my job."

"And you will. We will simply modify their requests to fit our own needs. For instance, why don't you install a kill switch for the kill switch?"

"Sterg, why didn't we think of that? It's a great idea. So, I would install the kill switch for them, but I would have my own means to disable said kill switch?"

"Precisely," Professor Dea said. "Also, while you're installing the upgrades, why don't you install a way to block them from specifically sensing Sterg?"

"I just built a device that chimes a warning signal when it detects certain frequencies. It could be something like that, where rather than sending a warning, it blocks that information from being sent. The problem is that Sterg's frequencies are far more complex than those simple drones."

"Drones? What drones?" Professor Dea asked.

"Oh, right, you've never been underground. Granted, I never saw one when I was underground, but I was told about them from—" He realized he had said too much, so he cut himself short.

"Navacus, who else knows about Sterg?"

"Only just, like, my entire team, plus Norman. So, eight others, not including us."

"And you questioned me about trust. That was not a smart thing to do. There are too many others who know. Someone is going to make a mistake."

"That's technically already happened, but it was with West, and we spoke about it already."

"You really need to be more careful," Professor Dea groaned. "It's no wonder Yilvin and the others are onto you."

"You know, now that you put it that way, I really have been quite careless, haven't I? And here I thought I was being so careful. But, at the same time, if I didn't tell my team, then I would have slipped up about it sooner or later. Them knowing is a good thing, even if you don't think so."

"There's nothing that can be done about it now, but you're right, it may be advantageous."

He nodded. "Right. Now, about West. Are you saying that you're going to help me with the upgrades?"

"Yes, if you have time, now would be a great opportunity to go through a few things. I know you have Sterg, but with me around, we can get this done much faster."

"Now? It's been a long day. I have another long day tomorrow, and it's already quite late," Navacus complained.

"All valid excuses. But Navacus, some things are more important than rest. Your life could depend on it. And, besides, the more work we get done now, the less you'll have to do later."

Navacus wheezed. He knew Professor Dea was right. This was one of the only opportunities he'd have to work closely with Professor Dea like this, and he could use the help. Sure, he could ask his own team for help, but they all had their own tasks to complete. He didn't want to overload them or distract them, especially the Harmertians. That was why he had specifically requested Lyd to keep quiet that he'd found Kate. If word got out, it would only distract everyone from the current goal. Of course, he would tell Norman and everyone else about it eventually. He just needed to wait for the right time while focusing on the moment at hand.

He nodded to Professor Dea. "Okay, sure, we can get some work done tonight. But if we're going to do this, then we gotta start soon."

"Great," Professor Dea exclaimed. "How about we start with the kill switch to the kill switch?"

***

There was only about an hour left until dawn by the time Navacus made it into bed. He was completely and utterly exhausted, yet he was proud of the work he'd accomplished with Professor Dea. While he was right that this helped to alleviate his workload, he still had a lot on his plate, even with Sterg's enhancements.

*How am I going to be rested enough to take on the next day?* he thought. *Sterg, is there any way that you can use your powers to give my body a full night's rest in only about an hour and a half? There is a way? Fantastic. You are an excellent companion.*

**21**

## ESCAPE FROM LOVE

Tyrona opened her eyes and stared at the ceiling. She was groggy, as if she had taken some tarnight the night before. As she lay there, she realized the ceiling she was staring at was not the gray ceiling she had grown accustomed to, but a white one. She didn't remember being moved, but she also didn't remember falling asleep.

The last thing she remembered was talking to Kate. She had been encouraging her to use magic to escape her cell.

*I must have been successful, for I'm now in a different room. And if I was drugged, then that would explain the grogginess. I guess this room must be more secure than the last one.*

Tyrona sighed and sat up, then nearly jumped out of her skin—if it could even be called her skin. The body she was in was not her body. She studied her hands, turning them over and rubbing her fingers together. She could definitely feel her thumbs running over her fingertips, but her hands were pale. These were not the dark umber hands she was born with.

Sudden movement caught Tyrona's attention. She turned to her left and saw a familiar woman looking back at her—Kate Thomas. She stood up and approached the mirror. As she placed her hand against the cool surface, her memories rushed back to her. Her consciousness had left her body, and she had seen herself lying next to Kate's body. She had then spoke with a small, gray humanoid. He had been frightened of her as she told him all about herself. She didn't know who it had been, but he was the last person she had communicated with before she faded away.

And yet, somehow, she was still alive. Only now, she was inside Kate's body.

*But wait… if I'm now in Kate's body, what happened to Kate? Is she in my body? Did we undergo some horrific experiment that caused us to swap bodies?*

A quiet response swam through her murky mind. *"No, Tyrona. I'm still here…"*

It was a strange sensation to watch someone else control your body through your own eyes. For some reason, Kate couldn't control her own movements, even though this was her body. She knew that she should have been scared, but Tyrona had been in her head for some time now, so that wasn't what was bothering her. Instead, the strangest part was absorbing Tyrona's thoughts. When Tyrona remembered her final moments, Kate saw it as well, as if she had lived those moments herself. This was more than just communicating telepathically; it was as if their two separate lives had been merged into one.

*"Kate, is that you?"*

*"I don't know what's happening. I don't have control over my body, so how do you, Tyrona?"*

In her confusion, Tyrona began looking around the room as if she was expecting to see her.

*"I'm just as confused as you are,"* Tyrona replied, although it didn't really need to be said. Kate could feel everything that Tyrona was feeling, just as Tyrona could feel everything Kate was feeling, now that she was aware she was here.

*"Tyrona… what I saw… I mean, what you—what we saw… our bodies were connected to all those wires and devices. They must have somehow melded our consciousnesses together into one body—my body. That's the only explanation I can think of."*

*"But why would someone want to do this? And what happened to my body then? Why was I the one that had to die? What is the purpose of this nightmare?"*

She didn't know what to say. Tyrona had died—she saw it as if she had been the one talking with that Harmertian. And yet, she didn't die, because she was still here. She felt so overwhelmed she didn't know what to do. She slumped down onto the bed and slid to the floor.

She looked up and stared at herself in the mirror. It felt like it had been weeks since she had seen herself, but what she saw she barely recognized. She stood up and approached the mirror to get a closer look at herself. Her head was completely shaved and her eyes were dark and sunken. She looked gaunt, as if she hadn't had a proper meal in while, which she supposed was true. They must have somehow fed them to keep them alive, but they hadn't fed her well.

Once her thoughts turned to food, her stomach rumbled and her mouth felt parched. Her knees buckled and she fell to the floor. In her surprise and confusion, she hadn't realized how weak she was.

She put her hand to her head, stood up, then froze.

*"I have control over my body again! Tyrona, what did you do?"*

*"I didn't do anything—we didn't do anything. It happened when you— I mean, we—fell to the floor."*

*"How odd... so, we both can control my body, only we can't do it at the same time?"*

*"I don't understand it either, how this all works. I mean, we don't understand..."*

*"Wow, is this confusing."*

*"Right? Your thoughts are my thoughts, and my thoughts are our thoughts."*

*"Our thoughts are our thoughts, but what about our feelings? What about Norman?"*

Norman—oh how she wished that he was safe. He may have been the reason she was on Melridion, but now, all she could hope for was that his situation was better than hers. And how could it not be? He was here to get his legs back—to get his life back, not to be melded with another person.

But, no, that wasn't right, was it? There was something important she was forgetting—Theodore! She had been mistaken; in her final moments, she had felt Theodore's presence. And he was here because of her, because she had been whisked away from Eklatros against her will. He had come for her, to save her, but now she feared he was trapped here himself. He needed to save himself; she wasn't worth saving.

Wait, what was she thinking? Of course she was worth saving! She was here for Norman, and she would not leave him behind! And what about Theodore?

Her head spun as the conflicting thoughts and emotions tumbled through her like a roller coaster. Part of her loved Norman and part of her had never met Norman, just like part of her loved Theodore and the other part of her didn't know who he was. Sure, they could feel how much each man meant to the other, and they could access many joyful memories about each of them, but still they loved who they loved.

She placed her back against the wall and slid to the floor then hugged her knees as she buried her head into them, then burst into tears. Not for Kate or Tyrona, not for their situation, but for Theodore and for Norman.

Theodore wouldn't recognize her. He wouldn't know who she was, even if she tried to convince him otherwise. But, as for Norman, she didn't love Norman. She loved Theodore—but she loved Norman more.

She screamed in agony as her tears ran down her legs. She couldn't face either of them, not like this. If she couldn't make heads or tails of who she was or who she loved, then how could her lover? How could either of them accept her? She had to let them both go, didn't she?

"*No, what am I thinking? I can't ever let him go. I can't... I won't!*"

"*But can we figure this out? Or will we go insane?*"

"How do you feel?"

She broke out of her daze and saw a man sitting on her bed across from her. He wore a white coat and slacks, and he stared at her through black framed spectacles.

*Spectacles? That's so archaic. Glasses is the modern term.*

"Kate, how do you feel?" the man repeated.

"Hungry... so hungry."

"We thought that would be the case. Here, this should help," he said as he handed her a plastic wrapped rice grain bar and a bottle of water. She took it, tore open the bar, and scarfed it down. Then she chugged the water and immediately felt better.

"Now, how do you feel?"

She pondered on his question for a few moments. As she had been eating, conflicting emotions had surged through her. Kate was familiar with the rice grain bar and had enjoyed it thoroughly. However, Tyrona had thought it was dry and bland. This proved to them that they actually were sharing one body, that this wasn't some strange trick or mind-bending illusion. "Kate feels strange... I honestly don't know how I feel. We don't really know how to deal with this situation. Also, am I a we?"

"I know you must be terribly confused. You have two different people living in one body, so I think you are both an I and a we, depending on the situation. Now, my name is Professor Randall, and I'm here to help answer whatever questions you may have."

"We have a lot of questions, but what I want to know is why us? Why was I taken from Norman, and why did you drain the life out of my body?"

"Tyrona, when you arrived, you took us all by surprise. When we realized how powerful you are, we wanted to help keep that power alive. You would not have survived for long on our planet. While you could breathe our air and, from what we gather, our gravity is similar to your own, there are a million other factors to consider. For all we know, our common cold could kill you. So, Professor Durrist, my colleague, decided that we should attempt to transfer your magical powers into another body.

"Now Kate, forgive my bluntness, but you were chosen because you were essentially hand-delivered right to us. Right when we were considering how to source that other body, you arrived."

"Um, seriously? How much colder could you people even be? You only ever saw us both as playthings you could experiment on!" she shouted as she stood up from the floor. For a moment, her vision flashed purple.

Professor Randall shirked back, leaning down onto the bed. "Now, please, it's only natural that you'd be angry. But you're still consciouses, right? Both of you are. Please settle down, and—"

"Settle down? No, I don't have to listen to a puny little man like you! If you say I can still use my powers, then there's nothing you can do to stop me from getting inside your head and causing you to lose your mind."

"I wouldn't be so sure about that," Professor Randall said hesitantly. "We can't be sure that you would have the same powers. You are in a different body, after all. Plus, we don't know how Kate will influence your powers either."

She looked down at her hand and turned it over. "You know, that's the first thing you've said that makes complete sense. You're right. I can't know what my powers are until I test them out... on you," she said as she glared at Randall. He gulped, and his eyes went wide.

"Durrist! Carl! Get me out of here!" he yelled.

Behind Professor Randall, a door she hadn't yet noticed opened, and a familiar face walked through. Her jaw nearly fell to the floor.

"Dasch? Is it really you? How can this be?"

Dasch looked down at Professor Randall and said, "You're free to leave. Go prepare for the meeting. I'd like to speak with her one-on-one."

"Absolutely. I'll see you again soon, Kate slash Tyrona, whichever you prefer," Professor Randall said as he stumbled over the bed. He quickly exited and shut the door behind him.

"Look at us, reunited again," Dasch said as he held his hands in the air.

"Dasch? What is this place? What have they done to us?"

"Right," he said as he clapped his hands together. "First things first. I'm not Dasch. I'm Gnudashar. I am the Gnusar that dwelt inside that man for millennia, biding my time. And now, my time has come."

She spat on the ground in front of her. "To the void with you then. I don't want to talk to you," she said as she turned away from him for a split second before turning back around. "What happened to Dasch then?"

The smirk that grew on her friend's face chilled her to her core. "He's still around. He's been banished to the space I was imprisoned in. Oh, what a pair we are! We've both come such a long way since our time with Ànifa. You know, she liked you, too. She was really looking forward to getting to know you."

"Who? You mean Ànifa? Did she say that? Where is she, anyway? Is she here, too?"

"Of course, you wouldn't know. No, Ànifa is not here. I hate to admit this, but she died a heroic death."

"What?" she said as she flung herself to her feet and threw her arms out. "Ànifa passed away?"

"Indeed, and in doing so, she really mucked up Gnusaramnii's plan."

"Good. At least she died doing something important," she responded and crossed her arms.

"That of course depends on the perspective. Now, before Ànifa died, she spoke with Yttendaus in a strange, ethereal realm. While that conversation was just between her and Yttendaus, everyone present could listen in, meaning myself, Theodore, Cecil, Druder, and the rest. During that conversation, Yttendaus unlocked all of Ànifa's memories, causing them to flow into our heads. Not everyone could handle the overload of information. Cecil and Vesten didn't remember any of it. However, Dasch could handle it, and those memories passed onto me."

She didn't know if she wanted to puke, scream, cry, or all the above. Not only did this monster take over Dasch's body, but it held Ànifa's memories as well. She didn't know how this situation could get any worse.

"I do have good news, though," the monstrosity continued after a few moments. "Your precious Dorie is here."

"Really? He's really, actually here?" she asked, then looked down at her pale hands. She folded her hands over themselves and held them to her chest.

"He is here, and so is Cecil and another, Druder. You never met him, but he's an actual elf and has been very interesting to observe."

"So, I really felt his presence," she closed her eyes and smiled, then opened them and glared at the creep. "Now, what about Norman? How is Norman, is he safe? Is he well?"

"Oh, am I speaking with Kate now? I have never met Norman, but from what I am told, he is doing quite well and has a brand-new pair of legs."

She closed her eyes and smiled, then opened them. "That's great to hear. I'm glad he got a new pair of legs. But he must be worried about me, right?"

"Again, I have never met Norman, and I only know what I am told. His emotional state is not part of those reports. But, if he loved you, I'm sure he misses you."

She shook her head slightly. "If you've never met him, then how do you know Norman has a new pair of legs? How can I trust you?"

"Fair enough," Gnudashar said as he pulled a tablet out of his coat pocket. He took a few moments to tap on it, then turned it to her. On the screen was a soundless video that showed Norman standing —he was actually standing—among a group of scientists, talking to them.

"So, as you can see, Norman is doing well and is getting along splendidly with Professor Clums and Professor Qymberkon, who are his caretakers."

"Thank you for showing me that," she said as he put the tablet back in his pocket. "When can I see him again? And Theodore—when can we visit Theodore?"

"All in due time. But first, we need to monitor you for a little longer. You have just been through a very intensive operation. Both your minds and your body need time to adjust and heal. Once you are ready, and once you've got a good grasp on your powers, then we can revisit this discussion."

She smiled as she hopped in joy and impatience. "Great! I'm ready now. I'd like to test out my powers."

Gnudashar smirked at her. "You're still too weak to practice your powers. Let's wait until another day."

She stopped hopping. "Oh."

"Believe me, I know how energy consuming it is to try and focus on multiple minds and memories at once. But I think I can make things a little easier on you. Rather than calling you Kate or Tyrona, as we won't know who we're speaking with, how about we come up with a new moniker for you?"

"You know... that's not a bad idea. Because I am Kate, and I am Tyrona, and Kate's thoughts are Tyrona's thoughts. It's quite confusing."

"I understand. That is why I now go by Gnudashar, as I am more than the sum of my parts. How about we call you... Tykate? No—Kaytrona."

"Kaytrona? I kinda like that, even if you are a monstrosity."

Out of nowhere, a fierce wave of exhaustion rushed over her. She stumbled, sat down on her bed, and placed her hand on her forehead.

"See what I mean?" Gnudashar continued. "You're exhausted. Rest up now, Kaytrona. We'll speak again soon."

Her vision blurred and the room swayed back and forth, then she collapsed on the bed.

*That bastard drugged us again,* she thought. *How do they expect me to test out our powers if they keep on drugging us? How can... How does... Theodore... Norman... I'll... I'll see you again...*

**22**

# ESCAPE FROM CONSTRICTION

Gnudashar stepped out of the room with a large smirk on his face, then gestured to Carl.

"Come. Let's report back to Lord Foxaire."

"Sure thing. I'm right behind you," Carl replied, forcing his face not to react to his master's creepy smile.

He followed Gnudashar through the winding path that took them through Professor Xergat's laboratory and to the gyroscope bay. Every time Carl was forced to walk this path, he kept his eyes forward. He never wanted to see what grotesque creatures Xergat was working on. It didn't matter how much he believed in Lord Foxaire's plan, nor that he knew these experiments were necessary; he still hated seeing them.

Once they were safely aboard the gyroscope, he breathed easier. As he watched the transparent sphere roll through the underground tunnel, his earpiece chimed.

"Mister Feng, Sid Heigel reporting for duty, sir."

"Sid, I'm glad to hear from you," Carl responded. "How was your last mission?"

"We secured four bounty hunters for the next job. We can discuss the details when you and Gnudashar arrive."

"Understood. We're on our way. ETA ten minutes."

"Good deal. Over and out," Sid said, and the line went dead.

"Sid got four IBHA agents," Carl informed Gnudashar.

His companion grumbled unhappily. "I suppose that will have to do. Kanaghar has gotten quite stingy."

"I'm sure Sid will let us know more soon."

With that, they passed the rest of the time in silence.

The gyroscope docked, and they took the elevator directly to Lord Foxaire's penthouse. Gazelle smiled as they entered the reception room.

"You're right on time. Lord Foxaire is waiting for you both," the lustrous Nioavellian said.

Carl nodded and followed Gazelle's smooth hips into Foxaire's room. The doors clicked into the locked position behind them.

Lord Foxaire was speaking with a tall, muscular Human. His bald head helped to show off his tanned skin, and his chiseled jawline was accentuated by light stubble.

"Gnudashar, Carl, welcome. How is our magical sorceress doing?" Lord Foxaire asked, his deep voice rumbling through the painting-covered room.

"She's confused and overwhelmed, as was expected. Overall, though, it seems like her mental state is strong. She's still getting a grip on her body, but it shouldn't take long for her to get accustomed to it. Ideally, the sedative we gave her will be her final one," Gnudashar answered. He stood with his chin held high and his hands clasped behind his back. In contrast, Carl stood informally with his arms crossed. He had been around Lord Foxaire long enough to know when formality was required, and this was not one of those times.

"Good. Let it be so. Once she wakes up, make sure the drugs pass through her as quickly as possible without the use of additional drugs. Her new room is being prepared for her arrival, so I need her to be in top shape for her first magic trial run," Lord Foxaire replied.

"Very good, my lord," Gnudashar answered with a slight bow. "Also, I decided upon a new name for her. Kaytrona."

"That's fine," Lord Foxaire said with a dismissive wave. "Sid, what did you make of the storage room?"

"Well, as Gnudashar said, there was an explosion. Debris was everywhere. Nothing could be salvaged, not even the white wand we found. It was the only thing still in one piece, and yet it was glued to the desk."

"Of course nothing could be saved. Everything in that backpack was essentially shrunken down by over two or three degrees. That's an exceptionally high amount of pressure, which was only being held together by Tyrona's strong magical willpower. Once she died, the hold on that magic vanished, causing everything in that backpack to be obliterated, along with the other contents of the room," Gnudashar said as if he was the smartest one in the room.

"It is a shame—I was hoping to study those items further. However, at least the wand is still intact. We will need to study it closer after the move."

"I apologize, sir. I should have seen it coming. I could have helped to prevent this," Gnudashar said as he looked down at the floor.

Lord Foxaire sighed. "You're still getting a grip on your multiple memories and personalities. At least no one was harmed. However, next time I won't be so lenient. Now, Sid here just finished informing me about our bounty hunter mercenaries. While only four agents could be secured, Kanaghar has assured us that these four agents are all highly skilled."

Gnudashar cleared his throat. "Sir, are you sure four will be enough? The request was for ten agents. I don't understand why we can't get all ten."

Lord Foxaire smiled, showing off his off-putting yellow teeth. "Do not be concerned, my good prophet. Kanaghar must have his reasons. And no matter what happens, I have him right where I want him."

"Sid, are the four we got actually good ones?" Carl asked.

"Yes, Mister Feng," Sid replied. "Two of them, Creson and Brock, have been a team for over seven years, which is close to a lifetime in their line of work. And while the other two, Anessti and Egimas, have only been partners for a short time, both have a history of successful jobs. Plus, Anessti is well known by someone that works for us. He was West Kilinder's partner before West joined our ranks."

"Ah, so he's the one that beat West to a pulp. I must thank him when I get the chance," Lord Foxaire replied.

Carl thought on that for a moment before replying. "We'll need to tread carefully. Judging by the way West and Anessti parted ways, I don't think they should be around each other. Let's have Creson and Brock on base while the other two patrol the upper atmosphere."

"Good idea. I'll let them know their assignments next time I speak with them," Sid replied.

"Great. How are your own soldiers holding up?" Carl asked.

"Impeccably. All fifteen of my Cyclones are up to speed on the situation and are ready to be deployed at a moment's notice."

"I'd like to personally inspect them after this. We can't allow for any holes in our security," Carl demanded.

"Of course."

Lord Foxaire looked back and forth between them and steadied his gaze on Carl. "Satisfied?"

After Carl nodded to his superior, Gazelle spoke up. "My lord, Anessti nearly killed his partner, West. How can we trust someone who literally broke their partner's back?"

Lord Foxaire grinned. "Ah, Gazelle, I understand your concern, but it only makes me trust him even more. Anessti was hired to take out West. The fact that Anessti didn't hesitate to severely maim his own partner ensures me he is only in it for the money. And I can trust those that only believe in money, for I will always be the highest bidder. And yes, while Anessti technically didn't finish the job, which shows some sense of sympathy, it also provided us with a valuable new team member."

Gazelle nodded. "Oh, okay, I understand now. Anessti shouldn't be a problem then."

"Good. Now, let's get into the meat of it," Lord Foxaire said, still addressing Gazelle. "Call Professor Durrist."

"At once, my lord," Gazelle replied as she walked over to a large monitor and typed on a nearby console. A few moments later, Professor Durrist and Professor Randall appeared on the screen.

"Lord Foxaire. It's good to see you," Professor Durrist said.

"Professor Durrist, Randall. Now that you're here, we can begin," Lord Foxaire said as he stroked his tentacle-like beard. "I've received the final confirmation from Chief Engineer Volvordime. The satellite station is officially ready for us to move into. This means our plan will go into motion immediately. Professors, I need you to prepare the Titans. I also want to move the Eklatros subjects as soon as possible. We must get them to a more secure location."

"Of course, my lord," Professor Durrist replied. "I will check in with the hangar crew to see if all three ships are fully prepared. And since we only have the three ships, we'll likely need to move the Titans in several batches. However, I see no problem moving the four Humans. They should all fit on the first round of transports."

"Very good," Lord Foxaire said with a smile. "Gnudashar, I'd like you to help facilitate the move for the Eklatros subjects."

"It would be my pleasure," Gnudashar replied.

"I have a question," Professor Durrist interjected. "What about Svetlana and West? Professor Clums will begin their enhancements in a few days. The timing will likely overlap on the day of the move."

"That should not be an issue, and it's part of the reason we are enlisting aid from the IBHA," Lord Foxaire replied. "Whoever is being worked on the day of the move will help to distract Professor Clums and his team. They must not catch wind of what is going on, especially in light of the strange occurrences surrounding the Yggdrazim lately."

"I don't know what has been going on, but Professor Clums is definitely up to something," Professor Durrist said. "The more I speak with him, the more I can tell there's something different about him. We need to keep a very close eye on him. Once the move is completed, I plan on allocating most of my resources into observing our Yggdrazim friend."

"That is why I am sending Gazelle down to the compound," Lord Foxaire announced and then turned to Carl. "You'll need to introduce her as my direct eyes and ears. We need to give him something to truly fear."

Carl smiled at the irony of that statement, since he and his specialized glasses were Lord Foxaire's direct eyes and ears, but of course, no one else knew that.

"Certainly, my lord," he replied, then turned to Gazelle. "I hope you can pick up some information on him."

"Oh, you don't need to worry about that. With my abilities, I should uncover the truth immediately," Gazelle boasted.

"Indeed, you will not fail me," Lord Foxaire said with a hard look. "Now, as soon as the first move is complete, we will immediately prepare for the next round, which will include any remaining Titans, along with Professor Randall, Bodeelch, and Professor Peal and his subjects. For the final round, we will move Professor Durrist, Professor Dea, and Professor Clums and his subjects, as well as Professor Xergat, Yilvin, the other successes, and any remaining drones or failures that we will want to bring along."

"My lord, are you sure it's wise to keep Professor Clums here for that long? What if he finds out what is going on?" Carl asked.

"Even if he discovers our plans, what can he do? Where can he go? The security cameras will catch him if he tries to escape through any of the underground passages. And he is a Yggdrazim. He cannot survive a day in the desert heat. He's got nowhere to run. Plus, the longer he's here, the more time we have to determine if he is a threat or not. While he is a brilliant scientist and his loss would be felt, together, Professor Qymberkon and Sylcertiverner can make up for it."

"I sure hope so," Carl replied. "West is something else entirely. We need Professor Clums to do more work like that."

"I already have four subjects being prepped at the satellite station. As soon as he and his team arrive, they will be put to work," Lord Foxaire replied. He turned to the screen and continued, "Professor Durrist, once you arrive, you will be briefed by Professor Ean to begin the transfer of taking over command."

"Of course. Ideally, Professor Randall will begin sending me reports once he gets there," Professor Durrist said as he turned toward his partner.

"That's the plan," Professor Randall replied.

"Very good," Lord Foxaire said.

"Is there news about the progress on the gate?" Carl asked.

"Yes. A very brief report, but I am told that work is going smoothly. The skeleton structure is nearly complete."

"That's great. Hopefully it will be completed by the time I arrive. With the arrival of our prophet," Carl said as he nodded to Gnudashar, "and the Eklatros messengers, the time of Gnusaramnii's return is nearly upon us. We need to be ready."

"And I know you will see to it that we will be," Lord Foxaire said. "Sid, how much longer until the bounty hunters arrive?"

"Approximately two hours."

"That gives us time to prepare," Lord Foxaire said. "Carl, once you're finished inspecting Sid's troops, hurry back to the compound and connect with West. He'll be waiting for you."

"I'll be sure to let West know," Professor Randall added.

"Now, if there's nothing else, let's adjourn this meeting. Gazelle, I need you to be ready to leave as soon as Carl is. You'll be going to the compound with him."

"I'm ready now," Gazelle said with a nod. "But who's going to take over for me while I'm gone? Surely you've found a better alternative to those three drones I've been babysitting?"

"For now, Sid will take over your duties until moving day. He'll keep an eye on those three drones and keep them in line."

"Are you sure you can trust the drones?" Carl asked.

"I know I cannot trust them," Lord Foxaire replied. "That's why I'm putting my trust in them, because they are untrustworthy. I can rely on them to perform exactly as expected."

"I suppose that makes sense," Carl replied as he scratched the back of his neck.

Lord Foxaire smiled. "Get to work, everyone. We're on a schedule."

Professor Durrist and Professor Randall's faces disappeared from the screen, and the monitor went black. Carl nodded and approached Sid. Gazelle sauntered over to them.

"If you don't mind, I'd like to inspect your troops as well," Gazelle said to Sid.

"Of course. We all take our job to protect Lord Foxaire very seriously. It's only natural you'd want to meet them. Now, right this way," Sid said as he led them to the door. He then waited awkwardly as Gazelle stepped over to unlock the doors.

Carl followed Sid and Gazelle in silence. His heart was beating excitedly in chest, and he controlled his breathing so it wouldn't show. They were finally leaving this dump behind. Sure, it was a useful place and served them well, but it was time to put it behind them. The compound was always meant to be a temporary place. It wasn't built for them anyway. Even the original builders had abandoned it before it had been completed because they knew the location was horrendous. But it had allowed them to remain hidden, which was the entire point.

Within a few minutes they arrived at a large hall. It was decorated similarly to the rest of the mansion, down to the elegant glass chandeliers and deep red carpeting. Standing at attention in three rows of five were Sid's personal soldiers. They went by the moniker Sid's Cyclones because of their unique ability to destroy a room and lead investigators down false paths.

They all wore heavy body armor, which was spray painted light blue. They wielded double barrel shotguns and plasma swords to accentuate their close-combat fighting skills.

"Attention, soldiers!" Sid barked. "Prepare for inspection."

The soldiers continued to stand as still as marble statues, as Carl and Gazelle looked them over. Carl found all weapons and armor were fully up to code. Gazelle informed them that while all the soldiers had no coherent thoughts, she detected that eight of them were attracted to her and only one showed a slight concern for their personal safety. After pointing out the latter soldier, Sid approached and barked in his face. After a few minutes, Gazelle proudly announced that all worries and desires had been wiped away.

"Your soldiers are in terrific condition," Carl said. "I'm confident they will perform admirably."

"They always do," Sid said with a grin. "Thanks for the help, Gazelle."

"My pleasure. I love watching minds fall into full obedience," she said with a sly smile that sent chills through Carl.

"That's... great," he replied. "Now, let's go. I'm sure our gyroscope is ready for launch. Sid, take care, and until next time."

"You do the same," Sid replied as they shook hands.

"Oh, how is everything going with our side project?" he asked Sid. With everything going on, he had nearly forgotten he'd asked him to spy on Gnudashar.

"Smoothly. Nothing new to report."

"Very good." Carl nodded, then led Gazelle out of the room and to the main elevator.

"Do you need to grab any supplies before we go?"

"No, I'm ready as is. I have a room prepared already," Gazelle answered.

He nodded and tried to ignore the alluring nature of his companion. He knew his lust was because of her powers, but part of him didn't care, and that was the part he needed to silence.

*It won't be much longer now*, he thought. *If all goes according to plan, by the end of next week I'll be settled into my new home and free from Gazelle's bewitchment and the prophet's insufferable presence. Then I will finally focus on Gnusaramnii's return.*

**23**

# ESCAPE FROM CONVICTION

If West had eyes, he'd be rolling them. Now that he had been away from the Intergalactic Bounty Hunter Association for several months, he realized he had grown quite insufferable toward them. Of course, it didn't help that he had always disliked Tag Creson and S.C. Brock. While he couldn't deny the fact that they were the best two-person team in the IBHA, their cruel and horrific methods to get the job done never sat well with him. It didn't matter that the IBHA subtly encouraged this type of behavior—West had never been one for torture. He had prided himself on killing his targets efficiently to give them the least painful death possible.

Now that he was out of the IBHA, he was finally able to criticize them to his heart's content. He didn't, of course, because he was simply too frightened of them. He still wasn't sure why they were here or why he was giving them a tour of the underground facilities, but he did his best to be civil—and it helped that he no longer had a head.

"Seriously? Another dead end? What the heck is wrong with this place?" Brock said. He was a dark-skinned Human with a bald head and a thin black goatee.

265

"As I've mentioned, this facility was abandoned in development by the first construction crew. When Lord Foxaire took over, he modified the structure the best he could, but as you can obviously see, much of the underground is unable to be used."

"You know, I heard a rumor that Lakinceitians like to build mazes. Are you sure that the whole construction thing isn't just a bullshit excuse?" said Tag Creson, a stark white Eusphyrchiian, who walked with his back straight to help compensate for his short stature.

West turned to his kin. "I wouldn't doubt that played a large part in them keeping it this way, but I'm not sure. I was just educated on the matter a few days ago."

"Yeah, how are you enjoying your new cushy job?" Creson asked.

"Don't you mean crushy? Anessti really did a number on you," Brock said, laughing, causing his entire muscular body to shake.

Another fierce, mental eye-roll ensued. "That's great you noticed, Brock. And I'm doing very well; thank you for asking. Professor Clums built LSS, this computer that helps keep me alive. It's also a multi-purpose device." He stopped and took off his hat, revealing his neck scars and hat stand. "As you can see, I need all the help I can get to keep on kickin'."

Brock's eyes grew wide, and Creson just smirked before replying. "I figured as much. Others may not notice your handicap as easily, but I knew that hat didn't grow three sizes."

"Yeah but... hot damn. I've never seen anything like this before. I didn't even know you could survive without a head," Brock said as he continued to gape and stare.

"It was always possible in theory," Creson said with a hint of fascination in his voice. "I may just need to try this for myself sometime."

West quickly put his hat back on. He wasn't happy he had given Creson inspiration for new torture methods, but part of him couldn't help but smile on the inside. Yes, he was gravely disfigured, but at least he was no longer a slave to the IBHA. Instead, he was a slave to Lord Foxaire which, so far, had been much better—and *cushier.*

"So, how is that blue backstabber doing, anyway?" West asked to break the growing silence.

"Just fine, just fine... maybe even better than you!" Brock joked. "But seriously, you know that he's here, too, right?"

"Wait, what?" West asked, causing him to stop in his tracks.

"Oh, uh, yeah. He and Egimas are patrolling the atmosphere, so it's likely you won't run into him," Brock said, trying to recover from his blunder.

"That's good. I really don't want to see him again. But Egimas, huh? I think I met her once. She's the Eusphyrchiian huntress, right? Just joined like three months ago?"

"That's the one," Creson confirmed. "She's been making quite a stir in the IBHA, and not just because of her sultriness. I hear she's ruthless on the job. I'd like to see her in action sometime."

"I'm sure you would," West said as he elbowed Creson.

Creson simply smiled awkwardly and slowly turned his gaze to the ceiling. West smiled internally—he didn't know Creson well, but he did know that he was terrible with the other genders.

Brock cleared his throat. "So, what else do you need to show us?"

"We've got only two more sections to visit. The one we're heading to now holds a few of Professor Durrist's successes, including an Ancilsan and a Yggdrazim. Then we'll visit the gate those otherworldly Humans came through."

"Ah, wonderful. More interesting people to meet," Creson said with a sly smile.

"So, why are you here anyway? I know I keep asking, but I really wish you could fill me in, especially for old times' sake," West prodded. He hoped the tour wasn't just for the bounty hunters' benefit.

Creson was stern faced as he shared a glace with Brock. Brock raised an eyebrow and shrugged, then turned toward West again. "Ah, this seems like a quiet area. We were told to keep this on the down-low, but we're here to protect several assets that will be moved to an off-site location. And the more we know about this place, the better we'll be able to do our jobs."

"Exactly. Though I don't know why *we* needed to tell him that. If his superiors wanted him to know, they'd tell him themselves," Creson said with his arms crossed.

"It's not my problem. I don't work here. We're just here for a job," Brock replied.

"Nothing is ever your problem," Creson quipped.

As the two brutes bickered, West's mind jumbled though dozens of questions. Who was being moved, and to where? What was the reason for the move? Would he be leaving? Were they all leaving? Brock brought him back to reality as he loudly cleared his throat.

"Hey, West. Can we pick up the pace? We don't got all day."

"Of course, my apologizes. Right this way."

*What does this all mean?* West thought. *If Lord Foxaire would turn to the IBHA for protection, then what's really going on? Brock mentioned that other agents are patrolling the atmosphere… Are they expecting some sort of attack? Are we all in danger? Oh stars, who can I even talk to about this?*

---

"I am thrilled that progress is going well on Norman," Professor Bodeelch said. "Especially now that you have solidified the idea for the retinal-scan lock mechanism. That's really a fantastic solution."

"Isn't it, though?" Navacus said enthusiastically. "We needed something that was hands free, and it didn't make sense to be voice activated either, so a retinal scan was the only clear winner."

"Indeed. Now, in light of all of this, I need to request that you turn your complete focus to the upgrades on West and Svetlana. Those upgrades are now a higher priority than working on Norman. Feel free to pull in any team members you may need to get the work done faster. Ideally, please keep some resources allotted to Norman, but again, West's and Svetlana's upgrades are more important."

Navacus skillfully hid his surprise with Sterg's residual help. In the meantime, Sterg was doing what it could to pull any extra information from Bodeelch. However, it couldn't learn much. The main thing Sterg could confirm was that Bodeelch really was in a rush to get these upgrades completed. There was also something he wasn't telling Navacus, something that created this new schedule. Navacus was certain Sterg would have been able to discern more if he wasn't forced to hide its presence, this time from an alluring Nioavellian that was watching over the lab. He didn't know what was going on with Gazelle, but he knew she would be able to detect Sterg.

"I understand," Navacus said. "And actually, I made a lot of progress on West's upgrades last night."

"Wonderful. Are any components completed?" Professor Bodeelch asked.

"Not at the moment, but it should only take me a few more hours to complete at least two or three of them."

"Great. It's 15 o'clock now, so would you say that you should be completed by 19 o'clock?"

"Sure, that shouldn't be a problem."

"Great, I'll send a message to West and ask him to head up to your lab then," Professor Bodeelch said.

"Oh, so you mean you want me to work on him today? I thought the plan was to install them tomorrow. I won't have much time to do any testing."

"Then test only what needs testing. As I said, our timetable has been moved, so it's highly important you complete these upgrades as soon as possible."

"Right, I understand. I will be ready by then."

"Wonderful. If you don't mind, I would like to ask Professor Dea to help you out as well."

Navacus couldn't help but smile. "His assistance will be much appreciated."

"Good. And another thing—since Norman is being worked on in this lab, we'll need to find a different space for you to perform West's upgrades. Now that Professor Peal's lab isn't in use any longer, would you mind doing your work there?"

"Uh, sure. I guess I would just need a hover-cart to move my tools and supplies, and I would need to move my computer as well."

"That's fine. Ask Gazelle to help out then."

Navacus wished he could keep an eye on her through Sterg, but Gazelle seemed to possess strange powers that allowed her to see far more than she should be able to. For all he knew, she was watching him right now, even listening in on their conversation. He didn't like having her around, not one bit.

"Right, Gazelle. How long will she be sticking around for?"

"As long as Lord Foxaire deems it necessary. I'm just the messenger here," Professor Bodeelch said. "He makes the rules."

"That's fine, I was just wondering."

Professor Bodeelch grinned and nudged him with his elbow. "Don't lie—I know you can't resist her either. To the void with the interspecies relationship stigma. If I were younger, I'd be all over that pretty little thing."

Navacus struggled to hide his disgust. He had felt Gazelle's false allure even before she entered his lab. He knew it was because of her powers, but luckily he had his own methods of getting around it, thanks to Sterg. Sadly, it seemed as if everyone else was being pulled in.

"Yeah, well, if there's nothing else, I'd like to check back in with her."

"I knew it! No, there's nothing else. I'll be sticking around for about an hour longer, but then I'll need to get to my other duties."

"Thanks for letting me know," he said as he opened the door to his office and stepped out into his lab. At the moment, Fumalli was hovering as close to Gazelle as possible while still being productive. Even Mac and Lyd were struggling to keep their eyes off her. Luckily, Syl and Grasberg were both gay, and Kurjon wasn't interested in other females. However, they were still quite entranced by Gazelle. As for Norman, he was unabashedly staring at Gazelle as she rattled off intelligent-sounding nonsense.

Navacus wheezed loudly as he stepped into the lab, causing everyone to turn and face him. Behind him, Professor Bodeelch stepped out of his office and clasped his hands together.

"Everyone, I would like your attention, please. Professor Bodeelch just informed me of a change in plans. Norman, I apologize, but we'll need to slow down working on you for the time being," he explained.

"What do you mean? I thought work was going well," Norman said as he looked around at the lab assistants.

"Work is going well," Navacus emphasized. "However, other projects have taken priority. That being said, I would like Lyd, Syl, and Kurjon to help me out. Professor Qymberkon will take the lead on Norman's attachments. That leaves Mac, Poi, and Grasberg to continue working on Norman."

Syl frowned. "Are you sure you need my help? I have a lot going on here."

Navacus thought for a moment, then nodded. "If that's the case, then you should stay here. I'll need to take Grasberg then."

Grasberg shrugged. "Sure, that's fine. What will we be doing anyway?"

"You'll be assisting me with West's upgrades tonight, and we'll be moving our operation to Professor Peal's old lab. Gazelle, would you kindly go grab a hover-cart for us in the storage room while we prepare things on our side?"

Gazelle squinted at him as if she was trying to pierce his soul. After a few moments, her intensity died down, and she shrugged. "I'll be back in two minutes," she said as she left the room. All eyes were on Gazelle's exit. Once she was gone, everyone jumped back into action.

"Right, so Lyd, Kurjon, and Grasberg, help me gather all the tools. We should grab whatever we can that they won't need here. Professor Qymberkon, what do you think you can spare? And Professor Bodeelch, if you've got nothing going on, could you also lend a hand?"

As promised, Gazelle returned with the hover-cart. Ten minutes later, the cart was loaded.

"Alright everyone," Navacus said as he slapped his feathery hands together. "Norman, if you need me, just say the word and Professor Qymberkon can buzz me over. Peace, love, and faith."

"P-L-F!" Syl replied. "Good luck!"

Navacus stepped out into the hallway and led his small party to Professor Peal's side of the compound. Grasberg and Kurjon helped to push the cart and Gazelle trailed behind them.

"This feels a little strange," Grasberg as he looked around the hallways. "I have never been to this side of the compound before."

"Me neither," Lyd said as he stood on the cart, watching over the breakable items. "Hopefully we'll have enough room to set everything up."

Navacus shrugged. "Well, let's find out, shall we?" When he opened the door to Professor Peal's lab, the first thing he noticed was how clean it was. The room was nearly barren of any equipment—it must have been moved underground. What little equipment was left was placed in the back corner of the room. A noise caught his attention, and he looked to see Professor Dea turn away from an open cabinet.

"Ah, Professor Clums, welcome. I took the liberty of clearing up the lab to give us room to work."

"Thanks a lot, Professor," Navacus replied with a shallow nod. "Now, let's get everything set up."

It wasn't long before they had the lab set up the way they needed it. "I'm glad you're here, Dea. We can now continue where we left off last night."

Lyd nodded in understanding as he stood on top of one of the tables. "I was wondering how you got so much accomplished."

Gazelle cleared her throat and smiled joyfully from a corner of the room. "I don't mean to interrupt, but we are on a schedule."

Navacus nodded. "Right, I understand. With Professor Dea's help, we should be able to complete all the upgrades in time. But first, we need to get everyone caught up. Also, Gazelle, are you going to be assisting?"

Gazelle giggled as she waved a hand in dismissal. "Oh, of course not, silly. I'm not qualified for such things. I can comfortably keep an eye on things from here."

Navacus wheezed, then explained to everyone about each of the four modifications. Lyd, Kurjon, and Grasberg each voiced their displeasure at West's kill switch and monitoring device. Gazelle cut in to explain that the upgrades were all meant to help protect West's best interests.

As Navacus had expected, they completed all the components and coding needed in under three hours. They then prepared the room for West and took a short break while they waited for his arrival.

*I really hope West understands,* he thought. *Aside from Gazelle, I know none of us want to install the kill switch or the remote-control movement device. I'm just glad that Dea and I worked on our own modifications last night to help counteract them. I just don't know when I'll be able get the chance to tell West about them.*

---

West stood outside the lab with his hand on the doorknob as he took a moment to collect himself. He had no idea what to expect. No one had informed him yet on what was going to happen. While he was dreading the worst, at least he got a break from Creson, Brock, Bsarg, and the other Lakinceitian security guards. It hadn't been long after the tour that Professor Randall had asked Creson and Brock to help fill everyone in.

Professor Randall had confirmed that in a few days' time, they were going to oversee moving several assets to an off-world location. They were planning to move Theesakin, Zadgarcolth, and Karkilver during the first trip, along with four of the Humans from the magical world, Eklatros. Each of the compound's security guards were going to play an integral role in ensuring that everything was successful. Bsarg, Nijork, and Jakog had been tasked with guarding Professor Peal's subjects while West had been asked to help with the Titan's move, since his connection with Theesakin was crucial.

As soon as his questions were answered, West had been pulled away and informed of immediate upgrades. It had come as a shock, as he hadn't even been informed that he was getting upgrades. While he delayed the inevitable, at least he was glad Professor Clums was performing them.

West tipped his hat and then stepped into Professor Peal's previous laboratory.

"West, it's so great to see you again," Professor Clums said as he waddled over to him. "I hope we're not interrupting anything important."

"I was in the middle of something, but I'll just get filled in on the rest later. To be honest, I didn't know this was even happening."

Professor Clums wheezed. "Why am I not surprised? I apologize —I wasn't aware that you weren't aware."

"It's not a problem. So, who's this?"

"I'm very pleased to meet you, West Kilinder. I'm Gazelle," the attractive Nioavellian said as she walked over to him with a hand out. He took her hand and shook it. "I'm actually like you. I was enhanced by a different professor, so you could say I have abilities of my own."

"Oh yeah?" he asked as he tipped his hat. "What kind of abilities?"

"That's on a need-to-know basis," she said slyly.

"Uh, okay then," he replied, then turned back to Professor Clums. "So, what are you going to be doing to me?"

"To start things off, we'll be installing a jetpack on your back. It will be connected to LSS at three different points, which will help support it while strengthening LSS."

West nodded in approval. "Wow, that sounds great. A jetpack? So I'll be able to fly? How is it even going to be powered?"

"It's a miniaturized version of what powers spaceships, but reworked to provide you with thrust. There will be a battery that we'll need to install, and it will be powered by your own body heat and residual energy, so it won't ever need to be replaced."

"That's a genius idea. You really think of everything, don't you?"

"Right, well, there's still three other modifications that we need to discuss, some of which will involve some software updates to LSS, as well as hardware improvements."

He could tell Professor Clums wasn't pleased about the situation.

He had paused slightly in hesitation at various times during his explanation. As West looked around the room, he seemed to pick up the faint signal that almost seemed to be the presence of another person. He shrugged. Maybe that would change after these upgrades.

"What are the changes?" he prompted.

"Well, we will need to install a monitoring device, a remote control of sorts, and a couple of switches," Professor Clums said, his voice wavering. Gazelle cleared her throat and glared at the professor.

West put his hand on his hat and shook his body back and forth. "Come again? A recording device and a remote control? For what, for me?"

Gazelle looked directly at him. "Please understand, West, all these updates are for your best interest. We need a way to keep an eye on you in case you find yourself in any dangerous situations. It would be a waste if you were to tragically die."

He tipped his hat, only partially in agreement, but mostly to himself. Of course they wanted a way to spy on him. In a way, he was surprised they were only now getting around to it.

"Alright, well, the sooner we get started, the sooner we get it over with, right?" West said.

"I wholeheartedly agree," Gazelle said in a sing-song voice, smiling. "Let's get back to work, everyone!"

*What am I getting myself into?* West thought. *I really don't want to be spied on, but I know I don't have any say in the matter, as I truly am a slave to Lord Foxaire. This and Gazelle's overbearing presence proves it.*

It was an hour and a half into work when his hunger hit him. They had just finished installing the jetpack and supports and were preparing to start on the last three upgrades.

Navacus wheezed and turned to Gazelle. "Hey, if you don't mind, would you go grab us our meals? Everything is back in the fridge and pantry in my lab. Sorry, in the rush to get over here I forgot them."

Gazelle rolled her eyes and her head. "I'll be back soon," she said as she left the lab.

He waited a few seconds, then turned to Professor Dea. "Is this a good time to explain?"

Professor Dea nodded. "Yes. Let's make it quick."

*Wait, Navacus,* Sterg's voice rang through his head. *Please, reveal me. Trust me, it will be faster this way. There's no time to hesitate.*

"Ah, but first—West, prepare yourself."

"Prepare for what?" West asked as he sat up on the operating bed. "Are there even more upgrades or surprises coming?"

"Uh, something like that." A moment later, he uncapped Sterg and let it expand out into the room. West let out a loud whistle.

"What in the void, Professor?" West asked. "This is what I have been sensing! And how strange is this—the dull ache I've been feeling is gone now, too. Who are you?"

"I am Sterg, and we'll need to keep the introductions short. But let it be known that I am Navacus Clums' personal guardian, and I have been helping around here as well. Now, as you all know, Gazelle cannot know about me or what Navacus will now explain to you."

"Right," Navacus said with a nod. "West, we made our own, secret modifications. We have a way to oversee, limit, and edit what gets transmitted from the monitoring device. We'll also install a way for you to override their remote control over your movements. Finally, we made a kill switch for their kill switch, so if their kill switch ever gets activated, then our kill switch will activate first to deactivate their kill switch."

"At least, we have an eighty percent certainty of our success," Professor Dea cut in.

"What? A kill switch? Why are you doing all of this?" West asked.

"Because I didn't build LSS for their benefit," Navacus answered. "I built LSS for you, and you alone."

"Gazelle is approaching, I must once again hide my presence," Sterg said, fading into the background.

"Oh, okay," West said as he held a hand on the rim of his white hat. "That was a lot to take in. But thank you."

A moment later, Gazelle walked in holding two bags worth of meals. She allowed them to continue their break to allow everyone to eat.

*It is quite a relief that West finally knows about you now, Navacus* thought as he dug into his mixed rice bowl with mediocre grilled fish. *This will make things easier moving forward. And yes, Sterg, I agree—we need to have another meeting. Tomorrow night. A lot is going on, and we need to stay on top of everything if we're to come out of this on top.*

**24**

# INTERLUDE: LOCATION - EKLATROS

```
Begin Replay of NIWAT Inner Datalog
Recording C-0000670333 S-001 N-01
```

*Francentia* burst into another unknown solar system. This was the fourth system since we'd left Theronior, and the planet we sat above was the first to contain a large blue ocean. The planet was small—I was almost tempted to classify it as a dwarf planet. *Francentia*'s quick scan confirmed that the mass of the water and the other objects on the planet were helping to maintain its spherical shape. I was so distracted by the composition of the planet itself that I had almost missed the most important detail.

"Maker, are you seeing this?" Blu-Dreem asked. "This planet is teeming with life! Even though the planet is small, it has a larger ratio of life than even Theronior did!"

"Yes. We'll need to be cautious. *Francentia*, can you detect any orbital defense systems or communication channels that we'll need to avoid?" Maker Denorad asked.

"Negative," *Francentia* softly announced. "My scanners are reading no signs of any advanced technology. This planet is still in its iron age."

"Does that mean that even our basic weaponry is more advanced than anything they have?" Zombu asked.

"If they really are in their iron age, then it's quite likely," I replied. "This means we'll need to be even more careful. We are not here to make enemies. If we are still on the Gnusars' trail, and they have also visited this planet, then we may be able to gain some valuable information."

"Not to mention that we have information they would also find valuable," Maker Denorad added. "I agree with you, Niwat. *Francentia*, disable all weapon systems, then begin our approach."

"Acknowledged. Powering down weapon systems."

"Hey, Maker, where are we trying to go? In my opinion, we'll need to avoid any large settlements," I said.

"I agree. I'm sure that with the right numbers, we could be overwhelmed," Zanzi added.

"Fair point, but that isn't what I was getting at. I don't want to make a big scene. It would be best if we made as little noise as possible here. We don't want to inadvertently cause any trouble for them."

"Also agreed," Maker Denorad nodded. "How about we stick to the oceans for now? Maybe we'll be able to come across a manned vessel."

"Good plan," I replied.

"Weapons offline. Beginning approach," *Francentia* announced.

"*Francentia*, take us down to the ocean. There—between those two landmasses. Beedee, keep us on course."

"Yes, Maker," Blu-Dreem replied. "Also, the battery is still working perfectly with no anomalies detected."

"That's great, thanks for the report," Maker Denorad replied.

*Francentia* expertly broke into the upper atmosphere and deployed its cooling mechanisms. Within a few seconds we were clear of the ozone and descending through the upper layer of clouds. Once through those, there were no other obstacles—only the wide blue ocean stretched out beneath us.

"*Francentia*, scan for any nearby vessels." Maker Denorad said.

"One vessel found, located three kilometers south-southeast."

"If it's that close, it's likely they can already see us. I mean, there's no cloud cover or anything to hide in," Zanzi complained.

"You're right," I replied. "At least it's only one vessel."

"*Francentia*, approach the vessel slowly and cautiously. Remember, they've never seen anything like us before. They may be hostile toward us, so if they do attack, don't do anything. Don't even try to dodge. We need to show them that we are not a threat," Maker Denorad commanded right before his stomach rumbled loudly. "Ah... sorry. I can't control that."

"Maker Denorad, when was the last time you ate?" Blu-Dreem asked. I nodded in concern.

Maker Denorad hummed to himself. "*Francentia*, how long until contact?"

"Five minutes."

"Okay, I'll grab a quick bite first. I am quite hungry."

Maker Denorad exited the cockpit and returned two minutes later with a kuafruit and a slice of flatbread.

"You know, times like this make me wish I didn't have to eat at all. Unfortunately, I can't modify any of my major bodily functions without killing myself."

"They may have food they can spare," I suggested. "Of course, we don't know anything about their species or if their food would be edible."

"Exactly. I'd rather not get my hopes up."

As we got closer, it became apparent that the ship we were approaching did indeed see us coming. *Francentia* identified twenty lifeforms on board, three of which were injured. That only increased the percentage that they would be hostile.

Even so, I couldn't help but admire the craftsmanship of the ship —it was a beautiful piece of work. It sported two large sails, and on top of the highest one was a basket that held two figures. The ship's keel cut through the water so perfectly, the wake the ship left behind barely caused any waves at all. Its figurehead was of a beautiful woman who looked extremely human-like. The only oddities were large, pointed ears. She wore a long-sleeved, button-up dress with a puffy hood and held her hands out to her sides. Her right hand held an arrow while her left hand held an orb.

It was a marvel of wooden engineering. I hadn't seen anything like it—I was used to metal and plastics.

"Three of them are injured," Maker Denorad said as he tossed the pit of the fruit in the bin. "We could use that to our advantage somehow."

"One minute until arrival," *Francentia* announced.

"Everyone, see the figurehead on the ship? It looks like a human woman."

"Because it is a human woman," Zanzi pointed out. "Niwat, look toward the deck. There are all sorts of people running around. Some are even carrying weapons."

"Stick to the plan," Maker Denorad said calmly. "*Francentia*, open communication systems. I want to talk to them."

"External communication activated," *Francentia* announced as she came to a halt, hovering forty meters above the ocean's surface.

A man with a large hat approached the head of the ship. He stood with one leg on a crate and his hands on his hips. Behind him stood two women and two men. While everyone else seemed on edge, the captain had a peculiar look on his face—one of eagerness, hopefulness, and surprise.

"Greetings. Please, do not be afraid. We mean you no harm. While our technology surpasses your own, I believe we can be friends," Maker Denorad said into the microphone.

"You speak our common tongue, and yet we can't fuckin' see you," the captain called back to us. Now that things had settled down, I could clearly see the captain's scruffy red beard and long, dirty red hair, which sat beneath a tall, pointed dark blue hat with a large rainbow feather. "How can we trust you? We don't fuckin' know where you came from."

"I think he's asking us to go out there," Blu-Dreem said.

"And we need to, right now, Maker," I insisted. "We cannot delay."

Maker Denorad nodded. "*Francentia*, lower us until our ramp can reach the deck, then deploy ramp."

"Acknowledged. Descending. Descending. Ramp deployed."

"Time to go," Maker Denorad said as he stood up.

"Do you mean for all of us to go?" Zanzi asked, hesitantly getting to his feet.

"Blu-Dream, you stay behind. We'll need a quick escape if things turn sour," Maker Denorad commanded, then turned to Zanzi and said, "and no complaining. I mean it. In fact, keep your mouth shut. They need to see us, but they don't need to hear a word from you."

"Yes, Maker," Zanzi said with a fierce nod. I smiled, then followed Zanzi, Zombu, and Maker Denorad to the ramp.

As we walked down the ramp, the stares we received clearly conveyed their shock and surprise. Maker Denorad, having most of his robotic parts covered up, was the best representative we had.

"Halt. Do not go any further. You will not fuckin' step aboard my ship unless I say so," the captain said sternly. "Please, give us a moment to convene amongst ourselves."

"Absolutely. Take your time," Maker Denorad said.

The captain and the four others nearest to him huddled together. Even though they spoke in hushed tones, my audio receptors could still hear the conversation.

"I know you don't fuckin' like this, but I need to hear them out."

"Vesten, are you fuckin' sure? Those are metallic people! They could be dangerous."

"But Patsy, they came from the sky—and they came directly to us."

"I know what you're thinking. But I don't see how they could possibly be connected to Cecil and the others."

"You never fuckin' know. That whole asinine situation with the deinonychus ranchers aside, this has been a long, strange day. I had a very vivid dream... and then there was that bright burst of light near the horizon at dawn. Plus, it's been three years since Ànifa's sacrifice. I don't fuckin' know why, but I think it's all connected."

"Vesten—"

"Whatever you say, Captain. We'll follow your command."

"Thank you, Bart. Now, once we break, I need everyone to follow my orders. Tushar, find Ashe, Gonth, and Arsona, and head to the navigation room. We must protect the information we have in there. Patsy, I need you to find Anqi and Martin. Tell them to prepare for a fight. And make sure Annalyse and Trevonn stay in the crow's nest. We need our eyes on them at all times."

"Got it."

"Then, Patsy, please go to Dale and let her, Finfoler, and the others know what's going on. And please, stay by Dale's side. She fuckin' needs you. She's stronger with you by her side."

"She really is. But Vesten, are you fuckin' sure?"

"Yes. Bart and Zi'ra are going to stay here with me. If anything happens, they'll protect me."

"They fuckin' better."

"I owe everything I am to Captain Vesten. I will protect him with my life," Bart confirmed.

"Zi'ra?"

"Oh, you know me, girl. I'm having a blast," said Zi'ra. "This is really exciting, no? I'll keep a close eye on those four weirdos. And yes, of course I'll protect your cousin."

"Thank you both."

"Now, let's get fuckin' to it," Vesten commanded.

As the huddle broke, the dark-skinned man and the red-haired woman ran down to the main deck and shouted orders.

"Now that we see you, we still can't fuckin' trust you," the captain said and stared us down. "Your ship is powered by a mysterious technology, and three of you aren't fuckin' human. Please, explain yourselves, and make it quick. We have places to be."

Maker Denorad nodded and motioned for us to back up a few paces. He then introduced each of us and briefly explained what an androbotix was while he conveniently omitted that he was a cyborg. As our maker recounted the harrowing journey we were forced to take as the Gnusar ravaged Theronior, the ship's captain stared at us with no visible emotion. Out of respect for their privacy, I refrained from scanning him beyond surface level.

When Maker Denorad finished, the captain stood still for several moments with his hands behind his back, then stepped forward.

"Anyone who has faced the Gnusar is a friend of ours. I am Captain Vesten Teixeira, and I welcome you aboard *New Horizons*."

Maker Denorad stepped down from the ramp, and I followed, leaving Zanzi and Zombu behind. Captain Vesten held out a hand, and Maker Denorad shook it. As he shook my hand, he didn't seem phased by my silico-metal skin. "And you're Captain Denorad and Niwat, right?"

"Yes. We are pleased to meet you, Captain Vesten," Maker Denorad replied. "So, are you actually familiar with the Gnusar? Did you fight against them?"

"I am pleased to meet you all," Captain Vesten replied with a polite smile as he ignored my question. "Behind me are Bart and Zi'ra, two of my most trusted advisers. Now, as much as I would love to continue this conversation, we really are in a rush. One of my crew is badly injured. We fear that if we do not make it to our destination by tomorrow morning, she will not make it. And unfortunately, the winds have not been kind to us."

Maker Denorad hummed. "How far do you need to go? Are you going to the large landmass, or the smaller island beneath it?"

"The island of Panna. We're headed to a town called Beetaramn."

Maker Denorad nodded. "We'll help you get there. Just give me a second."

Captain Vesten nodded with a confused smirk plastered on his face. Maker Denorad spoke into his communication device, activating the group chat on my screen. The faces of our ship's crew all popped into the sidebar.

"Blu-Dreem, report in."

"All is good here, Maker," Blu-Dreem replied, causing the yellow box to move from bordering Maker Denorad's square picture to bordering his own.

"Good. *Francentia*, how far are we to Beetaramn?"

"Calculating. Based on the limited knowledge I have, roughly one hundred seventy-seven kilometers with ninety-three percent accuracy."

"Good odds. *Francentia*, calculate how to create enough thrust to push this vessel quickly but safely."

I watched as Captain Vesten's face turned into a mixture of fear and confusion. Upon doing so, Maker Denorad stepped away for more privacy. "What does he fuckin' mean, push us?"

As *Francentia* replied, I turned down the volume of the chat and addressed Captain Vesten. "I believe the idea is to use *Francentia*—our ship—to use its thrusters to push you along. *Francentia* and Maker Denorad are currently calculating both the distance and the amount of thrust needed. From what it sounds like, you and *New Horizons* will be perfectly fine. Besides, I saw how cleanly your ship cuts through the water."

"Fuckin' right? Elven woodworking, man. It's beyond my understanding and truly is a fuckin' work of art. Makes it so I barely miss my old ship. Which is why I am very cautious of this plan. Who is *Francentia*? Is she your helmsman?"

"No. *Francentia* is the ship's artificial intelligence and is semi-sentient, which means she can make her own decisions and can anticipate our needs."

Captain Vesten scratched his tanned arm, which sported light red hairs. "Artificial intelligence? Semi-sentient? The fuck is all that?"

"If I may, Captain," Zi'ra, an almost space-black woman with long pointed ears said as she stepped forward. "To me, it sounds like they can combine magic and technology. I think we should give it a go. I'd love to see how their magic works, yeah."

I nodded in response to Maker Denorad's question from the group chat.

"You're the expert, especially when it comes to the Ekataramn," Captain Vesten said to Zi'ra, then turned to face me. "Fuck it, let's do it. But if you hurt us, trust me, we have powerful allies that will avenge us." As Vesten spoke, Maker Denorad and the others came to a final decision on the calculations.

"I understand. As we said earlier, we do not wish to harm you. And since your friend is in critical condition, we will do what we can to help," I said.

"Indeed," Maker Denorad said as he stepped back into the conversation. "Believe me, you're in great hands. And you're not doing this alone. Zombu is going to go assist Blu-Dreem, another androbotix, while Zanzi, Niwat, and myself stay aboard your ship. If that's alright with you, of course."

"It will put us all at ease, I believe," Captain Vesten replied, then turned to his crew. "Bart, take the wheel. I'll help if needed. Zi'ra, tell everyone to tie up any loose crates and equipment, posthaste. And make sure Tushar, Patsy, Annalyse, and Trevonn know."

"Yes, Captain," she replied as she ran down the stairs.

I turned my attention back to *Francentia* as the ramp finished retracting.

"We'll be fine, old friend," Maker Denorad said to me.

"Oh, I know we will be. I heard all the calculations; I just couldn't log any of it. I had to focus on listening to the vulgar captain."

"It's not a problem. He is quite vulgar, isn't he? As long as he's hospitable, though, it won't matter. Anyway, we better hold on. We may have some slight turbulence."

"Why did I have to stay behind again?" Zanzi said quietly.

"I'm impressed. You really restrained yourself. But now, if you need to scream, please position yourself far away from anyone else," Maker Denorad ordered. "We can't have our new friends go deaf on your account."

"Yes, Maker. And I'll even lower my volume," Zanzi said as he walked toward the end of the ship, sat down, and fiercely hugged a banister.

I walked behind the wheel of the ship and held on to the railing. Maker Denorad secured himself beside me.

"We're good to go on our end," Blu-Dreem said as his face popped onto my screen.

"Captain Vesten, is your ship secured?"

Captain Vesten looked down at Zi'ra, who gave a firm nod. From my vantage point, I could see that everyone on the deck was clinging to something.

"We're ready," Captain Vesten said with a slight waver of hesitancy in his voice.

"*Francentia*, engage thrusters. Retreat thirty-four meters, and then point side thrusters in our direction," Maker Denorad commanded.

"Acknowledged."

Three minutes later, *New Horizons* was flying at its top speed across the ocean. Even with Zanzi's reduced volume, I could hear his wailing from my position. I spun my head around to see Vesten and Bart gripping the wheel tightly. A look of shock and surprise crossed their faces when they saw me staring, so I swiveled my head back around to face forward.

I couldn't help but break out into a wide smile. This was my first time seeing an ocean up close, and soaring across one was an incredible experience. Plus, the sky was clear and unpolluted. It was a magical experience.

---

Begin Replay of NIWAT Inner Datalog
Recording C-0000670333 S-002 N-11

Thirteen of us approached an A-framed cottage as we hobbled through the town of Beetaramn. Zanzi and I wore dark cloaks to hide our true selves from the curious townsfolk. As we made our way down the road, Maker Denorad and Captain Vesten carried Dale, a blond woman whose swollen left leg was wrapped in a bloodied bandage; Zanzi and Zi'ra carried Disakorn, a man with short, messy black hair, a badly sprained ankle, and a recently dislocated shoulder; and Gonth—a man with radiant hazel skin and pointed ears—and I supported an annoying knight named Preston, who had a concussion and a broken right foot. Finfoler—the doctor—and another man with pointed ears and Patsy walked backward and kept fussing at us to walk straight, while two others, Anqi and Ashe, led the way.

The door to the A-frame burst opened as we reached the front gate, revealing an elderly woman with frizzled white hair and thick glasses.

"Hurry, get her inside! Quickly now, all of you!" the woman commanded with a firm voice.

Captain Vesten and Maker Denorad, carrying Dale, were the first ones through. Gonth, Preston, and I followed, and as I entered, a young woman in baggy clothing rushed around the wide-open room, preparing the bed for Dale. Once the three injured were settled in, the young woman and Finfoler tended to Dale, who was fading in and out of consciousness. Patsy knelt beside the bed and tightly clutched Dale's hands.

Vesten sat near me and sighed. I heard him quietly whisper to himself. "Joan... where are you, my love? We need you now... I need you now."

It was silent while everyone took the time to find a place to sit. The room wasn't meant to hold fifteen people comfortably, but we made it work. Once everyone was settled, the two local women handed out bowls of food. Zanzi and I both awkwardly declined, but Maker Denorad really enjoyed it. As everyone ate, Zanzi stepped outside to place his drones around the A-frame so we could monitor our surroundings.

When Zanzi returned, the elderly woman approached and stared me, Zanzi, and our maker down, then turned to Captain Vesten.

"Please explain her injuries," the elderly woman said.

"Of course, Tanaq Farag. Allow me to first apologize for..."

Tanaq Farag snorted as she waved a hand in dismissal. "I don't care about that formal crap right now. Out with it, Vesten. What happened?"

"Ah, well, she got fuckin' sliced up by a deinonychus' claws. There was blood everywhere. Finfoler did everything he could, but we were already running low on our medical supplies, and we also had to tend to Preston and Disakorn. But Fin will let Afyna know what he needs."

"They're already discussing it," Tanaq Farag said as she pointed to Finfoler and Afyna, who were whispering amongst themselves.

"Seriously, thank you for seeing us on such short notice. Since Sage Mason and Charlotte left on their journey, yours is the only place I can sail to directly for low-key medical assistance."

"And we're happy to help. Now, tell me everything. Why were you attacked by dinosaurs, and deinonychus no less?"

"Because of four stupid fucking idiot dino ranchers. We were wrapping up a job in Port Gall when we came across two frantic men. They explained how they lost four deinonychus in the Gatelceous Jungle. As much as I wanted to fuckin' turn them down, I am, often begrudgingly, the interim guildmaster of the Guild for Eklatros, so I had to agree to help them. They, of course, told us other bullshit details to explain why they were there in the first place, but what ends up happening is that they led us not only to the Gatelceous Jungle, but to the fucking Raptor Claw."

Tanaq Farag gasped in shock. "Oh my word, idiots indeed, for only their ilk would go there."

"Precisely," Captain Vesten said as he threw his arms out. "Let me tell you, we saw some scary fuckin' shit. But long story fuckin' short, we couldn't catch the four deinonychus using the methods we had originally planned, so the elves, being the expert woodworkers that they are—I mean, they helped build *New Horizons*—came up with what seemed like a great idea."

"In our defense," Gonth interrupted, raising his hand, "it was a great idea, and it was structurally sound for being a crudely put together rig."

"Oh, I fully fuckin' agree with that," Captain Vesten said as he grew more animated. "So, what we ended up fuckin' doing was digging a deep pit with a wooden rig above it. The idea was to trap the dinos in the pit and pull them out one by one with the lasso attached to the rig. And the whole fuckin' point of doing it this way, rather than just using manpower, was to keep everyone safe. The plan would've worked, too, if not for that fuckin' idiot rancher."

"Oh man, screw that guy," Disakorn said as he wiped his good hand across his face. "He should be the one in pain, not us."

"Yeah, that's the most fucked up part, is all the ranchers got out of it unscathed. So, we successfully trap all four deinonychus in the pit by luring them out of the jungle with some chickens. We were pulling up the first one and this fuckin' guy is leaning on the rig. So, we got the deinonychus all the way up to the fuckin' top and were about to sedate it with a drugged dart. But, because this guy is fuckin' leaning on it, the wood bends more than it should and fuckin' cracks. He immediately fuckin' backs off, and the four ranchers run back while a whole bunch of us run in to help. The rig ends up fuckin' snapping, and it collapses the hole and kills all three of the deinonychus at the bottom. And during this, Preston over there got hit in the head with a beam of wood and knocked out cold, and his foot got crushed in the process. Luckily, he was wearing his helmet, because if not he'd be fuckin' dead."

"Here, here," Preston said with a raspy voice as he raised a clenched fist. "My armor may be uncomfortable, but it has saved my ass many times."

"Really? I thought being a jailer was one of the cushier positions. I mean, you were at ease when you locked Cecil and me up," Vesten joked, then turned back to Tanaq Farag. "So, we start pulling Preston out of the rubble, not realizing that the last deinonychus was tangled in ropes and buried in debris nearby. It ends up springing up and slashing out with its claws and it cut Dale's leg deep. Then, as he tried to run back, Disakorn over there badly twisted his ankle and fell hard on a rock, dislocating his shoulder. It was a fuckin' mess. But Zi'ra was fuckin' on top of it and shot the dart before the dino could wreak any more havoc."

Zi'ra beamed and slapped Anqi on the shoulder. "Ah shucks, there was nothin' to it," she said as she twirled a strand of black hair.

"What matters is that everyone made it out alive," Tanaq Farag said, looking at each of Captain Vesten's crew with a warm smile that spread to her eyes. "Afyna, how's Dale?"

"Her body is going into overdrive, but Fin is working on a salve to help with that," Afyna replied with a soft voice. "We'll also need to give her a strong tea to fight off the infection when she's conscious. However, the main issue is her leg."

"What do you mean?" Patsy asked with tears in her eyes.

"We'll need to amputate it," Finfoler said sternly with sad eyes. "There's no other way. It's too far gone to save."

Patsy sobbed, then sucked in a breath and said, "Do what you need to, just save her life."

Anqi and Zi'ra approached Patsy and led her to an empty cot to let her rest. I turned my attention to the bottom right corner of my screen. Since I was near the drones Zanzi had set up, I could pick up on their feeds. Many of the cameras were pointed toward a large volcano that was emitting faint puffs of steam. The sun was low on the horizon, revealing a boulder hovering above the volcano. Before I could zoom in to investigate, Tanaq Farag cleared her throat and turned her attention to Maker Denorad, Zanzi, and me.

"I have never seen anyone like you before. Where did you come from?"

Maker Denorad spoke up firmly. He explained where we were from and how we got here. Tanaq Farag sat down in awe at the end of it and scratched her chin. "That's some story. While it is quite unbelievable, there are tales of your arrival in many ancient scrolls. While it could be a misinterpretation, I am the Tanaq, the religious leader, and I am here to witness the truth."

"Now, that is unbelievable—that you knew of our coming. We knew nothing about your planet before we arrived. Now, before I ask about your experiences with the Gnusar, I want to offer some aid to your friend Dale," Maker Denorad said calmly. "Our ship, *Francentia*, is currently in low orbit around your planet."

"Eklatros," Tanaq Farag added. "Her name is Eklatros."

Maker Denorad nodded and corrected himself. "*Francentia* is in low orbit around Eklatros. On board we have a fabricator for any parts we may need. As you may have noticed, my two companions don't have any bio-organic parts. So the fabricator is meant for replacing any parts at any time."

Tanaq Farag stared at me and Zanzi for a few long seconds before I removed my cloak, revealing my androbotix body. Tanaq Farag's eye widened, and her mouth hung open. She shook her head a moment later and composed herself. "Excuse my rudeness. I have never seen anything like you before."

"Right, your society is not as advanced as our own," I said in attempt to reassure her. "That is why we are doing whatever we can to keep a low profile."

"Good. It would be for the best if there weren't any whispers of you," she said with a nod and turned back to Maker Denorad. "Now, please continue."

"Yes. So, our fabricator can make Dale a new leg. We just need to scan it and send the specifications over. It should only take a few hours, so it could be delivered sometime during the night."

"I—I don't know what to say. You can make her a new leg using your advanced technology? Thank you for your generosity. You've already done so much for us."

"Think nothing of it. All we want in return is knowledge about your experience with the Gnusar," Maker Denorad said, then quickly added, "and food. If you have any food you could spare, that would be fantastic. I must admit, I was surprised to see other humans here. I wasn't expecting that."

"It's amazing, isn't it? That there are humans on other planets? As for your request, I'm sure we can scrounge something up," Tanaq Farag said with a smile, then turned to Dale and her caretakers. "Afyna, what needs to be done?"

Within ten minutes, it was over. Dale's leg was cleanly amputated, thanks to Finfoler's expert skills, and then Zanzi and I got to work preparing Dale for her new robotic leg. After a quick scan of the amputated leg, I sent it to *Francentia*, then settled in.

Vesten then dove into his story, starting with how he met a woman named Ànifa.

Begin Replay of NIWAT Inner Datalog
Recording C-0000670333 S-002 N-42

I stood in the moonlight and focused my vision on the boulder floating above the volcano's cauldron as I processed Vesten's story. There was a lot to take in, starting with the Gnuelry, Gnurargurts, Gnureavers, and even the Ekataramn, along with the existence of several races superior to humans, who lived on a floating island, and the gate that transported Vesten's friends to another world—the world where the Gnusar were from.

We were only four planets into our trek, and already we were blessed with a deluge of knowledge. We now knew our final destination, but we didn't know how long it would take to get there.

I shook my head and refocused on the moment. Out of all the fantastical things we were told tonight, the floating masses intrigued me the most. This boulder was where Tyrona had disappeared and apparently traveled to the Gnusar's home world. Eklatros really was a magical place.

Zombu descended silently from the sky, interrupting my thoughts. He held a silver box that encased Dale's new leg.

"Thanks for coming down, Zombu," I said.

"Well, that was some story. I didn't expect to learn so much already."

"That's what I was just processing. It's almost like we were meant to come here. Anyway, let's go. Everyone is waiting."

I led Zombu down the slope and to Tanaq Farag's A-frame. When we arrived, Dale was bouncing with excitement. Patsy stood over her with a frown and watery eyes. When we showed Dale the leg, everyone gasped. I had to admit, it was a good-looking piece of technology. It was black and gold—we don't have any human skin-tone paints—and sparkled in the candlelight.

We quickly installed the leg, and Dale could move it within seconds. She jumped to her feet and walked around the room twice before her exhaustion and pain caught up with her. When she was back on the bed, Afyna and Finfoler gave her some more medicine.

A text chat box appeared on my screen. It was just transparent enough to let me still see the others in the room.

Are you sure this is a good idea? — Zanzi

As our maker said, it's the least we can do.
The information they provided us is priceless.
— Niwat

I've only been here for twenty minutes, and I can already tell these are good people.
There's nothing to be concerned about. — Zombu

Looks can be deceiving. — Zanzi

Tanaq Farag interrupted our digital conversation. "Zombu, I know there's not much room, but I would be honored if you stayed the night."

"Thank you, but I—"

"It would be easier than going back and forth, right? You'll need to be present at tomorrow's celebration."

"What celebration?" I asked.

"I'll need to call in some favors come morning, but I'm going to rent out the community center so we can have a proper celebration before you return on your journey, to thank you for everything you've done for us."

Begin Replay of NIWAT Inner Datalog
Recording C-0000670333 S-003 N-17

I sat between Blu-Dreem and Maker Denorad at a large wooden table. Zanzi and Zombu sat beside Blu-Dreem, while Maker

Denorad sat next to Captain Vesten and Bart. We were in a large building—I'd say it was nearly the size of a large-size storage shack back on Theronior. In total, there were twenty-seven of us. It had been a while since I had been in such a large gathering of friends and acquaintances.

Four servers attended to the table, bringing out enormous platters of cooked meats, steamed vegetables, aromatic cheeses, and rolls of fresh bread. To drink, everyone had a glass of wine, a mug of ale, and a cup of water. Without needing to ask, they did not give me or my fellow androbotix any drinks and removed our tableware to make us more comfortable.

Zanzi leaned over and whispered to us, "I hope they're trustworthy."

"If Tanaq Farag trusts them, then we must as well," I replied.

The room grew silent as Captain Vesten stood on the bench to address the room. He looked like a proper captain today. He wore a white button-up shirt with brown slacks, a brown jacket embroidered with numerous patches, and his blue hat with the rainbow feather.

"My friends, new and old! I'm so fuckin' excited to be here with everyone and to celebrate with an amazing feast. The celebration, of course, is in honor of our new friends and saviors, the crew of *Francentia*," he said as urged us to stand. We got to our feet, and there was loud applause, and then we sat back down a few moments later. "Without them, Dale would have been much worse off, and she wouldn't have a fuckin' robotic leg! Also, a fuckin' huge shout-out to Finfoler and Afyna for being miracle workers. I mean, Dale can already fuckin' walk again. Thank you, everyone."

"Thank you, so, so much!" Dale said as she looked at us. "I know I've already said it a thousand times, but seriously, thank you."

"It wasn't a problem, really," Maker Denorad said as his cheeks grew red with everyone looking at him.

"Now, I want to thank the chefs, Dusit and Duangthip," Captain Vesten said as he pointed to the black-haired couple. "Without your magical cooking skills, and I fuckin' mean *magical*, we wouldn't be feasting on our enemies. For our main course tonight is deinonychus in three ways," he said with a wink, "grilled, roasted, and smoked. While I don't believe any of us have ever eaten deinonychus before, I'm told that they're fuckin' tasty. And speaking of magical skills, none of this could have happened without Zi'ra." At the mention of her name, Zi'ra stood up, waved to the room, and gave a shallow bow. She wore an elegant red dress that made her dark features pop. "For those that don't know, let me instill pure fear into your hearts. Zi'ra Shnuckeramn, our bubbly elf friend who is fascinated by new experiences and living life, has the stone-cold ability to control the dead." A mock-gasp filled the room, as nearly everyone in the room knew about her talents. On my screen, Zanzi sent a text message to the group chat.

> Those that control the dead can never be trusted. Her heart must be as black as her skin. — Zanzi

"Correction—I can only control the freshly dead. If they've been dead for longer than a day, I can't control them—unless I have a close, personal connection with the deceased," Zi'ra stated.

"Fuckin' scary shit, right? As I always say, I'm just glad she's on our side," Captain Vesten joked. "Now, to the point. The idiot ranchers didn't have any use for dead deinonychus, so Zi'ra here reanimated the three dead dinos, made them climb out of the hole, and led them onto *New Horizons*. At which point, of course, Dusit and Duangthip began their magic. And what a fuckin' great way to get back at those that harmed us, right?

"But enough from me, I know you all want to fuckin' tear in. But real fuckin' quick, another big shout-out to our new friends," he said as he pointed at us, "and to my fuckin' crew—it's been a long three years together, but I want to sincerely thank each and every one of you. You have all proven your worth—even you Preston." The room broke out in laughter. "But all jokes aside, I couldn't've fuckin' done it without you all. It's been a fuckin' long time since we've had the chance to sit down like this, so live it the fuck up! My deepest gratitude to our savior and my dear friend, Princess Ànifa. Thank you for three years of peace. To Eklatros!"

"To Eklatros!" The room echoed, then the table shook as everyone, including Tanaq Farag, banged their mugs on the table and drank deeply.

Excited conversations broke out between groups as they tore into their food. Beside me, Maker Denorad moaned in pleasure. "I don't know what a deinonychus is, but this is delicious. It's tender, it's juicy, it's just so... elegant."

"I'm so fuckin' glad you like it," Captain Vesten beamed. "Only half of the meat was cooked up for tonight. The rest of it has been cured, dried to make jerky, or otherwise prepared to perfection by our talented chefs."

"That is quite impressive. How did they do it all so quickly?" Maker Denorad asked through his mouthful of food.

"As I said, they're fuckin' magic. After we defeated Gnusaramnii, the elves left Yttendaus and traveled Eklatros. They reawakened the magic we all naturally possess. For Dusit and Duangthip, they were already master chefs, but now they can weave magic into their food, which makes it just so much fuckin' better."

"What about you then, Captain Vesten?" I asked. "Do you have magical abilities?"

"I do," he replied with a slow nod. "Luckily, I don't have to use it often, because it still scares me. I was considering using it before you all showed up, but I'm glad I didn't have to."

I decided not to follow up with another question. Before Captain Vesten could settle back into his meal, Dale sprang up from the bench and starting dancing, even though there was no music. In response, Patsy, Anqi, Zi'ra, Arsona, Ashe, Annalyse, Duangthip, and Afyna got up to dance with her while shouting incoherently.

"They're a lively bunch, aren't they?" I asked.

"They've been through a lot together," Captain Vesten replied. "And fuck—Dale is alive, and has a brand-new leg thanks to you all.

Again, I can't thank you enough for everything you have done for us. I mean it, truly. You are in my debt."

"It was the least we could do, Captain Vesten. You and Tanaq Farag have shown us such generous hospitality, despite our obvious differences," Maker Denorad said.

Captain Vesten puffed out a stream of air as he waved his hand. "Fuck, man, you're one of us now. Look around—there's people of all races here. We even have a faerie friend and an angel companion, but sadly they're back on Yttendaus."

Captain Vesten frowned at his halfway finished plate of food.

"You know, you'll need to make sure Dale keeps that leg out of sight, Captain Vesten. It may not be a good idea for others to see it," I said.

"Please, call me Vesten. There's no more need for formalities. As I said, we're all friends here," he said as he slapped Maker Denorad's shoulder, causing him to spit out some water. "And don't you fuckin' worry. I talked with Dale this morning. She knows that she needs to keep it under wraps, which will be easy enough to do."

The party of women laughed loudly as they made their way back to their seats.

"You see those four?" Vesten asked with his mouth full as he pointed at Disakorn, Dusit, Duangthip, and Damrong. "Well, three years ago, those four were local heroes in their hometown of Sathon, after it was ravaged by a terrible fuckin' attack from the Gnusar. You wanna know what I call them? I call them the four dynamos, you know, because of all the *D* names."

"Ah yes, I've been meaning to ask you more about your experience fighting the Gnusar," I said quickly to get him back on topic.

In response, Vesten dove deeper into his stories, telling us all about his battles with them. Just as Vesten was completing a tale of how they were nearly finished off by Gnurargurts in a slot canyon, Tanaq Farag squeezed herself between Maker Denorad and me.

"You'll grow tired of his war stories the longer you stick around," Tanaq Farag said with a hearty laugh. "Now, I'm sure you're wondering, so I wanted to reassure you that our four incredible servers won't say a word about you. They are my most devoted followers, so they are simply blessed to be in your presence and to be part of our gathering."

"Right, I was wondering about that," Blu-Dreem said as he leaned over me. "Back on our planet, religion had gone by the wayside five hundred sixty years ago."

"Really? What a shame. What caused the downfall?" Tanaq Farag asked.

"Well, my kind did," Blu-Dreem replied. "Once the humans' technology got so advanced that it created us, a philosophical debate consumed the populous. If we were sentient, emotional, caring, intelligent, and charismatic—all with our own unique personalities —and we were made by humans, then didn't that make them gods? So, the populous ultimately concluded that if they had become godlike, they had no reason to pray to a separate god."

"That's... well, I want to say that's surprising, but it really isn't," Tanaq Farag said sadly. "It really speaks to the truth of human nature. But it is disheartening. It sounds like humans on your planet truly lost their way."

"I can attest to that," Maker Denorad said. "I didn't much care for other people. Everyone was self-centered, and most of them treated their androbotix like tools to be used and discarded, not as actual living creatures. You know, maybe the Gnusar was the cleansing we all needed."

Zombu and Zanzi looked at him with shocked expressions. "I am still traumatized by our escape from Theronior. That was harrowing. Truly harrowing," Zanzi said.

Tanaq Farag laughed. "Destiny can be challenging, and it can be terrifying. But you are here, and I believe it is where you need to be. My apologies, I know all your companions' names, but I was never told your name."

"Oh, I'm Blu-Dreem, but they often call me Beedee for short."

Tanaq Farag smiled warmly as she looked to the ceiling, closed her eyes, and sighed. "Did you know that Blue Dream is an herb that my good friend Sage Mason cultivates?" She opened her eyes and looked right at Blu-Dreem. "It is best known for its calming effects, but it is also used to help one have more vivid dreams. That plant is among the most sacred and holiest plants on Eklatros.

"It is no coincidence that you are here, and that you are called Blu-Dreem. You, the one who is most content to be in the background, will bring great change to Eklatros. I have seen it, in my own visions. Blue Dream personified as it defends the oncoming darkness."

"I don't know, that doesn't sound like me," Blu-Dreem said. "I don't much like actual conflict, and I'm more comfortable behind the controls of a ship."

"Precisely," Tanaq Farag said with a grin and a wink, then turned to Maker Denorad. "You made him, right? Why did you name him Blu-Dreem?"

"Right, I made all of them," Maker Denorad said proudly. "Niwat here was my first, and still the sharpest. His name stands for Naturally Intelligent With Automated Technology. I thought it was a pretty spiffy acronym," he said as he momently closed his eyes and shook his shoulders before continuing. "Zanzi and Zombu were both created around the same time; however, as I briefly explained to you earlier, some of my organic organs were donated to Zombu, not only to reuse them, but to make him even more advanced. So Zanzi means 'of the mind' and Zombu means 'of the body' in our ancient language. Then, as I was working on Beedee here, since he was my fourth, I was having a hard time coming up with a unique name, but one of my favorite characters on a cartoon I grew up with was named Blu-Dreem, so I decided to name him that."

"What's a cartoon?" Tanaq Farag asked.

Maker Denorad started telling her all about television and animated cartoons. When she realized his explanation would take a while, Tanaq Farag stopped him and turned her attention to all of them.

"The five of you have a big part to play yet. Your destination is the source of Gnusaramnii, right?"

"Correct. And we even heard that some of your friends traveled there three years ago," Maker Denorad said.

"Yes, it's been a long time since they left. But if you're here, then I know we'll see them again," Tanaq Farag said solemnly.

"Fuck yes, we will!" Vesten exclaimed as he approached us. "Hey, so, if you do go to where Gnusaramnii is from and where my friends are, could you pass a long a message for me?"

"Sure, I can record that for you," I said as I stood.

"Great, thanks! Wait, what do you fuckin' mean? You'll write my letter for me?"

"Oh no, you don't need to resort to that," I said. "Just look into my eyes and speak your message to them. I'll show it to them if and when I see your friends."

"Fuckin' seriously? Great, thank you so much!" Vesten cleared his throat, took a deep breath, then looked into my eyes and recorded his message. As he finished up, he paused, then whispered, "Seriously, come back. I may be acting strong and invincible, but I need you back here. Eklatros needs you. I can feel it. There's been a lot of changes, and all have not been for the good."

I stopped the recording when Patsy slapped Vesten on the shoulder and pulled him over to where she and Dale were sitting. As he was leaving, Vesten looked back at me and nodded, and I nodded back in understanding.

As the feast winded down, most in attendance grew more and more intoxicated. Everyone grew louder and let loose, truly being themselves as they celebrated joyously together.

Just when I thought things were wrapping up, Martin and Anqi staggered over to me, supporting each other arm over arm. Martin had to hunch down a bit to allow Anqi to get her arm over his shoulder. They shared a laugh, then Anqi's face became serious as she looked into my eyes. "Hey, I want to ask you a really, really serious question. I want to go with you," Anqi said.

Martin laughed. "Anqi, seriously, how much longer are you going to keep up this joke?"

Anqi disarmed herself from Martin and stepped back with her

arms crossed. "I told you, honeybear, this is not a joke. I want to go with them," she said, then turned back to me. "I want to go with you. I've been thinking about it ever since you arrived. And after all that's happened since then, and now this party and reliving old times... I want to have my own new experiences again. I want to travel to different worlds and meet new people and see new animals and new sights! I want to live, to explore what our vast cosmos has in store for us!" she finished as she swirled in place.

By now, Maker Denorad, Zanzi, Zombu, and Blu-Dreem had approached. I turned to Maker Denorad and said, "He's the one you gotta ask. He's the boss."

Maker Denorad hummed. "This is quite unexpected. Just so you know, space is cold for humans, and it can be scary. Staring out into the dark void can put things into a different perspective."

"That's all fine! I don't mind the cold, and I want new perspectives," Anqi said, then turned to Martin who was huffing in annoyance. "Martin, I love you, and I will always love you. And I am so incredibly lucky to have been married to you for two and a half years now. But as much as I enjoy everyone, I was never meant for life on the sea. I mean, you know how long it took me to get over my fear of water. And because I have, I am ready for bigger and scarier things."

Martin looked into her eyes and embraced her. When he pulled back, he was in tears. He held Anqi's hands and looked deep into her eyes. "I know, honey. You have to go. I've known for a while now that you've been unhappy and getting restless. But I haven't known what to do—Vesten, Patsy, Dale, everyone... they're family. And I can't leave them. I need to stay and do my part."

"And I know you need to. That's why I love you, because you've always been there to protect your friends and family." She stood on her toes and kissed him. "Thank you for giving me your approval. It means a lot."

"I know you'd leave with or without it. But I do mean it. You do what you need to do, Anqi Gan. I love you."

"And you do what you need to do, Martin Greene. I love you more."

The knight with broad shoulders and a rainbow plume on his silver helmet approached. "In that case, allow me to accompany you, Anqi."

"Oh no, you don't need to do that, Mikhail. I'll be fine," Anqi said as she waved her hands.

"As a member of the Guild for Eklatros, it is my duty. Not only that, but I am a former member of the Guild of Chivalrous Knights. While I was happy to see the dissolution of the guilds, I am still chivalrous at heart. Besides, traveling to outer space sounds quite thrilling," Mikhail said while rubbing his hands together.

"I know, right? Well, if you want to come along, I can't freaking stop you," Anqi said.

"Then it is settled. Denorad, I humbly ask that you take Anqi and I aboard your fine ship."

Before Maker Denorad could reply, Gonth came running up to them.

"Wait! Wait, I say! I also want to go with you," Gonth exclaimed as he steadied his breathing. "I mean, you'll need an elf by your side, and even if you don't, it won't hurt. Besides, while I never met Druder, I would be honored to follow in his footsteps and take the brave plunge to the new world."

"What's the fuckin' commotion?" Vesten asked as he sauntered over to them. "By the looks of it, I've got three deserters on my hands. Whatever will I do with you?"

"My sincerest apology, Captain Teixeira," Mikhail said as he got down on one knee. "I should have asked your permission before I promised them my sword."

"Your sword, was it?" Vesten asked as he glared at Mikhail. He held his glare for several seconds, then broke out into a wide smile. "You're one of the best swordsmen I've ever seen, and that includes Dasch. They would be lucky to have you."

"Thank you ever so much, Captain," Mikhail said as he got to his feet.

"Yeah, thanks, Vesten. You know I'll always love you. I just really need to do this," Anqi said.

"I know. It's fine, it really is. You three should go with them. Go find Theodore, Cecil, Dasch, Druder, *and* Tyrona. Let them know we've got their backs and that we're ready for them to come home when their mission is through." Vesten then turned and addressed the room. "Is there anyone else who wants to abandon ship? How about you, Bart?"

Bart, a man with a red bandanna wrapped around his head, spoke up. "No, Captain. My place is by your side. I know I can be overbearing at times, but know that it's only because I care for you, our crew, and *New Horizons*."

"And you're the best bosun I could ask for. I would be a fuckin' mess without you," Vesten said, then turned back to Anqi, Mikhail, and Gonth. "You will be missed, but we've got your jobs covered. Besides, I'm sure I could pick up some more scalawags if the need arises. Not fuckin' saying that you three are scalawags, of course."

"Hold on, I need to cut in here," Zanzi said as they stepped up to Vesten. "We have yet to agree to anything. Besides, how do we know—"

"Zanzi, that's enough," Maker Denorad said. "Zanzi is just a little apprehensive. But from my viewpoint, we're all friends. So I will gladly take you three on board. As I was warning Anqi, space is cold, and you'll need to learn to adjust to lower levels of oxygen. The only thing I'm concerned about is our food stores."

No arguing about this, Zanzi. If you need to, keep your eyes on them. — Denorad

I believe this needs to happen this way. I understand your hesitation, but I know you'll come to see why soon enough. — Blu-Dreem

Alright then. I will keep them on surveillance. — Zanzi

As I read the text chats, Tanaq Farag and Afyna approached. "Your food and water are taken care of. Afyna and the servers just finished packing everything up. You've got thirty-four pounds of deinonychus meat in various forms—ground, jerky, brined, and so forth. We're also sending you off with twenty pounds of white rice, twenty pounds of dried black beans, ten pounds of mixed dried fruit, ten pounds of peanuts, seven pounds of salt, and two hundred twenty-five liters of water. If you can take it all, of course."

"Wow, that is extremely generous. That's a lot of food. I don't know what to say," Maker Denorad said.

Tanaq Farag laughed. "You just said it, my friend. I had a hunch you'd be taking on extra passengers, so I gave you what I could spare."

"Seriously, thank you so much. The only thing is that is a lot of water. We can harvest and recycle our own water. However, if it's anything like the water I had during my meal, I'll gladly take some. Just not that much."

"Understood. Our water is some of the best around. Don't let those mountain folk tell you any differently. Anyway, the water is packed in fifty-six-liter barrels. Take what you need."

As they spoke, Blu-Dreem had *Francentia* analyze the supply load. Denorad nodded when the final report came through. "It looks like we can carry two barrels of water."

"How should we get it on board?" I asked.

"How big is your ship?" Tanaq Farag asked.

"Oh, well if she gets close enough, *Francentia* won't need to land. She can hover over the building and her attractor beam can pull everything in," Maker Denorad said.

"Then it's settled!" Tanaq Farag declared victoriously.

"Fucking fantastic! I'll need to hear all about your travels when you return," Vesten said.

"Wait! Won't everyone see *Francentia*?" Zanzi asked. "We can't allow anyone to see us."

"We'll just wait until the dead of night," Tanaq Farag reasoned. "If people hear noises, they'll just assume it's from Nibelkaith. The volcano rumbles loudly from time to time and it's rarely threatening. They'll just sleep right through it."

"Alright, then it *is* settled," Maker Denorad said, then turned to the three new passengers. "Anqi, Mikhail, Gonth, I'm really looking forward to getting to know you better."

"Yeah, same on our side!" Anqi said. "Now, I don't want to be too forward, but what's our next stop? The more Martin knows, the less he'll worry."

"Then apologies to Martin, as we do not know," I explained. "Our jump drive is on the fritz and we can't control where it takes us."

"Destination unknown it is!" Anqi said excitedly.

"Wherever you go, destiny will guide you," Tanaq Farag said. "Be well and be safe, my good friends. Go with peace, go with love, and go with my faith in you."

**25**

# ESCAPE FROM AUTHORITY

Navacus drifted back and forth between consciousness and sleep. His alarm beeped and buzzed, but he couldn't care less. He knew Fumalli would turn it off for him.

*"Sterg, that was the most intensive dream-like vision yet. And all those people—they spoke of the otherworldly Humans that Professor Durrist has locked up down there. What does this all mean?"*

*"That the gears are turning faster now. We'll need to be prepared for what's to come."*

*"You keep saying that, but what is to come? After that dream, it seems like more of them are on their way. Is that what we need to be prepared for?"*

*"It's one of the many things, yes. Now, you know what you need to do to prepare for tonight, right?"*

*"Of course, you know I do. You're definitely right, though—things are speeding up."*

---

Norman coughed into his fist before using that same fist to softly knock on the door. After a few moments, Professor Qymberkon opened the door.

"Please, come in," Professor Qymberkon said, ushering him in.

Norman looked around the room. It looked like he was the third one here. Professor Clums was chatting with West and Professor Dea. As he stepped into the room, they turned to look at him.

"Ah, Norman! It's great to finally see you again," West said walking up to him.

Norman couldn't help but stare for a few seconds. Although they had met once, it had been rushed, so now he got a much better look at the former bounty hunter. Norman knew West didn't have a head, but the wide-brimmed, stark-white cowboy hat helped to hide that fact. However, it was the computer grafted into West's chest that Norman was most interested in.

West must have noticed him staring. "Yeah, LSS really is a masterpiece, isn't it?"

Norman shook his head, embarrassed. "I'm sorry, I didn't mean to stare."

"It's not a problem! LSS truly is a lifesaver." West explained more about how the Life Support System worked before turning the conversation to his legs. They didn't have long to converse before there was a knock was at the door.

*West, I'm glad that we'll be working together,* Norman thought. *Professor Clums really changed our lives, didn't he? But who would've ever expected us to be in a situation like this?*

---

Navacus clapped his feathery hands. "Please, settle down everyone. Let's get into it. We have a lot to discuss. It's only been five days since we last met up like this, but things are happening faster than any of us could have anticipated. I first want to welcome West and Professor Dea, and while there may be some confusion, everything should be clear by the end," he said as he addressed the packed room. Everyone was here now that needed to be part of the plan—Fumalli, all six of his assistants, West, Norman, Professor Dea, himself, and, of course, Sterg. Not everyone had room to sit, so West and Norman stood while Professor Dea hovered near Sterg.

"Indeed, our time is upon us," Sterg added.

"Yes, it really is. Everyone, thank you for gathering here tonight. Now, let's be clear, this is a rebellion, a mutiny—whatever you want to call it. We are breaking out of this place. If anyone wants to stay, now is the time to leave this meeting."

The room remained quiet, and no one moved. While Sterg sensed some traces of hesitancy, everyone wanted to escape from the compound.

"Wonderful. Now, before we dive into things, I wanted to reiterate why we are together and why we need to do this. I thoroughly studied my contract, and it does in fact declare that myself and all the other professors and assistants in this room are owned by Foxaire Biotech Industries."

"I found the same thing," Poi said. "It took me a few nights, but even Mac, Lyd, and I are Lord Foxaire's property."

"Right, we're all slaves for him. Me, Norman, and Svetlana especially so," West added.

"Exactly," Navacus said. "And since you mentioned her, to be clear, Svetlana is not part of this. I do not believe we can trust her. We must be cautious, and we must make smart decisions. And the best decision is an informed decision. So, I am going to ask several of you to speak—to tell everyone what you discovered since we last met. I want to start with Lyd, as I know you've been eager to present."

"My Vortex, yes, I need to get this off my chest," Lyd said, then dove into his last experience in the underground facility. While he covered little ground, he had met Cecil and had been witness to something truly divine.

"I still can't fully explain what happened, or even describe how it felt," Lyd said as Poi held him tightly. "But I did, I felt Tyrona die, and in her final moment she called out to Theodore—one of the other Humans that came through the gate. It was wild."

"Those Humans are vitally important. We will need to help them," Sterg said.

"Right! And if there are other Humans, maybe that's where Kate is!" Norman said excitedly.

"Ah... yeah, about that..." Lyd trailed off as he looked straight down at the end-table he was standing on.

"What is it? Tell me! Did you see Kate?"

Lyd looked up at Norman. "No, but Tyrona told me that her life was being drained from her body and... and was being given to someone named Katherine Padmashiri Thomas."

The room fell silent as everyone turned to Norman. His face flashed through a mixture of emotions, starting from confusion and shock, to sadness and anger, and ending on happiness.

"I don't know how to feel about that, but if that's true, then they aren't harming Kate, they're somehow giving her extra life—and that means she's alive. Thank you, Lyd, for letting me know. Everyone, Kate is alive!" Norman shouted in glee.

"Hush, keep it down," Navacus whispered. "While this is great news, we must remember to keep our heads straight, especially during these emotional times."

"Right, I'm sorry, it's just... she's alive," Norman said as he wiped tears from his eyes.

"And I'm glad she is. We will absolutely do what we can to save her and the Eklatros Humans," Navacus said.

"Right, but after that encounter," Lyd continued, "as I was trying to hide from everyone pouring into that room, I found a strange area that seemed to be an entirely separate structure. There were no wires or cables or ventilation shafts leading to this domed building. Not only that, but I saw Svetlana guarding it. Whatever is in there must be highly classified."

"That would be where the Titans are being kept, and Svetlana's only task is to stand guard over it," West said. "Also, I would presume that the last ventilation shaft you have yet to visit is where Durrist and Randall's offices are located."

"Now, there's something I need to mention, as this is a fine segue," Navacus said with a nod. "I haven't told anyone about this, not even you, Fumalli, well, not really."

"What's going on with you now?" Fumalli asked from his place at the kitchen counter. "There's already Sterg. What else could be happening?"

"Well, Sterg, you can explain better."

"On certain nights, I have been guiding Navacus' consciousness to witness the events of a group of people. One is Human, the others are robots that were built by the Human-Cyborg. They have a spaceship capable of interstellar travel by making hyper-jumps. They are currently following Gnusaramnii's devastation, going from planet to planet."

"Wait, so you're seeing what Gnusaramnii leaves behind?" Professor Dea asked.

"Yes. And what's more is that I'm seeing everything through the perspective of one of the robots. His name is Niwat, and in the last dream I had, they were on Eklatros and learned about Theodore, Cecil, Dasch, and Druder—the four that came through the gate. Niwat's goal is to arrive here, in the Vortex System. Not only that, but three people from Eklatros joined up with Niwat and his crew."

"Are they friends of theirs?" West asked. "I was there when they came through the gate. I couldn't place my finger on it back then, but something about them made it feel like they had just left something important behind."

"As far as I know, only one of them knew the four. But either way, they have reinforcements on the way, and their goals align with ours. They wish to see Gnusaramnii defeated."

"How can they get into the Vortex?" Grasberg asked. "All the wormholes are inactive."

"Possibly by using their jump drive. They found a very unusual battery on a planet that had some Gnusar left behind, and that battery could be the key."

"Well, all of this makes them even more important," Norman said.

"Plus, they can reunite with their friends, and I can reunite with Kate. It'll be a win-win for everyone."

"Indeed it will be," Navacus replied. "Now, I want to ask for West and Professor Dea to speak—whoever wants to go first."

"I want to hear from West first," Professor Dea said.

"Alright. Well, first of all," West began, "I wanted to thank you all for the enhancements. I haven't tried out my jetpack yet, but it seems like it'll be a lot of fun to use."

"If you get a chance tomorrow, try it out then, even if it's for five minutes. It could be useful," Professor Dea said.

"Yeah, great point. I also want to thank you for what you did to help block the monitoring device and the kill switch you installed. LSS has been running scans, and your countermeasures should work perfectly."

"That's great to hear," Kurjon said, her eyes full of relief. "I wasn't happy that we had to do that to you."

"You were only doing your job; I understand," West said, then addressed the entire room. "Everyone, Lord Foxaire is setting a plan in motion to move all assets out of the compound and to some off-world satellite station that could be anywhere."

"Hold on, what? We're being moved? Why?" Fumalli asked.

"I wasn't told why, but I was told a lot of information," West replied. "Rather than rehash it to you, let me play you this recording of Carl giving me and the other security guards our instructions."

West started the recording. The first to speak was clearly Carl, and he explained that a move was taking place and could happen any day now. Several assets would be moved, and the less they knew about who was being moved, the better. He then asked for West to help move a few of the Titans, as his connection with them would be invaluable, and told him about the underground gyroscope bay he would need to report to once the Titans were secured. Carl then addressed Bsarg, Nijork, and Jakog, and essentially asked them to stay out of the way by making them guard Professor Peal's subjects, who were not being moved but still needed to be watched. Since

Professor Peal and most of his team were helping with the move itself, Carl needed to make sure that the assets staying behind were protected.

The brief recording ended, and West looked around at the room of shocked and confused expressions.

"I don't understand, why would they suddenly move us?" Poi asked. "This seems so random."

"Or it's not random at all," Professor Dea said. "I'll let West finish, but I get the sense that this has been Lord Foxaire's plan for a long time now."

"Honestly, I am getting the exact opposite impression," West said. "Part of me feels like this is being rushed, and if it is, then there must be a good reason. I say this because there are four IBHA agents here."

"You mean the bounty hunters? Why are they here?" Mac asked.

"I think it's because they needed a fast security fix. I gave two of them a tour of the underground, and two others are monitoring the atmosphere from space—and one of those two is my old partner, Anessti, who nearly killed me."

"Ah, that's unfortunate. Hopefully you won't need to interact with him," Navacus said.

"I sure hope not. But at the same time, I wish I could see that bastard so I could give him a well-deserved punch to the face."

"I'd like to see that," Syl said. "But Carl mentioned a gyroscope bay? What's up with that?"

"Well, I did some digging with LSS after that meeting, and apparently there is a gyroscope bay that leads into Nalpetalis—likely where Lord Foxaire is. I also found information on a separate underground space."

"It's an underground spaceport," Professor Dea said. "I just learned about it earlier today."

"A spaceport? That's it—that's our ticket out of here," Navacus said as he brought his fist down into his palm. "I had a feeling this was all going to fall perfectly into place. How did you come to learn about this?"

"I had a meeting today with Carl, Professor Yilvin, and Professor Bodeelch. As the three top professors in the compound, Carl let us in on their plan. This is only phase one of three. In this phase, they are moving three of the Titans and the Eklatros Humans. And he told us that all the assets, as he called them, would be securely transported using this facility's underground space hangar. Now, this facility is just beyond Nalpetalis' radar. So, any space travel could theoretically go about undetected."

"That makes sense," West replied. "The bounty hunters had to arrive somehow, and they are keen on staying off the radar."

"Precisely. Now, Carl revealed another important detail. They had been holding off on doing several experiments until those specimens went to their off-world location. This, to me, means that they've known about this for some time and have been preparing for it for a while," Professor Dea explained.

"I suppose that is possible, but it still feels rushed," West said, adjusting his cowboy hat.

"Did Carl tell you any other important information?" Navacus asked.

"The most important thing—the exact time and date of the move: Tsenar ninth at ten o'clock."

"The ninth! That's only two days from now," Syl exclaimed and threw his arms up. "How can we do all that we need to do in two days?"

"Technically we only have tomorrow, and mainly tomorrow morning," Navacus replied. "This means we'll need to pick up our pace. Lyd, you'll need to go back underground and warn everyone down there of our plan."

Lyd sighed in exasperation. "If it's necessary, then I suppose I'll go back down there. It's just both times have really put me on edge. What, with witnessing someone's death in a strange, ethereal way, to being surprised by you, West."

West laughed. "Ah, you really gave us a shock. Newtus and I both sensed you at the same time."

"Yeah, well the point is that I would rather spend as little time as necessary down there."

"I can go down with you this time," Poi said.

"What? Are you sure?" Mac exclaimed. "Remember what happened last time?"

"Yeah, but now we're going to set them free, right? Is that what you're thinking, Professor Clums?" Poi asked.

"Yes, we'll need to save everyone we can," he replied.

"We must fully commit to this," Sterg emanated from the center of the room. "The time is now. We must prepare for Eklakiln, Tsenar ninth. If you fail, there will be no opportunity for a second chance. Eklakiln morning is the only window you'll get to escape from here and from Lord Foxaire's reach and dominance."

As the silence stretched on, Sterg could feel everyone's nerves rising, but at the same time, a sense of resilience was also forming.

"So, no pressure, then," West said, breaking the silence.

A bout of nervous laughter brightened up the room.

"Hey, isn't it odd that Eklatros sounds similar to Eklakiln?" Fumalli asked.

"I think all the days are named after some old Lakinceitian deity, but I couldn't tell you more than that," Syl replied.

"Either way, we need to come up with a plan," Navacus said with a firm nod. "Please chime in if anyone has any ideas, but I've been thinking that we'll need to split up into three groups. The first group should rescue the Titans, the second group can rescue the Humans, and the third group can free Professor Peal's subjects and the others, like the Yggdrazim and the Ancilsan."

"I'm all for this," Fumalli said. "You know I am, but I think you're rushing into things. We need to make informed decisions, remember? Now, I don't know what a Titan is, do you, Grasberg?"

Grasberg shook his head. "No, I do not."

"The Titans are Lord Foxaire's pet projects," Professor Dea explained. "From what I know about them, they are true abominations—chimeras created by blending together different DNA strands to make something new."

"That sounds horrifying," Kurjon said as she sniffled and wiped her nose.

"Oh, they are, and I've had the pleasure of meeting all five of them. There's Karkilver, the colossal bird; Ophertusc, the pale ghost; Zinartee, the gaseous entity; Zadgarcolth, the golden gorilla; and my personal favorite, Theesakin, the green dragon," West explained.

"And when you say your personal favorite, that's sarcastic right? They all sound like monsters," Grasberg asked.

"Actually, no," West replied. "I can communicate with Theesakin using a certain frequency LSS can produce. He's a surprisingly kind soul for having such an intense demeanor."

"Ah, well that's unexpected. Does that mean he'll be on our side?" Syl asked.

"I believe so," West said.

"That would be great if it's the case. So, which of these Titans are being moved? Is Theesakin one of them?" Navacus asked.

"Yes. Karkilver, Zadgarcolth, and Theesakin will be moved in the first round," Dea said.

"We'll need to rescue Theesakin for sure. The other ones I would not recommend aiding in any way. They really are monsters—which is why it would be beneficial to have Theesakin on our side," West said.

"I'll trust your judgement. If you don't think the others are worth saving, then I will agree with you. Now," he said, then turned to his oldest friend, "Fumalli, thanks for making me slow down. I have to apologize—Sterg's thoughts are blended with mine, so at times like this, it gets hard to see the difference. Sterg was the one calculating ahead like that; I was just speaking it, and as you said, rushing ahead of things."

"We've only been together for a short time. You'll learn to better discern my thoughts from yours soon enough," Sterg radiated.

"What about the other ones we're trying to save? Can we know more about them?" Poi asked.

West then told the room about Sassafrass, Blood Bat, Denoptace, Newtus, and Ivy—all of Professor Peal's subjects that he'd met so far.

There were still two rooms he had never entered, but West agreed to inform the group if he could.

"Well, now that we all know what's in store for us, if we are to break up into three teams, we'll need three team leaders," West suggested.

"And who would you suggest?" Navacus asked.

"You, Professor Dea, and myself. I think the three of us have the most leadership experience," West said.

"I have no problem with that," Syl replied.

"Yeah, I wouldn't want to be a team leader anyway," Lyd said.

"Great, but who goes where?" Professor Dea asked.

"I just want to interrupt this train real quick," Norman said as he stepped into the center of the room. "If we only have one day, what about my attachments? I don't mean to be stingy, but if we do this, I'll need the new bio-locking mechanism completed. I know we got the bare bones laid out today, but it would be great to have it working soon. Also, aren't there cameras in my wheels? Can Lord Foxaire access those?"

"Ah yes, thanks for bringing that up. We'll need to disable those cameras tomorrow, and that should only take a few minutes. Then, all work will need to be focused on Norman's retinal scan. We need to complete the wristbands and link them to the base. Is that feasible?" he asked.

"If it's our complete focus, then yes, we can get it done," Syl replied. "You're working on Svetlana's add-ons tomorrow, right?"

"Yes, and I was hoping to borrow Kurjon, Grasberg, and Lyd. But, if needed, I'll give you back Grasberg."

"That would be a big help," Fumalli said. "We'll need the extra set of hands."

"I know I don't get a say in this, but if I did, I would say that's fine with me, because I don't care either way," Grasberg added, showing his true sass.

"Thanks for agreeing to this, Grasberg," Navacus replied.

"Also, keep in mind that I am available to assist you tomorrow as well," Dea said. "Plus, I can help to keep Gazelle's mind tendrils at bay."

"That would be fantastic," Navacus replied.

"Mind tendrils? What do you mean by that?" Kurjon asked.

"Gazelle has several distinct, yet similar, abilities," Dea replied. "As you all know, one is to make her irresistibly attractive, but she can also reach out with her mind to detect hidden presences. In my culture, we visualize that ability with tentacles and tendrils that poke and prod around."

"That makes sense," Kurjon replied as she nodded in thought.

"Hey, so I don't mean to be nit-picky, but if we are trying to escape from this place, how will we transport all of my attachments? I don't believe we ever came up with a solution for that," Norman said.

"Easy. I'm an Eridavlos," replied Professor Dea. "I will simply come by tomorrow and use my natural talents to vacuum up the attachments and store them in my specialized organ."

"Wait a minute, that's real? I thought it was just a spacenet rumor," Poi said.

"Yes, it is real. It's not something I do often, as the objects I consume that way get shrunken down and condensed, and they weigh me down. I can't take too much with me this way, but I can take your attachments and any important tools and parts needed—as much as can fit, of course."

"Oh yeah, of course, I don't want to be a burden," Norman said as he retreated to his spot against the wall.

"It's fine. They are necessary because you are necessary, and they can't be left behind," Professor Dea said as he mentally accepted the task.

"And once we're away from this place, we'll work on a better solution. But that works for now. I'm glad we've got that settled, so let's get back into things," Navacus said as he looked to Sterg and nodded. "Oh, but real quick, about our work on Svetlana. I want to be clear that the idea is to get Svetlana completely out of order so she can't participate on the ninth."

"I still don't understand. Why aren't we taking her with us?" Poi asked.

"I will answer that, as it makes Navacus uncomfortable," Sterg replied. "He's conflicted about this, but she must not be allowed to come with us. I have never met her, but as my soul was arriving here, I passed Svetlana. All I saw was darkness. Her mind has been corrupted, either from the original technology you all used to install her eye or from being tampered with. Either way, she would only be a danger to us if she were to come along. She is not safe to be around.

"Are you serious? You're saying it's something we did that made her, what, evil?" Poi asked as she took a few steps forward and threw out her arms. "But that can't be, right? Our designs were flawless!"

"Poi, calm down," Mac said as he placed a hand on her shoulder. "It could have been the underground professors."

"I know. It's just... I don't want to be a part of this anymore. I don't want to hurt anyone."

"What you did saved my life," West said. "I thank you every day for the gifts you gave me. But I agree with this decision. Svetlana is not the person you knew. Her mind has been tampered with."

"Poi, you have made my life so much better," Norman said as he approached the table Poi was on. "You see? I can walk again. And it's all thanks to you and your team. I am forever grateful and in your debt. I have never met Svetlana, but at least the two of us are on your side, right?"

"Thank you, Norman and West," Poi said through her sniffling. "That means a lot."

"I have to say, we really did some good work here, Fumalli," Navacus said. "All of you—you've been a great team, and I couldn't have asked for a better one. I just wish that we weren't being used to benefit Foxaire's twisted fascinations. But, if we all make it out of here, then we can continue that work. We need to finish Norman's hover attachment, and I have been toying with an idea for another attachment as well. But we must first focus on what is most immediate. We need to determine who is going to be part of which team, and which team will go where."

"I think we should figure out where the leaders are going, and then decide from there," Lyd suggested.

"Makes sense," Navacus said with a nod.

"I think I should be where the Titans are. I mean, I'm supposed to be there anyway, and I have a good connection with Theesakin," West suggested.

"I disagree," he replied. "You are expected there, so if you show up, they'll expect you to perform certain tasks. But if you don't show up, they'll be frazzled. We need them to be frazzled. You need to go help Professor Peal's subjects. I know you are fond of Newtus."

"I am," West said as he tipped his cowboy hat forward. "And I think I'm one of the only people she would trust, so I can agree to that."

"Great. Then I will see to the Titans. Professor Dea, that leaves you to rescue the Humans," Navacus said.

"That's fine with me," Professor Dea replied. "But, off topic, you don't need to call me professor here. Dea is fine."

"Ah yes, of course. Soon we won't need to go by our titles at all. If that's the case, please just call me Navacus, and Fumalli is of course Fumalli. Now, the question is, who's going with me? I want to request, and I am sorry, but I need Norman with me."

"Aw, but can't I go with Dea? That's where Kate is!" Norman moaned.

"I know, but you're the most muscle we've got—other than West, of course. I need you with me in case something goes sour. And I'd like you to use your treads. You're much faster with those. Plus, then when Kate sees you again, I'm sure she'll be impressed with your new skills."

"You know, when you put it that way, she would be impressed, wouldn't she? Plus, if I had a good story to tell, that will help her forgive me for not being there for her," Norman said with a nod.

"I know where you're going is dangerous, but that's exactly why I need to come with you," Fumalli said. "I couldn't live with myself if something happened to you and I wasn't there."

"It will be dangerous, and I welcome your help. You're the one I trust the most. So, you'll watch my back, and I'll watch yours."

"Sounds like a plan, partner," Fumalli replied in a poorly attempted space-pirate accent.

"Great. Now, if it's not asking too much, I need one other with me —Sylcertiverner."

"Oh, uh, I don't know if I am interested in befriending giant monsters," Syl said, waved his hand in dismissal.

"Right, but you're quick and agile, and you're great in tight situations."

"When working on motherboards and electronics, not with monsters."

"Monsters they may be," West said, interrupting the exchange, "but they are misunderstood. If we had more time, I would have liked to see if Theesakin could help communicate with the others. At least, it was an idea I had."

"If we ever discover where they're being taken, it may just be possible," Navacus said. "And I understand your hesitation, but we will need your help, Syl."

Syl sighed and crossed his arms. "Then I'll do what I can."

"Alright, so that leaves the three of us Harmertians," Poi said as she pointed at Mac and Lyd, "and Kurjon and Grasberg."

"So it does. I don't think I should need too much backup, so I can take just two with me," West said.

"Well, we already decided before we arrived that if anything were to happen, the three of us would stick together," Mac said. "We need to stay together from here on out. Which is why I would like to go underground with you and Lyd tomorrow as well. The three of us work better together than apart."

"Great! I'm glad you're braving up, brother," Poi said, nudging him. Mac crossed his arms but couldn't help but smile.

"Then it's decided," Navacus said. "The Harmertians will go with Dea to assist the Humans, and Grasberg and Kurjon will go with West to assist Professor Peal's subjects. Remember, our goal is to save everyone we can."

"But not Svetlana, right?" Poi shot back.

He opened his beak, but before he could reply, West jumped in. "Poi, listen to me. Svetlana is not the same person she was when I first met her. She used to be a happy, bubbly person who loved to chatter away. But now she's stone cold and focused only on the job, and she is fully committed to Professor Durrist. She would do anything to defend him, including killing us if she had to."

Mac gasped in horror. "She hasn't killed anyone, has she?"

"Not that I am aware of, but she has the same demeanor as those I used to work with in the IBHA. I know that look well," West replied.

"Sure, it's just... I just wish there was something we could do to help her," Poi said with a heavy sigh.

"I do, too. I really do, Poi," Navacus replied. "I don't want to leave her behind, but I trust Sterg and West. And when I saw Svetlana last, she really was quite different. You don't have to be happy about it, but you do need to accept it."

Poi sat cross-legged on the table. "I just need some time."

"I understand."

"If you aren't ready to—" Lyd began before Poi cut him off.

"Don't even finish that sentence. I'm going underground with you. Mac, too. We're a team, right?"

"Right," Mac said with a nod.

"We are a team—all of us in this room," Navacus said, using his arms to create a circle. "We all need to trust each other with our lives. We don't know what kind of resistance we'll face. Even though we know where Bsarg and the others will be, it doesn't mean that there won't be even more added security."

"So how are we going to do this? Sure, we broke out into teams, but what are we going to actually do? What *can* we actually do?" Poi asked as she leaned forward and rested her elbow on her knee while holding her palm up to the air.

They talked well into the night as they solidified a general plan with the idea that it could be interrupted at any moment. They also decided that upon stealing two spaceships, they would regroup on Carange's resource-stripped moon, Termatyl. West had his own private hiding spot he could lead them to. Before they departed for the night, they reviewed their plans for the next day. Once everything was settled, the team departed one by one.

*I really hope we're not putting anyone in danger, Navacus thought. If anything were to happen to anyone... I don't know what I would do. Thank you, Sterg. That helps, but even so, I would rather die than see any of my friends die. Oh, so you'll protect me from a highly condensed blast of energy? As much as I would like to see that happen, I don't want to test that theory anytime soon.*

## 26

# ESCAPE FROM RESTRAINT

Lyd stood on the floor of Navacus' office and suited up to prepare to once again go underground. This would be the third and final time he would navigate the air ducts, and he was happy that he wasn't going alone. He watched Poi out of the corner of his eye as she secured her modified hazard suit. Almost as if he knew, Mac cleared his throat to get their attention.

"Hey, so is everyone ready to go? I'm assuming we'll need to use the same level of caution as before and only communicate via hand signing and umpty code?"

"For the short time that we'll be together, yes," Lyd nodded. "When we're separated, we'll send each other secure messages from our tablets. The encryption that I started running when you arrived should be completed."

"Ah, so that's what that was for," Poi said playfully. "When you said you were going to make them more secure, I thought you meant it was for sending lewd photos and videos."

Mac groaned. "I know you're nervous, but let's keep the sexual jokes to a minimum, please."

"You're never any fun," Poi teased.

"I am, too. I'm just practical. We need to be serious," Mac replied.

"Right, we do," Lyd said with a nod. "Remember, this should be quick, just in and out. Mac, you're going where you've already gone before to warn the Ancilsan and the Yggdrazim. Then I'll help to direct Poi to Professor Peal's area. Remember, West should already be there when you arrive and will do the communicating. Your job is to ensure nothing happens to him."

"Yeah, and I know I'm supposed to leave him behind if something happens, and I'd rather not be a hero, but I wouldn't feel right letting him get punished." Poi replied.

"That's why you'll send us a message via our tablets. Since we'll be split up, that's the only way we'll be able to communicate. You send me a message, and I'll relay that message to Prof—to Navacus."

"Right, okay," Poi said as she nervously tried to scratch her arm through the hazard suit.

"Good. And remember, West will speak aloud the signal when he's safely leaving the area. Finally, I will warn the otherworldly Humans, and Kate, if I find her. I'd like this to take no more than an hour, and if possible, under sixty minutes. When you're finished in your area, send a message to each of us and make your way up the elevator shaft. We'll rendezvous right here where we're standing. West ensured us that no one should be using the elevator near Navacus' lab, so we should be good. If not, then we'll convene at the elevator shaft."

"Sounds like a plan. I hope that we'll make it back up here without incident. I don't want to be down there any longer than necessary," Mac said.

"Neither do I. Now, let's do a quick run through of our system and security checks then head down there."

All security and communication checks were successful, so the three Harmertians used their jetpacks to get up into the ceiling. Just as West had confirmed, the elevator was fully descended. They made it down without incident. In the back of his mind, Lyd thought of the grate that was still sitting at the bottom of the elevator shaft, but knew it was the least of anyone's worries.

They fought their way through the pounding wind and took

refuge in the path that led to where the Ancilsan and Yggdrazim were being held. After a round of negative security checks, they breathed easier.

*Good luck*, Lyd signed to Mac, then clasped him on the shoulder.

Mac nodded and replied, *Same to you.*

*Be careful, Mac*, Poi signed.

Mac bid them a final farewell and headed down the ventilation shaft. He nodded at Poi, taking a few seconds too long as he looked into her eyes. She stared back and smiled before looking away. Lyd silently cursed himself and led the way back into the wind tunnel. He grabbed Poi's hand as an unusually strong burst of air passed over them, and she squeezed it back.

They couldn't help but quietly laugh as they found refuge in the shaft Poi would follow. They ran another round of security scans, and this time both of their scans came back positive. There would be three people passing by soon and they were being tailed by two others. Lyd motioned to Poi for them to hold up and not move. In response, Poi stepped close to him and wrapped her arm around his waist. He followed suit. They silently clung to each other, breathing heavily, as the threat passed by. After it was clear, Poi awkwardly stepped away from him.

*That was scary*, Poi said with hand signals. *Thanks for protecting me.*

*I'm always here for you*, he signed.

*This is my stop*, Poi signed. *Be safe, and check in with me when you get to your destination.*

Lyd nodded, then took out his tablet and wrote Poi a private message.

> Poi, no matter what happens, I just wanted to tell you I'm in love with you. I have been for a long time now. I just need you to know that.

He took a deep breath and hit send. Lyd looked up to find Poi looking between him and her tablet expectantly. After a painstaking few seconds, Poi looked up at him. Her face was hard to read. She put her tablet away, stepped up to him, and lightly kissed him. He was so stunned that she had already stepped back before he could react. Poi blushed and swiftly tapped a response on her tablet. As soon as she finished, a smile grew on her rosy cheeks, and then she looked at him one last time and waved. He waved back as she turned away and headed down the shaft.

> Sorry, I didn't know what to say, but I feel the same way. See you in a bit... gotta go!

He smiled and took one last look at Poi before turning away and heading back into the whirlwind.

---

Altun yawned lazily as he stared blankly at the wall. Even though he looked bored, his mind was sharp and alert. That was one of the most beneficial aspects of being a shape-shifter—he had full control of his outward appearance and the emotions that showed on his face and in his body language. At least, that was the idea. He was still practicing, as he knew it was a skill he would need.

He yawned again, showing off his large teeth and sharp canines, then reclined on his bench and scratched the fur on his belly. His ears perked up at a faint sound, then he heard it again. He morphed his ears to better tune into the sound. It sounded a lot like when those three Harmertians had visited him a few days ago, but this time, there seemed to be only one.

He continued to appear relaxed and at ease as the noise grew louder. As it drew closer, it stopped for about a minute, then it sighed heavily, as if in sadness. Soon a small gray face popped out of the grate above him. He looked up at the Harmertian and gave him a subtle grin.

"Oh, thank goodness, I'm relieved to see that you're safe and sound," the Harmertian whispered. "I'm sure you remember, but we met a few days ago. I'm Mac."

Altun yawned and said "Altun" mid-yawn.

"Right, Altun. Sorry, I had forgotten your name, but we obviously never forgot about you. I'm sorry to say, but there were two others around the last time I was here. Both are gone now."

Altun subtly nodded. "So that's what the commotion was. It is always hard to see someone pass nameless to the afterlife. In my culture, we have a term for that: Flohawkah'mon. It means honored deceased."

"That's beautiful," Mac whispered. "Let us share a moment of silence for our departed friends, the Yggdrazim and the Eridavlos."

*If they're gone, then I'm the last one left,* Altun thought. *I don't know if I should be happy or sad. I was one of twelve, and there had been two per species. So many innocent lives taken too early. If I can, I will avenge you all.*

After several moments, Mac broke the silence. "Altun, unlike last time, I'm here to help break you free."

Altun pretended like there was something stuck between his teeth, and he scratched at it. "I would be forever in your debt. I've been keeping a keener eye out since you and your kin were here. Aside from them removing the flohawkah'mon, security hasn't been very attentive as of late."

"That's great news," Mac whispered. "We plan to enact our escape early tomorrow morning."

Altun flicked his claw as if he got the bit of food out of his teeth and wiped his mouth. "Couldn't come soon enough."

"I agree," Mac whispered. "I won't be here tomorrow, but my friends will be. There will be a headless Eusphyrchii, a male Kolythoanthaean, and a female Nioavellian."

"A headless Eusphyrchii? Sounds interesting," Altun said mid fake-yawn.

"I'm not sure if we know how we'll actually break you free, but I'm sure—"

"No need. I have a plan. I've been waiting for the right time," Altun whispered.

"Oh, that's great. What will you do?"

Altun subtly shook his head as if to say "I can't tell you right now," and asked, "Where should I meet your friends?"

Mac explained the basic layout of the ventilation system, and how there were many dead ends and unused rooms. And while Mac didn't know how Altun would get to Professor Peal's section, the directions he gave him would have to do.

"I'm sure I'll figure it out. Either way, I can blend in," Altun whispered.

Mac nodded. "Right, your abilities—I was told about those. How quickly can you change?"

Altun shrugged, and within a second his face changed to a Human woman's. Mac's eyes widened in surprise. "That's impressive... and quite unsettling. Does it hurt?"

He shrugged again and shifted his position, relaxing an arm underneath his head as he nodded. "Every time, but don't be concerned. I'm used to it."

"I— Well, I guess that's good. But be prepared for tomorrow," Mac said as he tried to hide his unease.

"I am. If my plan doesn't work, don't come looking for me. I can take care of myself," he said, only half-believing it. Sure, he had a plan to escape, but he wasn't confident it would work.

"Good. I assume we'll be setting off multiple alarms. That will be your signal," Mac whispered.

Altun nodded in response. Mac nodded, gave him a wave, and slid away from the grate. He heard Mac tap on a tablet before making his way down the ventilation shaft.

Altun smiled widely while shaping his face into a bored look of contentment.

*This is it*, he thought. *Thank you, Mac, for including me in your plan and for quickening my escape. This plan is much better than my own, and I will be glad to have friends to assist.*

Cecil breezed through two hundred push-ups, sit-ups, and squats. He was winded, but his body wanted more. He had never experienced this type of high before coming to this dreadful planet, and in many ways, it was more addicting than alcohol or star-weed. He took a long sip from his water cup and jumped around a few times to get back into it.

Five push-ups in, a soft voice interrupted his rhythm, and he held himself upright to ensure he had heard correctly.

"Cecil, are you there? It's Lyd," the voice whispered. Cecil got to his feet, sat on the bed, looked up for a moment, then rolled his head back and forth.

"Hey, I'm glad you're back. Did you speak with Theo and the others?" he asked.

He could hear Lyd stutter before he responded. "Oh, uh, no. I haven't talked to Theodore, only you and another—Tyrona."

He couldn't help but shoot to his feet and jump around in excitement. "Tyrona! She's here—she's actually here!"

Again, Lyd hesitated before responding. "I... well... I'm not sure how to say this, but she spoke to me telepathically, like her voice was in my mind."

"That sounds like something Tyrona could do," Cecil nodded as he took a sip from his water cup.

"Right, well, she was fading away... Cecil, I witnessed her final moments of life."

He choked down the water, then coughed and sputtered out the bit that came back up. After his coughing fit ceased, Cecil took a deep breath to calm his wild emotions.

"Are you sure of this?" he asked when he was ready to respond. Tyrona couldn't be dead. It would destroy Theodore.

"Yes, I am. And she called out to Theodore before she passed, so I believe she knew he was here," the Harmertian whispered.

In spite of it all, that made him smile. "That's good. I'm glad she knew he came for her—that we all came for her."

"Yes, I believe she was at peace knowing that. However, she also told me her life force was being drained and given to someone else."

Cecil stared at the wall as he tried to wrap his mind around what he had been told. "Tyrona's life was drained from her? What... how?"

"I don't know, but I'll find out more soon, I'm sure. You are my first stop."

He wasn't sure what to think. Dasch had lost the war to the Gnusar and was working for the enemy, and now Tyrona's life force was drained from her and placed into another. Cecil didn't know how it could get much worse. All he knew was that he needed to escape—and he needed to get Theodore and Druder out as well. It wasn't safe here.

"Okay," he responded. "Is that why you've come back, to tell me this news?" Cecil asked.

"Not the whole reason. I bring good news along with the ill."

Cecil sat down on the bed as he listened to Lyd's story. By the end of it, he was feeling so pumped up that he couldn't help himself—he had to do some squats. There was no way he could sit still now, not after everything that he'd just been told.

"Tomorrow... we'll be free of this place tomorrow? This is better than anything I could ever ask for," he said breathlessly through his squats. "You have given me something to look forward to. Let's hope that this Professor Dea will be able to unlock our cages."

"He's really smart, he should be able to. And if not, he's an Eridavlos. Plus, like I said, me and my kin will be here."

"I don't know what an Eridavlos is, but I thank you all the same," Cecil said as he transitioned to jumping exercises.

"Of course. We can't leave you behind. Besides, I was told that you and your friends are important. Which brings me to my next point—I need to find the others and let them know what's going on."

"Then go. Inform the others. Theodore and Druder need to know," he said through his heavy breathing.

"Yes I... what are you doing?" Lyd asked with confusion in his voice.

"Working out," he replied, then stood up and let out a deep breath. "Lyd, please don't tell Theodore about what happened to Tyrona. He can't find out that way. I need to be the one to tell him."

"I understand. I'll see you bright and early tomorrow," Lyd said. "Until then."

Cecil heard Lyd tapping on a hard surface before he disappeared from earshot. He took a deep breath and let it out, and then a wide smile overtook him. He stretched his arms out and restarted his round of push-ups.

*I need to be ready,* he thought. *Ànifa, we're finally getting out of this place. Maybe this all wasn't in vain. I don't want it to be true, but maybe us coming here was part of a bigger plan somehow, and that Tyrona's death…*

*I just don't know how I'll tell Theodore. But I must. I'm the leader… but not only that, we've been together the longest. It was just me and Theo, back when we were first exiled together. Man, how we used to bicker and fight. But now he's my closest friend. So, I'll do everything I can to get you out of this place and to break the news the best I can.*

*Now, after this, I really need to rest. I just hope nothing happens to Theodore or Druder by the time we escape tomorrow.*

---

Lyd held his breath as another group of people passed by below him. He wasn't sure if he was passing by the same group multiple times as they patrolled the underground, or if there were multiple groups patrolling, but either way, his progress was slow.

He had spoken to Theodore, Druder, and even Kaytrona, as she was calling herself now. Yet, he had dawdled—he shouldn't have chatted for so long. Just as they had predicted, security had gotten stronger in the short time since he'd arrived underground. Thankfully, both Poi and Mac had made it upstairs unharmed. Lyd had barely any time to respond to let them know he was on his way.

The latest surge of security passed, and he was finally free to continue. He walked along slowly, all the while thanking Navacus for the noise-dampening boots—he was doing his best not to make a sound. Just five meters from the wind box, and he was once again interrupted by activity from below.

It took him nearly triple the time it would normally to get back to the elevator. He glanced at the time. Navacus and the others would likely be in the lab by now.

He typed a quick message directly to Poi and stepped onto the top of the elevator. Just as he was about to activate his jetpack, the elevator lurched into motion as it sped up the elevator shaft. Lyd pushed himself flat as he rode the elevator up to the top. Once it stopped, he continued to lie flat as he waited to see what would happen. After a few moments, the elevator lurched down again. He got up on his knees and activated his jet pack.

He breathed a sigh of relief as he exited the ceiling and descended into Professor Clums' lab. Just as he had predicted, everyone was there.

"Lyd, you're back!" Poi cried as she ran up and gave him a big hug. Mac walked up to them and laughed.

"She wouldn't let us leave this table until she knew you were back."

Syl walked up to them, breaking their moment together. "Lyd, welcome back, but you need to hurry and get ready. I believe Professor Bodeelch may be—"

Syl was interrupted as Professor Bodeelch stepped into the lab, followed by Gazelle. A moment later, Professors Clums and Dea stepped out of the office to greet them. All the while, Syl stood still, giving Lyd a chance to use a toolbox as cover to change his clothes.

"And how are you doing today, Syl?" Professor Bodeelch asked as he approached. As the toolbox lid shut, Professor Bodeelch locked eyes with Lyd. "Ah, and the Harmertians are here, too. I don't mean to be rude, but I didn't see you when I walked in."

"Sorry about that, we have a lot to do to prepare for today," Mac said as he gathered up some nearby supplies.

"Yes, you all sure have a busy day ahead of you. I won't bother you for long, as I have a lot to do today myself."

Gazelle approached while Professor Bodeelch had been talking and gave them an odd look. "Why do you three smell funny?"

"Uh, excuse me?" Poi asked loudly as she marched to the edge of the table and put her hands on her hips. "How rude of you. We were up all night and didn't get a chance to shower, so I'm sorry if our body odor displeases you."

Gazelle continued to glare at Poi. "Why were you up all night?"

"Like we said, we have a lot of work to do, and we were celebrating an important holiday last night," Lyd said as he tried to rack his brain for a Harmertian holiday that was close to this time of year. Between all the different species and religions and cultural groups, there were a lot of holidays.

"That's right, we sure were," Poi said. "Aurora Sworous may not have been a Harmertian, but the three of us have always revered and respected the good she did for all refugee species."

Lyd smiled and nodded. That's right—it was Aurora Day.

Gazelle stared at them for another few seconds and sighed. "I'm sorry, I'm just a bit frazzled. We'll leave you all to it then."

"That's right. Professor Clums, please send us a detailed report on Svetlana's upgrades by twenty-two o'clock," Professor Bodeelch reiterated.

"Will do, Professor," Professor Clums responded. Professor Dea nodded in agreement.

"I plan to check in with you later on as well," Gazelle told them. Professor Clums simply nodded in response.

Lyd waved them goodbye as they left the lab and everyone could breathe easier. Even Sterg was out and about, checking in with everyone.

*It's going to be a long day, but at least Poi, Mac, and I are safe,* Lyd thought. *That was a close call, though. Gazelle really has some impressive senses. I'm just glad that our plan is officially in motion.*

**27**

# ESCAPE FROM RESISTANCE

West walked behind the barracks. It was dawn, and all he could see was the orange light streaming over the flat, open desert. What little shrubs and cacti there were stretched long shadows toward him.

*I hope this thing isn't loud, but it should be early enough—everyone else should still be asleep,* he thought as he took a deep breath. He activated the jetpack and was launched half a meter off the ground.

He couldn't help but laugh in excitement. "Wow, this is really cool. I've always secretly wanted something like this," he said quietly to himself.

The jetpack was nearly silent. He wasn't sure how Professor Navacus did it, but what he created was on another level. It was like technological magic. He was still getting used to calling Professor Clums by his first name.

West shook his head to clear his mind and looked around. He was alone. He nodded and pushed himself a few meters higher and traveled east, away from the compound. After about a hundred meters, he spun around in the air and looked back at where he had started from.

*This is unreal,* West thought. *I can control this jetpack as if it had always been a part of me. LSS is incredibly adaptable, but I suppose I must be, too, then. If this were any other day, I would probably stay out here longer, but I need to get my ass in gear now that I know this thing works.*

---

West waved to Jakog as he passed through the automatic sliding doors and entered the compound. He stood in the atrium for a moment and used his enhanced vision to check on the status of the elevator in Navacus' wing. It was descended, so he sent a quick confirmation message to Lyd and then made a beeline to Professor Peal's end of the hall so he would have a quicker path to Newtus, Ivy, and the others. It was still early, but he had a lot to do.

Things were quiet as he strolled quickly through Professor Xergat's section. Thankfully, the lights were still dimmed, so he couldn't see into the tubes that were scattered about the narrow hallway. All were active experiments, and all were horrific, but Xergat enjoyed showing off.

Before he knew it, West was strolling through the door and into Professor Peal's section. Surridge and Kamarial looked up from a large tablet and were surprised to see him.

"West, what are you doing here so early?" Kamarial asked.

"Uh, hey, Kamarial. Hey, Surridge. I wasn't expecting to see you," he said as he tipped his hat to greet them.

"Are you here to see Newtus?" Kamarial asked.

"That's part of it," he said as he shifted his weight nervously. "I'm also here to talk to Ivy again, and it's been a while since I've said 'hi' to Sassafrass, Blood Bat, and Denoptace, so I wanted to pay them a visit, too."

"Ah, I see. Did Professor Peal or Kalosse approve this?" Surridge asked with her arms crossed and her left foot tapping the ground.

"That again? I thought I could come by whenever, as long as I'm not interrupting. Am I interrupting?"

"No, well, not particularly," Kamarial replied.

"It's just the fact that you always talk to them alone. I'd like to accompany you today. As long as we're not intruding, of course," said Surridge.

West panicked for a quick second before logic took control. He couldn't turn them down, but he had to warn everyone what was coming.

"Is there anyone else around?" he asked in response.

"No, it's just us. We wanted to check in on ol' Salty Susan early today. She's been really active lately, and we're seeing complex patterns in her dances and movements," Kamarial answered enthusiastically.

"Who's Salty Susan?"

"Oh, she's a Curik—you know, like a stag beetle. She can't talk. At least, not with words. That's what we've been trying to figure out—if she's trying to communicate through her dancing."

"But we record everything, so we can review those videos at any time. What we're interested in is why all the videos of your visits are corrupted. It looks like most of the time you two are just staring at each other," Surridge said as her deep blue eyes pierced right through him.

"Huh, that's really odd. It could be something to do with LSS' frequencies. I'll need to look into it," West said, doing his best to sound convincing. LSS was growing more adept at reading his emotions and expressing them accordingly.

"Well, in the meantime, we'd like to join you," Surridge reiterated.

"Yeah, I wouldn't mind saying hi to everyone. I feel like we don't do it as often as we should," Kamarial said.

West nodded in resolution. "Come along, then. Let's visit with Newtus first."

"I thought you'd want to see her last, so you could get more time with her," Kamarial teased as she led them over to Newtus' door.

"What? We just get along well," West said.

Surridge unlocked the door and turned to him. "Oh yeah, we've noticed."

"Good morning, Newtus! How are you doing today?" Kamarial

asked as she entered Newtus' room. West followed her to find Newtus sitting in her usual spot, waiting for them.

"Good morning, Kamarial. It's nice to see you again. And, good morning, West and Surridge," Newtus said as she twisted a flower stem in her hand, causing the flower to spin and create a blur of white and pink colors.

"Good morning, Newtus," Surridge said with a wave. West tipped his cowboy hat at her and telepathically said, "*Newtus, it's good to see you. You need to help me with them.*"

"I'm sorry; it's been a few days since I came by. It's just been so hectic," Kamarial said.

Newtus nodded along. "It's not a problem. West, it's been a few days since I've seen you, too. What's been going on with you?"

"Oh, you know... the usual. But there is something I need to talk with you about. And please, I hope that you have my back on this, Newtus," he said, then turned to Kamarial and Surridge.

"Oh, what's going on?" Kamarial asked, her voice reaching a higher pitch with nearly every word.

"Yes, what is going on, West?" Newtus asked.

"Please, I need you to stay quiet about this. I really don't know if I can trust you, but right now, I need you to trust me and hear me."

He then dove into it and explained what he and his team had discussed last night while accentuating that they needed to escape from this place. He could tell most of it truthfully—the only real omission was Sterg.

Surridge and Kamarial were stunned and stood in silence for several long seconds after he finished.

"I mean, this place is a cesspit—seriously, why are we in the middle of this stinkin' desert?" Kamarial asked as she raised her hands toward the surface. "At least it stays cool down here. But what you're doing is madness. You're going to get everyone hurt or killed. I don't see how this could end any way but badly."

"I wholeheartedly agree," Surridge said. "I need to let Professor Peal and the others know—"

West grabbed the tablet out of the brunette Human's hands. "I'm sorry, it's just—we need to do this. I just hope our actions don't cause you two any harm."

"Whether or not you actually pull off your stupid stunt, there will be major consequences for all of us," Surridge said as she threw her arms out in the air.

"But if what he says is true, we're slaves here, too," Kamarial whispered. "I may not have had much of a life back on Ijurvoll, but I want to go back someday. Sooner than later."

"Then come with us," West urged. "Both of you could come with us. We are trying to save as many as possible, and that includes you."

"And what, just leave Professor Peal and the others behind?" Surridge asked.

"The fewer people that know about this, the better. If Carl or Durrist catch wind of this, it'll be over before it even starts."

"I just... This doesn't seem right," Surridge said.

"It's okay, it really is," Newtus said in a reassuring tone. "Both of you need to decide what you need to do on your own."

"Right. Take the day to decide. And please, do not tell Professor Peal or the others," West urged.

"But you mean to take all our subjects? Newtus, Ivy, Sassafrass— all of them? All our hard work?" Surridge asked.

"Elizabeth, I cannot move in this cage," Newtus said as she stood up straight. "I am stifled and wasting away. I need to breathe the fresh air, I need to feel the leaves and the grass and the wind, and I need to *hunt*. I'm through being hand-fed, and I am not yours to own. I don't care what your contracts say—I am a free soul of this universe, and I deserve to go home, back to my kirwach. I can assure you, if you were in my position, you would want to escape just as much as I do."

"Liz, look at her," Kamarial said as she held her arm out toward Newtus. "She's a highly intelligent creature that's locked up underground. That's not right."

"No, but it's our job. We work for Professor Peal—*and* for Lord Foxaire. I don't like the situation we are in—of course I don't. But rules are rules, and if we mean to survive, we must play by the rules," Surridge said.

"I always found that rules were made to be broken," West said. "That's part of the reason the IBHA drew me in when I was young and stupid. But I still believe that sentiment now, especially when the rules literally take your freedom away from you."

"West, let me talk to them some more. You need to inform the others," Newtus said.

"Right, thank you, Newtus. I knew you would have my back. I owe you one."

"Are you insane? I owe you a thousand times more. You're going to break me out of my cage," Newtus said as she flicked her tail affectionately.

"I'll do everything I can to set you free. Speaking of, you mentioned a beetle earlier. Is there anyone else down here I don't know about?" West asked.

"Room number three is vacant. Its former occupant died three days ago. And, aside from Susan, there's only Penny, the Dark Therid. She's very dangerous. I would not suggest setting her free. And please, don't take Susan with you. We just started making real progress with her," Kamarial pleaded.

"How about this. If you decide to come with, then we'll take her with us. But if you stay behind, then I'll let her be."

"Sure. I mean, I just... I still don't think I agree to this," Surridge said.

"I understand your hesitation, but you have seen the tanks in Professor Xergat's section, no doubt."

"That's another reason why I like to get here early," Kamarial replied. "They make me very uncomfortable, so I prefer when the lights are dimmed."

"Precisely. Have you ever considered why Xergat displays his abominations out in the open? Besides him being an egotistical ass, of course. But it's because it tells him and likely even Lord Foxaire who has empathy and who doesn't. At least, that's my best guess. All I really know is that if someone can harm intelligent beings like he does and get praised for it, then I really don't want any part in it."

"I know. It's horrible what Professor Xergat is doing," Surridge said, "but what we're doing—it's not as horrible as that, isn't it?"

Kamarial shrugged. "I don't know, Liz. This has really put things in a new perspective for me."

"Right, I'm just... I don't know what to do."

Now it was West's turn to plead with them. "Then talk to Newtus some more. Get to know her better. And please, let me speak with the others."

"I'll allow it," Kamarial answered without hesitation. "I'm sure Denoptace would be much happier if he were anywhere but here. And Sassafrass and Blood Bat don't deserve whatever cruel fate is in store for them—just like you don't deserve your fate, Newtus." Newtus nodded in response. "As for Ivy—Professor Peal will not be pleased if you take Ivy. But I'm a Eusphyrchiian, too, just like you are, West. It's really hard to see my own like that, you know?"

"That's why I need to help him. He's my kin—just like Newtus is now my kin. I have to save them."

"Right, so the lone Human of this group seems to be the only one who wants to obey the rules," Surridge said with a heavy sigh. "That being said, I do heavily sympathize. And you know what? I'm not officially on the clock yet. We've still got thirty minutes. Use your time wisely, West."

"Thank you. I really appreciate having your approval. Newtus, if I don't see you again today, then I'll see you tomorrow."

"See you then," Newtus said out loud, then continued telepathically. "*I will ensure neither of them tells anyone else what you said, even if it means using my special abilities.*"

"*Thank you, just don't harm them, please.*"

"*Eh, it shouldn't hurt them physically,*" Newtus replied.

"*Well, just don't hurt them then,*" West said as he strolled out of the room. Standing in the hallway, he now had two options. He tipped his hat and walked to the first room.

When he entered, the lights were dimmed. He didn't want to wake them, and he hoped they would forgive him. He found the control panel and increased the amount of light a few notches. Blood Bat and Sassafrass responded immediately.

"West, how good of you to visit once again," Sassafrass said in her oddly soothing voice. The large red snake broke her sleeping coil and stretched her long muscular body.

"Hello! See you!" Blood Bat squawked as he flapped his batwings and reared up his scorpion legs in greeting.

"The living fuck is all the racket? And who turned the brightness up early?" Denoptace shouted from his dimmed enclosure. West couldn't see the stick bug, but he figured it was likely making crude gestures.

"It's West. I apologize I haven't gotten the chance to visit with you again sooner. I hope you have been well."

"For us, days are the same," Sassafrass replied.

"Yeah, it's the freaking worst. It's so tediously boring here," Denoptace replied.

"Right, well, that's why I'm here. I have a way to free you from captivity."

"Me? Free? Sassafrass! Rude one!" Blood Bat squawked.

"Then get us the void out of here," Denoptace said. "And please, get me as far away from this squabbling freak as soon as you can."

Sassafrass hissed threateningly in response. West cut in before tensions could rise, then dived into his story. To speed things up, he told an abridged version of what he told Newtus, Surridge, and Kamarial.

"I see," Sassafrass said as if she was deep in thought when he was finished. "It sounds like a risky planses, but if its gets us out of heres, then I'll slither to the tasks."

"Free! Free!" Blood Bat squawked.

"Thanks for thinking of us. At least you're not a total bonehead," Denoptace added.

West let the racist comment go and replied, "As I said, our goal is to save as many as possible. Even Surridge and Kamarial may join us."

"As long as Professor Peal doesn't joins, then I'm games," Sassafrass replied.

"Yeah, I don't really give a shit as long as I get the void out of this freaking place," Denoptace said as he finally unshaded his enclosure. The stick bug was standing at attention with a strong sense of eagerness around him.

"Trust me, I'll do everything I can. Now, I have one more to see before Peal and the others arrive, and I need to talk to him as well. I will be back tomorrow, I promise."

"I sure hope so," Sassafrass said.

"Tomorrow! Free!"

"Just don't leave us behind," Denoptace said.

West tipped his cowboy hat and left the room. He checked the time—twenty minutes to go. He took a second and used his infrared vision to see through the walls. Newtus was still speaking with Surridge and Kamarial, and just as she had said, there was no one behind door number three. Behind door number four, he identified the beetle and the spider. All were accounted for.

He turned his attention to the air ducts and identified Poi as she sat hidden in a position where she could overhear the conversations. He nodded in contentment and entered Ivy's room.

He couldn't tell if Ivy was asleep or awake, as there was no movement. Just when he was about to say something, dual voices spoke to him. "West, it's so good to see you again. I was hoping you'd be back soon." Once of the voices sounded feminine and the other masculine, and the combination of both simultaneously was quite odd.

"Ivy, is that you? I haven't heard you speak out loud yet."

"Ah, you're correct. Last time we spoke, I was just coming into consciousness, which again, I thank you endlessly for."

"Oh, it was nothing. I was just looking out for other Eusphyrchiians."

"As you should be."

"I don't mean to be rude, but how do you have two voices?"

The dual laughter startled him for a second. "What you hear is Adok and Ados speaking telepathically simultaneously."

"You can speak out loud telepathically? I wasn't aware such a thing was possible."

"Is that not what you do, brother West?"

"I speak through my computer, LSS. But this is not why I'm here. I have something important to say."

"I'm listening," Ivy replied as he moved closer to the barrier, his ivy legs wreathing unnaturally across the ground. West nodded, mainly to himself, and for the third time today told the story of what was going to happen.

"I understand. Thank you for thinking of me. I can be of great assistance in your escape. My silk strands are quite diverse, and there are a few lethal ones."

"That's good to know. And of course, I couldn't leave you behind. We're the same, you and I. Two headless Eusphyrchii, one alive thanks to technology and one alive thanks to the power of nature."

"I would say I'm far more unnatural than not," Ivy said with a chuckle. "But I am what I am now. If you have a way to get me out of here, I will do everything I can to make sure we all escape unharmed."

"I appreciate that, but that's my line," he joked.

"It's as you said, we are the same," Ivy said with another chuckle.

"But in all seriousness, what we are trying to pull off is very dangerous and risky. I can't guarantee that—"

"West, with us together, we can move mountains. Believe me, I can sense it."

"I believe you, my kin."

"I am pleased," Ivy replied.

"I wish I could stay for longer, but if all goes well, we'll have time to talk. I really must be going, though."

"I understand. Until tomorrow, West."

He tipped his cowboy hat and departed.

As soon as he stepped out into the main room, Surridge and Kamarial emerged from Newtus' room.

"West, great timing," Kamarial said. "Professor Peal is due by here any minute."

"Yes, I better be on my way," West replied. "Have you made a decision?"

Surridge shook her head. "Not yet, but we'll think about it. If we see you tomorrow, we'll let you know. And if not, then that's our answer."

"Understood," West said. "I hope you come with us. I don't know either of you well, but you both seem kind. You don't deserve what's coming to you either."

"If what you're hinting at ever comes to pass," Surridge replied.

"I'd be grateful if it doesn't. As Professor Clums likes to say: peace, love, and faith." West nodded and then headed to the exit.

"West," Kamarial called out. He turned around, and she approached a few steps and clasped her hands together. "Please, be safe tomorrow. I don't want to see anyone harmed."

"Neither do we," West said. "That will be up to Lord Foxaire and his goons."

He tipped his hat toward the ceiling and saw Poi tapping on her tablet. She had gotten the signal. He stepped out of Professor Peal's area and took a deep breath.

*It really is a shame that we can't let Professor Peal know about this*, he thought. *But there are a lot of parties involved in this plan. It's already risky and dangerous, and there's no need to make it even more so. Not when there are no guarantees.*

West stood before Theesakin. Even though they communicated telepathically, he would have preferred to be alone. Instead, he was surrounded by a dozen others. There were Professor Durrist and Professor Randall, Carl, Creson, Brock, four security guards dubbed Sid's Cyclones, and three Lakinceitian drones. He took a deep breath. Now it was time to test the device Professor Clums installed that would jumble up his outgoing frequencies just enough to cover his tracks.

"*Greetings, West.*"

"*Good day, Theesakin. How has everything been?*"

"*Normal, for the most part,*" Theesakin replied. He was swiftly mastering the language. "*But now is not normal. Why are there others, and why do they wield dangerous weapons?*"

"*Because tomorrow they plan on moving you to an off-site location. I have yet to uncover where you're being taken, though.*"

"*Ah, if that's the case, hopefully the next cage will have more room than this.*"

"*Ideally, there will be no next cage. We mean to set you free. Several of us are planning an escape, and we're going to take you along.*"

Theesakin closed his eyes for a moment and opened them while remaining unmoving. He sat on his butt with his knees raised and his tail curled around him with his four arms crossed. From Professor Durrist's and Professor Randall's reactions, they weren't getting anything useful from their interaction.

"*Now, I don't know how much time we have before we get interrupted,*" West continued. "*But I will not be here to break you out tomorrow. I am needed elsewhere. Instead, my good friends will be here. There's Navacus Clums, an Yggdrazim—like a white bird-man with a large and flat orange beak. Then there's Fumalli Qymberkon, a Nioavellian, and Syl, a Kolythoanthaean. So, those two gray guards are Kolythoanthaean and that blue one is a Nioavellian.*"

"*I understand. Thank you for letting me know, and for taking me with you. I will not harm your friends, but I will not show anyone else the same mercy.*"

"*And I don't expect you to. That's why the guards and the bounty hunters are here—*"

"Hey West, are you done painting each other's nails?" Brock yelled. "How much longer are you just going to stand there?"

Professor Durrist turned to the bounty hunter. "Have patience, please."

"It's okay," West replied. "He's not very talkative today, anyway. All the firepower is making him nervous."

"Really? A magnificent beast such as this is afraid of us?" Creson said in astonishment. "What I would give to have one such as this by my side."

"Yeah, we'd be unstoppable," Brock replied.

"That's not why you're here, of course," West cut in. "You're here to assist, not to steal."

"West is right. I don't appreciate your comments," Professor Durrist said. "I would have thought the two of you would understand that. Sid's Cyclones sure do."

West could see all four of them subtly grin in response. Creson, however, was unfazed.

"How powerful do you think its arms are? I bet it could easily rip an Ancilsan's arm off."

"What did I just say, Tag?" Professor Durrist said as he stared him down.

"I got this," Carl said as he stepped in between them. "Let's take this outside, shall we? We have other Titans to see."

*"I'm sorry our time together is always so rushed,"* West thought. *"But once we're out of here, I'll have time to really get to know you."*

*"I look forward to that, my friend. I will anticipate your allies' arrival,"* Theesakin responded.

"Right, let's move on, then," Professor Randall said.

*Theesakin, Ivy, Newtus, Sassafrass, Blood Bat, and Denoptace, you will all be free,* he thought. *I will make sure of it. We will get you out of this dreadful place.*

## 28

# ESCAPE FROM THE MUNDANE

arl watched Gnudashar and Sid as they conversed before the meeting. Lord Foxaire still hadn't arrived but was due in shortly. While he knew he shouldn't, he missed Gazelle's presence. Even if he was being influenced by her powers, Carl still liked to see her.

He let his mind wander, and his attention drifted to his favorite painting in the room. It was called *Aspirations* by the famed Eusphyrchiian artist Kala Lang and was the lesser-known companion piece to her most famous painting, *Visionaries. Aspirations* depicted a forest clearing that was full of people from various species and all nine species were represented. Above the clearing, the blue sky quickly faded to a black sky filled with stars, a place unlike their own.

"So, what's the most outrageous thing that Dasch or Ànifa did?" Sid asked as he leaned in to Gnudashar.

Gnudashar laughed, then stood in thought for a moment. "You know, I have one for each. First, when Ànifa was still a child, she used her guardian angel to help her plot several elaborate pranks on her two younger sisters. My favorite one involves flowers called pollen-bursters, a cockatrice foot, and—"

Before Gnudashar could finish, the rumbling floor interrupted him. Red flashing lights appeared as a klaxon blared. They stepped back against the wall, each of them brushing against one of the many paintings. A loud scraping noise accompanied the sudden jolt of movement as two large panels slid away, revealing a large rectangular hole in the floor and the large elevator as it rose into the room. On the elevator platform was the colossal bulk of Lord Foxaire, looking sharp and alert from his rest.

"Carl, Gnudashar, Sid. Good morning to you all," Lord Foxaire greeted them as the platform came to a rest.

"Good morning," the three of them replied off canter.

"Are the others ready?"

"Yes, Professor Durrist and Gazelle checked in a few minutes ago. I'll bring them up now," Carl said as he activated the main television screen while simultaneously calling up Professor Durrist.

The line rang only once before it was answered. Professor Durrist's dark green face appeared on the screen. It was all they could see before he leaned back to show Professor Randall and Gazelle standing behind him.

"Hello everyone," Professor Randall said with a wave.

"Good morning. Does anyone over there miss me?" Gazelle said playfully.

"I sure do," Sid blurted out. Carl smiled to himself, as he had nearly done the same. In response, Gazelle kissed her hand and blew it to them with a wink.

"Alright, let's get to it." Lord Foxaire's deep voice rumbled throughout the room. "As you all know, tomorrow is the first of three large moves. We have a lot to do today to prepare."

Carl listened attentively as Lord Foxaire gave each of them their primary duties for the day. The first thing Carl was asked to do was contact Professor Ean to see if they were ready to receive everyone for transfer. After that, he was to contact Chief Engineer Volvordime and ask about the progress on the space-gate; this task had been his personal request, as he wanted to stay on top of things. After that, he was to meet with the two bounty hunters and have them follow him throughout his final inspections of all the specimens.

Sid, Gnudashar, Gazelle, Randall, and Professors Durrist all received their own set of tasks. As the meeting wound down, Gazelle spoke up.

"Excuse me, I have a request."

"Make it quick," Lord Foxaire replied.

"Of course. I would like to interview Professor Clums' assistants. I want to—"

"Absolutely not," Lord Foxaire said harshly. "I do not want you interfering with Professor Clums' affairs today. I need you to simply stand in the room and keep an eye on them while they work on Svetlana. They have a lot of work to do, and it will likely take them several days, so make sure they stay focused. Aside from that, only speak when spoken to. Do not engage with them."

"If I may, wouldn't it be valuable to learn more about—"

Again, Lord Foxaire interrupted Gazelle. "Leave them alone until after this move. They are scheduled to be moved at a later date. Our goal is to keep Professor Clums distracted, even if it means taking Svetlana out of the mix, and that is precisely why the bounty hunters are here." Lord Foxaire clapped his hands together, which was the maximum reach for his arms. "Get to work, everyone."

Before Gazelle could speak up again, Lord Foxaire turned off the screen.

"Good luck with your tasks," Sid said as he left the room, leaving Carl, Gnudashar, and Lord Foxaire behind.

"I must reiterate to the two of you that everything must go as planned. We cannot afford any hiccups. I need the two of you to stay on top of everyone, including Sid, Gazelle, and the professors."

"I will not let you down, Lorphax, for everything depends on this," Gnudashar said, using Lord Foxaire's true name. "I know this to be the true path forward for us. I had a vision last night that showed our ultimate victory, and that vision will not be far off from reality as long as we succeed."

"I am pleased to hear this," Lord Foxaire replied. "I'm glad your soothsayer abilities are finally materializing."

"Agreed. It definitely took a few days to get used to the conflicting personalities and memories, but now that I've gotten things sorted out, I can finally come into my true power."

"Fantastic. Now, go. Get to work and ensure that Gnudashar's vision comes true."

———

"Oh boy, today is finally the day we get to meet these allusive Titans," Brock said as he rubbed his hands together in excited anticipation. Creson nodded his bony white neck in agreement.

"Right, but that won't be until a few hours from now," Carl said impatiently. He didn't enjoy having the bounty hunters around, but he knew they were necessary. He had yet to interact with them much, but today they would be together for nearly the entire day.

At least the conversations with Professor Ean and Chief Engineer Volvordime were fruitful. Ean and her team had nearly all the containment cells prepped and ready. She assured that everything would be fully prepared when everyone arrived. As for Volvordime, they were successful at ramping up the incoming supply of raw materials. They were pulling from multiple sources—Mishunaed, Carange, Clendenic, and Ijurvoll—and each operation was done using a different shell company. Lord Foxaire had personally set up the shell companies, which meant that it would be nearly impossible to trace any activity back to Foxaire Biotech Industries.

"As I'm sure you've noticed, this underground space is quite confusing," Carl continued.

"Yeah, it's like a mind-fry," Brock said. "West showed us a few places, but I'm not sure if I could get back to them easily. Plus, he didn't show us anything interesting."

"I remember where West went... but it would be better if you led the way," Creson said in his perpetually creepy voice.

"Of course. We'll start by visiting the lone survivor of one of Professor Durrist's original experiments. He wanted to see if other species could obtain the ability to shape-shift, like how some Lakinceitians still can."

Creson hummed to himself. "A very powerful ability, indeed. Besides the two of us, the best bounty hunter in the IBHA is a Lakinceitian who can shape-shift. It's fascinating to watch him change forms."

"That sounds like a dangerous advantage," Carl said, mostly to himself.

"Oh, it really is," Brock replied with a twinkle in his eye.

He led them through the twisty path to where Altun was held. "Right. Altun is really one of a kind. He has nearly more control over his transformations than Lakinceitians do. It's too bad Durrist could never replicate it."

"What species is Altun?"

"He's an Ancilsan. One of the biggest and most powerful ones I've seen. So, in total, there were twelve specimens that underwent these experiments. There were six species, one of each gender. They used Yggdrazim, Human, Nioavellian, Eridavlos, Kolythoanthaean, and Ancilsan. And actually, we had the female Yggdrazim survive until just a few days ago. Her transformations weren't always complete, and sometimes she transformed erratically and unprompted, so we had to keep her drugged. We also let go of the final Eridavlos specimen recently as well."

Creson hummed in interest. "It's fascinating that an Ancilsan was successful. It must be due to their primitive bodies. I need to speak with Durrist more, as we seem very like-minded."

"Right, only your 'experiments'," Brock said, using finger quotes, "always involve how slowly you can torture someone."

"One of art's finest forms," Creson said, his voice full of pride.

*These two are batshit*, Carl thought. *I can't wait until they're out of our hair.*

Creson and Brock only spoke with Altun for a short time, as Altun wasn't talkative. At least Carl got Altun to show off—Altun had shape-shifted into a male teenage Human, an elderly female Kolythoanthaean, and a stern-faced Lakinceitian. Creson and Brock had been highly impressed.

"Why do you keep someone with such useful abilities locked away like this?" Brock asked as they were leaving Altun's area.

"Because we can't control him. You talked to him; he is highly uncooperative. That is why we are planning to have Professor Navacus Clums build a mind-control device similar to Svetlana's, so we can control him like we do her," Carl said. "Those plans have been put on the back-burner until after the move to the satellite station."

"Ah, Svetlana. It's too bad that she's being worked on today. I was really looking forward to getting to know her," Brock said.

As Carl led the chatty bounty hunters back through the main halls and to Professor Peal's area, they had to squeeze around several squadrons of Sid's Cyclones as they practiced their route for tomorrow.

*It's been a while since I've been over here, but Ivy should be awake now,* Carl thought. *He will be interesting to meet, and I'm sure these two bozos will agree.*

---

Ivy Hedera was idly shooting various strands of silk from Adok and Ados while simultaneously stretching out his ivy legs as he thought about what West had told him. He was going to escape from this place, which meant he had to be prepared for anything. Luckily, he had full control over all his components, and together, all four pieces made him stronger than he had likely ever been. He still didn't remember his life before, but he had concluded that he didn't much care, since he was alive and that's what mattered. It was this moment and every moment after that was important, not his lost past.

The sound of the exterior door opening brought him back to reality. He stopped shooting his silk strands and retracted his ivy, then turned his attention to the seven people walking in. He recognized Professor Peal and his team, but he wasn't familiar with the other three. He stayed quiet, letting them approach and settle into the observation room.

To Professor Peal's right stood an unknown Human with short

black hair and glasses, while the other two new faces stood to his left —a muscular, dark-skinned Human and a short Eusphyrchiian. The Eusphyrchiian stared at him with a look of hungry desire. Behind them were Kalosse, Kamarial, and Surridge, who each held tablets.

Professor Peal cleared his throat. "Ivy, I hope you are doing well today. This is Carl Feng. He's a representative of the company we work for, Foxaire Biotech Industries. He's here to take some assessments of you. These other two are Tag Creson and S.C. Brock."

"It's a pleasure and an honor to finally meet you," Carl said, his eyes wide with wonder. "You are far more impressive in person. The photos and videos don't do you justice."

"Uh, thank you, I suppose?" Ivy replied, speaking through both Ados and Adok. It produced the desired effect—all three newcomers jumped in surprise. Ivy always enjoyed when that happened. "So, what can I do you for, Carl?"

"As Professor Peal said, we're here to assess you. I'd first like to know about your voice," Carl said.

"It's simple really," Ivy replied using only Ados. He switched to Adok and continued. "It's easier to speak through both spiders instead of one at a time, like this."

"I don't even know..." Tag said as he looked at him like a puzzle to be solved.

"Hey, Tag, what don't you know? Never seen one of us that was missing its head and most of its limbs?" he asked, once again speaking with both spiders.

"Oh no, I am acquainted with West Kilinder, but you are far more impressive than he is in several ways," Tag said, his voice quivering in excitement.

"Right, so who are these guys? And what kind of name is *S.C.*?" Ivy asked.

"We're here on active security duty. And S.C. stands for Supreme Carnivore. I had my name legally changed the first chance I got," the macho Human said with a grin.

"And here I thought I had a silly name," Ivy said with a laugh, prompting the Carnivore Supreme to glare at him.

"Let's settle down and get back to business," Carl said in a stern voice.

They asked several questions that Professor Peal and the others could have easily answered for him, such as how his ivy worked. They also wanted to see him demonstrate several of his silk strands, so he showed off some of the more impressive-looking ones, including a mild acidic strand, a weak electric strand, and a thin metallic strand. All the strands Ivy showed them were highly diluted. He knew he couldn't show off his true strength, not when he had less than a day to wait before he could actually use them.

After that, he was made to perform tests on his ivy legs, and once again he held back significantly. All the while, the three newcomers looked at him with smiling faces; they couldn't hide the fact that they wanted to use him to their own advantages.

After what felt like close to an hour, everyone left except for Kamarial and Surridge. They turned off their tablets and approached the glass so they could talk to him quietly.

"I want to apologize for that," Kamarial whispered and bowed slightly. "I didn't realize they were going to ask so much of you."

"Yeah, well, that's why I was created, right? To perform when asked—to be used as a tool. I could see it in their eyes."

"I can assure you, we weren't thinking about the ramifications of what would happen to after we made you. I mean, we're just scientists. All we wanted to do was push science past its perceived limits," Surridge replied, her voice filled with shame and regret.

"Oh, I don't blame either of you, or even Professor Peal. I know you were just doing your jobs," Ivy replied.

"Right, well, we know West talked to you this morning, and we wanted to give you our support," Kamarial said. Surridge shot her a glare, then Kamarial continued, "Well, I wanted to give you my support. What they are doing to you doesn't sit well with me, especially as a Eusphyrchiian myself."

"I appreciate that," Ivy replied. "So, are you coming with us? West mentioned that there would be others."

Kamarial hesitated before answering. "We're still deciding."

"I'm the one who's the most torn. I just can't leave Max—Professor Peal—behind," Surridge said. "He is too good of a friend to abandon."

"I can sympathize with that," Ivy replied. "Just do what you think is right, then. You must decide for yourselves. Of course, keep in mind I'm new to pretty much everything, so take my advice as you'd like."

"Ivy, just because you've only been conscious for a short time doesn't mean you aren't highly intelligent. Whoever you were before—"

"—helped me become who I am now. That's all I care about," Ivy replied, finishing Kamarial's sentence for her. A moment later, Surridge's and Kamarial's tablets chimed at the same time. Surridge turned to face Kamarial.

"We're being summoned," Surridge said.

"Sorry, we need to get back to work," Kamarial said. "We wish you the best of luck, and if I do not see you again, know that I only want the best for you, whatever that may be."

"Thank you, Kamarial and Surridge. I wish the same for you both. I won't forget you."

The women gave him one last nod then left the observation room.

*West, I sure hope you know what you're doing,* Ivy thought. *There is a lot at stake here, not just for the ones that are escaping, but for the ones staying behind. All I know is that even if I was made to be used, I will not submit—I will live my life on my own terms.*

Carl still couldn't believe how talkative the two bounty hunters were. He had been expecting them to have quiet demeanors, but the truth was the complete opposite. Everything they did was to show off and brag about themselves.

After they visited with the Titans, Carl had to stay with the bounty hunters while they prepared for tomorrow. He knew he had been assigned to them so Lord Foxaire could watch them as well. They still didn't fully trust them, so it was good to keep an eye on them. Yet, Carl was getting antsy—he still had a lot to do back at Lord Foxaire's mansion. At this point, he was waiting for Sid to finish up with his squad so he could relieve him.

Currently, Creson and Brock were having a civil disagreement about which of the Titans were their favorites. They unanimously agreed Theesakin was the best, so they were fighting over who ranked second place. Brock's second favorite was Zadgarcolth, while Creson was torn between Zinartee and Ophertusc. Either way, they both were vastly underestimating Karkilver, which was Carl's favorite. He liked how simple Karkilver was—a pure killing machine, even more so than Zadgarcolth or Theesakin.

Carl breathed a sigh of relief when he received the message from Sid confirming he was inbound. He was more than ready to part ways with the bounty hunters. He led them to the space where they would spend the night. It was a tight fit, but it would have to do, as it was the only ventilated space that wasn't in use.

"I hope this is okay. Remember, it'll be just for tonight, then you'll be back in the rooms you've been staying in," Carl said.

"Oh, this is just dandy," Brock said. "We've had much, much worse."

"Indeed, we have. Like the time we were hiding in the sewers beneath Kokorocco for nearly two weeks," Creson suggested.

"Ah, that was bad, but I think that the worst for me was—"

"If that's everything, then I need to be on my way," Carl said, cutting off Brock.

"Oh, so that's it then?" Brock asked. "We have nothing else to do? The night is still young."

"Yes it is, which is why I must be going. Sid Heigel will be by soon to take over for me, but in the meantime, I still need to prepare for tomorrow."

"I understand," Creson said.

"Right, later then," Carl said as he walked away as quickly as possible. He made a beeline to the gyroscope bay. His hand was centimeters away from pressing the button to call a gyroscope when Lord Foxaire's voice came through his earpiece.

"Carl, I'm glad I caught you. Do not press that button," his boss demanded.

"Okay, what's going on?"

"I need you to head upstairs on the double. I've asked Bsarg, Nijork, and West to meet you up there. Gazelle has taken over Professor Yilvin's lab, and she must be stopped. Drag her back here— she is in serious trouble."

"Understood. On my way now," he said as he turned on his heels and sped down the winding hallway to the closest elevator.

*Good gracious Gazelle*, Carl thought. *What have you gotten yourself into? You better not screw anything up. This operation is far too important.*

## 29

# ESCAPE FROM BOUNDARIES

Kaytrona awoke and lazily opened her eyes. Something had roused her out of her unnatural slumber, but she didn't know what it was. She tried to sit up, but her spinning head forced her to lay back down.

"Damn grogginess, this is seriously messing with me," she said with an arm over her forehead. "If they keep this up, I don't know how we'll have any strength to do anything at all."

A tinny-sounding foreign voice caused her to sit straight up in bed. "Kate, is that you?"

"Who's there? Show yourself!"

"I can't see into your cell; I can only speak to you. I'm Lyd, I don't know—"

"Holy Eklatros, Lyd!" she blurted louder than she meant to. "You're the one who I spoke to in my final moments. I apologize for unloading on you like that."

"Tyrona, is that you?" Lyd replied with some hesitation in his voice. "Don't even worry about it. So, you are both really in there, huh?"

"Yes. Both Kate and I are living in her body. I have to say, this is not how I envisioned my afterlife would be," she said with a chuckle. "And *I* never expected to be a host to a Human from an alien world."

"Uh, right," Lyd said, sounding unsure of how to respond. "Anyway, I'm here because I need to talk to you both, or just you, I mean. If possible, please try to minimize your reaction just in case they're watching. Now, we are going to escape from this place tomorrow."

Lyd's warning was the only thing that stopped Kaytrona from jumping for joy. Instead, she smiled deeply and sat down on the bed, then laid down while Lyd explained the plan. Of her Eklatros kin, she was the last one to learn of it.

"I'm glad everyone else knows. But can you clarify about Norman's vehicular device? Are you saying that he's essentially his own car?"

"That's one way to look at it, sure," Lyd replied.

"Oh Norman, of course you'd get something like this," she said to herself out loud. "And Theodore, tomorrow we will be reunited. I only hope you'll recognize me, that you'll recognize my soul. And Norman, I suppose I can forgive you for not being there for me. Your task sounds exciting."

"Yeah, hey, so I've got to get moving, and—"

"Oh fiddle-sticks, I'm sorry, I keep on talking to myself, or like, we keep on talking... Anyway, thank you so much, Lyd. Take care, and journey back safely."

"Thank you, Tyrona, or is it Kate?"

"Please, call me Kaytrona."

"Okay, Kaytrona. Thank you, and see you tomorrow."

She grabbed her pillow, squeezed it, and yelled into it. "Whoo-hoo! Theodore, Norman! We're coming for you!"

After several minutes of celebrating, the reality struck her. If she was going to be escaping, then she would need a way to use her magic. She tried to focus, but her mind was still hazy from the drugs. Even so, she did what she could to push through it.

*This would be far easier if I had my wand*, she thought. *This planet may have done horrific things to us, but at least we have some allies on our side. I wonder how we got so lucky. I suppose that if it comes down to it, we may just need to rely on those allies. Dorie, I hope that you're able to use magic still. And Cecil, I hope that you have something up your sleeve, too. We need to use everything we have to our advantage, which is why I'm happy to hear that you have new legs, Norman. And, apparently, you're like a car now, too. This I really need to see for myself.*

<hr>

Theodore smiled as he looked at the stack of books. While he didn't read every word in the six volumes he received on the Nishna Delta, he had gained an immense amount of knowledge from them.

It was early into the second volume when he started to uncover similarities in how water flowed through the delta and the energy he felt coursing through his body every time he used magic. Since he didn't have any mastery over water, he had never thought to study its other properties. He was ever so thankful for the reading material that had been forced upon him, for it was making him view everything in a whole new light. He knew they were only giving these volumes to him to mess with him and bore him, which made his discoveries even more exciting.

Several of the volumes spoke about how the local people would shape the rivers and the land to their own benefit. They would build various structures called dams, dikes, and levees to control how the water flowed. They would also build irrigation channels to funnel the water from the delta into farmland, which created new pathways for water to flow.

So, while he did not have any usable conduit, he could still practice by navigating the flow of energy throughout his body. He would create dams, causing his exteriors to go numb, and upon releasing the dams his skin felt like it was being prickled by thousands of tiny needles. In a similar sense, he could do the same with his magic—he could hold it back while it built up to produce even more powerful attacks.

Yet the most insightful epiphany came from thinking about

irrigation channels. He knew that electricity was everywhere, even within his own body, so if he had a way to divert that electricity into his fingertips, he could potentially shoot electric shocks. First, he had to move the energy into his fingertips, then practice on damming it back to release charged bursts.

While he had been practicing, a voice interrupted him. He called himself Lyd and informed Theodore that he was going to be escaping from this place. Upon hearing the news, he had an invigorated desire to get his new trick to work. For all he knew, it could make all the difference. Plus, he needed to get to Tyrona as soon as he could. He had felt her call out a few days ago before her presence disappeared. He had to know why she had reached out and why she hadn't tried since.

Once Lyd was gone, Theodore sat on the floor and put his hands on his cross-legged knees. He took a deep breath, coughed, then scratched at the stubble growing on his chin. It was nothing compared to the thick beard he once knew and loved, but it was something.

He shook his head and refocused. He began with his base, then moved up his spine until he felt his energy billowing out of his crown. He then diverted the energy from his heart into his arms and then into his fingertips. After a few seconds, he could feel static electricity in his fingertips. He let some out, causing his fingertips to sparkle.

Theodore smiled to himself. "It works. Just like I knew it would." He spent the rest of the day practicing, and by his evening meal, he was producing controlled bolts of electricity.

*Tyrona, I'm coming for you,* Theodore thought. *I cannot believe I will see you again so soon. It feels like a lifetime ago that you were taken away, even if it has only been a few weeks. Well, a few weeks in my time—I can't say for sure if time would even move the same on this planet.*

*Cecil, Druder… Tyrona. Let's rid ourselves of this horrible place and find a way back home to Eklatros. With all of us together, I know we can make it out of here. And we will not forget you, Dasch. Once we have some breathing room, I plan to find a way to save you. I know we can help you find your way back to your true self. We will not abandon you.*

Druder stood on his hands in the center of the dark room. He took a deep breath and felt it invigorate the large amount of energy flowing within him. It nearly burst from him as it flowed with his bloodstream, delivering warmth to every corner of his body. He was finally ready. His preparation throughout the past few days had led to this point. He took another deep breath, and as he exhaled, pushed his consciousness out with it. In his mind's eye, he saw himself in the dark. He couldn't help but smile. Standing on his hands really helped him concentrate, but it looked ridiculous, now that he could see himself.

He took another deep breath and pushed his consciousness out further, then he did it one more time. He did not dare to push himself further than this, for this was just a trial run.

It took a few moments for Druder to gain his bearings, and what came into focus confirmed several of his theories. First, his cell was one of many, and his companions were in other cells around him. The cell block was situated in a straight line. At the start of the line was Cecil, next was Theodore, then himself, and finally, at the very end, was a presence that he couldn't quite understand. It was clearly one person, but it felt like two, and one of them contained traces of Eklatros. He assumed it was Tyrona, but he wasn't sure why there was another presence with her.

While he was studying his surroundings and trying to hone in on how his friends were faring, he sensed five new presences approaching. One he recognized well—Dasch, or rather, Gnudashar, the vile infestation. Then there was Carl, the human that had visited him before. The other three presences he didn't recognize, but one of them was highly concerning. She radiated an energy he had never felt before. The moment he turned his focus on her, a chill ran down his spine and he immediately backed away. As he rushed back into his body, he felt her presence searching for his own.

*What in Eklatros was that?* he thought. *How did she do that? That was horrifying. I can only assume that she'll visit me in due time. Then, hopefully, I can learn more.*

*In all, though, that was well worth it. I found Theodore and Cecil, and what could be Tyrona. And, not only that, but it worked. I could successfully go outside my body. This will be useful, I'm sure of it. If only I had mastered this sooner, then maybe I could have seen Lyd while I spoke with him. Either way, tomorrow will be a great day, I am sure of it.*

Cecil lounged on his bed as his muscles pulsed and ached from his workout. He had pushed himself harder than he'd meant to, especially considering he needed his full strength tomorrow.

He smiled as he reflected on how strong he had become. He hadn't even known he was capable of this much strength, and the best part was that he didn't use any tools to accomplish the task—no barbells or punching bags, only his own body. Even if he couldn't reclaim his armor, he didn't really feel like he needed it anymore. Of course, that could just be his overconfidence talking. Also, he wasn't sure if he'd still fit in his old armor. He was much bulkier now.

His plan to doze the day away was rudely interrupted when his window to the outside world was opened. Peering through it was the face of his old friend, but behind those eyes he could see the evil festering within.

"Cecil, so good to see you again. I'm sure you remember me—Gnudashar."

He spat on the ground. "You're a monster. I don't want to speak with the one who is possessing my friend's body."

"You know, I could easily argue that this is my true body, but I have a feeling it won't change your opinion."

"Yeah, that I can agree with. Look, why are you here?"

"We're just checking in," Gnudashar said as more of the wall became transparent, allowing him to see four people standing behind his frenemy. He recognized the bespectacled black-haired man, but he didn't recognize the dark-skinned man standing beside him. There was also an alien with an egg-shaped head and indigo-colored skin and a shorter alien with skin that reminded him of eggshells.

"You already know Carl Feng," Gnudashar continued. "Joining us today is Gazelle—" the indigo alien batted her eyes playfully, "—Brock and Creson." The man and the eggshell alien waved at him accordingly.

"Are you here to show off your new friends? You know I'm not impressed. Our group is the best," Cecil replied as he tried to annoy Gnudashar. He knew he probably shouldn't taunt him, but this was likely his final chance to. Unfortunately, Gnudashar didn't seem fazed.

He grunted, sounding just like Dasch for a moment before he opened his mouth. "*Colleagues* is the word I would rather use in this case."

"Right, look, can we get to the point? This is kinda sad," Brock said.

"Are you sympathizing with me?" he asked.

"Oh black-holes no. I'm saying this is tedious to listen to. I don't give a crap about your little feud."

"Brock, calm down. Maybe it is important," Creson said.

Cecil nodded to himself. This strange man was right—now was not the time to mess with them, even if he still wanted to. "You know, I agree. Can we get to the point? There's gotta be more to this than just checking in."

Gnudashar grunted like Dasch again, making Cecil second guess himself. "Gazelle, do your thing."

"With pleasure," Gazelle said as she strut up to the transparent barrier. He couldn't help but stare into her twinkling eyes, and as he did so, he felt like he was drowning in love. He didn't know why, but suddenly, all he wanted was this alien creature. It was all he desired—nothing else mattered. She was the only thing that he cared about in the whole wide—

*Wait a minute*, he thought. *This isn't right... these aren't my true thoughts. Besides, I don't like women.*

He tried to fight it, but Gazelle's presence overcame his senses, and he once again fell into her honey-trap. Then, as soon as he questioned if he lost his mind, it stopped. The alien presence melted away as if it had never even been there.

"What was that?" he yelled as he squeezed at his arms. "What did you just do to me?"

"Oh, don't be such a baby. I barely even did anything," Gazelle said with a pouty lip, then turned to her colleagues. "Keep in mind I am not a mind reader, as much as I want to be. What I can do is sense feelings and desires. And he has something on his mind, like a big event that he is looking forward to. There is also a strong desire to escape from this place."

"Well, that's not surprising. When Dasch was in the cell, he wanted to be free of it, too," Gnudashar said. "I wonder what this big event could be, though."

"My death," he said as straight-faced as he could. "If I can't leave this place, then I just want to die. I don't want to be used, and I don't want to waste away into nothingness."

"I wouldn't call your sexy body nothingness," Gazelle said with a wink.

Cecil put a hand over his mouth and visually gagged. "I didn't do this for your eyes."

"No? You don't desire me? Most do, even after I caress them," Gazelle said playfully.

"What you did to me was abusive and wrong," he said firmly. "Besides, I'm attracted to men."

Gazelle rolled her eyes and sighed. "That just figures. I don't have a strong sway over male homosexuals."

"Let's move on, then," Carl said, speaking for the first time.

"Right. Let's hurry through these guys so we can finally meet the Titans," Brock said.

"That would be great, since it wouldn't matter if I pried deeper, anyway. Besides, I think I felt the next guy trying to examine my aura. I want to ask him about that," Gazelle said. Cecil wasn't sure if she was talking about Theodore or Druder, but he hoped they would play it safe.

"You only have time for the next one anyway," Carl said. "You need to meet up with Svetlana and head upstairs after this."

"Alright then, let's go," Gnudashar said with a wave of his arm before turning back to Cecil one last time. He looked at him with his dead eyes and the smile of a cheater who knew he was going to win. "Cecil, do take care of yourself now."

The wall suddenly turned completely opaque and Cecil was alone again.

*They didn't say it, but they must be checking up on us before they enact their plans*, he thought. *I'm just glad I didn't reveal anything to them, and if Lyd spoke to the others, then I hope they don't reveal anything either. That Gazelle... I feel like I was mind-fucked by her, and it just feels wrong in every way possible. She's dangerous, that one. I hope we won't have to deal with her tomorrow.*

*That all being the case, though, it's odd that they just revealed so much to me, probably because they believe I can't do anything about it. But come tomorrow, I'll show them something to fear.*

<hr>

Dasch was having trouble tearing himself away from the screen. The monster controlling his body was messing with his dearest friends. It was overconfident, like it had absolutely no doubt that it was going to win. And, honestly, it had every right to think that. The vision they had last night was still bothering him.

It began on a charred world he didn't recognize. The blackened plants and rocks were littered with corpses. There were many humans but even more aliens, some he had seen before and some were unfamiliar. As the body count grew, he noticed there were no Gnusar or Lakinceitians among the fallen. The field of death then focused in on hundreds of creatures standing in the center of the destruction. Countless Gnusars, Gnuelry, Gnureavers, and Gnurargurts cheered and shouted as they gave thanks and honor to their leader—Gnusaramnii.

This was now the second time he had laid eyes on the evil

monster, and it looked quite different from how he had remembered it. It was still a towering, massive slug-like creature, but now it was covered in spikes. Also, surrounding its head was a ring of tusks that created a bone collar, which only accentuated how hideously ugly its face was. It was like Gnusaramnii had evolved into an even stronger version of what it had been, which was quite unsettling.

And, even though he knew this was only a vision, Gnusaramnii had locked eyes with Dasch and belted out a string of its hideous laughter, along with a message for him. "Dasch, how fitting that you are now imprisoned in this way. It must be from the immortality I granted you so long ago. But this is a fate worse than death, and it suits you better."

Even if he hadn't been struck with pure terror, he wasn't sure if he could've responded. It didn't matter, though, because that was where the vision had ended.

The most curious part about the vision was that Gnudashar had received a different message from Gnusaramnii, one he had learned upon Gnudashar's awakening. Essentially, Gnusaramnii had told Gnudashar that the key to their victory was within reach and if they followed the true path, they would manifest it. Dasch wasn't sure how to interpret that, as he knew the various Eklatros prophecies got some details wrong, but Gnudashar took it as a sign that everything would go smoothly.

He smiled to himself. Gnudashar's pride would be his downfall. And the best part was that he still wasn't fully aware of his presence, or that Gnusaramnii had spoken to him separately.

*I don't know how, but the next chance I get, I will do whatever I can to ensure Gnudashar's plan fails,* Dasch thought. *I cannot allow my friends to be moved to an even more secure location. I need to get them out of here. I just hope I'll have the strength to do it—to gain control of my body as long as it takes. But I cannot call myself a solider of Kieth's Golden Army, nor a friend and ally of Ànifa's, if I do not try.*

**30**

# ESCAPE FROM CONTROL

Navacus wheezed as he read over the requests for Svetlana's upgrades, which had dropped into his inbox earlier. As he had been warned a few days ago, they were quite extensive. Even if he wasn't trying to dawdle, it would take him at least two to three days to complete the upgrades, and that didn't include the time it would take to prepare the components they needed to install. While he had known what to expect, the designs that were included differed from what Carl had talked to him about way back at the end of Caranar—the helmet and the extra limbs were not listed.

He opened a blank document and drafted the message he needed to send to Professor Bodeelch later that night.

*"I wish you could help me type faster, Sterg."*

*"I wish this as well. Your short arms and hands inhibit you from using your tablet efficiently."*

*"Wow, thanks so much for the support,"* Navacus replied, rolling his eyes.

A knock at his door interrupted him. He wheezed, stood up, and opened the door to find Fumalli, who was smiling at him. Behind his dear blue friend was a flurry of movement.

"Nava, your team is ready to head over to Professor Peal's lab, and we are all are set to go on my end."

"Good, I'm glad to hear it," Navacus said. "Sorry, I was just reviewing the work, and time got away from me. They're really asking for a lot. It'll take multiple days to complete."

"You know, I think that's why you were assigned this task," Fumalli said.

"I suspect you're right," he said with a nod, then smiled at his friend. "Well, we better get to it. I know you're busy today as well."

Navacus stepped into his lab as his assistants settled down. Poi sat at her computer with Mac beside her, and they studied the screen together, while Syl and Grasberg stood between Norman, and the three discussed the plan amongst themselves. Dea, Lyd, and Kurjon stood by the door, the hover-cart fully loaded with supplies. Navacus approached Syl, Grasberg, and Norman while Fumalli trailed behind him.

"Syl, Grasberg, all set for the day then?"

"Yes, Professor," Grasberg replied as he looked up from his tablet.

"It sounds like they've got everything under control," Norman said. "They've assured me my retinal scan device will be operational by tonight."

"It will be, as long as we get started now," Syl said briskly.

"Well, don't let me keep you," Navacus replied, then looked at Fumalli. "Work hard, everyone. Norman is going to need his retinal scan. And don't forget to lay out the other attachments for Dea to grab tonight."

"Of course," Fumalli replied. "We won't forget."

"Right, I'll be back later for those," Dea said from his place by the door.

"Good. Peace, love, and faith." Navacus nodded and said goodbye to his friends. His gaze lingered on Fumalli for a few seconds before he turned away.

*Take care of everyone for me, Fumi,* he thought. *We need to keep our heads straight today so we can be successful tomorrow.*

Svetlana Slesarenko sat on the metal operating table with her hands placed firmly on her lap. They were just about ready to begin.

Before Svetlana and Gazelle had arrived, Navacus and his team had quickly thrown together a basic outline for the new eye, as they had a pretty good idea of how to replicate their previous work. Navacus was missing having his whole team together—he could really use one of Poi's designs right now. But, Dea really helped to fill in the gaps.

Gazelle coughed into her hand, and he took the hint. While she was just there to observe, Navacus still had to hide Sterg's presence. He hoped this would be the last time.

"Alright, we better get started," Navacus said. "First, I want to review the upgrades that were requested. Then, for today, we'll focus on only one of the four requests, and get as far as we can. There may be a possibility that you'll need to stay the night here, as we'll need to disassemble a few things."

"If that's what it takes. I was assured you knew what you were doing," Svetlana replied coldly.

"Did you already forget how we worked together the first time around?" Navacus asked, his eyes narrowed.

"I was different then. Everything is better now—I have a clearer mind. I see things in a different way."

"Right, well your vision will be changing again—we are replacing your final Human eye."

"Finally. This old eye has really been causing me issues and headaches. I'll be glad to be rid of it."

Navacus took a sharp breath and held it for a second as he stared at his table with wide eyes. *It really is like talking to a completely different person.* "Well, you won't be rid of it now; we need time to build the new eye first. For today, we'll prepare you for your new shield plating armor. This means tightening and strengthening the structural foundations throughout your spine and body to support the extra weight. Once that is completed, we'll begin work on your eye. Then we have instructions to install various weaponry in your arm so you can be a better security guard." Svetlana nodded along to everything and even cracked the faintest of a smile when he mentioned her firepower. "We also have instructions to create a body suit for your remaining Human parts that will grant your biological parts the same power your mechanical parts can wield."

"Good, then I will be fully complete," she said.

"Well, not fully, since there's still more. They want us to install a way to download information directly to your brain. Then, that's it. I suspect this will take us a week to ten days total."

"Yeah, it's like project 2.0," Lyd said. "Are you sure your timeline is right? We are only half a team. For something as extensive as this, we really should have our whole team."

"I know, but we've got to work with what we have. Professor Qymberkon, Syl, and the others need to focus on Norman. And you're right. That's why it'll take us over a week."

"That's longer than I expected," Svetlana said.

"I agree. I need to run this past my superiors," Gazelle said. They all turned their attention to her and she waved her hands. "Oh please, don't mind me. You have a lot to do."

"Alright, we're going to have to put you under, Svetlana," he said.

"Just don't keep me under the whole time," Svetlana replied. "I still need to reply to my messages."

"We can't keep you under for that long—your body still requires sustenance. Now, let's get to it."

Navacus handed the bottle of anesthetic to Kurjon and nodded.

*You know what to do,* he thought. *Make sure you give her enough to keep her under until tomorrow afternoon.*

---

Navacus and his small team were well into hour eight when they could finally take their first break. They had just finished fortifying Svetlana's internal support system, closed her up, and sutured the wounds with a healing gel.

"Alright, here's the plan," Navacus said with a nod. "Lyd and Kurjon, you two take your break first. Then come relieve us after about twenty or thirty minutes."

"Sounds great. I really need a snack," Lyd said as he stretched his arms above his head.

"Same here. Let's get going. We'll be back," Kurjon said with a smile and a wave.

"Hold on, you two," Gazelle said from her spot against the wall, causing them all to jump in surprise.

"Damn, I forgot you were here," Lyd said, clutching his heart.

"Ah yes, I toned down my presence to let you focus," Gazelle replied. "I would like to accompany you. I need a break myself."

"Sure, that's fine with me," Kurjon replied.

"Then let's get going," Gazelle said as she opened the door to Professor Peal's lab. Lyd and Kurjon headed into the hallway first. Before she followed, Gazelle glared at Navacus and Dea, as if to say, "don't do anything funny."

Once they were alone, Navacus breathed a sigh of relief and pushed Sterg back out.

"I thought Gazelle would never leave. She was standing so still, I thought she turned into a statue," Dea said with a laugh.

"The way she masks her presence is highly impressive," Sterg said in its deep, rumbling voice.

"Yeah, I can agree with that. But we have little time. She won't be gone for long. Sterg, watch for her presence," Navacus said, then hesitated as he looked down at Svetlana. Her blond hair was cropped short, and she let out small sounds every time she exhaled. Like this, she looked like she wouldn't harm a gnat.

"Navacus, I can assure you; we cannot save her. Not with the limited time we have," Sterg said.

"Are you sure? I know talking to her is like talking to a lifeless chatbot, but looking at her now... she just looks so peaceful."

"She is heavily sedated," Dea said, pointing out the obvious.

"Yeah, but—"

"Navacus, I know you trust me. You know why we need to do this.

She is simply too dangerous to take with us. She could report back to Lord Foxaire, and our escape would be over before it even started," Sterg said.

"Yes, of course, you are right. And we have limited time. Dea, what do you suggest we start with?" Navacus asked, fully resigning to the fact that he had to leave Svetlana behind. He vowed that if the opportunity arose, he would save her from herself.

"Her arm. We need to disassemble it anyway, right? Why not cut some wires we aren't supposed to?"

"Sounds like a plan. I don't like the idea of making her a living weapon. What we're installing is far more firepower than any security guard should ever need."

"That's because we're making a soldier," Dea said sadly, as his greenish pronosua worked at the plating on Svetlana's mechanical arm. The arms attached to the ghostly hands trailed back into Dea's underside.

"That would make sense, wouldn't it?" Navacus replied as he cut the first batch of wires. This was it—the first time he'd actively sabotaged his own work.

"I didn't mention this last night, as I didn't want to upset the others, but the entire purpose of the compound is to create a squad of enhanced individuals to join the army Lord Foxaire is building."

"An army?" Navacus asked, too stunned to finish cutting through the yellow wire. In his mind's eye, Sterg turned to him and everything fell into place. "You're right, Foxaire is building an army. Between everything I saw, or was told about in the underground, and what Professor Peal has been doing..."

"Indeed. Lord Foxaire is pulling out all the stops to make powerful soldiers to support Gnusaramnii when it returns. And the arrival of the Humans from Eklatros was the sign they needed."

"Are you referring to that prophecy I heard about? What's the deal with that?" Navacus asked.

"I don't know much about it myself; I just know that it heralds Gnusaramnii's return to the Vortex System, and ultimately the complete destruction of the system," Dea explained. "Again, the

Humans were some of the first signs, but there were other minor signs that came before, which led Lord Foxaire to purchase the compound. I may technically be your superior, but I am still just a pawn in his plans, so I am not told much. Everything I just told you is not anything I was told directly."

"I see. I just don't know why anyone would want to help Gnusaramnii return."

"That's why they wanted to use you to create mind-control devices for all of Professor Durrist's subjects. What you did with Svetlana helped ensure them that you were the one for the job."

"They really are controlling her mind then," Navacus said, his heart aching for her. If only he had known this before, then maybe things would be different. While they had been working on strengthening Svetlana's inner support, he realized it must have been the wiring they added to her brain for her eye and her ear that allowed Lord Foxaire and the others to control her.

"Right, Svetlana is part of this army now. But remember, Navacus, we are saving many more tomorrow. Between West and Norman, Peal's subjects and the Humans, we are going to deal Lord Foxaire a heavy blow. Not to mention, he'll be losing us, and his professors are some of his most valuable assets. I mean, we're making his army for him."

Navacus felt physically ill. "I can't believe I've been deceived. I mean, obviously I knew something was wrong with this place, hence the plan, but this is worse than I thought. I guess I'm glad they never asked me to go underground again."

"Right, the coming of the Humans was unexpected, and only sped up Lord Foxaire's plans for us, hence the sudden decision to move us to a different location."

"And you don't know where everyone's being moved to, right?"

Dea shook his head. "No one does. I don't even think Carl knows, and Lord Foxaire tells Carl everything. This is beyond top secret."

"I don't like the sound of that, or the thought of Svetlana being used as a soldier for Gnusaramnii. That's why I plan to save her, if I get the chance, of course."

"And I'll be there right beside you if that time comes," Dea said. "Sterg, anything yet?"

"Negative. All is clear," Sterg replied.

"Then let's see how much more we can do before Gazelle returns."

They moved on to sabotage Svetlana's left leg. About halfway though, they realized something was wrong.

"It's been too long," Sterg said, echoing his own thoughts. "They should have been back by now."

"I agree," Navacus said. "I'm going to take a peek outside."

He walked up to the door, but it wouldn't budge. He tried again just to make sure. "Hey, we're locked in here."

Dea floated to him. "It must be locked from the outside," he said as he tried to get his green pronosua tendrils under the door. After a moment, he pulled them back quickly with a sharp hiss. "Dang, that hurt. It was like an electric shock. Gazelle has sealed us in."

"Either she doesn't want us to leave, or she's doing something to Lyd and Kurjon."

"Or both," Dea suggested.

"I don't like this. Sterg, is there anything you can do to help us get out of here?"

"Unfortunately, I am not strong enough yet to influence the physical world, aside from messing with the frequencies to disrupt the camera feeds," Sterg replied. "Additionally, I sense no one else within my sphere of awareness."

"Shoot. What can we do? There's got to be *something* we can do," Navacus said as he aimlessly rushed around the room.

"Calm yourself," Dea said. "We won't get anywhere by making rash decisions. We must think about this with cool heads."

A moment later, a cold, calming sensation flowed through Navacus. "Thanks Sterg; that helps. Now, let's see if we can figure something out."

*Please be okay*, Navacus thought as he took a deep breath. *If Gazelle does anything to either of you, I'm going to lose it.*

Lyd's attention was fully focused on Gazelle. He couldn't tear his eyes from her, even if he wanted to, and a small part of him did, but his senses were being completely overwhelmed. His love for Poi seemed inconsequential now that Gazelle was in his life. He now knew she was the one he had been waiting his entire life for. Screw the fact that he stood to her knees; there had been stranger interspecies couplings.

Beside him, Kurjon was pleading with him, but her words sounded like they were coming from far away. It was as if they were separated by an ocean of vast empty space.

"That's right, Lyd. Focus on me. Now, please, tell me what you're planning. Tell me—" Gazelle turned her gaze away from him and looked at Kurjon. "Would you please pipe down? You'll get your turn next."

Kurjon's frantic movements ceased as her body relaxed. "Lyd, please... you must fight her," Kurjon said with a slight slur.

Gazelle locked eyes with Lyd. His heart nearly jumped out of his chest. He was so happy that the woman he loved only wanted his attention as well.

"Tell me what's going on, Lyd."

He breathed in deep, taking in her sweet scent. He could live in that scent and be content for eternity. The combination of her natural odors and her perfumes was intoxicating.

And yet, a small part of him continued to scream at him to adhere to reason. With immense effort, he turned his head toward the lounging Kurjon. He looked in her eyes and saw her fear.

"No, focus on me, you dimwit," Gazelle said as she grabbed his head and turned it back toward as she stared at him impatiently.

"If I tell you," he said slowly at first, then picked up his pace, "then promise me you won't harm Kurjon."

"Is that all you want?" Gazelle asked as she batted her eyes.

"No, definitely not. I want to be with you, Gazelle. I want to escape from this place, just the two of us, so we can live together in peace."

Gazelle's smile got wider and wider as he spoke. Her lips parted slowly. "You want to kiss me?"

"Absolutely I do," Lyd said, his mouth watering. He swallowed. The part of him screaming inside made him look at Kurjon once more.

"Please, Lyd," Kurjon whispered softly. She sounded like she was in pain despite her relaxed posture.

"Damn women," Gazelle said as she rolled her eyes. "You really are the playboy, aren't you, to have all these beautiful women lusting for you. But I'm your sweet-pea. I'll take care of you in ways no one else can."

"My sweet-pea... You want to know what the scheme is?"

"Yes, that's what I want," Gazelle said as she leaned in closer. She put her hands on either side of him and pecked him on the lips. She pulled back slowly, her eyes closed, and as they slowly opened, her gaze pierced right to his heart. She leaned in close and whispered in his ear. "Why did you and your Harmertian buddies not check in this morning with Jakog?"

Whatever part of him wanted to resist was melting away under the intensity of his burning desire for her. "Oh, to the void with it. Now, here's the deal, my sweet-pea—"

Before he could finish, the door slammed open. Gazelle screamed in distress, and Lyd felt her sway over him recede just enough for his rational mind to kick back in.

*Damn this temptress!* he thought. *Anyone that can make me push Poi to the side cannot be trusted. Poi, I love you, and after all of this, I just want to be with you.*

*Kurjon, thank you for helping me. Now, let's see if I can help you.*

---

It had been nearly a half-hour since they'd realized they were locked in. To pass the time, Navacus finished his report and scheduled it to send to Bodeelch at twenty o'clock, as requested. Dea had been growing increasingly anxious. He needed to vacuum up Norman's attachments, and he wanted to do it sooner than later, just in case there were any additional unforeseen circumstances. Of course, that was dependent on leaving Professor Peal's lab. As for Svetlana, they had fully sabotaged everything they had planned to.

"I am sensing activity in the hallway," Sterg said.

"Really?" Navacus said as he jumped out of his chair and hurried to the door. Professor Dea was right behind him.

"Sterg, who is it?" Dea asked.

"There are four people. One is West, and he is approaching us now. The others, Carl, Bsarg, and Nijork, are on the edge of my awareness. I cannot decipher exactly what they are doing."

"Carl, West, and the other security guards?" Dea said. "Gazelle really must be up to something."

"Right. As soon as West sets us free, we need to find her," Navacus said while preparing himself for what was to come.

*Whatever happens, I just hope this doesn't jeopardize our plan for tomorrow,* he thought. *I hope Lyd and Kurjon are safe, but as you said, Sterg, this is our only opportunity. We can't let anything get in the way of our escape.*

**31**

# ESCAPE FROM ARROGANCE

Even this deep into working with them, Norman was still surprised by how fast they worked. While it took nearly the full day, his retinal scan unlocking mechanism for his attachments was completed. Now it was time to sync the wristbands to his metallic base unit, test it out, and address any potential issues.

He snapped both wristbands on and admired them. They had been thrown together, and Grasberg promised that if he had time, he would make them more visually striking, but as far as Norman was concerned, they were perfection. Each wristband could scan either of his eyes to unlock his attachments. Not only that, but they even had a special cover over the scanner to prevent accidentally unlocking anything. All he had to do to remove the cover was stare into it for seven seconds without moving or physically slide back the cover.

"You are all incredibly impressive. This is amazing. Thank you so much," Norman said in awe, turning his arms over to study the different sides of the wristbands with the aid of the ceiling lights.

Syl shrugged, but his smile revealed displayed his delight. "We're just doing our job. Thank you for being such a wonderful person to work with."

"No doubt," Professor Qymberkon said. "You really make our

work easier by staying calm and collected throughout the process. Now, let's start the syncing. This should only take a minute or two."

Professor Qymberkon gently grabbed hold of Norman's wrists one at a time and began to sync them using a specialized, unique frequency.

"Will I need to re-sync them often? And what happens if they unsync randomly at inopportune times?"

"Ideally, once synced up, they shouldn't need to be reconnected. But, as with any piece of technology, that's not completely guaranteed," Poi said. "As much as I hate to admit it, even our designs can have unforeseen flaws in them."

"That's not a problem, because again, these are amazing," Norman said.

"Just remember that the frequency we're using to sync them should be safe from outside forces," Syl explained. "That being said, if Lord Foxaire were to discover the frequency we are using, I have no doubt they could inhibit the communication between the components."

"If that's the case, we can't give them the opportunity," he replied.

"That's the spirit," Mac said. "The sync is nearly complete—seventy-four percent already."

"Great, just a few more moments," Professor Qymberkon said with pride.

Just then, there was a knock on the door. It opened with a creak, and West stuck his cowboy hat inside.

"Hey, I'm sorry to interrupt, but I'm just checking in."

"West! What a surprise," Professor Qymberkon said. "What's going on?"

"Has Gazelle been by here recently?"

"No, I haven't seen her since first thing this morning," Mac said.

West leaned his body forward to nod in approval. "What about Professor Clums, Lyd, or Kurjon?"

"Nope, and Professor Dea hasn't been by either. It's just been us all day long," Syl said.

"What's the matter? Is there a problem?" Norman asked as he used his mechanical legs to jump off the operating table.

"That's what I'm here to find out," West said.

"Swing by Professor Peal's lab then. That's where they're set up at," Professor Qymberkon said.

"Will do. Please remain calm and stay put. I'll be back with an update shortly," West said. He shut the door behind him and left the lab.

"Um, should we be concerned?" Poi asked. "What if they're in trouble?"

"I sure hope they're all okay and that it's nothing more," Professor Qymberkon said. "Let's just stay out of the way and let West handle it for now."

"I'm willing to help if the situation calls for it," Norman said.

"If it comes down to that," Syl said. "The syncing is complete. Let's just focus on running these tests."

Norman nodded and hopped back up on the operating table. He pulled his legs up so they weren't dangling and held on to the supports with his free hand. The tests went smoothly; he scanned both of his eyes with his wristbands to detach his legs. They then successfully tested it out on his vehicular attachment. A short time later, they were wrapping up for the day.

"Shouldn't West be back by now?" Poi asked nervously.

"Let's give him a few more minutes. Again, we don't want to cause any problems," Professor Qymberkon replied.

Norman tried to maintain a straight face, but he could see the worry in the Nioavellian's eyes.

*I'm all fired up*, Norman thought, nodding to himself. *This retinal scan unlocking system is fantastic and will really come in handy. I just want to use it for real now. West, you better show up soon, because if not, I'm going out there. Professor Clums and the others have done too much for me. I won't allow them to be harmed.*

———

West walked by Professor Peal's area of the underground, performing his nightly walkthrough. He smiled and sent a wordless message of hope to Newtus, Ivy, and the others. Suddenly, an unexpected noise from LSS caused him to stop in his tracks. A voice was speaking to him.

"West, this is Lord Foxaire," the deep, rumbling voice said through his speakers. It was an odd sensation and felt quite intrusive. He only assumed it was part of the feature that Navacus and the others had been forced to install. The voice continued. "I need you to head upstairs and check in with Carl. There's a security incident happening in Head Professor Yilvin's lab."

West wasn't sure how to respond, so he just spoke back. "I'll be up there on the double."

The only reply was a grunt. He didn't know if Lord Foxaire was still watching or listening, but he hurried to the elevator near Professor Clums' office. If there was something going on upstairs, he had to make sure that everyone was okay. Then he would need to process what had happened with Lord Foxaire. He was still uneased by it.

After the elevator ride, West quickly checked in with Professor Qymberkon, then hurried over to Carl, who was standing outside the closed door.

"Thanks for coming," Carl said with a curt nod. "Bsarg and Nijork will be here momentarily. In the meantime, let's head into the lab."

"Real quick, can I make sure that Professor Clums is okay? I hear he's working out of Professor Peal's lab."

Carl nodded. "Make it quick."

West tipped his hat in thanks and sped off. When he made it to the door to Professor Peal's lab, he noticed it was locked up tight. There was also a standard Electra-Block device creating a temporary electrical field. He had used many of these devices himself while in the IBHA. He just wasn't sure how Gazelle got her hands on one. Only the Intergalactic Police Department supplied them.

He turned off the Electra-Block device and unlocked the door.

Before he could open it, Dea's ethereal arms yanked it open, revealing Dea, Navacus, and Sterg's ghostly presence in the doorway.

"Thanks for setting us free," Navacus said. "How are Lyd and Kurjon? Have you seen them?"

"Not yet. I wanted to free you first," West answered as he eyed Svetlana. She was splayed open with many wires and internal structures showing. They had completely disabled her. He turned his focus back to the two anxious professors and continued. "Follow me —it's going down in Head Professor Yilvin's lab."

West waved an arm and led them down the hallway. After only a few steps, he felt Sterg's presence fade away.

"Was Yilvin swayed by Gazelle, too?" Navacus asked as he followed him.

"It's possible, but I can't say for sure. Yilvin has always been mysterious to me. His mind is often blank when it should be active," said Dea.

"What does that even mean?" Navacus asked in response.

They halted their brief conversation when they reached Yilvin's lab. They could hear Carl screaming at Gazelle inside, while Bsarg and Nijork stood outside the open door.

Bsarg approached and put an arm out. "Professors, I need you to step back for a moment and let us handle the situation. West, Carl could really use you in there."

"Of course," West said before turning back to them. "I'm sorry, but this should be over soon."

The moment he stepped through the doorway, he felt Gazelle's tendrils creep over him.

*Carl, I have your back*, West thought.

---

Navacus stood in the hallway outside Head Professor Yilvin's office. Through the open door, all he saw right now were West's and Carl's backs. Bsarg and Nijork blocked the way in, projecting an imposing presence with their thick bodies. However, the argument between

Carl and Gazelle was loud and clear. Carl was furious with Gazelle, Gazelle was doing anything she could to defend herself.

Dea leaned in close and whispered in his ear. "I can't sense much about what's going on."

"I'll see what I can find out," Navacus replied. It was an enormous risk to use Sterg around Gazelle, but he felt it was worth it. Besides, Gazelle was already in deep trouble, and Carl clearly wasn't listening to any of her excuses.

He took a deep breath and projected Sterg out. Gazelle's aura immediately turned its attention to him, and he heard her shout, but Carl and West fired back at her, not giving her a chance to be heard. He smiled at his good fortune in this calamitous situation, not to mention at their unexpected ally.

There were six people inside of Head Professor Yilvin's Lab, three of which were West, Carl, and Gazelle. He also sensed Lyd and Kurjon nearby and frowned. Gazelle's foul influence was coursing through them. Lyd was nearly drowning in her aura, but Kurjon had a much better hold on reality. She was acting like she had taken a heavy sedative, but there were no traces of medicine—only Gazelle. He was sickened, but also ecstatic that they were otherwise unharmed.

The sixth presence in the room was Head Professor Yilvin. He was simply standing in a corner of the room, watching the commotion. As Dea had mentioned, there was no mental activity. It was like Yilvin was brain-dead, as only his vital bodily functions were performing. Yilvin's complete lack of thoughts or emotions made Navacus' spine crawl. He withdrew Sterg as quickly as he could and once again hid its presence. Again, he felt Gazelle's aura track Sterg's movements. For better or for worse, Gazelle now knew his secret.

Navacus wheezed and quietly relayed what he had discovered to Dea. Dea nodded and floated away from Yilvin's office. Navacus followed, giving them a chance to speak with a little more privacy.

"What do you think is going on with Yilvin?" Navacus whispered to his floating friend.

"My best guess is that he is one of Professor Durrist's

experiments. It's like Yilvin is being used as a puppet, meaning someone can completely control his actions," Dea replied quietly.

"Yilvin is a puppet? Like, a living automaton? That only makes this place a thousand times worse."

"Agreed. It's been my fear for a long time, but Sterg confirmed everything I have been thinking. Just be thankful we have not been subjected to the same conditioning."

The sound of a projectile firing from Yilvin's lab ended their conversation. A second later, a body thumped to the ground. They rushed over to the Lakinceitian guards, who held their arms out to stop them.

"Please, stand back," Bsarg said firmly, his eyes bristling with authority.

*Damn Lakinceitians*, Navacus thought as he growled at the guards. *Sterg, what can you sense? What's going on in there now?*

---

Carl put away the small, hand-held tranquilizer gun.

"Good shot, Carl," Lord Foxaire's voice said through his ear-piece. "Now, grab a hover-cart, load her on a gyroscope, and get her here now."

Carl nodded, which was the visual cue to Lord Foxaire that he'd acknowledged the command. He then blinked his eyes, which meant he was ending their conversation, then shook his head. His body still tingled from Gazelle's lingering presence, but his feelings of desire didn't matter, only the end goal. That was the first thing that Lord Foxaire had drilled into him all those years ago.

"Will she be okay?" West asked as he bent down to examine the unconscious Nioavellian.

"She'll be just fine," Carl answered, then stepped out into the hallway. Bsarg and Nijork were effectively holding back Professors Dea and Clums.

"You two, thank you for your assistance. Now, could one of you grab a hover-cart? We need to carry Gazelle out of here."

"How are Lyd and Kurjon?" Professor Clums asked, his voice shaking with worry.

"They seem fine to me. Just give me a second, and I'll let you in to see them," Carl said. He stepped out of the way to let Nijork fetch the hover-cart. He went back inside Yilvin's lab, glanced at Lyd and Kurjon—both of whom stared back at him—then walked up to the brainless Kolythoanthaean.

"Did Gazelle get to him, too?" Kurjon asked.

Carl nodded as a smile crept over his face. He was glad his back was turned to them. It was a fitting way to cover up the truth. "Yes, it would seem so. Let me see if I can snap him out of it." Carl snapped his fingers in front of Yilvin's face, then slapped him on the cheek, knowing that both things would elicit zero reaction.

"Professor Yilvin. Professor Jaffe Yilvin, can you hear me? I need you to give me an answer."

Yilvin's eyes blinked, and his eyes lit up. He turned to face him. "Head Professor Yilvin reporting in."

"Good. Tell me, are you alright? Did Gazelle hurt you?"

Yilvin stared at him blankly for a quick second then shook his head. "I don't know. My mind is fuzzy. If you don't mind, I'd like to go take a seat. My legs are aching."

"No problem. I'll speak with you tomorrow then."

Yilvin nodded, then awkwardly moved himself out of the corner before heading into his private office.

"Feel better, Head Professor Yilvin," Kurjon said. Yilvin turned around, waved, and closed the door behind him.

"Okay, Professor Clums, you can head in," Carl called out, then turned to Lyd and Kurjon. Lyd was sitting on a small book in the center of a lab table, while Kurjon slouched in a chair. "How are you two feeling?"

"Really gross," Kurjon replied as Professor Clums rushed into the room, causing a few of his feathers to fall off and spin to the floor. Professor Dea hovered in the doorway.

"Kurjon, Lyd, I'm so glad you two are okay," Professor Clums said as he approached them.

Carl nodded to Dea, who retreated as he stepped into the hallway. "How's everything going on your end?" he asked the Eridavlos.

"Just fine, now that this is resolved," Dea replied as Nijork approached with the hover-cart. "Let me help you get Gazelle onto the cart."

"Oh, I would appreciate that," Carl replied. He always enjoyed seeing an Eridavlos use their pronosua. It was the entire reason Professor Dea held the position he did—Lord Foxaire enjoyed studying his natural talents.

As always, Dea did not disappoint. The ghostly green substance that flowed out of Dea wrapped around Gazelle, lifted her off the floor, and placed her gently on the hover-cart, before retreating back into Dea's body.

"Alright, I need to take her to Lord Foxaire. Now, listen up, everyone. Professor Clums." The chattering in the room stopped as everyone looked at him. "Please, do not speak of this incident to anyone. That includes Professor Qymberkon and any of your other assistants, Professor Clums. The events of this night are to be erased from your memories. Act as if nothing ever happened here. So please, carry on with what you were doing."

"Alright then. Professor Clums, stay with them. I'll go check in on Professor Qymberkon and the others," Dea said. "And I won't say a word about this."

"Good. West and Nijork, with me. Bsarg, it's your shift, right?"

"Yes, I'll get back to my post," the deep blue Lakinceitian said as he headed to the atrium.

He let Nijork take the hover-cart as they headed to the elevator in Professor Peal's wing so he could make it to the gyroscope bay faster.

"West, I need to ask a favor of you," Carl said when they were descending to the underground.

"What is it?" West's slightly mechanical voice replied.

"Keep an eye on Professor Clums and his team. Don't let them say anything about what happened. We can't let this situation blow up in our faces."

"I absolutely agree with that," West replied.

"Good," Carl replied as the elevator doors opened. Once they exited, he added, "I need to get back to Lord Foxaire. Check in with Sid before you head out for the night."

"Will do," West replied as he tipped his white cowboy hat forward.

Carl nodded to Nijork, and they hurried to the gyroscope bay.

*I'm finally heading back home,* Carl thought as he watched Gazelle's unconscious body rattle around on the cart. *This one caused us way too much trouble tonight. We can't allow this to happen again. We really need Professor Clums to build those mind control devices. Luckily, he and his team will be on the next shipment out of this shithole. And the sooner we're all out of here, the sooner I can get to work on my true cause.*

*Master Gnusaramnii, I will see to your return. I will be the one to lead you back to your rightful home.*

**32**

# INTERLUDE: LOCATION - OMALOHA

```
Begin Replay of NIWAT Inner Datalog
Recording C-0000670334 S-001 N-01
```

Anqi, Mikhail, and Gonth's hollers and gasps filled the cockpit as we jumped to the next solar system. Anqi sat in Zombu's chair, Gonth sat in Zanzi's chair, and Mikhail sat in my chair. I disengaged the electromagnetic grips on my soles and detached from the floor.

"It's really quite something, isn't it?" I said.

"That blew my mind," Anqi said slowly. "I know you warned me... but damn, that was seriously mind-blowing."

"I am overwhelmed," Gonth said as he wiped a tear from his eye. "That was almost beyond comprehension, even for an elf like me."

"Then a knight like me has better comprehension than an elf like you," Mikhail quipped back. "We saw the divine one's true powers."

"Uh-huh. And you worship the *porcupine* god, right?" Gonth replied.

As the Eklatros humans bickered, I turned my attention to the planet we hovered above. Its atmosphere was saturated with smoke, which obscured the surface. The atmosphere also was littered with debris.

"*Francentia*, can you detect any life?" Maker Denorad asked.

"I sense a small cluster of life in a mountainous valley on the equator," *Francentia* replied.

"Wow, really? Your ship is smart!" Anqi said, excited.

"I am more than a ship, but I appreciate the compliment," *Francentia* replied.

"Don't get her started," Maker Denorad said with an eye roll. "Can you take us there? Is it even worth scanning for security measures first?"

"No, that would not be necessary. The only life I sense is in that valley," *Francentia* replied.

Zanzi and Zombu's faces popped into the right side of my screen.

"Hey, how did the humans react? Can you send us a recording?" Zombu asked.

"Yeah, send us the recording," Zanzi said. "It's so boring back here. Watching it on my internal screen is just not the same. Remember, I need to keep an eye on them."

"Oh, they enjoyed it. And it's nothing that impressive, but okay," I replied.

"Who are you talking to?" Gonth asked.

"Just Zanzi and Zombu. They're in their bunks, so they are video chatting with me," I replied as I sent them the video clip.

"I still don't fully understand how that works, but gotcha," Anqi replied with a grin and a finger gun.

"Trajectory found for safe travel into the planet's atmosphere," *Francentia* announced.

"Niwat, prepare for our descent into the atmosphere," Blu-Dreem said without looking at me. His focus was completely on the consoles.

"Right, buckle up," Maker Denorad said as he turned back to Anqi. "There's still even more to see."

"Oh, I'm ready," Anqi said. "This is why I left. I needed an adventure like this."

"I'm glad you've been enjoying yourself. Now, *Francentia*, start your dive."

"Hang on tight," I said to Zombu and Zanzi as I re-secured my electromagnetic locks.

"We're still strapped down," Zanzi complained. "We can't go anywhere."

As *Francentia* entered the upper atmosphere, the dark, ashen smoke immersed the ship.

"It's almost as if the entire planet was on fire," Maker Denorad said quietly.

"Hopefully it's not still on fire," Anqi replied.

"There are several isolated areas that are burning, but nothing near where we are headed," Blu-Dreem said.

We broke free from the smoke several minutes later. The valley we approached was surrounded by towering mountain peaks. A steady stream of gray-white ash fell from the sky, adding to the blankets that covered everything in sight, except for one clearly marked path.

*Francentia* set down near the path with a soft thud.

"Are we going out there?" Anqi asked. "Is the air breathable?"

"I'm not sure. We'll need to take filtration masks, considering all the ash in the air," Maker Denorad said as he stood up and stretched, his body popping in several places.

"Good point. I'd rather not get cancer," Gonth said with a grin.

---

Begin Replay of NIWAT Inner Datalog
Recording C-0000670334 S-002 N-03

"Alright, everyone," Maker Denorad said once they had disembarked from *Francentia*. He pointed toward the middle of the valley. "*Francentia* said that she sensed life in this direction. As always, we should use caution. We have no idea what to expect."

*Francentia*'s robotic voice chimed out of the ship's speakers. "Alert. Gnusar detected directly underground. They are functioning at limited capacity."

"Maybe they're hibernating, like on Eklatros," Mikhail said as he fiddled with his breathing mask. He had left his helmet behind; it was the only way the mask would work.

"That's right, I remember Vesten saying that. We saw something similar on a different planet, before we got to yours. And cut it out, Mikhail, you'll mess up the seal," Maker Denorad said. "*Francentia, are they a threat?*"

"There is a four percent chance of an attack," *Francentia* replied.

"Almost no chance at all then," Blu-Dreem said. "Even so, are you sure I can't stay with *Francentia*?"

"She'll be fine on her own. Besides, remember what Tanaq Farag said? She thinks you're important, so having you around could be beneficial," I replied.

"Yeah, maybe you're the good luck charm we need so we don't get attacked," Zanzi said.

"Where's the threat?" Mikhail asked as he drew his sword.

"There won't be one. Right, *Francentia*?" Maker Denorad asked.

"Unknown," the ship replied. "The life on the valley's surface are not Gnusar, but they have strong signals. There are sixteen presences, but likely, there are quadruple that amount. My readings indicate they are strong in the magical arts, even stronger than Mikhail and Gonth combined."

"If you weren't our mode of transportation, I would show you how strong I am," Gonth replied as he took out a leather-bound book from his vest's inner pocket.

"That's not necessary. We need to be cautious, not start a ruckus," Zanzi said.

"Right, let's proceed," Maker Denorad ordered.

I followed Maker Denorad as the eight of us made our way through the ashen valley. The path we were on was covered in a fine layer of ash, ensuring we left footprints. However, the steady stream of ashen rain would cover them in no time. The ash was unrelenting —it was even messing with my joints.

After a few minutes, we came across a campsite. Seven tents of various sizes surrounded a fire-pit, which was still burning. The plastic tents were covered in ash, indicating they had been here for a while. We wordlessly approached the fire and surrounded it, almost like a mystical power was drawing us in.

"I know this is an alien planet, but this fire isn't what's causing all the ash, right?" Anqi asked.

"No, of course not. Look at the mountains. I can clearly see scorching, even on the summits of the tallest peaks. A massive firestorm must have engulfed the entire planet," Zanzi replied.

"I mean, I can kinda make that out, but it's really hard to see—what with all the ash and my non-robotic eyeballs," Anqi replied.

"Ah, my apologies. I forget you are not enhanced, as even Maker Denorad has upgraded from his original eyes," Zanzi said.

"Oh-ho! So, what does it say that even one without eyes can clearly see the burn marks?" said an unfamiliar voice.

I used my senses to find the source. Standing in front of the smallest tent was a peculiar pair of creatures. One was bipedal, with brownish skin, large floppy ears, and a long hose-like nose. It only had pockets where its eyes should have been and wore a deep blue cloak. Standing to its right was a quadrupedal beast with thick black-and-red-striped fur and three long, skinny tails. It had a mane of brown hair and black whiskers, a pink nose, and large, greenish-yellowish eyes.

"Everyone, we are being surrounded," Mikhail said as he drew his sword. "We must prepare for conflict."

"Why did we walk into the center of this campsite again?" Zanzi asked.

Around us, several other creatures had stepped out of the tents. There were two more pairs of creatures like the one that had spoken. Each of the bipedal creatures looked nearly the same, except one had no ears. The quadrupedal beasts accompanying these creatures were taller than the red and black one, and each had their own coloring—one was yellow and green and the other was purple and gray. Coming out of the largest tent were a dozen of short bipedal reptiles that had dark green scales and long, thin tongues that flicked out of their mouths randomly.

"There is no need for violence, Mikhail, but I know you are now even more on edge. Especially you, Zanzi," the creature replied.

"What the fuck? Who are you? How do you know who we are?" Anqi cried as she drew two throwing stars.

"Oh-ho! That could have gone better, couldn't it? You'd think those that can see the future like ourselves would have more tact, right?" the creature asked.

"Hold on. You can see the future?" Maker Denorad said as he stepped forward.

"Indeed we can, Denorad. But please, allow us to introduce ourselves. My name is Tiresias, and this is my temporary familiar, Noiyanit. And if you can't tell, I'm blind."

"It's nice to make your acquaintances," the red-and-black-striped beast, Noiyanit, said with a slight bow.

The purple and gray beast that stood beside the earless creature bowed. "Hello, I'm Ledjo. My familiar is Mosi. She's deaf, but don't worry, she can follow everything that is going on. And, for the most part, I speak for her."

"And I am Yai'rah," the yellow-and-green-striped beast said. "My familiar is Baroine. He is mute, so I must speak for him."

"Over here! We are the Kirbitas," one of the small reptilian creatures said, stepping forward. "My name is Raza, and we all are pleased to meet you. We've been waiting for your arrival."

"But how? This is the second time in a row now that our coming was foreseen, and yet we never have any idea where we are going," Maker Denorad said. "How can you know where we'll be when we don't even know?"

"Come, Denorad," Tiresias said as Noiyanit led her toward them. "Let's take a seat and I will explain everything."

---

```
Begin Replay of NIWAT Inner Datalog
Recording C-0000670335 S-001 N-03
```

We gathered around the fire as Tiresias spoke.

"Let's start from the beginning, shall we? All of us—the Kirbita, Ligthera, and Propoli—come from different planets in the same solar system that's in a completely different galaxy than the one we're in."

"I know it might not help, but what galaxy are we even in?" Blu-Dreem asked.

"We do not give names to galaxies, as there are simply too many. But we are in a different one than you started in."

"How is that possible? We're following something called the Gnusar, and this is only our fifth stop since we left our home planet. We couldn't have jumped far enough to make it to another galaxy," I said.

"I know you have many questions, but please, allow me to first tell my story," Tiresias said with a hand on Noiyanit's back as the familiar sat beside her. "Now, while we don't give names to galaxies, we gave a name to the solar system we are from. It is a simple name —the Magicks System. We call it so because it is where all magical power in the universe originated, including the Ekataramn."

"Wow, really?" Anqi said. "So, they really are aliens, just like Vesten said."

"So, my home is an alien tree?" Gonth asked.

"It's a bit complicated on that matter," Tiresias said. "Now, back to the story. I am a Propoli, and ever since we can remember, we have bonded with the Ligthera. It is believed that the Ligthera were once Light Beings—divine spirits of awesome power—that took physical forms. As for the Kirbita, they come from their own planet in the Magicks Solar System—the planet where the Ekataramn also originate from. Their species are the ones who tend to the Great Ones. They help raise the saplings and ensure the fully matured ones are well taken care of."

Tiresias cleared her throat and continued. "A very long time ago, well before any of us were born, there was an incident of immense proportions. The Kirbita were experimenting with the Ekataramn's ability to levitate above the ground they're rooted to. While there are many versions of this story, I believe the Kirbita put too much magical energy into the Ekataramn, causing it to float into outer space. It was many hundreds of years later when we realized the significance of the Ekataramn that traveled through the stars.

"Before I go any further, I must explain something about my species. We are soothsayers; we can see into the future using a technique unique to our skill sets. As for myself, I can read the future from the sounds of the fire, the odor of the smoke, and from the energy it produces. That's why I always have a fire nearby. Also, if you haven't noticed, all Propoli are born with some kind of disability which allows us to better focus on our visions. When we are young, we bond with a Ligthera, to the point where I can feel when my Ligthera companion steps on a sharp rock. However, Noiyanit is not my true familiar, and I will explain more about that later."

Tiresias scratched Noiyanit's chin. "One more thing you must know about my species is that, at times, we can leave our bodies and travel to different worlds. I've spent time on many planets, interacting with many different species for years at a time, only to come back into my body mere seconds after leaving it. So, we live far longer than our physical bodies show. We can also be reborn at any time in any place, as to us, time is not fixed.

"Now, on one fateful occasion, I was reborn as a Lakinceitian, a slug-like species. I helped support my friend at the time, Gnusar, in his quest to leave his home planet, and I was lucky enough to be among those that Gnusar took with him. Another notable companion of ours was called Mau. About a year into Gnusar's journey through the vastness of space, we discovered an asteroid with mysterious properties. It contained a divine power—a power Gnusar had been searching for. So, we directed the asteroid to crash into a small planet, and we discovered a large seed hidden deep inside it. We planted that seed and it became a giant tree. It communicated with us, telling us about its journey and how it had to cocoon itself to keep itself alive. After we saved it, this tree performed one final task before it died, and that task was to create seven new Ekataramn.

"So, Gonth, Yttendaus was born of this original Ekataramn; it's technically not an alien, as it was born on Eklatros."

"Ajenti—the mighty Ajenti University—is that original Ekataramn. It must be," Mikhail said as he looked at Tiresias with a sense of wonder.

"That is correct. Now, I should clarify that Gnusar, myself, and the other Lakinceitians lived alongside these young, budding Ekataramn for a long time. Much like the Kirbita back in the Magicks System, we helped protect them from the natural elements, animals, and the humans who had arrived after we did. We allowed the Ekataramn to grow into what they needed to be. And, in turn, the Ekataramn helped Gnusar become Gnusaramnii. As the Ekataramn grew, Gnusar evolved as he absorbed their power, and it slowly became Gnusaramnii.

"As for the non-immortals, we started to die off. Not only that, but one of our own, Mau, rebelled against Gnusaramnii. In response, Gnusaramnii did everything it could to hunt down and kill Mau. However, Mau was able to allude Gnusaramnii and survived. Shortly after Gnusaramnii gave up its chase, Gnusaramnii left Eklatros for its neighboring planet, where it built its next home while it allowed the Ekataramn to fully mature."

"Are you really telling us that Gnusaramnii raised the Ekataramn, and the Ekataramn made Gnusaramnii?" Gonth said with a horrified look on his face.

"I am, because that is fact," Tiresias said. "All is one, and one is all. Everything is interconnected. After I re-awoke into my true body, only then could I fully comprehend the magnitude of what I helped Gnusaramnii do. For as I said, we can be reborn at any time, and the Propoli and Ligthera already had Gnusaramnii on their radar. And so, I began my journey to find Gnusaramnii. Baroine, Yai'rah, Mosi, and Ledjo have accompanied me from the beginning, as did Mahki, my true familiar."

"What happened to Mahki?" Blu-Dreem asked.

"He was taken from me by one of Gnusaramnii's most vile henchmen—a dark wizard from an even darker corner of the universe. I dare not speak their name, for this dark wizard's power is beyond anything I have ever witnessed before. And all it wants is for Gnusaramnii to complete its goal.

"However, that's beside the point. The six of us have been tracking Gnusaramnii, and through our visions, we have learned of your journey, Denorad. We're here to guide you to your next destination."

"That's great, but earlier you said something about how we're in a different galaxy from Theronior's," Maker Denorad pressed. "How is that possible?"

"Right, thanks for reminding me of that point," Tiresias said with a nod as Noiyanit leaned against her. "After you left Theronior, you found a powerful battery. Is that correct?"

"What? Yeah, we found a battery. How did you know that?" Zanzi asked.

"Because Baroine made that battery. Well, not Baroine as you see him now, but as a citizen of that planet before it was overrun by Gnusaramnii. We knew you were coming, and we knew you would find that battery. That battery is the reason you have been jumping so far through space."

"But then, how does Gnusaramnii travel those distances?" Gonth asked. "This is making my head hurt."

"Gnusaramnii has various means to travel. One is using the dark wizard I mentioned, but that entity is still slumbering. We have been keeping a close eye on it, as we believe it will awaken soon, and no matter what we do, we will not be prepared for that day. So, in the meantime, I suspect Gnusaramnii must be using its own personal spacecraft."

"But if Gnusaramnii had a spacecraft, why didn't it use it to attack Eklatros?" Anqi asked.

"Gnusaramnii does not want to harm Eklatros. Remember, it helped raise the Ekataramn. It now needs them to complete its ultimate goal, but it knows it cannot do it alone. It needs a key. Your friend, Ànifa, was that key," Tiresias explained.

"But she died. Does that mean Gnusaramnii can't complete its mission? There's still one more Ekataramn that needs to be awoken, right?" Anqi asked.

"That's what Vesten told me," Mikhail replied.

"Again, that's complicated. As I said earlier, time is not fixed. Even though we can see into the future, there is always a possibility that future will never happen, at least not in our timeline, which goes down a whole other rabbit hole I don't need to get into."

"So, even though your methods aren't an exact science, you still created that battery and waited for us on this charred planet. Where are we anyway?" Maker Denorad asked after a few moments of silence.

"This planet's name is Omaloha. This name was given to it by the local species—Kolythoanthaeans," Tiresias said.

"And did all the locals die?" Mikhail asked.

"Almost completely," Tiresias said with her trunk to the ground. "We only found one survivor. He is resting now, but we'd like you to speak with him once he is up for it. He's currently resting in our ship, as he's been sick from the ash."

"What ship?" I asked, looking around. "I don't see anything, and *Francentia* didn't see any ships on her scans."

"That's because our ship is not made from metal, but stone. See that large boulder? We have several rooms set up in there, and we use our magic to continuously build up the exterior so we can continue going in and out of various atmospheres, as rocks are extremely common."

"Using rocks to fly through space? Now that's something I never even considered," Blu-Dreem said.

"We've found it works best for us, as it has allowed us to remain undetected from the Gnusar."

"They're slumbering beneath our feet, right?" Zanzi asked.

"Yes, they are hibernating. All Gnusar enter this state after a planet is taken over so they can wait for Gnusaramnii's master plan to be enacted."

"I wish we could do something about it," Gonth said. "I don't like the idea of Gnusar crawling around here."

"And why is that?" Tiresias asked. "They are not inherently evil. They only follow Gnusaramnii's will, but if not for that, they would be just like you or me."

"Right, that makes sense," Anqi said. "I mean, Eric Mason, a friend of Vesten's, befriended a Gnusar, and now he's an advocate for Gnusar rights."

"How intriguing. I've never heard of someone befriending a Gnusar before," Tiresias said thoughtfully.

"Yeah, well, he traveled around with this Gnusar and some real weirdos for a while, and that journey really changed him, from what I hear," Anqi replied. "I only met Eric once myself, very briefly... kinda like how I only met Ànifa for a few brief moments."

"And now you've been swept into the current," Tiresias said. "Everyone is always where they are meant to be. Whether or not you believe it, destiny has a ring of truth to it. The way time works is truly mysterious."

"Right, you mentioned time is not linear—can you explain that more?" I asked, my interest piqued. To me, time was linear; otherwise, all my internal systems couldn't run properly.

Tiresias echoed his thoughts. "As a sentient machine—for all intents and purposes, I mean no disrespect—I fully understand how you would see time as strictly linear. But, being a product of science, you must know that gravity affects how time flows."

"Yes, of course," Maker Denorad chimed in. "I programmed all my androbotix to automatically adjust to the changes in gravity and the flow of time. Otherwise, space travel could really mess up their internal systems."

"And only one as brilliant as yourself could do something like that," Tiresias said as she scratched Noiyanit behind the ears. Noiyanit's face grew content as she relaxed. "However, let me take it one step further. Time flows in the fourth dimension, and yet our ability to awaken into other bodies across time and space does not adhere to the fourth dimension. We use the higher dimensions to travel to where we need to be. Of course, we don't have control over where we are going, we just go with the flow. And yet, space itself has its own ways of distorting and warping time. That means, from the start of our conversation to now, in a distant corner of space, an entire star system could have been born and died.

"Now, we have no way of knowing how this time distortion truly works. We just know it's dictated by the Universal Consciousness, the entity that oversees everything. Only the Universal Consciousness has the power to warp time in large swaths of the universe."

"This is getting a bit much for me, I must admit," Anqi said as she clutched her head.

"Ah yes, my apologies," Tiresias said. "Let us enjoy the meal Baroine and Mosi prepared, then we'll visit with Jurhon."

***

```
Begin Replay of NIWAT Inner Datalog
Recording C-0000670335 S-002 N-01
```

The interior of Tiresias' nameless rock ship was quite humble. The walls, floors, and ceiling were all carved out of rock, and everything was perfectly smooth. Most of the furniture, including the tables, chairs, shelves, and beds were also carved from the asteroid. At various points along the floor, walls, and ceiling were handholds that must allow them to travel through the ship in zero-gravity. It made sense that a ship like this didn't have gravity stabilizers on it, as there was no technology in sight. Tiresias explained everything was done through magic, from lifting the ship into space to keeping a stable, livable atmosphere and temperature. The air levels were controlled by a wide variety of plants that had increased oxygen outputs.

After the tour, Tiresias led us to a room she did not show us earlier. In the room was a pale gray humanoid. He was tall, skinny, and had six fingers on each hand. He wore a mask over his mouth and plain brown robes. When we arrived, Jurhon sat up and introduced himself, and after the introductions were through, he explained how Omaloha got to be in such a sorry state.

"You must first understand the history of my species' time on this planet," Jurhon said with a raspy voice. He coughed and continued. "We Kolythoanthaeans did not originate from this planet. We arrived ages ago and terraformed it to suit our needs. Also, this was only the second planet that the Kolythoanthaeans ever terraformed. We know this from the detailed archives our forebears left behind.

"When I was born, it was well into the age that the Kolythoanthaeans knew the terraforming had gone wrong and had set up a rigorous process to manage it. This process used few resources, so we could keep it running indefinitely. Most of my kind had grown complacent and thought it would protect us forever. However, the Gnusar had other plans. When they arrived, they destroyed the facilities that kept our atmosphere and water supply in check. Once those shut down, the fires began. Omaloha was engulfed in fire for nearly a full month. I only survived with the support of other people, all of whom have passed on now. I alone remain to tell the tale."

"I can't even imagine what you went through," Anqi said with tears in her eyes. "I applaud you for your courage."

Jurhon coughed before he replied. "Thank you, I appreciate that."

"I'm curious about what you said regarding how you arrived on this planet," Maker Denorad said. "I ask because my culture has a similar story of how we arrived from the stars. I honestly never gave it a second thought until this trip."

"Are you a human?"

"Yeah, I'm human," Maker Denorad replied.

"So are we," Anqi said for her Eklatros crew.

"I'm an elf, by the way," Gonth chimed in.

Jurhon coughed then nodded. "I understand now. I have never seen a human before today. It is said that our species arrived as part of a space race with another species called the humans."

"Do you know where the space race originated?" I asked.

"The archives don't give it a true name, it is only referred to as home or other similar terms," Jurhon replied.

"I was a human once," Tiresias said. "It was quite a peculiar time in my life."

"So you've said before," Jurhon said, then looked at us. "As for you all, I am happy you are finally here. Now I can get off this horrible place—that is, if you'll take me with you."

"Oh no, we already took on three people. I don't know if *Francentia* can hold anymore. We're quite packed in as it is," Zanzi said.

"While that is true, we can make *Francentia* expand," Maker Denorad said. "She was always capable of becoming a larger ship."

"That makes a lot of sense, actually," Blu-Dreem said. "I've always wondered about the function of certain parts, but they must be to facilitate that expansion."

"Correct," Maker Denorad said, then called up *Francentia* and gave her the order to expand the ship.

"It should take about twelve cycles to complete," Maker Denorad said.

"Wonderful news," Tiresias said. "If that's the case, and if you don't mind, can you take two more? They're small—two of the Kirbita you met earlier."

"What are we, a public transit system now?" Zanzi asked.

"Zanzi, don't be rude," Maker Denorad snapped back. "We'll take as many as it takes to gets us to our destination. What are their roles here?"

"Great, thank you for agreeing. The Kirbita are our helpers. They help us clean up after the Gnusar, and they manage the tasks around the campsite. Now, Raza and Raff already met Kingau, the one you'll meet at your next destination," Tiresias said.

"Oh right, you said you'd help lead us to our next system. How is that going to work?" Maker Denorad asked.

"Again, your battery," Tiresias answered. "It was programmed to direct your ship onto a specific path. Your next destination is the last one we programmed in."

"So, the next destination is where Gnusaramnii is from? I wasn't expecting to get there so soon—not that I'm complaining or anything like that," Mikhail said as he waved his hands in front of him.

"No, fair knight," Tiresias said. "However, orbiting the planet called Thorpi is a gate, one that has been kept hidden from Gnusaramnii for centuries. It will allow you all to pass into the Vortex Solar System. It is one of the last existing routes into the system."

"And you're keeping it open for us?" I asked. "Why are we so important?"

"Because you will bring many needed gifts into the Vortex when you arrive," Tiresias replied, absentmindedly scratching Noiyanit's back. "We know little more than that, as the future is uncertain. We just know that you're needed there."

"How did we get caught up in this mess?" Zanzi asked as he placed a hand on his forehead.

"Fate often chooses those that have no desire for the challenges ahead of them," Tiresias said, then looked directly at me. "Especially you, Navacus Clums." I had no idea why she called me that.

---

Begin Replay of NIWAT Inner Datalog
Recording C-0000670335 S-005 N-01

I stepped into *Francentia's* expanded cockpit. Before, there were only five seats in the cockpit, and now there were nine, allowing all of us to fit snugly. Each of us had our own seat, except for Raza and Raff, who were strapping in with me.

"Thank you again for letting us into the cockpit with everyone," Raff, the male Kirbita, said. He had a dark blue stripe running down his back to indicate his gender, while Raza, the female, didn't have any stripes.

"It wouldn't be fair to leave you two alone in the interior," I said. "Besides, it's always a treat to show newcomers space travel."

"Yeah, this I am dying to see," Raza said as she bounced in her seat. "You can't see a dang thing through all that rock in the other vessel."

"Are you sure we're going where you think we're headed?" Zanzi asked.

"We are certain of it," Raff replied. "We may not have the same abilities as the Propoli or the Ligthera, but we have our own magical talents. And we trust Tiresias and the others."

"Who is this Kingau that we are meeting with, anyway?" I asked. "Are they someone like you or your companions?"

"No, Kingau is a Harmertian. She's even shorter than us," Raza said. "You'll meet her soon enough."

"Alright *Francentia*, take us out to our next jump point," Maker Denorad said. "Thorpi, here we come."

**33**

# ESCAPE FROM COMMAND

Carl yawned and used his coffee mug to cover his mouth, and then he took a sip of his hot, bitter drink. He had been forced to stay up later than he would have liked. He didn't sleep well and really needed the caffeine today. There was no room for any residual drowsiness—he had to be sharp and alert. That's why he continued to stand behind his chair while Sid and Gazelle sat at theirs.

The room they were in was small, so it was a tight fit. Lord Foxaire took up nearly all the available space, but it didn't matter as their attention was focused on the wall of screens in front of them. They displayed live video feeds from across the compound, both upstairs and downstairs. All three of the main screens were tuned to the underground laboratory. One was focused on the Titan's enclosure, another was focused on the areas where the Humans were being kept, and the third of the largest screens showed the hangar bay. There were three ships in the hangar, and they were each being prepared to house a Titan. Everyone else they were transporting would be divided between the remaining containment cells on each of the ships.

Carl noted that while the bounty hunters, the Lakinceitian guards, and all of Sid's Cyclones were at their posts, West and

Gnudashar were still nowhere to be found. He shook his head and turned to Lord Foxaire as he chewed out Gazelle.

"You put our entire operation in jeopardy, and you completely betrayed my trust," Lord Foxaire was saying. "Your actions may have dire consequences, and I will deal with you accordingly when those take place."

"I'm so sorry, my lord, I really am," Gazelle pleaded to her master. "But believe me, I sensed a foreign presence with Professor Clums. He is not to be trusted."

"I trust Professor Clums more than I trust you at the moment, because I can at least trust him to do his job. At least, I could, until you intervened. Who's to say what's on his mind now?"

"My lord—"

"Save it, Gazelle. I don't want to hear another word from you. Just sit there and be quiet," Lord Foxaire said, then turned his attention to Carl. "How's everything looking?"

"Fine, my lord," he said. "Gnudashar just arrived, and from what it looks like, all three spaceships are just about ready to be loaded. However, West Kilinder is absent."

"I see. Can we use the newly installed monitoring system to see where he is? Or his remote-control function?" Lord Foxaire asked.

"Let's see," Carl said as he sat in his chair. He took another sip, set his coffee mug next to his console, then booted up the program that controlled West.

"Alright, here it goes. Let's see if this works," Carl said as he pressed the button to activate the monitoring device.

He stared at the black screen for several long seconds.

"It doesn't seem to be working," he said as he tried again and the black screen remained.

"Last night I spoke to him through LSS—can we try that?" Lord Foxaire asked.

"No—the monitoring system needs to work in order to give him commands."

Lord Foxaire grumbled. "Well, it was working last night. Just keep an eye out for him and let me know when you see him. Sid, ask Professor Durrist to start sedating the three Titans."

"Shouldn't we wait for West?" Carl asked. "His relationship with Theesakin could be incredibly useful."

"It would be if he were here. He'll certainly be reprimanded for this, yet we cannot delay. I do not have time for technical issues. Sid, give the order."

"Very good, my lord," Sid said.

Carl took a sip of his coffee and let out a deep breath. Now was the moment he had been waiting all morning for. He spun around in his chair and faced his protector. "My lord, forgive me, but I must ask you a question."

"Go ahead, Carl."

"Why am I not in the hangar? I am your eyes and ears. I could take control if something went wrong, especially since West is still missing."

"I appreciate that, but I need you here with me. As important as today is, I cannot allow myself to be left alone. I need someone by my side at all times, and you are the one I trust the most," Lord Foxaire answered.

"I understand, my lord," he replied.

"If something does turn sour, I'll send Sid into the field. As for you, Gazelle, only if the situation gets completely out of hand will I ask you to go. But it will be the last resort."

Gazelle nodded in agreement. Carl smiled to himself—she was wise enough to remain silent, even after Lord Foxaire's wrath was no longer directed at her.

"Sid, Carl, keep an eye on the front door to the compound and for that ex-bounty hunter. We also need to ensure that Professor Clums and the others remain on task. I will continue to focus on the Titans."

Carl nodded, then glanced at the large screen. He watched as a dozen Lakinceitian drones shot Zadgarcolth with a specialized tranquilizer. Zadgarcolth lashed out at the drones, slamming three of them against the wall and stomping on two more before crashing to the ground and crushing two more drones.

*What a monster. I'm sure they'll enjoy their new larger cells—they certainly need the extra space.*

Carl turned his gaze to the compound doors where one of Sid's Cyclones stood at attention. This one was a brunette female Human that looked far more alert than he felt.

*At least she looks to be fully awake*, Carl thought as he took a sip of his coffee. *I just need more caffeine, then I'll be on her level.*

---

Lyd approached the door and quietly performed his secret knock. A few moments later, Mac opened the door and ushered him in.

"Thanks for getting here so early," Mac whispered. "I still need to get ready, but Poi should be just finishing up."

"Sure, no problem," he said with a nod and a smile. When he noticed Mac looking at him, he smiled even wider. "Today's the day we finally escape from this place."

"Aye, I just hope we all make it," Mac said as he placed a hand on his shoulder. Lyd placed a hand on Mac's shoulder in response.

"We will make it, my brother. I have faith in Professor Clums' plan."

Mac smiled and broke away as Poi stepped out of the bathroom. It didn't matter that it was still over an hour before dawn—Poi still managed to look absolutely radiant. Her bold red shirt and white pants blended perfectly with her orange eyes, which were glowing with excitement.

Mac nodded to his sister, then turned back to Lyd. "I'll be right out," Mac said as he stepped into the bathroom and shut the door.

A moment later, Poi was in his arms. He squeezed her for a few long moments before breaking away.

"Are you okay?" Poi asked. "How are you after what happened last night?"

"Oh, right," he replied slowly. He had nearly forgotten about the private message he had sent Poi when he got back to his room. He scratched his right arm and quietly continued. "I'm not really sure.

It's hard to describe, but it felt like Gazelle poured herself into my mind and my body. She was making me think thoughts that were not my own, but that I firmly believed in at the time. I... I just don't know, Poi. I just want to get through today, and once we're safe, I'll be able to better process everything."

Poi gave him a peck on the cheek. "Always the tough guy, aren't you?" she smiled, then yawned. "I'm exhausted. I didn't sleep well last night. I was far too excited."

"You look just fine to me—you're just as beautiful as you always are," he replied.

"Oh, you," Poi said as she leaned against him. Lyd wrapped an arm around her and closed his eyes. A moment later, Mac unlatched the door and they quickly stepped away from each other.

"Alright, are we all ready?" Mac asked as he nervously rubbed his hands together.

"Are you ready?" Poi asked with a raised eyebrow. "Don't tell us you're going to wimp out now."

"Nothing of the sort," Mac replied with a nervous laugh. "I mean, it's not like I have much of a choice, anyway. If we're to succeed, we all need to pull our weight, right?"

"Right. Now, we're meeting Professor Dea behind the barracks?" Lyd asked.

"Yeah," Poi said with a nod, then looked him in the eye. "Let's do this."

*I love you, Poi,* Lyd thought as he returned her smile. *Once this is all over, we can finally be together. Because I do love you. I want nothing to do with Gazelle.*

---

Navacus lay in his soft bed and watched several of his feathers float to the floor. Fumalli quietly snored beside him, causing the bed to shake lightly. In contrast, Navacus was wide awake and his mind was buzzing.

*"Sterg, what in the void happened? Did Tiresias really look me in the eye and speak directly to me? How is that even possible?"*

*"Tiresias may have sensed us. She is one of the most divine souls in the entire universe. All my fellow Light Beings deeply revere her. That is why she can have a temporary familiar. Most Propoli or Ligthera that lose their familiar can never bond with another again."*

*"That's great and all, but I'm still quite freaked out over here. I was absolutely not expecting that. Also, what's with the dreams basically two nights in a row now? What does that even mean?"*

*"That things are continuing to accelerate. Today is a good example of that."*

*"Sterg... is everything that Tiresias said true? Are they really paving Francentia's way through the cosmos?"*

*"They are, and Francentia will be here before you know it; of that I am certain. And you now hold knowledge that will be of dire importance soon."*

*"You mean how those Ekataramn things basically brought Gnusaramnii into existence?"*

*"Indeed."*

Fumalli snorted loudly in his sleep, interrupting Navacus' silent conversation. He looked at his slumbering friend. It was still dark and Fumalli's dark blue skin made him hard to see, but he could make out his features.

*This is the last time we'll be together in this specific bed. Give me a few more moments, and then I'll wake him up. I just want to savor this moment for as long as I can. This peaceful and humble moment before the thrill of the day begins.*

Navacus took a sip of his hot tea while Fumalli rushed around the kitchen to prepare a quick breakfast.

"You know Syl and Norman will be here soon, right?" Navacus whispered.

"I do," Fumalli replied, his voice full of stress. "That's why I'm trying to prepare something. We need to have enough energy to get through today."

"I appreciate that. What are you making?"

"Your favorite—toast and salted fish," Fumalli said as he opened the can of fish.

"Oh, I can smell it now!" Navacus replied, his mouth watering. "You're the best, Fumi. I don't know what I'd do without you."

"You wouldn't eat as well, that's for sure," Fumalli replied with a smile. He got quiet for a moment before he continued. "Hey Nava, if something happens, and I don't make it, please tell my parents that—"

"Tell them yourself, Fumi. I know they've been hard on you, but believe me, you will be fine. You'll speak with them again. I mean, we have Sterg with us, plus West, Norman, Dea, and our entire team—what could go wrong?" he said, partially to reassure himself. There were a plethora of things that could go wrong today, but Navacus couldn't focus on that. He needed to focus on visualizing their escape.

There was a soft knock at the door and Navacus quickly opened it. He wordlessly greeted Syl and Norman and invited them inside. The four of them ate a quick breakfast and drank some tea in the few minutes they had to spare. Once everyone was finished, he saw Fumalli eying his favorite kitchen knife.

"Hey, Fumi, bring it along. We don't have any weapons, so that will need to do," he told his best friend.

"I was thinking it could be useful. Do you want to take yours?"

"Might as well," Navacus said as he took his knife out of the holder and wrapped it in a hand towel. He handed Fumalli a towel, and they soon had both knives safely tucked away in their lab coats. He turned to Norman and Syl. "I'm sorry we don't have any extra knives."

"That's fine," Syl said. "If we can swing by the lab real quick, I have something I can grab."

"I'm ready," Norman said with a firm nod. He was wearing his treads, having swapped out his legs with Dea last night. "Let's do this thing. I want to reunite with Kate and get the void off this planet."

It wasn't much longer before they were headed out the door.

Navacus stood in the hallway with his hand on the doorknob, taking one last look at their apartment.

"Ready, Nava?" Fumalli whispered as he looked back at him.

"You know, it's strange. I think I'll miss our apartment. It was quite cozy," he whispered back.

"I'm sure we can find a nice apartment on a better planet than this one. Come on, let's escape from Melridion and never return to this wretched planet. Because you're right—we will be fine. We'll all make it," Fumalli whispered as he looked into Navacus' eyes.

"Agreed. Peace, love, and faith," he whispered in reply as he closed the door firmly.

*Let's get off this rock together and make new lives for ourselves,* he thought as he nodded to his friend. *Right, I know, Sterg. But we can still prepare for our battle with Gnusaramnii while having a posh apartment. We can have both things. Of course, it all comes down to how today plays out. I truly hope Gazelle hasn't been able to tell anyone about Sterg. I suppose that's true, huh? At this point, it may not really matter much.*

# 34

# ESCAPE FROM THE ROUTINE

Navacus opened the door to the barracks and stepped out into the dark desert. The sun had yet to rise, but for them, the day had already begun. He held the door open, letting Fumalli, Norman, and Syl through.

They walked halfway down the covered walkway when Navacus stopped them.

"Hang on a second. Let me and Sterg gauge the situation," he whispered.

He felt Sterg reach out and probe the atrium of the compound. As he had suspected, the Lakinceitian guards weren't present, which meant they were already stationed in Professor Peal's lab. And that meant it was highly likely that the other parties were in their positions as well. Standing in for the Lakinceitians was a Human woman. She was physically strong, yet mentally unstable. Sterg could sense that her mind was heavy with various burdens that she hid from the rest of the world.

*"Navacus, if you let me, I can erase her short-term memories to allow her to have no recollection of why she is here."*

*"Um, is that safe?"*

*"Absolutely not. In doing so, I could inadvertently erase long-term*

*memories, which could influence her personality. She may never be the same after we do this to her."*

*"You know, none of us will be the same after today, in one way or another. And there is a price to pay. Lord Foxaire needs to learn he can't get away with what he's doing. They messed with ours, let's mess with theirs. We've already sabotaged Svetlana, right? So, if messing with this woman's mind will ensure that all three teams can make it through here safely, then I guess I'm all for it. Unless, of course, there is another, non-invasive way."*

*"I could put her to sleep, but once I am out of range, she could wake up at any time. This would be a more permanent solution."*

*"This is the best option then. Okay, go ahead, Sterg."*

It took only a few moments, but the sensation was unlike anything Navacus had ever felt before. He literally felt Sterg enter her mind and pull at various strings. It felt wrong, and it was a power he hoped he'd never need to use again.

Sterg appeared beside him when it was finished. "We're clear," Sterg said.

"What just happened?" Fumalli whispered.

"There is a Human guard watching the door. I've ensured we can get past her without alerting the others," Sterg replied.

"We need to move," Navacus said to the others. "Let's not forget that there are cameras everywhere, and Lord Foxaire could be watching."

They hurried into the compound and were greeted by a pleasant woman with short, brown hair. She wore light blue body armor with a long-sleeved silver shirt underneath.

"Oh, hello everyone. I'm Courtney. Could you tell me where I am? I seem to be lost. I don't even know how I got here," she rambled.

"This is what Sterg meant? He wiped her memories?" Fumalli said in shock.

"Does that mean we can take her with us?" Syl asked. "With that armor, she could be useful."

"Oh, are we going somewhere?" Courtney asked.

"We are, but you are not," Navacus said firmly. "You must not leave this spot. We can't allow anyone to get suspicious. You'll see some other people come through this door, and when they do, let them through. But other than that, just sit here and act normal. Oh, and if anyone asks, we were never here."

"Okay, I think that sounds doable. How am I talking with you all if you're not here, though?" Courtney asked.

"I'm sure someone will come by to give you more directions later, and if they ask, tell them all is normal. That's all you need to say."

"Sure, I suppose that's fine," Courtney said, then straightened up. "Everything is normal. Have a great night, you who was never here."

"Are you sure she's okay?" Fumalli whispered as they hurried away.

"She'll be fine," Navacus replied, slightly doubting his own confidence in the matter, then stopped in his tracks.

"What's going on?" Fumalli asked.

"I sense two more guards—well, Sterg senses the guards. There's one stationed at each elevator. Sterg can take both out at the same time."

"Then we should do that, right?" Norman asked. "The more we take down now, the less we need to deal with later."

"Depending on how we take them down. I don't want a repeat of what happened to scatterbrain over there," he said, pointing to Courtney.

"Noted," Sterg said out loud to the group. "The one to the north, I can force into a deep sleep. The one to the south, I can trap in a suspended state of time that will allow us to move past him completely unnoticed."

"Huh, okay," Navacus replied. "So the one by Professor Peal's office can fall asleep, which should give West and the others enough time to slip by. Then, the one by my lab will essentially be unknowingly caught in a time loop. They won't be able to see or hear us."

"That's certainly crazy, but it sounds like it could work," Fumalli said.

"Agreed. Good thinking, you two," Syl said with a thumbs up.

Once again, Navacus felt Sterg slip into one of the guard's minds to lull them to sleep. As for the other guard, the barrier of time surrounding them would last until Sterg was out of range, which would allow them to meet up with Dea and his team.

"It's done. Let's go." He led his team into his laboratory, where Syl sped to a table in the back and picked up a nail gun. "I modified this last night. Theoretically, it will mimic a normal gun and shoot nails at much higher speeds."

"I'm sure it will come in handy," Navacus said. "Now, let's head over to the elevator and wait for Professor Dea and the Harmertians to arrive."

As they approached the end of the hallway, they saw the Kolythoanthaean guard enshrouded in a translucent sphere. He was standing still but wasn't suspended in time, as he was still shifting his weight.

"So, he can't see or hear us, right?" Norman asked as he cautiously approached the time shroud.

"Correct," Sterg replied.

"This is unreal," Norman replied. "I've never seen anything like this before."

"And this is the first time I've done this. I have a lot of powers I haven't used yet," Sterg said.

"I'm sure a lot of them will be used today," Navacus said.

*Sterg, please do everything that you can do to keep everyone safe,* Navacus thought. *This really is going to be a true test of your abilities and our connection with each other. If we can make it through this, then we can do anything together.*

---

Professor Dea was waiting for them behind the barracks when the Harmertian trio arrived.

"Good morning, and great timing, everyone," Professor Dea said. "Before we head into the compound, I have a gift for you."

"Like a going-away present?" Poi asked.

"You could say that," Professor Dea replied. There was an odd noise that sounded almost like a suction cup being released, and a moment later their three modified hazard suits fell to the sand below the Eridavlos.

"Oh wow, thank you so much for grabbing these for us," Lyd said. "They will be of great help to us today."

"I thought so, too. I only got a glimpse of them yesterday morning, but I knew I had to grab them," Professor Dea replied.

"Can you show us that again sometime, Professor Dea?" Mac asked. "What you just did was wild."

"Sure, when we get away from this place, I'll show you how my abilities work. And remember, just call me Dea from now on."

"No problem, Dea," Poi said with a smile. "Now, give us a moment to put these on."

"I think I'm going to need to take off my lab coat and some other layers," Mac replied. "These suits are very tight."

"No problem. I can vacuum up your clothes and take them with us," Dea said.

"Oh, let me watch when you do that!" Mac said excitedly.

"Hush now," Poi said to her brother. "Let's just get on with it."

As they undressed, Lyd caught Poi glancing at him. Of course, it meant she also caught him looking at her. Once they had their suits on, they watched in fascination as Dea hovered over their clothes. A pale green light washed over them and they lifted off the ground. When they approached Dea's body, there was a whooshing sound and they disappeared.

"That's so cool," Mac said quietly. "I wish I could do that."

Dea smiled sadly. "And you have no idea what I would give for a proper pair of arms and legs. Now let's get going."


They passed into the compound and approached a Human woman who was looking anywhere but directly at them.

"Hello newcomers," the guard said. "You are not here. I am here, but you are not. Have a great night, nobodies!"

"Okay... you, too, lady," Mac said with an awkward wave.

They hurried down Professor Clums' wing. Lyd waved to them as they approached, but when he noticed the Kolythoanthaean guard, he yelped in surprise.

"Hey—what's going on with him?" he asked.

"Oh, he's just suspended in a time loop. Don't worry about him, he can't hear us," Navacus said with a smile.

"Smart move," Dea replied. "What's going on with the one at the front?"

"Sterg messed with her memories and made her go all loopy," Norman said. "It was wild."

"Right, well we shouldn't dally," Navacus said with a loud wheeze. "Dea, can you activate the elevator?"

"Yes, just give me a moment," Dea said as he floated to a hidden console. Soon, the wall at the end of the hallway split in half. One half slid into the right side of the wall, and the other half slid into the left side of the wall, revealing a chrome elevator door and a side panel with only one button on it, and it was already lit up.

"Let's go. We can all fit, right?" Navacus asked.

"It will be a tight fit, but it will work," Sterg replied.

"Wonderful," Navacus said. "I'm glad we get to see you guys off for the day. And look, you're even wearing you suits!"

"It was Dea's idea," Mac said with a grin.

"And it was a great idea," Navacus replied. "Now, let's all cram in here."

They stepped into the elevator. As promised, it was a tight fit. Poi, Mac, and Lyd sat on Norman's treads in the corner of the elevator, while Dea hovered beside them. Syl, Fumalli, and Navacus fit into the other half of the elevator, while Sterg rose to the top. As the doors closed, Lyd couldn't help but laugh.

"Oh no, you're not having a nervous breakdown, are you?" Fumalli asked.

"No, nothing of the sort," he replied, catching his breath. "It's just crazy. We did everything we could to avoid this elevator prior to today, and now we're riding in it. And we even have our suits on."

Poi smiled and placed a hand on his leg. "It is kinda funny, isn't it?"

"Yeah, exactly. Life flows in mysterious ways," Mac replied.

"I wholeheartedly agree, but let's settle down and say sharp," Navacus whispered. "Sterg, keep an eye out."

"Will do," the Light Being replied.

Lyd grabbed Poi's hand and squeezed it. She smiled.

*And here we are*, Lyd thought as he gazed at Poi. *This is the moment. Let's rescue Kate and the other Humans, and ideally not die in the process. Then we can celebrate.*

As soon as West stepped into the compound, he felt Sterg's presence. He assumed Sterg was actively tampering with the cameras, and had influenced the guard who introduced herself as Courtney. She told him in an odd voice that she knew he wasn't here. He shrugged and hurried into Professor Peal's lab. He was the first to arrive, so he spent a few seconds using LSS to mess with the camera feeds in the room. He figured Carl was having a headache dealing with the various technical glitches, and assumed it was only a matter of time before the bounty hunters were let loose upon them. They would have to move quickly. At least he had disabled the monitoring system and remote-control device. That would give them a slight advantage.

It was only then that he turned his attention to Svetlana. Her mechanical parts were splayed open, and he could see where Navacus and Dea had cut wires and disconnected various components.

*I'm sorry, Svetlana*, West thought. *This isn't right, I know it, but it is for the best. Having you out of the picture today will be an immense help for us. So again, I apologize it's at your expense.*

He heard the door creek open and saw Grasberg and Kurjon peek their heads in. He tipped his hat and hurried over to them.

"Are you ready?" West whispered.

"Yeah, we're ready," Grasberg replied.

"Hey, is that Svetlana?" Kurjon asked.

"Yes, but it's best you two don't see her. She's in a sorry state."

"So it seems. It looks like they messed with her way more after Gazelle kidnapped me and Lyd," Kurjon replied as she pushed herself into the room.

"Ah, perhaps so. Now, let's go," West said as he opened the door wider and stepped into the hallway, nudging Kurjon out of the lab.

He closed the door behind him and motioned for them to follow him. As they reached the end of the hallway, the trio approached a Nioavellian guard who was snoring loudly. West quietly approached the wall, then tapped a button that was camouflaged into the white wall, revealing a panel. He typed in the six-digit code, and the elevator doors were revealed.

"What in the void?" Grasberg whispered. "This is crazy."

Once they were in the elevator and descending to the underground, he addressed his team.

"I must warn you both that where we are headed is not for the faint of heart. If either of you are squeamish, please keep your eyes on the ground."

"What do you mean? Why?" Kurjon replied, tensing up. "What's down there?"

"We will pass through Professor Xergat's lab. He is an unusually eccentric Lakinceitian who proudly displays his grotesque experiments. I've seen species of all kinds suspended in those tanks, and each one is a new level of horror."

"What in the void? I thought this place couldn't get more messed up, but this tops it," Grasberg said.

"The void sees you," Kurjon whispered back. "You know, like in the children's tale. Those that cursed the void were swallowed by it."

"Why did you have to bring that up now?" Grasberg shot back.

"I don't know. I'm really freaking nervous," Kurjon responded, rubbing her hands together.

"We all are. Now, get ready, we're nearly there," West whispered to his teammates. He really hoped nothing would go wrong.

The elevator doors slid open, revealing Professor Xergat standing next to a monstrous creature. Xergat was large for a Lakinceitian and had a dark brownish-green hide, and the creature looked to be a Human covered in bloodied, black feathers. A beak had been surgically grafted onto the bird-man's face.

"Good morning, West. You're quite late, and I see you brought guests," Professor Xergat said in a bored tone with a hint of menace. The bird-man squawked in agreement.

"I'm working on my own schedule from now on," West said as he stepped out of the elevator and motioned for the others to do the same.

"You want me to go out there with *that* thing?" Kurjon whispered as she pointed at the bird-man. The elevator doors began to close, but West pressed the console to keep it open.

West turned back to their foes and held out a hand. "Professor Xergat, listen to me, I need you to—"

As he was speaking, Professor Xergat quickly reached into his pocket. West directed his energy weapon and shot a focused blast at Professor Xergat. The bird-man lunged, which he had been anticipating. He timed his dodge perfectly and shot another blast of energy. The bird-man crumpled to the ground, while Professor Xergat dropped his tablet to the floor with a loud smack. Grasberg and Kurjon screamed, then simultaneously whispered, "Sorry!"

West turned around to face his team. "Are you okay? That was unexpected, but it's what we've got to expect from now on. We need to anticipate being surprised so we don't get caught. And that means we must keep our cool, alright?"

"Yes, sorry again, West. Will he be okay, though?" Kurjon asked, pointing to Professor Xergat.

West turned back and saw that the brownish-green Lakinceitian's body was smoking. He walked over and placed a hand on top of his head and shuddered in repulsion. He could feel the professor's pulse. West quickly pulled his hand back and stepped over the body.

"He'll be fine. Now, it's time to get out of the elevator."

Grasberg and Kurjon looked at each other and laughed nervously, then stepped out of the elevator.

"We need to hurry," West continued. "We've got to—"

"What is *that*?" Kurjon whispered loudly as she pointed to the nearest tank. Inside was an abomination. The poor soul had the body of a Eusphyrchiian, the arms of a Kolythoanthaean, and the head of a Human.

"I warned you of this. Please keep your heads down if you don't want to see anything else. We must stay sharp, and that means doing everything you can not to get psyched out," West commanded.

Grasberg and Kurjon nodded, then lowered their heads toward the ground. "Yeah, this is definitely the worst I've ever seen," Grasberg said.

"I can't believe we work here," Kurjon whispered, her voice filled with sadness.

West held his hand out to Kurjon. "Let's hold hands—I'll lead you."

Kurjon took his hand, and West gave it a squeeze. As he led them along, they passed by several Lakinceitian drones. Luckily, none of them paid them any attention because they were fixated on their tasks. The trio made it to the end of the lab without any other confrontations.

West opened the door and peeked out into the hallway. It was only a few dozen meters to Professor Peal's area, and yet, due to the twisting architecture, he couldn't see the doors from where he was standing. However, the coast was clear, at least for the moment.

*Kurjon and Grasberg, I'm sorry for how I'm treating you,* West thought. *I know you're not bounty hunters, but you are professors and scientists, so you understand the meaning of discipline. Please be strong— this should all be over soon. Let's just hope we don't run into Creson or Brock.*

"Hey Sid, are you seeing this? Something wonky is going on with the cameras near the compound entrance," Carl said as he pointed to the group of screens.

"What do you think it is?" Sid asked.

"It's similar to what happens every time Navacus Clums is around a camera," Lord Foxaire said.

Carl watched as Gazelle sat straight up, only to receive an intense glare from Lord Foxaire. She wisely stayed silent. Carl really did like to watch her squirm. But, what if Gazelle was right? What if the knowledge she had could help prevent this from going sour? And yet, it wasn't his decision, nor his place to question Lord Foxaire's orders. However, seeing these screens going haywire was only raising his suspicions of the Yggdrazim professor.

"Sid, give your soldier a call," Carl said to his Human companion.

"Right away," Sid said as he tapped on his tablet. "Courtney. Cyclone Courtney, come in."

A slightly dazed-sounding voice spoke through Sid's tablet. "Oh, hello! Who is this?"

"This is Captain Heigel. What is your status?"

"Everything is normal," Courtney replied.

"Did anyone come through the entrance recently?" Sid asked.

"Nobody was here," Courtney said.

"What about West? Have you seen him yet?"

"No, nothing from the west, only nobodies. Is there anything else you want me to do?"

Sid looked at Carl, who shrugged and shook his head in response. "No, just hold your position, and call in the moment you see West, Professor Clums, or anyone else," Sid said.

"Okie-dokie."

"Does she seem off to you?" Carl asked once the call ended. A moment later, the screens refocused, and they could once again see Cyclone Courtney. She was standing still in the middle of the atrium, and there was no one else around.

"Yeah, but she's always been a bit more charismatic than the others."

"That may be all that's going on then," Lord Foxaire said, "but keep a close eye on the entrance, everyone."

"Look, now the screens are acting up around Professor Clums' office," Sid said, drawing his attention from Courtney.

Carl scanned the rest of the screens and noticed something strange happening with the cameras around Professor Peal's upstairs lab, as well, and pointed it out to everyone.

"The sooner we leave this place, the better," Lord Foxaire said. "Everything is crapping out."

Carl stared at the screens, trying to make sense of what was going on. Maybe he could still get a glimpse of something useful.

"We have a situation—Professor Xergat is down," Sid announced.

Carl blinked his eyes a few times to clear the dryness, then looked at the screen Sid was pointing to. It showed Professor Xergat on the ground next to a feathered abomination.

"Shit," Carl said, then looked to Lord Foxaire. "Permission to send the bounty hunters to investigate?"

"Send only one," his Lord replied with a low growl. "We must protect our ships at all costs."

"Can you spare a few Cyclones?" he asked Sid.

"Just two."

He nodded and contacted Brock. "Brock, I need you to investigate a situation in Professor Xergat's lab. He's down, by the elevator. Take two of Sid's Cyclones with you."

"Sounds like fun," Brock replied.

"Good. Do we know where the perpetrators are?" Lord Foxaire asked.

"The cameras around Professor Peal's underground lab are going haywire," Carl replied. "It could be connected."

"Then ask Brock to go there after Xergat's."

Carl nodded and passed the order to Brock.

"Stay vigilant, everyone," Lord Foxaire said. "The Titans are almost ready to be loaded onto the ships. Theesakin will be first. The Eklatros Humans will be ready to be moved shortly as well. No interruptions can be permitted."

"Yes, sir," he replied.

*Part of me really wishes that we had listened to Gazelle, Carl thought. What if she had uncovered a plot that is unfolding right under our noses? And if that's the case, there's little that can be done about it now.*

**35**

# ESCAPE FROM LIES

"There's another guard nearby," Navacus said to everyone in the descending elevator. "Not only that, but we are approaching quickly."

"Can Sterg do another one of those time loop thingies?" Poi asked.

"Okay, it's done," Sterg replied as the elevator came to a halt. The doors opened, revealing a female Ancilsan standing at attention and surrounded by a time loop field. Her large frame was blocking the way out.

"Oh man, am I glad we don't have to deal with her," Fumalli said with a sigh of relief.

"Yeah, but her hairy fat-ass is blocking the way," Norman said. "Can she be moved?"

"Sterg?" he asked.

In response, he felt Sterg create a small noise further down the hallway. The Ancilsan moved and the time loop moved with her. They quickly piled out of the elevator and slid by the large guard as she made her way back to her position.

"Alright, do you know where you're going?" Navacus whispered to Dea.

"West gave us directions," Dea replied.

"Yeah, we got the map on our tablets," Poi said as she walked forward, tablet in hand. "It'll be just like our time in the air ducts, only this time we're actually here."

"Good," Navacus replied. "Take care, and remember, peace, love, and faith."

"P-L-F," Mac said in response, while Lyd and Poi held up peace signs with their fingers.

"See you soon," Fumalli said to them. "And do be careful."

"Well, at this point, all four of us can technically fly," Lyd said. "I think that will give us a good advantage."

"You might just be right," Norman said. "I would be right there with you all if my attachment was complete."

"After this, we'll have ample time to finish. I'm sure of it. Now, let's get going," Navacus said to the group.

They split off in opposite directions, with Fumalli, Norman, and Syl following him. After a few hundred meters, Navacus felt the time loop surrounding the Ancilsan dissipate. As they neared the Titan enclosure, Sterg prompted them to stop.

"Something is wrong. There are far fewer presences than there should be. They must have already been moved to the hangar," Navacus exclaimed.

"Which way do we go, then?" Syl asked. They had three options— a path to their right, a path to their left, or they could turn around and head back to the elevator.

Within seconds, Sterg had scanned all three directions. "We go left," Navacus replied. "Come on, we need to hurry!"

"Everyone, please wait," Sterg commanded. "Three people are approaching. There is nowhere to hide, so let me hide you. I will mask our presences; they will walk right by us none the wiser."

They squeezed against the wall, and Sterg placed a shroud over them. Moments later, a dark-skinned Human wearing a white suit and two pale Humans wearing blue body armor ran past them.

"Do you feel that?" the dark-skinned Human asked.

"Negative," one of the other Humans replied.

"Then come on. We don't got all day."

Sterg waited a few seconds after the Humans passed before dropping the shroud.

"That was amazing," Norman whispered. "What a great trick."

"My heart is only pounding out of my chest, but yeah, all good otherwise," Fumalli said as he clutched his breast.

"The threats have passed. We are clear to continue," Sterg said.

"I just hope Dea and the others don't get found," Navacus whispered.

They hurried to the next set of doors—Professor Durrist's lab. They gathered outside the entrance while Sterg scanned the area. Navacus could feel three presences. One was in the lab directly before them, and two others were in a back room. The one in the lab seemed weak. Sterg could also detect the path that led to the hangar.

"If we hurry, we can make it through the next room," Navacus whispered to his team. "Now, there is someone in the lab, but it seems to be one of the professor's subjects."

"It's your call," Fumalli said, nodding.

"Right, let's move stealthily," Navacus said as he quietly opened the door to the lab.

The room was fully lit, completely revealing them. He nodded to his team and made his way through the lab, keeping his eyes on the door he was shooting for.

"Navacus... Fumalli... is that really you?" a raspy voice rumbled through the silent room.

Using Sterg to identify the source, Navacus spun around and his beak dropped to the ground in surprise. Sitting in a metal cage was Professor Bodeelch. He was skin and bones, and his eyes were sunken deep into his leathery, wrinkled face.

"Professor Bodeelch!" Navacus exclaimed, far louder than he had meant to. He led his equally surprised team to the cage, and Sterg covered them all in a shroud, allowing the group to converse without being heard by other parties.

"What are you doing here, Venkatt? You look awful! How did this happen?" Navacus asked. Beside him, Fumalli was holding back tears.

"Navacus, Fumalli—it is so good to see you after all this time. I thought I would die here," Venkatt Bodeelch replied in a tired voice. It was as if his soul was exhausted to its very core.

"What do you mean? We just saw you yesterday!" Syl said.

"Unfortunately, that was not me. At least, that wasn't the real me."

"What do you mean? I am so confused," Syl said as he placed a hand on his forehead.

"Allow me a few moments to explain as quickly as I can. At the beginning of the year, I accompanied Durrist, Randall, Carl, and others to Acampachetli. Our main goal was to identify a suitable area where we could send Professor Peal to collect samples. However, our trip had a secondary purpose. Navacus, Fumalli—there is a gate on Acampachetli, hidden deep in the jungle. It only allows those to find it who need to, and apparently it deemed only me worthy. When I was at the gate I spoke with an odd creature with big, floppy ears and a long hose-like nose. A feline-like creature with blue and white fur accompanied her. She told me I needed to tell the chosen one this message: 'Deep in the kirwach lies the road to Eklatros.' I relayed this message to Durrist and the others. They searched for that gate for two full days, dragging me along with them, and we never found it again. So, they locked me up so I couldn't talk about the incident."

"The road to Eklatros... that's where those Humans came from. It must be significant," Navacus whispered excitedly to the others.

"And you must be the chosen ones. I believe this is the moment I've been waiting for—the only reason I am still alive," Venkatt said solemnly.

"I don't know about that, but this explains the sudden shift in your personality and demeanor. You're kind of a massive asshole now. But who has been acting in your place?" Navacus asked.

A klaxon started blaring as the lights flashed red.

"We've been found out!" Syl exclaimed.

"There's no more time. You must go!" Venkatt cried.

"At least let us free you first," he demanded. "We need to take you with us!"

A door crashed open behind them, causing each member of the group to turn around. Standing in the doorway were Professors Durrist and Randall. Sterg's shroud had only hidden their voices—they could clearly be seen.

"It's too late," Venkatt whimpered.

Sterg dropped the shroud as the two professors hurried over to them. Without a second thought, Sterg sent a wave of energy over them. Professor Randall slumped to the floor and instantly fell asleep. Professor Durrist simply laughed and shook it off.

"I am more than the average thin-minded person. My mind is impenetrable—it has to be." Durrist laughed, and his body began to morph. The process was sickeningly fascinating to watch. A few seconds later, Professor Bodeelch stood before them.

"It really has been you," Navacus said in awe.

"Yes, it has. It's been an annoying task and took a lot of time away from my real duties, but I suppose it wasn't an entire waste of time. Now, whatever you're planning on doing, it seems to be going quite badly. Was it your friends who just got caught?" Durrist said as he morphed back into his own skin. He reached into his lab coat pocket and took out his tablet. "All I need to do is call Lord Foxaire."

Despite everything Sterg tried, they could not persuade Durrist to do anything. "I could use some assistance," Sterg demanded.

In response, Norman lurched forward. He smirked and said, "So who's stopping you? I am."

A moment later, Norman crashed into a wide-eyed Durrist, who was far too slow to move out of the way. Durrist's tablet fell to the ground, and Norman quickly used his treads to crush the device. Norman chuckled to himself as he reversed his treads. Before Professor Durrist could get up, Syl used his nail gun to shoot two nails into his tail, pinning the professor to the floor.

"Curse you all!" Durrist shouted, pain and anger in his voice, and then he pulled a small gun out of his lab coat and quickly shot it off.

Before he had time to think, Navacus sprinted forward and snatched the gun out of Durrist's hand.

"Navacus!" Fumalli shouted.

Fearing the worst and sensing that someone had been shot, Navacus turned around. Fumalli fanatically pointed at the cage. Venkatt Bodeelch had been hit in the chest. He lay eerily still.

Durrist shouted curses at them as they stared at the fallen Kolythoanthaean. Sterg pulled at every seam of his body. "We must move as quickly as we can!" Sterg said.

Navacus nodded as he wiped a tear from his eye. "We must continue. With the alarms going off, we don't know what could be happening in the hangar."

"Can we at least shut him up?" Syl asked, annoyed.

Navacus quickly located a roll of durable tape and thew it to Syl with his feathery hands. Syl placed a strip of tape over Durrist's mouth, then rapidly taped up Randall's hands and feet.

The group hurried through the next door, where they faced a long hallway with two moving walkways. They got on the one moving away from them and sprinted. All the while, the klaxon continued to blast while the lights flashed red.

*I hope everyone is safe*, Navacus thought, wheezing while he ran down the moving walkway. *But there is no time to stop now. We must continue forward, and yet, we have our first casualty. I am so sorry we couldn't save you, my mentor and friend, Venkatt Bodeelch. I only wish I had seen through the lies sooner. But what you told us today will be of great importance once we escape from this place. I truly thank you for your sacrifice. Wait, yeah, I sense them, too, Sterg*, he nodded to himself as he drew his knife. *We've got company!*

**36**

# ESCAPE FROM PRISON

Lyd used his jetpack to hover in the air alongside Mac and Poi. Dea was several meters in front of them, using his pronosua to access the panel that opened the door to where Kate and the Eklatros Humans were being kept.

"Dea, we've got three signatures incoming," Mac said as he studied the security scans.

"I've got it!" Dea whispered triumphantly as the door slid open. The four of them silently floated into the room and quickly shut the door behind them. They found themselves in a small hall that turned to the left. Lyd held his breath as he watched the three people pass by on his tablet. One of them stopped in front of the door for a few seconds before moving on. He breathed a sigh of relief.

"They're gone," he whispered. "Wait! I'm sensing three signatures down that hallway." Lyd pointed at the only other path available to them.

"There's no avoiding them then. At least your suits are stealthy." Dea said. "Can each of you break open a door and free someone? If we can pull this off, we'll have the element of surprise."

"I think we can try that," Lyd replied confidently. "How do we open the doors?"

"It's hard to say without being able to see them. However, if all else fails, do what you can to hack the console."

"Sounds like a plan," Mac whispered.

"Yeah, we got this," Poi added.

Lyd nodded to everyone. "Dea, if you hear something, can you distract them?"

"Sure, I'll do what I can."

Lyd looked at Mac and Poi. "Let's do this on three. One, two—"

Before he could finish the countdown, a loud rumbling shook the hallway.

"Crap, they must already be moving them to the hangar! We're running out of time," Dea whispered.

Lyd nodded, then rushed around the corner, followed by Poi and Mac. He let Poi and Mac take the nearest consoles while he stopped at what he assumed was Theodore's room. A shout, and the three people approached. He glanced in the direction of the sound, never taking his focus from the console in front of him. A moment later, Dea flew around the corner and confronted their opposition.

*Whatever happens, I love you, Poi and Mac,* Lyd thought as his fingers danced across the keyboard. *You're the family I never had.*

---

Sir Cecil Kloud, guildmaster of the Guild for Eklatros and team leader in Ànifa's stead, stood at attention. He took a deep breath, calming his nerves. He wished he could do more, but he had no way to tamper with the cage he was in, and his body was still sore from his workout session the day prior.

Without warning, his cage began to vibrate. A moment later, a loud siren blared and he fell to his knees. He covered his ears. They were still raw from when his eardrums had ruptured during the fight with the diprotodon and the other ferocious animals.

"What's going on? What is this?" he shouted as he scanned the small cage he was in.

Movement caught his eye, and he turned to look as a door opened, revealing a small gray humanoid alien in an orange suit floating in the air.

"Come on, we've got to get out of here!" the alien called to him as they waved their arms.

Cecil nodded and jumped to his feet. There was no time to waste. He had to gather his team—he couldn't allow anyone to be left behind.

*This is it*, he thought. *Theodore, Druder, Tyrona… let's get out of this damn place!*

---

The S-Class Sorcerer Theodore Henry Caldwell braced himself as his prison violently shook. He could only hope that this was part of the plan and that Lyd and the others were coming to save him and the rest of his team.

He built up a layer of condensed energy just beneath his skin that surrounded his entire body, then let the flood gates loose. The energy shot out around him like a sensor beam. Surprise and glee washed over him. This was the first real magic he had performed since leaving Eklatros. He first sensed a small figure working on a device outside his cell, as well as several other presences in the hallway. His sensor sphere was dissipating quickly, but he picked up on Cecil's presence. Right before his sensor sphere vanished, he sensed Druder. His black-skinned elf friend was terrified and moved quickly away from them. His imagination filled in the gaps and showed him what Druder's horrified face probably looked like. The image seared into his mind.

*Hang on, Druder! We'll save you! But first, and I'm sorry, but where is Tyrona?*

Out of nowhere, sirens screamed into the room. He looked around in surprise and saw his door whoosh open. A small gray-skinned person hovered in the air and waved at him. Over the cacophony, Theodore could make out several people shouting at each other in the hallway.

"You must be Theodore! I'm Lyd. Now let's go! We don't have much time."

Theodore gathered himself, then marched toward Lyd and stepped into a stark white hallway. As soon as he left his cell, it started moving quickly away from him, likely going to the same place Druder was headed. In the hallway, the sirens were significantly quieter and were accompanied by flashing red lights. He looked to his right and saw Cecil step into the hallway.

"Theodore, is that you?" Cecil shouted and rushed to him. Cecil was wearing a thin white robe—the same thing he was wearing. Beneath Cecil's clothes he could see muscles that weren't there before.

"Cecil!" he cried as he embraced his friend, wrapping him in a hug.

"I almost didn't recognize you without your beard!" Cecil said.

Theodore teared up, and his smile reached his eyes. He was overjoyed to be reunited with his good friend.

"My door had nothing behind it, just an empty space," he could hear one of the small aliens saying as they approached.

"That would be my old room." The familiar voice sent a chill down Theodore's spine.

He stepped away from Cecil and looked at his former comrade. Dasch—now going by Gnudashar—was flanked by two aliens, one with deep blue skin and one with dark gray skin. They both wore sky-blue body armor and had on silver shirts underneath. He squinted at them in anger—the color reminded him of Ànifa's hair, and he would not allow them to defile her name. A levitating human torso wearing a white coat rushed toward them. His face was shockingly human, and even had a bit of black stubble on his chin.

"We're all on your side," the torso said. An ethereal green tentacle came out of the levitating torso and pointed at three small aliens. A strong desire to react to the ghostly appendage flashed through Theodore, but passed half a second later as he heard Lyd shout.

"Cover us!" Lyd and his kin whooshed by him as they flew around their foes. He smiled as he felt the static electricity build in his fingertips. Beside him, Cecil screamed and charged forward, knocking a sword that appeared to be made of solidified energy out of the blue alien's hands. Cecil threw himself to the ground, dodging a retaliating strike from the other alien. As he got up, Gnudashar kicked Cecil hard in the stomach. Cecil grunted but remained on his feet, only to be knocked to the ground by a smack to the head by the blue-skinned alien's other weapon.

"Are you really just going to stand there, Theodore?" Gnudashar taunted with a wide grin, holding his arms out to his sides.

He grinned. "I'm all charged up." Theodore held out his hands and shot streams of electricity from his fingertips. He felt the electricity plunge into his three opponents and tear across their bodies. Then, for a sickening second, he felt their life forces drain away. Before he could cease the flow of energy, the body armor the two aliens were wearing exploded, ripping the aliens to pieces. He shielded his face from the bloody spray, but it was no use.

"Holy starlight!" the levitating alien said as he turned away from the carnage.

A wave of shock, sorrow, and regret washed over Theodore. He had released far too much energy—he'd only meant to stun them. He looked down at Cecil, who was getting up from the ground. The shock must have shown on his face, but Cecil said reassuringly, "There was no way you could have known, Theodore."

Maniacal laughter sliced through the moment. "My, have you both gotten strong," Gnudashar said as he withdrew a long, thin, metal sword. "But it won't help you—"

"Theodore!" a female voice cried, interrupting Gnudashar.

The wizard's chest swelled with love, only to wrench at his heart when he saw an unfamiliar woman running toward him. As Gnudashar turned in her direction, Cecil stepped up and punched their former comrade in his left cheek, sending him careening into the wall. Gnudashar smacked his pale, bald head hard on the white surface and slid to the ground, his sword clattering to the floor.

Theodore turned his attention to the unknown woman. As she approached, she slowed down and stopped a few meters away from him. Behind her, the three small gray aliens flew toward them.

"One of them got away!" one of the small aliens said in a soft voice.

"It was Druder," Theodore said, not taking his eyes off the pale woman. He didn't understand why, but her aura reminded him of Tyrona.

"Then we must go after him! Where's Tyrona?" Cecil asked as he looked around the hallway.

"I'm right here," the pale woman said.

Once the words left her mouth, a wave of emotions sent Theodore to his knees. Even though he didn't recognize her face or voice, he knew she was telling the truth. His mouth hung open in shock, but no words came out.

*Tyrona, how can this be?* he thought. *What happened to your beautiful body?*

---

Theodore gaped at her with wide eyes. If she didn't love him as much as she did, she would have thought it comical. But the reality was anything but humorous. This was the moment she had been dreading—the one-sided reunion with Theodore. As much as she wanted to jump into his arms, she restrained herself. She needed to let him processes everything first.

As for Cecil, he was squinting at her like he could see past her new skin.

"It's me, Tyrona. Well, I go by Kaytrona now. I know you don't recognize me... but it's me, Dorie. Well, it's us, since as you can tell, this is not my body. This is Kate's body. Hi!" she said with a smile and a wave as Kate's personality took over. "It's nice to meet you. I've heard a lot about you. Oh, sorry girl, I'm interrupting your moment."

"No, actually I am," an Eridavlos said as he floated over to her. "We must hurry along."

"Professor Dea? Oh, and you guys are Professor Clums' Harmertian helpers! I remember you three," Kaytrona said as Theodore looked at her strangely.

"As heartfelt as this is, we must get out of here," Lyd said over the clamor of the alarm.

Professor Dea lifted the fallen soldier's plasma swords with green, ghostly hands and handed one to Kaytrona and one to Cecil. She cautiously took the sword in her hand. As the ghostly green limb retreated, it brushed against her wrist. It had felt like a long tongue was licking her, only there was no wetness left behind. A shiver of repulsion ran down her spine as soon as the sensation subsided.

The alarm and flashing lights stopped, causing Kaytrona's vision to momentarily blur. Everyone sighed in relief. Cutting through the newfound silence was a slight ringing sound.

"Wait, give me a moment, if you can spare it," Gnudashar grunted as he sat up against the wall.

"Why should we listen to you?" Cecil said with a snarl.

"Because, Cecil, this is Dasch speaking. I was able to take control, in part thanks to your punch. I know you don't believe me—I wouldn't believe me either. But trust me when I say you need to make a quick stop first. There is a storage room near the doors to the main hallway. That's where your supplies were placed."

"Our supplies—my staff!" Theodore said as a glimmer of hope returned to his eyes.

"I just—ugh! I can't hold it at bay much longer. I sincerely apologize for my failure. Go now and save Druder, if he can still be rescued. Don't waste your time with me. I can feel Gnudashar slipping back in control. I don't have much time left. Ack!" Dasch said as he writhed on the ground.

Kaytrona nodded to the others. "I believe him. Either way, it won't hurt to check it out, right?"

Theodore nodded. "If you really are Tyrona, you'll need your wand."

"That's the spirit, Dorie!"

She turned back and glanced at Gnudashar. He really was like her

—multiple individuals living in one body. She sympathized with him, knowing how maddening it was.

"Farewell, Dasch, if it is you," Cecil said.

"Just go, there's no time to waste!" Dasch cried as he clutched at his head.

The seven of them hurried down the hallway and approached the only door that didn't have a computer console next to it. It was locked.

"Use the energy sword," Professor Dea offered.

Cecil nodded and asked everyone to step back. He took a deep breath and swung the sword at the door. It seamlessly cut through the lock.

"Now, you can press that button to retract the sword," Professor Dea said. Kaytrona looked down at her own sword and pressed the button. Cecil did the same while Theodore stepped up to the door and pushed it open, then gasped in surprise.

Kaytrona glanced inside. It looked like a bomb had gone off. She nearly laughed when she realized that a bomb of sorts really had gone off.

"This mess must have been caused by the backpack. When Tyrona's—when my body died and my consciousness moved into Kate's body—our body—the spell holding the backpack together must have ended. And if it was shrunken down, then everything inside of it would have immediately become its original size and caused this to happen."

"But it's all destroyed!" Theodore cried as he picked up a pile of reddish sand that had once been his staff and let it run through his fingers. "My scarlet staff, my clothes, even Cecil's armor... everything is gone."

"Wait, I see something," Cecil said. "Tyrona—or whoever you are —look over there!"

She looked to where Cecil was pointing and he was right. Lying on a wooden desk was her ivory wand. Surrounding the wand was a ring of cleanliness before the piles of debris began, as if the wand had protected itself. And of course it did—her wand had cast the spell on the backpack, and no catalyst could be harmed by its own magic.

Kaytrona handed her energy sword to Theodore and walked into the room. Her bare feet crunched through the debris as she approached the desk and grabbed her wand. She felt the wand's familiar power flow into her body. She looked around at the mess and sighed.

"If I had time, I could likely repair some of the items," she said.

"And yet, we don't have any time," Lyd urged. "If there's nothing else, we really must get a move on."

She nodded, then used her wand to push the debris aside, giving her a clean path to the exit.

"Exactly, we must save Druder," Cecil commanded, then turned to look at Kaytrona, eyeing her curiously. "We'll need a proper explanation after that. But first, let's save our friend."

"I agree on both accounts. I want to get to the bottom of who you are. However, if you can use that wand, then..." Theodore trailed off, his pain and confusion glistening in his eyes.

"Let's *go*. We can chat later," Lyd said. "We must regroup with the others!"

"Right, I'm coming for you, Norman!" she said as she followed Lyd, Mac, Poi, and Professor Dea.

"Norman? Who the fuck is Norman?" Theodore asked as he stopped in his tracks. A shove from Cecil prompted him to continue.

"Uh, yeah, I'll explain everything later," Kaytrona replied.

*This is really strange, she thought. My two worlds are colliding—my Eklatros companions and Norman's professors. Theodore, I really do love you, and I hope I can make you understand my new reality. What's going to be even more anxiety-inducing will be talking with both Norman and Theodore. That being said—Norman, I cannot wait to see you again! At the very least, I know you'll recognize me.*

---

Druder sat in a corner of his room as the world itself shook. At least, that's what it felt like. Having lived among Yttendaus' roots on a floating island for most of his life, he had never experienced a ground-quake. So, while he couldn't say that's what was happening, it certainly felt like a ground-quake.

When the quaking started, Druder had reached out to feel for the others. Strangely, he had only sensed Theodore, and the wizard had shared his confusion. Druder hadn't been able to sense anyone else.

He began to ache from all the shaking. It had been several minutes, and there was no end in sight. At least the blaring alarm had stopped. In its absence, Druder had hoped Lyd would appear and make good on his promise, but he knew something had gone wrong.

*Seriously, what is going on?* he thought. *Could my entire room be in transit? If so, is this what Lyd had warned us about? Because how else does this make sense? If it really was a ground-quake, would the alarms really have stopped? And if I am being moved, then why does it seem like I'm the only one? And yet, if it means that Cecil and Theodore are safe, then that's what matters.*

*This is simply not what I expected when I walked through that gate. We only had a few seconds before we were put to sleep with those strange darts. The entire rest of the time, this is where I've been—in this dark jail. And sure, darkness may be what I'm used to, but I've never been away from the natural world for so long. I miss Yttendaus. I miss Eklatros. Why did I come here?*

---

Everything was falling to pieces before their eyes.

It started when Nijork activated the alarm. That had drawn their attention to Professor Peal's section. Even though the cameras were quite fuzzy, Carl could still identify West, Kamarial, Surridge, and many others gathering together. Sid had ordered Brock and his Cyclones to move on from Xergat's area to prevent the situation from getting any worse.

As soon as they thought that was resolved, they received notices that containment cells were being accessed where the magical Humans were being kept. Only one of them was moving to the hangar.

And now, on top of all that, Professor Clums, Qymberkon, Norman, and Sylcertiverner were charging into the hangar.

Lord Foxaire was furious, shouting incoherently in Lakinceitian. He stopped, took a deep breath, and leaned down to Sid. "Go. Now. Do whatever you can to stop these mutineering bastards!"

Sid jumped to his feet. "At once, my lord!"

Lord Foxaire turned to Gazelle. "Don't disappoint me again. I need you to go with Sid."

Gazelle's lips curled into a sinister-looking smile. "Of course, my lord. Thank you for giving me another chance."

Lord Foxaire grunted. "Just get out of my sight."

Sid and Gazelle had to squeeze around Lord Foxaire's bulk to get out of the room. When they were alone, Carl's master turned to him and sighed. "Gazelle was trying to tell us about this, wasn't she?"

"I believe she was. But sending Sid and Gazelle out was a good call. We need all the hands we can get."

"Agreed. What do you think we should do, Carl?"

He nodded. "Right. We need to defend the hangar. I think we should recall Brock to the hangar as well. We must protect the assets at all costs."

"If things weren't moving so slowly in the hangar, I would ask them to take off now. But only Theesakin is loaded. They're moving too damn slowly," Lord Foxaire reiterated. "Either way, hold off on recalling Brock. I want to see what's going on with West first."

"Can we at least fly Theesakin out of there?" Carl asked. "And what about the Human?"

"Good idea. Contact the pilot and see what the situation is."

"Yes, my lord," he replied.

*Damn you, Gazelle,* Carl thought as he picked up his tablet. *Had you uncovered the information in a less extreme way, we would have listened to you. We would have trusted you. All this madness could have been prevented. And yet, even with Sid's Cyclones we need more security.*

*It's too bad we halted the production of the mind-control devices; then we could have far more assets in play. However, Professor Clums seems to be leading the charge, and would have been the one making those devices.*

*This is just so unexpected. We should have been more careful. We should've put more stopgaps in place.*

37

# ESCAPE FROM THE ARTIFICIAL

They made it to the entrance of Professor Peal's area without running into any other foes. West took a moment to let Kurjon and Grasberg catch their breath. With all of LSS' scans reading normal, they had a few seconds to spare. Besides, he knew what was waiting for them and wasn't looking forward to it. While West didn't like the Lakinceitian guards, he also didn't want to harm them.

"Remember, once we go through that door, we'll come face to face with Bsarg, Nijork, and Jakog. While they have been civil to you in the past, there is no telling what they may do."

"Are they going to attack us like that Lakinceitian professor?" Kurjon asked quietly as she clutched her arms.

"They might. We must be prepared for anything," West said.

In response, Kurjon sniffled, and Grasberg stepped up and wrapped her in a hug. "We're with you, Kurjon," he said, holding her tight.

"Thank you," Kurjon said as they parted. "I know you are, and I thought I could handle this, but what Gazelle did last night... it's still bothering me."

"What she did to you was horrible," West said softly. "Her vile aura is really strong; she even affected me. Yet, while he may be our

455

oppressor, Carl saved us last night. How strange is that? Carl helping us with Gazelle."

Kurjon smiled as she snorted with laughter. "It's quite ridiculous. That's one part I can't make sense of yet. But honestly, everything we're doing is just insane."

"And we're not in the clear yet. Come, we should hurry on," West said as he tipped his hat.

As he turned to the door's console, Kurjon placed a hand on his arm. "Thank you for giving us a moment. I needed that."

"Yeah, well, a good leader knows when to slow down," West said. "But once I open this door, we won't have a moment like this until we're far away from this place."

"Then let's get to it," Grasberg said with a smile as he patted Kurjon's back. Kurjon nodded in approval.

West tipped his cowboy hat in approval and tapped the console. A moment later, the door opened with a hiss. As expected, they were greeted by Bsarg, Nijork, and Jakog. They each held an energy rifle in their stubby hands.

"West, what are you doing here?" Bsarg asked. "Aren't you supposed to be in the hangar?"

"Look who's with him," Nijork grumbled. "Something's not right."

"Everyone, I don't wish to harm you, but we need to release Professor Peal's subjects."

Nijork and Jakog inched closer. "What's that? You're trying to steal company property?" Jakog asked as he lifted his rifle.

"Hey, come on, it's us," Kurjon said as she raised her hands. "We just want what's best for everyone."

Nijork spat on the ground. "We have our orders."

West shot a blast of energy at Nijork the moment his gun started glowing red. A second shot rang out, and a body thumped to the ground. West looked back and forth between Kurjon and Grasberg, and both were unharmed.

His attention focused on Bsarg, who's gun was still steaming. Jakog lay dead on the ground, next to a stunned Nijork.

"Bsarg, what did you do?" West asked in disbelief. "Why would you shoot your own?"

"You think I don't see how corrupt this place is? That I don't feel guilty for the things I've done and been witness to?" Bsarg said passionately as he lowered his rifle. "I have never been okay with the mindless drones. And remember Sharg? She was my friend, and they twisted her into something that can no longer be called Lakinceitian. I'm as disgusted with this place as you are."

"What happened to Sharg?" Kurjon asked, her eyes wide with surprise and horror.

"I only saw her once after she was taken, but—" a loud alarm sounded, interrupting Bsarg. West looked at Nijork. He was grinning as he proudly held his tablet. "You're not getting away with this," the light blue Lakinceitian said from the floor.

West grabbed the tablet and threw it against the wall and Bsarg charged his weapon up again. "Get out of the way, West. You're blocking my shot."

West looked down at Nijork, who simply grinned back at him. West shot a weaker energy blast at Nijork, and it seemed to do the trick. He turned back to Bsarg.

"Come on, we've got to hurry."

"Wait, can you do something about the alarm?" Bsarg asked. "There could be reinforcements coming as we speak!"

"Never mind the fact that I don't trust you, you are correct, which is why we can't waste time on superfluous things," West said as he hurried to the second door, where Newtus was kept.

"Kurjon and Grasberg, start working on door number one. Bsarg, if you could help with door number five, that would be great," West commanded.

They jumped into action. West attempted to open the door to Newtus' terrarium, but his normal way of opening the door wasn't working. He realized the alarms must have kicked in an extra layer of security. It was no matter—LSS was on the job and already had seventy-five percent of a solution.

As West fiddled with the console and cursed the security

mechanisms, Kamarial and Surridge emerged from door number four. They each held a transparent cube that held a creature.

"What's all the ruckus? And what happened to them?" Surridge shouted over the alarm while pointing at the fallen Lakinceitians.

"We did what we had to do," West replied over the cacophony.

"We're trying to get into these rooms, but the door won't budge," Grasberg said, running over to them.

West looked around the room. While Kurjon pounded at the console, Bsarg got into Ivy's room.

"I can help you with that," Surridge said as she led Grasberg to the console while Kamarial approached him. In the transparent cube was a large beetle, scurrying in circles around its cage.

"Let me see that. Hold Susan," Kamarial said as she handed West the beetle. He took it and held it close to LSS to get a better look. After a few seconds, the door hissed open.

West stepped into the room. "I'll need to ask one more favor, Kamarial."

"Sure, that's fine," the Eusphyrchiian said, following him into the room.

Newtus stood in front of the transparent barrier, alert and ready. She smiled and nodded to him when they entered.

"West, so good to see you again. You too, Kamarial," Newtus said.

"Hey, Newtus. Now, how do we set her free?" West asked his fellow Eusphyrchiian.

"Right," Kamarial said with a firm nod. "I'll just need a few seconds."

"Great, thank you so much for your help," West said as he tipped his hat toward her.

"I'm just doing what I can," Kamarial said as she revealed a console on the wall he didn't know was there. She typed in a code and a door appeared. Kamarial pushed open the door. Newtus bounded out of her containment cell and nearly knocked West over when she embraced him.

*"Thank you so much. I will never forget your kindness,"* Newtus said to West telepathically.

"It's no problem," he said out loud, patting her on her smooth, scaly back with his free hand.

"We've got to hurry if we mean to escape this place," Kamarial said as she took the beetle back from West.

"Does that mean you're coming with us?"

"Yes, I am," Kamarial said firmly.

"Wonderful!" West said, giving her a brief hug.

"Is the Curik coming with us?" Newtus asked as she licked her lips.

"Yes, and I'll be looking after Susan," Kamarial said as she shielded the beetle from Newtus. "Now, let me see what I can do about this alarm."

---

Ivy stood in the center of his containment cell. His ivy legs were spread around the room, and he had dozens of spider webs placed strategically on the walls. While he couldn't hear what was going on, especially because of the loud alarm, he could feel all sorts of activity through the vibrations.

He felt someone approaching before the door opened. Ivy had been expecting West. Instead, a dark blue Lakinceitian he had never met entered the room.

"What in the void," the Lakinceitian said in deep, rumbling tones as he stared at Ivy in awe.

"Uh, are you with West?" Ivy asked.

"You have a dual voice? How odd. Yes, I am here to set you free. I'm Bsarg."

"I'm called Ivy Hedera, and I greatly appreciate it," he replied as he retracted his ivy and condensed it into his legs. At the same time, Ados and Adok broke their connections with their silk strands.

Bsarg approached the wall and tapped at something. After a few moments, a door appeared in the transparent wall. Ivy pushed it open, exited his stale, artificial cell, and approached the Lakinceitian, but he backed away, intimidated.

"Sorry," Ivy said, "I know I don't look like any Eusphyrchiian you've ever seen before."

Bsarg stared at him with wide eyes. "I had only heard the stories. Seeing you is something else entirely."

"I understand. Is West here?"

"Yes, he's helping the others. We need to regroup with them," the Lakinceitian said as he moved to the door. Ivy followed and entered a large, circular room. The room was even more barren than the one he'd just left, having no furniture at all. Two Lakinceitians lay on the floor. One was dead, and he could feel the other one's shallow breathing through the vibrations it gave off.

While he scanned the room, West appeared from a doorway, followed by a large purple lizard.

"That's a Neutortous," Adok whispered to Ivy. "They can be exceptionally dangerous."

"Ivy, I'm glad to see you!" West said.

"And same to you, West. Your friend Bsarg was nice enough to help me out."

"I'm glad he followed my orders," West replied over the loud alarm.

A moment later, Surridge, a Kolythoanthaean, and a Nioavellian entered the circular room, followed by more creatures from Acampachetli that Adok informed Ivy about. There was a Zubba, a Loxocemae, and a Phasmatodaedalus. The stick bug was loudly cursing about the noise. A moment later, the alarms ceased and Kamarial ran out of the room West had come from.

"Phew! I'm glad I could take care of that—the noise was driving me crazy," Kamarial said.

"Better!" the Zubba screeched.

"You're coming with us?" Kamarial asked as she looked at Bsarg.

"Yes. We need to leave now," Bsarg replied.

"I agree," West said. "Is this everyone?"

"Hold on, I'm not going," Surridge said as she stepped into the center of the room. "However, someone should take Penny. She doesn't deserve to be left behind."

"I'll take her," Ivy said. "She may feel more comfortable around other Dark Therids."

"Here you go, then," Surridge said as she handed him the spider encased in a transparent cube.

As soon as Ados and Adok took hold of the cube, Penny calmed down.

"You're sure you want to stay?" West asked.

"I can't abandon Max Peal or anyone else. I know this looks really bad," Surridge said as she waved her hands around the room, "but I'll be fine. Go on now, you better hurry. Take care, everyone. I wish you all the best of luck."

"Be safe, Liz," Kamarial said, giving Surridge a quick hug.

"Go, my friend. I'll be fine," Surridge replied.

*What a strange group this is,* Ivy thought. *Of course, I am the strangest of the bunch. I'll just need to keep an eye on that Neutortous, even if it seems like it's on our side.*

*Either way, I'll do whatever I can to ensure we make it out of this horrible place. Even though I don't know what I am, all my assets will come in handy.*

Altun waited patiently in his cell as he practiced transforming his hair into a key. He had successfully hidden that part of his abilities from the professors who watched over him. He had known from the moment he first transformed that he could do almost anything with his new abilities. And, even though his powers were helpful, especially now, he still couldn't call it a gift. The pain he had endured to obtain these powers still overshadowed their benefits. It had felt like his body had been broken down atom by atom and then rebuilt, and this torturous process happened countless times. His life was pure agony.

And yet, once the ordeal was over, Altun could transform into anything he wanted. He had spent the previous few days transforming his hair into small, unnoticeable items, like pebbles and pine needles. He learned that after transforming his hair into an inanimate object, he only had a few seconds until that object turned back into a clump of hair. And the best part was he could regrow that hair back instantly.

He had to time his escape perfectly. Altun knew he could transform his hair into the proper key without fail, but the tricky part was making the handle agile enough to bend into the keyhole. That is what he was practicing while ensuring his back was to the camera.

Without warning, a loud klaxon blared. This was the moment he'd been waiting for. He turned to the metal door and transformed his hair into a key with a long, flexible handle. While the key was still attached to him, he stuck it through the slot he received his meals from. It took him a few panicked seconds until he found the keyhole, then from there, he easily turned the key and unlocked the door.

He severed the key from his body and dashed out of the cell. He had a vague idea of what direction he needed to go, as he had been awake once when he was transported to and from the laboratory he had been tortured in.

The hallways twisted and turned, as if whoever had built this place had been on drugs. When he reached a fork, he quickly dashed down the hall to his right. After a few paces, he heard someone approaching.

"Who's there?" a voice called out to him.

He stopped in his tracks, as the voice sounded like it was a female Ancilsan. He had not been expecting to run into another Ancilsan—few of his kind leave their home on Strutheine. Most Ancilsan didn't want to leave their pack.

Sure enough, a female Ancilsan wearing light blue armor came around a bend. In contrast, he wore nothing but his naturally hairy hide. She stopped when she saw him.

"Who are you? Where did you come from?" she demanded as she pointed a rifle at him.

He didn't want to hurt her, but he knew she wasn't going to let him pass. Drawing from his memories of home, he transformed himself into a bromorg—a ferocious beast. Bromorgs have sharp teeth, two deadly tusks, and are covered from head to toe in venomous spikes. However, since he was the one controlling his transformations, Altun ensured his spikes would only cause her drowsiness.

The Ancilsan in blue armor stared at him with wide eyes as her gun lowered to the floor, likely due to her shock. He crashed into her, ensuring that several of the spikes punctured her flesh that lay underneath her protective layer of thick hair.

His opponent crashed to the ground. As he quickly morphed into her likeness, the full weight of what he had done stuck him. He had controlled the venom he had secreted. The possibilities of what he could produce were endless.

Altun shook his head and focused on the matter at hand. He awkwardly unlatched the armor from his slumbering kin and donned it. He double checked her body, found an ear-piece, and took that as well. He then headed in the direction she had come down, hoping that no one was behind him to stumble upon the body.

After a few minutes of navigating the twisting path, the alarm silenced and the lights returned to normal. After a few more paces, Altun heard voices. He turned around a bend and almost collided with a large purple lizard.

"Hey, watch it," the lizard hissed.

"Oh crap, I think it's an enemy!" a Nioavellian cried.

"No, wait! My name is Altun," he said as he transformed his face back to normal. "Are you allies with Mac, Lyd, and Poi?"

"Yes, they are our friends," a female Kolythoanthaean said. "If you know their names, then you must be the one we were told about."

As the Kolythoanthaean was talking, he scanned the large group. While there were a lot of strange beings, the oddest were two headless Eusphyrchiians.

"So, you're a friend?" the Eusphyrchiian wearing a large white cowboy hat asked, then looked at him. "You're not actually one of the guards?"

"No, I transformed myself into—"

"Hold on," the same Eusphyrchiian said as he held a hand out to silence him. "Brock is approaching—one of the bounty hunters. Two others accompany him. They're closing in on us fast."

Altun nodded and stepped forward. "I'll distract them."

"Are we going to trust him?" a male Nioavellian asked.

"I think we can trust him," the six-legged purple lizard said as she looked him over with her strange reptilian eyes.

"Doesn't seem like we have much of a choice," the Eusphyrchiian wearing the cowboy hat said.

"Stay safe, everyone," Altun said as he broke into a jog. He made only two twists around the hallway before he ran into a large, dark-skinned Human and two light-skinned Humans.

"Henela! What are you doing here? Shouldn't you be back at the elevator?" one of the light-skinned Humans asked.

"I received an order to check out the area back there," Altun replied, posing as Henela.

"As did we," the dark-skinned Human said. "We're heading there now."

"That's not necessary, there's nothing of significance to report."

"We were told West Kilinder was in Professor Peal's bay."

"I didn't see anyone of interest. They must have passed you somehow."

Before anyone could reply, a voice broke through their earpieces. "All Cyclones, please report to the hangar. Repeat, all Cyclones report to the hangar at once."

"What's going on now? Are we really missing the action?" the dark-skinned Human complained. "Come on, we better go. Wait, I'm getting new info." The Human stood with a finger to his ear for a few moments. "You three head back, Carl needs me to double-check Peal's area."

Before anyone could move, the lights blacked out momentarily and everything shook.

"What in the void? Did someone set off a bomb?" one of the Humans wearing blue armor said.

"Something like that. Carl just changed his mind—come on, we need to hurry back to the hangar, now!"

"Norsir is coming down the elevator now. We'll regroup with him soon," one of the other Humans announced.

Altun followed the Humans. He turned and looked behind him after a few paces.

*I'll forge on ahead,* Altun thought. *As long as everyone makes it out of this place alive, it will be worth it.*

---

Carl couldn't believe his eyes. Moments after Gazelle and Sid left the security room, pure chaos broke loose in the hangar. He was furious that they were forced to ignore West and the large group he had gathered.

*This has gone from bad to worse, then worse to a complete shitshow,* he thought. *I don't think there will be any coming back from this. I don't think Sid and Gazelle will make it in time.*

**38**

# ESCAPE FROM BELIEF

"Prepare yourselves, everyone, we've got six incoming," Navacus said as he ran down the moving walkway, gripping his knife. As a scientist, he had been the target of bullies when he was growing up, and those encounters had taught him how to defend himself. Plus, his connection with Sterg made him something even the phantoms should fear. He also had Fumalli, Syl, and Norman to back him up. What could go wrong?

"I see them," Norman said. "I can take out some of them."

"Go ahead, just be careful," he replied.

"Same to you," Norman said, then accelerated down the moving walkway. A moment later, the walkway lurched to a stop. Syl was thrown forward, but grabbed the handrail before he could be thrown face first onto the track. Meanwhile, Norman continued to charge at their foes in light blue armor as energy blasts streamed past him.

"Get down!" Norman cried.

"*Sterg, what do you suggest we do?*" Navacus thought—their silent conversation taking place triple as fast as talking out loud.

"*I am already redirecting each energy projectile the best I can. For our offense, I can blind them with a flash of light, though it will only disable them for a few moments,*" Sterg replied.

"*That may be all the time we need,*" he thought, then shut his eyes and shouted, "Everyone shut your eyes!"

Beside him, Syl screamed and fell to the ground. At the same time, a blast of bright, radiant light shot out of Sterg. Navacus opened his eyes and watched the guards writhe in agony on the ground. A moment later, Norman bowled over two of the guards, then turned back to face them.

"Let's go, c'mon! Eyes open," Norman yelled as he waved his arm.

Navacus turned his attention to Syl, who lay moaning on the ground. His left arm was smoking—he had taken a hit from an energy rifle.

Fumalli gasped. "Oh my word, Syl!"

"Help me get him to his feet, Fumi," Navacus said.

"I'm sorry Syl," Sterg said. "I was your shield, and I let you down."

"It's not your fault," Syl said through gritted teeth as he clutched at his wound.

Navacus put away his knife and helped to get Syl on his feet, causing the Kolythoanthaean to scream in pain.

"I think my ankle got twisted when I fell," Syl said breathlessly.

"Fumalli, you'll need to carry him," Navacus ordered.

"Of course. I got you, Syl."

Norman helped Navacus hoist Syl onto Fumalli's back. With his three legs, Fumalli was the best one to support Syl. Navacus grabbed his best friend's hand and pulled him along. The guards were still blinded, but could recover at any moment.

"*Hey Sterg, any other ideas?*"

As they ran past the guards, Sterg made him stop as it encased all six guards in a large time loop bubble, effectively forcing them to remain blinded until the group was out of range. Navacus turned and nodded to Fumalli as they continued. A little while later, the alarms silenced and the lights stopped flashing red. He wheezed in contentment.

The hallway was longer than he had expected, but they made it to the hangar not long after the encounter. It was massive—far larger than he would have imagined. Three gleaming white spaceships sat near each opposing wall with a large open space in the middle of the hangar bay. Each ship was the same. They had large black-windowed cockpits with straight middle sections, breaking off into two prong-like sections that could hold people, or in this case, large, monstrous creatures he assumed were the Titans. For the moment, Navacus could only see two, and they both lay unconscious in metal cages nearby two of the ships. One of the Titans was a large muscular humanoid with dark gray skin and bright yellow hair, and the other was an enormous bird with reddish-brown feathers. Sterg informed him that the third one was already loaded onto the spaceship directly in front of them.

Aside from the Titans, the hangar was full of Lakinceitian drones. Professor Peal was directing the drones, while his team—Kalosse, Mahlvern, and Walverm—were rushing about, ensuring each drone was on task. Navacus also spied at least eight more of the blue-armored guards and a short Eusphyrchiian in a red suit, who had a sour look on his white face. Finally, out of sight was the presence of a creature that had a strong aura surrounding it. This one seemed to be moving toward the spaceship on his right. Navacus wasn't sure who it was, but he had a strong feeling it was one of the Humans from Eklatros.

For the moment, no one had noticed them yet. He took another look at the cages the Titans were in.

*"Those cages were definitely not built for them. Sterg, can you wake them up? Let's see if we can cause a distraction."*

*"On it,"* Sterg replied.

Navacus felt Sterg rush over to the closest of the Titans—the giant avian—and pass through its mind. Sterg quickly identified the wide assortment of drugs coursing through its system and counteracted them. The massive bird began to stir.

"Hey! We've got intruders!"

Navacus looked around and saw a Eusphyrchiian wearing light blue armor pointing at them. A moment later, a deafening screech filled the hangar.

"It's awake! Karkilver is awake!" Mahlvern shouted in terror.

Sterg rushed to the yellow-haired Titan and woke it up a split second faster than the last. As soon as this one was awake, it rivaled the bird's screech with its own.

"Holy wormholes, what's going on?" Fumalli cried, Syl gasping in shock on his back.

Navacus shrugged. "I figured we needed a distraction."

"What now?" Norman asked, his voice filled with awe.

"We need to secure the spaceship directly in front of us. I believe that's where Theesakin is—the Titan West wanted us to save," Navacus replied.

"You must run as fast as you can," Sterg said in its deep, rumbling voice. "These chimeras won't be encaged for much longer."

"Red alert," Professor Peal shouted over a loud speaker. "Both Zadgarcolth and Karkilver are awake. I repeat, the Titans are awake! Where in the void are you, Durrist?"

"No one's listening!" Kalosse cried, then looked right at Navacus and the others and gasped.

"Let's move!" Navacus said, sprinting to the spaceship. Fumalli cursed and followed him. "Give Syl to Norman!"

Norman nodded, scooped Syl off Fumalli's back, and laid him down between himself and his treads. Norman wrapped an arm around Syl and revved forward. At the same time, the angry-looking Eusphyrchiian wearing red shouted orders at the blue-armored guards to attack.

All the while, Zadgarcolth and Karkilver screeched at each other, creating a deafening cacophony. They only made it a few dozen meters when a loud metallic snap rang through the air. Everyone's attention—even the guards'—turned to the large yellow beast. Zadgarcolth had broken two of the bars and was bending three more.

Across from Zadgarcolth, Karkilver attempted to flap its massive wings, causing the cage to vibrate. A moment after Zadgarcolth tore through three more bars, Karkilver's cage tipped over and crashed to the ground. Karkilver burst from its cage, shooting metal shards in every direction. Sterg quickly encased them in a protective bubble made from condensed vibrations. However, others weren't so lucky.

Navacus watched in horror as the two armored guards closest to them were impaled by metal bars. Five of the Lakinceitian drones were also struck. One of the projectiles narrowly missed cutting Professor Peal's head clean off.

The armored guards who were still standing fired their energy rifles at the Titans, but their weapons had no effect. Neither of the Titans were even remotely bothered by the energy blasts.

"Keep moving, everyone!" Navacus shouted, urging his team forward. He focused on the spaceship in front of him and blocked out everything else—even the thundering of the Titans. His body wasn't made for running, but he threw himself forward nonetheless. It was all that mattered.

*We need to move faster, Sterg*, Navacus thought. *Is there anything you can do to speed us up? I mean, at this point, I'm down to try anything, even that. Go for it.*

---

The artificial lights flickered and the ground beneath him shook as Theodore followed the strange aliens through the winding maze. He attempted to feel through the ground, but he realized he couldn't sense anything. This was not Eklatros—this was not the planet he knew and loved. Instead, he rather disliked this planet. During his time here, he had lost all his hair, his staff and clothes had been destroyed, and he'd been imprisoned for Eklatros knows how long. Worst of all, the love of his life was no more.

While the woman calling herself Kaytrona reminded him of Tyrona, she looked nothing like the woman he fell in love with. And yet, Kaytrona could wield Tyrona's wand without any issues, and the wand wouldn't respond to just anyone. It was incredibly confusing, and it tore at his heart, breaking it in ways he didn't know were possible.

He was one of the last ones in the group. Only the floating Human torso trailed behind him. It didn't matter that the alien was his ally—it really creeped him out.

One of the three small gray aliens that were floating through the air turned around to face them as the lights continued to flicker and said, "Dea, can you tell what's causing this?"

"It's hard to say," the limbless creep replied from behind him. "I sense a lot of activity coming from just ahead, though."

"I hope Navacus, West, and the others are all okay," another one of the small aliens said. He still wasn't sure which one was which.

"I'm sure they're all okay, Poi," one of the aliens said, while scooting closer to the other.

"We're approaching the door. It's slightly ajar," the other small alien said as it flew forward.

"Right, I can sense two presences in the next room. One is asleep and the other is extremely agitated," the floating torso said.

A small gray alien rushed forward. "I'll take a peek."

"Be careful, Lyd!"

The small alien flew through the open doorway and reappeared after a few seconds. "There's a taped up Lakinceitian professor and he's not pleased. The Human professor is the one that's asleep."

"Alright, let's—wait, I'm sensing something else now," the torso said.

Theodore turned around and looked past the creepy limbless alien, peering down the hall. It was faint, but he could feel several individuals moving quickly toward them. Cecil stepped up next to him.

"Are they on our side?" Cecil asked.

"It's hard to say," the limbless alien replied.

"I guess that means we should prepare for a fight," Kaytrona said as she stepped up to Theodore's other side and held out Tyrona's ivory wand.

He looked at the pale woman and she returned his gaze.

"Theodore, I want to explain, it's just—"

"Let's wait until we're away from this place, please," he said. "It's too painful."

"I should probably say something here as the leader, but I don't have much relationship experience," Cecil said quietly.

"Hush, all of you," the limbless one said. "They're near."

*Seriously, who is this woman?* Theodore thought as he prepared himself for possible conflict. *Why can't Tyrona just be Tyrona? Why did she have to be the one the Ekataramn had to take? Why couldn't it have been me?*

---

Lyd turned his attention away from the laboratory and stared down the twisted hallway they had just came from. Poi floated next to him and grabbed his hand.

"I sure hope it's West and his team," she whispered.

"Same here," he replied.

Mac looked at them quizzically, but before he could say anything, Dea broke the silence.

"I sense six approaching, none of them friendlies. They'll be here momentarily."

A deep, forced laugh sounded before he saw a muscular Human in a red shirt approaching. He was flanked by two pale Humans, a large Ancilsan, a Nioavellian, and a Kolythoanthaean—all wearing light blue armor.

"I get to have some fun after all," the muscular Human said as he took out a pair of spiked metal knuckles.

Lyd watched in awe as the Ancilsan dropped their rifle, grabbed the Kolythoanthaean and one of the Human guards by their heads, and smashed them together. They crashed to the floor. The Ancilsan then turned to the other Human in blue armor and ruthlessly clawed him to the ground.

While that was happening, Kaytrona had been muttering a spell with her wand held out in front of her. As the Human in blue armor fell, a burst of purple electricity shot out of the wand and hit the Nioavellian and the red-shirted Human in the chest, causing them to crumple to the floor. The elderly Human next to her gasped in shock.

The Ancilsan guard raised their hands while something strange happened to its face and body.

"I'm on your side. My name is Altun. There is a large group of other friendlies behind me."

"Altun, it really is you!" Poi cried as she rushed toward him. "I'm so happy to see that you're safe."

"And same with all of you. I'm happy to finally meet you face to face," Altun replied.

"Several others are approaching. I'm sensing West, Kurjon, Grasberg... and Bsarg," Dea announced.

"Bsarg? Why is he with them?" Mac asked.

"We'll find out soon enough," Dea replied.

*I thought we were done for*, Theodore thought. *Altun really took them by surprise. If things keep on progressing like this, we may actually make it out of here alive.*

---

West started running once he heard the commotion ahead of him. Everyone behind him picked up their paces as well.

"I really hope the others are okay," Kurjon said.

They came around a bend and saw Brock and five of the blue armored guards on the ground. Standing on the other side of the bodies was Dea, his team, an Ancilsan, and some of the Humans he had seen walk out of the gate.

"Good, you're all here now," Dea said as he floated to them. "We've got to hurry."

A moment later, the lights flickered and the ground shook.

"Agreed. It sounds like there's a war going on," West said. "Navacus and the others will need our help."

"You fools," Brock said as he pushed himself up and spit a bloody wad on the floor. "You'll never get away with this. Lord Foxaire will see to you one way or another."

"As long as he uses fools like you, we'll be just fine," West said. He charged his energy weapon and shot Brock in his side. The brute moaned and collapsed to the floor, piling onto the other bodies. "Damn, you really are nothing without Creson." West turned his attention to Dea and the others. "Looks like you all took care of yourselves pretty well."

"Thank Altun for the heavy lifting," Poi said as she floated closer, using a jetpack similar to his own.

"It was nothing. Humans and Kolythoanthaeans are weak," Altun said with a shrug.

"Compared to you, most definitely," the Human woman said.

"Hold on, are the lizards and snakes and things with us?" the elderly Eklatros Human asked.

"Yes. We're all in this together. I wish we had time for introductions, but for now, you can trust Newtus, Sassafrass, Blood Bat, and the rest. Kamarial here is with us as well."

"And the rest?" Denoptace said as he jumped in the air and waved his stick-like arms in an agitated manner. "What do you mean, and the rest?"

"Oh wow, they can talk!" the muscular red-haired Human said excitedly.

"And Denoptace, too," West said. If he had eyes, he'd be rolling them.

"And Penny and Susan," Kamarial added.

"Me! Me!" Blood Bat screeched.

"What about Bsarg?" Dea asked.

"I'm with you," Bsarg replied. "This place is a cesspit. I don't want to be here any longer either."

"We need to hurry. We've got to meet up with Navacus and the others!" West said as he stepped over Brock and the others. "Come on, everyone. Follow me, I'll lead the way."

"I don't normally follow anyone, but you I will follow," Newtus said.

"Same here," Sassafrass added.

"Who are you now, exactly?" the Human with red hair asked.

"My name is West. I was an experiment within these walls once, then was hired by Lord Foxaire, and now I rebel against him."

"Okay then. I'm Cecil."

"Cecil, could you watch my back? I could use someone like you."

"No problem, West." Cecil said and then turned to his companion. "Hey, Theodore, *West Wind* and now West... how strange is that?"

"*Newtus, keep an eye on Bsarg,*" West asked telepathically.

"*I'm watching everyone,*" she replied.

*Good,* West thought to himself. *There really are a lot of us now. I just hope we can overcome any obstacles we face with a group this large and diverse.*

<hr>

At this point, there was nothing more Carl could do but watch the chaos unfold on the screens. Sid and Gazelle still had ten minutes of travel time to get to the compound. At this rate, they'd be arriving to rubble.

Professors Durrist, Randall, and Xergat were all down. Most of Sid's Cyclones were incapacitated, and none of the ones standing had any tranquilizers strong enough to take the Titans down. Only Sid had the proper equipment.

Currently, Zadgarcolth was ripping the rest of his cage to shreds as Karkilver flapped its large wings. For the moment, all three transport-class spaceships were still untouched, which was a small blessing, even though Professor Clums, Norman, and others ran toward one of them. Luckily, they were directly in the path between the two Titans.

Zadgarcolth, finally free of its cage, screeched and pounded its yellow-haired chest. In response, Karkilver lunged forward. Everyone in its path scrambled to get out of the way, but Mahlvern wasn't so lucky. Karkilver's talons ripped Professor Peal's assistant to shreds. Lord Foxaire cursed, his voice seething in anger.

Zadgarcolth pounded its fists into the ground, causing all three ships to rock back and forth. The yellow ape-like beast charged, leaving two craters behind.

The screens flickered momentarily as the monsters met. Zadgarcolth raised an arm as thick as a tree trunk and readied its sharp claws. In response, Karkilver thrust its sharp beak at its foe. Zadgarcolth dodged and slammed its arm against Karkilver's neck. Long wings covered in dense plumage enveloped the yellow ape, and Karkilver lifted its head off the ground and screeched.

Zadgarcolth struggled for a few seconds before it forcefully shoved the large bird to the ground, breaking free from Karkilver's wings. Zadgarcolth panted heavily and turned just in time to block Karkilver's sharp beak.

Carl's attention turned to Professor Clums as he and his rebels made it to the ship that contained Theesakin.

"Do you think they mean to free that one as well?" Carl asked.

"They mean to escape. As long as Theesakin is asleep, he won't be a problem for them—for now, at least," Lord Foxaire replied. "But Carl, look here."

Lord Foxaire pointed to Professor Durrist's lab as dozens of figures streamed through it.

"Ah, West is finally making it to the hangar," Carl said, his voice heavy with sarcasm.

Lord Foxaire growled. "You know I don't like that."

"I'm sorry, my lord. This situation is just completely out of control. Like, there goes all of Professor Peal's subjects, and the magical Humans. They broke everyone free. And why is Bsarg with them? Is he revolting against us as well?"

"We needn't be concerned with Bsarg," Lord Foxaire growled. "He's Lakinceitian. He's only doing what he thinks will ensure his survival. I doubt he has any allegiance to any of them."

"I hope that's the case," Carl responded as the Titans continued to brawl. A ping sounded in the room.

"Well, at least the one Eklatros Human we held onto is finally loaded into one of the spaceships."

"We need to order the pilots to get to their positions," Lord Foxaire replied.

Carl quickly brought the info up on his tablet, then frowned. "Sir, two of Sid's Cyclones were the pilots, and they are deceased, and the third and last one is unresponsive."

Lord Foxaire growled deeply. "Contact the bounty hunters. We need them to be the pilots, and once Sid gets to the hangar, he can be the other pilot. We need to salvage what we can."

"Agreed," Carl said as he contacted Tag Creson.

*Man am I glad Lord Foxaire ordered me to stay behind*, Carl thought. *I don't know what I'd do if I were in that mess.*

# 39

# ESCAPE FROM THE COMPOUND

To his utmost surprise, Navacus made it to the spaceship with his team and encountered no further opposition. As soon as they arrived, Norman set Syl down on the floor of the receiving bay and leaned him against the wall. In the module with them was a large, green dragon-like Titan—Theesakin. It lay in a metal cage like the ones the other Titans broke free from.

*"He still slumbers—he is heavily drugged,"* Sterg said telepathically to Navacus.

*"Should we wake Theesakin up?"*

*"Negative. There's no need and would only draw unnecessary attention to ourselves."*

*"Yeah, we've already been noticed. That Eusphyrchiian was not happy about us taking this ship."*

*"They have their hands full; we're okay for now,"* Sterg replied.

While they waited for the others to arrive, Navacus and his team watched in awe as the two Titans continued to fight.

For the moment, Zadgarcolth had Karkilver in a headlock and was pounding its fist into the side of Karkilver's face. Karkilver screeched in pain, but right before the fourth strike, Karkilver's body began taking on a light sheen. An electric shock burst from

Karkilver's plumage, causing Zadgarcolth to jump back in surprise. It pounded its fists into the floor and roared.

"This is unreal," Norman said.

"Yeah, I knew today was going to be intense, but this is beyond insane," Syl said, the pain creeping into his voice.

"Right, did you see what happened to Mahlvern?" he asked.

"That made me sick to my stomach," Fumalli said.

"Rest in peace, Mahlvern," Syl said. "You did not deserve such a violent end. At least Professor Peal and the others are safe."

"So, you woke the Titans up?" Norman asked, turning to Sterg.

"Indeed. It was a simple procedure to counteract the drugs that had been coursing through their bodies," Sterg replied out loud.

"That doesn't sound simple to me," Fumalli said.

"Yeah, right?" Syl added.

"Wait, look! I think I see the others. They're all together in one large group," Navacus said, pointing.

"Really? That's great," Norman said.

"They better hurry. I fear these monsters will destroy everything in their path to kill each other," Fumalli said.

"Luckily, we haven't been hit yet," Norman said.

A moment later, a deafening screech drowned out everything else. Karkilver flapped its wings and lifted off the ground. Zadgarcolth jumped into the air and pounced on the giant bird. Before Zadgarcolth could strike, Karkilver slashed with its beak, cutting deep into the yellow-haired beast's chest. Zadgarcolth covered its wound with one arm as it howled, displaying its long and deadly fangs.

*"Sterg, can you help West, Dea, and the others? Are they in range?"*

*"Yes, they are. Leaving now."*

*Thank you, Sterg,* Navacus thought. *Let's make sure no one else gets hurt.*

West entered Professor Durrist's lab and found Durrist and Randall bound and gagged. Nails were pinning down Durrist's tail. As he raged, he tried to transform, but the nails were preventing him from completely changing.

"Holy Eklatros, is that one okay?" Cecil asked.

"Whoa, it looks he can shape-shift, too," Poi said as she floated next to their Ancilsan companion.

"And yet he cannot fully transform. How pathetic," Altun said. He still wore the light-blue armor.

Professor Durrist tried to talk to them, but it was impossible to understand him through the tape. They passed through another door and started down a long hallway. There were two moving walkways, but both were stagnant.

"I don't mean to brag, but if I was in the position that Lakinceitian is in, all I would need to do is enlarge the holes in my tail so I could slip from the nails and turn my mouth into a surface that the tape couldn't adhere to," Altun said with a note of smugness in his voice.

"I cannot shape-shift myself, so I can't speak much on the topic," Bsarg replied, "But it sounds like you have better transformation skills than even the most talented Lakinceitian shape-shifters."

"Quite so. Now, observe," Altun said as they approached a group of fallen soldiers wearing light blue armor. Altun approached and transformed his large, muscular body into a thin stick and the blue armor slipped right off. He quickly returned to normal.

"Wow, that would save time dressing and undressing," Grasberg said thoughtfully as he looked down at his three legs.

"Hush everyone, we're approaching the hangar," West said to the group.

"It sounds like two giants are fighting each other," Lyd whispered.

"If the Titans got loose somehow, then that could be what's going on," West whispered.

After a few moments, the hangar came into view. It was soon clear that two of the Titans were indeed fighting. A moment later, an orb of light approached them.

"Sterg!" West exclaimed. "What are you doing here? Is Navacus okay?"

"Navacus is fine. I'm here to protect you," Sterg replied.

"Uh, West? Who are you talking to?" Cecil asked.

"Oh right, you can't see or hear it. Sterg is a Light Being and is here to protect us."

"A Light Being, is it?" the elderly man said thoughtfully. "That's how Yttendaus appeared to Ànifa."

"We must move swiftly and efficiently," Sterg replied. "Those of you who can hear me, ensure the others stay close. We can't allow for anyone to get separated from the group once I encase you in my protective barrier."

"No problem," Dea said.

"Sure thing," West said, then relayed the message to everyone else.

"Like you said, West, I can't hear or see it, but I can feel a strange presence. Ados and Adok are sending me crazy signals, and same with the spider in the cube I'm holding," Ivy said, surprising several of them with his double voices.

"Whoa, who said that?" Kurjon asked with wide eyes.

"That was me. My apologies. I didn't mean to surprise anyone," Ivy replied.

"Right, we'll have time to chat later," West said as Sterg enveloped them in a protective barrier. The barrier was transparent and yet shimmered with a silvery hue. "Sterg has wrapped us in its protective bubble. We'll need to move as fast as we can past the Titans. We cannot stop and must not get separated," he reiterated.

"I've got your back," Cecil said as he opened and closed his fists.

"Let's do this," Newtus said with a firm nod.

They burst into the hangar just in time to witness Zadgarcolth shove Karkilver into one of the three identical spaceships, completely severing one of the ship's tail sections.

West stopped in his tracks, only to be pushed forward by Newtus.

"Weren't you the one that said not to stop?" Newtus said playfully.

"Right, sorry," he replied, picking up his pace.

"Our goal is the spaceship directly in front of us," Sterg said.

"We're headed to the ship right before us," Dea repeated to the group. "That's where Navacus and the others are."

As they ran across the open hangar, they passed several fallen drones and guards. West caught Creson's eye, who squinted at him and started running. A blast from an energy weapon scorched the ground in front of Creson, stopping him in his tracks. He spied Syl holding the smoking rifle as he leaned against the interior of the ship they were fast approaching.

All the while, Sterg reflected several energy rifle blasts and flying debris with the protective barrier.

*This is chaos*, West thought. *Thank you, Sterg. I'm not sure how we would be faring without you.*

---

Norman could barely contain himself. He spied Kate among the group West was leading. She had yet to meet his gaze, and his heart swelled as he watched her focus on getting to him safely.

He revved slightly toward the ramp and Navacus gave him a stern look. "Stay put, Norman. Sterg is doing everything it can to ensure they make it here safely."

"Right, I know. It's just—"

"Norman!"

He snapped his attention back to Kate. She waved at him while she pushed her way toward the front of the diverse group. Within moments, they reached the ramp and Norman charged down it before anyone could stop him. Kate knelt and embraced him in her warm arms. He squeezed her back, fully aware of his treads beneath him as it made for an awkward hug. Awkward or not, he finally had Kate back in his arms.

"Dagnabbit, what's all this now?" an elderly Human said as he approached them. "What's the meaning of this, Tyrona?"

Kate pulled out of his arms and looked back and forth between him and the unknown man. "Um, Norman, meet Theodore, and

Theodore, meet Norman. Norman, please call me Kaytrona—I am your Kate, but I am also his Tyrona."

It took Norman several long moments before her words fully hit him. "Wait, what? What do you mean—Kaytrona?"

"Everyone, I know emotions are running rampant right now, but so are the Titans," West said.

"Navacus, what's the situation?" Dea asked as the Eridavlos floated over to the Yggdrazim professor.

"Right, now that we're all here, we need to take control of the other ship—the one that is still undamaged," Navacus replied as he pointed at the spaceship that was being pounded to pieces by the raging monsters.

"What about Druder? Where is he?" the red-haired Human asked.

"Who's Druder?" West asked.

"He's our companion from Eklatros," Theodore said.

"Everyone, I am sensing a presence in the destroyed spaceship, and I believe it to be Druder," Sterg said.

Navacus quickly repeated the message. "I'm sorry, but I don't think we can do anything about him," Navacus said as he placed a feathery hand on Cecil's arm.

"Allow me to try," the Ancilsan said. "I believe I can sedate the Titans using my unique abilities."

"That would be helpful, thank you. Our distraction has become a hindrance," Navacus said.

"I'm only here to help," the Ancilsan said. He waved and started to walk away from the group.

"So, what about Druder?" the red-haired Human reiterated.

"I'll do my best to get to him," the Ancilsan replied.

"Altun, hold up. When you're done, run as fast as you can to the closest ship. We won't leave you behind," West said.

"You must if we do not make it in time. Depart as soon as you are ready to. I will make sure your friend Druder remains safe, no matter what happens," Altun said. Before anyone could argue, Altun turned and ran toward the battling monsters.

"We must trust in him. Now, who's coming with me?" Navacus asked.

After a quick discussion, it was decided. Norman would stay back with Kate, Syl, Grasberg, and the others while Navacus, Dea, West, and anyone else who wasn't staying behind would run to the other ship. As for the slumbering Titan in the ship with them, Bsarg insisted he could watch over him until they regrouped at their rendezvous point. Sterg confirmed that would be fine, as Theesakin was still heavily sedated.

"Norman, I have your attachments. Follow me, and I'll give them to you."

"That would be fantastic, thank you."

Dea led him into the primary hull of the ship and regurgitated Norman's attachments. It was odd to watch his legs emerge from a legless being; though, it may not have been the strangest thing he had seen all day.

*Kate, what's going on with you?* Norman thought as he detached his treads and prepared his legs. *Why are you calling yourself by a different name now? I can only assume you were experimented on, and I mean to get to the bottom of this once we have a moment to breathe.*

---

Ivy had volunteered to help to take the second spaceship. Among his companions were several Acampachetlian species, including the Loxocemae, the Neutortous, and the Zubba. He had given the encaged Dark Therid spider to Kamarial, who was staying behind on the other ship.

As they set off, he once again felt a strange presence grace them with a protective aura. He positioned himself near the back of the group to ensure everyone made it to the second ship safely.

They only made it a few dozen meters when the ground shook violently. He focused his out-of-body viewpoint behind him and saw the two Titans were unconscious. Their Ancilsan companion's abilities rivaled even his own, as there was nothing he could have done to stop them.

"Come on, we're almost there!" West called from the front of the group.

Without warning, the Nioavellian in front of him tripped and fell flat on his face. Ivy stopped to help him up, but as he did so, an energy blast grazed his right arm.

"Don't you dare run from me again," the short Eusphyrchiian wearing the red suit yelled, rage burning in his eyes.

"Try to stop us, then," Ivy replied as he commanded Ados and Adok to fire off their most acidic silk strands. The acidic strands flew toward the Eusphyrchiian foe. At the last second, his enemy drew an energy sword and sliced through the silk, cutting them out of the air.

The Eusphyrchiian laughed. "You'll need to be faster than that!"

The Eusphyrchiian ran toward him and the Nioavellian, who was now back on his feet. The Nioavellian drew a kitchen knife with a shaking hand. Ivy whipped out his ivy legs and tripped the approaching Eusphyrchiian. He readied Ados and Adok, but a painful blast to his back sent him sprawling. He fell to the ground, his gaze focused on the Human in light-blue armor who had shot him.

He couldn't move his body. In response to his paralysis, Ados, Adok, and his ivy forced him to crawl away from the Nioavellian. No matter how hard he tried, he couldn't help the trembling Nioavellian as he faced the bounty hunter alone. Since his body was in shock, his synergistic connection with his parts was out of sync. All he could do was watch as energy blasts whizzed over him and struck the guards in blue armor.

*I'm so sorry,* Ivy thought. *I don't even know your name, but you were one of us, and I let you down.*

---

Altun took a deep breath and morphed into a Lakinceitian drone. He slowly moved his bulky body into the center of the hangar. Even though the hangar was quite chaotic, he had a clear path. Plus, no one was paying attention to him, just as he had planned.

He faced the two monstrous beasts. At the moment, the large yellow-haired one had the massive bird in a chokehold while it stood on both of the bird's wings. He wondered if he should intervene or allow the bird to be killed. Before he could decide, the bird shocked the yellow beast with a jolt of electricity, and within seconds, the tables were turned. At the expense of the spaceship, the large bird tilted its head back and screeched victoriously.

The bird then aimed its beak and lunged in an attempt to stab the yellow beast in the face. However, Altun was faster. He shot two modified hairs at each monster. Each spike had a concentrated sedative, and he figured a double dose each would do the trick.

The Titans immediately slammed to the ground. The large bird fell into the middle section of the hangar bay, while the yellow-haired beast fell into the already damaged ship, turning the cockpit to pure rubble. Altun moved his Lakinceitian body as fast as he could toward the undamaged modular sections. He hoped Druder was safe.

*I'm coming for you, my unmet friend,* he thought. *However, while the main threat has been neutralized, there are foes about. It's unlikely that we'll make it out of here today, but if anyone had to be left behind, I'm glad it's me. With my talents, I can blend right in, which means that, in time, I may be able to stage another prison break. If all goes according to my hastily put together plan, of course.*

The violent shaking and cacophony of sounds finally ceased. Druder sat cross-legged on the floor and breathed a sigh of relief. He had no idea what was going on, but he was still alive, even if it meant he was still a prisoner.

As he mulled everything over, a door opened. The sudden stream of light blinded him, so he turned away and covered his eyes. As he did so, a foreign presence slithered into the room with him.

"I'm sorry for the sudden intrusion. My name is Altun. Are you Druder?"

"Yes. What do you want with me?" he asked without looking at the creature.

"I'm allies with your friends. I didn't catch all their names, but Cecil was asking about you. I promised him I'd keep you safe."

At the mention of Cecil, Druder turned and peered at the creature. It was similar to a Gnusar, which meant this must be one of the Lakinceitians. As he studied the alien creature, he watched in disbelief as the creature's ugly, leathery face suddenly sprouted brown hair. Within seconds, two sharp fangs and two large eyes appeared within the fur.

"This is my true face—I am not a Lakinceitian. I am in a similar position as you, so I must lie low," Altun said as he morphed his face back into a Lakinceitian's.

"What did you just do? Was that real?" Druder asked.

Before Altun could answer, three others stormed into his cell. They rushed over to him, completely ignoring Altun.

"Get on your feet and hold out your hands," the blue, three-legged alien barked.

Druder stood up and did as he was told. A moment later, a human wearing light blue armor snapped metal shackles to his hands, then bent down and shackled his legs.

"Now, move your ass," the gray alien said. "And how did this drone get in here? My word, everything has gone to shit. How could this day get any worse," the alien sighed then pointed a device at Altun and tapped on the screen. "Come along, you."

"Hey, at least the Titans got put down," one of the ones in blue armor said.

"Yeah, but how? What even happened? They didn't just fall asleep on their own in the middle of a life-or-death struggle."

"Maybe Sid knows what happened. He'll be arriving any minute now."

The chain connecting Druder's feet together was quite short, forcing him to shuffle. As he was pushed out of his room, he looked back and saw Altun silently following them.

Druder's eyes were still adjusting, so the shackles actually helped to ensure he didn't trip over anything. As things came into focus, he thought he could make out the forms of two large beasts. One reminded him of a dire sloth and the other was some kind of massive eagle. He shrugged and focused on his shuffling.

*Those monsters must have caused all the ruckus,* he thought. *And yet, what in Yttendaus is happening? Where are Cecil and Theodore? Did they escape? I really hope so. I wish I could have spoken to Altun more, but at least I have an ally.*

Navacus ran as fast as he could toward the ship as he fought back tears. Every ounce of him wanted to turn back and help Fumalli. And yet he had to continue on and ensure that everyone else made it to the second spaceship safely.

After an agonizing amount of time, they made it to the spaceship without any further incidents. They ran up the main entrance ramp, and Dea immediately rushed to the cockpit to start up the ship.

Now that he had completed his task, Navacus turned and ran back down the ramp with West in tow. He watched as their Eusphyrchiian ally used its ivy to crawl toward the ship, then focused on Fumalli. Navacus watched in horror as his closest friend in the world faced the bounty hunter with a kitchen knife.

"Shit, Creson is going after Professor Qymberkon!" West exclaimed.

Navacus was too focused to respond. As Fumalli stepped up to Creson, Creson expertly unarmed Fumalli by grabbing the knife out of his hands. Creson lunged at Fumalli and stabbed him in the chest.

"No!" Navacus screamed.

Creson, drawn to the noise, turned to Navacus and smiled, as if the pain excited him.

Without warning, stands of ivy shot out of the Eusphyrchiian and wrapped around the ship's landing gear while another strand of ivy wrapped around Fumalli. At the same time, numerous strands of silk shot from the two large black spiders and encased Creson in webbing. The Eusphyrchiian propelled itself toward them, causing it and Fumalli to slide up the ramp.

"Ivy, that was amazing!" West cried as he ran back up the ramp.

Navacus followed and knelt next to Fumalli.

"Hey, Nava," Fumalli said in a weak voice. Dark red blood trickled out of the wound in his chest where the kitchen knife remained.

"Fumi, I'm here," he said, tears welling in his eyes.

"Nava, did everyone make it?"

"I think so, yes. Hush now, don't speak. Save your strength."

"Navacus... tell my parents I forgive them..." Fumalli whispered. His head drooped as the strength left his body.

Activity buzzed around him as Navacus felt the spaceship lurch forward. They were finally moving—finally leaving the compound. They had accomplished their goal, and yet Fumalli Qymberkon lay dead in his arms.

He burst into tears and felt someone place a hand on his back. He curled into a ball and cried.

*Fumalli... why you?* Navacus thought. *Why couldn't it have been me? Out of the two of us, you deserved to live, not I. How did this happen? I know, I don't blame you, Sterg. It's only thanks to you that we made it this far. No, I blame myself. If only I could have done more, then maybe you'd still be alive.*

*With peace, and love, and faith... rest easy now, Fumalli, my dearest friend. I'll always love you.*

## 40

# INTERLUDE: LOCATION - THORPI

```
Begin Replay of NIWAT Inner Datalog
Recording C-0000670336 S-001 N-01
```

We emerged into the newest star system and hovered above a barren, rocky planet orbited by a large oval ring. Situated at the top of the oval was a space station.

"Whoa, so that's what we've been missing out on," Raff said as he bounced around in my seat. "Now I really wish our previous vessel had windows. I could watch us jump through space all day long and never grow tired of it."

"It's pretty neat, huh?" I replied.

"It was the definition of stellar," Raza said, her voice filled with wonder.

"I'm glad I could witness such a miraculous sight," Jurhon said, tears glistening in his eyes.

"What is that?" Anqi asked as she pointed at the ring station.

"It looks like a typical space station to me, and the ring must be the space-gate," Zanzi said.

"My mind is completely blown right now," Gonth said. "This

spaceship is one thing, but people *living* in space full-time? Who knew such a thing was even a possibility?"

"*Francentia*, run a scan of the planet and the space station," Maker Denorad ordered.

"Affirmative. Scanning. Scanning. Scan complete. The planet is completely uninhabitable. The atmosphere is too thin to support life. However, I am sensing a large cluster of life on the space station."

"Right, that's Kingau's garden. All sorts of plants and animals live there," Raza said.

"So, not only people, but even plants and animals can live in space? That is a wondrous feat," Mikhail said.

"Eh, it's overdone, especially in the dramas I used to watch," Zanzi said with a wave of his hand.

A soft ping sounded. "Incoming transmission, Maker," Blu-Dreem said. "The signal is coming from the space station."

"Patch them through," Maker Denorad responded.

"At once," Blu-Dreem said.

A moment later, an unknown voice came through *Francentia*'s speakers.

"Hello, can you hear me?" the voice asked.

"We hear you loud and clear," Maker Denorad replied.

"Kingau! We're back," Raff said, bouncing in the seat. I laid a hand on him to calm him down.

"Is that you, Raza and Raff?"

"Right, it's us," Raza replied. "We've brought new friends. They're the ones you've been waiting for."

"What a relief. I'm so happy you're back after all this time. Please, make your way to the landing zone. I'll meet you in the hangar bay."

Maker Denorad cleared his throat. "Right, will do. This is Captain Denorad speaking. Bringing in *Francentia* now."

"Wonderful. See you in a jiffy."

<hr>

```
Begin Replay of NIWAT Inner Datalog
Recording C-0000670336 S-002 N-01
```

*Francentia* touched down in the barren hangar. There were no other spacecrafts and the machinery was sparse, which gave us a lot of room.

"This feels a little like home," Zombu said sadly.

"I don't know what your home is like, but this is something I've never seen before," Gonth said as he stood up from his chair and stretched his arms above his head.

"Right, let's cut the chatter. I'm not sure what to expect, but let's try to be presentable," Maker Denorad ordered.

"I'm sure she'll appreciate that," Raza replied.

All eleven of us made our way down the ramp. A small gray humanoid wearing a purple spacesuit waited for us at the bottom.

"Holy smokes, there's a lot of you. I wasn't expecting this many. I'm sorry, where are my manners? I'm Kingau, and it's so nice to finally have someone else to talk to again," she said, bowing.

"Kingau! It's so great to see you," Raff said as he ran up to Kingau, wrapping her in a hug. Kingau was almost a head shorter than Raff.

"You look good, Kingau," Raza said.

"Thank you. I don't feel too great, though. But that's no matter. What's important is that you're all here now."

"Thank you for your hospitality, Kingau. I'm Captain Denorad and this is my crew," Maker Denorad said, then introduced everyone, including the Eklatros humans and the Kolythoanthaean, Jurhon.

"Please, follow me to a place where we can speak more comfortably. I can offer fresh fruits and nuts for refreshments," Kingau said.

"Thank you, but I don't need any sustenance, and neither do my companions," I said as I indicated to Blu-Dreem, Zanzi, and Zombu.

"No problem," Kingau replied.

"Fresh fruit sounds divine," Jurhon answered.

"I second that," Anqi chimed in.

Kingau led us into a well-furnished room that had several large couches and comfortable chairs. Scattered around the room were various potted plants. In the center of the room was a round table where there were several bowls of various foods.

"Is this the garden you were talking about?" Zanzi said, causing Kingau to chuckle.

"Oh no, this is not my garden. I just like to have as many plants around me as I can. They really help to freshen up the air. Now please make yourselves comfortable, as we have a lot to discuss."

***

Begin Replay of NIWAT Inner Datalog
Recording C-0000670336 S-002 N-07

I watched Anqi inspect an orange fruit before popping it in her mouth. Her eyes lit up, and she quickly grabbed several more of the bite-sized fruits.

"Before I tell my story, I again want to thank all of you," Kingau said. "I was honestly getting a little stir crazy being cooped up in here all by myself. Well, I'm not alone; I have the animals and plants to talk to, but they can't talk back, you know?"

"I understand. Isolation isn't easy," Jurhon replied.

"No, it is not. Now, is everyone ready?"

"Mikhail is still using the lavatory," Gonth said.

"I'm just now finished," Mikhail said as he stepped out of the restroom. "That's the nicest lavatory I've ever seen."

"That's because it never gets used. That one was meant for humans and Kolythoanthaeans, not for me. Everything in there is too big; that's why I have my own.

"But now that everyone is ready, let's dive into this." Kingau cleared her throat and continued. "This is not a story I enjoy telling, but I must, in order for you all to better understand your roles.

"My story begins when Thorpi was still a beautiful planet that supported a wide variety of life."

"So, Thorpi is the planet we're orbiting?" Blu-Dreem asked.

"Indeed. Thorpi was my home planet, and I miss it dearly. But I can never go back there—no one can."

"Right, we noticed there's basically no atmosphere," Maker Denorad said.

"Correct. I'll explain what caused that soon enough. Now, when I was young, Thorpi thrived with life. And yet, there was always a foreboding cloud hanging over everyone. For every Harmertian knew that one day our planet would be destroyed. And yet, that knowledge ensured that every Harmertian lived their life to the fullest. If someone wanted to do something, they'd do it, and it rarely mattered if it was legal or not. It really was a beautiful time. A time I call the golden age of the Harmertians.

"You see, several hundred years before I was born lived a highly revered Harmertian named Rej'jah, or Rej of the Jah clan. Rej'jah became a highly revered deity among my people. Rej'jah told us they had foreseen our demise, and that if the Harmertian species were to survive this devastating attack, we would need to be prepared.

"And so, four contingency plans were enacted and constructed over the next few hundred years. The first to start construction was the fortified city of Sai. This city was constructed deep underground and was designed to indefinitely sustain a large population of Harmertians. The second contingency plan was an ark—a large spaceship that could hold thousands of Harmertians and sustain them for several years. The third plan was to create incubation pods for all the Harmertians that would be unable to make it to Sai or the ark in time. I myself used one of these pods, and it is the only reason I still breathe. Now, the last and final contingency plan caused our planet's destruction—a biological weapon that had the power to completely destroy our atmosphere and render Thorpi uninhabitable."

"What? You destroyed your own planet? That's unthinkable!" Anqi cried.

"Many of us also felt that way. But when faced with our own extinction, that was the only way to ensure we would destroy the thing that would destroy us. The other three contingency plans would help to assure the Harmertians' survival in multiple ways.

"Before the attack, no one thought they would live to see it. We were taken by such surprise that our planet fell in less than a day. Gnusaramnii and its minions completely overwhelmed us. Millions died before they could reach a safety zone. But the ark successfully left our planet, though I don't know anything about the status of Sai. I'd say there's as much of a chance that no one is alive as there is that it's now a flourishing city."

Kingau paused and took a sip of water before continuing. "As I mentioned, I used one of the incubation pods to survive the attack. However, I was the only survivor from those pods. You see, I was awoken by a group of humans and Kolythoanthaeans and was quickly taken to a medical bay. I was the only one they found."

"A group of humans and Kolythoanthaeans, you say? That's sounds a lot like our group now," Jurhon said.

"Indeed, and it is no coincidence. Of course, not all of you are human."

"Yeah, I'm an elf, which are better than humans," Gonth said as he crossed his arms, eliciting a sharp look from Mikhail and Anqi.

"I'm not human, but I do have human parts that Maker Denorad donated to me," Zombu said.

"How interesting. How have your human parts not withered away in your artificial body?"

"They're encased in special sacks filled with a specific solution of chemicals," Maker Denorad said.

"Ah, I see. Your technology is beyond anything my species was capable of. Though we did accomplish great feats. Our weapon successfully eliminated our invaders. I saw the piles of slug-like bodies myself as I was taken off-planet. That was my last time on Thorpi.

"But, to the point. I apologize for rambling. The humans and Kolythoanthaeans that saved me also had members of my own species with them. Several Harmertians greeted me when I awoke and told me all about their escape from Thorpi and how they found refuge in a place called the Vortex Solar System. They convinced the humans and Kolythoanthaeans to lay aside their differences and put their space race to good use.

"Now, this was way back when the space-gates were still operational. For you see, around each terraformed planet, a space-gate was built that utilized the natural ring of wormholes that surrounded the Vortex System. And even though my planet was destroyed, they began to build a space-gate around Thorpi. However, construction was abandoned shortly before the gate was finished. The wormholes surrounding the Vortex System were acting up and causing the space-gates to malfunction. So, this gate was abandoned and all the workers returned to their homes."

"So, this gate isn't functional then?" Maker Denorad said. "Tiresias had promised us that this gate would take us to the Vortex System."

"Oh it can, and it will. The first time Raza and Raff were here, they and many others of their kind completed the gate. After that, Tiresias and Mahki recalibrated the gate, so now one ship can pass through the gate before that calibration is broken."

"Ah, that's right. Mahki was still with Tiresias at that time," Raza said.

"Oh? What happened to Mahki?" Kingau asked in horror.

"He was stolen by a dark wizard. At least, that's what Tiresias tells us," Raff replied.

"Then it must be true," Kingau said and placed a hand over her heart. "I mourn for them."

After a moment of silence, Maker Denorad spoke up. "So, when can we use this gate?"

"In due time. We first need to activate the gate, and that can take several hours," Kingau replied, then started to cough. As soon as her coughing fit ceased, she took a long drink of water.

"Is it your cancer?" Raza asked in concern.

"It's been getting worse. I honestly don't know how much longer I can hold out, which is why your timing is impeccable."

"If you don't mind me asking, what kind of cancer do you have?" Maker Denorad asked.

"It's practically everywhere. This morning I tested in at sixty-seven percent cancerous. The only reason I still live is because of the temporary medical treatments the humans and Kolythoanthaeans gave me, and from a healing energy that Tiresias wrapped me in.

"You see, I was in that incubator for years. Those that found me have no idea how I survived, as everyone else had succumbed to the intense radiation. However, even though I survived, I did not come out of it unscathed. The cancer that ravages my body will never go away. I will never be healed from it," Kingau explained.

"Even so, I have anti-cancer pills back on *Francentia*—our spaceship," Maker Denorad said. "I regularly take them to help with the radiation. I'm sure they could help."

"If you can spare some, that would be most kind," Kingau said as she placed her palms together.

"Certainly, it's no problem. *Francentia* can always generate more pills."

"You speak of your ship as if she were a person," Kingau said.

"Well, she is quite unique," I said. "Even though her creativity and AI are much less capable than my own, she has a pleasant personality and can even come up with some good ideas."

"How fascinating. You must tell me more about how that all works. But first things first—I better go get the gate activated. I could use some assistance."

"We'll help!" Raza replied, slapping Raff on the back.

"I can also help," Blu-Dreem said.

"I would like to as well," I replied. "I'm very interested to see how this works."

"Can we all go?" Anqi asked.

"That's fine with me," Kingau replied with a smile.

"In that case, I'll go fetch some anti-cancer pills for you," Maker Denorad replied. "I'll meet up with you guys."

"How will you know where to go?" Kingau asked.

"We can let him know through our chat," Zombu replied.

Begin Replay of NIWAT Inner Datalog
Recording C-0000670336 S-002 N-12

I stood in the space station's control room near the panel that would activate the gate. I also spied consoles that monitored the internal temperature, humidity, water filtration, air purification, gravity stabilizers, and more. Much of the information was easy to understand, despite this facility being constructed by people who originated from a completely different planet.

As I studied all the different components, I became more and more impressed. The calculations needed to calibrate a machine such as this was almost beyond my comprehension.

"Alright. Now, Raza and Raff, do you two remember your way around here?" Kingau asked.

"Oh yeah, most definitely," Raff replied.

"Great. I'll need your help coordinating the keystrokes then," Kingau said.

"Right, we set this place up so the gate can only be activated if there's more than one person on board," Raza replied.

"Is that for security purposes?" Blue-Dreem asked.

"Yes. There are also a few fail-safes in place that we must correctly bypass, otherwise the gate will be locked for a predetermined duration," Kingau said.

"That all makes sense," I said with a nod. "This is highly advanced—I honestly don't know if I could recreate something like this."

"It still amazes me to this day how the humans and Kolythoanthaeans created this," Kingau replied.

Maker Denorad's face popped into the corner of my screen. "Hey Niwat, I got the pills for Kingau. Where are you?"

"Maker Denorad is contacting me. He should be here soon," I said, addressing the room before I stepped off to the side to reply to

Maker Denorad. "I'm sending you my location and the route we took to get here."

"Thanks. Be there soon," Maker Denorad said as he signed off.

As I walked back over to the others, Kingau, Raza, and Raff were working on booting up the process to activate the gate.

"So, I know you said this thing is calibrated, but could you show us that data?" Zombu asked.

"Unfortunately, that would be a bit tricky," Kingau replied. "Give us a few minutes to get past these fail-safes and I'll explain."

---

```
Begin Replay of NIWAT Inner Datalog
Recording C-0000670336 S-002 N-14
```

Maker Denorad arrived with a container of pills right when Raza, Raff, and Kingau completed the final fail-safe, which involved them pressing a specific sequence of buttons simultaneously.

"Kingau, here are the anti-cancer pills. *Francentia* made a special batch just for you. If these don't work, she may need to scan you herself to better understand your condition," Maker Denorad said.

"Thank you so much. I'll let you know how they work. Can I take one now?" Kingau asked.

"Certainly. You should take one every day for ten days, then every other day after that," Maker Denorad replied.

"What a truly amazing spaceship you have," Kingau said, then swallowed one of the small capsules.

"Great. Now, as I was saying earlier. When Tiresias and Mahki calibrated this gate, we ran dozens of tests with probes. Each probe returned with positive readings from the Vortex Solar System. However, they each provided vastly different readings. So, while the probes made it into the Vortex System, they arrived in completely different locations. So, there is no way of knowing exactly where you will end up."

"In other words, we could go through the gate and immediately get pulverized by a star, is that correct?" Zanzi asked.

"Theoretically, yes. That is a possibility," Kingau replied. "Also, from our tests, we were able to determine that this system has three stars that rotate extremely close to each other."

"Oh, great. Three stars. That means that there's an even a higher probability of us being pulverized. Fantastic," Zanzi said.

"I don't know why you always need to focus on the negative," Maker Denorad said.

"Hey, someone has to analyze and report the dangers of our plans, right? We need to know what to expect," Zanzi replied.

I sensed an argument brewing, so I spoke up, interrupting Maker Denorad's reply. "No matter what, we need to prepare for the worst. I believe that's what Zanzi is getting at."

"Yeah, basically," Zanzi replied.

"As frightening as this is, I agree," Mikhail said. "As an Ajentian Knight and a member of the Guild for Eklatros, I believe that one can never be too prepared. That being said, how do we prepare?"

"We'll need to chat with *Francentia*—she's the one that needs the data," Maker Denorad said.

"And as the official pilot, I need to be in on this discussion," Blu-Dreem said.

"Either way, we're done here now," Kingau said. "The gate should be activated in a few hours. While we wait, would anyone like to accompany me to my garden?"

Everyone spoke up in agreement, even Maker Denorad. "If we have a few hours, I can check it out for a bit. *Francentia* shouldn't need long to prepare her safety protocols."

Begin Replay of NIWAT Inner Datalog
Recording C-0000670336 S-003 N-01

The garden held a completely different energy compared to the rest of the space station. The air was far more humid and carried a plethora of fragrances and pollens. There was even an artificial breeze, which helped to carry the sounds of the garden to us.

Even though it was called the garden, it was more akin to a bio-dome back on Theronior, which had artificial nature-filled environments that were perfectly balanced. From where I stood, I could only see the field of dark green grass in front of us, which led into a forest full of deciduous trees. I could also see a variety of insects, birds, and some rodents. It was hard to say how balanced this environment was, but it sure was serene.

"Holy Eklatros, this place is absolutely breathtaking," Anqi said as she gaped at the scenery.

"This is not what I was expecting," Mikhail said with wide eyes.

"This is... this is..." Jurhon couldn't finish his thought as he fell to his knees and sobbed in joy.

Kingau walked over and patted him on the back. "It's sure is a sight, isn't it?"

"I haven't seen anything green since before the fall of Omaloha," Jurhon said quietly.

"This place is amazing; how did it come to be?" I asked. "Didn't you tell us that Thorpi's atmosphere was destroyed and you were found by the ones who made this station long after the fact?"

"Yes, that's exactly right," Kingau said with a nod. "However, the incubation pods were for more than just Harmertians. We made incubation pods for many animals and eggs of all kinds—birds, reptiles, insects, you name it. We also had a cache of seeds containing a large variety of plants. What you see here is only a small fraction of the seeds we have saved.

"I asked the humans and the Kolythoanthaeans to build this place, and they happily agreed. They wanted to see Thorpi's splendor with their own eyes as much as I wanted to. And the garden was one of the first areas completed when they were building this place. However, the station was abandoned before they could see the plants fully take root. And now, look at this place. I know I call this a garden, but it really is so much more."

"It's beautiful," Maker Denorad said as he plucked a strand of grass and inhaled the scent. "My home world didn't support much natural life, but we had bio-domes that were kinda like this. But this is better than any of the ones I ever visited."

"Yeah, the one closest to us wasn't properly managed. It was in a really sad state," Blu-Dreem said.

"Everything is worse off now, though," Zanzi said, creating an awkward silence.

"So, Kingau, are you coming with us?" asked Anqi.

"If you'll all have me. That being said, I wouldn't be upset if you said no," Kingau said with a chuckle.

"We'll gladly take you on board," Maker Denorad said.

"And I agree with your call, for once," Zanzi said. "I would feel bad leaving her alone."

"I wouldn't truly be alone, but thank you. As much as I love this place, I want my final days to be exciting ones. I want to see new sights and meet new people. I want to live again," Kingau said as she wiped a tear from her eye.

"I'm glad to hear it," Maker Denorad said.

"What's going to happen to this place, then?" Gonth asked.

"That was my question as well," Anqi said. "Don't tell us that all of this will wither away."

"Oh, of course not," Kingau said. "Do you think I water each and every tree? Everything is fully automated. Even the potted plants you saw in the lounge are on an automatic watering system. Even after I leave, as long as the solar panels continue to power the station, this place will live on."

"That's good. Knowing there's a place like this... a haven of life drifting around in space is kinda comforting," Anqi said.

"I agree," Kingau said with a firm nod. "Of course, while I can't take any of this with me, I will take seeds and eggs with me. If we truly are going into the Vortex System, I would like to reintroduce our natural flora and fauna to the Harmertians there."

"I think that's a grand idea," Mikhail said with a wide smile. "I now wish I had thought of the same thing."

"Why would you need to bring seeds from Eklatros with you?" Anqi asked.

Mikhail shrugged. "There's no guarantee we'll ever return, you know? So, if we don't, that means I'll never see Eklatros' majesty again."

"Wow, way to bring down the mood," Anqi replied.

"I mean, he has a fair point," Zanzi said.

"As for me, I never want to come back here," Kingau said. "As grand as this place is, every time I lay eyes on Thorpi, all I see is death. This place is a good respite from that, but I crave more. I want to speak with a member of my own kind again and leave Thorpi behind me."

"Then it shall be so," Maker Denorad said. "Beedee, are you ready? We should start prepping *Francentia*'s defense and security systems."

"Sure. Just one last look," Blu-Dreem replied.

I smiled, knowing that we were all recording what we were experiencing into our memory vaults. It was strange that this was the first life we've seen like this since we started our journey. Even though Eklatros was a lush planet, we only experienced a fraction of it. The volcano had been impressive, but this was on a different level. Knowing that it was artificial made it even more impressive.

---

Begin Replay of NIWAT Inner Datalog
Recording C-0000670336 S-005 N-08

*Francentia* stared down the active space-gate. It was a surge of whirling energy that was almost too bright to look at, even for me. Thankfully, *Francentia* darkened the windshield to ensure we wouldn't be blinded.

Once again, I hosted a passenger in my seat—Kingau. Raza was strapped in with Anqi, and Raff was strapped in with Zombu.

"Prepare for interstellar travel by space-gate," *Francentia* announced. "ETA to jump point: one hundred seconds."

"This is it, everyone!" Maker Denorad said excitedly as he gazed into the swirling mess of time and space. "Prepare to face the unknown!"

"Wow, this is *so* exciting," Anqi said, clasping her hands together.

"I know, isn't it?" Raza replied. "I'm so happy that Tiresias entrusted us with this mission, right Raff?"

Raff was so entranced with the gate, he could only murmur in reply.

"I just want to say that I'm glad everyone is with us," I said. "You've all made this journey much more special."

"Let's please not get burnt up by the stars, or plunge into any atmospheres, or run into any moons or asteroids or space stations," Zanzi said.

"Seconded!" Kingau replied. "I can't die before I get a chance to live again. Onward, my new friends. Let us dive into the Vortex!"

**41**

# ESCAPE FROM MELRIDION

They watched the monitors in disbelief, unable to tear their eyes from the screens. The Titans had been neutralized, and yet no one, not even Professor Peal, knew how. And in the chaos, Professor Clums and his ragtag band of mutineers commandeered two of their prisoner transport ships. The third ship had been completely demolished. It would take a while for Lord Foxaire to build up favor with the Intergalactic Police Department again.

Carl shook himself out of his daze and sent the prisoner transport ships' tracking codes to Egimas and Anessti.

The communication line blinked. Carl sighed and pressed the button to activate it.

"Hey, what the shit happened?" Sid growled. "Who took down my Cyclones?"

"Where are you, Sid?" Carl asked.

"Outside Professor Durrist's lab. My soldiers and Brock, the bounty hunter, need medical attention," Sid replied.

"No, I'm fine," a deep voice growled through the speaker. "I need to regroup with Creson and pursue them!"

"Settle down for a moment," a softer voice said in response.

"That was Brock and Gazelle. Did you catch what they said?" Sid asked.

"Yeah, and I can see you all, too," Carl said as he finally found the screen. Sid was standing with a hand on his hip and the other to his ear, and he was clearly agitated. Meanwhile, Gazelle was on her knees, tending to the wounded. "It looks like Gazelle is already helping."

He watched as Gazelle laid her hands on two of Sid's Cyclones and woke them up. She moved on to Brock and the others.

"What are you doing?" Sid asked.

"What's it look like? Healing them. I'm the medic you asked for—I can use my powers to send waves of soothing energy that help cells repair faster." Gazelle's voice was faint, but Carl and Lord Foxaire could hear her.

"Sid," Lord Foxaire said, "tell Gazelle to move on to Professor Durrist's lab next. We need you to hurry into the hangar. Professor Peal could use your assistance. Just ignore Durrist for now."

"Copy that," Sid replied, then relayed the message to Gazelle.

Carl watched as Sid hurried through the doors and ran right past Durrist, who was still nailed to the floor. He couldn't believe how incompetent everyone had been. Sure, they could have used a dozen extra hands, but their forces still performed horrendously.

"Did this just happen?" Sid asked, running down the hallway toward the hangar. They still couldn't activate the moving walkways due to the fallen soldiers. "And what's Peal need help with, anyway?"

"Cleaning up the mess. I am absolutely astounded at what happened," Lord Foxaire said, echoing Carl's thoughts. "You need to pay for your soldier's failures. We relied on your Cyclones, and it is because of their inadequacy that we lost nearly all of our assets. Carl, disconnect transmission."

"Wait, Lord Foxaire, please—"

Carl flipped off the communication feed, cutting Sid off mid-sentence.

"Carl, what's Professor Clums' status? Can we track them?" Lord Foxaire asked.

"We already are," Carl said as he brought the info up on the largest screen. "I sent the tracking codes to Egimas and Anessti. I hope they'll make up for their colleagues' disappointment. I still can't believe Creson ignored a direct order from us."

"I'll take it up with Kanaghar. For now, tell them to use nonlethal force," Lord Foxaire commanded. "I want those ships disabled, not destroyed. If we can recover our lost assets, then maybe we can turn this day around somehow. And if they disobey our orders again, I'll hunt them down and kill them."

"Understood. Relaying your message now."

"Did you know Gazelle had healing powers?" Lord Foxaire asked after a few seconds.

"No, I did not. I think we need to reevaluate everyone after this."

"Agreed. Even Gnudashar," Lord Foxaire said. "He may be our prophet, but he allowed his former friends to escape. We need to make sure he's on our side."

*What a mess we have on our hands*, Carl thought. *We'll be dealing with the fallout from this for a long time, even if we recover the ships. No matter which way you slice it, today was a complete disaster.*

---

West hurried to the cockpit to join Dea. Even with no limbs, Dea was still able to expertly navigate the ship out of the hangar and into the long underground runway by using his green translucent hands.

"How is everyone? Did we all make it?" Dea asked.

"Almost," West replied. "The shapeshifting Ancilsan and the other Eklatros Human were left behind, and Professor Qymberkon was killed in action."

Dea turned to face him. "What, really? What happened?"

"Creson got to him, but we got Professor Qymberkon's body on board thanks to Ivy. Navacus is really hurting. Newtus and the Harmertians are doing what they can to comfort him."

"I understand. I'll go see him once we're out of this mess."

"Let's not forget that we have two bounty hunters waiting for us. Anessti—my old backstabbing partner—and Egimas," West said.

"Right. These ships don't have any weapons, but hopefully we can outmaneuver them," Dea replied.

"Agreed. Now, we're approaching the exit."

Sunlight streamed through the large opening to the underground runway and illuminated the short, steep ramp they were jetting toward.

"Hold on, everyone!" Dea said into the ship's intercom.

They shot out from the underground passageway and soared into the indigo sky. West pulled back the throttle with everything he had. They encountered some slight turbulence as they entered the upper atmosphere. It was nothing to fear, but he clenched the throttle even tighter. The events from today had him shaken up.

A communication line blinked and he flipped it on. "Hey, that was intense!" a soft voice said over the ship. "This is Kurjon and Grasberg, by the way. I found the direct communication line between our ships. It should be private."

"Great, but even so, let's keep the chatter to a minimum. Just do your best to stay on our tail. This is West and Dea," West replied.

"No problem." Grasberg's reply came as they got their first true glimpse of space. Yet, they had no time to enjoy the beautiful sights, as warning bells immediately started to chime.

"Electromagnetic pulse detected," the robotic voice announced.

"Damn, these ships can talk? This is far more advanced than my old personal skipper," West said.

"That's what you took away from that interchange?" Dea said in surprise. "They're trying to shut down our electronic systems!"

"Yeah, I've dealt with these before. Well, one singular pulse on one singular occasion."

"And what happened?"

"I got lucky," he replied honestly. "But experience is experience, so at least I know what to expect. That being said, I didn't have LSS last time. I just hope we can pull this off, otherwise I'll be fried. Tell everyone to strap in if they're not already. We're in for a very bumpy ride."

Kurjon's voice came through the intercom. "Hey, West? Someone is trying to speak with us." Before she finished speaking, his second communication line started blinking.

"Same here. Let me deal with these pricks. Stay safe," West replied, then swapped channels. "Is that you, Anessti?"

"West," Anessti said, drawing out each sound. "I offer you a choice because of our history together. Surrender now and prepare to be boarded, or we'll take out all electrical systems, including your oxygen supply."

West wanted to laugh but restrained himself. He didn't want to aggravate his former partner from the get-go. "Considering our history, you owe me a huge favor if you mean to make up for what you did to me."

"Oh, I have no issue with what happened. I completed my job and you survived. I think it was a win-win, don't you agree?" Anessti asked.

"No, I don't. You owe me one, which means we'll be taking option three," West said as he cut off the communication line. "Dea, let's punch it! We need to jet toward the nearest public highway."

West checked the map and smiled inwardly. This time, luck was on their side. They were only a few units away from the Carange-Melridion Freeway, which would take them right past Termatyl.

West opened communications to the other ship. "Don't lose sight of us. We're heading to the CarMel Freeway."

"We're right behind you," Grasberg replied. "Do you have a plan for our friends?"

"Run," he replied, then turned off the communication line.

"Here comes the first EMP!" Dea shouted.

"Change rotation forty-five degrees by twenty-degrees, then punch the throttles," West commanded. He had inadvertently slipped into the captain's role and had no qualms about it. It was finally time for him to save lives rather than take them.

Dea did as instructed, and they jolted away from the EMP at just the right angle to use its shockwave to further propel them forward. The ship groaned as it accelerated, pushing them back in their seats.

"Whoa! That was close! I could literally feel the shockwave through LSS."

"I could feel it as well, and I am glad you're alright," Dea replied.

"Dea, what's Kurjon and Grasberg's status?"

"They made it. Their trajectory is in line with ours."

"Great, because it looks like we've got another EMP coming. This time change rotation to fifteen degrees by fifty degrees. We'll zig-zag our way out of this if we have to," West said.

"Are you sure we'll be safe on the freeway?" Dea asked.

"I mean, unless those two are stupid enough to throw the entire IBHA into peril, I'm sure we'll be fine. All public transit ways are completely off-limits to bounty hunters. That's the deal they struck with—" The shock from the EMP cut West off as the fringes of the magnetic field coursed through LSS. Luckily, they were just far enough out of range for the blast to be nonlethal and have no effect on the ship.

He took a moment to scan through his systems. Everything was functioning at half capacity, but it was good enough. "Suffice it to say that we shouldn't have anything to worry about. If they attack the freeway, the entire IBHA will be shut down."

"Good. We'll be there soon. However, this time we have two EMPs coming our way," Dea replied, his voice slightly shaking. "It looks like one is headed directly toward us, and the second is directed at the others."

West swiftly flipped on the transmission to speak to Kurjon and Grasberg. "Change of plans. Kill all engines and cut off all power, now! No time for arguments."

"No arguments here," Kurjon said before West flipped off the communications.

"But West! What about LSS?" Dea said.

"I have you! Just do it!"

Dea quickly followed orders. A second after all major power systems were shut off, the shockwave arrived. West gripped the edges of his seat as LSS flickered on and off until all power was completely lost.

He was thrust into complete nothingness—he couldn't see, hear, or feel anything at all, not even any pain.

*This better not be it. It can't end this way. I—*

A pulse of energy washed over him, and LSS kicked back on. He sucked in a breath as his heart began to beat once again.

"West! Are you okay?" Dea asked, his eyes brimming with tears.

"Ugh, yeah, thank you for that. I'm glad my assumption was right —that you could restart LSS if it failed."

"You knew that was going to happen? What if it didn't work?"

"Then I'd be dead. Now, enough arguing about this—I'm still kickin'. How long has it been since the EMP hit?"

"Just a few seconds," Dea responded.

"Alright. We need to make it look like they won," he whispered. "Let's lie low for a bit longer."

"How can you be sure that they didn't win?" Dea asked. "There was still power running to the auxiliary systems."

"We'll be fine as long as the main engines aren't fried."

West looked out the window and saw the bounty hunters approaching.

"I think it worked. Now, turn everything back on and start warming the engines back up."

Dea nodded as he quickly got their ship running again. West flipped on the communication channel again. "Kurjon, Grasberg, if you can hear me, we need to fly."

"The ship should be ready for us to accelerate in fifteen seconds," Dea announced.

"Perfect. Just hold all systems still until we're fully powered back up."

"West, we're here. We'll be a few seconds behind," Kurjon said over the communication line.

"Great. Once we start moving, be sure to keep up. You've done a great job so far, so don't fall behind now."

"We won't," Grasberg replied.

*I hope you take this personally, Anessti,* West thought as their ship accelerated. *I can see you getting chewed out now. Your use of nonlethals was your downfall.*

---

Cecil had his eyes glued to the window. He never imagined he would ever travel through space, and now he was in a convoy with other ships all travelling in the same direction—ships of all shapes and sizes. His favorite part had been when they broke free of the planet's atmosphere. He had even shed a few tears of happiness, despite the dangerous situation they had been in. The aliens piloting the ship had done a fantastic job getting them out of that mess.

However, through all the excitement, they left Druder and the shape-shifting alien behind. The entire situation had been out of his control, and yet he wished he had done more. Druder should be escaping with them. Instead, they had abandoned him with no clue where to find him. He really was an awful leader.

Beside him, Theodore quietly growled as the woman called Kaytrona embraced the red-head with mechanical legs nearby. Cecil tore his focus away from the window and looked at the pair. He thought they were being a bit inconsiderate, even though there was nowhere else to go.

"It feels so good to hold you again."

"I missed you, too, Norman," Kaytrona replied with her eyes closed. She opened them and broke away from Norman.

"Do you need to do that right here?" Theodore growled.

Kaytrona looked at him and frowned. "Dorie, I'm so sorry. This all must be so very confusing for you."

"I'm just as confused," Norman said. "How do you know this old man?"

Theodore huffed. "Why don't you ask her?" He said, crossing his arms and turning away from them.

"Please don't be like that, Dorie. If you only knew how conflicted I am right now. I love you, just as Kate loves Norman. I am both Tyrona *and* Kate, and yet I am now only one woman where once there had once been two. It's maddening."

Kaytrona was interrupted by a disembodied voice that echoed throughout the small room. "This is Grasberg speaking. West has asked us to look for a tracking device. We need to disable it before we reach the outskirts of Carange's electromagnetic field. Kurjon and I are searching the cockpit, but we need all hands on deck here. Unfortunately, we don't know what it would look like or how big or small it could be. If West finds it before us, he is going to let us know. Thanks for your cooperation."

Kaytrona awkwardly looked back and forth between Theodore and Norman. "It sounds like we need to help. I'll explain everything later when we have a chance to breathe."

"I wish that we had an idea of what we need to be looking for, though," Norman said.

"Well, we can't do much," Cecil said with a wave of his hands. "Theodore and I have never seen any of this before. I wouldn't be able to tell a doohickey from a thingamajig."

"I've been on a ship like this before, and even I don't know where to start looking," the alien with a hard white exoskeleton said as she held onto two transparent cubes. One held a spider and one held a beetle.

"I can help," the deep blue Lakinceitian said as he slithered over to them. "I don't know much about this particular ship, but I know it was borrowed from the police. All police spacecrafts place their trackers in the engine room."

"Wait, are you saying we technically just stole from the police?" the white alien asked.

"Yes, which makes it even more important we find the tracker. Come on, Kamarial. I'll need your help."

"We'll help, too," Norman said. Next to him, Kaytrona nodded.

"Okay. I'll be right back. Be good, Denoptace," the alien named Kamarial said.

"Shit, whatever. I'll just hang out here then," the stick bug said. For some reason, the insect reminded Cecil of Vesten.

"Great," Kamarial said.

The two aliens exited the room with Norman and Kaytrona in tow, leaving them alone with the insects.

"What are you staring at? Don't you have your own shitty problems to worry about?" the stick bug said as it turned its back to them.

"What did we get ourselves into?" Theodore asked, his voice filled with sadness.

"Stay strong, my dear friend," Cecil replied. "This is not what we expected, but in all reality, we shouldn't have expected anything. But, I still believe we're here for a reason, even if we don't understand what's going on. What's important is that we're alive and we've escaped from our cells."

"And we've been reunited, somewhat, at least," Theodore said with a sad smile. "I just... Tyrona."

"I know. I don't understand how Tyrona is in that woman's body either. Let's just try to stay positive," Cecil said as he rubbed Theodore's back.

"I don't know how. I don't think I can be around her. She's not Tyrona, even if she can wield her wand. She's not the woman I fell in love with," Theodore said as a tear slowly slid down his cheek.

Cecil leaned over and gave his friend a hug. "Hopefully this will all make more sense soon."

A moment later, the blue, three-legged alien emerged from the helm of the ship. "Hey, West disabled their tracker," the alien said.

"Okay, well, the others went to the engine room," Cecil replied.

"Great, that's where the tracker was," the alien replied. A moment later, the opposite door opened and everyone returned to the central room.

"Hey, Kurjon, we disabled the tracker," Kamarial said.

"Great, I'll let Grasberg know. I believe we'll be arriving soon," Kurjon said as she exited the room.

"Nice, that was a short trip," Cecil said.

"All ships can travel faster in the freeway lanes," the blue slug-like alien said. "The ships get pushed along by an electromagnetic field."

"I don't understand all that, but great," he replied.

*Stay strong, Cecil,* he thought to himself. *I need to heed my own advice and stay strong for Theodore.*

*Druder, we'll find you. I promise. No matter what happens next, we are not leaving the Vortex without you.*

---

Navacus held Fumalli's cold hand. Mac, Poi, Lyd, and the large purple lizard named Newtus had helped him strap Qymberkon into a seat at a round table.

Navacus remained strapped in as well, and his eyes had rarely left Fumalli. Grief clouded his vision to everything else around him. He barely registered the condolences from his friends. Even Sterg was having a difficult time getting through to him.

"Navacus, I have no words," Dea said. "Fumalli Qymberkon was a generous and caring soul. He was as intelligent as he was passionate about his job, and I know how much he cared for you."

"Thank you, Dea," Navacus mumbled.

"Do you want me to help take the knife out?"

"The knife—Fumi's favorite kitchen knife. Dea, that bastard killed him with his own knife. What kind of sick person does such a thing?"

"A murderer," Dea replied flatly. "Shall I take it out?"

"Ah, yeah, I think that would be for the best. But don't clean it. I—"

"I know of the Nioavellian traditions," Dea said, cutting him off. He choked back tears of his own before continuing. "I will be sure to leave any residue alone. Poi, can you find me a container?"

"Sure," Poi replied as she activated her jetpack and flew off to search the small kitchen area.

"I'm sorry I've been such a mess," Navacus said.

"There's nothing to apologize for," Dea replied. "He was your dear friend."

A moment later, Navacus was gently pressed back in his seat as the ship decelerated.

"Ah, we must have exited the freeway," Dea said. "We'll reach Termatyl soon. West promised to bring us to a safe place where we can lie low for a while."

"What about the bounty hunters that attacked us?" Poi asked as she returned with a plastic container.

"West is certain they're following us, even without the tracking devices. Now, here I go," Dea said as his pronosua emerged and gently pulled the knife out of Fumalli's chest. Navacus' heart lurched the moment the knife came free. He still couldn't believe Fumalli was gone. His best friend in the entire world, his rock and support, was gone.

"There, now that's better," Dea said as he gently placed the knife into the container Poi had brought them.

"Thank you, Dea. I couldn't have done it myself."

"It's no problem. What shall I do with this?"

"I'll take it," Navacus replied with a firm nod. "Before he died, Fumalli told me that he forgives his parents. I don't know if you know, but that's huge. When he was young, Fumalli's parents constantly hovered over him and pushed him into studying science. At first he loathed it, but that changed when he discovered biomechanics. But even after he discovered his passion, he still never forgave his parents for how harshly they had treated him. Once he left Clendenic, he never returned. And now... now I need to present this knife to them, and tell them of the wonderful person he became."

Tears rolled down his feathery cheeks, wetting his already dampened facial plumage even further. "And you know how I always say peace, love, and faith? That was inspired by Fumalli. His peaceful and graceful nature; his love for life and new discoveries; and his faith in science and our friendship."

"That's so sweet," Poi said.

"Yeah, if you keep going on like that, you're going to make me cry," Lyd said.

A crackle of static sounded over the loudspeakers before West's voice came through. "Dea, I need you back up here. Everyone else, strap in. We're going for a ride through the abandoned mines."

"See you again soon, everyone," Dea said before returning to the cockpit.

*Thank you, everyone, Navacus thought as he looked around the room. We certainly have some strange companions, don't we, Sterg? Newtus is incredible; I've never seen such a huge lizard before. Then there's the Loxocemae and the Zubba, who are quite content chatting with each other. Finally, there's the quiet Eusphyrchiian with the spiders and the ivy that saved Fumalli's body. But even so, I'm thankful for everyone here with me. Dea, West, Mac, Lyd, and Poi... thank you for supporting me through this.*

*And Sterg, I'm sorry. I didn't realize my sadness would cause you to retreat into me, but I thank you for your support as well. I think I'm doing a little better now.*

*Fumalli, I'll forever love you. Go with peace, embrace the divine love, and your faith will see you onto your next journey.*

**42**

# ESCAPE FROM HARM

"It looks like the bounty hunters used the same exit we did. They're hot on our tails," Dea announced.

"So, we haven't lost them yet," West said. "Just as I was expecting. No matter; we should be diving into the mine soon. Once we're under the surface, they can't deploy EMPs without the risk of affecting their own ships. For now, we just need to focus on getting to the main mine entrance."

"Are you sure we can lose them? And that we'll even fit?" Dea asked.

"True, these ships are much larger than the personal craft I used in the IBHA. But these caverns are wide—made for large mining vessels. Even if it gets tight, we should be fine. I hope, at least," he added.

West eagerly watched as they approached Termatyl. Behind it loomed the large cloudy blue world of Carange, the Human's home world. Hundreds of years ago, the Humans nearly stripped Termatyl bare of its natural resources. They stopped all production when they discovered that their intensive mining was affecting the tides and global weather. The scientific community reported that mining was halted just before the moon would have collapsed in on itself, which would have had dire consequences for not only Carange, but the entire Vortex System.

When the mining companies abandoned Termatyl, they left behind thousands of kilometers of zig-zagging mazes. Even so, it took a gutsy pilot to maneuver in the mines. West had confidence in Dea and himself, but he wasn't sure how Grasberg and Kurjon would handle such precise movements.

He hailed their companion ship. "What's the plan, West?" Kurjon asked right off the bat.

"First of all, you've both done a fantastic job so far. However, how much piloting experience do you actually have?"

"For myself, absolutely none," Kurjon replied.

"I played several spaceflight simulation games, and I was allowed to sit in the cockpit of a past flight, but this is the first time I've ever piloted in real life," Grasberg said.

"Wow, you could have fooled me," West replied.

"Yeah, we were chosen because we had the most experience," Kurjon replied. "If Syl wasn't injured, he would be here instead of me."

"Understood. Again, you've both done a great job, especially considering the circumstances. But navigating the mines is something even expert pilots fear. This is going to be a trial by fire of sorts. I don't mean to frighten you, but I need you to understand the gravity of the situation we're in," he warned.

After a moment of silence, Grasberg replied. "We understand, West."

"Good. Do not—I repeat—do not leave our tail. Some of the turns will be tight and narrow. If we're successful, it shouldn't take us long to lose our party crashers," he said.

"Good, because they're closing in on us," Dea reported.

"Alright, keep it up, guys. We're almost at the home stretch. Over and out," West said as he flipped off the communication channel.

A moment later, Sterg appeared in the cockpit, its shimmering ethereal presence surprising them both.

"Sterg, I wasn't expecting you," West said.

"I hope I am not interrupting, but I have an idea," Sterg said.

"Lay it on us," West replied.

"I believe I can create a delayed burst of light that should effectively blind and disorient our pursuers."

"That would be brilliant, thank you," West replied.

"Agreed. That sounds like a good plan," Dea said.

"Tell me when you're ready for it," Sterg said.

"Will do. Now, brace yourselves, here we go," West said.

Their stolen prisoner transport ship dived into the deep tunnel. Grasberg, Kurjon, and the others followed close behind.

The main shaft they were in was the widest entrance to the mines on the moon. It led to an interchange that went to nearly every mine entrance within Termatyl. West had likely only explored a small fraction of the mines, as they were exceptionally treacherous. Many ships—civilian, police, military, even the IBHA—never returned to the surface. Not only could one get lost within the tunnels, but if a ship ran out of fuel or solar energy, they would be done for. Luckily, their ship was full up on fuel, and it ran on a hybrid battery and a solar powered system, another newer feature that West wasn't used to.

He shook his head and focused. As they approached the first off-shoot tunnel, Egimas and Anessti's ships dove into the entrance. Luckily, the bounty hunters' window of opportunity for using EMPs had passed. Now all they had to do was employ Sterg's plan and lose them in the mines.

"Alright Dea, we're going in," West said.

"I thought we were already inside," Dea replied.

"This is just the beginning."

West maneuvered the ship into the same tunnel he'd always used. He smiled—it was nice to be back here. In a way, Termatyl was a second home to him. Even though Anessti had been his partner, they always went to their own spots. That was for an extra layer of security —if they had been pursued, at least one of them could potentially get away unharmed.

This meant that while Anessti knew several of the turns West would make, he also didn't know where to go once they passed their off-shoot fork. They just had to make it there before they were stopped.

"How are the others doing?" he asked Dea.

"Just fine. They're staying close. Almost too close, in my opinion."

"Good, that's just the way they need to be. Damn are they fearless for new pilots."

"I'm sure it's purely situational," Dea replied.

"Even so, they're flying better than most. They must have some natural skills."

"That being the case, our other friends are getting close," Dea said, clearing his throat.

"We've only got a little further to go. We'll make it," West said, more to reassure himself than anyone else.

"At this proximity, I can check in on the other vessel," Sterg said.

"That would probably frighten them more than help them," West said. "You should stay put for now."

"Understood," Sterg replied.

He flipped on the communication device. "Good job, guys," West said. "We've only got a little further to go until we should be in the clear. Sterg has a flawless plan. Coming up real soon now will be a series of four very sharp curves. And in these ships, it's going to be a tight fit."

"Thanks for the warning," Grasberg replied. It sounded like he was panting.

"Alright, sharp left, now!" West commanded as they plunged into the dark tunnel, their headlights the only thing lighting their way. "Now, go right! After that will be a left, then it will straighten out, and then another hard left."

There was a loud crash followed by a blinking alarm. "Warning. Satellite dish damaged," the ship's robotic voice announced.

"Shit, I think we just lost our communication array," West said. "We're going to have to trust in their skills now. Sterg, get ready."

"Just give the word," Sterg replied.

"The bounty hunters have caught up to us," Dea said.

"It's alright. We've made it."

They turned the final bend and approached a fork. West headed straight to the path on the left. That led to a chamber with three paths. He dove into the middle one, turned left, and entered a wide-open space containing fifteen different paths.

"Now, Sterg, do your thing!"

Sterg's luminous form pulsed, creating a copy that swiftly flew through the ship. Or, rather, the copy stayed in place while their ship flew through it. He watched the rear-view monitor and saw Sterg's ball of light pass through Grasberg and Kurjon's ship. A second later, an extremely bright light burst out behind them. In response, West dove into the tunnel that led to his private cavern.

"I think we lost the Bounty Hunters, and Kurjon and Grasberg are still following," Dea said.

"Good. With all the different passages, they're sure to be stumped now," West replied.

*We're almost there now*, West thought. *I think everyone is going to need a nice long break after today. And yet, I'm sure we haven't seen the last of Anessti and Egimas.*

---

Ivy sat at one of the oval windows lining one side of the small general use area and watched as they descended into a large, wide cavern. There was enough room for nearly a dozen similar-sized spaceships. Their ship rocked gently as they landed. He raised his arms so Ados and Adok could get a better view of the other spaceship when it landed nearby.

Ivy was still getting used to his multiple viewpoints. Even though Ados and Adok gripped his wrists with their mouthparts, he could use their eyes to look in nearly every direction. Plus, while his ivy legs didn't have eyes, they could see in other ways. They could detect vibrations of all kinds, which would alert his spider hands to direct their gazes in the source direction. And, watching over everything was his omnipotent viewpoint, which continuously hovered above him.

Ivy had been toying with his new vision for most of the journey. While he still didn't know anyone well, everyone seemed like they would be easy to get along with, including the Neutortous, the Zubba, and the Loxocemae. As it were, Ivy sat alone while the others chatted with each other in pairs. Even the mourning Yggdrazim seemed to be in fine spirits.

West and the Eridavlos entered the room. The Eridavlos was grinning from ear to ear. "Everyone, we've safely arrived. We can finally breathe easy. We are no longer being pursued and we are, for the moment, out of Lord Foxaire's clutches. We're finally free!"

The room burst into cheers and exultations.

"That being said," West said, his robotic voice cutting through the excitement. "The two bounty hunters, Anessti and Egimas, may not be able to find us now, but they will be waiting for us when we leave. And by that point, Creson and Brock may join them as well. Yes, we are safe for now, and we can finally relax, but sooner or later we will need to face our foes.

"So please, enjoy this time. We will plan to convene outside in an hour, after I get the artificial atmosphere acclimater set up. We need to go through introductions and get everyone on the same page. So just sit tight for now."

"Just let us know if you need our help," one of the Harmertians said as they used their jetpack to float in the air.

"It should be fine. I've done this dozens of times before," West replied with a wave of his hand. "Thank you, though. Now, once I get the acclimater set up, I will need some help to wake up Theesakin— the Titan we took with us."

"We can help with that again," the Yggdrazim said, though Ivy was unsure as to whom the 'we' referred to.

"I would like to see this for myself," Newtus said.

"Yeah, I agree," Ivy said, speaking up for the first time. "If you don't mind, of course."

"Not at all. I actually think that you two, Newtus and Ivy, may have a few things in common with Theesakin. And thank you as well, Navacus and Sterg. I'll come and get you all soon then," West said. He walked up to him and said, "Ivy, I'm sorry we haven't gotten a moment to speak, but I wanted to thank you for what you did for Navacus and Fumalli."

"Oh, about that. I could have done more had my body not been paralyzed. It was only after I fully regained control of myself that I was able to grab the Nioavellian, but by that point it was too late," he replied.

"It's not your fault, if that's what you're thinking. Tag Creson is a monster. He would have killed every last one of us if he had gotten his way," West replied.

"I don't know if that makes me feel much better, but thanks for your condolence," Ivy replied.

"Sorry, I've never been the best at this," West replied with a chuckle. "I'll come get you soon, Ivy."

West tipped his cowboy hat at him, then left the room. A strange sensation made Ivy turn to his right. The Eridavlos was floating next to him.

"Ivy, is it? I'm Dea. It's a pleasure to finally meet you."

"Dea, I'm Ivy, though you just said that."

"If you don't mind, and I'm sorry to even ask this, but—"

"You want to know how this all works, don't you?" Ivy said, using Adok to motion to himself.

"It's just... I only heard the reports from Professor Bodeelch, but seeing you in person is even more extraordinary. Sorry, I didn't mean it how it sounded. I may be a scientist, but you're fascinating for even more reasons than that. I don't know if that makes it any better, and wow, now I am rambling."

Ivy laughed for the first time, surprising himself at the dual, hearty laugh the two spiders produced.

"Thank you, Dea. I really needed that. I don't mean to laugh at you, it's just you don't need to be so uptight. I'm not going bite, especially since Ados and Adok here are already biting onto me. Sure, I'll tell you about myself, and anyone else who would like to listen."

"Yes, I am interested," the Loxocemae said as it slithered up, prompting everyone else in the room to agree.

"Okay, then. Looks like we've got a full house," Ivy said with a chuckle. "Now, as you may know, I was created by Professor Peal, Kalosse, Kamarial, and the rest of Peal's team. However, it wasn't until I first met West that my existence began."

*This is actually kind of nice*, Ivy thought. *It feels good to be surrounded by friends.*

———

Lyd followed West, Ivy, Newtus, and Navacus onto the moon's rocky subsurface. Only Dea, Sassafrass, and Blood Bat stayed behind. Both ships used their lights to illuminate the part of the cavern they were in. Lyd, Poi, and Mac all wore Harmertian-sized breathing masks, as the acclimater wasn't finished creating its perimeter. They were the only ones who required the masks, as they had the smallest lungs of the group. Lyd continued to use his jetpack to make traveling around easier.

He hadn't used his real legs since before Ivy began telling his story, and what a story it was. What Professor Peal had accomplished was more impressive than what they had done with West. But watching the two walk together side-by-side was something else entirely. It was like the best of both worlds, even if both those worlds had been seething with wickedness.

Lyd was happy to be free of Lord Foxaire, but part of him really missed his old job and his old life. As exciting as the day had been, his future was saturated with uncertainty. He had no idea what he would do next. No matter what he decided, he would make sure that Poi was by his side, just like she was now.

The group made their way to the other spaceship and entered the open pod. Inside was Bsarg and a Titan that was enclosed in a cage with metal bars, even though the pod had its own built-in containment unit.

The creature in the cage was curled up in a ball of dark green scales. It was hard to see much else, but Lyd could tell it would be similar in height to the large yellow Titan they had just escaped from.

"Good to see you all made it safely," Bsarg said.

"It's good to see you, too, Bsarg. I'm glad you came with us, even if you don't always understand my humor. Now, everyone, this is Theesakin. I know we're in a cramped space, so let's please give him some room when we wake him up," West said.

"Can't we just move the cage down into the main area?" Mac asked.

"The acclimater is still doing its thing," West replied. "It should be done soon, but until then, it's best we stay in here for now."

"Are we sure this is a good idea?" Poi asked.

"I second that," Newtus said. "This is not what I was expecting."

"Theesakin is my friend. As long as I'm here, he should remain calm," West said.

"If you say so," Navacus said. "Sterg is ready whenever you are."

"Huh, who is Sterg?" Ivy asked. The strange Eusphyrchiian's dual voice still weirded Lyd out.

"I'll explain later," Navacus replied.

"Right, now wake Theesakin up, please," West said.

A soft, radiant light pulsed near Theesakin, and the large green-scaled beast abruptly opened its eyes.

"Remember to stay back, everyone," Bsarg said as he waved Newtus and Ivy back. Poi approached Lyd and put her hand in his.

The beast stood up, but the cage was shorter than it was, so it had to hunch down. Even so, it's four strong arms, two long wings, and thick tail could all clearly be seen. It looked at them with big black eyes that were hard to read, with a face that was surrounded by horns.

It growled and continued to stare at them silently.

"Uh, West, what's going on?" Lyd asked after a few awkward seconds.

"Oh, sorry, I should have explained that we communicate telepathically. Theesakin says—"

"He says that he is glad we saved him, and thanks us for getting him out of there. I can hear you guys, too, you know," Newtus said.

"So could I, actually," Ivy said. "It was a bit surprising at first."

"I'm impressed, though not wholly surprised," West said. "I mean, I've spoken to both of you telepathically before."

"I wonder why Theesakin can't project its voice out loud telepathically like Ados and Adok do," Ivy said.

"Maybe you can teach him one day," West said, then turned back to Theesakin, who was looking back and forth between all of them.

"Oh, how wonderful," Ivy said. "He said he would like that."

"Phooey, I'm feeling a bit left out," Poi said. She removed her hand from Lyd's and crossed her arms. "I want to hear what's going on."

"So do I," Lyd agreed.

"Theesakin apologizes that he can't speak to you yet," West said.

"At the very least, what you're saying is true, right? It really is speaking to you?" the blue Lakinceitian asked.

"Yes, he's really speaking to us," West said. "And he has a question for you, Bsarg."

"Oh? What's its question?" Bsarg asked.

"*His* question is this—why did you come with us? I know you told us earlier that you thought the compound was corrupted, and yet you shot and killed Jakog without any hesitation," West said.

"I did what I had to do. Isn't that the same with all of you?" Bsarg said.

"It wasn't necessary. I could have easily disabled him with LSS like I did with Nijork," West replied. "Besides, I thought you were friends. How could you so easily turn your back on him?"

"We were never friends, just coworkers," Bsarg replied. "Besides, I just did what I thought was right in the moment. It all happened so fast. Also, why am I being singled out?"

"Theesakin's only experience with Lakinceitians are negative ones. He associates much of his pain and torment with your kind, so he's wary of you," said West.

"I suppose I can't blame him for that. Durrist is quite cold-hearted," Bsarg said.

A noise chimed from West's Life Support System. "Ah, the acclimater is completed. That means we can get Theesakin out of this cage. Can anyone pick locks?"

"I'm not sure that is necessary," Mac said as he floated over to a set of compartments. "You should check in here first."

"Good thinking," West said as he walked over and opened the cabinet. Inside was a long metal key dangling from a hook. "Here we go. Let's hope this works."

"Why are they using these cages, anyway? Why not just put them in the actual containment pods?" Lyd asked.

"I believe it's because of how the Titan's enclosure was constructed," Bsarg answered. "Unlike the other cells in the underground, which can be moved around, the Titan's cells were built into the structure. These cages must have been all Lord Foxaire could get his hands on."

"They really made our escape quite easy, honestly," West said.

"Not easy enough," Navacus said sadly.

"Agreed. Now, if everyone can head down into the cavern, I'll get this cage opened," West said.

Lyd nodded, found Poi's hand again, and they flew out of the pod. Once everyone was out, they heard metal clanking, followed by large footsteps that shook the entire ship. In response, the ramp leading into the main body of the ship descended.

Theesakin thundered out of the ship and roared. The noise was deafening, especially considering the echo the chamber was creating. Theesakin jumped into the air and soared around above them, displaying his long green and yellow wings.

"What a sight that is," Poi whispered in his ear.

"None of this would have seemed possible a week ago," Lyd replied.

*Life sure is crazy*, he thought. *This has been one wild day. Rest in peace, Professor Qymberkon. I wish you were here with us.*

There was a scattering of nervous and excited chatter as everyone arranged themselves into a large circle. To help everyone see each other, three of the talking animals—the stick bug, snake, and Zubba —positioned themselves in front of the largest among them, Theesakin. Next to Theesakin stood Bsarg, who looked tiny in comparison. Even Syl, who was still in pain, was present. Flanking Navacus were Norman and Dea.

While there were a lot of them, twenty-four by Navacus' count, there were a few missing faces, including Altun and a missing Human named Druder. Most notably, Fumalli was absent, and the void continued to make his heart ache. But he couldn't curl up in a ball and hide from the world. Navacus was the one who had convinced everyone to take part in the mad escape plan, so he was responsible for making sure everyone continued to stay civil with each other.

That's why he had to stay strong and set an example. With help from Sterg, he knew he could get through this. Navacus wheezed, shook his feathery hands, and addressed the diverse crowd.

"Everyone, I welcome you to our safe haven! Once again, thank you, West, for setting up the artificial atmosphere acclimater. Being able all be together like this is absolutely amazing. All twenty-four of us just stood up to Lord Foxaire, and now we are finally free." A loud cheer erupted. After everyone settled down, he continued. "We worked together to make our grand escape happen. And yet, I don't think there is a single one among us who knows all of us, and so we need to change that.

"So, I'm going to introduce myself, then we'll go around in a circle, starting with Norman here. So, right, I am Navacus Clums, a former professor. We... Fumalli Qymberkon and I... we helped Norman and West by building them mechanical enhancements that have changed their lives. I don't regret my time at Foxaire Biotech Industries, but I do regret being used without my knowledge. And I regret Fumalli is not among us right now. After this... after this I want to hold a ceremony for Fumalli, for anyone that would like to join in.

"Again, my name is Navacus Clums, and I'll pass the baton to Norman Harrison."

Norman introduced himself. He was using his mechanical legs and stood proudly as he described how they changed his life. Next, the Human woman calling herself Kaytrona explained how she was both Kate Thomas and Tyrona Knorse. It was confusing and hard to understand, but she really did seem to have two different personalities.

The circle continued from there. When they arrived at Theesakin, there were three translators that helped at different parts—West, Newtus, and Ivy. Essentially, they said that Theesakin was incredibly thankful for the help and he would do whatever he could to help pay it back.

It really was quite astounding, having a Titan in their mix. And yet, Theesakin was extremely friendly. Even Sassafrass and Newtus said as much as they explained how Theesakin's aura was exceedingly calming. Not only that, but it was interesting to see how well Newtus was getting along with Sassafrass and Blood Bat, even though she explained how they would typically be her prey.

When it was time for Kamarial to speak up, she explained how she was familiar with the spaceships that they had stolen. She had ridden in a similar one when she had visited Acampachetli with Professor Peal and the rest of her previous team. She told of hard-to-find compartments that could have hidden supplies in them and agreed to help search the two ships.

The circle ended with Dea, who apologized for his role back at the compound. "I regret I didn't do more with the information I had," Dea finished, a tear running down his cheek.

"You did exactly what you needed to do," Navacus assured him. "We're all here, aren't we? Who's to say we would all still be here if anything had gone differently? All twenty-four of us are alive, and that is what matters."

"You know, you keep saying twenty-four. By my count, there's only twenty-three, if we include Penny and Susan. Who is the twenty-fourth?" Kamarial asked.

"I'm glad you asked. Many of you have met Sterg, but most of you have not. It's time you all become aware of its presence."

*Alright Sterg*, Navacus thought. *Let's try not to startle them too badly, shall we?*

---

It was a lot to process, but Cecil could still remember nearly everyone's names. Navacus was the one Ànifa had dreamed about, and the three small Harmertians—Mac, Lyd, and Poi—along with the two Kolythoanthaeans, Syl and Kurjon, and the blue alien, Grasberg, were all members of Navacus' former crew. Then there were all the different animals; Penny, Salty Susan, Sassafrass, Blood Bat, Newtus, and Denoptace, four of which could speak. Never would he have imagined that he would meet a talking animal, but he never imagined he would leave Eklatros either. But here he was, standing in a circle with a large green monster named Theesakin. The other strangest one, in his opinion, was the Eusphyrchiian with spiders for hand and ivy for legs, who went by Ivy. There were several other strange aliens as well, including Dea, Bsarg, and Kamarial.

Cecil stood between Theodore and his new Eusphyrchiian friend, West. Next to Theodore were Kaytrona and Norman. No matter how much Kaytrona confused Theodore, Cecil knew that the old wizard still had to be near Tyrona.

There really were a lot of them, a lot more than he had been expecting. And now Navacus was going to introduce them to someone else, and yet there was no one else in sight.

"Alright, are you ready, everyone? Don't be alarmed—the light you are about to see will not harm your eyes," Navacus said.

A moment later, a radiant light burst into the center of the circle. Cecil reflexively shielded his eyes, but the moment he covered them, a strong sense of familiarity washed over him. He lowered his arm and looked into the orb of light as a deep voice emanated from it.

"Greetings, everyone. Please do not be frightened. I am Sterg, a Light Being that is bound to Navacus Clums."

As soon as he heard the words *Light Being*, Ànifa flashed through his mind. When Ànifa had spoken to Yttendaus, Yttendaus had taken the form of a Light Being. Sterg was similar to how Yttendaus had appeared that day.

Theodore leaned in to whisper in his ear. "Do you feel it? That familiar presence? I've felt it before; once when we first entered our cells, and just before our escape."

"I can't explain why, but it reminds me of Ànifa in more ways than one," Cecil whispered back.

"You feel the same as well?" Theodore whispered excitedly. "This Light Being is strongly reminiscent of Ànifa."

They had been whispering to each other while Sterg had continued to explain how his link with Navacus worked when it addressed them. "Cecil and Theodore, you are reminded of your friend, Ànifa, is that right?"

"Holy Eklatros, Ànifa! That's who you remind me of," Kaytrona said excitedly. "But how is this possible?"

"I do not know myself," Sterg replied. "I have lived many lifetimes on many planets. The memories of all those lifetimes are not accessible to me. And yet, if three of you are reminded of your friend, then it's possible I was your friend during my last lifetime."

"It would be fitting if it were true," Theodore said proudly. "Ànifa was always the one to light the way forward."

"Right, and you're connected to Navacus? Ànifa used to have dreams of Navacus and his team."

"Wait, what?" Navacus said. "Your deceased friend used to dream about me?"

"Not just you," Theodore replied, "but many of those here. She saw West, Norman, and even Ivy being worked on, and so she saw your entire team as well. She also saw Sassafrass, Blood Bat, Newtus, Denoptace, and the others."

"Even myself?" Sassafrass replied. "How strange and unexpected."

"Yeah, this is starting to get a little weird," Poi said.

"And yet everything is coming full circle," Sterg said. "If my previous lifetime had these dreams, then that helps to explain why I am connected to Navacus. If this is true, then there was a bond between us well before I entered this state."

"So, you really are Ànifa, then?" Cecil asked.

"I am Sterg, not Ànifa, even if I am her soul."

"But even so, that makes me really happy," Cecil replied. "That means you truly did lead the way, and that you were always watching over us."

"Yes, this must be the case," Theodore said, his eyes wet with tears.

"You know, that all being said, I'm quite confused. Who is Ànifa?" Kamarial asked.

"It's been a long day. We should rest now and reconvene in the morning after we've all had time to process everything," Navacus said.

"What does morning even mean in a place like this?" Cecil asked. "All the light is artificial."

"Precisely. We can program the ships to turn their lights on in a way that mimics Melridion's sunrise at the time that we would normally have experienced it," Dea said.

"For those who were able to experience it," Newtus said harshly.

"You'll see a real sunrise again soon, I'm sure of it," Navacus replied.

*Wouldn't that be an amazing thing, Cecil thought. But more than that, I miss the wind on my face and the sun warming my armor. Armor that I will never wear again. I don't know how, but if there is a way to obtain some armor in this very alien place, I would love to get my hands on some.*

**43**

# ESCAPE FROM RESPONSIBILITIES

Altun watched the guards around him with two hidden eyes while he kept his main vision focused on the containment cell in front of him. Since he was still disguised as a Lakinceitian drone, he couldn't move around freely without being heavily questioned. He was forced to mimic the other four drones he was with, who were sitting still since they weren't being controlled.

As far as Altun knew, no one suspected anything. Since he could shape-shift into nearly anything, he was able to control even the finest body's movements. That allowed him to breathe freely and sprout several hidden eyes, which lay hidden beneath the leathery bulk of his current Lakinceitian hide.

The spaceship he rode in was Lord Foxaire's personal vessel, which was nearly twice the size of a public spacebus. It made sense, since Lord Foxaire was more than twice the size of a typical Lakinceitian. Even the rumors didn't do his sheer size justice. Altun had only caught a glimpse of Lord Foxaire, and now that he had, he could put a face to his enemy. For in the end, everything led back to Lord Foxaire.

Altun was currently in the large, open cargo bay. He and the other Lakinceitian drones had been ordered to keep an eye on the only assets Lord Foxaire had been able to hold onto, and one of those was Druder. It didn't matter that Altun had only just met Druder—his only goal now was to make sure Druder stayed safe. Altun had always been highly protective—he had to be, as the eldest brother of eleven younger siblings. As much as he missed his family, he couldn't abandon those that needed him. He knew his family must be worried, but he couldn't risk blowing his cover or endangering his family by sending them a message.

"All crew, we are thirty minutes out to our destination. Prepare for docking. Repeat, prepare for docking," a voice projected through the loudspeakers.

"What, are we really there already?" a Human wearing light blue armor asked.

"Who knows? No one tells us anything," a Nioavellian replied.

"You heard the captain, get to work you good-for-nothing losers," a bald, muscular Human said as he marched toward the chatty guards.

"Hey, Sid—"

"Don't you dare 'hey Sid' me, Hector. Get your ass in gear. We're docking at a refueling and resupply bay. Spread the word, then prepare the cargo bay. We'll be taking on some more supplies."

"Why can't the drones do it?" Hector complained as he looked in Altun's direction.

"Think of it as the first part of your long punishment. Each of you cost Lord Foxaire large amounts of time and money, not to mention the irreplaceable specimens that were stolen. You're supposed to be Sid's Cyclones—the greatest private ops team in the Vortex System, and you behaved like clowns. So, this tells me that some reeducation is in order. Now, you better start hustling, or I'll whip some ass."

"Sir, yes sir!" the two guards said with simultaneous salutes, then hurried off.

The space around Altun was soon bustling with activity. A few minutes before they docked with the resupply station, Carl arrived and barked out orders. Then, over the course of a few hours, they took on multiple crates, filled with both raw ore and processed minerals and alloys. No explanation was given as to the purpose of the materials.

All throughout the loading and reshuffling, Altun kept a keep an eye on Druder's cage. It was easy to spot, as it was the smallest one of the bunch. The other four belonged to the Titans, including the ones he had helped to put down.

The new cargo only served to further pique his interest. In more ways than one, Altun was happy that he was still in the mess of things, especially since he was free. Not completely free, but free from a cage. As soon as he could, he would abandon his current skin for another one. Plus, he needed to ensure he always had access to Druder. Not only that, but he wanted to be more involved, to learn as much as he could about Lord Foxaire's plans. The more he knew, the more he could do to hinder their progress.

*What a wild ride it's been*, Altun thought. *Who would have ever thought that a solo vacation to Clendenic would be so utterly life-changing? Sure, I was searching for meaning in my life, but getting kidnapped in the dead of night from my warm, cozy bed was not ideal. No matter what, I am where I am, and I am who I am now. For all I know, I received these powers and lived through the pain for a reason, and that reason could be to protect this Human, Druder, in whatever way I can.*

West stretched his arms over his head as he worked on waking himself up. It was early, but he wanted to check the perimeter scanners. Even with the artificial atmosphere acclimater and its built-in security sensors, they were still vulnerable. Egimas and Anessti could find them if they happened to look in the right place, and the longer they stayed, the more likely they would be found. At the same time, he didn't want to cause a panic. This was the first chance they had to relax in a long time, so West wanted to ensure everyone was well rested before the inevitable.

He tapped the console on the acclimater, and as expected, they were completely alone. Even so, he breathed a sigh of relief. With that task complete, he wanted to learn more about the ships they had stolen. While the tracking devices had been disabled, they could still be emitting signals that could be picked up by unwanted parties.

As he turned away from the acclimater, he briefly turned his attention to Theesakin, who lay on the ground with his tail wrapped around him. Theesakin's body slowly rose and fell with each deep breath as he slumbered. West smiled at his large, dragon-like friend. They had gotten lucky with him. If he hadn't already been loaded onto the spaceship, they never would have saved him, and Theesakin deserved to live a life free from poking and prodding.

West approached the ship he had piloted and quietly walked up the main ramp. Each ship had only four individual bedrooms for the limited crew that was needed. Between the two ships, the eight rooms had filled up fast, which meant that the rest of them slept in the small general use area—the pods, like the one Theesakin had been in, weren't used. Even though the pods contained beds, no one wanted to use them, as they were a reminder of what they had just escaped from.

With as many of them as there were, people were sleeping anywhere they could. West had to creep through the ship as quietly as he could so he wouldn't wake anyone up.

He opened the cockpit door and closed it with the control panel, then settled into the captain's chair. The spaceship was off, and he didn't want to completely turn it on for several reasons, but he could flip on some of the basic controls.

West's fingers danced across the touchpad and activated the basic functions. More than anything else, West wanted to speak with the ship to learn as much as he could about it.

"Hello, hello. Can you hear me?" he whispered.

"Affirmative. How may I serve you today?" the robotic ship's voice responded.

*How cool is this*, he thought. *I've always wanted a ship with voice activated controls. What an amazing add-on.*

"I'd like to know if you or the other ship nearby have been sending or receiving any radio signals since we arrived."

"Negative. The satellite dish broke off and we can no longer receive long-range communications."

"Oh right, I had almost forgotten about that. What about short-range communications?" he asked.

"Short-range communications are still functional."

"That's good at least. Now, are you recording this conversation?" West asked.

"Negative. Would you like to start a recording?"

"No, I don't. I'm just making sure we really are in the clear. Do you have any directives programmed by Lord Foxaire?"

"Negative."

"What about any other tracking signals we aren't aware of that can lead the police to us?"

"Negative."

"Great. Can you tell me anything about where you were headed? Do you have any coordinates?"

"The most recent coordinates are from 239 Pine Echo Drive, Nalpetalis, Sotaraag, Melridion to 101 Desert View, Volgash, Sotaraag, Melridion."

"Hmm, it looks like that's the address of the Intergalactic Police Department's headquarters on Melridion, and the second address must be the compound," West replied. "Does that mean these ships were loaned out by the IPD?"

"Affirmative. This interplanetary prisoner transport spacecraft is property of the Intergalactic Police Department."

"How ironic is that? We were essentially prisoners, and our key to escape is an actual prison transport. If you are property of the IPD, why was there no police escort?"

"That would be due to Lord Foxaire's large monetary payment."

"Of course he bribed them. Duh," West said, more to himself than to the ship. "Well, this may put us in even more hot water if we'll need to avoid the IPD and the IBHA. What a pain in the ass."

"I am happy to have been of use. Is there anything else I may assist you with?" the ship asked after a few moments of silence.

"Hey, do you have a name?"

"Yes. You may call me *Dalorent*."

"*Dalorent*? Where does that name come from?"

"From the individual that named me."

"I should have expected that," he said as he tipped his cowboy hat up. "*Dalorent*, is there anything you'd like to share with me today?"

"There are three unread messages in my inbox. Would you like to hear them?"

"Yes, please. Now we're getting somewhere."

The first message was a short one from the IPD to take care of the ship. The second message was from Carl, telling the captain to keep a close eye on the prisoners, and to notify him if anyone woke up. The final message was from Lord Foxaire himself:

> To whomever I may be speaking to, know that this little escapade of yours will not last long. We will find you, and you will be severely punished to the point where you'll wish you were dead. You'll regret ever crossing me.

"Hey, *Dalorent*, when did you receive the last message?" West asked.

"Thirteen hours, twenty-seven minutes, and sixteen seconds ago."

"That must have been when we were in the freeway. Thank you, *Dalorent*. This has all been very helpful."

"It was my pleasure," *Dalorent* replied.

West was about to get up when another thought struck him.

"Hey, *Dalorent*, do you know the name of the other spaceship?"

"The other spaceship's name is *Karna*."

"*Dalorent* and *Karna* it is then. Thank you. Please power down all systems, including yourself."

"Affirmative. Powering down now."

After a few seconds, all the lights on the console turned off. West took a deep breath and leaned back in his chair.

*Oh man, as awesome as our escape has been, we're really in a mess of a situation,* he thought. *We've stolen from the IPD and angered both the*

*IBHA and Lord Foxaire. Once everyone is awake, I want to make sure we have a solid plan in place for our next steps.*

---

Lyd wandered down the ramp of the spaceship with Poi by his side. It appeared as if they were the last ones to get up, as there was a buzz of activity. However, the important thing was that there was a caffeine station set up already. As they approached, Kamarial was finishing up making herself a drink.

"I know, I'm bad. I'm on my third cup already. But it's just so nice not to have anything to do for once," Kamarial said as she added sugar to her streaming cup.

"Ah, well, we just got up. It sounds like we slept in," Lyd said as he scratched the back of his neck.

"That's just fine! You do what you want to do now. Isn't that the whole point? What are you two having this morning?"

"Do we have any lo-cha tea?" Poi asked.

"Yes, absolutely. Let me give you a hand with those," Kamarial said with a smile.

"Oh, it's fine, we—" Lyd began, but Kamarial jumped in before he could finish.

"It's not a problem, really. As nice as it is not having anything to do, it also feels really strange. I want to start searching the ships soon for any hidden cargo we may have. Mac already agreed to help us."

"Mac! Where is he?" Poi asked, looking around.

"He's helping with Syl. They're in *Karna*."

"Huh? *Karna*?" Lyd asked, unsure what the Eusphyrchiian was talking about.

"Oh, that's right. You wouldn't know. West found out the names of the two ships. That one is *Karna*," Kamarial said, pointing one of the ships, "and that one is *Dalorent*."

"Ah, alright then. We should go check up on Syl," Lyd said.

"I'll come with you," Kamarial said. "I don't know you all well, but I really appreciate that you've let me come with you."

"Of course! We're all in this together, right?" Poi said.

With their steaming hot teas in hand, the trio slowly made their way over to *Karna*, where they found Syl, Kurjon, Grasberg, and Mac crammed into one of the small bedrooms.

"Ah, hey everyone, we're a bit over capacity in here, sorry about that," Grasberg said with a wave.

"It's no problem," Lyd replied as he sipped on his tea. "How's Syl doing?"

"He's doing alright. He still can't walk yet, but he's in good spirits," Grasberg replied.

"I can hear you, you know," Syl said from within the room.

"I'll step out so you two can come in," Kurjon said as she slid past Grasberg.

"Good morning, dear sister. Did you sleep well?" Mac asked with a smirk on his face.

"Just fine, thank you," Poi replied, beaming.

He watched as Poi placed her tea on the floor, approached the bed, and climbed up the blankets. Lyd followed. Neither of them were wearing their suits today. Once he was on the bed, Lyd could finally get a proper look at Sylcertiverner. The Kolythoanthaean had a few bruises on his face, but Lyd could see in his eyes how grateful he was.

"Ah, good morning, Poi and Lyd. Thanks for coming by. And you too, Kamarial. I can see you out there," Syl said as he waved his six-fingered hand.

"Good morning, Syl. And, I mean, it really is a grand morning as it's our first away from the compound," Poi replied.

"Indeed. I never realized how much that place was crushing my soul until now. Sure, my body aches everywhere, but I'd rather be where I am now than back in the compound," Syl replied.

"Isn't that the truth?" Lyd said.

After a few minutes of chatting, Lyd said goodbye to Syl, reclaimed his tea, and followed Poi, Mac, and Kamarial out of the room. Kurjon and Grasberg followed.

"So, are you ready to search the ships now?" Kamarial asked.

"Oh yeah, you said there could be hidden things. Can I help, too?" Kurjon asked.

"I'd like to as well," Grasberg said. "It's not like there's anything else to do, now that we've finished replacing Syl's dressings."

"Of course. The more of us there are, the quicker it'll go. Here, let me show you what we're looking for. Follow me," Kamarial said with a wave.

Kamarial led them into the first pod on the left side of *Karna*. The small transport pod was seemingly empty at first sight, but Kamarial revealed a hidden touchpad in the wall.

"Now, from what I was told the first time I rode on one of these spaceships, the idea is that these pods can hold four to eight prisoners each, depending on what species is being held. While keeping hidden compartments where the prisoners are kept may not seem like a great idea, it's also one of the last places the prisoners would search. Not only that, but the guards in charge of the pods use these hidden compartments to store weapons and other supplies that would be easy to access if the situation called for it," Kamarial explained.

"Huh, that's quite unexpected," Poi said.

"But how do we crack into the compartment? Do you know the code?" Mac asked.

"No, that's where I was hoping you all could come into play. You know computers and technology better than anyone else here, right?" Kamarial asked.

"I mean, I guess you could put it that way," Kurjon replied. "While hacking into security systems isn't one of my main skills, I'll see what I can do."

"Do we know if attempting to access these compartments will send a security message to the IPD?" Grasberg asked.

"Whoa, wait, what? What's this got to do with the police?" Lyd asked.

Mac quickly explained what they had missed earlier when West explained the situation to everyone.

"Yeah, are we sure we want to be doing this?" Poi asked.

"West assured me it should be fine. He made sure the ships weren't sending or receiving any messages or frequencies. Of course, it may not be a bad idea to have someone in the cockpit while you all work on getting into the compartments. I'll go find West and speak to him about that," Kamarial said.

"Alright, just let us know when we're okay to start tinkering with these things," Lyd said, rubbing his hands together. Even with the chance that the IPD could find them, they were already on the run. Plus, he loved surprises.

Once they got the go-ahead, they split up into groups of two. While Mac wanted to go with Poi, Poi insisted she wanted to go with Lyd, so Mac was paired with Kamarial.

When they were alone, Poi embraced Lyd and gave him a soft kiss. "I know we were tired last night, but if you're feeling up to it..."

"Is the desert hot? Of course I'm interested," he replied with a smirk.

Poi hummed seductively. "I'll just need to give Mac an excuse not to come look for us."

"Well, let's see if we can find anything to distract him," Lyd replied, turning his attention to the touchpad. Within ten minutes, they had the compartment open. All that was inside were three pairs of universal handcuffs and a baton.

They carefully removed the items and placed them in the middle of the pod before moving to *Karna*'s next pod, which happened to be the same one Theesakin had been in. *Karna* and *Dalorent* had six pods each, and Lyd and Poi had four pods left to search.

The second and third pods didn't yield exciting results—a metal chain, an energy rifle magazine, and a taser. As they revealed the last of the hidden touchpads, they didn't have high expectations. They had moved onto *Dalorent*, the second ship, and were almost one whole pod faster than the other groups.

"This one will probably contain the normal police junk like the other ones," Poi said with a sigh.

"I wouldn't call it junk. Just because we're too small to use those items doesn't mean that the others can't," Lyd replied as he easily hacked into the console.

"I just wish they made more things Harmertian sized, you know?" Poi said, then flexed her right bicep. "We may be small, but we're mighty."

Lyd laughed. "You've got that right."

The compartment hissed open.

"Alright, let's see what we've got," Lyd said as he peeked into the compartment. From his position, standing on the small elevated surface, he could see a small object at the bottom of the compartment. "Shoot, it's too far down in there. We'll need some help with this one."

"Case in point—if these were Harmertian sized, we wouldn't need help in the first place," Poi complained.

"I'm sorry to interrupt, but I hear you need help with something?" Dea said as he poked his head into the pod.

"Ah, Dea, great timing. Can you help us get whatever is in this compartment?" Lyd asked.

"Sure," Dea said as he floated into the room and used his green pronosua to reach into the slot. A moment later, the objects were revealed.

"Holy smokes, you two struck gold," Dea said as he showed them the two small vials.

"What? Are those seriously nanobots?" Poi asked in surprise.

"That's what they look like to me," Dea said. "If these are brand new, then we should be able to program them to do anything we want for us."

"Damn, we really did win the jackpot," Lyd said with a laugh. "These things are the most valuable substance per milligram in the universe."

"Right, especially since Lord Foxaire doesn't manufacture them anymore, at least that's the last I heard," Dea said.

"I wish we could have worked with these," Poi said. "Norman's attachments would make so much more sense if they were built using nanobots."

"Right, but the idea there would be that Norman could turn his attachments into anything, including highly advanced weaponry," Dea said. "Something like that would be much more difficult to control."

"Ah, of course. It's all about the control," Poi replied.

A shout from outside alerted them that the others were also finished with their search. They exited the pod and regrouped with the others. It turned out that Kurjon and Grasberg had also found a vial of nanobots, which meant they had three in total. The vials were small, but Dea estimated each one held a hundred-thousand nanobots. And while it sounded like a big number, Dea explained it took nearly that amount to create even the simplest of devices.

"I only worked with nanobots a few times during my introductory trainings with Foxaire Biotech, but experience is experience. Let me study these to see what we can do with them," Dea said.

*Well, this search was much more fruitful than I would have imagined,* Lyd thought. *Hopefully we'll find a way to use these nanobots to our advantage.*

---

Navacus looked at the group before him and realized everyone was present. Kamarial held both of the caged Acampachetlian creatures as she chatted quietly with Grasberg. It didn't matter that many of those present never knew Fumalli Qymberkon—having everyone here made the small ceremony all the more meaningful.

Traditionally, Nioavellians were cremated, but they didn't have the proper equipment to do that. Instead, they decided to bury Fumalli. While he didn't much like the idea that he could never visit his best friend's grave again—as he would have to find his way back here to do that—it seemed fitting to bury him within a moon. Fumalli had always been a guiding light, like how moonlight can illuminate the dead of night. The next time Navacus visited Carange, Fumalli would be smiling down upon him, and that was a comforting thought.

Of course, the other option would have been taking Fumalli with them, and that wasn't feasible for a multitude of reasons. To Navacus, the most important of those was that he couldn't dishonor his friend by letting him slowly decompose in one of the pods.

Navacus wheezed and straightened his back before addressing his friends. He stood on *Dalorent's* main ramp, elevating him a little. "Everyone, thank you so much for being here. I know you don't have anywhere else to go, or even anything else to do right now, but even so, I really appreciate it. It means a lot, so again, thank you.

"I know some of you didn't know Fumalli well, but know that if you had gotten a chance to know him, you would have loved him. He was a kind, gentle being and was always highly considerate of others. He was the shoulder you could lean on in dark times, and his laughter could turn any frown upside down. Plus, his cooking skills were exceptional.

"While I could spend hours telling you stories of Fumalli, I don't want to put you to sleep either," Navacus said, forcing himself to chuckle to help prevent him from breaking down. "What I will say is that without the genius of Professor Fumalli Qymberkon, West and Norman wouldn't be here. It is only because of his brilliance that my team and I were able to succeed. I may have been the head professor, but I was nothing without Fumalli. I *am* nothing without him.

"Fumalli was my best friend, and my bed will forever be cold without him. I love you, Fumalli. Go with peace, be remembered with love, and may your faith in living life to its fullest rub off on us all."

He paused for a moment so he could take a deep breath and calm his racing heart. A tear rolled down his feathery cheek. He shook his head, wheezed, and concluded his eulogy. He smiled and pointed to the freshly dug hole to everyone's left. "Now, I want to thank everyone that pitched into help dig the grave and get everything prepared. As I said, you've all helped to make this a truly special ceremony. I want to let anyone else step up and say a few words, but no pressure."

Navacus walked down the ramp and stood beside it. Taking his place on the impromptu stage was Grasberg, who was helping the injured Sylcertiverner up the ramp to join him.

"I'll make this quick, since I really shouldn't be out of bed yet," Syl began. "Professor Qymberkon was more than just my mentor and friend. He was my family. He was a constant in my life for so long, I will miss him dearly."

"Fumalli was my Nioavellian buddy," Grasberg said. "It was nice having someone of my own species to talk to. He understood the pains of having three awkward legs, and I could laugh with him whenever I tripped over myself. He really was the best mentor I could have asked for—Navacus Clums included, of course. Rest in peace, buddy."

After Syl and Grasberg, Kurjon said a few words, and then Mac, Poi, and Lyd told a few stories about Fumalli. West and Norman closed out the eulogies, and they both thanked him dearly for his role in their new lives.

Navacus reclaimed his position on *Dalorent*'s ramp and dried his eyes before speaking. "Thank you, everyone for your kind words. Now, let us gather around Fumalli Qymberkon one last time."

He walked down the ramp and to Fumalli, who lay under a sheet beside the two-meter-deep grave. "Ivy, I hope it's not asking too much of you, but could you lower Fumalli into his grave?"

"Yes, it's no problem," Ivy said. The modified Eusphyrchiian unfurled its ivy legs and wrapped its vines around Fumalli.

Before Navacus was ready, it was time to complete the task. "I'm sorry we can't cremate you, but you will forever be the heart of Termatyl. May your light guide us all through dark times."

He grabbed a handful of silt and dropped it into the grave, watching the fine gray silt run off the sheet. One by one, anyone that was able followed suit. Finally, Dea concluded the ceremony by using his levitation powers to quickly cover the grave with the rest of the dirt and silt. Once it was fully filled in, Navacus picked up a smooth rock to mark the grave.

Navacus remained long after everyone left. Even Sterg knew to leave him alone. Instead, Sterg was off with West, his old team, and others, coming up with a plan for next steps. Even though he wasn't around them, if he wanted to, Navacus could tune into Sterg at any time and listen in. He chose to keep to himself, as he knew he would absorb the information though Sterg when he was ready for it.

*I'm really not okay with this, you know, Navacus thought. In no way am I ready to say goodbye to you. I know that it only makes sense to plan for the future, especially considering our circumstances, but I just can't right now. I need to be as close to you as possible.*

*You were my everything, Fumalli. I don't think I'll ever be the same after this.*

## 44

# ESCAPE FROM THE PAST

"Are you ready, my lord?"

"I am. Let's get this over with."

Carl nodded to Lord Foxaire and pressed the button to let him speak to the next room.

"Gazelle, we're ready for you," Carl said, then lifted his finger off the button, disconnecting the feed.

A moment later, the door opened and Gazelle strode into the small room. Only a metal table adhered to the floor took up the space between them. Carl straightened his back to ensure he was standing as tall as he could.

"Please, take a seat," he said as he used his open-palmed hand to refer to the only metal chair in the room. Gazelle smiled, displaying her pearly white teeth, which contrasted well with her indigo skin, and gracefully sat down, placing all three of her legs neatly side by side.

"I hope your travels are faring well, my lord," Gazelle said smoothly.

"Don't use your seductive powers on me, witch. This is not a friendly chat," Lord Foxaire shot back.

"My, my—"

"Gazelle, please, this is not the time," Carl said, cutting off Gazelle before she could anger Lord Foxaire further. "Understand that Lord Foxaire does not wish to be here. He did not plan on traveling to our satellite station anytime soon. However, your actions had a role to play in our utter humiliation, and that is why you are here now. We mean to sort things out with you, one way or another."

"Oh, spooky," Gazelle said playfully. However, Lord Foxaire's deep growl and mean stare killed her smile. "Look, I thought we already went through this. I'm sorry for how I reacted with Kurjon and Lyd."

"We believe your actions that night spurred Professor Clums to lead his mutiny against us. Had you not treated them in such a way, none of this may have ever happened," he said.

"I don't fully agree with that. I believe they would have mutinied either way. They were plotting something, and that's what I was trying to get to the bottom of. Not only that, but Professor Clums had a presence around him that could see far more than a Yggdrazim should. Had you let me do my thing, I could have prevented your utter humiliation."

"And I do not doubt that is a possibility," Carl replied, "but it cannot be denied that your actions that night did not sit well with Kurjon, Lyd, or any of Professor Clums' team. Yes, had I not stopped you, you could have uncovered more information, but at what cost? Gazelle, you do not get to decide when you use your powers. We made you, and you work for us. We own you. So, you will do what we tell you, or we will see to it that you will never use your powers again. And that includes your healing abilities. Do we make ourselves clear?"

For once, Gazelle seemed to grasp the gravity of the situation. She sat up straight and replied, "Crystal."

"You will remain on high security watch for the duration of our journey," he continued. "Once we arrive at the satellite station, you will be assigned a set of personal caretakers to watch your every move. They will remain by your side day and night. When you regain our trust, we can talk about alternatives to your situation."

"I understand."

"Now, we have one more question. We were unaware of your healing powers. Why did you keep such useful powers a secret from us?" Carl asked.

Gazelle furrowed her brows. "I... what? How did you not know? Professor Durrist knew. I think. And if he did, I'm sure he would have told you. But I have had healing powers since Durrist made me who I am; though, I've only ever used them on myself. I'm sorry you were unaware."

"Is there anything you want to say to us before we dismiss you?" Lord Foxaire asked.

Carl smiled and leaned in to watch the show.

"Yes. I want to thank you for your kindness and generosity. If I think of anything else you are not aware of, I will inform you immediately. I greatly apologize for my actions, and I am looking forward to my life of servitude."

Carl couldn't tell if she was being serious or not, but it wasn't up to him.

"Your apology will be accepted at a later date," Lord Foxaire replied. "Now, leave us, and go straight back to your quarters."

"Yes, my lord," Gazelle said, then stood up and bowed before leaving the room.

"There's a chance her sentiments could have been sarcastic," Carl said when he and Lord Foxaire were alone.

"Be that as it may, we have her exactly where we want her. She will be of great importance in the future," Lord Foxaire said.

"Can the same be said about Elizabeth Surridge?" Carl asked.

"Let's find out. Send her in."

Carl pressed the call button. "Surridge, you're next."

The door opened, and the brunette Human entered the room. Her hair was disheveled and her eyes were sunken, as if she hadn't slept in days.

Carl cleared his throat. "Please, take a seat."

Surridge sat down, then craned her neck to look up at Lord Foxaire. They stared at each other for a few moments before Lord Foxaire spoke up.

"Elizabeth Surridge, under your watch, every single one of Professor Peal's test subjects were taken. We even have you on camera handing the last Dark Therid over to the mutineers. Not only that, but your colleague, Kamarial, escaped with Professor Clums. What do you have to say for yourself?"

"M-my lord," Surridge said, stumbling over her words. "Kamarial is my friend, and I was powerless to stop her from joining them."

"Did you know of Professor Clums' plot?" Carl asked.

"Actually, I did. West told me and Kamarial about it the day before. At the time, Kamarial and I decided to keep quiet about it, as we both felt pity for our test subjects, and knew that it was morally right to allow them to be taken from your, uh, ownership. I know how bad that sounds, but I stayed behind because despite my feelings and mistakes, I still firmly believe in science, and I want to continue working alongside Professor Peal and push the boundaries of what we think is possible."

"I'm confused. You want to do your job, and yet you take pity on those you experiment on. If you truly want to work for us, then you must disassociate yourself from your emotions. Only logic and science can remain. Do you understand?" Lord Foxaire growled.

"I do. As much as I was looking forward to setting my test subjects free, now that they are free, I really do regret it. I just wish that, at the very least, I had kept Salty Susan and Penny for myself. I wish that we still had at least some of our test subjects left."

"Fortunately for you, we do," Carl said.

"Wait, what? Did Sassafrass or someone fall behind?" Surridge asked.

"It's funny that you mention the Loxocemae, because you seem to have forgotten about the other three survivors," Lord Foxaire said.

"Oh my word, I *did* forget about those three," Surridge said excitedly. "Where are they?"

"I took them for my personal collection," Lord Foxaire replied. "You may not know this, but snakes are my favorite animal. I have been taking good care of Sage, Saffron, and Sesame."

"Could I... could I see them again sometime? I know my specialty is in botany, but I can't help but look back at those days and smile. It wasn't long ago, but so much has changed since then. We did our best work when we were still in our original lab, above the ground," Surridge said.

"Elizabeth Surridge, understand you are in deep trouble," Lord Foxaire said. "We will not forgive nor forget what you did. However, you have been remorseful, and for that, I will give you one last chance. Continue your work with Professor Peal. If you slip up again, we will not be so lenient."

"Thank you, Lord Foxaire," Surridge said as she bowed her head.

"Don't you mean 'my lord?'" Carl asked.

"Yes, of course, my lords," Surridge said.

"You may go. Please return to your quarters," Carl said.

"Thank you, my lords. Thank you so much. I will not forget your kindness," Surridge said as she left the room.

"Why did you go soft on her, my lord?" Carl asked.

"She's got nowhere to run, and the professors have no way to send messages to the outside world. If she steps out of line, kill her."

"Of course, my lord. Now, last up we have Gnudashar."

"That deceiving prophet," Lord Foxaire growled. "Let's see how he can worm his way out of this one."

Carl nodded, then pressed the call button. "Gnudashar, we're ready for you."

The freakishly pale Human entered the room. Today he wore a deep red suit with yellow and black accents.

"Hey, Lorphax. How's it going?"

"Spare us your pleasantries and take a seat," Lord Foxaire demanded.

Gnudashar looked at them in shock for a moment, then sat down.

"Gnudashar, you are our prophet, and we respect and revere you for all that you are," Carl said. "You assured us nothing would go wrong, and that you had a vision to prove it."

"I did have a vision of us succeeding. However, looking back at the vision now, it's possible that vision had been for Dasch. It's likely that the vision helped Dasch break free from his prison and take control of my body."

"Which was his body originally," Carl said.

"That's just a technicality. It's my body now," Gnudashar replied.

"I agree. That is why we will work on purging Dasch from you when we arrive at the satellite station," Lord Foxaire said.

"Okay... so what does that mean, exactly?"

"Our top professors will put their heads together to see if they can come up with a way to kill Dasch Valentine once and for all, leaving only Gnudashar behind."

"And how can you be certain that it won't kill me in the process?"

Carl shrugged. "We can't. That's up to the professors"

"Is there another option?" Gnudashar asked.

"Why do you even ask? Do you not want to be free from Dasch? Are you keeping him around for an ulterior purpose?" Lord Foxaire pressed.

"No, it's nothing like that. It's just that I never even considered the idea of separating myself from Dasch. I mean, I lived inside of him for thousands of years. The least I can do is give him a couple hundred years of the same torture I endured."

"No. That will not be happening. We will remove Dasch from you, which will ensure you will only receive visions pertaining to Gnusaramnii and not this leech of a Human. He must be eliminated," Lord Foxaire demanded.

"Alright. If there is no other way—"

"There is no other way," Carl said with a smirk. He was enjoying this interrogation the most. He loved watching Gnudashar squirm. "When you arrive at the satellite station, a new set of caretakers will be assigned to you. They will remain by your side before, during, and long after your procedure. Is that understood?"

"Yes, Carl, I understand," Gnudashar replied, his unhappiness with the situation clearly displayed in his tone.

"This is not Carl's decree," Lord Foxaire said. "It is my own. You will report to us only when you have a vision, and if we discover you are withholding your visions from us, severe punishment will follow."

"Yes, Lorphax."

"That is the last time you will ever use that name. I am Lord Foxaire."

"Alright, if you say so, Lord Foxaire."

"Get out of my sight," Lord Foxaire growled.

Gnudashar nearly tripped over the chair as he sped from the room.

"I don't know what I would do without you, Carl. Your steadfast loyalty will soon be heavily rewarded," Lord Foxaire said. "I appreciate your help with this matter."

"Of course, my lord. It's my genuine pleasure," Carl said.

"Now, I am in dire need of a long rest. I will see you when we arrive," Lord Foxaire said.

"Have a relaxing time, my lord. I will take care of everything from here," he said, then bowed and walked out of the room.

He entered the waiting area that the others had sat in and took a seat himself. He needed a moment before he got back to his duties. It was always one thing after another. The first thing he wanted to do was check up on Svetlana's condition, as Professors Durrist, Randall, and Xergat had been tasked to put her back together.

*Good stars, everything is just a massive pile of rubbish, just like Svetlana was when we found her*, Carl thought. *Oh, how I wish I had my own assistant. If Gazelle hadn't fucked up as badly as she did, she would make a great assistant.*

*At least Lord Foxaire and I can rely on each other. No matter what compensation I get, it's all about doing everything I can to herald Gnusaramnii's return. If I live to see it, that is all the reward I'll need.*

<hr>

"So, to wrap things up, Dea and I will remain the pilots of *Dalorent*. We will do what we can to distract the bounty hunters while *Karna*, piloted by Grasberg and Kurjon, will go to Mishunaed. There, they will lay low in Sylcertiverner's uncle's bar, The Fallen Heroes, until *Dalorent* can regroup with them. Is everyone agreed?" West asked the small group. Only Grasberg, Kurjon, Ivy, Dea, Newtus, Bsarg, and Sterg were present, besides himself. They stood between the two spaceships.

"Sounds like a great plan to me," Kurjon said.

"Agreed," Sterg said as it floated directly across from Dea. "I want to reiterate that Navacus and I will be on *Dalorent*, so Newtus here will be Theesakin's caretaker, as she is the only other one who can speak to him."

"I humbly take on this responsibility," Newtus said as the large six-legged lizard bowed.

"Don't forget I'll be watching Theesakin as well. I may not be able to speak to him, but with my experience as a security guard, I'll make sure nothing happens to him," Bsarg said.

"That would be wonderful, thank you," West said as he tipped his white cowboy hat forward in thanks. "Now, if there's nothing else, I say we conclude our meeting, then spread the word to everyone else so they can decide which spaceship they want to be on. And please keep in mind that we won't be able to communicate once we go our separate ways, at least until we get *Dalorent*'s satellite dish replaced."

Kurjon and Grasberg were the first ones to leave the group, followed by Sterg and Ivy.

"I don't know if you're stupid, brave, or both, but you've got to be at least one or the other if you truly mean to face four bounty hunters at once. I wish you all the best," Bsarg said.

"Thank you. And Bsarg, thanks for being here. I didn't expect you to turn against Lord Foxaire. I mean, you are Lakinceitian after all," West replied.

"I may be Lakinceitian, but that doesn't mean I like the idea of being mind-controlled by Professor Xergat or Gnusaramnii. I'm still in disbelief at what they did to Sharg, so I'm glad I escaped before the same fate befell me."

"I still don't understand how someone can treat members of their own species in such gruesome ways," he said as he shook his cowboy hat from side to side.

"Neither can I. Now, if you don't mind, I want to relax while I still can," Bsarg said as he left, leaving West behind with Newtus and Dea.

Dea looked back and forth at West and Newtus and nodded. "I should be going as well. I want to familiarize myself with *Dalorent's* controls the best I can before we're thrust into another intense situation."

Once West and Newtus were alone, they wordlessly retreated to a more private location. Newtus swayed as they looked at each other.

"I really don't want to be separated from you, West. You're my only true friend among this group," Newtus said, her big round eyes filling with tears.

West embraced Newtus, hugging her neck. "Remember when you influenced my thoughts when I was lying in bed? Even though we were apart, you were still able to communicate with me."

"That won't work when we'll be worlds apart from each other," Newtus replied, then broke away from West.

"I suppose that makes sense. Well, I'm sure you'll get along just fine with your shipmates," he said as he tipped his hat in affirmation.

"Sure, but they're not you. I can't speak to them telepathically, well, aside from Theesakin, and I still don't know how I feel about him. As calm and carefree as he is, his mind has a darkness I do not like."

"I feel this as well, but as long as we treat him with kindness and respect, I believe he will remain on our side. He is a powerful ally."

"I don't doubt that, but what if Theesakin is as unhappy about your absence as I will be?"

"I wish I could do something about that, but you are much safer on *Karna* than on *Dalorent*. If we get captured by the bounty hunters, they would hand-deliver Theesakin right back to Lord Foxaire."

"Or Theesakin would rip those bounty hunters to shreds, just like I would if I got the chance," Newtus said with a deep, rumbling growl.

"Or Theesakin would rip *Dalorent* apart and kill us all. I don't think he fully understands the extent of his power, just like we don't.

We've never seen him in action before. We don't know what he can do. Until we find out, we must be as cautious as possible."

"I know you're right, but even so, I want to be with you," Newtus said.

"I would love to have you by my side as well. But I must ask, do you not want to return to home to Acampachetli, to your kirwach you told me so much about?"

"West, look at me. I am not the same Neutortous I was after being forcefully taken from my kirwach. As much as I miss it, I don't think I can go back. Too much has changed. I will forever miss the natural world, but it is not a life I want to return to. I mean, don't you feel the same way?"

"I do. I don't think I can ever live a normal life again. That's why I will devote myself to taking down Lord Foxaire and rescuing those we left behind. Then, ultimately, I will stand against Gnusaramnii, and if I die fighting, so be it."

"Don't speak like that. You'll make it through this," Newtus replied as she placed a hand on his back.

"I wouldn't be so sure. Had that EMP hit any sooner, I would have been fried. I mean, I basically died, but Dea was able to restart LSS in time. I live only due to LSS, and it is vulnerable."

"It doesn't have to be. Navacus built it, didn't he? Why can't he build you some protective armor or something?"

"I can ask him about that, sure," West said with a firm nod. "Thanks for the great idea."

"Of course. I just wish we could still talk when we're apart."

"I'm sure there's a way to fix our long-range communications. As soon as we do, I'll be in touch."

He remained with his lizard friend for a few more minutes before they were interrupted by Kamarial, who apologized profusely.

"*No matter what happens, I'm sure we'll see each other again soon, Newtus,*" West said telepathically.

"*We better,*" Newtus replied.

*We will,* he thought.

She took a deep breath and shook her hands to let out her nerves. At the moment, she couldn't recall if this nervous tick was Kate's or Tyrona's, but she supposed it didn't matter anymore. Each day, her two separate lives blurred together more and more. She feared the day when she would only be Kaytrona.

She turned around and faced Theodore and Norman. She had been having trouble planning out what she wanted to say, but now she knew.

"Dorie... Norman," she said, nodding to each of them. "I know that you're both confused and in pain. I wish I could help you both ease your consciousness, but I fear our conversation may only make things worse."

"Can you spare us the warnings? As much as I appreciate your concern, we're grown men. We can handle it," Norman said.

"Ah, yes. We can handle it, sure," Theodore mocked while sounding unsure of himself.

"Dorie, I know you're hurting the most. In the flesh, I am not Tyrona. But I am Tyrona, and I do still love you, just like I still love you, Norman. I have strong feelings for both of you, so please understand that I am probably more confused than either of you."

"You love me, and you love him, and we both love you. But only one of us can be with you," Theodore said sadly.

"I mean, not necessarily," Norman said. "Sure, polygamy is frowned upon, but it's not banned on Strutheine. Not that I'm saying I want to do that, but I am saying that it's technically an option for our situation."

"I will never entertain that notion, not even if it means I don't get to be with Tyrona," Theodore said firmly.

"I figured as much," Norman said.

"I didn't even consider that, but I have to agree with Theodore," Kaytrona said. "I don't want to go down that road. However, I know what my next step is. I need time to figure everything out. And I want to ride on *Karna*—I don't want to get involved with those bounty hunters. I'm hoping to sort things out on Mishunaed. If the two of you want to come with, that's fine. If you don't, that's fine, too. I will respect whatever each of you decides to do."

"Before I decide that, can you tell me what happened to you? I watched you, Tyrona, burst into a bright light and disappear. I still haven't fully come to terms with what happened that day. I hoped finding you would erase that, but it's only made things worse. I just... please, I need to know," Theodore said as his eyes welled with tears.

"Of course, you both deserve to know what happened to Tyrona and Kate. I haven't gotten a chance to tell you yet, so let me tell you now.

"Dorie, I remember that fateful day as well. We spent that night together, then found our way up the volcano with help from those dire wolf spiders."

"Wait, hang on. What's this about spiders?" Norman asked.

Kaytrona looked at Norman. "In order to reach Panabeeta, we needed to each ride upon a dire wolf spider. Not only did they help us climb Nibelkaith, the spiders allowed us to pass over the bridge and onto the slick surface of the floating island."

"Okay, that raises even more questions, but I'll hold those for later. Please, continue," Norman said.

"Eklatros is a magical place. It is truly unique from any of the worlds I visited here in the Vortex. But as for Tyrona, I remember when I disappeared as well, Dorie. I remember feeling an overwhelming sense of freedom. And then I remember an underground stone door with intricate carvings."

"No way. Are you serious?" Theodore asked. "Were you really there at the door to Bugenaluf? I remember feeling your presence, but there is no way you would even know about that had you not been there. That made my spine tingle."

"I was there. And then I emerged from some gate and arrived in a room. I was attacked, so I used my powers and took down most of my foes using a high-pitched frequency, but then Svetlana got to me. The next thing I remember, I was in a gray room and Kate was in my head. At that point, I was still in my own body. But what I thought was real was a lie. Upon the moment of my death, I discovered I was never in a gray room. My mind was being fused with Kate's while they drained my life from me and gave it to Kate. That is why I am now Kaytrona—I am both Kate and Tyrona, just as I am neither Kate nor Tyrona. I am Kaytrona."

"So, what happened to Kate, then?" Norman asked with tears in his eyes.

"I was deceived. After they made me leave your side, a Kolythoanthaean called Professor Bodeelch offered to give me a tour of the facility. I agreed because I wanted to see where they would be working on you, Norman. And, I suppose, he did show me Professor Clums' lab. Then he led me into an elevator, and I thought nothing of it. It must have happened then, as we were descending. Because the next thing I remember is being alone in a gray room with Tyrona in my head."

"Those bastards! That's why I never heard from you. I was worried sick. Part of me wished you were back home and just didn't get a chance to write to me, or that they were censoring your messages. I just... I am so sorry that I even let you come with me in the first place."

"Um, I wouldn't have stayed behind even if you tried," she said with a laugh.

"Yeah, that's true, isn't it? Either way, I feel horrible that you were subjected to such cruel experimentation. And I'm sorry for you as well, Tyrona, and for you, Theodore. The situation we're in is not natural. It's not right."

"It's not fair. It's just not fair at all," Theodore said as he wiped tears from his eyes.

"No, none of us deserve this. But I cannot change who I am now, and that's why I need time to think," she said.

"That much I can fully understand," Theodore said. "I'll give you all the time you need. In the meantime, Cecil and I should go on *Dalorent*. We can't sit on our hands while Druder is somewhere out there. He came with us through the gate, and we're not leaving him behind. And the same with Dasch. I can't give up on Dasch yet either."

"I understand. You've always been a loyal friend and companion, and I wouldn't expect anything less. What about you, Norman?"

"I just want to get out of this mess. I want nothing to do with bounty hunters or going anywhere Lord Foxaire can touch me. I'm riding aboard *Karna* to lay low. I think it's the best option we have to reclaim a semblance of our past lives," Norman said.

"So that means we'll be together. This doesn't change the fact that I need time away from you, too, Norman."

"Sure, I get that. I just want to be near you. I think it's different for me, because you are the spitting image of Kate. And I know you are still Kate, but as you said, you are Kaytrona now. And I'll respect that."

"I'm glad to hear it," Kaytrona said with a smile. "Thank you, both of you, for understanding."

"It's fine. I have a lot to think about, especially considering I'm thinking about giving up magic," Theodore said.

It was as if a bomb had gone off. Kaytrona was in complete shock. "Dorie, what are you even talking about? I know you lost your staff, but I'm sure you can make a new catalyst here in the Vortex. I'll help you, if needed, and if I feel up to it."

"Thank you, but it's not about that. I killed two people with my raw power. I literally felt their life drain away as I blasted them with untamed energy. I thought I was being clever, damming up my powers and releasing it. I thought it would compensate for my lack of a catalyst, but instead I became overpowered. I never want to do that again. So, I decided I am going to give up magic, for now at least. I need to figure out my life here, and it gives me a chance to start fresh. Besides, I'll have Cecil by my side through thick and thin."

"And what does he think about this decision of yours?" she asked, still unsure of how to process what he was telling her.

"I haven't told him yet. You're the first ones I've told. I honestly wasn't even fully sure of myself until now. I think it will be good to spend time away from you, too, Kaytrona. I don't think being around you right now is good for me."

"Then all I can do is wish you the best. I hope you figure out what you need to," she said.

"And I hope the same for you," Theodore replied.

"And I hope the same for both of you, and I mean it," Norman said.

Soon after that, they each went their separate ways. Kaytrona retreated to *Karna* and found an empty bedroom. She crawled into the bed, curled into a ball, and cried.

*Is this really the right call?* she thought. *My heart aches. I don't want to be parted from Theodore... I mean, we just found each other again. But at the same time, I understand where he's coming from. So, maybe space away from both of them is what I need. I just hope Norman will respect my wishes. He usually is very caring, but what worries me is that The Fallen Heroes is a bar. His mind can go to dark places when he drinks. But I suppose we'll cross that bridge when we get there.*

## 45

# ESCAPE FROM CONCEALMENT

Lyd was the happiest he had ever been. He and Poi had finally mated, a moment they had both been looking forward to for a long time. It had been magnificent, better than he could have imagined. And now, hopefully, he would soon be a father.

Lyd was propped up, lying next to Poi as they stared into each other's eyes. "You're so wonderful, you know that, right?" Poi said softly.

"Not as wonderful as you are. I love you, Poi."

"And I love you, Lyd," she said as she sat up and kissed him. "And soon, we'll be a family."

"We didn't jump into things too quickly, did we?" Lyd asked.

"No, I don't think so. We'll be on Mishunaed soon. A large population of Harmertians live there. Maybe we can make a new life there and put all of this behind us," Poi said, her eyes shining with hope.

"You know what, that sounds really nice. We'll need to come up with new identities, but I'd like to try and make that work," Lyd replied with a firm nod.

"Do you really think that would be necessary? I don't want to leave my clan behind," Poi replied.

"It will be only for appearances. You will always be Poi of the Sai Clan, just as I will always be Lyd of the Yan Clan."

"Then that sounds perfect. It's just... what do we tell Mac? The two of us have always been together. Can we invite him to live with us?"

"That's his choice, but I'll happily extend the invitation to him as well. We're family now, and that means that Mac is my brother just as much as he is yours."

"Yes, that's right. But even so, I think I need to talk to him one-on-one. Would you be okay with that? I think he'll take the news better if it's from only me."

"If you feel like that's the right approach, then I agree. After you speak with him, maybe we can talk to him together."

"That sounds like a plan."

Poi leaned in and kissed him again, then stood up and stretched.

"Oh, do you mean to talk with him right now?" Lyd asked.

"Yeah, the sooner the better," Poi said. "I don't mean to spoil the moment, but we'll have our whole lives to be together after this."

"Then you better get it over with, then come right back here to me. Deal?"

"Deal," Poi replied with a smile.

Lyd watched as Poi donned her underclothes and slid into her orange jetpack suit.

"I'll be back shortly," she said, then blew him a kiss.

Poi activated her jetpack and lowered herself from the ceiling to the floor of the ship. After they had left Professor Qymberkon's funeral, the two had gone back to *Karna* and searched the ship for any hidden spaces they could fit into. They discovered the ceiling panels in the main hallway had storage spaces meant to store small bags and boxes, but was also a secluded place for Harmertians.

*I love you Poi,* Lyd thought. *Hopefully we can leave this moon soon, because at this point, I just want to be with you on Mishunaed, safely hiding in Syl's uncle's bar.*

———

Navacus wheezed as he munched on a canned fish sandwich. He stood outside and looked at *Dalorent*, the spaceship that was his new home. Sterg had made the decision for them, and Navacus was happy about it. Had he gone to Mishunaed, he would likely have too much downtime, which could lead him down a dark path.

"That was exactly why I decided we needed to go with West. We cannot sit still, not now, at least," Sterg responded to his thoughts.

"Yeah, it really is for the best, I think. You can be of great assistance with the bounty hunters."

As Navacus took another bite, Poi approached, soaring toward him using her jetpack.

"Prof—Navacus, have you seen Mac? It's important," Poi said, her face full of joy.

"Yeah, he's on *Dalorent*, in the general use area getting some lunch. There are a few sandwich options if you're hungry," he replied.

"That sounds really good right now, thank you," Poi replied, then waved as she headed up *Dalorent*'s ramp.

"She recently mated," Sterg announced.

"Ah, how nice for her and Lyd. You know, in Harmertian culture, that means they're bonded for life now."

"Is their bond similar to ours?" Sterg asked.

"Well, in a way, yeah. The only difference is that if they get separated, it's only emotional pain they feel, not physical pain."

"But pain all the same. All species have their own unique cultures," Sterg replied.

A moment later, West's voice rang out, echoing throughout the cavern.

"Code red! The bounty hunters are almost upon us. Everyone, strap into a ship now and prepare for immediate retreat!"

As West's message emanated from *Dalorent*, Navacus sent Sterg out to scout the grounds.

"Newtus and Bsarg are securing Theesakin in his in-flight cage now. Kurjon and Grasberg just made it on board *Karna*. We're now the last ones not on a spaceship," Sterg announced.

"Then let's book it!"

Navacus ran to the acclimater and smashed the emergency shutdown button. He spun on his heels and ran toward *Dalorent's* ramp. As he approached, he saw a figure emerge from the ramp.

"Poi! No, get back on board!" he yelled.

Poi looked at him, her face awash in shock and anguish. As he approached, Poi remained floating in one spot, and he grabbed her and pulled her into *Dalorent*. The moment they were on board, the ramp quickly shut behind them.

"No! Lyd, I... I needed to get back to Lyd!" Poi cried.

"I'm sorry, Poi. There's no time. I'm sure we'll meet up with them soon enough."

"But, you don't understand..." she said, then got quiet.

"Navacus, Poi is pregnant," Sterg said out loud, causing Poi to hide her face in her hands.

"Oh! I see. Then let's make sure we find you a comfortable place to rest," he said awkwardly as Mac emerged from the general use area.

"Poi! I'm glad you're safe! Don't scare me like that again," Mac lectured.

"Mac... I'm sorry," Poi said.

"You're safe, and that's what counts. I know Lyd isn't here, but I am. I'm your brother, and I'll take care of you through your pregnancy," Mac said softly.

"Mac..." Poi said, then embraced him in a hug and cried into his shoulder.

"I don't mean to spoil the moment, but we really need to strap in," Navacus said as the ship rocked violently back and forth.

"Come on, Poi," Mac said. He was also wearing his jetpack suit. Mac activated his suit and Poi did the same, and they flew into the general use room.

Navacus followed them in and spied an open chair next to Ivy. He waddled over, sat down, and quickly strapped himself in. "We're in for one wild ride," he said to Ivy.

"That's why I'm here," Ivy responded using his dual voice.

*I hope everyone is where they want to be*, Navacus thought. *The bounty hunters didn't really give us any time to think. At least we got the word out beforehand. Now I just wish the best of luck to West and Dea. May they ensure our survival.*

---

West was glad he had been sitting in the spaceship's cockpit, as it had given them an extra few seconds to prepare. The moment he saw the warning message from the acclimater flash onto the monitor, he activated the coms and sent out the message.

Luckily, nearly everyone had already been on one of the two spaceships. As soon as he saw Navacus and Poi make it on board, he closed the ramp and quickly secured the ship for spaceflight.

"Everyone is safely strapped in," Dea reported as he worked through his own set of checks.

"Let me know when you're ready to fly," West replied.

"I just need a few more seconds... there! *Dalorent* is ready for spaceflight, West."

"Hold on tight!" West said as he punched the throttle. *Dalorent* shot into the air and lurched forward as West directed it toward the main exit he liked to use.

"Dea, activate the ship-to-ship coms."

"Coms activated," Dea replied.

"*Karna*, come in. What's your status?" West asked.

"We're right behind you," Grasberg replied. "Just let us know when our paths will split."

"It won't be long, especially with your natural piloting skills," he replied.

"Warning. Missiles detected," *Dalorent* said.

"Did you catch that?" West asked.

"*Karna* announced the same thing," Kurjon replied. "Where are the missiles coming from?"

"I'm not sure," West replied. "I don't see any other ships on my monitors. It's possible they don't even know where we are." An explosion rocked a chamber behind them, confirming West's theory.

"They must have shot at the space we just left," he continued. "They'll be on our tails soon."

"Got it," Grasberg replied as West weaved *Dalorent* through a string of different chambers. As he turned down a particularly tight bend, two signals appeared on his monitor, coming in fast from behind them.

"They've found us, and we're approaching the main shaft where we are certain to have even more company," West said. "On my mark, go right, then release your trash." The fork he was gunning toward was just around the next bend. "Three, two... Mark!"

A moment after West pointed *Dalorent* toward the left chamber, he emptied *Dalorent*'s trash chutes, just as two signals appeared on his monitors.

"Good luck, *Karna*. We're signing off. Take care of each other," West said.

"Same to you. Good luck, *Dalorent*, and stay safe," Grasberg replied as the coms cut out.

"West, it looks as if the bounty hunters split as well. One is following us, and the other is following *Karna*," Dea reported. "Was that the point in releasing the waste?"

"I wanted both of them to follow me," West said. "I just hope that the others can handle it."

"I'm sure they'll be alright," Dea said. "As you said, Grasberg and Kurjon are natural pilots."

"That they are. Activate ship-wide communications," West ordered. A moment later, a light turned on, indicating the coms were open. "We're moments away from entering the main shaft. We have one behind us and two that are trying to block our exit. Brace yourselves; this may get bumpy. Over and out."

Dea nodded and flipped off the communication array with his ghostly green hands. A moment later, Sterg appeared between them.

"What's your plan?" Sterg asked.

"I don't really have one," West said. "Prepare for breech, now!"

*Dalorent* shot out of the mine tunnels and into the wide main shaft they had used to enter Termatyl. A moment later, *Dalorent* announced they had missiles incoming.

"I believe I can ward off the missiles," Sterg said.

"Great! Go right ahead. You don't need my permission," West replied.

Sterg's light pulsed brighter, and the Light Being sped out of the cockpit and into the tunnel. West watched in awe as Sterg got the missiles' attention and directed them into the side shaft. As the explosion rocked through the mineshaft, Sterg emerged from the inferno. A moment later, the Light Being was once again by their side.

"Great job!" West said.

"Thank you, but it was foolish. I pushed my limits with Navacus. That was quite painful for both of us."

"Sometimes that's what it takes to not die, though," West replied. "I truly appreciate it."

"West, we're being hailed," Dea announced.

"Patch them through," West replied as he slowed *Dalorent* down. Within moments, they were surrounded by three bounty hunter spacecrafts.

"West, are you there?" the voice said over the coms. He recognized it as Tag Creson.

"I'm here. How are you all doing this fine day?" West replied.

"Just fine, now that we've got you in our grasp. I'm not sure what trick you used to deflect our missiles, but know that at this range, there's little you can do to stop us from blowing you to smithereens," Creson replied.

"Then what's stopping you?" West asked.

"You know why. You're harboring valuable assets, and you're more valuable to us alive. But again, we will kill you if you give us a reason to."

"I suppose I better not antagonize you then. Where's my old partner at? Can I speak to him?"

"He's perusing your allies," a soft female voice said over the coms.

"Ah, so you're here, Egimas. I'd rather it be this way anyway—Anessti can go get himself killed for all I care," West replied.

"If you're finished chattering, please follow us out of Termatyl. We will escort you back to Melridion, understand?" a third voice said—Brock.

"No problem. Lead the way," West said, then muted the communications.

"Are you sure about this, West? This wasn't the plan, was it?" Dea asked.

"Oh, void no, this is not the plan, but I figured something like this would happen," he said.

"We still have a chance," Sterg said.

"That we do. We just need to wait for the right moment. It will be a slim chance, but it will be all we got."

"Then we'll take it," Dea said. "I don't want to die, but I also don't want to get caught either."

"I feel you there," West said. "The good news is I'm not planning on dying today. As soon as we break free from this shaft, we're going to shoot for Carange's atmosphere. We'll try to lose them in the mess of traffic, satellites, and space junk."

*Of course, no one really plans out their deaths, do they?* West thought. *I just wish we had better options.*

---

*Karna* rocked violently back and forth as Norman clenched his eyes shut and gripped the armrests. When the turbulence passed, he opened his eyes and took a deep breath.

"We're not out of the woods yet," Kaytrona said. She was strapped into the seat across from his and was peering out the oval window.

"What do you see?" Norman asked. He didn't really want to know. He was scared shitless—one of his biggest fears was dying in the cold vacuum of space, and he hoped that didn't become a reality today.

"Just rocks. We're still going through mine shafts. That should be familiar for you, right Norman?"

"Yes, I'm fine with mine shafts, but not in space. My old mines had atmosphere," he replied. "Plus, the way we're flying, it's just—"

he was interrupted by another bout of shaky maneuvering as they weaved through the tunnels. "—it's just so darn unsettling."

"I mean, that was a fun one, in my opinion," Kaytrona replied with a smile. Beside her, Kamarial looked at her in shock. The three of them were the only ones in the room—everyone else was off on their own or piloting the ship.

A moment later, there was a loud thud. Norman peeked out the window. "What was that?" he asked.

"Hey everyone, Kurjon here," Kurjon said through the loudspeakers. "We're being pursued. Luckily, they can't fire on us in these tunnels because it's too tight—they'd also get caught up in the blast. But we could pop out into space at any moment now, so hold on tight."

"Is she serious?" Kamarial asked.

"Oh, she's serious. Kurjon isn't one to make light of bad situations, unlike someone I know," Norman said as he glanced at Kaytrona and placed a hand on his metal knee. It was colder to the touch than he had been expecting, but he refrained from jerking his hand away.

"This sucks," Kamarial said.

Norman silently echoed her sentiment as they broke free from the rocky chasms and flew from Termatyl's surface.

"I wonder if Dorie is getting space sickness right now," Kaytrona said, giggling softly to herself.

"What? How can you even—"

"Oh, don't be so serious. If we die in the next two minutes, would you rather have spent your last moments strung up in anxiety or laughing your ass off? I mean, come on, does anyone know any good jokes?"

"Kate—shit, sorry, Kaytrona, I know you love teasing me, but this is serious."

"Exactly why we need to laugh! We're still alive, so we should be living, right?"

"We're in missile lock!" Kurjon shouted from the speakers as *Karna* began to spin wildly. "Hang on! Prepare for collision!"

"Fuck!" Norman shouted, drawing out the word. He closed his eyes, expecting the worst, but no impact came.

"I don't believe it! We've been saved!" Grasberg said excitedly over the speaker.

Norman turned to the window, and his jaw dropped in disbelief. Out of nowhere, an unknown spaceship had appeared. It looked like nothing he had ever seen before, and it was ripping the bounty hunter's ship to shreds.

"What in the void was that?" Norman shouted. "Both ships should've been done for!"

"Did you not see it? That ship appeared out of nowhere! One second there was nothing, and a moment later, it was just there!" Kaytrona said excitedly.

*Is this even real life right now?* Norman thought. *We were seconds away from death, and somehow this* one *ship not only took the missile strikes head on, but it also tore that ship to pieces? What is that ship even made of, and where did it come from?*

**46**

# ESCAPE FROM FATE

"Alright, come on you stupid drones. It's time to move out," Professor Xergat said as he tapped on his tablet.

Altun responded with the real Lakinceitian drones and fell in as the last one in the group. They had only just arrived at the satellite station and were among the first ones off. Altun took one last look at Druder's containment cell and followed the drones off the spaceship.

As they disembarked the ship, Professor Durrist nodded at Professor Xergat. "I'll try to meet up with you after I'm done here."

"Professor Durrist, please pay attention. Now, Professor Peal, I need you and your team to connect with Professors Sareyse and Poulson—" Carl was saying to the remaining professors on the tarmac.

"Wait, they're alive? I thought they died years ago," Professor Peal said in surprise.

"That was just a ruse to get the public off our asses. They've been working here at the satellite station, for years now. At first, it was quite barren. Now that more facilities have come online, they are in dire need of extra hands."

Altun didn't get a chance to listen in on the rest of the conversation, as he and the drones were being herded deeper into the

579

station. Professor Xergat was moving quite slow due to his recent injuries, which gave Altun a chance to study his surroundings. He made a mental note of everything they passed, including the number of unmarked doors. After several turns, they were led to a set of double doors. Professor Xergat pressed the button next to them and the doors swung wide open, revealing a Harmertian wearing blue-rimmed glasses and a white lab coat, standing at attention.

"Ah, thank you for bringing me such grand gifts," the Harmertian said, then looked at Professor Xergat. "My apologies, but who are you again? I thought I was meeting with Professor Durrist."

"Professor Durrist has been given other assignments due to recent poor performance. I'm Professor Xergat, and I made these drones."

"Ah, Professor Xergat, it's a pleasure to meet the mastermind behind these drones. I'm Professor Ean, and I'm excited to see them in action. Are you certain you won't be needing them any longer?"

Professor Xergat grunted. "I am more than happy to hand them off to you. Besides, if I ever need one, I can always go grab one from my old underground lab."

"What do you mean? Are you saying you had more that you didn't take with you?"

"Yeah, I think about fifteen or so got left behind. I mean, who can keep track of all of them, anyway?" Professor Xergat responded. He yawned, as if he was getting bored with the conversation.

In contrast, Professor Ean's face was one of pure shock. "Couldn't you have taken more with you?"

The large brownish-green Lakinceitian shrugged. "Yeah, sure, but why bother? These drones are so dumb. They're really not worth the hassle."

The Harmertian was lost for words.

"Get over it, Ean. They'll survive for a while on their own; it's really not a big deal. If you have a problem with it, take it up with Lord Foxaire," Professor Xergat continued.

"Well, I suppose I'll just have to take good care of the five you've given me," Professor Ean said, then leaned in and started sniffing Altun.

"They don't have much of an odor, do they?"

"That was one of the first things I rid them of. Otherwise, their stench would be completely unbearable," Xergat replied.

"I see," Ean said, then stepped back from the drones. "So, what do I need to know about them?"

"Right. First of all, remember that even though each of them are chipped, they're still alive, which means that you can't expect them to perform at full capacity like a machine would. To control them, you'll need to use this tablet. If you need others made, let Carl or someone know and they can provide you with more. Now..."

As Professor Xergat rattled off, Altun took the time to scan the room he was in. Once again, he used hidden eyes to take in even more. However, there wasn't a whole lot to see. The small lab seemed to be made for Lakinceitians, which made it easier on Professor Ean as well—the table and chairs were all smaller than ones built for Humans, Nioavellians, Kolythoanthaeans, and even Ancilsans. On the tables was a scattering of unused lab equipment, including several empty beakers, some microscopes, and a few torches.

*This may become my new life for a while,* Altun thought. *I never got the opportunities to change into something else. I was hoping to keep a close eye on Druder, but that may be difficult, depending on what I'm tasked to do. The good news is that Ean seems to have a conscience, which may work in my favor.*

---

Norman watched as they dove into Mishunaed's dense atmosphere. The darkness of space was soon lost in a stream of fire and vapor.

After the initial excitement back at Termatyl, the rest of the short journey to Mishunaed was relatively boring, especially after the news that *Dalorent* had gotten away safely. Apparently, *Dalorent* had received help from the same unknown party that had helped *Karna,* but they couldn't communicate with them to find out any more information. They were out of range from *Dalorent,* at least until they replaced their satellite dish.

Norman had been to Mishunaed twice; it was the closest planet a typical Carangian could travel to. Both times he had gone to the same city, Abison, and both times had been for a mining convention. This time around, they headed for Balkisune, the capital city of Mishunaed. At first, Norman had been concerned about going to the largest city on the planet, but Kamarial had brought up the point that it gave them a lot of extra cover. While there were dozens of different ship models out there, a prison transport ship like the one they were in was a rare sight. They flew over the city's skyscrapers, using the busiest of skyways to hide in plain sight. However, as they reached the outskirts of the city, the traffic thinned out considerably.

The door to the cockpit opened, and Kurjon stepped into the common area. She stretched, raising her hands above her head, then yawned.

"Oh my, I'm sorry about that. Does anyone know where Syl is?" Kurjon asked the room, breaking the long bout of silence. Norman shrugged. Besides himself, Kaytrona, Lyd, Newtus, and Kamarial were now in the room with him.

"I believe he's still resting in his containment unit," Lyd replied, his eyes still red from crying.

"Okay, I'll go get him," Kurjon replied as she passed through the narrow room and out the other door.

"That went pretty well," Kamarial said. "I thought we were all gonna die back there."

"Yeah, we got really lucky," Norman replied.

"I wonder who helped us, though. And how did they appear out of nowhere without a portal to pass through?" Kaytrona asked. "I mean, you guys all saw it too, right?"

"I didn't see it," Lyd replied.

"Neither did I," Newtus said.

"I think I saw it," Norman replied as Kurjon and Syl entered the room. Syl had one arm over Kurjon, and she helped him along. "I don't know for sure, though. It all happened so fast."

"Are you talking about that ship that came out of nowhere? I've never seen anything like that before," Kurjon said.

"Wait, what happened?" Syl asked.

"I'll tell you all about it later. For now, we need you to contact your uncle," Kurjon said as she led Syl into the cockpit. She opened the door and Grasberg stepped out so they could fit.

"What happened, Grasberg?" Lyd asked.

"I don't even know. What I do know is that those missiles were coming right for us. We should all be dead, but out of nowhere that mysterious ship took the missiles head on and survived, and then it collided with one of the bounty hunters. My best guess is that they came from beyond the Vortex System, since I've never seen anything like that before."

"That's not possible though, is it?" Kamarial asked.

"I mean, I came from outside of the Vortex System," Kaytrona said. "Well, at least Tyrona did. One minute, Tyrona was just casually riding a giant spider while it clutched onto a platform floating over a massive volcano, and the next minute she was standing beside a gate of some kind. So, it is possible."

"It sounds like you arrived in the Vortex through the gate I saw once," Lyd said. "I would love to hear more about it."

"Right, and the ship that rescued us didn't use a gate," Grasberg pointed out. "It just arrived miraculously in the path of those missiles."

"Unless they used a gate on the other side to come here," Newtus said. Everyone in the room looked at the large purple lizard. "What? If it can happen from one direction, why can't it happen from the other?"

"That's a fair point," Lyd said thoughtfully.

Kurjon's voice from the loudspeakers interrupted the conversation. "Hey, strap in, everyone. We'll be landing soon. Grasberg, please switch out with Syl."

The door to the cockpit opened, revealing Syl leaning against the door frame, putting weight on his injured leg. Grasberg helped Syl to one of the chairs, then headed into the cockpit.

"Hey everyone, how's it been going in here?" Syl asked as he strapped in.

"Great. I mean, we're getting off this ship soon, and I don't plan on ever stepping aboard again," Kamarial said.

"You're planning on staying in Mishunaed?"

"For a while at least," Kamarial said with a nod. "I really don't have anyone to go back to on Ijurvoll. And if I do travel again, I'd just use one of the public transports."

"I'm sure my Uncle Sive could help get you set up with a job here. He has a lot of contacts and is skilled at scrubbing the books," Syl said. "That's why we're going to go see him. If anyone can hide us from Lord Foxaire, it's Uncle Sive."

"I'm glad to hear it," Norman said. "I don't want to be told what to do anymore."

"None of us do," Kaytrona said.

Norman watched as they approached a landing pad. Grasberg and Kurjon set them down smoothly.

"Woohoo! We're finally here," Kaytrona whooped.

"I need to stand up and stretch," Norman said. As soon as he unstrapped himself from the chair, they started moving again. He quickly sat down.

"Why does it feel like we're descending?" Kamarial asked.

A moment later, Kurjon and Grasberg stepped out of the cockpit. "Hey, yeah this isn't us," Grasberg said.

"We're being moved underground to keep us out of sight," Kurjon said. "We can disembark once we reach the final platform, at least that's what we were told."

"So, what exactly does your uncle do, Syl?" Lyd asked. "Storing spaceships underground isn't the conventional method, right?"

"I'm not really sure," Syl said with a shrug. "As far as I know, he helps to run a bar."

"It must be one popular place," Norman said as he gazed out the window, watching the moving rock wall.

A few minutes later, they reached the final platform and came to a complete stop.

"Alright, we're good to go," Grasberg said.

Norman nodded and finally stood up and stretched, raising his arms high above his head. He yawned as he followed everyone off the ship.

They stepped out into a darkly lit hangar, and there wasn't a soul in sight.

"Syl, where is everyone? This is starting to creep me out," Kurjon said.

"I don't know... Uncle Sive said he'd be here. You heard the conversation, right?" Syl said.

"Um, this isn't a trap, right?" Lyd asked. "I didn't get separated from Poi only to die here, right?"

The sound of static crackled to life, causing all of them to jump.

"What in the void is that?" Grasberg shouted over the noise.

"Greetings and apologies," a voice said over a staticky loudspeaker. "Please, make your way to the stairs. Sive will be waiting for you at the top level."

The voice and static cut out, leaving them in silence.

"Okay, I don't think I like that," Norman said as he wrung his hands together. "We should have a few of us stay behind with Theesakin, Bsarg, and the others."

"I'd like to stay behind," Lyd volunteered as he shuffled back toward the ship.

"I'll keep an eye on Theesakin," Newtus said. "I mean, it's my job, and I don't want to leave Bsarg alone with him."

"Good point," Norman said. "Whoever is moving forward, follow me. Let's just get this over with."

"I hope there aren't too many stairs," Syl said.

"It's okay, I can help you," Norman said as he turned around and put an arm around Syl.

"Thank you, Norman," Syl replied.

"It's not a problem. I mean, you helped construct these legs, so it's only fitting they help support you now," he replied.

"Aw, that's so sweet," Kurjon said as she clasped her hands together and followed.

With Syl leaning on him, Norman led Grasberg, Kurjon, Kamarial, and Kaytrona up the spiral staircase.

*What have we gotten ourselves into?* he thought. *I really hope we can trust these people.*

---

Everything happened fast. West thought they were all goners as the three bounty hunters converged upon them. Even though Sterg had helped them out, they couldn't rely on him to protect them now.

West clutched the controls as tightly as he could as he dodged and weaved around in an attempt to make *Dalorent* a harder target to hit. Then, when they broke free from the mine shaft, a nearby explosion caught his attention. For a moment he feared the worst, especially since there was a new unknown spaceship coming right toward them. However, instead of firing on them, the new ship sent a stream of lasers at the bounty hunters.

"What in the void is happening, Dea?" he asked his copilot.

"I haven't the foggiest," Dea replied. "That spaceship did not originate from the Vortex. It's faint, but I am sensing traces of unknown atmospheres on that ship."

"How can you sense that from so far away?" West asked. "I thought you had to use your green mist stuff to feel around."

"I use my pronosua to interact with the world around me, yes, but I can pick up energies through other means," Dea explained.

"Is it horrible that I never knew it had a word? What was it, pronosua?" West asked.

"Yes, but that's not what's important right now," Dea said, redirecting his attention to what was unfolding before them.

The unknown ship shot down one of the bounty hunters, and the remaining two were retreating. The ship before them was quite odd. It didn't conform to any of the conventional ship models. It really didn't look much like a spaceship at all—instead, it looked like a large, round bird with a short neck and a small head. The ship had two long wings, each holding several guns and other components.

As West was gawking at the ship, the communication line started to blink. "Is that them? Should we take it?" he asked.

"Yes. I am not sensing any malice coming from them," Dea replied.

"That's good, at least. Alright, here goes nothing," West said as he flicked on the communication line.

"Hello, and thank you for your assistance. My name is West, and with me is my friend Dea. Who do we have the pleasure of speaking with?"

---

While the others were fighting for spots at the windows, Navacus had the benefit of using Sterg. Now that they weren't running for their lives, he sent Sterg outside their ship to get an unobstructed view of their saviors.

"Where do you think they came from?" Ivy asked.

"It's certainly doesn't look like any ship I've ever seen before," Mac said as he floated next to Poi.

"Yeah, everything here is alien, but that looks like some kinda giant metal turkey to me," Cecil said.

"I'm just glad we're safe and sound. That was way too stressful," Poi said as she rubbed her belly.

"*Sterg, can you see who's in that ship?*" Navacus asked his Light Being companion telepathically.

"*Not at this distance. But they are sending signals to our ship—they're communicating with West and Dea,*" Sterg replied.

"*Go find out what they're saying.*"

Sterg slipped into the cockpit and tuned into the conversation. Dea nodded at Sterg as a familiar voice was speaking.

"We thoroughly apologize for the surprise; we ourselves had no idea where we were going to end up."

"A rather curious detail, if I may add. However, right now I'd like to know why you're sparing us," West replied.

"*Francentia*—our ship—quickly analyzed the situation and let us know we needed to rescue your ship and the other one, as you have passengers on board that we need to talk to."

"What are you even talking about? How do you know who is on our ship? Are you in cahoots with someone?" West asked, grilling the voice.

"No, nothing of the sort. Allow us to approach so we can link up with you, and we will explain more."

"Give me a minute to consult my crew," West said.

"Of course, take your time."

West flipped off the communication line and turned his body toward Dea and Sterg. "So, what do you think we should do?"

"I wish they told us more about who they want to talk to," Dea said.

"I believe they want to speak with our passengers from Eklatros," Sterg said.

*Right, that makes sense. Must be why they protected* Karna. *Speaking of, how are they doing?* Navacus thought. Sterg relayed his thoughts to West and Dea.

"Let me call them up really quick," West said.

While West spoke with Grasberg and Kurjon, Mac and Poi approached Navacus. He turned his attention from Sterg and focused on the Harmertians.

"How are you holding up?" Mac asked.

"I'm alright. I really miss Fumalli, but at least everything has been rather distracting," Navacus replied. "How are the two of you?"

"I just hope Lyd is okay," Poi said with a sad smile.

"West is speaking with Grasberg and Kurjon now. It sounds like they're all safe," Navacus replied.

"How do you... Oh, of course. Sterg is eavesdropping for you, huh?" Mac said, squinting at him.

Navacus shrugged his feathery shoulders. "Is it really eavesdropping if West and Dea know Sterg is there?"

"I guess not," Mac replied.

"What's going on with that strange ship?" Ivy asked, joining the conversation.

"They want to link up with us so we can talk face to face."

"Do we know who they even are?" Poi asked. "I'm glad they saved us, but what are their intentions? What if Lord Foxaire is behind this, too?"

"I don't think that's the case. Rather, we believe it has something to do with you two—Cecil and Theodore," Navacus said as he turned to face the otherworldly Humans.

"Wait, us? What about us?" Cecil asked.

"We believe there's someone on that ship you're familiar with," Navacus said. He didn't want to reveal too much yet. Not until he was certain.

"How is that possible? Eklatros does not have any of the technological advancements that you do. Our planet is a humble one," Theodore said.

"Well, either way, I'll be sure to ask about you two. West is starting to speak with the other ship again. Let me focus on that so I can find out more." Navacus nodded to the others in the room with him, then turned his attention to Sterg.

"West, hold on," Sterg said as West reached for the switch to swap back to *Francentia*.

"What's up?" West asked.

"Navacus wants to ask them about Cecil and Theodore to see if they know anything about them."

"Sure, if they're okay with it," West said, then tipped his hat. "Now, I'm going to switch to the unknown ship. Alright, hey Captain Denorad, are you there?" West asked.

"I'm here. Have you decided?"

"Well, for one, you didn't harm our companions, and so we thank you for that. Two, can you tell us why you are so interested in Cecil and Theodore?"

A muffled sound of excited chatter came from the other end before the line went silent for a few seconds.

"It seems like they definitely know them," Dea said as the communication line sounded with static.

"Sorry about that. Tell Cecil and Theodore that Anqi says hi."

"Will do," West replied. "We're ready to link up."

Navacus brought his full attention back into his own body once again. He wheezed then looked at Cecil and Theodore.

"Anqi says hi. You've met her before, right?"

"Wait, Anqi? Like the woman that was on Patsy's crew?" Cecil said as he looked at his elderly companion.

"I remember Anqi; she had been quite upset with Ànifa at the time," Theodore replied with a chuckle, then pointed out the window. "Does this mean she's on that spaceship?"

"It seems like it," Navacus replied.

Francentia *is actually here*, Navacus thought. *After all those dreams, we finally get to meet with them in person. I just wasn't expecting them to save us and the others from the bounty hunters. You're right, at least Theesakin isn't here for this. Who knows how he would react. Right, of course, Sterg. Let's officially meet some aliens.*

# EPILOGUE
## PROTECT THE VORTEX

*Francentia*'s sirens blared as the space-gate folded them into the Vortex Solar System. Niwat looked around the bridge at all his companions. Anqi, Zanzi, and Kingau were screaming, some out of fear and some from pure excitement. Jurhon muttered to himself with closed eyes while Zombu tightly gripped the edges of his seat.

As they neared the exit of the space tunnel they were in, Niwat turned his full attention back to the screens.

"Warning. Proximity alert," *Francentia* announced.

"Shit, brace for impact!" Maker Denorad shouted.

As they were thrown out of the gate, they were immediately pelted with missiles. Luckily, the projectiles weren't strong enough to cause any damage to *Francentia*'s shield.

"Warning. Excessive speeds. Proximity alert," *Francentia* announced again.

Before anyone could react, their trajectory caused them to collide with a small, single-passenger ship. Whoever had been in there never had a chance.

"What the fuck just happened?" Anqi yelled. "Did we enter into a war zone?"

"Something like that. Look at that ship weaving around over

there. It looks just like the other ship that's going in the opposite direction," Blu-Dreem said as he did everything he could to slow *Francentia* down.

"Scanning. Scanning. Scan complete. Both of the medium-class ships have someone on board with powerful magical abilities," *Francentia* announced.

"That must be them!" Anqi cried. "Cecil, Theodore, Dasch, Tyrona, and Druder!"

"Right, *Francentia*, reverse engines and accelerate toward them," Maker Denorad said. "Zombu, get on the guns. We may need to assist our allies. Now, let's see where fate has taken us!"

<hr>

Cecil gripped the back of a chair as the ship shook violently. A moment later, the turbulence stopped and a robotic voice sounded over the loudspeakers. "Ship-to-ship connection secure. However, the..."

The rest of the details were lost on him as he turned his attention to Theodore.

"Shall we go and see what's in store for us this time around?"

"We might as well, right? I just wish it wasn't just the two of us," Theodore replied.

"What do you mean? We're all here with you," Ivy said. Cecil couldn't resist the urge to shudder. He still wasn't used to the dual male and female voices.

"Right, of course. He just meant that we once had a party of our own. And now it's just the two of us," Cecil replied.

West and Dea emerged from the cockpit and looked at them. "Alright, are you two ready? And is there anyone else who would like to come with us?" West asked.

"I mean, I think we're all going, right?" Mac said as he looked around the room. "I think we all want to see this."

"It may be a tight fit since they're linked to the exterior door with one of the containment modules. We're going to have to squeeze in there," Dea said.

"That's fine. We're small," said Poi. Blood Bat squawked in agreement.

"Lead the way, West," Cecil said. The strange headless alien nodded at him, if it could be called that, and opened the door that led to the rest of the ship.

With Theodore by his side, Cecil and the rest of the crew followed West into the containment module. Two strange individuals greeted them. One was a man who looked to be made completely of metal, and beside him stood a human that had multiple mechanical enhancements.

"Greetings, I am Niwat, and this is my maker, Denorad. We are pleased to meet you all."

"It's great to meet you as well. I'm West." He tipped his hat and introduced everyone.

"So, where's Anqi? I thought Anqi said hi," Cecil asked.

"She is back on the ship with her companions, Mikhail and Gonth. Do you know them as well?" Niwat asked.

"I don't know Mikhail or Gonth, but we know Anqi," Theodore replied as West, Navacus, and the others chatted with Denorad.

"Wonderful," Niwat replied. "I don't want to delay your reunion much longer, but first I have a message for you from your friend, Captain Vesten."

Cecil was at a loss for words. How did this robot alien have a message from Vesten?

"Could you back up for a moment?" Theodore asked. "How do you know Vesten?"

"Of course, my apologies," Niwat said. "My companions and I visited Eklatros during our journey. That is when we met Vesten, Anqi, and many others."

"Wait, you were actually on Eklatros? That's wild," Cecil said.

"That is one way to view it," Niwat said. "Now, are you ready to hear Captain Vesten's message?"

"Right, yes. How is that going to work exactly?"

"Just like so," Niwat said. A beeping noise sounded and suddenly Vesten's voice began flowing from Niwat's mouth.

"Fuckin' seriously? Great, thank you so much!" Vesten's voice said before he cleared his throat. "Hey everyone! I, uh, I don't fuckin' know if I'm doing this right... okay fuckin' great. So, how are you all doing? I miss you all so much. I mean, a lot has changed for me since we last saw each other—I'm the fuckin' captain of nearly twenty crew! But even with all these great people around, I miss our group, you fuckin' know? The seven of us. It only lasted a short time, but honestly? That's what made it so fuckin' great.

"Cecil, I think you'd be happy to know that in these past three years, I have been living true to my duty as interim guildmaster for the Guild for Eklatros. We've helped hundreds, if not thousands, of people by now. And I couldn't have done it without your guidance and friendship. I hope your own journey is going well, and come back soon! I'm fuckin' more than ready to relinquish this title back to you.

"Theodore, I fuckin' hope you've found Tyrona by now, and I hope she's safe. You do everything you can to protect her, you hear? Protect her as if your life fuckin' depends on it. Wait, why am I saying all this? I fuckin' know that you will. If you found her, like how I found Patsy, I know you'll never let her out of your fuckin' sight again.

"Tyrona, keep Theodore in line, alright? I want to hear all about what happened to you, too, so fuckin' come back, you hear?

"Dasch, you grumbly old man. I hope you're still fighting that good fight. You were the fuckin' backbone we all needed. We wouldn't have succeeded without you by our side. So, I'm glad you're there with Cecil, Theodore, Tyrona, and Druder. I know you're fuckin' protecting everyone. So, keep it up, buddy.

"Speaking of, Druder. I know we didn't get to know each other well, but know that each and every day I am so fuckin' thankful you are over there with everyone. Just knowing that they have someone else to support them is reassuring. For all I know, you'll become the fuckin' glue that holds them all together." Vesten took a breath and wiped a tear from his eye.

"Seriously, come back. I may be acting strong and invincible, but I need you back here. Eklatros needs you. I can feel it. There's been a lot of changes, and all have not been for the good."

By the end of it, Cecil was doing everything he could to hold back his tears while his mind swirled with questions. What did Vesten mean, three years? It had only been a month or two at most since they had left Eklatros. Not only that, but what was going on with Eklatros? Were the Gnusar returning? Had they been gone for too long?

Theodore broke the silence that stretched on between them, snapping him back to the moment. "Thank you very much for delivering that message. That was Vesten, alright. With everything that's happened recently, hearing his voice was reassuring."

"Sure, but he needs our help. Didn't you hear him? We need to return to Eklatros as soon as we can," Cecil said firmly, then looked at Niwat. "Can you take us back?"

"I'm sorry, but we have no way of returning."

"That's okay. I know we'll find a way back. We'll rescue Druder and possibly even Dasch, then we'll return to Eklatros. I just hope it won't be too late by the time we do all that," Cecil said, his tone uncertain.

"And Tyrona, too... I need more time to get to Tyrona. Well, Kaytrona now, I suppose," Theodore said.

"I'm sure we can help you out," Niwat said. "Our goal was reaching the Vortex Solar System. Now that we're here, I'm sure we can do what we can to help you. I'd just need to talk with Maker Denorad first, of course."

"We will absolutely accept any assistance that comes our way. Thank you," Cecil said as he placed his palms together.

"Of course," Niwat replied.

"Alright, here's the situation," West said, gathering everyone together. "We can't leave the ships linked together for long, plus we need to get a move on. The bounty hunters could return at any time, and we should wait a bit before we meet up with *Karna* on Mishunaed in case we're being tracked somehow. So, does anyone have any ideas? Captain Denorad and Niwat, feel free to chime in, too."

"Well, I would like to go to Clendenic to visit with Fumalli's parents, but that might be too much of a risk right now," Navacus said.

"I think it's too soon for that, too," Dea said.

Cecil smiled and let his new companions discuss the plan. He didn't know anything about this place, so anywhere but here sounded fine by him.

*No matter what everyone else decides, I must stay on mission,* Cecil thought. *As far as I'm concerned, Druder is our highest priority. I will not let him suffer. Then, we need to find a way back to Eklatros. I wonder if Anqi knows how to get back?*

*Of course, we may be stuck here forever. I know it's a fool's hope that we can return to Eklatros. But even so, I will devote the rest of my life to finding a way home. We need to prepare Eklatros for Gnusaramnii's return. We must protect our friends.*

# GLOSSARY

**Time Period:** Rikiln, Ohocinar 38th to Sarkiln, Tsenar 10th
[read like Monday, June 24th]

**<u>Dramatis Personae – Vortex Solar System</u>**

**<u>Professor Clums' Team</u>**
Professor Navacus Clums (*nah-vuh-kuhs klooms*) [Yggdrazim]
Sterg (*sterg*) [Light Being]
Professor Fumalli Qymberkon (*foo-mall-ee quim-burr-con*) [Nioavellian]
Sylcertiverner (*sil-sir-tiv-er-ner*) [Kolythoanthaean]
Grasberg (*gras-berg*) [Nioavellian]
Kurjon (*kur-jon*) [Kolythoanthaean]
Poi of the Sai Clan (*poy*) [Harmertian]
Mac of the Sai Clan (*mack*) [Harmertian]
Lyd of the Yan Clan (*lid*) [Harmertian]

**<u>Professor Clums' Test Subjects</u>**
Svetlana Slesarenko (*sfet-lah-nuh sles-ah-ren-koh*) [Human Cyborg]
West Kilinder (*west kill-en-dur*) [Eusphyrchiian Cyborg]
Norman Harrison (*nor-men hair-es-son*) [Human Cyborg]

**<u>Professor Peal's Team</u>**
Professor Maximilianus Peal (*max-uh-mill-ee-an-us peel*) [Human]
Professor Kalosse (*kuh-laows*) [Nioavellian]
Elizabeth Surridge (*ee-liz-uh-beth sur-ridge*) [Human]
Kamarial (*kuh-mar-ee-ul*) [Eusphyrchiian]
Walverm (*wall-verm*) [Kolythoanthaean]
Mahlvern (*mall-vern*) [Kolythoanthaean]

**<u>Professor Peal's Test Subjects</u>**
Newtus (*new-tuss*) [Neutortous]
Denoptace (*duh-nopt-ace*) [Phasmatodaedalus]
Stick-Brain (*stick brain*) [Phasmatodaedalus]
Blood Bat (*bluhd bat*) [Zubba]
Sassafrass (*sass-uh-frass*) [Loxocemae]
Sage (*sage*) [Loxocemae]
Saffron (*saff-ron*) [Loxocemae]
Sesame (*ses-ah-me*) [Loxocemae]

Salty Susan (*sahl-tee soo-suhn*) [Curik]
Penny (*pen-ee*) [Dark Therid]
Ados (*a-dos*) [Dark Therid]
Adok (*a-dock*) [Dark Therid]
Ivy Hedera (*eye-vee head-er-ah*) [Eusphyrchiian]

## Compound Security Guards
Bsarg (*buh-sarg*) [Lakinceitian]
Nijork (*nee-jork*) [Lakinceitian]
Jakog (*juh-cog*) [Lakinceitian]
Sharg (*sharg*) [Lakinceitian]

## Other Compound Staff
Head Professor Jaffe Yilvin (*jaf yill-vin*) [Kolythoanthaean]
Professor Dea (*dee*) [Eridavlos]
Professor Venkatt Bodeelch (*venn-cat boh-dealch*) [Kolythoanthaean]
Professor Xabio Durrist (*sha-bee-oh dur-wrist*) [Lakinceitian]
Professor Randall (*ran-daal*) [Human]
Professor Xergat (*zer-gat*) [Lakinceitian]

## Titans
Ophertusc (*oh-fur-toosk*) [Chimera]
Zinartee (*zin-are-tee*) [Chimera]
Karkilver (*car-kill-vur*) [Chimera]
Zadgarcolth (*zad-jer-colth*) [Chimera]
Theesakin (*thee-sake-in*) [Chimera]

## Professor Durrist's Test Subjects
Altun (*all-toon*) [Ancilsan]
Unnamed female [Yggdrazim]
Unnamed female [Eridavlos]
Katherine Padmashiri Thomas (*kath-rin pad-muh-sure-ee tom-us*) [Human]
Kaytrona (*kay-troh-nuh*) [Human]

## Foxaire Biotech Industries Leadership and Staff
Lord Foxaire (*fox-air*) [Lakinceitian]
Carl Feng (*kaarl fung*) [Human]
Gazelle (*guh-zell*) [Nioavellian]
Sid Heigel (*sid hi-gel*) [Human]
Gnudashar (*new-duh-shar*) [Gnureaver]
Chief Engineer Volvordime (*voll-vor-dime*) [Kolythoanthaean]
Professor Ean of the Col Clan (*een*) [Harmertian]
Professor Sareyse (*sar-eye-see*) [Nioavellian]
Professor Poulson (*poul-son*) [Human]

## Travelers from Eklatros

Sorcerer Theodore Henry Caldwell (*thee-oh-door hen-ree cald-well*) [Human]
Sir Cecil Johnathan Kloud (*sess-sul john-a-thun cloud*) [Human]
Dasch Valentine (*dah'sh val-en-tyn*) [Half-Elf]
Druder Nanasazii (*dru-dur nah-nuh-saw-zee*) [Elf]
Sorcerer Tyrona Claire Knorse (*tie-roe-nuh claire norse*) [Human]

## Bounty Hunters

Kanaghar (*can-ah-gar*) [Lakinceitian]
Tag Creson (*tag cress-en*) [Eusphyrchiian]
Supreme Carnivore 'S.C.' Brock (*ess see brock*) [Human]
Egimas (*egg-ee-maas*) [Eusphyrchiian]
Anessti (*ah-ness-tee*) [Nioavellian]

## Original Lakinceitians

Gnusaramnii (*new-sar-raam-nee*) [Lakinceitian]
Mau (*mao*) [Lakinceitian]

## Dramatis Personae – Francentia's Travels

## Crew of *Francentia*

Maker Denorad (*den-ore-add*) [Human Cyborg]
Niwat (*nigh-watt*) [Androbotix]
Zanzi (*zaan-zee*) [Androbotix]
Zombu (*zom-boo*) [Androbotix]
Blu-Dreem 'Beedee' (*blue-dream*) [Androbotix]

## Crew of *New Horizons*

Captain Vesten James Teixeira (*vest-en james tay-shay-ruh*) [Human]
First Mate Patricia Judith 'Patsy' Matros (*pat-see muh-trows*) [Human]
Second Mate Dale Lovett (*dale love-it*) [Human]
Bosun Bartholomew Hobbs (*bar-thawl-oh-mew hobbs*) [Human]
Quartermaster Tushar Kothari (*too-shar koh-thar-ee*) [Human]
Assistant Navigator Zi'ra Shnuckeramn (*zigh-ruh shnuck-er-raam*) [Elf]
Chef Duangthip Wihok (*doo-oong-tip wee-hock*) [Human]
Sous Chef Dusit Wihok (*do-sit wee-hock*) [Human]
Medic Finfoler Dithear (*fin-foll-er dith-ear*) [Elf]
Trevonn 'Money' Hillside (*trev-on mun-ee hill-side*) [Human]
Annalyse Skye (*ann-uh-lease sky*) [Human]
Damrong Nakhon (*daam-rong nah-con*) [Human]
Disakorn Nakhon (*dis-ah-corn nah-con*) [Human]
Gonth Crescent (*gonth cress-cent*) [Elf]
Mikhail Kohmoon (*mik-hail koh-moon*) [Human]
Preston Cherry (*press-tun chair-ree*) [Human]

Arsona Fig (*are-soh-nuh fig*) [Elf]
Ashe Walker (*ash walk-er*) [Human]
Martin Greene (*mar-tin green*) [Human]
Anqi Gan (*ahn-chee gahn*) [Human]

**Citizens of Beetaramn**
Tanaq Jayne Farag (*tah-nock jane far-raag*) [Human]
Afyna Lucarieo (*ah-figh-nugh loo-care-ee-oh*) [Human]

**Travelers from afar**
Tiresias (*tie-ree-see-us*) [Propoli]
Noiyanit (*noy-yan-it*) [Ligthera]
Baroine (*bar-oh-in*) [Propoli]
Yai'rah (*yai-ruh*) [Ligthera]
Mosi (*moh-see*) [Propoli]
Ledjo (*led-joe*) [Ligthera]
Raza (*rah-zuh*) [Kirbita]
Raff (*raff*) [Kirbita]

**Omaloha's Lone Survivor**
Jurhon (*jurr-hon*) [Kolythoanthaean]

**Thorpi's Lone Survivor**
Kingau; Kin of the Gau Clan (*king-gau*) [Harmertian]

**Eklatros' Saviors**
Princess Ànifa Tataluynnia Ekataramnii (*uh-niff-uh tat-tuh-loo-nee-uh e-khat-ah-raam-nee*) or (*uh-nee-fa*) [Human-Ekataramn Hybrid]
Joan de Ligtheramnii (*joan duh lig-thur-raam-nee*) [Angel]
Quaant Yttenramnii (*k'wah'nt yit-ten-raam-nee*) [Faerie]

## Universal Terms

### Variations of the Gnusar

Gnusar (*new-sar*): aka Scaly Monsters. These creatures are covered in hard green scales. They have the power of speech and are immune to fire. They have two small feet that hide beneath their bulk.

Gnuelry (*new-el-ree*): aka Jelly Monsters. These creatures come in many variations and colors, depending on their viscousness.

Gnurargurt (*new-rar-gurt*): These creatures are animals and gods that have been killed and reanimated as minions for the Gnusar.

Gnureaver (*new-ree-ver*): These creatures are mostly humans and elves that have been possessed and corrupted to become fiercely intelligent warriors. Can appear to be grotesque creatures or can look like normal humans or elves, depending on the circumstances in which the individual was possessed.

### Intelligent Species

Androbotix (*an-drough-bot-icks*): All Androbotix are robotic beings created by Humans and are highly intelligent. They vary in size and shape depending on who made them. They are native to the planet Theronior.

Ancilsan (*an-sill-san*): Refugee Species that moved into the Vortex System, hailing from the planet Strutheine. Humanoid species, covered in light- to dark-brown fur with short, squat bodies and strong limbs and jaws. They are more comfortable in trees than on land.

Angels (*ayn-jlz*): The third and final variation of Humans, hailing from Eklatros. Angels are the most divine form of Humans / Elves, and there are only seven in existence. Their wings are similar to swan wings. They have an innate ability to heal wounds and illnesses. They have light- to dark-brown skin. They evolved after the Great War of Eklatros to be a higher governance of all living things.

Ekataramn (*e-khat-ah-raam*): Divine beings, originally hailing from the Magicks System. They are tree-like and root into the ground, but can unroot and travel if in duress. They can contain elements of all walks of life, including animals, plants, and fungi.

Elves (*elvz*): The first variation of Humans, hailing from Eklatros. Their skin tone ranges from light brown to pitch black. They have long, pointed ears and live many times longer than Humans.

Eridavlos (*air-ee-daav-lows*): Refugee Species that moved into the Vortex System, hailing from the planet Strutheine. Humanoid species with no limbs. They use a mysterious organ, called a pronosua, to levitate above the ground.

Eusphyrchii (*yous-fur-chee*): Native Species to the Vortex System, hailing from the planet Ijurvoll. Humanoid species with hard white or gray exoskeletons. They have the ability to regrow lost limbs.

Faeries (*fae-rees*): The second variation of Humans, hailing from Eklatros. Faeries began as Elves and evolved into winged creatures. They can change their body size at will, but mainly stay about the size of a typical songbird. Their wings are similar to butterfly wings. They have light- to dark-brown skin.

Humans (*hyoo-muhn*): Native Species to the Vortex System, hailing from the planet Carange. Regular humans.

Harmertians (*har-mur-tian*): Refugee Species that moved into the Vortex System, hailing from the planet Strutheine/Mishunaed. Humanoid species. They are short, growing only about fifty to seventy centimeters tall. They have light- to dark-gray skin.

Kirbita (*kir-bit-ah*): Small bipedal reptilian creatures. They are covered in light- to dark-green scales. They stand about seventy to ninety centimeters tall. Kirbitas can naturally use magic and hail from the Magicks System.

Kolythoanthaean (*koly-tho-anth-ee-ā-an*): Native Species to the Vortex System, hailing from the planet Mishunaed. Humanoid species standing on average around 180 centimeters with light- to dark-gray skin and have six digits on each of their hands and feet.

Lakinceitian (*lake-in-set-ee-an*): Native Species to the Vortex System, hailing from the planet Melridion. Gastropod species with two small arms and two legs that are essentially useless as they are hidden beneath their bulk. They also have small, short tails.

Ligthera (lig-thair-ah): Quadrupedal creatures that hail from the Magicks System. They are feline-like and have three skinny tails. Each Ligthera is dual colored, such as green and blue or pink and orange. However, all Ligthera have pink noses, greenish-yellow eyes, and a brown mane. Most Ligthera are bound to a Propoli as lifelong companions. They can speak and are powerful magic users in their own right, but rarely use their magic.

Nioavellian (*nigh-oh-ah-vell-ee-an*): Native Species to the Vortex System, hailing from the planet Clendenic. Humanoid species with blue to light purple skin tones and egg-shaped heads. They have two arms and three legs.

Propoli (*pro-pole-ee*): Hailing from the Magicks System, they are some of the strongest magic users in the cosmos. Each Propoli is born without one of their senses in order to heighten their other senses. They can live many lifetimes during their long lives as they are reborn into other bodies on other planets. They are bipedal and elephant-like, with big ears and a long trunk. Their skin tone ranges from brown to dark gray.

Yggdrazim (*yigg-druh-zem*): Refugee Species that moved into the Vortex System, hailing from the planet Strutheine. Avian-based species, with large flat beaks and white to light gray plumage.

## Acampachetlian Species

Aldagos (*al-dog-os*): Large amphibians with hard shells.

Bahamus (*bah-ha-moos*): Snakes that can grow to be hundreds of meters long. They are mostly immobile.

Curik (*curr-ick*): Beetle-like insects that are unable to fly.

Dark Therid (*there-id*): Specialized spiders that have about thirty spinnerets and four extra silk glands. A single bite from a Dark Therid can kill a fully grown Ancilsan.

Grumantrus (*grum-an-trus*): Praying mantis-like insects.

Loxocemae (*locks-oh-sem-eh*): Snakes with blood-red scales. They are independent from birth and eat their fellow hatchlings as their first meal.

Neutortous (*new-tur-toos*): Giant lizards. They are deep purple to dark blue in color. They prey on Loxocemae.

Phasmatodaedalus (*fas-mat-oh-day-dahl-us*): Stick bug-like insects that do not stop growing. While mostly independent, they live in social groups with a queen.

Zubba (*zoo-bah*): Zubba have the body of a bat, with the bat's wings and furry head. The bat half is fused onto the back of a large scorpion. The scorpion part does not have a head. The scorpion's and the bat's coloring are always different, and each one seems to have their own personality.

Zubula (*zoo-boo-luh*): Zubula are very similar to Zubba. The main difference is the scorpion part has a head, and they command the Zubba.

**<u>Planets of the Vortex Solar System</u>**

<u>Acampachetli</u> (*a-comp-ah-chet-lee*): Jungle world where Dark Therids, Zubba, Loxocemae, etc. reside

<u>Mishunaed</u> (*me-shoo-naid*): Kolythoanthaean home world

<u>Carange</u> (*cuh-raange*): Human home world

<u>Termatyl</u> (*term-a-till*): Carange's moon

<u>Melridion</u> (*mel-rid-ee-on*): Lakinceitian home world

<u>Clendenic</u> (*clen-den-ick*): Nioavellian home world

<u>Strutheine</u> (*struth-eyen*): Home world for refugee species, such as Yggdrazim, Harmertian, Ancilsan, and Eridavlos

<u>Ijurvoll</u> (*idge-or-vull*): Eusphyrchiian home world

<u>Dunartera</u> (*do-nar-terra*): Gas giant

**<u>Cities and Regions</u>**

*<u>Mishunaed</u>*
Abison (*abb-ee-son*)
Balkisune (*balk-uh-soon*)

*<u>Melridion</u>*
Nalpetalis (*nall-pet-all-us*)
Volgash Desert (*voll-gash*)
Nishna Delta (*nish-nuh*)
Krefna Mountains (*kreff-nuh*)
The Compound

*<u>Carange</u>*
Bahutenrut (*bah-hut-en-rut*)
Delgrious (*dell-gree-us*)
Kokorocco (*coh-coh-rock-oh*)
Starofsky (*star-off-ski*)

*<u>Strutheine</u>*
Yolavien (*yo-lah-veen*)
Ligthuria (*lig-thur-ee-uh*)

*<u>Ijurvoll</u>*
Warae (*war-ay*)

*<u>Clendenic</u>*
Kelhorr (*kell-hoor*)
Kelhorr University

## Planets outside the Vortex System
Eklatros (*ek-luh-trohs*)
Theronior (*ther-ron-ee-ore*)
Omaloha (*oh-muh-loh-ha*)
Thorpi (*thor-pee*)
Alfah'moosai (*al-fuh-moo-sai*)
Beeta'zo (*bee-tuh-zoh*)

## Businesses and Organizations
Foxaire Biotech Industries
Intergalactic Bounty Hunter Association
Intergalactic Police Department

## Spaceships
*Dalorent* (*duh-lore-ent*)
*Karna* (*car-nuh*)
*Francentia* (*fran-sen-tee-uh*)

## Miscellaneous Terms
Acclimater (*ack-luh-mat-er*): A device that can create a temporary artificial atmosphere in places that have no atmosphere.

Electra-Block (*uh-lek-truh-blok*): A device that can create a temporary electric field to keep someone from passing through an area. These are highly regulated by the Intergalactic Police Department.

Flohawkah'mon (*flow-haak-uh-mon*): A person that passes away without a name. Roughly translates to honored deceased in the Ancilsan's native language.

Kirwach (*kur-wash*): An Acampachetlian term that roughly translates to home or one's territory.

Pronosua (*pro-no-sue-uh*): The mysterious organ that Eridavlos' use to interact with the world around them. Looks like a green ghostly mist.

## Melridion Time

### Days - Each day is 25 hours long with 80-minute hours:

1. Eklakiln (*ek-luh-kiln*)
2. Sarkiln (*sar-kiln*)
3. Melrikiln (*mel-ree-kiln*)
4. Dunakiln (*doo-nuh-kiln*)
5. Pjorkiln (*puh-jor-kiln*)
6. Rikiln (*ree-kiln*)
7. Gnuakiln (*new-ah-kiln*)
8. Ramnkiln (*raam-kiln*)

### Months - Each month is 40 days long:

1. Vuhardeena (*voo-har-dee-nuh*)
2. Heinineara (*hey-in-air-uh*)
3. Lakinar (*lake-in-ar*)
4. Teinianar (*tay-nee-an-ar*)
5. Kampanar (*kamp-uh-nar*)
6. Julinar (*jool-in-ar*)
7. Caranar (*car-in-ar*)
8. Ohocinar (*oh-hock-in-ar*)
9. Tsenar (*tsen-ar*)
10. Drazineara (*drazz-in-air-uh*)
11. Zaltrineara (*zal-trin-air-uh*)
12. Kiliranar (*kee-lee-ruh-nar*)
13. Gardevinar (*gar-dev-in-ar*)

# ACKNOWLEDGMENTS

First of all, thank *you*. Whether you are a returning fan or a new reader, thank you for taking the plunge into the cosmos.

Even though this is the second book in the *Rebalancing the Cosmos* series, this story is much older than Eklatros'. This is the story I have been working on since I was six or seven years old, and I will forever thank LEGO for giving me the tools to make my imagination bloom. Among the oldest of my LEGO characters are Navacus Clums, West, and Ivy, and their stories are only just beginning.

I want to thank my wonderful editor, Erika M. Weinert, dba The Werd Nerd, for your continued guidance, support, and friendship. *Rebalancing the Cosmos* wouldn't be what it is today without you.

Thank you, BMR Williams, for continuing to make such great maps. You really brought Melridion and the Vortex System to life. BMR also illustrated the map of Eklatros, and I'm sure he'll illustrate my future maps as well. To find BMR Williams on Fiverr, search for mitsumightous.

To Walter Robinson, author of the *State of Vesta Fortuna* series, thank you for creating the initial illustrations of *Dalorent* and *Karna*. It was so amazing to finally see the ships I had envisioned for decades. You illustrated them perfectly. Check out Robinson's book series if you're interested in an epic science fiction series.

Many thanks to the amazingly talented Tom Edwards Design for illustrating the absolutely stunning cover. It came out better than I had ever imagined.

Thank you, Eric, Ashton, and Roscoe, for being amazing adventurers in my custom Dungeons & Dragons campaign. Each of you are helping to shape this series in ways I never would have dreamed possible, and it's awesome.

I'm not sure how many authors thank their book's interior designers, but seriously, Bryan Canter is the best. I am so thankful for having someone that can go in and make little tweaks and edits to the PDFs even after the project is done.

Finally, I need to thank my family, friends, and everyone I have known and befriended throughout my life. All of you have influenced my life in one way or another and, in turn, many of you had an effect on this book and the entire series in more ways than one.

# ABOUT THE AUTHOR

Alex Galassi was born in Littleton, Colorado, in the early 1990s and has lived in Colorado his entire life. He received his Bachelor's Degree at the University of Colorado in Boulder at the School of Journalism and Mass Communication. He is the author of the *Rebalancing the Cosmos* series and the VP of Technology at Blue Zenith Design + Strategy, a small business founded and run by his mother. When he is not at work or writing fiction, Alex enjoys exploring Colorado's beautiful mountains, reading fantasy and science-fiction novels, attending concerts at Red Rocks, and playing Magic: The Gathering, Dungeons & Dragons, and video games.